T0366614

THE CLAY SANSKRIT LIBRARY
FOUNDED BY JOHN & JENNIFER CLAY

GENERAL EDITOR

SHELDON POLLOCK

EDITED BY

ISABELLE ONIANS

WWW.CLAYSANSKRITLIBRARY.ORG
WWW.NYUPRESS.ORG

*Artwork by Robert Beer.*
*Typeset in Adobe Garamond Pro at 10.25 : 12.3+pt.*
*Editorial input from Dániel Balogh, Ridi Faruque,*
*Chris Gibbons, Tomoyuki Kono & Eszter Somogyi.*
*Printed and Bound in Great Britain by*
*TJ Books Ltd, Cornwall on acid free paper*

# MAHĀBHĀRATA

## BOOK FIVE

# PREPARATIONS FOR WAR

## VOLUME TWO

TRANSLATED BY

Kathleen Garbutt

NEW YORK UNIVERSITY PRESS

JJC FOUNDATION

2008

Copyright © 2008 by the JJC Foundation
All rights reserved.

First Edition 2008

The Clay Sanskrit Library is co-published by
New York University Press
and the JJC Foundation.

Further information about this volume
and the rest of the Clay Sanskrit Library
is available at the end of this book
and on the following websites:
**www.claysanskritlibrary.org**
**www.nyupress.org**

ISBN 978-0-8147-3202-1

**Library of Congress Cataloging-in-Publication Data**
Mahābhārata. Udyogaparva. English & Sanskrit.
Mahābhārata. Book five, Preparations for war /
translated by Kathleen Garbutt. -- 1st ed.
p. cm.-- (The Clay Sanskrit Library)
Epic Poetry.
In English and Sanskrit (romanized) on facing pages;
includes translation from Sanskrit.
Includes bibliographical references and index.
ISBN: 978-0-8147-3202-1
I. Garbutt, Kathleen. II. Title. III. Title: Preparations for war.
BL1138.242.U39E5 2007
294.5'92304521-dc22
2007017336

# CONTENTS

# CSL CONVENTIONS

## Sanskrit Alphabetical Order

| | |
|---|---|
| Vowels: | *a ā i ī u ū ṛ ṝ ḷ ḹ e ai o au ṃ ḥ* |
| Gutturals: | *k kh g gh ṅ* |
| Palatals: | *c ch j jh ñ* |
| Retroflex: | *ṭ ṭh ḍ ḍh ṇ* |
| Dentals: | *t th d dh n* |
| Labials: | *p ph b bh m* |
| Semivowels: | *y r l v* |
| Spirants: | *ś ṣ s h* |

## Guide to Sanskrit Pronunciation

| | |
|---|---|
| *a* | b*u*t |
| *ā, â* | f*a*ther |
| *i* | s*i*t |
| *ī, î* | f*ee* |
| *u* | p*u*t |
| *ū,û* | b*oo* |
| *ṛ* | vocalic *r*, American p*ur*dy or English p*re*tty |
| *ṝ* | lengthened *ṛ* |
| *ḷ* | vocalic *l*, ab*le* |
| *e, ê, ē* | m*a*de, esp. in Welsh pronunciation |
| *ai* | b*i*te |
| *o, ô, ō* | r*o*pe, esp. Welsh pronunciation; Italian s*o*lo |
| *au* | s*ou*nd |
| *ṃ* | *anusvāra* nasalizes the preceding vowel |
| *ḥ* | *visarga*, a voiceless aspiration (resembling the English *h*), or like Scottish lo*ch*, or an aspiration with a faint echoing of the last element of the preceding vowel so that *taiḥ* is pronounced *taih*[i] |
| *k* | lu*ck* |
| *kh* | blo*ckh*ead |
| *g* | *g*o |
| *gh* | bi*gh*ead |
| *ṅ* | a*n*ger |
| *c* | *ch*ill |
| *ch* | mat*chh*ead |
| *j* | *j*og |
| *jh* | aspirated *j*, he*dgeh*og |
| *ñ* | ca*ny*on |
| *ṭ* | retroflex *t*, *t*ry (with the tip of tongue turned up to touch the hard palate) |
| *ṭh* | same as the preceding but aspirated |
| *ḍ* | retroflex *d* (with the tip |

| | |
|---|---|
| | of tongue turned up to touch the hard palate) |
| *ḍh* | same as the preceding but aspirated |
| *ṇ* | retroflex *n* (with the tip of tongue turned up to touch the hard palate) |
| *t* | French *t*out |
| *th* | ten*t h*ook |
| *d* | *d*inner |
| *dh* | guil*dh*all |
| *n* | *n*ow |
| *p* | *p*ill |
| *ph* | u*ph*eaval |
| *b* | *b*efore |
| *bh* | a*bh*orrent |
| *m* | *m*ind |
| *y* | *y*es |
| *r* | trilled, resembling the Italian pronunciation of *r* |
| *l* | *l*inger |
| *v* | *w*ord |
| *ś* | *sh*ore |
| *ṣ* | retroflex *sh* (with the tip of the tongue turned up to touch the hard palate) |
| *s* | hi*ss* |
| *h* | *h*ood |

## CSL Punctuation of English

The acute accent on Sanskrit words when they occur outside of the Sanskrit text itself, marks stress, e.g., Ramáyana. It is not part of traditional Sanskrit orthography, transliteration, or transcription, but we supply it here to guide readers in the pronunciation of these unfamiliar words. Since no Sanskrit word is accented on the last syllable it is not necessary to accent disyllables, e.g., Rama.

The second CSL innovation designed to assist the reader in the pronunciation of lengthy unfamiliar words is to insert an unobtrusive middle dot between semantic word breaks in compound names (provided the word break does not fall on a vowel resulting from the fusion of two vowels), e.g., Maha·bhárata, but Ramáyana (not Rama·áyana). Our dot echoes the punctuating middle dot (·) found in the oldest surviving samples of written Indic, the Ashokan inscriptions of the third century BCE.

The deep layering of Sanskrit narrative has also dictated that we use quotation marks only to announce the beginning and end of every direct speech, and not at the beginning of every paragraph.

## CSL Punctuation of Sanskrit

The Sanskrit text is also punctuated, in accordance with the punctuation of the English translation. In mid-verse, the punctuation will not alter the sandhi or the scansion. Proper names are capitalized. Most Sanskrit meters have four "feet" (*pāda*); where possible we print the common *śloka* meter on two lines. The capitalization of verse beginnings makes it easy for the reader to recognize longer meters where it is necessary to print the four metrical feet over four or eight lines. In the Sanskrit text, we use French *Guillemets* (e.g., *«kva saṃcicīrṣuḥ?»*) instead of English quotation marks (e.g., "Where are you off to?") to avoid confusion with the apostrophes used for vowel elision in sandhi.

### SANDHI

Sanskrit presents the learner with a challenge: *sandhi* (euphonic combination). Sandhi means that when two words are joined in connected speech or writing (which in Sanskrit reflects speech), the last letter (or even letters) of the first word often changes; compare the way we pronounce "the" in "the beginning" and "the end."

In Sanskrit the first letter of the second word may also change; and if both the last letter of the first word and the first letter of the second are vowels, they may fuse. This has a parallel in English: a nasal consonant is inserted between two vowels that would otherwise coalesce: "a pear" and "an apple." Sanskrit vowel fusion may produce ambiguity.

The charts on the following pages give the full sandhi system.

Fortunately it is not necessary to know these changes in order to start reading Sanskrit. All that is important to know is the form of the second word without sandhi (pre-sandhi), so that it can be recognized or looked up in a dictionary. Therefore we are printing Sanskrit with a system of punctuation that will indicate, unambiguously, the original form of the second word, i.e., the form without sandhi. Such sandhi mostly concerns the fusion of two vowels.

In Sanskrit, vowels may be short or long and are written differently accordingly. We follow the general convention that a vowel with no mark above it is short. Other books mark a long vowel either with a bar called a macron (*ā*) or with a circumflex (*â*). Our system uses the

## VOWEL SANDHI

| Initial vowels: | Final vowels: a | ā | i | ī | u | ū | ṛ | e | ai | o | au |
|---|---|---|---|---|---|---|---|---|---|---|---|
| a | ' â | " â | y a | y a | v a | v a | r a | e ' | ā a | o ' | āv a |
| ā | ' ā | " ā | y ā | y ā | v ā | v ā | r ā | a ā | ā ā | a ā | āv ā |
| i | ' ê | " ê | ' î | " î | v i | v i | r i | a i | ā i | a i | āv i |
| ī | ' ē | " ē | ' ī | " ī | v ī | v ī | r ī | a ī | ā ī | a ī | āv ī |
| u | ' ô | " ô | y u | y u | ' û | " û | r u | a u | ā u | a u | āv u |
| ū | ' ō | " ō | y ū | y ū | ' ū | " ū | r ū | a ū | ā ū | a ū | āv ū |
| ṛ | a' r | a" r | y ṛ | y ṛ | v ṛ | v ṛ | ' ṝ | a ṛ | ā ṛ | a ṛ | āv ṛ |
| e | ' âi | " âi | y e | y e | v e | v e | r e | a e | ā e | a e | āv e |
| ai | ' āi | " āi | y ai | y ai | v ai | v ai | r ai | a ai | ā ai | a ai | āv ai |
| o | ' âu | " âu | y o | y o | v o | v o | r o | a o | ā o | a o | āv o |
| au | ' āu | " āu | y au | y au | v au | v au | r au | a au | ā au | a au | āv au |

## CONSONANT SANDHI

| *Permitted finals:* k | ṭ | t | p | ṅ | n | m | *(Except āḥ/aḥ)* ḥ/r | āḥ | aḥ | *Initial letters:* |
|---|---|---|---|---|---|---|---|---|---|---|
| k | ṭ | t | p | ṅ | n | ṃ | ḥ | āḥ | aḥ | k/kh |
| g | ḍ | d | b | ṅ | n | ṃ | r | ā | o | g/gh |
| k | ṭ | c | p | ṅ | ṃś | ṃ | ś | āś | aś | c/ch |
| g | ḍ | j | b | ṅ | ñ | ṃ | r | ā | o | j/jh |
| k | ṭ | ṭ | p | ṅ | ṃṣ | ṃ | ṣ | āṣ | aṣ | ṭ/ṭh |
| g | ḍ | ḍ | b | ṅ | ṇ | ṃ | r | ā | o | ḍ/ḍh |
| k | ṭ | t | p | ṅ | ṃs | ṃ | s | ās | as | t/th |
| g | ḍ | d | b | ṅ | n | ṃ | r | ā | o | d/dh |
| k | ṭ | t | p | ṅ | n | ṃ | ḥ | āḥ | aḥ | p/ph |
| g | ḍ | d | b | ṅ | n | ṃ | r | ā | o | b/bh |
| ṅ | ṇ | n | m | ṅ | n | ṃ | r | ā | o | *nasals* (n/m) |
| g | ḍ | d | b | ṅ | n | ṃ | r | ā | o | y/v |
| g | ḍ | d | b | ṅ | n | ṃ | *zero*[1] | ā | o | r |
| g | ḍ | l | b | ṅ | l̃[2] | ṃ | r | ā | o | l |
| k | ṭ | c ch | p | ṅ | ñ ś/ch | ṃ | ḥ | āḥ | aḥ | ś |
| k | ṭ | t | p | ṅ | n | ṃ | ḥ | āḥ | aḥ | ṣ/s |
| gg h | ḍḍ h | dd h | bb h | ṅ | n | ṃ | r | ā | o | h |
| g | ḍ | d | b | ṅ/ṅṅ[3] | n/nn[3] | m | r | ā | a[4] | *vowels* |
| k | ṭ | t | p | ṅ | n | m | ḥ | āḥ | aḥ | *zero* |

[1]ḥ or r disappears, and if a/i/u precedes, this lengthens to ā/ī/ū. [2]e.g. tān+lokān=tāl̃ lokān.
[3]The doubling occurs if the preceding vowel is short. [4]Except: aḥ+a=o '.

macron, except that for initial vowels in sandhi we use a circumflex to indicate that originally the vowel was short, or the shorter of two possibilities (*e* rather than *ai*, *o* rather than *au*).

| | | |
|---|---|---|
| When we print initial | *â*, before sandhi that vowel was | *a* |
| | *î* or *ê*, | *i* |
| | *û* or *ô*, | *u* |
| | *âi*, | *e* |
| | *âu*, | *o* |
| | *ā*, | *ā* |
| | *ī*, | *ī* |
| | *ū*, | *ū* |
| | *ē*, | *ī* |
| | *ō*, | *ū* |
| | *ai*, | *ai* |
| | *āu*, | *au* |
| | ', before sandhi there was a vowel *a* | |

When a final short vowel (*a*, *i*, or *u*) has merged into a following vowel, we print ' at the end of the word, and when a final long vowel (*ā*, *ī*, or *ū*) has merged into a following vowel we print " at the end of the word. The vast majority of these cases will concern a final *a* or *ā*. See, for instance, the following examples:

| | | |
|---|---|---|
| What before sandhi was | *atra asti* is represented as | *atr' âsti* |
| | *atra āste* | *atr' āste* |
| | *kanyā asti* | *kany" âsti* |
| | *kanyā āste* | *kany" āste* |
| | *atra iti* | *atr' êti* |
| | *kanyā iti* | *kany" êti* |
| | *kanyā īpsitā* | *kany" ēpsitā* |

Finally, three other points concerning the initial letter of the second word:

(1) A word that before sandhi begins with *ṛ* (vowel), after sandhi begins with *r* followed by a consonant: *yatha" rtu* represents pre-sandhi *yathā ṛtu*.

(2) When before sandhi the previous word ends in *t* and the following word begins with *ś*, after sandhi the last letter of the previous word is *c*

and the following word begins with *ch*: *syāc chāstravit* represents pre-sandhi *syāt śāstravit*.

(3) Where a word begins with *h* and the previous word ends with a double consonant, this is our simplified spelling to show the pre-sandhi form: *tad hasati* is commonly written as *tad dhasati*, but we write *tadd hasati* so that the original initial letter is obvious.

### COMPOUNDS

We also punctuate the division of compounds (*samāsa*), simply by inserting a thin vertical line between words. There are words where the decision whether to regard them as compounds is arbitrary. Our principle has been to try to guide readers to the correct dictionary entries.

## Exemplar of CSL Style

Where the Devanagari script reads:

कुम्भस्थली रक्षतु वो विकीर्णसिन्धूररेणुर्द्विरदाननस्य ।
प्रशान्तये विघ्नतमश्छटानां निष्ठ्यूतबालातपपल्लवेव ॥

Others would print:

kumbhasthalī rakṣatu vo vikīrṇasindūrareṇur dviradānanasya /
praśāntaye vighnatamaśchaṭānāṃ niṣṭhyūtabālātapapallaveva //

We print:

kumbha|sthalī rakṣatu vo vikīrṇa|sindūra|reṇur dvirad'|ānanasya
praśāntaye vighna|tamaś|chaṭānāṃ niṣṭhyūta|bāl'|ātapa|pallav" êva.

And in English:

May Ganésha's domed forehead protect you! Streaked with vermilion dust, it seems to be emitting the spreading rays of the rising sun to pacify the teeming darkness of obstructions.

("Nava·sáhasanka and the Serpent Princess" 1.3)

# INTRODUCTION

The first volume of 'Preparations for War' (*Udyoga-parvan*) saw the Pándavas attempt to forge peace with Duryódhana and their relatives by requesting only five villages of their former kingdom. Sánjaya is sent back to the Pándavas by Dhrita·rashtra to negotiate, though in truth Duryódhana's unwillingness to compromise ensures that war is inevitable. Finally the Pándavas attempt one last-ditch effort to avoid war by sending Krishna, whom they hope their enemies will respect enough to take advice from. This second volume opens with Krishna traveling to Hástina·pura, the Kuru city, to attempt to convince Duryódhana to make peace.

But 'Preparations for War' is a book of gloomy realism. It highlights the manner in which greed for power eclipses any other considerations. It is a book which exposes the human condition in all its bleak depths. The problem of war-mongering dominating diplomacy is not limited to any particular age of human history. In the modern age we face the same problem: wise advice is ignored by the powerful, and so 'Preparations for War' is a book which can speak to us today as directly as it could speak to its first audience.

It is a cynical book, full of cynical characters. As this volume opens, Krishna is ostensibly going to fix the situation and create peace. However, he realizes only too well how futile his efforts will actually be. When Vídura tells him he should not have come (92.26), he replies by saying that though he knows he will achieve nothing, he must at the very least be seen to try. It is something of a formality on his part, though his attempts against all odds prove his utmost virtue (93.16–17).

While the first volume of 'Preparations for War' showed the unlikelihood of peace, this second volume completes the account of diplomacy's total failure. War is inevitable and finally accepted, and both sides ready their armies. Nevertheless, this book is not monotonously sombre. The first volume of 'Preparations for War' contained the *Sanatsujātīya*, a work of enormously important religious philosophy which brought hope by explaining that war is not the sin one might believe it to be, and that the heroes of the epic might save themselves. This teaching serves to balance the gloom of the reality in which the characters find themselves with the hopeful truth of its overall irrelevance. In the present second volume we also find elements set into the normally gloomy narrative to balance the whole: parables and tales, sometimes only loosely apposite, which serve to break up the cynicism and dread. While these stories may not be as crucial or as philosophically interesting as the *Sanatsujātīya*, they do serve to enhance this volume rather than merely embellish it.

## Mátali

The tale of Mátali, Indra's charioteer, is in many ways a diversion from the main narrative. Its point is to show Duryódhana that his insistence on challenging Árjuna, who has Vishnu-Krishna as his ally, is as idiotic as Gáruda's challenging Vishnu in heaven. However, this point is long in coming. The tale is in itself rather lovely, and gives us a highly cinematic vision of the underworld. Nárada acts as tour guide and shows us the wonders and marvels of the world below as he guides Mátali, but in the middle of an intense and important debate about the fate of the world it may seem peculiarly placed.

The story of Mátali, unlike the story of Indra's misery in the previous volume, is not Vedic in origin. Instead it is Puranic in character, with its lengthy and glorying descriptions. Generally speaking, Puranic myths highlight the otherness of the supernatural, thereby bringing human insignificance into sharp focus.

Duryódhana must be humbled. His arrogance is a matter of constant focus, and inspires another of the stories to come, that of Yayáti's fall. So the whole tale of Mátali, though not perhaps strictly relevant in every respect, serves to balance human conceit. The constant awe and wonder with which it depicts only minor characters in the supernatural order is designed to deflate the pomposity and arrogance of the human protagonists and show the beauty of reverence.

### Gálava and Horses

The moral of the story of Gálava is ostensibly that obstinacy brings bad consequences. Duryódhana's stubborn arrogance and refusal to give any consideration to the advice of others will lead to his own suffering and death in war, while Gálava's obstinacy leads him to consider suicide. But though there is a link to the main narrative, once again we find that the account grows beyond the bare minimum and draws on legend and myth to become a substantial tale in its own right. For example, the story of Vishva·mitra, who ascended to brahminhood through asceticism, is worked into this tale.

But while known Vedic stories are weaved in and manipulated to have fresh relevance, we once again also find elements of the Puranic literature with its cinematic images of wonderment. Gáruda describes the regions of earth to Gálava in poetic detail, and the vivid descriptions of their flying are a fanciful and delightful flourish in an otherwise largely bleak book.

Many threads and styles are brought together in this story and there is often more meaning than one might believe at first glance. The price of eight hundred moon-hued horses with a single black ear each is rather unusual, but this highly specific breed has family significance as it is the very kind paid to Vishva·mitra's father by Richíka for Sátyavati, daughter of Gadhi (119.4 and for the actual story 'The Forest,' Critical Edition (CE) III.115). So the same horses are used to buy both Vishva·mitra's sister and his eventual wife, Mádhavi. This lady is a figure of interest in her own right. Dumézil recognizes a link to Medb, the legendary queen of Ireland, in the name Mádhavi, especially since the roots of both names are associated with alcohol. In the Sanskrit case here, the word *madhu* is used of a honey-sweet liquor. Both women are also sources of royalty, for Mádhavi produces four famous lineages through her four marriages, while Medb is sometimes considered the very personification of royalty.

## Yayáti's Fall

Moreover, Mádhavi is the link which allows this tale to veer onto the subject of Yayáti's fall. She is Yayáti's daughter; it is through her that Yayáti acts as original king, as Dumézil sees him, by creating the kingdoms and lineages of earth, and it is she who ensures Yayáti's return to heaven by introducing him to his grandsons and granting him her merit.

Yayáti himself is a well-known figure. He is mentioned in the Vedas and even used in early Upanishads as an example to explain the transmigration of the soul. He was also the son of Náhusha, Indra's usurper as king of the gods in the first volume of this book. In fact, both father and son suffer the same failings, for it was Náhusha's arrogance which caused his downfall, and Yayáti too falls from heaven because of his pride. This thread links up the tales interspersed throughout these two volumes, for just as Yudhi·shthira was compared to Indra—usurped but eventually victorious, leaving Duryódhana represented by the arrogant human king Náhusha—so here Duryódhana is compared to Yayáti. Duryódhana's arrogance is highlighted as his undoing throughout the entirety of 'Preparations for War.' Every character remarks upon it, even Karna (as discussed below), and the stories also comment upon its consequences, be it in direct comparison, as in the tales of Yayáti's fall and Náhusha's fall, or in specifics and general style as in the narrative of Mátali.

### Amba

The tale of Amba is certainly intriguing. It is unusual, and it is easy to believe that it could exist merely to explain the references elsewhere in the "Maha·bhárata" to Shikhándin's having been born a girl. The story is a good antidote to the seriousness of the main narrative, though it is ridiculous in places. Nevertheless, it is satisfying and fitting that Bhishma's undoing comes as the result of a woman after he has spent his entire life in chaste abstinence.

There is seemingly no reference to Amba outside the "Maha·bhárata," and so VAN BUITENEN may well be correct in assuming it was an ingenious product of the epic itself: a new tale invented to fill in the back-story and embellish and explain the main narrative. The elements of the story, as VAN BUITENEN points out, are in fact all borrowed from the "Maha·bhárata" itself. We are reminded of Bhishma's heritage as a Vasu, of Drúpada's wish to have a child to kill Bhishma, of Rama Jamadágnya's atagonism with kshatriyas, and of many other details which appear elsewhere in the epic.

If the theory is correct, and Amba was dreamed up to explain Bhishma's certainty that Shikhándin is in fact a woman, then it only serves to demonstrate the flexibility of creation in the "Maha·bhárata." The universe of the "Maha·bhárata" has shown that it is able to borrow from outside itself and manipulate for its own ends, but its ability to build a whole history and self-contained world within its own confines is testament to its enormous scale, not merely in size but in vision.

## Vídula and Son

This tale is the most didactic of the stories in 'Preparations for War.' As Kunti bids Krishna farewell, she asks that he remind her son Yudhi·shthira of this story, in which another mother lectures her son and urges him to war. The comparison is clear: Vídula like Kunti is keen to see her son regain his lost kingdom, defeat his enemies, and live in luxury. Vídula has nothing but contempt for living on charity (134.12–13), and so too Kunti mentions her hatred for such compromise (132.33). Vídula points out that her son was prophesied to suffer disaster but rise victorious again (134.8), and so too Kunti had earlier told Krishna of the prophecy made about Árjuna and his brothers:

> *The night I gave birth to Savya·sachin a voice told me: "Your son will conquer the earth and his fame will touch upon heaven. Once he has killed the Kurus in a great battle and regained the kingdom, Dhanan·jaya Kauntéya and his brothers will offer three sacrifices."* (90.65)

So, like Vídula's son Sánjaya, the Pándavas too are fated to triumph in the end.

Vídula's words match the current situation precisely, and are highly didactic in nature. This idiomatic and rousing passage is the sort of speech one would expect to hear on the battlefield itself. Its harshness and immediacy imply that it is an example of early epic: oratory from a purer strain of kshatriya storytelling.

### Karna

After Kunti has sent this martial message to her sons, both Krishna and Kunti herself try to sway Karna from his loyalties. Here perhaps lies one of the most intriguing passages of this volume. So often Karna is presented as a mere echo of Duryódhana. Here we see him as a true tragic hero, as we later will again in his eponymous book.

As pointed out in the first volume's introduction, 'Preparations for War' is a book of frequent inversion. The norms are reversed and we see the corrupting influence of war all too often. For example, Yudhi·shthira underhandedly convinces Shalya to demoralize Karna in battle, and in a most surprising turn of events Bhima says that all the Pándavas would be willing to live as slaves to Duryódhana in order to avoid war. Here again we see how 'Preparations for War' digs a little deeper at the characters of its protagonists.

Krishna tries to secretly manipulate Karna by bribing him with the offer of his usurping Yudhi·shthira's position as eldest Pándava, making him effectively king of the world, and taking Dráupadi, the most beautiful of women, to be his wife (Canto 140). This sly attempt to divide the Kurus and steal Duryódhana's closest ally shows how Krishna, the avatar of Vishnu, is willing to act questionably. It is arguably to Karna's credit that he stays allied to the Kurus. He makes it clear that he knows he could win the world at the head of the Pándavas, and that it is his right, but he chooses to support the men who have always supported him and refuses to betray his friends. Here we realize that Karna is not the villain we have supposed, no mere copy of power-lusting Duryódhana, but a loyal and rigidly moral man. His situation reveals him to be a tragic hero, caught in between differing loyalties. That he chooses to respect those who have respected him, and in so doing accepts death and rejects wealth and power, is an astonishing revelation.

Epic sometimes risks slipping into one-dimensional characterization by the very fact of its repetitious nature, but here, on the brink of war, the audience's sympathies are suddenly torn. One of the most criticized villains turns out to be a disciplined and loyal friend, able to resist Krishna's temptations. Nothing is black and white in 'Preparations for War': the normally righteous are sly, the normally wicked are moral, and the normally truculent are submissive. Karna is no longer a deserving victim, and he sacrifices his life willingly. His dream (143.30–45) makes it clear that he knows he will lose, and that his boasts are designed to boost the morale of the Kurus rather than merely being a sign of his arrogance. He even apologizes for his previous behavior.

But it is not only Krishna who attempts to sway Karna. Now that war is imminent, his real mother, Kunti, also tries to influence her son (Canto 145). This is an interesting passage to contrast with the story she quotes for Yudhi·shthira. Whereas Kunti and Vídula urge their sons to war, Kunti urges Karna to withdraw and change his allegiance. While Yudhi·shthira and Vídula's son Sánjaya are both fated to triumph, Karna is destined to die, and he knows it. Kunti and Vídula encourage their sons to support their families, while Kunti asks Karna to abandon the people whom he knows as his family. Though he is aware he could technically be called a Pándava, his true family are those who raised and loved him, so he refuses to betray them. He even promises not to harm any of his brothers, bar Árjuna (146.20–21).

## Psychoanalysis

There is another intriguing aspect to consider when discussing the "Maha·bhárata." Psychoanalysis has inspired men such as Otto Rank and Robert Goldman to investigate the epic from a different perspective. In the case of Karna, Rank, a colleague of Freud, sees the struggles of childhood enacted. Karna's three father-figures, Surya, the *suta*, and Pandu, represent the three stages of a male child's emotion toward his father. Surya is the earliest figure of a "hero" father, Ádhiratha is the father for whom Karna feels affection, while Pandu is the father-figure against whom

Karna rebels. Karna's affection for his foster-mother Radha over Kunti also fits with RANK's patterns. Interestingly, RANK raises the point that the traditional psychology of the tragic epic hero bears more than a passing resemblance to those with paranoiac and delusional mental diseases. His observations on the heroes of ancient epic are a fascinating and unusual reading of the subject.

ROBERT GOLDMAN has used Freudian theory to explain the problem of Amba. Though VAN BUITENEN believes she was devised merely to fill in a missing back-story, GOLDMAN believes her part is far more vital to the entire epic. She becomes the female character of two Oedipal triangles: one is described in this book, and the other provides a psychological basis for Bhishma's allowing himself to be defeated by his "son"—that is, Árjuna. In this volume of 'Preparations for War,' Amba enlists the help of Rama Jamadágnya to help her destroy Bhishma. However, the younger man, Bhishma, the pupil and "son" of Rama, defeats his father-figure, thereby ensuring that Rama's relationship with the girl is destroyed. The word *ambā* itself in Sanskrit usually means "mother," and it is in this light that GOLDMAN sees her when she is reincarnated as Shikhándini in the triangle between Bhishma, the "father," and Árjuna, the "son."

'Preparations for War' is far more complex than a mere cursory glance may indicate. Behind the conventions and repetition of epic there lies a far more delicate treatment of its protaganists. Black and white unexpectedly gives way to shades of gray, and so the book can keep surprising the reader. The bleak tone of this book of despair can suddenly give way to the secret of emancipation or beautiful visions of wonderful lands. The same message is constantly portrayed, but through very various means, and just when one imagines one can predict how a character will react, one's expectations are proved wrong. Overall, however, 'Preparations for War' reveals to us the detailed breakdown of diplomacy and the power of greed to overwhelm sense and morality. War is inevitable, and the book ends with the armies arrayed on Kuru·kshetra, ready for battle.

## Note on the Sanskrit Text

I have used KINJAWADEKAR's edition of the "vulgate" established by Nila·kantha as the main text for my translation. On occasion it was felt necessary to emend the text, usually due to a transparent case of typographical error, but also in cases where it seemed faulty or incomprehensible. In such cases, emendations have been made with reference to the text of the Critical Edition and its extensive critical notes.

## Concordance of Canto Numbers with the Critical Edition

| CSL | CE |
|---|---|
| 84–150 | 82–148 |
| 151–152 | 149 |
| 153–159 | 150–156 |
| 160 | 157* |
| 161–167 | 158–164 |
| 168 | 165–166.13 |
| 169 | 166.14–166.39 |
| 170–174 | 167–171 |
| 175 | 172–173 |
| 176 | 174–175 |
| 177 | 176 |
| 178 | 177–179 |
| 179–196 | 180–197 |

* CE canto 157 (125 vv.) excludes a large portion of the corresponding CSL canto (18 vv.).

## Abbreviations

| | |
|---|---|
| CE | *Mahābhārata* Pune Critical Edition |
| conj. | conjecture |
| CSL | *Mahābhārata* Clay Sanskrit Library edition |
| K | Kinjawadekar |

## Bibliography

### THE MAHA·BHÁRATA IN SANSKRIT

*The Mahābhāratam with the Bharata Bhawadeepa Commentary of Nīlakaṇṭha*. Edited by RAMACHANDRASHASTRI KINJAWADEKAR. Poona: Chitrashala Press, 1929–36; reprint, New Delhi: Oriental Books Reprint Corporation, 1978 (2nd ed. 1979). Vol. 5 Udyoga Parva. [K = CSL]

*The Mahābhārata*. Critically edited by V.K. SUKTHANKAR, S.K. BELVALKAR, P.L. VAIDYA et al. 1933–66. 19 vols. Poona: Bhandarkar Oriental Research Institute. [CE]

### THE MAHA·BHÁRATA IN TRANSLATION

VAN BUITENEN, J.A.B. (1978). *The Mahābhārata: Book Four, The Book of Virāṭa; Book Five, The Book of the Effort*. Chicago: University of Chicago Press.

### SECONDARY SOURCES

AGRAWALA, V.S. (1956). "The Mahabharata: A Cultural Commentary." *Annals of the Bhandarkar Oriental Research Institute* 37, pp. 1–26.

BROCKINGTON, J.L. (1998). *The Sanskrit Epics*. Leiden: Brill.

SHULMAN, D.D. (1985). *The King and the Clown in South Indian Myth and Poetry*. Princeton: Princeton University Press.

DUMÉZIL, GEORGES (1986). *Mythe et Épopée*. Paris: Magazine Littéraire.

GOLDMAN, ROBERT P. (1978). "Fathers, Sons, and Gurus: Oedipal Conflict in the Sanskrit Epics." *Journal of Indian Philosophy* 6.4, pp. 325–92.

HILTEBEITEL, ALF (1977). "Nahuṣa in the Skies: A Human King of Heaven." *History of Religions* 16.4, pp. 329–50.

HILTEBEITEL, ALF (1984). "The Two Kṛṣṇas on One Chariot: Upaniṣadic Imagery and Epic Mythology." *History of Religions* 24.1, pp. 1–26.

Olivelle, P. (trans.) (2006). *Five Discourses on Worldly Wisdom* (*Pañcatantra*). New York: New York University Press and JJC Foundation.

Rank, Otto (1914). *The Myth of the Birth of the Hero: A Psychological Interpretation of Mythology*. New York: Journal of Nervous and Mental Disease Publishing Company.

# MAHA·BHÁRATA

BOOK FIVE

# PREPARATIONS FOR WAR

VOLUME TWO

# 84–94

# KRISHNA'S JOURNEY

VAIŚAMPĀYANA uvāca:

84.1 PRAYĀNTAṂ DEVAKĪ|putraṃ para|vīra|rujo daśa
mahā|rathā mahā|bāhum anvayuḥ śastra|pāṇayaḥ,
padātīnāṃ sahasraṃ ca sādināṃ ca, paraṃ|tapa,
bhojyaṃ ca vipulaṃ, rājan, preṣyāś ca śataśo 'pare.

JANAMEJAYA uvāca:

kathaṃ prayāto Dāśārho mah"|ātmā Madhu|sūdanaḥ?
kāni vā vrajatas tasya nimittāni mah"|âujasaḥ?

VAIŚAMPĀYANA uvāca:

tasya prayāṇe yāny āsan nimittāni mah"|ātmanaḥ
tāni me śṛṇu sarvāṇi daivāny autpātikāni ca:
84.5 an|abhre 'śani|nirghoṣaḥ sa|vidyut samajāyata,
anvag eva ca parjanyaḥ prāvarṣad vighane bhṛśam.
pratyag ūhur mahā|nadyaḥ prāṅ|mukhāḥ Sindhu|saptamāḥ.
viparītā diśaḥ sarvā, na prājñāyata kiṅ cana.

prājvalann agnayo, rājan, pṛthivī samakampata
udapānāś ca kumbhāś ca prāsiñcañ śataśo jalam.
tamaḥ|saṃvṛtam apy āsīt sarvaṃ jagad idaṃ tathā,
na diśo n' ādiśo, rājan, prajñāyante sma reṇunā.
prādur āsīn mahāñ chabdaḥ khe, śarīraṃ na dṛśyate;
sarveṣu, rājan, deśeṣu tad adbhutam iv' âbhavat.
84.10 prāmathnādd Hāstinapuraṃ vāto dakṣiṇa|paścimaḥ
ārujan gaṇaśo vṛkṣān paruṣo 'śani|niḥsvanaḥ.

VAISHAMPÁYANA said:

As Dévaki's long-armed son set out on his journey, ten 84.1
powerful warriors, the crushers of enemy heroes, followed him, weapons in hand, while a thousand infantrymen and a thousand cavalrymen shadowed him, enemy-scorcher. So too did hundreds of other servants, bringing with them ample supplies, my king.

JANAM·ÉJAYA asked:

How did high-souled Dashárha, slayer of Madhu, make his way? What various portents marked the occasion of the highly energetic hero's journey?

VAISHAMPÁYANA replied:

Listen to me as I describe all the varied heavenly and prodigious omens that presented themselves during the
high-souled hero's journey. Deafening peals of thunder 84.5
echoed in a clear sky, and lightning flashed. Immediately afterward the cloudless firmament rained heavy downpours. The seven mighty rivers that flow east, including even the Indus, flowed backwards. All directions were inverted and nothing could be discerned.

Fires blazed, my king, and the earth shook. Water overflowed from hundreds of wells and jars, and this entire universe was veiled in darkness. All points of the compass were rendered invisible by dust, my king. In every land an astounding marvel occurred: a booming din erupted in
the sky, but the body producing it could not be seen. A 84.10
south-westerly wind with a rough thundering roar pulverized Hástina·pura, uprooting groups of trees.

yatra yatra ca Vārṣṇeyo vartate pathi, Bhārata,
tatra tatra sukho vāyuḥ sarvaṃ c' āsīt pradakṣiṇam,
vavarṣa puṣpa|varṣaṃ ca kamalāni ca bhūriśaḥ,
samaś ca panthā nirduḥkho, vyapeta|kuśa|kaṇṭakaḥ.

saṃstuto brāhmaṇair gīrbhis tatra tatra sahasraśaḥ,
arcyate madhu|parkaiś ca vasubhiś ca vasu|pradaḥ.
taṃ kiranti mah"|ātmānaṃ vanyaiḥ puṣpaiḥ su|gandhibhiḥ
striyaḥ pathi samāgamya sarva|bhūta|hite ratam.

84.15 sa Śālibhavanaṃ ramyaṃ sarva|sasya|samācitam
sukhaṃ parama|dharmiṣṭham abhyagād, Bharata'|rṣabha,
paśyan bahu|paśūn grāmān ramyān hṛdaya|toṣaṇān,
purāṇi ca vyatikrāman, rāṣṭrāṇi vividhāni ca.

nityaṃ hṛṣṭāḥ su|manaso Bhāratair abhirakṣitāḥ,
n' ôdvignāḥ para|cakrāṇāṃ, vyasanānām a|kovidāḥ,
Upaplavyād ath' āgamya janāḥ pura|nivāsinaḥ
pathy atiṣṭhanta sahitā Viṣvaksena|didṛkṣayā.
te tu sarve samāyāntam agnim iddham iva prabhum
arcayām āsur arc"|ârhaṃ deś'|âtithim upasthitam.

84.20 Vṛkasthalaṃ samāsādya Keśavaḥ para|vīra|hā
prakīrṇa|raśmāv āditye vyomni vai lohitāyati,
avatīrya rathāt tūrṇaṃ, kṛtvā śaucaṃ yathā|vidhi,
ratha|mocanam ādiśya sandhyām upaviveśa ha.
Dāruko 'pi hayān muktvā, paricarya ca śāstrataḥ,
mumoca sarva|yoktr'|ādi, muktvā c' âitān avāsṛjat.

But in contrast, Bhárata, wherever Varshnéya traveled on his journey, the breeze was thoroughly pleasant and auspicious, while frequent showers of lotuses and flowers rained down. The road was smooth, unproblematic, and free of thorns and tough grass.

On his route, thousands of brahmins worshipped him with praise, revering the giver of wealth with gifts of honey, milk and riches. Women came out onto the road and scattered the high-souled man—who desired only what is good for all creatures—with bewitchingly fragrant forest flowers. He saw charming cattle-rich villages that gladdened his
heart, passed through cities and various kingdoms, and then 84.15
reached Shali·bhávana, a pleasant and happy place of impeccable virtue that abounded in every kind of crop, bull of the Bharatas.

The invariably happy and amenable people who lived in Upaplávya, protected by the Bháratas, unaware and unconcerned about the calamities of enemy hordes, came out of their city and stood together on the path, eager to see Vishvak·sena. They all revered the blazing, fire-like lord, who had come and stayed in their land as a guest, with the honor he deserved.

As Késhava, destroyer of enemy heroes, reached Vrika· 84.20
sthala, the sky flushed red from the sun's widespread rays. So he got down from his chariot, quickly washed according to the custom, had his chariot unyoked, and took his seat for the evening rites. Dáruka untied the horses, tended to them as laid down in the shastras, and, after having removed all their harnesses and so on and untied them, he let them roam free.

abhyatītya tu tat sarvam uvāca Madhu|sūdanaḥ:
«Yudhiṣṭhirasya kāry'|ârtham iha vatsyāmahe kṣapām.»
tasya tan matam ājñāya cakrur āvasathaṃ narāḥ,
kṣaṇena c' ânna|pānāni guṇavanti samārjayan.

84.25 tasmin grāme pradhānās tu ya āsan brāhmaṇā, nṛpa,
āryāḥ kulīnā hrīmanto, brāhmīṃ vṛttim anuṣṭhitāḥ,
te 'bhigamya mah"|ātmānaṃ Hṛṣīkeśam arin|damam,
pūjāṃ cakrur yathā|nyāyam āśīr|maṅgala|saṃyutām.

te pūjayitvā Dāśārhaṃ sarva|lokeṣu pūjitam
nyavedayanta veśmāni ratnavanti mah"|ātmane.
tān prabhuḥ «kṛtam! ity» uktvā, sat|kṛtya ca yath"|ârhataḥ,
abhyetya c' âiṣāṃ veśmāni punar āyāt sah' âiva taiḥ,
su|mṛṣṭaṃ bhojayitvā ca brāhmaṇāṃs tatra Keśavaḥ,
bhuktvā ca saha taiḥ sarvair avasat tāṃ kṣapāṃ sukham.

VAIŚAMPĀYANA uvāca:

85.1 TATHĀ DŪTAIḤ samājñāya prayāntaṃ Madhu|sūdanam
Dhṛtarāṣṭro 'bravīd Bhīṣmam arcayitvā mahā|bhujam,
Droṇaṃ ca Sañjayaṃ c' âiva, Viduraṃ ca mahā|matim,
Duryodhanaṃ sah'|âmātyaṃ hṛṣṭa|rom" âbravīd idam:

Once the slayer of Madhu had finished all his chores, he said: "For the sake of Yudhi·shthira's mission, we will spend the night here." Understanding that he had made his decision, his servants set up camp and quickly gathered food and drink of excellent quality.

Now in this village, my lord, there were eminent brah- 84.25
mins who were noble and descended from distinguished lineages; scrupulous men who observed the brahmanic code of behavior. These men came to high-souled, foe-destroying Hrishikésha and rightly paid him their respects, adding benedictions and auspicious blessings.

Once they had honored Dashárha, worshipped in all worlds, they then offered their jewel-filled houses to the high-souled man. The lord replied "That's enough!" and treated them well, as they deserved, by going to their homes and then returning with them once more. Késhava treated the brahmins to mouthwatering food, and once he had eaten in the company of all these men, he spent the night happily.

VAISHAMPÁYANA continued:

NOW IT HAPPENED that Dhrita·rashtra discovered 85.1
through messengers that the slayer of Madhu was on his way, so, honoring him properly, he addressed long-armed Bhishma, as well as Drona, Sánjaya, highly intelligent Vídura, and Duryódhana and his ministers. Bristling with joy, he said:

«adbhutaṃ mahad āścaryaṃ śrūyate, Kuru|nandana!
striyo, bālāś ca, vṛddhāś ca kathayanti gṛhe gṛhe,
sat|kṛty' ācakṣate c' ânye, tath" âiv' ânye samāgatāḥ,
pṛthag|vādāś ca vartante catvareṣu sabhāsu ca:
85.5 upāyāsyati Dāśārhaḥ Pāṇḍav'|ârthe parākramī!

sa no mānyaś ca pūjyaś ca sarvathā Madhu|sūdanaḥ,
tasmin hi yātrā lokasya, bhūtānām īśvaro hi saḥ;
tasmin dhṛtiś ca vīryaṃ ca, prajñā c' âujaś ca Mādhave.
sa mānyatāṃ nara|śreṣṭhaḥ, sa hi dharmaḥ sanātanaḥ;
pūjito hi sukhāya syād, a|sukhaḥ syād a|pūjitaḥ.
sa cet tuṣyati Dāśārha upacārair arin|damaḥ
Kṛṣṇāt sarvān abhiprāyān prāpsyāmaḥ sarva|rājasu.

tasya pūj'|ârtham ady' âiva saṃvidhatsva, paraṃ|tapa,
sabhāḥ pathi vidhīyantāṃ sarva|kāma|samanvitāḥ
85.10 yathā prītir, mahā|bāho, tvayi jāyeta tasya vai,
tathā kuruṣva, Gāndhāre—kathaṃ vā, Bhīṣma, manyase?»

tato Bhīṣm'|ādayaḥ sarve Dhṛtarāṣṭraṃ jan'|âdhipam
ūcuḥ «paramam! ity» evaṃ pūjayanto 'sya tad vacaḥ.
teṣām anumataṃ jñātvā rājā Duryodhanas tadā
sabhā|vāstūni ramyāṇi pradeṣṭum upacakrame.
tato deśeṣu deśeṣu ramaṇīyeṣu bhāgaśaḥ
sarva|ratna|samākīrṇāḥ sabhāś cakrur an|ekaśaḥ.
āsanāni vicitrāṇi yutāni vividhair guṇaiḥ,

"Descendant of the Kurus, there is news of a great and extraordinary marvel! Women, children, and the elderly are gossiping about it from house to house. Some discuss it respectfully, and others chatter about it in groups. It is the talk of each and every person congregating at crossroads and assemblies: the mighty Dashárha is coming here for the 85.5
Pándava cause!

We should respect and honor the slayer of Madhu in every way, for the path of the world rests within him and he is the lord of living creatures. Resolve, heroism, wisdom, and energy reside in Mádhava. He ought to be esteemed as the greatest of men, for he is eternal law. Assuredly, when paid homage he brings happiness, but when he is not, misery ensues. If Dashárha, tamer of enemies, is pleased with our ministrations, then through Krishna we will attain all our hearts' desires in the midst of all kings.

Arrange matters to honor him at once, enemy-scorcher, and erect courts on the road, equipped with everything he could wish for. Make sure he feels affection for you, long- 85.10
armed son of Gandhári—or do you have any thoughts on the matter, Bhishma?"

At this, Bhishma and all the rest praised Dhrita·rashtra, the lord of his people, and honored his speech by pronouncing it "Perfect!" Once King Duryódhana knew they agreed, he ordered pleasant sites to be designated for the courts. So it was that in one bewitching spot after another they built numerous halls, strewn with every kind of riches. Painted thrones covered with various decorations, women, perfumes, ornaments, exquisitely delicate clothing,

striyo, gandhān, alaṅkārān, sūkṣmāṇi vasanāni ca,
85.15 guṇavanty anna|pānāni, bhojyāni vividhāni ca,
mālyāni ca su|gandhīni—tāni rājā dadau tataḥ.
viśeṣataś ca vās'|ârthaṃ sabhāṃ grāme Vṛkasthale
vidadhe Kauravo rājā bahu|ratnāṃ mano|ramām.
etad vidhāya vai sarvaṃ dev'|ârham atimānuṣam
ācakhyau Dhṛtarāṣṭrāya rājā Duryodhanas tadā.
tāḥ sabhāḥ Keśavaḥ sarvā, ratnāni vividhāni ca
a|samīkṣy' âiva Dāśārha upāyāt Kuru|sadma tat.

DHṚTARĀṢṬRA uvāca:

86.1 UPAPLAVYĀD IHA, kṣattar, upāyāto Janārdanaḥ
Vṛkasthale nivasati, sa ca prātar ih' âiṣyati.
Āhukānām adhipatiḥ, puro|gaḥ sarva|Sātvatām,
mahā|manā, mahā|vīryo, mahā|sattvo Janārdanaḥ,
sphītasya Vṛṣṇi|rāṣṭrasya bhartā goptā ca Mādhavaḥ,
trayāṇām api lokānāṃ bhagavān prapitāmahaḥ.
Vṛṣṇy|Andhakāḥ su|manaso yasya prajñām upāsate,
Ādityā, Vasavo, Rudrā yathā buddhiṃ Bṛhaspateḥ.
86.5 tasmai pūjāṃ prayokṣyāmi Dāśārhāya mah"|ātmane
pratyakṣaṃ tava, dharma|jña; tāṃ me kathayataḥ śṛṇu.
eka|varṇaiḥ su|kḷpt'|âṅgair Bāhli|jātair hay'|ôttamaiḥ
catur|yuktān rathāṃs tasmai raukmān dāsyāmi ṣoḍaśa.
nitya|prabhinnān mātaṅgān īṣā|dantān prahāriṇaḥ
aṣṭ'|ânucaram ek' âikam aṣṭau dāsyāmi, Kaurava.
dāsīnām a|prajātānāṃ śubhānāṃ rukma|varcasām

food and drink of the highest quality, various delicacies, 85.15
and beautifully fragranced garlands—these were the items the king provided.

In the village of Vrika·sthala the Kuru king made a particular effort and erected a charming hall studded with vast numbers of jewels for Krishna to lodge in. So it was that King Duryódhana arranged these matters, and told Dhrita·rashtra of all the superhuman accommodation fit for a god. But Késhava Dashárha did not so much as spare a glance at all the halls and various treasures; instead, he went straight to the seat of the Kurus.

DHRITA·RASHTRA said:

CHAMBERLAIN VÍDURA, Janárdana is on his way here 86.1
from Upaplávya. He is spending the night at Vrika·sthala and will arrive here in the morning. The lord of the Áhukas, leader of all Sátvatas, the high-minded, mightily strong and great noble Janárdana is Mádhava, the defender and supporter of the rich kingdom of the Vrishnis, and the blessed grandfather of the three worlds.

The Vrishni-Ándhakas gladly obey his wisdom just as the
Adítyas, Vasus, and Rudras follow Brihas·pati's advice. In 86.5
your presence I will pay homage to high-souled Dashárha, law-wise Vídura, so listen as I tell you what I plan to do.

I will present him with sixteen golden chariots yoked with four pure-hued and excellent Báhlika-bred steeds with well-formed limbs. I will give him eight pole-length tusked battle elephants with permanently rent temples and eight keepers for each beast, Káurava. I will give him a hundred

śatam asmai pradāsyāmi, dāsānām api tāvatām,
āvikaṃ ca sukha|sparśaṃ pārvatīyair upāhṛtam—
tad apy asmai pradāsyāmi sahasrāṇi daś' âṣṭa ca.
86.10 ajinānāṃ sahasrāṇi cīna|deś'|ôdbhavāni ca—
tāny apy asmai pradāsyāmi, yāvad arhati Keśavaḥ.
divā rātrau ca bhāty eṣa su|tejā vimalo maṇiḥ—
tam apy asmai pradāsyāmi, tam arhati hi Keśavaḥ!
eken' âbhipataty ahnā yojanāni catur|daśa,
yānam aśvatarī|yuktaṃ dāsye tasmai tad apy aham.
yāvanti vāhanāny asya, yāvantaḥ puruṣāś ca te,
tato 'ṣṭa|guṇam apy asmai bhojyaṃ dāsyāmy ahaṃ sadā.
mama putrāś ca pautrāś ca sarve Duryodhanād ṛte
pratyudyāsyanti Dāśārhaṃ rathair mṛṣṭaiḥ sv|alaṃkṛtāḥ.
86.15 sv|alaṃkṛtāś ca kalyāṇyaḥ pādair eva sahasraśaḥ
vāra|mukhyā mahā|bhāgaṃ pratyudyāsyanti Keśavam.
nagarād api yāḥ kāś cid gamiṣyanti Janārdanam
draṣṭuṃ kanyāś ca kalyāṇyas, tāś ca yāsyanty an|āvṛtāḥ.
sa|strī|puruṣa|bālaṃ ca nagaraṃ Madhu|sūdanam
udīkṣatāṃ mah"|ātmānaṃ, bhānumantam iva prajāḥ!
mahā|dhvaja|patākāś ca kriyantāṃ sarvato|diśam
jal'|âvasikto virajāḥ panthās tasy'!—êti c' ânvaśāt.
Duḥśāsanasya ca gṛhaṃ Duryodhana|gṛhād varam
tad adya kriyatāṃ kṣipraṃ su|saṃmṛṣṭam alaṃkṛtam!
86.20 etadd hi rucir'|ākāraiḥ prāsādair upaśobhitam
śivaṃ ca ramaṇīyaṃ ca sarva'|rtu su|mahā|dhanam.
sarvam asmin gṛhe ratnaṃ mama Duryodhanasya ca,
yad yad arhati Vārṣṇeyas tat tad deyam a|saṃśayam!

golden-complexioned beautiful slave girls with bodies unstretched in childbirth, and as many male slaves again. I will present him with eighteen thousand sheepskins, soft to the touch, presented by mountain tribesmen. I will give 86.10
him thousands of black antelope skins from the lands to the north-east—as much as Késhava deserves!

Then there is this flawless jewel which sparkles so magnificently day and night—I will give him this as well, for Késhava deserves it! I will give him a mule-yoked carriage with which one can cover fourteen *yójanas** in a single day, and I will always give him eight times the food which the men and animals in his convoy require.

All my sons and grandsons, barring Duryódhana, will go out beautifully adorned to greet Dashárha with polished chariots. Thousands of exquisitely ornamented and beau- 86.15
tifully countenanced royal courtesans will go out on foot to meet illustrious Késhava. And the bewitching girls from the city who set out to see Janárdana will do so unveiled. Let the whole city of men, women, and children gaze at the high-souled slayer of Madhu just as creatures gaze at the sun!

Let his path be decorated everywhere with enormous flags and banners. Let the road be sprinkled with water and cleared of dust!—he ordered. Duhshásana's house surpasses Duryódhana's, so quickly decorate it at once and embellish it! That lovely, pleasant house gleams with its beauti- 86.20
ful structures and terraces, and is filled with great wealth all year round. All my treasure, and that of Duryódhana as well, is within that house, and whatever Varshnéya deserves should be given him without hesitation!

VIDURA uvāca:

87.1 RĀJAN, BAHU|MATAŚ c' âsi, trailokyasy' âpi sattamaḥ,
saṃbhāvitaś ca lokasya, saṃmataś c' âsi, Bhārata.
yat tvam evaṃ|gate brūyāḥ paścime vayasi sthitaḥ,
śāstrād vā su|pratarkād vā; su|sthiraḥ sthaviro hy asi.
lekhā śaśini, bhāḥ sūrye, mah"|ōrmir iva sāgare,
dharmas tvayi tathā, rājann, iti vyavasitāḥ prajāḥ.
sad" âiva bhāvito loko guṇ'|âughais tava, pārthiva,
guṇānāṃ rakṣaṇe nityaṃ prayatasva sa|bāndhavaḥ.
87.5 ārjavaṃ pratipadyasva, mā bālyād bahu nīnaśaḥ,
rājan, putrāṃś ca pautrāṃś ca, su|hṛdaś c' âiva su|priyān.
yat tvam icchasi Kṛṣṇāya, rājann, atithaye bahu,
etad anyac ca Dāśārhaḥ, pṛthivīm api c' ârhati.
na tu tvaṃ dharmam uddiśya, tasya vā priya|kāraṇāt
etad ditsasi Kṛṣṇāya, satyen' ātmānam ālabhe!
māy" âiṣ", â|satyam ev' âitac, chadm' âitad, bhūri|dakṣiṇa,
jānāmi tvan|mataṃ, rājan, gūḍhaṃ bāhyena karmaṇā.

pañca pañc' âiva lipsyanti grāmakān Pāṇḍavā, nṛpa,
na ca ditsasi tebhyas tāṃś—tac chamaṃ na kariṣyasi.
87.10 arthena tu mahā|bāhuṃ Vārṣṇeyaṃ tvaṃ jihīrṣasi,
anena c' âpy upāyena Pāṇḍavebhyo vibhetsyasi.
na ca vittena śakyo 'sau, n' ôdyamena, na garhayā,
anyo Dhanañjayāt kartum—etat tattvaṃ bravīmi te.

VÍDURA replied:

SOVEREIGN LORD, you are held in high regard as the best 87.1
of men throughout the three worlds, and you are honored and respected in this world of men, Bhárata. Now that you have reached the last stage of life, whatever you say goes, regardless of whether it comes from the scriptures or from wise reasoning, for you are a very assured old man. My king, the people are as convinced that law resides within you as they are that there is a mark on the moon, that light exists within the sun, and that vast waves lie within the ocean. The world is constantly furthered by your throng of virtues, king, so always attempt, with your relatives, to preserve those virtues.

Act sincerely, my lord, to prevent idiocy causing the great 87.5
destruction of your sons, grandsons, friends, and dear ones. However much you want to give Krishna as your guest, my king, Dashárha deserves that and more, even the earth itself! But I'd swear, hand on heart, that you don't really want to give all this to Krishna for the sake of mere virtue or even as a means to please him! This is really just deception—a lie, a disguise, granter of great wealth! I recognize your secret intention through your external gesture, king.

The Pándavas want to take just five villages, my lord, but you have no intention of giving them to them—you will
not make peace. You want to win long-armed Varshnéya 87.10
over with wealth, and to divide him from the Pándavas by this strategy. But I tell you truly: this man cannot be alienated from Dhanan·jaya through wealth, perseverence, or abuse. I understand Krishna's magnanimity, I understand

veda Kṛṣṇasya māhātmyaṃ, ved' âsya dṛḍha|bhaktitām,
a|tyājyam asya jānāmi prāṇais tulyaṃ Dhanañjayam.
anyat kumbhād apāṃ pūrṇād, anyat pād'|âvasecanāt,
anyat kuśala|saṃpraśnān n' âiv' êkṣyati Janārdanaḥ.
yat tv asya priyam ātithyaṃ mān'|ârhasya mah"|ātmanaḥ,
tad asmai kriyatāṃ, rājan, mān'|ârho 'sau Janārdanaḥ.
87.15 āśaṃsamānaḥ kalyāṇaṃ Kurūn abhyeti Keśavaḥ
yen' âiva, rājann, arthena, tad ev' âsmā upākuru.
śamam icchati Dāśārhas tava Duryodhanasya ca,
Pāṇḍavānāṃ ca, rāj'|êndra; tad asya vacanaṃ kuru.
pit" âsi, rājan, putrās te; vṛddhas tvaṃ śiśavaḥ pare.
vartasva pitṛvat teṣu—vartante te hi putravat.

DURYODHANA uvāca:

88.1 YAD ĀHA VIDURAḤ Kṛṣṇe, sarvaṃ tat satyam Acyute;
anurakto hy a|saṃhāryaḥ Pārthān prati Janārdanaḥ.
yat tat satkāra|saṃyuktaṃ deyaṃ vasu Janārdane
aneka|rūpaṃ, rāj'|êndra, na tad deyaṃ kadā cana!
deśaḥ kālas tath" â|yukto; na hi n' ârhati Keśavaḥ;
maṃsyaty Adhokṣajo, rājan, «bhayād arcati mām iti.»
avamānaś ca yatra syāt kṣatriyasya, viśām pate,
na tat kuryād budhaḥ kāryam, iti me niścitā matiḥ.
88.5 sa hi pūjyatamo loke Kṛṣṇaḥ pṛthula|locanaḥ
trayāṇām api lokānāṃ viditaṃ mama sarvathā,
na tu tasmai pradeyaṃ syāt tathā kārya|gatiḥ, prabho.

his sure devotion, and I know that he will not abandon Dhanan·jaya, for he holds him as dear as life itself.

Janárdana will look for a jar full of water, some water with which to wash his feet, and your asking after his health, and nothing else. So treat the high-souled hero who deserves respect to the kind of hospitality which he holds dear, my king, for Janárdana is worthy of honor. Késhava is coming 87.15
to the Kurus for one reason: hoping for a happy ending. So give it to him, my king. Dashárha wishes for peace between you and Duryódhana and the Pándavas, lord of kings; so do as he says. You are their father, my king, and they are your sons. You are old and they are young, so behave like a father towards them—for they certainly behave as sons toward you.

DURYÓDHANA said:

EVERYTHING VÍDURA has said about Krishna the imper- 88.1
ishable is quite true: Janárdana is inseparably attached to the Parthas. All the various gifts you want to give to Janárdana in the name of hospitality, lord of kings, should never be given to him at all! This is neither the time nor the place. It is not that Késhava does not deserve it, but Adhókshaja will imagine that you are bestowing gifts upon him because you are afraid, my king.

Lord of men, it is my belief that a wise kshatriya should not do anything which results in him being held in contempt. I am well aware that lotus-eyed Krishna is most de- 88.5
serving of worship in this world and indeed in all three and in all respects, but it would not be the proper course to give

vigrahaḥ samupārabdho na hi śāmyaty a|vigrahāt.

VAIŚAMPĀYANA uvāca:

tasya tad vacanaṃ śrutvā Bhīṣmaḥ Kuru|pitāmahaḥ
Vaicitravīryaṃ rājānam idaṃ vacanam abravīt:
«satkṛto '|satkṛto v" âpi na krudhyeta Janārdanaḥ.
n' âlam enam avajñātuṃ, n' âvajñeyo hi Keśavaḥ.
yat tu kāryaṃ, mahā|bāho, manasā kāryatāṃ gatam,
sarv'|ôpāyair na tac chakyaṃ kena cit kartum anyathā.
88.10 sa yad brūyān mahā|bāhus, tat kāryam a|viśaṅkayā;
Vāsudevena tīrthena kṣipraṃ saṃśāmya Pāṇḍavaiḥ.
dharmyam arthyaṃ ca dharm'|ātmā
dhruvaṃ vaktā Janārdanaḥ.
tasmin vācyāḥ priyā vāco
bhavatā bāndhavaiḥ saha.»

DURYODHANA uvāca:

na paryāyo 'sti yad, rājañ, śriyaṃ niṣkevalām aham
taiḥ sah' êmām upāśnīyāṃ yāvaj|jīvaṃ, pitā|maha!
idaṃ tu su|mahat kāryaṃ śṛṇu me yat samarthitam:
parāyaṇaṃ Pāṇḍavānāṃ niyacchāmi Janārdanam.
tasmim baddhe bhaviṣyanti Vṛṣṇayaḥ, pṛthivī tathā,
Pāṇḍavāś ca vidheyā me! sa ca prātar ih' âiṣyati.
88.15 atr' ôpāyān yathā samyaṅ na budhyeta Janārdanaḥ,
na c' âpāyo bhavet kaś cit, tad bhavān prabravītu me.

him gifts now, my lord. Once war has begun, peace cannot be forged through cordiality.

VAISHAMPÁYANA said:

When Bhishma, the grandfather of the Kurus, heard what Duryódhana had to say, he addressed King Vaichitravírya. He said: "Regardless of whether he is treated properly or improperly, Janárdana will not become angry. Késhava cannot be treated contemptuously, for he is not contemptible. The plans he decides upon cannot be thwarted by anyone, even if they were to use every means at their disposal, mighty-armed man. Whatever the long-armed man 88.10
advises must be done without hesitation, so we should quickly make peace with the Pándavas, using Vasudéva as our advisor. Janárdana has a law-abiding soul and will surely speak virtuously and profitably. You and your relatives must speak so as to please him."

DURYÓDHANA replied:

My king, for as long as I live there will be no situation in which I will share my exclusive fortune with those men, grandfather! Listen to the great plan I have devised: I will take Janárdana prisoner, for he is the Pándavas' last refuge. When he is imprisoned, the Vrishnis, the earth, and the Pándavas will submit to me! He will arrive here in the morning. Tell me, sir, by what means we can ensure that 88.15
Janárdana does not get wind of this, so no disaster should befall us.

VAIŚAMPĀYANA uvāca:

tasya tad vacanaṃ śrutvā ghoraṃ Kṛṣṇ'|âbhisaṃhitam
Dhṛtarāṣṭraḥ sah'|âmātyo vyathito viman" âbhavat.
tato Duryodhanam idaṃ Dhṛtarāṣṭro 'bravīd vacaḥ:
«m" âivaṃ vocaḥ, prajā|pāla! n' âiṣa dharmaḥ sanātanaḥ,
dūtaś ca hi Hṛṣīkeśaḥ sambandhī ca priyaś ca naḥ!
a|pāpaḥ Kauraveyeṣu sa kathaṃ bandham arhati?»

BHĪṢMA uvāca:

parītas tava putro 'yaṃ, Dhṛtarāṣṭra, su|manda|dhīḥ!
vṛṇoty an|arthaṃ n' âiv' ârthaṃ yācyamānaḥ suhṛj|janaiḥ.
88.20 imam utpathi vartantaṃ pāpaṃ pāp'|ânubandhinam
vākyāni su|hṛdāṃ hitvā tvam apy asy' ânuvartase!
Kṛṣṇam a|kliṣṭa|karmāṇam āsādy' âyaṃ su|durmatiḥ
tava putraḥ sah'|âmātyaḥ kṣaṇena na bhaviṣyati.
pāpasy' âsya nṛśaṃsasya tyakta|dharmasya dur|mateḥ
n' ôtsahe 'n|artha|saṃyuktāḥ śrotuṃ vācaḥ kathañ cana.

ity uktvā Bharata|śreṣṭho vṛddhaḥ parama|manyumān
utthāya tasmāt prātiṣṭhad Bhīṣmaḥ satya|parākramaḥ.

VAIŚAMPĀYANA uvāca:

89.1 PRĀTAR UTTHĀYA Kṛṣṇas tu kṛtavān sarvam āhnikam
brāhmaṇair abhyanujñātaḥ prayayau nagaraṃ prati.
taṃ prayāntaṃ mahā|bāhum anujñāpya mahā|balam
paryavartanta te sarve Vṛkasthala|nivāsinaḥ.
Dhārtarāṣṭās tam āyāntaṃ pratyujjagmuḥ sv|alaṃkṛtāḥ
Duryodhanād ṛte sarve Bhīṣma|Droṇa|Kṛip'|ādayaḥ,

VAISHAMPÁYANA said:

When he heard Duryódhana tell of his horrific plans for Krishna, Dhrita·rashtra and his counselors were troubled and disturbed. Dhrita·rashtra then addressed Duryódhana, saying: "Defender of your people, don't say such things! This is not eternal law! Hrishikésha is an envoy, and our relative and friend! He has done the Káuravas no harm, so how does he deserve imprisonment?"

BHISHMA said:

Dhrita·rashtra, your idiotic son is possessed! He chooses catastrophe rather than profit, even when his friends be-
seech him. You follow this wicked man and his evil support- 88.20
ers even though he has gone off the rails, and you ignore the advice of your friends! If your utterly evil-minded son and his advisors lay a hand on pure-acting Krishna they will die instantly. I do not dare to listen to any more of the disastrous ideas that this evil, cruel, and wicked-minded man who has abandoned all morality may propose.

Having said this, aged Bhishma, the best of the Bharatas, whose strength was his truth, rose from his seat, utterly enraged, and left.

VAISHAMPÁYANA said:

AT DAWN KRISHNA got up, performed all the morning 89.1
rituals, said his farewells to the brahmins, and set off for the city. The entire poplulation of Vrika·sthala said their goodbyes to long-armed and indomitable Krishna as he left, and then they returned to their homes. All the finely ornamented Dhartaráshtras except Duryódhana, with Bhishma,

paurāś ca bahulā, rājan, Hṛṣīkeśaṃ didṛkṣavaḥ
yānair bahu|vidhair anye, padbhir eva tathā pare.
89.5 sa vai pathi samāgamya Bhīṣmeṇ' â|kliṣṭa|karmaṇā
Droṇena Dhārtarāṣṭraiś ca tair vṛto nagaraṃ yayau.

Kṛṣṇa|sammānan'|ârthaṃ ca nagaraṃ samalaṃkṛtam,
babhūva rāja|mārgaś ca bahu|ratna|samācitaḥ.
na ca kaś cid gṛhe, rājaṃs, tad" āsīd, Bharata'|ṛṣabha,
na strī na vṛddho na śiśur; Vāsudeva|didṛkṣayā.
rāja|mārge narās tasmin saṃstuvanty avaniṃ gatāḥ
tasmin kāle, mahā|rāja, Hṛṣīkeśa|praveśane.
āvṛtāni vara|strībhir gṛhāṇi su|mahānty api
pracalant' îva bhāreṇa dṛśyante sma mahī|tale,
89.10 tathā ca gatimantas te Vāsudevasya vājinaḥ
pranaṣṭa|gatayo 'bhūvan rāja|mārge narair vṛte.

sa gṛhaṃ Dhṛtarāṣṭrasya prāviśac chatru|karśanaḥ
pāṇḍuraṃ puṇḍarīk'|âkṣaḥ prāsādair upaśobhitam.
tisraḥ kakṣyā vyatikramya Keśavo rāja|veśmanaḥ
Vaicitravīryaṃ rājānam abhyagacchad arin|damaḥ.
abhyāgacchati Dāśārhe prajñā|cakṣur nar'|âdhipaḥ
sah' âiva Droṇa|Bhīṣmābhyām udatiṣṭhan mahā|yaśāḥ,
Kṛpaś ca Somadattaś ca mahā|rājaś ca Bāhlikaḥ
āsanebhyo 'calan sarve pūjayanto Janārdanam.

Drona, Kripa, and so on, came out to greet him, and numerous townspeople also came out, keen to see Hrishikésha, my king; some by various types of carriage and others by foot. He met them on the road and made his way to the 89.5
city surrounded by pure-acting Bhishma, Drona, and the Dhartaráshtras.

Out of respect for Krishna the town had been decorated, and the royal road was covered with many treasures. No one stayed in their homes, bull-like Bharata sovereign, not women, nor the elderly, nor children; for they were all eager to catch a glimpse of Vasudéva. The men on the royal road prostrated themselves on the ground and sang praises when Hrishikésha entered, great king. Even the grandest houses filled with high-born women seemed almost to shake on their foundations from the weight, and Vasudéva's swift 89.10
horses traveled slowly, their progress impeded, for the royal road was teeming with people.

The lotus-eyed tormentor of his enemies entered Dhrita·rashtra's brilliant white, terrace-adorned palace, and Késhava, the destroyer of his enemies, marched through three palace enclosures until he finally approached King Vaichitravírya. As Dashárha drew near, the greatly famous king whose only vision was wisdom stood up, and so too did Drona, Bhishma, Kripa, Soma·datta, and mighty King Báhlika. Everyone rose from their seats and paid homage to Janárdana.

89.15 tato rājānam āsādya Dhṛtarāṣṭraṃ yaśasvinam
sa Bhīṣmaṃ pūjayām āsa Vārṣṇeyo vāgbhir añjasā.
teṣu dharm'|ânupūrvīṃ tāṃ prayujya Madhu|sūdanaḥ
yathā|vayaḥ samīyāya rājabhiḥ saha Mādhavaḥ.
atha Droṇaṃ sa|Bāhlīkaṃ sa|putraṃ ca yaśasvinam,
Kṛpaṃ ca Somadattaṃ ca samīyāya Janārdanaḥ.
tatr' āsīd ūrjitaṃ mṛṣṭaṃ kāñcanaṃ mahad āsanam
śāsanād Dhṛtarāṣṭrasya tatr' ôpāviśad Acyutaḥ.
atha gāṃ madhu|parkaṃ c' âpy, udakaṃ ca Janārdane
upajahrur yathā|nyāyaṃ Dhṛtarāṣṭra|purohitāḥ.
89.20 kṛt'|ātithyas tu Govindaḥ sarvān parihasan Kurūn
āste sāmbandhikaṃ kurvan Kurubhiḥ parivāritaḥ.
so 'rcito Dhṛtarāṣṭreṇa pūjitaś ca mahā|yaśāḥ,
rājānaṃ samanujñāpya nirakrāmad arin|damaḥ.
taiḥ sametya yathā|nyāyaṃ Kurubhiḥ Kuru|saṃsadi
Vidur'|âvasathaṃ ramyam upātiṣṭhata Mādhavaḥ.
Viduraḥ sarva|kalyāṇair abhigamya Janārdanam
arcayām āsa Dāśārhaṃ sarva|kāmair upasthitam.
«yā me prītiḥ, puṣkar'|âkṣa, tvad|darśana|samudbhavā
sā kim ākhyāyate tubhyam? antar'|ātm" âsi dehinām.»
89.25 kṛt'|ātithyaṃ tu Govindaṃ Viduraḥ sarva|dharma|vit
kuśalaṃ Pāṇḍu|putrāṇām apṛcchan Madhu|sūdanam.
prīyamāṇasya su|hṛdo viduṣo† buddhi|sattamaḥ
dharm'|ârtha|nityasya sato gata|roṣasya dhīmataḥ
tasya sarvaṃ sa|vistāraṃ Pāṇḍavānāṃ viceṣṭitam
kṣattur ācaṣṭa Dāśārhaḥ sarvaṃ pratyakṣa|darśivān.

Varshnéya approached illustrious King Dhrita·rashtra 89.15
and Bhishma, and immediately paid them his respects. Mádhava, the slayer of Madhu, then met the kings, following the lawful order in greeting them according to age. Next Janárdana met famous Drona and his son, as well as Báhlika, Kripa, and Soma·datta.

A huge and prestigious polished golden throne stood in the hall, and at Dhrita·rashtra's bidding Áchyuta took his place upon it. Then Dhrita·rashtra's priests offered a cow, a honey dish, and water to Janárdana, according to the custom. So it was that Govínda, treated hospitably, laughed 89.20
with all the Kurus as they surrounded him, and sat making friendly conversation.

Honored and paid homage by Dhrita·rashtra, the great glorious enemy-tamer bid the king farewell, and left. Once he had met the Kurus in the proper fashion in the Kuru assembly, Mádhava left for Vídura's delightful home. And Vídura approached Janárdana with all auspcious blessings, paid his respects to Dashárha, and provided him with all he desired. "What would be the point of my telling you of the joy I feel at seeing you, lotus-eyed one, when you are the inner soul of embodied creatures?" he exclaimed.

Then, when Vídura, aware of all law, had treated Go- 89.25
vínda hospitably, he asked the slayer of Madhu after the health of the Pándavas. Highly intelligent Dashárha, blessed with the gift of foresight, told the whole detailed story of the Pándavas' trials to his dear friend, the wise and attentive steward, a good man of constant virtue and profit but devoid of anger.

VAIŚAMPĀYANA uvāca:

90.1 ATH' ÔPAGAMYA Viduram apar'|âhṇe Janārdanaḥ
pitṛ|ṣvasāraṃ sa Pṛthām abhyagacchad arin|damaḥ.
sā dṛṣṭvā Kṛṣṇam āyāntaṃ prasann'|āditya|varcasam
kaṇṭhe gṛhītvā prākrośat smarantī tanayān Pṛthā.
teṣāṃ sattvavatāṃ madhye Govindaṃ saha|cāriṇam
cirasya dṛṣṭvā Vārṣṇeyaṃ bāṣpam āhārayat Pṛthā.
s" âbravīt Kṛṣṇam āsīnaṃ kṛt'|ātithyaṃ yudhāṃ patim
bāṣpa|gadgada|pūrṇena mukhena pariśuṣyatā:
90.5 «ye te bālyāt prabhṛty eva guru|śuśrūṣaṇe ratāḥ,
paras|parasya su|hṛdaḥ sammatāḥ sama|cetasaḥ,
vinīta|krodha|harṣāś ca, brahmaṇyāḥ, satya|vādinaḥ,
tyaktvā priya|sukhe Pārthā, rudatīm apahāya mām,
ahārṣuś ca vanaṃ yāntaḥ sa|mūlaṃ hṛdayaṃ mama,
a|tad|arhā mah"|ātmānaḥ kathaṃ, Keśava, Pāṇḍavāḥ?
ūṣur mahā|vane, tāta, siṃha|vyāghra|gaj'|ākule,
bālā vihīnāḥ pitrā te, mayā satata|lālitāḥ,
a|paśyantaś ca pitarau katham ūṣur mahā|vane?
śaṅkha|dundubhi|nirghoṣair, mṛdaṅgair, veṇu|nisvanaiḥ
90.10 Pāṇḍavāḥ samabodhyanta bālyāt prabhṛti, Keśava,
ye sma vāraṇa|śabdena, hayānāṃ heṣitena ca,
ratha|nemi|ninādaiś ca vyabodhyanta tadā gṛhe,
śaṅkha|bherī|ninādena veṇu|vīṇ"|ânunādinā,
puṇyāha|ghoṣa|miśreṇa pūjyamānā dvi|jātibhiḥ,

VAISHAMPÁYANA continued:

AND IN THE AFTERNOON, after having visited Vídura, Janárdana, the tamer of his enemies, went to see his paternal aunt, Pritha. When she saw Krishna coming towards her, his face gleaming like the sun, Pritha threw her arms around his neck and cried out as she remembered her children. Pritha wept upon seeing Varshnéya Govínda, her courageous sons' companion, after such a long time. And once Krishna was seated and had been treated to the proper hospitality, she addressed the lord of warriors with her shriveled mouth, stuttering and choked with tears: 90.1

"Késhava, how are those high-souled Pándavas, so undeserving of their fate, who from childhood on have delighted in obedience to teachers, who were respected friends to each other and of one mind—the Parthas who suppressed their anger and joy, who were honestly spoken and brahmanic, who abandoned pleasure and happiness and left me crying, taking my heart and its very roots with them as they wretchedly made their way to the forest? 90.5

My son, how did they live in the great forest filled with lions, tigers, and elephants? As children they lost their father, and so it was always I who cared for them. How did they 90.10
live in the great forest when they couldn't see either parent? From childhood onward the Pándavas were woken by the blares of conch shells, the beats of kettledrums and tambourines, and the sounds of flutes, Késhava. In their house they used to be woken by the trumpeting of elephants, the neighing of horses, the clatter of chariot wheels, the blares of conch shells and trumpets, and the notes of flutes and guitars, mingled with the mutterings of morning blessings

vastrai ratnair alaṅkāraiḥ pūjayanto dvi|janmanaḥ,
gīrbhir maṅgala|yuktābhir brāhmaṇānāṃ mah"|ātmanām,
  arcitair arcan'|ârhaiś ca stuvadbhir abhinanditāḥ
prāsād'|âgreṣv abodhyanta rāṅkav'|âjina|śāyinaḥ,
krūraṃ ca ninadaṃ śrutvā śvāpadānāṃ mahā|vane
90.15 na sm' ôpayānti nidrāṃ te na tad|arhā, Janārdana!
bherī|mṛdaṅga|ninadaiḥ śaṅkha|vaiṇava|nisvanaiḥ
strīṇāṃ gīta|ninādaiś ca madhurair, Madhu|sūdana,
bandi|māgadha|sūtaiś ca stuvadbhir bodhitāḥ katham
mahā|vaneṣv abodhyanta śvāpadānāṃ rutena ca?
  hrīmān, satya|dhṛtir, dānto bhūtānām anukampitā
kāma|dviṣau vaśe kṛtvā satāṃ vartm' ânuvartate,
Ambarīṣasya, Māndhātur, Yayāter, Nahuṣasya ca,
Bharatasya, Dilīpasya, Śiber Auśīnarasya ca
rāja'|rṣīṇāṃ purāṇānāṃ dhuraṃ dhatte dur|udvahām,
90.20 śīla|vṛtt'|ôpasampanno, dharma|jñaḥ, satya|saṅgaraḥ
rājā sarva|guṇ'|ôpetas trailokyasy' âpi yo bhavet,
Ajātaśatrur dharm'|ātmā śuddha|jāmbūnada|prabhaḥ,
śreṣṭhaḥ Kuruṣu sarveṣu dharmataḥ śruta|vṛttataḥ,
priya|darśo, dīrgha|bhujaḥ—kathaṃ, Kṛṣṇa, Yudhiṣṭhiraḥ?

and accompanied by the cries of the worshipping brahmins. They honored the twiceborn with clothes, jewels, and ornaments, while in return the high-souled brahmins honored them with praise and auspicious benedictions.

They used to wake up in the best palaces, on beds of 90.15
*ranku* hides, greeted by praise from those who are honored and those deserving of honor. Surely those undeserving men couldn't get any sleep in the great forest, listening to the pitiless shrieks of beasts of prey, Janárdana! How
could men who were woken by the sounds of trumpets and
tambourines, by the blares of conch-shells and the music
of guitars, by the sweet sounds of women's songs, by praise
from heralds, bards and minstrels, wake up in the great
forests to the screech of predators, slayer of Madhu?

What of the modest man, firm in truth, disciplined,
kind to living creatures, who had brought desire and hatred under his control, who took the path of good men,
and who bears the same heavy yoke as Ambarísha, Mandhátri, Yayáti, Náhusha, Bharata, Dilípa, and Shibi Aushínara, the ancient royal sages? Embellished by his charac- 90.20
ter and behavior, he was law-wise, true to his promises,
and could have been king of the three worlds, endowed
with every virtue as he was. So Krishna, how is righteous-
souled Ajáta·shatru, bright as pure gold, the best of all Kurus in morality, learning, and conduct—that handsome,
long-armed Yudhi·shthira?

yaḥ sa nāg'|âyuta|prāṇo vāta|raṃhā mahā|balaḥ
s'|â|marṣaḥ Pāṇḍavo nityaṃ priyo bhrātuḥ, priyaṅ|karaḥ;
Kīcakasya tu sa|jñāter yo hantā, Madhu|sūdana,
śūraḥ Krodhavaśānāṃ ca, Hiḍimbasya Bakasya ca;
parākrame Śakra|samo Mātariśva|samo bale
Maheśvara|samaḥ krodhe Bhīmaḥ praharatāṃ varaḥ;
90.25 krodhaṃ balam a|marṣaṃ ca yo nidhāya paraṃ|tapaḥ
jit'|ātmā Pāṇḍavo '|marṣī bhrātus tiṣṭhati śāsane;
tejo|rāśiṃ mah"|ātmānaṃ variṣṭham a|mita'|âujasam
bhīmaṃ pradarśanen' âpi Bhīmasenaṃ Janārdana;
taṃ mam ācakṣva, Vārṣṇeya, katham adya Vṛkodaraḥ?
āste parigha|bāhuḥ sa madhyamaḥ Pāṇḍavo balī
Arjunen' Ârjuno yaḥ sa, Kṛṣṇa, bāhu|sahasriṇā
dvi|bāhuḥ spardhate nityam atīten' âpi, Keśava,
kṣipaty ekena vegena pañca bāṇa|śatāni yaḥ
iṣv|astre sadṛśo rājñaḥ Kārtavīryasya Pāṇḍavaḥ;
90.30 tejas" āditya|sadṛśo, maha"|rṣi|sadṛśo dame,
kṣamayā pṛthivī|tulyo, Mahendra|sama|vikramaḥ;
ādhirājyaṃ mahad dīptaṃ prathitaṃ, Madhu|sūdana,
āhṛtaṃ yena vīryeṇa Kurūṇāṃ sarva|rājasu;
yasya bāhu|balaṃ sarve Pāṇḍavāḥ paryupāsate,
sa sarva|rathināṃ śreṣṭhaḥ Pāṇḍavaḥ satya|vikramaḥ,
yaṃ gatv" âbhimukhaḥ saṃkhye na jīvan kaś cid āvrajet,
yo jetā sarva|bhūtānām a|jeyo Jiṣṇur, Acyuta,

What of the mightily powerful and truculent son of Pandu, ever dear to his brother and bringing him joy, swift as the wind and as forceful as a thousand elephants; the man who killed Kíchaka and his kin, the heroic slayer of the Krodha·vashas, Hidímba, and Baka, O Madhu·súdana; Bhima who matches Shakra in prowess, matches the wind god in power and Mahéshvara in fury, and is the greatest of fighters? What of the tamer of his enemies who disciplined 90.25
his fury, strength, and impatience and took control of his soul; the intolerant son of Pandu who abides by his brother's commands, the mass of brilliance, the high-souled, greatest, boundlessly energetic and terrifying-looking Bhima·sena, O Janárdana? Tell me, Varshnéya, how is Vrikódara doing now?

And what of the middle Pándava, the mighty Árjuna with two arms like iron bars, who ever competes with thousand-armed Árjuna* though his rival is long dead, Krishna Késhava? What of the man who shoots five hundred arrows in a single burst, the son of Pandu who is a match for King Kartavírya in archery; the man who rivals the sun in 90.30
brilliance, the great seers in self-discipline, the earth in patience, and great Indra in prowess? What of the man whose strength brought the Kurus their great, celebrated, blazing sovereignty over all kings, Madhu·súdana; the man whose strength of arms all the Pándavas praise, who is the greatest of all warriors and the son of Pandu whose power lies in his truth? What of the man against whom no challenger in battle ever survives, Jishnu the invincible conqueror of all living creatures, Áchyuta? What of the man who is the Pándavas' last resort just as Vásava is the last resort of the

yo 'pāśrayaḥ Pāṇḍavānāṃ devānām iva Vāsavaḥ,
sa te bhrātā sakhā c' âiva katham adya Dhanañjayaḥ?
90.35 dayāvān sarva|bhūteṣu, hrī|niṣevo, mah"|âstravit,
mṛduś ca su|kumāraś ca, dhārmikaś ca priyaś ca me;
Sahadevo mah"|êṣv|āsaḥ śūraḥ, samiti|śobhanaḥ
bhrātṝṇāṃ, Kṛṣṇa, śuśrūṣur, dharm'|ârtha|kuśalo yuvā;
sad" âiva Sahadevasya bhrātaro, Madhu|sūdana,
vṛttaṃ kalyāṇa|vṛttasya pūjayanti mah"|ātmanaḥ;
jyeṣṭh'|ôpacāyinaṃ vīraṃ Sahadevaṃ yudhāṃ patim
śuśrūṣuṃ mama, Vārṣṇeya, Mādrī|putraṃ pracakṣva me.

su|kumāro, yuvā, śūro, darśanīyaś ca Pāṇḍavaḥ,
bhrātṝṇāṃ c' âiva sarveṣāṃ priyaḥ prāṇo bahiś|caraḥ;
90.40 citra|yodhī ca Nakulo mah"|êṣv|āso mahā|balaḥ,
kac cit sa kuśalī, Kṛṣṇa, vatso mama sukh'|âidhitaḥ?
sukh'|ôcitam a|duḥkh'|ârhaṃ, su|kumāraṃ mahā|ratham
api jātu, mahā|bāho, paśyeyaṃ Nakulaṃ punaḥ?
pakṣma|sampāta|je kāle Nakulena vinā|kṛtā
na labhāmi dhṛtiṃ, vīra—s" âdya jīvāmi, paśya mām.

sarvaiḥ putraiḥ priyatarā Draupadī me, Janārdana,
kulīnā rūpa|sampannā, sarvaiḥ samuditā guṇaiḥ;
putra|lokāt pati|lokaṃ vṛṇvānā satya|vādinī
priyān putrān parityajya Pāṇḍavān anurudhyate;
90.45 mah"|âbhijana|sampannā, sarva|kāmaiḥ su|pūjitā
īśvarī sarva|kalyāṇī Draupadī katham, Acyuta?

gods? How is Dhanan·jaya, your brother and your friend, doing now?

What of the man who is merciful to all creatures, the man 90.35
who practices modesty and is a great master of weaponry, the gentle, highly delicate, and moral man who is dear to me—the great archer Saha·deva; the hero who gleams in battle, the youth who is skilled in virtue and profit and obeys his brothers, Krishna? His brothers always honor high-souled and well-behaved Saha·deva's conduct, Madhu·súdana. Tell me about the hero Saha·deva, lord of warriors, who obeys his elder brothers and obeys me, Varshnéya.

What of that very tender youth, the brave and handsome Pándava, as dear to all his brothers as their own lives?
Krishna, is Nákula in good health—the powerful and great 90.40
archer, the warrior of varied styles, my child who was raised in luxury? Will I really see uncommonly tender Nákula again, long-armed man? My great warrior was used to luxury and didn't deserve his misery. I can find no contentment when I am without Nákula for even the blink of an eye, hero, and yet look—I am still alive today.

What of Dráupadi, dearer to me than all my sons, Janárdana? She is nobly born, endowed with beauty and every virtue; an honestly spoken woman, who chose her husbands' world over that of her sons, and so abandoned her
dear boys and followed the Pándavas. How is utterly stun- 90.45
ning Queen Dráupadi, the lady of great noble descent who is honored with her every desire, Áchyuta?

patibhiḥ pañcabhiḥ śūrair agni|kalpaiḥ prahāribhiḥ
upapannā mah"|êśvāsair Draupadī duḥkha|bhāginī.
catur|daśam idaṃ varṣaṃ yan n' âpaśyam, arin|dama,
putr'|ādhibhiḥ paridyūnāṃ Draupadīṃ satya|vādinīm!
na nūnaṃ karmabhiḥ puṇyair aśnute puruṣaḥ sukham,
Draupadī cet tathā|vṛttā n' âśnute sukham a|vyayam!

na priyo mama Kṛṣṇāyā Bībhatsur, na Yudhiṣṭhiraḥ,
Bhīmaseno yamau v" âpi. yad apaśyaṃ sabh"|āgatām
90.50 na me duḥkhataraṃ kiñ cid bhūta|pūrvaṃ tato 'dhikam,
strī|dharmiṇīṃ Draupadīṃ yac chvaśurāṇāṃ samīpa|gām
ānāyitām an|āryeṇa krodha|lobh'|ânuvartinā
sarve praikṣanta Kurava eka|vastrāṃ sabh"|āgatām;
tatr' âiva Dhṛtarāṣṭhraś ca, mahā|rājaś ca Bāhlikaḥ,
Kṛpaś ca Somadattaś ca nirviṇṇāḥ Kuravas tathā.

tasyāṃ saṃsadi sarveṣāṃ kṣattāraṃ pūjayāmy aham.
vṛttena hi bhavaty āryo, na dhanena, na vidyayā.
tasya, Kṛṣṇa, mahā|buddher gaṃbhīrasya mah"|ātmanaḥ
kṣattuḥ śīlam alaṅkāro lokān viṣṭabhya tiṣṭhati.»

VAIŚAMPĀYANA uvāca:

90.55 sā śok'|ārtā ca hṛṣṭā ca dṛṣṭvā Govindam āgatam
nānā|vidhāni duḥkhāni sarvāṇy ev' ânvakīrtayat.

«pūrvair ācaritaṃ yat tat ku|rājabhir, arin|dama,
akṣa|dyūtaṃ, mṛga|vadhaḥ kaccid eṣāṃ sukh'|āvaham?
tan māṃ dahati yat Kṛṣṇā sabhāyāṃ Kuru|sannidhau
Dhārtarāṣṭraiḥ parikliṣṭā yathā na|kuśalaṃ tathā,
nirvāsanaṃ ca nagarāt, pravrajyā ca, paraṃ|tapa,

Dráupadi has five heroic husbands, great archers and warriors like fire, but still she suffers her share of unhappiness. This is the fourteenth year in which I have not seen honestly spoken Dráupadi, enemy-tamer, and her anxieties for her sons must be making her miserable! Surely no man finds happiness from his pious deeds if Dráupadi, with such high conduct, cannot find eternal bliss!

Even Bibhátsu and Yudhi·shthira are not as dear to me as
Krishná, nor Bhima·sena or the twins. Never before have I 90.50
known anything more pitiful than seeing Dráupadi come to the court, led before her father-in-law, during her monthly bleeding, by an ignoble man entertaining his fury and greed. All the Kurus gawped at her when she came to the assembly in her single garment! Dhrita·rashtra, great King Báhlika, Kripa, and Soma·datta were there, and the Kurus despaired.

Of those who were at court, the only one I respect is Vídura the steward. For it is not through one's wealth or learning that one becomes noble, but through one's conduct; and that high-souled, highly intelligent, and deep-charactered steward's conduct is an ornament which stands as support to the worlds, Krishna."

VAISHAMPÁYANA continued:

So, pained by her grief, but full of joy at seeing Govínda 90.55
arrive, she poured out all her many and various troubles.

"Do the practices of ancient and wicked kings, such as gambling and hunting, bring them pleasure, enemy-tamer? It burns me that Krishná was assaulted by the sons of Dhrita·rashtra in the assembly before the Kurus in such a sick manner! Then the exile from the city, and their life

nānā|vidhānāṃ duḥkhānām abhijñ" âsmi, Janārdana.
ajñāta|caryā, bālānām avarodhaś ca, Mādhava,
na me kleśatamaṃ tat syāt putraiḥ saha, paraṃ|tapa.
90.60 Duryodhanena nikṛtā varṣam adya catur|daśam!
duḥkhād api sukhaṃ na† syād yadi puṇya|phala|kṣayaḥ.
na me viśeṣo jātv āsīt Dhārtarāṣṭreṣu Pāṇḍavaiḥ,
tena satyena, Kṛṣṇa, tvāṃ hat'|âmitraṃ, śriyā vṛtam
asmād vimuktaṃ saṅgrāmāt paśyeyaṃ Pāṇḍavaiḥ saha.
n' âiva śakyāḥ parājetuṃ, sattvaṃ† hy eṣāṃ tathā|vidham!
pitaraṃ tv eva garheyaṃ, n' ātmānaṃ na Suyodhanam,
yen' âhaṃ Kuntibhojāya dhanaṃ vṛttair iv' ârpitā.
bālāṃ mām āryakas tubhyaṃ krīḍantīṃ kandu|hastikām
adāt tu Kuntibhojāya, sakhā sakhye mah"|ātmane!
s" âhaṃ pitrā ca nikṛtā, śvaśuraiś ca, paraṃ|tapa,
atyanta|duḥkhitā, Kṛṣṇa, kiṃ jīvita|phalaṃ mama?
90.65 yan māṃ vāg abravīn naktaṃ sūtake Savyasācinaḥ:
‹putras te pṛthivīṃ jetā, yaśaś c' âsya divaṃ spṛśet.
hatvā Kurūn mahā|janye, rājyaṃ prāpya Dhanañjayaḥ
bhrātṛbhiḥ saha Kaunteyas trīn medhān āhariṣyati.›
n' âhaṃ tām abhyasūyāmi. namo Dharmāya vedhase,
Kṛṣṇāya mahate! nityaṃ dharmo dhārayati prajāḥ.
dharmaś ced asti, Vārṣṇeya, yathā vāg abhyabhāṣata,
tvaṃ c' âpi tat tathā, Kṛṣṇa, sarvaṃ saṃpādayiṣyasi.

of banishment, enemy-scorcher—I know a wide range of troubles, Janárdana.

Nothing is more painful to me and my sons than their life in disguise and their estrangement from their children,
enemy-scorching Mádhava. It is now the fourteenth year 90.60
since Duryódhana tricked us! If happiness does not develop from this misery, then the fruit of meritorious acts is destroyed. Knowing that I have never made any distinction between the sons of Dhrita·rashtra and the Pándavas, by that truth, Krishna, I will see you and the Pándavas escape from battle with your lives, with your enemies dead, and surrounded by good fortune! But then, men such as they—with such a true nature—cannot be defeated!

I blame my father, rather than Suyódhana or myself, for he gave me to Kunti·bhoja just as rich men give away money. I was a child playing, ball in hand, when my honorable father gave me to high-souled Kunti·bhoja, one friend to another! I have been humiliated by my father and my father-in-law, enemy-scorcher, to the point of unbearable misery; so what good has come of my life, Krishna?

The night I gave birth to Savya·sachin, a voice told me: 90.65
'Your son will conquer the earth, and his fame will touch heaven. Once he has killed the Kurus in a great battle and regained the kingdom, Dhanan·jaya Kauntéya and his brothers will offer three sacrifices.'

And I do not doubt it. I bow to Dharma, to the creator, and to mighty Krishna! Law supports its subjects eternally. And if law really exists, Krishna Varshnéya, then you will achieve everything, just as the voice foretold.

na māṃ, Mādhava, vaidhavyaṃ, n' ârtha|nāśo na vairatā
tathā śokāya dahati, yathā putrair vinā|bhavaḥ!
90.70 y" âhaṃ Gāṇḍīva|dhanvānaṃ sarva|śastra|bhṛtāṃ varam
Dhanañjayaṃ na paśyāmi, kā śāntir hṛdayasya me?
itaś catur|daśaṃ varṣaṃ yan n' âpaśyaṃ Yudhiṣṭhiram,
Dhanañjayaṃ ca, Govinda, yamau, taṃ ca Vṛkodaram.
jīva|nāśaṃ pranaṣṭānāṃ śrāddhaṃ kurvanti mānavāḥ,
arthatas te mama mṛtās,
tesāṃ c' âhaṃ, Janārdana.
brūyā, Mādhava, rājānaṃ
dharm'|ātmānaṃ Yudhiṣṭhiram:
‹bhūyāṃs te hīyate dharmo. mā, putraka, vṛthā kṛthāḥ!›
par'|āśrayā, Vāsudeva, yā jīvati, dhig astu tām!
vṛtteḥ kārpaṇya|labdhāyā a|pratiṣṭh" âiva jyāyasī.
atho Dhanañjayaṃ brūyā, nity'|ôdyuktaṃ Vṛkodaram:
90.75 ‹yad|arthaṃ kṣatriyā sūte, tasya kālo 'yam āgataḥ.
asmiṃś ced āgate kāle mithyā c' âtikramiṣyati,
loka|saṃbhāvitāḥ santaḥ su|nṛśaṃsaṃ kariṣyatha,
nṛśaṃsena ca vo yuktāṃs tyajeyaṃ śāśvatīḥ samāḥ;
kāle hi samanuprāpte tyaktavyam api jīvanam.›
Mādrī|putrau ca vaktavayau kṣatra|dharma|ratau sadā:
‹vikrameṇ' ârjitān bhogān vṛṇītaṃ jīvitād api;
vikram'|âdhigatā hy arthāḥ kṣatra|dharmeṇa jīvataḥ
mano manuṣyasya sadā prīṇanti,› puruṣ'|ôttama.

O Mádhava, widowhood, the loss of our wealth, and the current quarrel do not burn me with such grief as being separated from my sons! What peace is there in my heart 90.70
when I cannot see Dhanan·jaya, the Gandíva bowman, the greatest of all who wield weapons? Govínda, this is the fourteenth year that I have not seen Yudhi·shthira, Dhanan·jaya, the twins, or Vrikódara. People perform *shraddha* rites* for those who have gone, assuming they are dead, and to all intents and purposes they are dead to me and I to them, Janárdana.

Mádhava, tell righteous-souled King Yudhi·shthira: 'Your righteousness is fast diminishing. Don't let it decrease further, my son!' Shame on the woman who lives dependent on others, Vasudéva! Insecurity is still better than a life of accepting charity.

Then tell Dhanan·jaya and ever-ready Vrikódara: "There 90.75
is a purpose for which a lady of the kshatriya class gives birth. Its time is at hand. But if when the time comes it passes in vain, then no matter how highly the world regards you at present, you will be behaving very cruelly. I will abandon you forever should you become involved with something base, for when the occasion demands it one must abandon even one's life.'

Best of men, tell the twin sons of Madri, who have always taken pleasure in warrior law: 'Choose the pleasures which are found only through prowess, even over your life, for the gains won through heroism always delight the mind of the man who lives according to the warrior code.'

gatvā brūhi, mahā|bāho, sarva|śastra|bhṛtāṃ varam

90.80 Arjunaṃ Pāṇḍavaṃ vīraṃ: ‹Draupadyāḥ padavīṃ vara!›
viditau hi tav' âtyantaṃ kruddhau tau tu yath" ântakau
Bhīm'|Ârjunau nayetāṃ hi devān api parāṃ gatim!
tayoś c' âitad avajñānaṃ yat sā Kṛṣṇā sabhāṃ gatā,
Duḥśāsanaś ca Karṇaś ca paruṣāṇy abhyabhāṣatām.
Duryodhano Bhīmasenam abhyagacchan manasvinam,
paśyatāṃ Kuru|mukhyānāṃ tasya drakṣyati yat phalam!
na hi vairaṃ samāsādya praśāmyati Vṛkodaraḥ.
su|cirād api Bhīmasya na hi vairaṃ praśāmyati,
yāvad antaṃ na nayati śātravāñ chatru|karśanaḥ.

90.85 na duḥkhaṃ rājya|haraṇaṃ, na ca dyūte parājayaḥ,
pravrājanaṃ tu putrāṇāṃ na me tad duḥkha|kāraṇam,
yat tu sā bṛhatī śyāmā eka|vastrā sabhāṃ gatā
aśṛṇot paruṣā vācaḥ. kiṃ nu duḥkhataraṃ tataḥ?
strī|dharmiṇī var'|ārohā kṣatra|dharma|ratā sadā
n' âbhyagacchat tadā nāthaṃ Kṛṣṇā nāthavatī satī.

yasyā mama sa|putrāyās tvaṃ nātho, Madhu|sūdana,
Rāmaś ca balināṃ śreṣṭhaḥ, Pradyumnaś ca mahā|rathaḥ,
s" âham evaṃ|vidhaṃ duḥkhaṃ saheyaṃ, puruṣ'|ôttama,
Bhīme jīvati dur|dharṣe, Vijaye c' â|palāyini.»

Long-armed man, go and tell the hero Árjuna, son of Pandu, the best of all who wield weapons: 'Choose Dráupadi's path!' For you know that when Bhima and Árjuna are immeasurably angry they are like death, and they could lead even the gods onto their last path! It was a sign of contempt for those two men when Krishná was brought to the assembly and Duhshásana and Karna hurled insults at her. Duryódhana attacked spirited Bhima·sena while the leading Kurus looked on, but he will see what reward that will yield him! For Vrikódara does not smooth over a quarrel once it has begun. No, Bhima certainly does not smooth over a quarrel, no matter how long it lasts, until the enemy-plower has brought an end to his enemies! 90.80

Not the painful seizure of the kingdom, not the defeat at gambling, nor even the exile of my sons causes me such pain as the fact that tall, dark Dráupadi was taken to the assembly wearing only a single garment, and was forced to listen to vile insults. What could be more painful than that? The shapely-hipped lady always took delight in the duties of her warrior class, but during her monthly bleeding Krishná the wife of champions could find no one to protect her. 90.85

But my sons and I have you as our champion, Madhu·súdana, and Rama, the greatest of powerful men, as well as the mighty warrior Pradyúmna. And so I will prevail over this misery, best of men, as long as invincible Bhima and unretreating Víjaya are alive."

VAIŚAMPĀYANA uvāca:

90.90 tata āśvāsayām āsa putr'|ādhibhir abhiplutām
pitṛ|ṣvasāraṃ śocantīṃ Śauriḥ Pārtha|sakhaḥ Pṛthām.

VĀSUDEVA uvāca:

kā tu sīmantinī tvādṛg lokeṣv asti, pitṛ|ṣvasaḥ?
Śūrasya rājño duhitā Ājamīḍha|kulaṃ gatā
mahā|kulīnā bhavatī hradādd hradam iv' āgatā.
īśvarī sarva|kalyāṇī, bhartrā parama|pūjitā.
vīra|sūr vīra|patnī tvaṃ, sarvaiḥ samuditā guṇaiḥ,
sukha|duḥkhe, mahā|prājñe, tvādṛśī soḍhum arhati.
nidrā|tandre, krodha|harṣau, kṣut|pipāse, him'|ātapau—
etāni Pārthā nirjitya nityaṃ vīra|mukhe ratāḥ.
90.95 tyakta|grāmya|sukhāḥ Pārthā nityaṃ vīra|sukha|priyāḥ
na tu svalpena tuṣyeyur mah"|ôtsāhā mahā|balāḥ.
antaṃ dhīrā niṣevante, madhyaṃ grāmya|sukha|priyāḥ;
uttamāṃś ca parikleśān, bhogāṃś c' âtīva mānuṣān.
anteṣu remire dhīrā, na te madhyeṣu remire.
anta|prāptiṃ sukhām āhur, duḥkham antaram etayoḥ.

VAISHAMPÁYANA said:

Shauri, the Parthas' friend, soothed Pritha, his paternal aunt, as she grieved, drowning in her woes for her sons. 90.90

VASUDÉVA replied:

Is there any woman like you in the worlds, aunt? You are the daughter of King Shura, and a high-born lady who passed, through marriage, into the line of Aja·midha, moved like a lotus from lake to lake. You are a queen blessed with every conceivable mark of beauty, whose husband worshipped her absolutely. You are the mother of heroes, the wife of a hero, and you are endowed with every virtue. A woman like you, wise lady, ought to cope with both happiness and misery.

The Parthas have defeated sleep and laziness, anger and joy, hunger and thirst, and cold and heat, and they always
take delight in the chief aims of heroes. The Parthas have 90.95
abandoned the joys of being villagers and always enjoy the pleasures of heroism. They are not satisfied with merely a little, but are highly energetic and tremendously powerful. The resolute push themselves to the limit, but those who enjoy the pleasures of village life are happy with the mundane. Determined men take pleasure in the most total human catastrophes and utterly blissful pleasures, but they do not enjoy humdrum experiences. They say that happiness lies in reaching the limits, and the range in between is misery.

abhivādayanti bhavatīṃ Pāṇḍavāḥ saha Kṛṣṇayā;
ātmānaṃ ca kuśalinaṃ nivedy' āhur an|āmayam.
a|rogān sarva|siddh'|ârthān kṣipraṃ drakṣyasi Pāṇḍavān
īśvarān sarva|lokasya, hat'|âmitrāñ, śriyā|vṛtān!
90.100 evam āśvāsitā Kuntī pratyuvāca Janārdanam
putr'|ādhibhir abhidhvastā nigṛhy' â|buddhi|jaṃ tamaḥ:

KUNTY uvāca:

yad yat teṣāṃ, mahā|bāho,
pathyaṃ syān, Madhu|sūdana,
yathā yathā tvaṃ manyethāḥ,
kuryāḥ, Kṛṣṇa, tathā tathā,
a|vilopena dharmasya, a|nikṛtyā, paraṃ|tapa.
prabhāva|jñ" âsmi te, Kṛṣṇa, satyasy' âbhijanasya ca,
vyavasthāyāṃ ca mitreṣu
buddhi|vikramayos tathā.
tvam eva naḥ kule dharmas,
tvaṃ satyaṃ, tvaṃ tapo mahat,
tvaṃ trātā, tvaṃ mahad Brahma, tvayi sarvaṃ pratiṣṭhitam.
yath" âiv' āttha, tath" âiv' âitat, tvayi satyaṃ bhaviṣyati.

VAIŚAMPĀYANA uvāca:

90.105 tām āmantrya ca Govindaḥ, kṛtvā c' âbhipradakṣiṇam
prātiṣṭhata mahā|bāhur Duryodhana|gṛhān prati.

VAIŚAMPĀYANA uvāca:

91.1 PṚTHĀM ĀMANTRYA Govindaḥ kṛtvā c' âbhipradakṣiṇam
Duryodhana|gṛhaṃ Śaurir abhyagacchad arin|damaḥ,
lakṣmyā paramayā yuktaṃ, Purandara|gṛh'|ôpamam,
vicitrair āsanair yuktaṃ praviveśa Janārdanaḥ.

The Pándavas and Krishná pass on their greetings to you, the queen. They say that they are well, and they ask after your health. Soon you will see the Pándavas as healthy masters of the whole world, surrounded by good fortune, with their enemies dead and all their aims successfully achieved!

So it was that Kunti, overwhelmed by her anxieties over 90.100
her sons, was consoled. And taking control of the darkness that had been born of her lack of information, she replied to Janárdana.

KUNTI said:

Long-armed Krishna, slayer of Madhu, do whatever you think will benefit the Pándavas, without harming moral law or resorting to trickery, scorcher of the foe. I understand the power of your truth and your lineage, Krishna, as well as your intellectual prowess, in making arrangements for your friends. In our family you are the law, the truth, and great austerity. You are the rescuer, the great Brahman, and everything resides within you. It will be as you say, and truth will reside in you.

VAISHAMPÁYANA said:

Long-armed Govínda bade her farewell, circumambu- 90.105
lated her, and then left for Duryódhana's palace complex.

VAISHAMPÁYANA continued:

ONCE GOVÍNDA HAD said goodbye to Pritha and walked 91.1
around her, Shauri the enemy-tamer went to Duryódhana's palace—a palace that resembled Indra's dwelling, decked as it was with the most exquisite treasure, and adorned with ornamented thrones. Janárdana made his way to this palace, and entered.

tasya kakṣyā vyatikramya tisro, dvāḥ|sthair a|vāritaḥ,
tato 'bhra|ghana|saṃkāśaṃ, giri|kūṭam iv' ôcchritam,
śriyā jvalantaṃ prāsādam āruroha mahā|yaśāḥ.
tatra rāja|sahasraiś ca Kurubhiś c' âbhisaṃvṛtam
91.5 Dhārtarāṣṭraṃ mahā|bāhuṃ dadarś' āsīnam āsane,
Duḥśāsanaṃ ca Karṇaṃ ca, Śakuniṃ c' âpi Saubalam
Duryodhana|samīpe tān āsana|sthān dadarśa saḥ.
abhyāgacchati Dāśārhe Dhārtarāṣṭro mahā|yaśāḥ
udatiṣṭhat sah'|âmātyaḥ pūjayan Madhu|sūdanam.
sametya Dhārtarāṣṭreṇa sah'|âmātyena Keśavaḥ
rājabhis tatra Vārṣṇeyaḥ samāgacchad yathā|vayaḥ.
tatra jāmbūnada|mayaṃ paryaṅkaṃ su|pariṣkṛtam,
vividh'|āstaraṇ'|āstīrṇam abhyupāviśad Acyutaḥ.
tasmin gāṃ madhu|parkaṃ c' âpy udakaṃ ca Janārdane
91.10 nivedayām āsa tadā, gṛhān rājyaṃ ca Kauravaḥ.
tatra Govindam āsīnaṃ prasann'|āditya|varcasam
upāsāṃ cakire sarve Kuravo rājabhiḥ saha.
tato Duryodhano rājā Vārṣṇeyaṃ jayatāṃ varam
nyamantrayad bhojanena, n' âbhyanandac ca Keśavaḥ.
tato Duryodhanaḥ Kṛṣṇam abravīt Kuru|saṃsadi
mṛdu|pūrvaṃ śaṭh'|ôdarkaṃ Karṇam ābhāṣya Kauravaḥ:
«kasmād annāni, pānāni, vāsāṃsi śayanāni ca
tvad|artham upanītāni n' āgṛhīs tvam, Janārdana?
ubhayoś ca dadat sāhyam, ubhayoś ca hite rataḥ,
91.15 sambandhī dayitaś c' âsi Dhṛtarāṣṭrasya, Mādhava.
tvaṃ hi, Govinda, dharm'|ârthau vettha tattvena sarvaśaḥ;
tatra kāraṇam icchāmi śrotuṃ, cakra|gadā|dhara!»

The famous hero strode through three enclosures, unimpeded by the doorkeepers, and then climbed up to the palace which blazed with glory, gleaming like a dense cloud
rising on a mountain peak. And there it was that he saw 91.5
strong-armed Dhartaráshtra, sitting on a throne, surrounded by thousands of Kuru kings; and he saw Duhshásana, Karna, and Shákuni Sáubala sitting in seats near Duryódhana.

When he approached, far-famed Dhartaráshtra and his ministers got up and honored Dashárha Madhu·súdana. Késhava Varshnéya met Dhartaráshtra, and his advisors, and all the kings in order, according to their age. Áchyuta then sat down on a beautifully decorated gilt couch which was strewn with various covers, and the Káurava offered
Janárdana a cow, a plate of honey, and some water; and next 91.10
he offered his home and kingdom.

All the Kurus and kings paid homage to Govínda as he sat, glorious as the tranquil sun. Then King Duryódhana invited Varshnéya, the best of conquerors, to have some food, but Késhava refused. So Duryódhana Káurava addressed Krishna in the midst of the Kuru gathering, glancing at Karna and speaking gently to begin with, signaling his future deceit:

"Why do you refuse the food, drink, clothes, and beds which have been brought for you, Janárdana? You gave your alliance to both sides, and wish for the advantage of both
sides. You are Dhrita·rashtra's dear relative, Mádhava. In- 91.15
deed, you truly know law and profit in all cases, Govínda, so I want to hear your reason, discus and mace wielder!"

VAIŚAMPĀYANA uvāca:

sa evam ukto Govindaḥ pratyuvāca mahā|manāḥ
udyan|megha|svanaḥ kāle pragṛhya vipulaṃ bhujam,
a|laghū|kṛtam, a|grastam, a|nirastam, a|saṃkulam
rājīva|netro rājānaṃ hetumad|vākyam uttamam,
«kṛt'|ârthā bhuñjate dūtāḥ, pūjāṃ gṛhṇanti c' âiva ha.
kṛt'|ârthaṃ māṃ sah'|âmātyaḥ samarciṣyasi, Bhārata.»
evam uktaḥ pratyuvāca Dhārtarāṣṭro Janārdanam:
«na yuktaṃ bhavat" âsmāsu pratipattum a|sāmpratam.
91.20 kṛt'|ârthaṃ v" â|kṛt'|ârthaṃ ca tvāṃ vayaṃ, Madhu|sūdana,
yatāmahe pūjayituṃ, Dāśārha, na ca śaknumaḥ,
na ca tat kāraṇaṃ vidmo yasmin no, Madhu|sūdana,
pūjāṃ kṛtāṃ prīyamāṇair n' âmaṃsthāḥ, puruṣ'|ôttama.
vairaṃ no n' âsti bhavatā, Govinda, na ca vigrahaḥ;
sa bhavān prasamīkṣy' âitan n' ēdṛśaṃ vaktum arhati.»

VAIŚAMPĀYANA uvāca:

evam uktaḥ pratyuvāca Dhārtarāṣṭraṃ Janārdanaḥ
abhivīkṣya sah'|âmātyaṃ Dāśārhaḥ prahasann iva:
«n' âhaṃ kāmān, na saṃraṃbhān,
na dveṣān, n' ârtha|kāraṇāt,
na hetu|vādāl, lobhād vā
dharmaṃ jahyāṃ kathañ cana.
91.25 saṃprīti|bhojyāny annāni, āpad|bhojyāni vā punaḥ.
na ca saṃprīyase, rājan, na c' âiv' āpad|gatā vayam.

VAISHAMPÁYANA said:

When he said this, high-minded and lotus-eyed Govínda grasped his strong arm and replied in a voice which boomed like looming thunderclouds. His response was phrased with excellent words full of reasoning. They were not rushed, not swallowed, not dropped or confused, and they ran as follows: "Envoys eat and accept honor when they have accomplished their aims. So, when I have achieved my aim, you and your advisors will pay honor to me, Bhárata."

Addressed in this manner, Dhartaráshtra replied to Janárdana: "It is not appropriate for you to treat us improperly. Regardless of whether or not you achieve your aims, 91.20
Madhu·súdana, we are trying to honor you, but apparently we are unable to do so, Dashárha. We do not know what reason you have to refuse the honors paid to you by friends, Madhu·súdana, best of men. We have no argument with you, Govínda, nor any quarrel, and, reflecting on this, you ought not to speak to us in such a manner."

VAISHAMPÁYANA said:

Spoken to in this way, Janárdana Dashárha almost laughed as he surveyed Dhartaráshtra and his counselors, and he said to them:

"I would never contravene law out of desire, anger, or hatred, for gain, to argue the point, or out of greed. Eating 91.25
food is done for reasons of either affection or distress. But you inspire no affection, king, and no disaster has befallen me.

a|kasmād dvekṣi vai, rājañ, janma|prabhṛti Pāṇḍavān
priy'|ânuvartino bhrātṝn, sarvaiḥ samuditān guṇaiḥ.
a|kasmāc c' âiva Pārthānāṃ dveṣaṇaṃ n' ôpapadyate.
dharme sthitāḥ Pāṇḍaveyāḥ; kas tān kiṃ vaktum arhati?
yas tān dveṣṭi sa māṃ dveṣṭi; yas tān anu sa mām anu;
aikātmyaṃ māṃ gataṃ viddhi Pāṇḍavair dharma|cāribhiḥ.

kāma|krodh'|ânuvartī hi yo mohād virurutsati,
guṇavantaṃ ca yo dveṣṭi, tam āhuḥ puruṣ'|âdhamam.
91.30 yaḥ kalyāṇa|guṇāñ jñātīn mohāl lobhād didṛkṣate,
so '|jit'|ātm" â|jita|krodho na ciraṃ tiṣṭhati śriyam.
atha yo guṇa|saṃpannān hṛdayasy' â|priyān api
priyeṇa kurute vaśyāṃś, ciraṃ yaśasi tiṣṭhati.
sarvam etan na bhoktavyam annaṃ duṣṭ'|âbhisaṃhitam;
kṣattur ekasya bhoktavyam, iti me dhīyate matiḥ.»

evam uktvā mahā|bāhur Duryodhanam a|marṣaṇam
niścakrāma tataḥ śubhrād Dhārtarāṣṭra|niveśanāt.
niryāya ca mahā|bāhur Vāsudevo mahā|manāḥ
niveśāya yayau veśma Vidurasya mah"|ātmanaḥ.

91.35 tam abhyagacchad Droṇaś ca,
Kṛpo, Bhīṣmo, 'tha Bāhlikaḥ,
Kuravaś ca mahā|bāhuṃ
Vidurasya gṛhe sthitam.
ta ūcur Mādhavaṃ vīraṃ Kuravo Madhu|sūdanam:
«nivedayāmo, Vārṣṇeya, sa|ratnāṃs te gṛhān vayam.»
tān uvāca mahā|tejāḥ Kauravān Madhu|sūdanaḥ:
«sarve bhavanto gacchantu; sarvā me 'pacitiḥ kṛtā.»

From the moment they were born you have hated the Pándavas, king, and without any good reason. Your brothers treated you kindly and were endowed with every virtue. This irrational hatred for the Parthas has no justification. The Pándavas abide firmly by moral law, so who ought to speak against them? The man who hates them hates me, and the man who follows them, follows me. Understand that I have become one soul with the morally acting Pándavas.

They say a man is the lowest of the low if he acts out of desire and fury, if he hates a virtuous man, or if in his idiocy
he wants to destroy him. Should a man fail to control his 91.30
soul and his anger, and should he wish to view his noble and virtuous relatives with foolishness and greed, he will not keep his good fortune for long. But then there is the man who wins control over virtuous men through affection, even though his heart feels no love for them—he will rest on his fame for a long time to come. So, all this food is tainted with wickedness and I should not eat it. My mind is made up: I must only eat the food which Vídura the steward offers me."

Having said these things to unforbearing Duryódhana, the long-armed man left Dhartaráshtra's gleaming palace. Mighty-armed and high-minded Vasudéva went on his way, and coming to high-souled Vídura's home, he stayed there.

Drona, Kripa, Bhishma, Báhlika, and other Kurus came 91.35
to visit the long-armed lord as he stayed in Vídura's house. The Kurus said to the hero Mádhava, the slayer of Madhu: "We offer our houses and jewels to you, Varshnéya." But great glorious Madhu·súdana replied to the Káuravas: "You may all leave, for every honor has been paid to me."

yāteṣu Kuruṣu kṣattā Dāśārham a|parājitam
abhyarcayām āsa tadā sarva|kāmaiḥ prayatnavān.
tataḥ kṣatt" ânna|pānāni śucīni guṇavanti ca
upāharad an|ekāni Keśavāya mah"|ātmane.
91.40 tais tarpayitvā prathamaṃ brāhmaṇān Madhu|śūdanaḥ
vedavidbhyo dadau Kṛṣṇaḥ prathamaṃ draviṇāny api;
tato 'nuyāyibhiḥ sārdhaṃ, marudbhir iva Vāsavaḥ
Vidur'|ânnāni bubhuje śucīni guṇavanti ca.

VAIŚAMPĀYANA uvāca:

92.1 TAṂ BHUKTAVANTAM āśvastaṃ niśāyāṃ Viduro 'bravīt:
«n' êdaṃ samyag vyavasitaṃ, Keśav', āgamanaṃ tava.
artha|dharm'|âtigo, mandaḥ, saṃraṃbhī ca, Janārdana,
māna|ghno, māna|kāmaś ca, vṛddhānāṃ śāsan'|âtigaḥ,
dharma|śāstr'|âtigo, mūḍho, dur|ātmā, pragrahaṃ gataḥ,
a|neyaḥ śreyasāṃ, mando Dhārtarāṣṭro, Janārdana!
kām'|ātmā prājña|mānī ca, mitra|dhruk, sarva|śaṅkitaḥ,
a|kartā c' â|kṛta|jñaś ca, tyakta|dharmā, priy'|ânṛtaḥ,
92.5 mūḍhaś c' â|kṛta|buddhiś ca, indriyāṇām an|īśvaraḥ,
kām'|ânusārī, kṛtyeṣu sarveṣv a|kṛta|niścayaḥ,
etaiś c' ânyaiś ca bahubhir doṣair eva samanvitaḥ
tvay" ôcyamānaḥ śreyo 'pi saṃraṃbhān na grahīṣyati.

When the Kurus had left, Vídura the steward strove to pay homage to undefeated Dashárha, providing for his every desire. The steward fetched numerous delicious types of food and drink of the highest quality for high-souled Késhava. Krishna, the slayer of Madhu, first satisfied the 91.40
brahmins and gave wealth to those who were learned in the Veda; then, like Vásava together with the Maruts, he enjoyed Vídura's delicious and excellent food.

VAISHAMPÁYANA continued:

THAT NIGHT, ONCE he had eaten and relaxed, Vídura said 92.1
to him:

"Késhava Janárdana, your coming to visit wasn't a sensible decision, for the irascible fool Dhartaráshtra transgresses profit and moral law. He destroys the honor of others while desiring honor for himself. He contravenes the orders of his elders, he fails to obey the scriptures of moral law, and he is a wicked-souled idiot who has become obstinate! He is a fool, who cannot be governed by his betters, Janárdana.

His soul is lustful, he considers himself wise, he betrays his friends, he is suspicious of everyone, he does not do his job, he is ungrateful, he has abandoned morality, and he delights in deception. He is a fool of undeveloped intelli- 92.5
gence, a man with no lordship over his senses, a slave to lust, and a man incapable of making decisions about anything that needs doing. He possesses these and many other faults, and in his anger he will not accept what you tell him, even if it is in his best interest.

Bhīṣme, Droṇe, Kṛpe, Karne, Droṇa|putre, Jayadrathe
bhūyasīṃ vartate vṛttiṃ, na śame kurute manaḥ.
niścitaṃ Dhārtarāṣṭrāṇāṃ sa|Karṇānāṃ, Janārdana,
Bhīṣma|Droṇa|mukhān Pārthā na śaktāḥ prativīkṣitum!
senā|samudayaṃ kṛtvā pārthivaṃ, Madhu|sūdana,
kṛt'|ârthaṃ manyate bāla ātmānam a|vicakṣaṇaḥ.
92.10 ‹ekaḥ Karṇaḥ parāñ jetuṃ samartha, iti› niścitam
Dhārtarāṣṭrasya dur|buddheḥ sa śamaṃ n' ôpayāsyati.

samvic ca Dhārtarāṣṭrāṇāṃ sarveṣām eva, Keśava,
śame prayatamānasya tava saubhrātra|kāṅkṣiṇaḥ,
‹na Pāṇḍavānām asmābhiḥ pratideyaṃ yath" ôcitam,›
iti vyavasitās; teṣu vacanaṃ syān nir|arthakam.
yatra s'|ûktaṃ dur|uktaṃ ca samaṃ syān, Madhu|sūdana,
na tatra pralapet prājño, badhireṣv iva gāyanaḥ.
a|vijānatsu mūḍheṣu nirmaryādeṣu, Mādhava,
na tvaṃ vākyaṃ bruvan yuktaś, cāṇḍāleṣu dvijo yathā.
92.15 so 'yaṃ bala|stho mūḍhaś ca na kariṣyati te vacaḥ
tasmin nirarthakaṃ vākyam uktaṃ sampatsyate tava.

teṣāṃ samupaviṣṭānāṃ sarveṣāṃ pāpa|cetasām
tava madhy'|âvataraṇaṃ mama, Kṛṣṇa, na rocate.
dur|buddhīnām a|śiṣṭānāṃ bahūnāṃ duṣṭa|cetasām
pratīpaṃ vacanaṃ madhye tava, Kṛṣṇa, na rocate.
an|upāsita|vṛddhatvāc, chriyā darpāc ca mohitaḥ,
vayo|darpād a|marṣāc ca na te śreyo grahīṣyati.

He puts the highest faith in Bhishma, Drona, Kripa, Karna, Drona's son, and Jayad·ratha, and his mind will not set itself on peace. Janárdana, the Dhartaráshtras and Karna have convinced themselves that the Parthas are incapable even of looking directly at Bhishma, Drona, and the Kuru leaders! He has turned the earth into his assembled army, Madhu·súdana, and the fool believes he has already achieved his aim, for his soul is ignorant. The foolish- 92.10
minded Dhartaráshtra has concluded that Karna is able to defeat his enemies singlehandedly, and so he will not go for peace.

You are striving for peace, hoping for brotherly love between the two parties, Késhava, but be aware that the Dhartaráshtras as a whole have decided not to give the Pándavas what they deserve, and so your advice to them will be futile. Where good or bad counsel amounts to the same thing, slayer of Madhu, a wise man does not talk fruitlessly as though he were singing to the deaf. Speaking to ignorant, wicked fools, Mádhava, would be as improper as a brahmin advising *chandálas*—the very lowest kind of people.
Duryódhana is a fool. He relies on power, and will not make 92.15
use of your advice. The counsel you give him will be given in vain.

It doesn't please me that you will appear in the midst of all those evil-minded men as they sit together, Krishna. It doesn't seem right for you to speak against them in the midst of those numerous wicked-thinking, ill-behaved, and evil-minded men, Krishna. He will not accept what is in his best interest because he has never respected his elders. He

balaṃ balavad apy asya; yadi vakṣyasi, Mādhava,
tvayy asya mahatī śaṅkā, na kariṣyati te vacaḥ.
92.20 ‹n' êdam adya yudhā śakyam Indreṇ' âpi sah' âmaraiḥ›
iti vyavasitāḥ sarve Dhārtarāṣṭrā, Janārdana.
teṣv evam upapanneṣu kāma|krodh'|ânuvartiṣu
samartham api te vākyam a|samarthaṃ bhaviṣyati.
madhye tiṣṭhan hasty|anīkasya mando
rath'|âśva|yuktasya balasya mūḍhaḥ
Duryodhano manyate vīta|bhītiḥ
‹kṛtsnā may" êyaṃ pṛthivī jit" êti.›
āśaṃsate vai Dhṛtarāṣṭrasya putro
mahā|rājyam a|sapatnaṃ pṛthivyām.
tasmiñ śamaḥ kevalo n' ôpalabhyo,
baddhaṃ santaṃ manyate labdham artham.
paryast" êyaṃ pṛthivī kāla|pakvā.
Duryodhan'|ârthe Pāṇḍavān yoddhu|kāmāḥ
samāgatāḥ sarva|yodhāḥ pṛthivyāṃ,
rājānaś ca kṣiti|pālaiḥ sametāḥ,
92.25 sarve c' âite kṛta|vairāḥ purastān
tvayā rājāno hṛta|sārāś ca, Kṛṣṇa,
tav' ôdvegāt saṃśritā Dhārtarāṣṭrān
su|saṃhatāḥ saha Karṇena vīrāḥ.
tyakt'|ātmānaḥ saha Duryodhanena
hṛṣṭā yoddhuṃ Pāṇḍavān sarva|yodhāḥ;
teṣāṃ madhye praviśethā yadi tvaṃ,
na tan mataṃ mama, Dāśārha vīra!

has become foolish on account of the pride he takes in his good fortune, his pride in his youth, and his irascibility.

He also has a powerful army, and if you give him advice, Mádhava, he will be extremely suspicious of you, and
he will not accept your counsel. All the Dhartaráshtras are 92.20
convinced that not even Indra and the gods could defeat their warrior force now, Janárdana. No matter how powerful your words, they will have no power over men with their conviction, led by their desires and anger.

The idiotic fool Duryódhana stands in the midst of his elephant army, a force equipped with chariots and horses, and without a trace of fear he thinks to himself, 'I have defeated the whole world!' Dhrita·rashtra's son expects a mighty kingdom on earth, free of competition. No, complete peace cannot be attained with a man of his sort, who believes that all he owns is secure and that his aim is achieved.

This earth is inverted, and the time has come. All the warriors on earth have gathered, with the kings and the rulers of this world, eager for war against the Pándavas in Duryódhana's cause. All these kings have longstanding quarrels 92.25
with you, for you stole their property, Krishna, and it is because they fear you that these heroes rely on the Dhartaráshtras and are so closely united with Karna. Each and every warrior would forsake his life, happy to fight the Pándavas with Duryódhana, and so, should you enter their midst, hero Dashárha, it would be against my better judgment!

teṣāṃ samupaviṣṭānāṃ bahūnāṃ duṣṭa|cetasām
kathaṃ madhyaṃ prapadyethāḥ śatrūṇāṃ, śatru|karśana?
sarvathā tvaṃ, mahā|bāho, devair api dur|utsahaḥ,
prabhāvaṃ, pauruṣaṃ, buddhiṃ jānāmi tava, śatru|han.
yā me prītiḥ Pāṇḍaveṣu bhūyaḥ sā tvayi, Mādhava,
premṇā ca bahu|mānāc ca sauhṛdāc ca bravīmy aham.
92.30 yā me prītiḥ, puṣkar'|âkṣa, tvad|darśana|samudbhavā
sā kim ākhyāyate tubhyam? antar'|ātm" âsi dehinām.»

ŚRĪ|BHAGAVĀN uvāca:

93.1 YATHĀ BRŪYĀN mahā|prājño, yathā brūyād vicakṣaṇaḥ,
yathā vācyas tvad|vidhena bhavatā mad|vidhaḥ su|hṛt,
dharm'|ârtha|yuktam tathyaṃ ca, yathā tvayy upapadyate,
tathā vacanam ukto 'smi tvay" âitat pitṛ|mātṛvat.
satyaṃ prāptaṃ ca yuktaṃ v" âpy
evam eva yath" āttha mām
śṛṇuṣv' āgamane hetuṃ,
Vidur', âvahito bhava.
daurātmyaṃ Dhārtarāṣṭrasya, kṣatriyāṇāṃ ca vairatām,
sarvam etad ahaṃ jānan, kṣattaḥ, prāpto 'dya Kauravān.
93.5 paryastāṃ pṛthivīṃ sarvāṃ s'|âśvāṃ sa|ratha|kuñjarām
yo mocayen mṛtyupāśāt, prāpnuyād dharmam uttamam.
dharma|kāryaṃ yatañ śaktyā no cet prāpnoti mānavaḥ,
prāpto bhavati tat|puṇyam, atra me n' âsti saṃśayaḥ.
«manasā cintayan pāpaṃ, karmaṇā n' âtirocayan,
na prāpnoti phalaṃ tasy', êty» evaṃ dharma|vido viduḥ.

Why should you go into the midst of your many evil-minded enemies as they sit together, enemy-plower? You are impossible for even the gods to defeat, long-armed man, in every respect, and I am aware of your power, manly prowess, and intelligence, destroyer of your enemies. My affection for the Pándavas matches the affection I feel for you, Mádhava, and I speak with love, out of great esteem
and friendship. But then what is the point of my telling 92.30
you of the love I feel when I see you arrive, lotus-eyed man, since you are the inner soul of embodied creatures?"

THE BLESSED LORD said:

YOU HAVE SPOKEN as an exceptionally wise man, and you 93.1
have spoken as a perceptive man would speak. You have spoken to me as someone like you ought to speak to a friend like me. You have spoken to me in words which comply with moral law and profit and are truthful, just as it is appropriate for you to do. You have spoken to me like a mother or father. What you have said to me is true, serves its purpose well, and is fitting; but listen to the reason for my visit, Vídura, and be attentive.

I arrived here to see the Káuravas today, fully aware of the wickedness of Dhartaráshtra's soul and the hostility of the
warrior kings, steward. But the man who releases the whole 93.5
topsy-turvy earth, with its horses, chariots, and elephants, from the shackles of death would attain to the very highest law. I have no doubt that a man who strives to carry out law with all his ability gains the merit of the law, even if he does not manage to accomplish the task of law itself. Indeed, scholars of moral law know that a man who contemplates

so 'haṃ yatiṣye praśamaṃ, kṣattaḥ, kartum a|māyayā
Kurūṇāṃ Sṛñjayānāṃ ca saṅgrāme vinaśiṣyatām.
s" êyam āpan mahā|ghorā Kuruṣv eva samutthitā
Karṇa|Duryodhana|kṛtā; sarve hy ete tad anvayāḥ.
93.10 vyasane kliśyamānaṃ hi yo mitraṃ n' âbhipadyate
an|arthāya yathā|śakti, taṃ nṛśaṃsaṃ vidur budhāḥ.
ā keśa|grahaṇān mitram a|kāryāt saṃnivartayan
a|vācyaḥ kasya cid bhavati kṛta|yatno yathā|balam.
tat samarthaṃ śubhaṃ vākyaṃ dharm'|ârtha|sahitaṃ hitam
Dhārtarāṣṭraḥ sah'|âmātyo grahītuṃ, Vidur', ârhati.
hitaṃ hi Dhārtarāṣṭrāṇāṃ, Pāṇḍavānāṃ tath" âiva ca,
pṛthivyāṃ kṣatriyāṇāṃ ca yatiṣye 'ham a|māyayā.
hite prayatamānaṃ māṃ śaṅked Duryodhano yadi,
hṛdayasya ca me prītir, ānṛṇyaṃ ca bhaviṣyati.
93.15 jñātīnāṃ hi mitho bhede yan mitraṃ n' âbhipadyate
sarva|yatnena madhya|sthaṃ, na tan mitraṃ vidur budhāḥ.
na māṃ brūyur a|dharmiṣṭhā mūḍhā hy a|suhṛdas tathā,
«śakto n' âvārayat Kṛṣṇaḥ saṃrabdhān Kuru|Pāṇḍavān.»
ubhayoḥ sādhayann artham aham āgata, ity uta
tatra yatnam ahaṃ kṛtvā gaccheyaṃ nṛṣv a|vācyatām.

a wicked act in his mind, but does not follow through with the deed itself, does not attain the ill result of the act.

So, without resorting to deception, I will strive to make
peace, steward, between the Kurus and Srínjayas who are
destined to meet their destruction in battle. This great horrifying calamity is now upon the Kurus, and it is Karna and
Duryódhana who have caused it. All the rest merely follow
those two. The wise understand that someone who does not 93.10
go to the aid of a friend in torment, and does not try to
prevent it with every power he possesses, is indeed cruel.
But no one can blame someone who does everything he
can to prevent a friend from doing something bad, making
every effort, even grabbing him by the hair. Dhartaráshtra
and his ministers ought to accept my advice, Vídura, since
it is effective, pure, beneficial, and conforms to morality
and profit.

I will try my best to accomplish what will benefit the
Dhartaráshtras, the Pándavas, and the kshatriyas on earth,
without using any deception; and if Duryódhana perceives
that I am striving for his benefit, then my heart will be
pleased, and I will be released from my debt. The wise un- 93.15
derstand that a man who does not do everything he can
to help a friend when there is a rift between relatives, but
instead stands in the middle, remaining neutral, is not a
true friend.

I have come here to benefit both sides, and to prevent the most wicked of people, fools, and enemies from talking about me, saying "Krishna did not prevent the furious Kurus and Pándavas even though he had the power to do so." And when I have tried my best in there, I will be

mama dharm'|ârtha|yuktaṃ hi śrutvā vākyam an|āmayam
na ced ādāsyate bālo, diṣṭasya vaśam eṣyati.

a|hāpayan Pāṇḍav'|ârthaṃ yathāvac
chamaṃ Kurūṇāṃ yadi c' ācareyam,
puṇyaṃ ca me syāc caritaṃ, mah"|ātman,
mucyeraṃś ca Kuravo mṛtyu|pāśāt.

93.20 api vācaṃ bhāṣamāṇasya kāvyāṃ,
dharm'|ārāmām, arthavatīm, a|hiṃsrām
avekṣeran Dhārtarāṣṭrāḥ śam'|ârthaṃ,
māṃ ca prāptaṃ Kuravaḥ pūjayeyuḥ,

na c' âpi mama paryāptāḥ sahitāḥ sarva|pārthivāḥ
kruddhasya pramukhe sthātuṃ, siṃhasy' êv' êtare mṛgāḥ!

VAIŚAMPĀYANA uvāca:

ity evam uktvā vacanaṃ Vṛṣṇīnām ṛṣabhas tadā
śayane sukha|saṃsparśe śiśye Yadu|sukh'|āvahaḥ.

VAIŚAMPĀYANA uvāca:

94.1 TATHĀ KATHAYATOR eva tayor buddhimatos tadā
śivā nakṣatra|sampannā sā vyatīyāya śarvarī,
dharm'|ârtha|kāma|yuktāś ca vicitr'|ârtha|pad'|âkṣarāḥ
śṛṇvato vividhā vāco Vidurasya mah"|ātmanaḥ
kathābhir anurūpābhiḥ Kṛṣṇasy' â|mita|tejasaḥ
a|kāmasy' êva Kṛṣṇasya sā vyatīyāya śarvarī.

beyond reproach among men. If that childish man listens to my sound advice, compliant with moral law and profit, but doesn't accept it, then he will become a victim of his own fate.

If I make peace between the Kurus and Pándavas without doing any harm to the latter's cause, then I will have won merit, high-souled man, and I will have freed the Kurus
from the shackles of death. If the Dhartaráshtras take the 93.20
advice I give into consideration—advice which is inspired, important, harmless, and delights in morality—then my aim of peace may be accomplished, and the Kurus will worship me for having come.

Then again, all kings united are not enough to stand against me in battle when I am angry, like deer facing down a lion!

VAISHAMPÁYANA said:

Once he had said this, the bull of the Vrishnis, the bringer of joy to the Yadus, lay down on a couch which was soft to the touch.

VAISHAMPÁYANA continued:

SO IT WAS THAT the auspicious, star-studded night passed 94.1
as those two intelligent men conversed. The night slipped by though Krishna and Vídura were unwilling for it to do so, as Krishna of immeasurable splendor discussed topics consistent with morality, profit, and desire with varied syllables, words, and meanings, and high-souled Vídura listened as he spoke, and replied with similar types of conversation.

tatas tu svara|sampannā bahavaḥ sūta|māgadhāḥ
śaṅkha|dundubhi|nirghoṣaiḥ Keśavaṃ pratyabodhayan.
94.5 tata utthāya Dāśārha ṛṣabhaḥ sarva|Sātvatām
sarvam āvaśyakaṃ cakre prātaḥ|kāryaṃ Janārdanaḥ
kṛt'|ôdak'|ânujapyaḥ sa, hut'|âgniḥ, samalaṃkṛtaḥ
tataś c' ādityam udyantam upātiṣṭhata Mādhavaḥ.

atha Duryodhanaḥ Kṛṣṇaṃ, Śakuniś c' âpi Saubalaḥ
sandhyāṃ tiṣṭhantam abhyetya Dāśārham a|parājitam
ācakṣetāṃ tu Kṛṣṇasya Dhṛtarāṣṭraṃ sabhā|gatam,
Kurūṃś ca Bhīṣma|pramukhān rājñaḥ sarvāṃś ca pārthivān:
«tvām arthayante, Govinda, divi Śakram iv' â|marāḥ.»
tāv abhyanandad Govindaḥ sāmnā parama|valgunā.
94.10 tato vimala āditye brāhmaṇebhyo Janārdanaḥ
dadau hiraṇyaṃ, vāsaṃsi, gāś c' âśvāṃś ca paraṃ|tapaḥ.

visṛjya bahu|ratnāni Dāśārham a|parājitam
tiṣṭhantam upasaṅgamya vavande sārathis tadā.
tato rathena śubhreṇa mahatā kiṅkiṇīkinā
hay'|ôttama|yujā śīghram upātiṣṭhata Dārukaḥ.
tam upasthitam ājñāya rathaṃ divyaṃ mahā|manāḥ
mah"|âbhra|ghana|nirghoṣaṃ sarva|ratna|vibhūṣitam
agniṃ pradakṣiṇaṃ kṛtvā brāhmaṇāṃś ca Janārdanaḥ,
Kaustubhaṃ maṇim āmucya, śriyā paramayā jvalan
94.15 Kurubhiḥ saṃvṛtaḥ Kṛṣṇo Vṛṣṇibhiś c' âbhirakṣitaḥ
ātiṣṭhata rathaṃ Śauriḥ sarva|Yādava|nandanaḥ.

In the morning, many melodious heralds and bards woke Késhava with the blares of conch shells and the booms of kettledrums. Dashárha Janárdana, bull of all Sátvatas, got 94.5
up and went through his morning routine. Once he had washed and whispered mantras, made an offering to the fire, and adorned himself, Mádhava then devoted himself to the rising sun.

Later, Duryódhana and Shákuni Sáubala came up to undefeated Dashárha as he stood before the morning light; and they told Krishna that Dhrita·rashtra had gone to court and that the Kurus, with Bhishma at their helm, and all the kings were there as well: "They are there for your sake, Govínda, just as the immortals in heaven wait for Shakra." Govínda greeted the two men with conciliatory and extremely charming replies. Then, once the sun was bright, Janárdana, 94.10
the scorcher of his enemies, gave gold, clothes, cattle, and horses to the brahmins.

Once he had given away a great deal of wealth, his charioteer, Dáruka, joined undefeated Dashárha where he stood, and greeted him. Then Dáruka quickly approached him with his large gleaming chariot, decorated with little bells and yoked with excellent horses. Knowing that the celestial chariot, which clattered with the roar of a great monsoon thundercloud and was ornamented with every kind of jewel, was ready, Janárdana circled the fire and the brahmins, attached his Káustubha jewel, and then, blazing with supreme glory, Krishna Shauri, the joy of all Yádavas, got 94.15
onto his chariot surrounded by Kurus and protected by Vrishnis.

anvāruroha Dāśārhaṃ Viduraḥ sarva|dharma|vit
sarva|prāṇa|bhṛtāṃ śreṣṭhaṃ, sarva|buddhimatāṃ varam.
tato Duryodhanaḥ Kṛṣṇaṃ, Śakuniś c' âpi Saubalaḥ
dvitīyena rathen' âinam anvayātāṃ paraṃ|tapam.
Sātyakiḥ, Kṛtavarmā ca, Vṛṣṇīnāṃ c' âpare rathāḥ
pṛṣṭhato 'nuyayuḥ Kṛṣṇaṃ gajair aśvai rathair api.
teṣāṃ hema|pariṣkārair yuktāḥ parama|vājibhiḥ
gacchatāṃ ghoṣiṇaś citrā rathā, rājan, virejire.
94.20 saṃmṛṣṭa|saṃsikta|rajaḥ pratipede mahā|patham
rāja'|ṛṣi|caritaṃ kāle Kṛṣṇo dhīmāñ śriyā jvalan.
tataḥ prayāte Dāśārhe prāvādyant' âika|puṣkarāḥ,
śaṅkhāś ca dadhmire tatra, vādyāny anyāni yāni ca.
pravīrāḥ sarva|lokasya yuvānaḥ siṃha|vikramāḥ
parivārya rathaṃ Śaurer agacchanta paraṃ|tapāḥ.
tato 'nye bahu|sāhasrā vicitr'|âdbhuta|vāsasaḥ
asi|prās'|āyudha|dharāḥ Kṛṣṇasy' āsan puraḥ|sarāḥ.
gajāḥ pañca|śatās tatra, rathāś c' āsan sahasraśaḥ;
prayāntam anvayur vīraṃ Dāśārham a|parājitam.
94.25 puraṃ Kurūṇāṃ saṃvṛttaṃ draṣṭu|kāmaṃ Janārdanam
sa|bāla|vṛddhaṃ sa|strīkaṃ rathyā|gatam, arin|dama.
vedikām āśritābhiś ca samākrāntāny an|ekaśaḥ
pracalant' îva bhāreṇa yoṣidbhir bhavanāny uta.
sa pūjyamānaḥ Kurubhiḥ, saṃśṛṇvan madhurāḥ kathāḥ,
yath"|ârhaṃ pratisatkurvan prekṣamāṇaḥ śanair yayau.
tataḥ sabhāṃ samāsādya Keśavasy' ânuyāyinaḥ
sa|śaṅkhair veṇu|nirghoṣair diśaḥ sarvā vyanādayan.

Vídura, a scholar of all law, climbed up after Dashárha, the greatest of all creatures of breath and the foremost of all wise men. Duryódhana and Shákuni Sáubala followed Krishna the enemy-scorcher on a second chariot. And Sátyaki, Krita·varman, and other Vrishnis followed behind Krishna with elephants, horses, and chariots. The decorated cars, yoked with superb horses, rattled as they rolled along and flashed with their golden adornments, my king.

After a while wise Krishna, who blazed with glory, made 94.20
his way to the main road, which was cleared of dust and sprinkled, and upon which royal seers were walking. As Dashárha traveled, cymbals were played, conch shells were blown, and other musical instruments also resounded. Young hero enemy-scorchers from every corner of the world walked around Shauri's chariot, striding like lions. In front of Krishna went many thousands of men in wonderful multicolored outfits, brandishing swords, spears, and other weapons. Following behind the undefeated hero Dashárha, as he went on his way, came five hundred elephants and thousands of chariots.

The Kurus' whole city had come out onto the road, in- 94.25
cluding women, children, and the elderly, and they swarmed around, desperate to catch a glimpse of Janárdana, O enemy-tamer. The grand houses were packed with so many women resting on the balconies that they appeared to be tipping under the weight. Krishna traveled slowly, looking around, being honored by the Kurus, and listening to their charming words, and where it was deserved he returned the

tataḥ sā samitiḥ sarvā rājñām a|mita|tejasām
saṃprākampata harṣeṇa Kṛṣṇ'|āgamana|kāṅkṣayā.
94.30 tato 'bhyāśagate Kṛṣṇe samahṛṣyan nar'|âdhipāḥ
śrutvā taṃ ratha|nirghoṣaṃ parjanya|ninad'|ôpamam.
āsādya tu sabhā|dvāram ṛṣabhaḥ sarva|Sātvatām,
avatīrya rathāc Chauriḥ Kailāsa|śikhar'|ôpamāt,
nava|megha|pratīkāśāṃ jvalantīm iva tejasā
Mahendra|sadana|prakhyāṃ praviveśa sabhāṃ tataḥ.

pāṇau gṛhītvā Viduraṃ Sātyakiṃ ca mahā|yaśāḥ
jyotīṃṣy ādityavad, rājan, Kurūn prācchādayañ śriyā.
agrato Vāsudevasya Karṇa|Duryodhanāv ubhau,
Vṛṣṇayaḥ Kṛtavarmā c' âpy āsan Kṛṣṇasya pṛṣṭhataḥ.
94.35 Dhṛtarāṣṭraṃ puras|kṛtya Bhīṣma|Droṇ'|ādayas tataḥ
āsanebhyo 'calan sarve pūjayanto Janārdanam.
abhyāgacchati Dāśārhe prajñā|cakṣur nar'|ēśvaraḥ
sah' âiva Droṇa|Bhīṣmābhyām udatiṣṭhan mahā|yaśāḥ.
uttiṣṭhati mahā|rāje Dhṛtarāṣṭre jan'|ēśvare
tāni rāja|sahasrāṇi samuttasthuḥ samantataḥ.
āsanaṃ sarvato|bhadraṃ jāmbūnada|pariṣkṛtam
Kṛṣṇ'|ârthe kalpitaṃ tatra Dhṛtarāṣṭrasya śāsanāt.

smayamānas tu rājānaṃ Bhīṣma|Droṇau ca Mādhavaḥ
abhyabhāṣata dharm'|ātmā, rājñaś c' ânyān yathā|vayaḥ.
94.40 tatra Keśavam ānarcuḥ samyag abhyāgataṃ sabhām
rājānaḥ pārthivāḥ sarve, Kuravaś ca Janārdanam.

favor. Then, when he reached the assembly hall, every direction resounded with the sounds of lutes and conch shells from Késhava's entourage.

The whole assembly of immeasureably splendid kings quivered with joy in eager expectation of Krishna's arrival. And as Krishna came closer the kings were thrilled, listening 94.30
to the clatter of his chariot which boomed like a thundercloud. Shauri, the bull of all Sátvatas, approached the door of the assembly and alighted from his chariot as though descending from a peak of Mount Kailása. Then he entered the assembly, which resembled mighty Indra's seat, blazing with splendor and glowing like a new cloud.

The great glorious man took Vídura and Sátyaki by the hand and overshadowed the Kurus with his glory, my king, the way the sun outshines the stars. Karna and Duryódhana went before Vasudéva and the Vrishnis, and Krita·varman followed behind Krishna. Letting Dhrita·rashtra take the 94.35
lead, Bhishma, Drona, and the others all rose from their seats and paid homage to Janárdana. When Dashárha entered, the great glorious king whose only sight was wisdom stood up along with Drona and Bhishma, and when great King Dhrita·rashtra, lord of his people, rose, then so too the thousands of kings stood up on all sides. And there stood an utterly charming and gilt-ornamented throne, set up for Krishna at Dhrita·rashtra's order.

Virtuous-souled Mádhava smiled and greeted the king, Bhishma and Drona, and the other kings in order of age. The Kurus and all the kings on earth paid their respects 94.40
to Késhava Janárdana once he had arrived in court. And as Dashárha the enemy-scorcher and sacker of enemy cities

tatra tiṣṭhan sa Dāśārho rāja|madhye paraṃ|tapaḥ
apaśyad antarikṣa|sthān ṛṣīn para|puraṅ|jayaḥ.
tatas tān abhisaṃprekṣya Nārada|pramukhān ṛṣīn
abhyabhāṣata Dāśārho Bhīṣmaṃ Śāntanavaṃ śanaiḥ:
   «pārthivīṃ samitiṃ draṣṭum ṛṣayo 'bhyāgatā, nṛpa,
nimantryantām āsanaiś ca sat|kāreṇa ca bhūyasā;
n' âiteṣv an|upaviṣṭeṣu śakyaṃ kena cid āsitum.
pūjā prayujyatām āśu munīnāṃ bhāvit'|ātmanām.»
ṛṣīn Śāntanavo dṛṣṭvā sabhā|dvāram upasthitān
94.45 tvaramāṇas tato bhṛtyān «āsanān'! îty» acodayat.
āsanāny atha mṛṣṭāni mahānti vipulāni ca
maṇi|kāñcana|citrāṇi samājahrus tatas tataḥ.

   teṣu tatr' ôpaviṣṭeṣu gṛhīt'|ârgheṣu, Bhārata,
niṣasād' āsane Kṛṣṇo rājānaś ca yath"|āsanam.
Duḥśāsanaḥ Sātyakaye dadāv āsanam uttamam;
Vivimśatir dadau pīṭhaṃ kāñcanaṃ Kṛtavarmaṇe.
a|vidūre tu Kṛṣṇasya Karṇa|Duryodhanāv ubhau
ek'|āsane mah"|ātmānau niṣīdatur a|marṣaṇau.
Gāndhāra|rājaḥ Śakunir Gāndhārair abhirakṣitaḥ
94.50 niṣasād' āsane rājā saha|putro, viśāṃ pate.
Viduro maṇi|pīṭhe tu śukla|spardhy'|âjin'|ôttare
saṃspṛśann āsanaṃ Śaurer mahā|matir upāviśat.

   cirasya dṛṣṭvā Dāśārhaṃ rājānaḥ sarva eva te,
amṛtasy' êva, n' âtṛpyan prekṣamāṇā Janārdanam.
atasī|puṣpa|saṅkāśaḥ pīta|vāsā Janārdanaḥ
vyabhrājata sabhā|madhye hemn' îv' ôpahito maṇiḥ.
tatas tūṣṇīṃ sarvam āsīd Govinda|gata|mānasam;
na tatra kaś cit kiñ cid vā vyājahāra pumān kva cit.

stood in the midst of the kings, he saw sages led by Nárada standing in mid air, and keeping his gaze on those seers he spoke gently to Bhishma, the son of Shántanu, saying:

"My lord, the sages have come to watch this earthly meeting. Let them be offered seats and lavish hospitality, for no one can sit if these sages are not seated. Let honor quickly be paid to the perfect-souled sages." Shántanava saw the
sages standing at the door of the court, so, directing the 94.45
servants, he speedily said "Seats!" and they brought large, spacious thrones, polished and gleaming brightly with gold and jewels.

Once these sages were settled in their seats and had accepted the offerings made to them, Bhárata, Krishna sat on his throne and the kings took their correct places. Duhshásana gave Sátyaki a magnificent chair, and Vivínshati gave Krita·varman a gilt stool. Not far from Krishna, Karna and Duryódhana, those two impatient and great-spirited men, were sharing the same seat. Lord Shákuni, king of the
Gandháras and guarded by Gandháras, took his place with 94.50
his son, lord of earth. Great-minded Vídura sat on a jewel-studded chair spread with the finest white antelope skins, touching Shauri's seat.

All the kings watched Dashárha at length, but they could not satisfy themselves with staring at Janárdana, just as drinkers of ambrosia are never sated. Janárdana, dressed in yellow, resembled flaxen flowers as he sparkled in the middle of the court, as though he were a gem set in gold. Absolute silence fell as the assembly focused their attention upon Govínda; no one anywhere in the hall said a word.

95–96

# THE MEETING BEGINS

VAIŚAMPĀYANA uvāca:

95.1 TEṢV ĀSĪNEṢU sarveṣu
tūṣṇīṃ bhūteṣu rājasu
vākyam abhyādade Kṛṣṇaḥ
su|daṃṣṭro dundubhi|svanaḥ.
jīmūta iva gharm'|ânte sarvāṃ saṃśrāvayan sabhām
Dhṛtarāṣṭram abhiprekṣya samabhāṣata Mādhavaḥ.

ŚRĪ|BHAGAVĀN uvāca:

«Kurūṇāṃ Pāṇḍavānāṃ ca śamaḥ syād iti, Bhārata,
a|praṇāśena vīrāṇām,» etad yācitum āgataḥ.
rājan, n' ânyat pravaktavyaṃ tava naiḥśreyasaṃ vacaḥ;
viditaṃ hy eva te sarvaṃ veditavyam, arin|dama.
95.5 idaṃ hy adya kulaṃ śreṣṭhaṃ sarva|rājasu, pārthiva,
śruta|vṛtt'|ôpasampannaṃ, sarvaiḥ samuditaṃ guṇaiḥ.
kṛp", ânukampā, kāruṇyam, ānṛśaṃsyaṃ ca, Bhārata,
tath" ārjavaṃ, kṣamā, satyaṃ—Kuruṣv etad viśiṣyate.
tasminn evaṃ|vidhe, rājan, kule mahati tiṣṭhati,
tvan|nimittaṃ viśeṣeṇa, n' êha yuktam a|sāmpratam.
tvaṃ hi dhārayitā śreṣṭhaḥ Kurūṇāṃ, Kuru|sattama,
mithyā pracaratāṃ, tāta, bāhyeṣv ābhyantareṣu ca.
te putrās tava, Kauravya, Duryodhana|purogamāḥ
dharm'|ârthau pṛṣṭhataḥ kṛtvā pracaranti nṛśaṃsavat.
95.10 a|śiṣṭā, gata|maryādā, lobhena hṛta|cetasaḥ
sveṣu bandhuṣu mukhyeṣu, tad vettha, puruṣa'|rṣabha.
s" êyam āpan mahā|ghorā Kuruṣv eva samutthitā

VAISHAMPÁYANA continued:

WHEN ALL THE kings were sitting in hushed silence, 95.1
Krishna started to speak, booming like kettledrums,
and his teeth flashed. Mádhava directed his gaze towards
Dhrita·rashtra and spoke so that the whole assembly could
hear, thundering like a stormcloud at the end of the summer heat.

THE BLESSED LORD said:

Bhárata, I came here to beg for peace between the Kurus
and Pándavas without the destruction of heroes. My lord,
there is nothing else that I need tell you for your future happiness, since you are already aware of everything you ought
to know, enemy-tamer. This lineage of yours is currently 95.5
the most noble of all royal families, my king, for it is endowed with learning and good conduct, and augmented by
every virtue.

Compassion, pity, kindness, a lack of cruelty, sincerity, forgiveness, and truth distinguish the Kurus, Bhárata. Impropriety is out of place in a line as great as yours, my king, particularly if perpetrated by you. For you are certainly the best curb upon the Kurus when they behave deceitfully towards outsiders or relatives, my friend and greatest of the Kurus.

Your sons, led by Duryódhana, have turned their backs
on moral law and profit, Kaurávya, and they turn to cruelty. They are ill-disciplined, they have overstepped their 95.10
bounds, and when it comes to the foremost of their own
relatives they are robbed of sense by their greed, bull-like
man, and you know it. There is an awesomely horrifying

upekṣyamāṇā, Kauravya, pṛthivīṃ ghātayiṣyati.
śakyā c' êyaṃ śamayituṃ tvaṃ ced icchasi,† Bhārata,
na duṣ|karo hy atra śamo mato me, Bharata'|rṣabha.
tvayy adhīnaḥ śamo, rājan, mayi c' âiva, viśāṃ pate;
putrān sthāpaya, Kauravya, sthāpayiṣyāmy ahaṃ parān.
ājñā tava hi, rāj'|êndra, kāryā putraiḥ sah' ânvayaiḥ,
hitaṃ balavad apy eṣāṃ tiṣṭhatāṃ tava śāsane.
95.15 tava c' âiva hitaṃ, rājan, Pāṇḍavānām atho hitam
śame prayatamānasya mama śāsana|kāṅkṣiṇaḥ.
svayaṃ niṣphalam ālakṣya saṃvidhatsva, viśām pate,
sahāya|bhūtā Bharatās tav' âiva syur, jan'|ēśvara.
dharm'|ârthayos tiṣṭha, rājan, Pāṇḍavair abhirakṣitaḥ;
na hi śakyās tathā|bhūtā yatnād api, nar'|âdhipa.
na hi tvāṃ Pāṇḍavair jetuṃ
rakṣyamāṇaṃ mah"|ātmabhiḥ
Indro 'pi devaiḥ sahitaḥ
prasaheta, kuto nṛpaḥ!
yatra Bhīṣmaś ca Droṇaś ca Kṛpaḥ Karṇo Viviṃśatiḥ,
Aśvatthāmā Vikarṇaś ca Somadatto 'tha Bāhlikaḥ.
95.20 Saindhavaś ca Kaliṅgaś ca Kāmbojaś ca Sudakṣiṇaḥ.
Yudhiṣṭhiro Bhīmasenaḥ Savyasācī yamau tathā,
Sātyakiś ca mahā|tejā, Yuyutsuś ca mahā|rathaḥ—
ko nu tān viparīt'|ātmā yudhyeta, Bharata'|rṣabha?

catastrophe impending for the Kurus, and if disregarded, Kaurávya, it will destroy the earth.

However, this situation can be calmed if that is what you want, Bhárata, for in my opinion peace is not difficult to achieve, bull of the Bharatas. Peace depends on you, king, and on me, lord of earth. Keep your sons in check, Kaurávya king, and I will restrain your enemies. Your sons and their followers should do what you order, lord of kings, and what's more, it would be extremely beneficial for them to abide by your command.

What benefits you, king, also benefits the Pándavas, and 95.15
they are eagerly awaiting your commands as I strive for peace. Consider this for yourself, lord of earth, and act accordingly. Let the Bharatas become your allies, lord of your people. Abide by moral law and profit, king, protected by the Pándavas, for you are certainly unable to defeat them as you are, lord of men, however much effort you put into it.

Even Indra and the gods would not be able to defeat you, let alone earthly kings, if you were defended by the high-souled Pándavas! Which perverse-souled man would fight against you if you had Bhishma, Drona, Kripa, Karna, Vivínshati, Ashva·tthaman, Vikárna, Soma·datta, Báhlika,
the Sáindhava king, the Kalíngan king, and Sudákshina of 95.20
the Kambójas, as well as Yudhi·shthira, Bhima·sena, Savya·sachin, the twins, great glorious Sátyaki, and the mighty warrior Yuyútsu, O bull of the Bharatas?

lokasy' ēśvaratāṃ bhūyaḥ, śatrubhiś c' âpy a|dhṛṣyatām
prāpsyasi tvam, amitra|ghna, sahitaḥ Kuru|Pāṇḍavaiḥ.
tasya te pṛthivī|pālās tvat|samāḥ, pṛthivī|pate,
śreyāṃsaś c' âiva rājānaḥ sandhāsyante, paran|tapa.
sa tvaṃ putraiś ca pautraiś ca, pitṛbhir bhrātṛbhis tathā,
su|hṛdbhiḥ sarvato guptaḥ sukhaṃ śakṣyasi jīvitum.
95.25 etān eva purodhāya sat|kṛtya ca yathā purā
akhilāṃ bhokṣyase sarvāṃ pṛthivīṃ, pṛthivī|pate.
etair hi sahitaḥ sarvaiḥ Pāṇḍavaiḥ svaiś ca, Bhārata,
anyān vijeṣyase śatrūn; eṣa sv'|ârthas tav' âkhilaḥ.
tair ev' ôpārjitāṃ bhūmiṃ bhokṣyase ca, paran|tapa,
yadi sampatsyase putraiḥ sah' âmātyair, nar'|âdhipa.
samyuge vai, mahā|rāja, dṛśyate su|mahān kṣayaḥ—
kṣaye c' ôbhayato, rājan, kiṃ dharmam anupaśyasi?
Pāṇḍavair nihataiḥ saṅkhye putrair v" âpi mahā|balaiḥ
yad vindethāḥ sukhaṃ, rājaṃs, tad brūhi, Bharata'|rṣabha.
95.30 śūrāś ca hi kṛt'|âstrāś ca sarve yuddh'|âbhikāṅkṣiṇaḥ
Pāṇḍavās tāvakāś c' âiva; tān rakṣa mahato bhayāt.
na paśyema Kurūn sarvān Pāṇḍavāṃś c' âiva saṃyuge,
kṣīṇān ubhayataḥ śūrān, rathino rathibhir hatān.
samavetāḥ pṛthivyāṃ hi rājāno, rāja|sattama,
a|marṣa|vaśam āpannā nāśayeyur imāḥ prajāḥ.
trāhi, rājann, imaṃ lokaṃ, na naśyeyur imāḥ prajāḥ!
tvayi prakṛtim āpanne śeṣaḥ syāt, Kuru|nandana.

You will attain supreme lordship over the world and invincibility from your enemies when you are united with both the Kurus and Pándavas, destroyer of your enemies. The kings of this world who are currently your equals, lord of earth, or even your betters, will then seek alliances with you, enemy-scorcher. Protected on every side by your sons, grandsons, fathers, brothers, and friends, you will be able to live happily.

By putting them first and treating them kindly as you did 95.25
before, you will enjoy the whole earth in its entirety, lord of earth. Indeed, united with the Pándavas as well as your own sons, Bhárata, you will conquer your other enemies; it is entirely to your advantage. You will enjoy the land they will have won for you, enemy-scorcher, if you with your sons and advisors join with them, lord of men.

But if this ends in war, mighty king, then you will see an overwhelming annihilation—an annihilation of both sides, king, and what morality do you see in that? Tell me, sovereign bull of the Bharatas, what happiness you will find when the Pándavas or your own mightily powerful sons are
killed in battle? They are all heroes, the Pándavas and your 95.30
sons, trained in weaponry, who eagerly anticipate war, so protect them from grave danger.

We would no longer see all the Kurus and Pándavas, but rather heroes on both sides diminished in number—chariot warriors killed by chariot warriors in battle. The kings of this earth have assembled, greatest of sovereigns, and having fallen under the power of intolerance, they will destroy mankind. Save this world, king, and prevent mankind from being destroyed! If you return to the normal state of affairs

śuklā, vadānyā, hrīmanta, āryāḥ, puṇy'|âbhijātayaḥ,
anyonya|sacivā, rājaṃs—tān pāhi mahato bhayāt!
95.35 śiven' ême bhūmi|pālāḥ samāgamya paras|param
saha bhuktvā ca pītvā ca pratiyāntu yathā|gṛham,
su|vāsasaḥ sragviṇaś ca sat|kṛtā, Bharata'|ṛṣabha,
a|marṣaṃ ca nirākṛtya vairāṇi ca, paraṃ|tapa.
hārdaṃ yat Pāṇḍaveṣv āsīt prāpte 'sminn āyuṣaḥ kṣaye,
tad eva te bhavatv adya; sandhatsva, Bharata'|ṛṣabha.
bālā vihīnāḥ pitrā te tvay" âiva parivardhitāḥ;
tān pālaya yathā|nyāyaṃ, putrāṃś ca, Bharata'|ṛṣabha.
bhavat" âiva hi rakṣyās te vyasaneṣu viśeṣataḥ;
mā te dharmas tath" âiv' ârtho naśyeta, Bharata'|ṛṣabha.
95.40 āhus tvāṃ Pāṇḍavā, rājann, abhivādya prasādya ca:
«bhavataḥ śāsanād duḥkham anubhūtaṃ sah' ânugaiḥ,
dvā|daś' êmāni varṣāṇi vane nirvyuṣitāni naḥ,
trayo|daśaṃ tath" âjñātaiḥ sa|jane parivatsaram,
‹sthātā naḥ samaye tasmin pit" êti› kṛta|niścayāḥ
n' âhāsma samayaṃ, tāta, tac ca no brāhmaṇā viduḥ.
tasmin naḥ samaye tiṣṭha sthitānāṃ, Bharata'|ṛṣabha,
nityaṃ saṅkleśitā, rājan, sva|rājy'|âṃśaṃ labhemahi.
tvaṃ dharmam arthaṃ sañjānan samyaṅ nas trātum arhasi;
gurutvaṃ bhavati prekṣya bahūn kleśāṃs titikṣmahe.

then the vast majority of mankind will survive, descendant of the Kurus.

Protect these pure, generous, modest, noble, and high-born heroes who are currently allies, king: protect them from grave danger! Let these kings of earth gather together 95.35
with one another in a spirit of kindness, eating and drinking together, and let them return to their homes in exquisite clothes, garlanded and treated well, bull of the Bharatas, so that they put aside their intolerance and quarrels, enemy-scorcher.

Let the love you had for the Pándavas return now that so much of your life has passed, bull of the Bharatas, and ally yourself to them. As children they lost their father, and so it was you who brought them up. Protect them as well as your own sons, bull of the Bharatas, as is right. You ought to protect them, especially in times of disaster, so that your virtue and profit are not destroyed, bull of the Bharatas.

The Pándavas pass on their greetings to you, king, and 95.40
they appease you. They have this to say to you:

"At your command, sir, we and our followers experienced misery for twelve years living in the forest, and during our thirteenth year living unknown in Viráta's community. We have abided by the agreement, for we believed that our father would do the same. The brahmins who were with us know that we did not break our promise, father.

So now abide by our agreement, just as we abided by it, bull of the Bharatas, for we have suffered constantly, king, and we should receive our share of the kingdom. Understanding moral law and profit as you do, you ought to save us, as is fitting. We have looked upon you as our

95.45 sa bhavān mātṛ|pitṛvad asmāsu pratipadyatām.
guror garīyasī vṛttir yā ca śiṣyasya, Bhārata,
vartāmahe tvayi ca tāṃ, tvaṃ ca vartasva nas tathā;
pitrā sthāpayitavyā hi vayam utpatham āsthitāḥ;
saṃsthāpaya pathiṣv asmāṃs, tiṣṭha dharme su|vartmani.»

āhuś c' êmāṃ pariṣadaṃ putrās te, Bharata'|rṣabha:
«dharma|jñeṣu sabhā|satsu n' êha yuktam a|sāmpratam;
yatra dharmo hy a|dharmeṇa, satyaṃ yatr' ân|ṛtena ca
hanyate prekṣamāṇānāṃ, hatās tatra sabhā|sadaḥ.
viddho dharmo hy a|dharmeṇa sabhāṃ yatra prapadyate,
95.50 na c' âsya śalyaṃ kṛntanti, viddhās tatra sabhā|sadaḥ;
dharma etān ārujati yathā nady anukūla|jān.»

ye dharmam anupaśyantas tūṣṇīṃ dhyāyanta āsate
te satyam āhur dharmyaṃ ca, nyāyyaṃ ca, Bharata'|rṣabha.
śakyaṃ kim anyad vaktuṃ te dānād anyaj, jan'|ēśvara?
bruvantu te mahī|pālāḥ sabhāyāṃ ye samāsate.
dharm'|ârthau saṃpradhāry' âiva
yadi satyaṃ bravīmy aham,
pramuñc' êmān mṛtyu|pāśāt
kṣatriyān, puruṣa'|rṣabha!
praśāmya, Bharata|śreṣṭha,
mā manyu|vaśam anvagāḥ.
pitryaṃ tebhyaḥ pradāy' âṃśaṃ
Pāṇḍavebhyo yath" ôcitam,

teacher and suffered numerous hardships. Please treat us 95.45
like a mother or father would. The behavior of a teacher towards his pupils should be very honorable, Bhárata, and we as pupils behave respectfully towards you, our teacher—so treat us properly. If we stray from the correct path, it is assuredly our father who should rein us in; so keep us on the correct paths, and by so doing, stay on the good path of virtue yourself."

Your sons also have this to say to the assembly, bull of the Bharatas: "Inappropriate behavior is not fitting here in an assembly of men who understand moral law. The courtiers who watch while law is destroyed by illegality and truth by deception, are also destroyed. When righteousness is struck
by unrighteousness and comes to the court for help, but the 95.50
courtiers do not tear out the spear, then those very courtiers are also wounded. Moral law uproots them, just as a river uproots the plants growing on its banks."

Sitting in silent thought, they look to the law; they speak the truth, bull of the Bharatas, and it is moral and right. What else could you possibly tell them but that you will grant them their share, lord of your people? Let the kings of earth who are sitting as courtiers in this assembly have their say. If I have given proper consideration to moral law and profit, and if I have spoken the truth, then release these kshatriya warriors from the shackles of death, bull-like man!

Make peace, greatest of the Bharatas, and don't fall prey to your rage. Give the Pándavas their paternal share, as is
right. Then, once your task has been successfully accom- 95.55
plished, enjoy the pleasures of life with your sons, enemy-scorcher. You are aware that Ajáta·shatru always abides by

95.55 tataḥ sa|putraḥ siddh'|ârtho bhuṅkṣva bhogān, paraṃ|tapa.
Ajātaśatruṃ jānīṣe sthitaṃ dharmaṃ satāṃ sadā,
sa|putre tvayi vṛttiṃ ca vartate yāṃ, nar'|âdhipa.
dāhitaś ca nirastaś ca tvām ev' ôpaśritaḥ punaḥ,
Indraprasthaṃ tvay" âiv' âsau sa|putreṇa vivāsitaḥ.
sa tatra vivasan, sarvān vaśam ānīya pārthivān,
tvan|mukhān akarod, rājan, na ca tvām atyavartata.
tasy' âivaṃ vartamānasya Saubalena jihīrṣatā
rāṣṭrāṇi dhana|dhānyaṃ ca, prayuktaḥ param'|ôpadhiḥ.
sa tām avasthāṃ samprāpya, Kṛṣṇāṃ prekṣya sabhā|gatam,
95.60 kṣatra|dharmād a|mey'|ātmā n' âkampata Yudhiṣṭhiraḥ.
aham tu tava teṣāṃ ca śreya icchāmi, Bhārata,
dharmād arthāt sukhāc c' âiva.
mā, rājan, nīnaśaḥ prajāḥ.
an|artham arthaṃ manvāno 'py
arthaṃ c' ân|artham ātmanaḥ,
lobhe 'tiprasṛtān putrān nigṛhṇīṣva, viśāṃ pate.
sthitāḥ śuśrūṣituṃ Pārthāḥ, sthitā yoddhum arin|damāḥ;
yat te pathyatamaṃ, rājaṃs, tasmiṃs tiṣṭha, paraṃ|tapa.

VAIŚAMPĀYANA uvāca:

tad vākyaṃ pārthivāḥ sarve hṛdayaiḥ samapūjayan.
na tatra kaś cid vaktuṃ hi vācaṃ prākrāmad agrataḥ.

VAIŚAMPĀYANA uvāca:

96.1 TASMINN ABHIHITE vākye Keśavena mah"|ātmanā
stimitā hṛṣṭa|romāṇa āsan sarve sabhā|sadaḥ.
«kaś cid uttaram eteṣāṃ vaktuṃ n' ôtsahate pumān,»

the morality of good men, as does his behavior towards you and your sons, lord of men.

The man who was burned and exiled, the man whom you and your sons banished to Indra·prastha, relies upon you again. He brought all the kings under his control and made you their leader while living in Indra·prastha, king, and he did not cross you. Even though he was behaving in this manner, Sáubala employed the worst deceptions against him because he wanted to steal his kingdoms, wealth, and grain. But even when he had fallen into such circumstances,
and when he watched Krishná dragged to court, Yudhi· 95.60
shthira, a man of immeasurable soul, did not budge from his duty as a kshatriya.

I wish the best for you and for them, Bhárata, out of considerations of moral law, profit, and pleasure. Don't destroy your people, king. Lord of earth, hold back your sons who have transgressed their bounds in their greed, believing in their souls that a useless plan is profitable but a profitable plan is useless. The enemy-taming Parthas are ready to obey, but they are also ready to fight; so abide by what is most beneficial to you, enemy-scorching king.

VAISHAMPÁYANA said:

All the kings honored his words in their hearts, but no one stepped forward to give their opinion.

VAISHAMPÁYANA continued:

WHEN HIGH-SOULED Késhava had said this, all the mem- 96.1
bers of the assembly remained motionless, covered with goosebumps. All the kings were thinking to themselves in their minds, "No man would dare to say anything in

iti sarve manobhis te cintayanti sma pārthivāḥ.
tathā teṣu ca sarveṣu tūṣṇīṃ bhūteṣu rājasu
Jāmadagnya idaṃ vākyam abravīt Kuru|saṃsadi,
«imāṃ me s' ôpamāṃ vācaṃ śṛṇu satyām a|śaṅkitaḥ.
tāṃ śrutvā śreya ādatsva, yadi sādhv iti manyase.
96.5 rājā Dambhodbhavo nāma sārvabhaumaḥ pur" âbhavat.
akhilāṃ bubhuje sarvāṃ pṛthivīm, iti naḥ śrutam.
sa sma nityaṃ niś"|âpāye prātar utthāya vīryavān
brāhmaṇān kṣatriyāṃś c' âiva pṛcchann āste mahā|rathaḥ:
‹asti kaś cid viśiṣṭo vā, mad|vidho vā bhaved yudhi,
śūdro, vaiśyaḥ, kṣatriyo vā, brāhmaṇo v" âpi śastra|bhṛt?›
iti bruvann anvacarat sa rājā pṛthivīm imām
darpeṇa mahatā mattaḥ, kañ cid anyam a|cintayan.
taṃ ca vaidyā a|kṛpaṇā, brāhmaṇāḥ sarvato '|bhayāḥ
pratyaṣedhanta rājānaṃ ślāghamānaṃ punaḥ punaḥ.
96.10 niṣidhyamāno 'py a|sakṛt pṛcchaty eva sa vai dvijān.
atimānaṃ śriyā mattaṃ tam ūcur brāhmaṇās tadā
tapasvino mah"|ātmāno veda|pratyaya|darśinaḥ
udīryamāṇaṃ rājānaṃ krodha|dīptā dvijātayaḥ:
‹aneka|jayinau saṃkhye yau vai puruṣa|sattamau,
tayos tvaṃ na samo, rājan, bhavit" âsi kadā cana.›
evam uktaḥ sa rājā tu
punaḥ papraccha tān dvijān:
‹kva tau vīrau? kva|janmānau?
kiṃ|karmāṇau ca? kau ca tau?›

response to that speech." But while all the kings remained silent, the son of Jamad·agni voiced his opinion in the Kuru assembly.

"Listen to this example and be confident about its truth. Then once you have heard it, take what would benefit you most, if you think my advice is good. Long ago there was 96.5
a universal monarch by the name of Dambhódbhava, who enjoyed rule over the whole earth in its entirety, or so tradition tells. The heroic and mighty warrior would always rise in the morning, once the night had passed, and sit asking questions of the brahmins and kshatriyas:

'Is there any man, be he a shudra, a vaishya, a kshatriya, or a brahmin, who is as good a warrior or better than me in battle?' The king traveled the earth repeating this, intoxicated by his enormous pride, without giving a thought to anything else.

The scholarly brahmins all around, who were far from feeble or afraid, tried to prevent the king from boasting repeatedly. However, though he was prohibited from doing 96.10
so, he kept on questioning the twiceborn, overly proud and drunk with his good fortune, and the ascetic, high-souled brahmins, who could see the certainty of the Veda, blazed with fury and replied to that excessively arrogant king, saying: 'King, you will never match either of the two most excellent victors in numerous battles.' When he was told this, the king again questioned the brahmins, saying: 'Where are these two heroes? Where were they born? What did they do? Who are they?'

BRĀHMAṆĀ ūcuḥ:

Naro Nārāyaṇaś c' âiva tāpasāv iti naḥ śrutam
āyātau mānuṣe loke; tābhyāṃ yudhyasva, pārthiva.
96.15 śrūyete tau mah"|ātmānau Nara|Nārāyaṇāv ubhau
tapo ghoram a|nirdeśyaṃ tapyete Gandhamādane.

sa rājā mahatīṃ senāṃ yojayitvā ṣaḍ|aṅginīm
a|mṛṣyamāṇaḥ saṃprāyād yatra tāv a|parājitau.
sa gatvā viṣamaṃ ghoraṃ parvataṃ Gandhamādanam
mṛgayāṇo 'vagacchat tau tāpasau vanam āśritau.
tau dṛṣṭvā kṣut|pipāsābhyāṃ kṛśau, dhamani|santatau,
śīta|vāt'|ātapaiś c' âiva karśitau puruṣ'|ôttamau,
abhigamy' ôpasaṅgṛhya paryapṛcchad an|āmayam.
tam arcitvā mūla|phalair, āsanen' ôdakena ca;
96.20 nyamantrayetāṃ rājānaṃ: ‹kiṃ kāryaṃ kriyatām iti?›

tatas tām ānupūrvīṃ sa punar ev' ânvakīrtayat:
‹bāhubhyām me jitā bhūmir, nihatāḥ sarva|śatravaḥ.
bhavadbhyāṃ yuddham ākāṅkṣann upayāto 'smi parvatam.
ātithyaṃ dīyatām etat, kāṅkṣitaṃ me ciraṃ prati.›

NARA|NĀRĀYAṆAV ūcatuḥ:

apeta|krodha|lobho 'yam āśramo, rāja|sattama.
na hy asminn āśrame yuddhaṃ; kutaḥ śastraṃ kuto 'n|ṛjuḥ

THE BRAHMINS replied:

They are Nara and Naráyana, both ascetics, according to our information, who have come to the human world. Fight them, king. Rumor has it that both high-souled Nara and 96.15
Naráyana are practicing indescribably horrific asceticism on Mount Gandha·mádana.

So the king drew up an enormous six-winged army, and, unable to tolerate their superiority, he set out for the place where those two undefeated heroes were staying. He went to the jagged and horrifying Mount Gandha·mádana, and as he hunted for them he found the two ascetics living in the forest. Seeing that the two most excellent men were emaciated from hunger and thirst, that their veins were popping out, and that they were tormented by heat and by the cold winds, he went up to them, took hold of their feet, and enquired after their health. In return they honored him with roots and fruit, a seat, and water; then they called to the 96.20
king, saying: 'What may we do for you?'

So in reply he told them the phrase he repeated time and again: 'I have conquered the earth by my arms, I have killed all my enemies, and I have come to this mountain hoping to fight against you. Grant me this favor as an act of hospitality, for I have been eagerly anticipating it for a long time now.'

NARA AND NARÁYANA replied:

Greatest of kings, anger and greed are cast out from this hermitage. There is certainly no fighting in this hermitage. Where would one find weapons or anything wicked here?

anyatra yuddham ākāṅkṣa; bahavaḥ kṣatriyāḥ kṣitau.

RĀMA uvāca:

ucyamānas tath" âpi sma bhūya ev' âbhyabhāṣata
punaḥ punaḥ kṣamyamāṇaḥ sāntvyamānaś ca, Bhārata,
96.25 Dambhodbhavo yuddham icchann āhvayaty eva tāpasau.
tato Naras tv iṣīkāṇāṃ muṣṭim ādāya, Bhārata,
abravīd, ‹ehi, yudhyasva, yuddha|kāmuka kṣatriya!
sarva|śastrāṇi c' ādatsva, yojayasva ca vāhinīm.
ahaṃ hi te vineṣyāmi yuddha|śraddhām itaḥ param!›

DAMBHODBHAVA uvāca:

yady etad astram asmāsu yuktaṃ, tāpasa, manyase,
eten' âpi tvayā yotsye, yuddh'|ârthī hy aham āgataḥ.

RĀMA uvāca:

ity uktvā śara|varṣeṇa sarvataḥ samavākirat
Daṃbhodhbhavas tāpasaṃ taṃ jighāṃsuḥ saha|sainikaḥ.
tasya tān asyato ghorān iṣūn para|tanu|cchidaḥ
96.30 kad|arthī|kṛtya sa munir iṣīkābhiḥ samārpayat.
tato 'smai prāsṛjad ghoram aiṣīkam a|parājitaḥ
astram a|pratisandheyaṃ. tad adbhutam iv' âbhavat;
teṣām akṣīṇi, karṇāṃś ca, nāsikāś c' âiva māyayā
nimitta|vedhī sa munir iṣīkābhiḥ samārpayat.

Expect battle elsewhere, for there are many kshatriyas on earth.

RAMA said:

Even though he was refused in this manner, he pestered them a great deal, and though they excused themselves and soothed him repeatedly, Bhárata, Dambhódbhava re- 96.25
mained keen to fight, and challenged the pair of ascetics. And so Nara took a fistful of reeds, Bhárata, and said: 'Come on, then! Fight, you battle-crazed warrior! Take up all your weapons and draw up your army. I will indeed strip you of your confidence in battle forever!'

DAMBHÓDBHAVA replied:

If you believe that is a suitable weapon to use against us, ascetic, then I will fight you, for I did indeed come here with battle as my aim.

RAMA continued:

Having said this, Dambhódbhava showered him on all
sides with a shower of arrows, for he wished to kill the 96.30
ascetic with his army. The sage disposed of Dambhódbhava's horrific enemy-tearing arrows with his reeds, rendering them futile, and then the undefeated ascetic launched his horrifying and invincible reed-weapon at the king. What followed next was almost supernatural. The sage, with a perfect aim for his target, hit the army's eyes, ears, and noses with his reeds, by means of his magic.

sa dṛṣṭvā śvetam ākāśam iṣīkābhiḥ samācitam,
pādayor nyapatad rājā, ‹svasti me 'stv, iti› c' âbravīt.
tam abravīn Naro, rājañ, śaraṇyaḥ śaraṇ'|âiṣiṇām:
‹brahmaṇyo bhava dharm'|ātmā,
mā ca sm' âivaṃ punaḥ kṛthāḥ.
n' âitādṛk puruṣo, rājan,
kṣatra|dharmam anusmaran
96.35 manasā, nṛpa|śārdūla, bhavet para|purañ|jayaḥ,
mā ca darpa|samāviṣṭaḥ kṣepsīḥ kāṃś cit kathañ cana,
alpīyāṃsaṃ viśiṣṭaṃ vā tat te, rājan, samāhitam.
kṛta|prajño, vīta|lobho, nirahaṃkāra, ātmavān,
dāntaḥ, kṣānto, mṛduḥ, saumyaḥ prajāḥ pālaya, pārthiva.
mā sma bhūyaḥ kṣipeḥ kañ cid a|viditvā bal'|âbalam.
anujñātaḥ svasti gaccha m" âivaṃ bhūyaḥ samācareḥ
kuśalaṃ brāhmaṇān pṛccher āvayor vacanād bhṛśam.›
tato rājā tayoḥ pādāv abhivādya mah"|ātmanoḥ
pratyājagāma sva|puraṃ, dharmaṃ c' âiv' ācarad bhṛśam.
96.40 su|mahac c' âpi tat karma yan Nareṇa kṛtaṃ purā,
tato guṇaiḥ su|bahubhiḥ śreṣṭho Nārāyaṇo 'bhavat.
tasmād yāvad dhanuḥ|śreṣṭhe Gāṇḍīve 'straṃ na yujyate,
tāvat tvaṃ mānam utsṛjya gaccha, rājan, Dhanañjayam.
Kākudīkaṃ, Śukaṃ, Nākam,
Akṣisantarjanaṃ tathā,
Saṃtānaṃ, Nartakaṃ, Ghoram,
Āsyamodakam aṣṭamaṃ—
etair viddhāḥ sarva eva maraṇaṃ yānti mānavāḥ.
kāma|krodhau, lobha|mohau, mada|mānau tath" âiva ca,

When the king saw the sky turned white with reed-weapons, he fell at the ascetic's feet and said, 'May I be blessed!' Nara, a refuge for those who long for protection, replied to him, my king, saying:

'Be friendly to brahmins and righteous in your soul. Do 96.35
not do this again. Tiger-like sovereign, a sacker of cities keeps his warrior duties in mind and should not be a man such as you. Don't ever abuse someone when puffed up with pride, regardless of whether he is better or worse than you—or that's what you'll deserve, king.

Perfect your wisdom, dispense with greed, do not be selfish, have some self-discipline, be generous, forgiving, gentle, safe, and protect your subjects, king. Don't check for anyone's strength or weakness or insult anyone again. Go with our leave and blessing, but don't act like this anymore. At our particular command, ask after the brahmins' health.'

So the king saluted the feet of those high-souled ascetics, and, returning to his own city, he practiced law incessantly.

It was an enormous achievement that Nara accomplished 96.40
so long ago, but his numerous virtues ensured that Naráyana surpassed even him. Therefore, let go of your pride, king, and go to Dhanan·jaya before he attaches a missile to Gandíva, the greatest bow, such as the missiles Kakudíka, Shuka, Naka, Akshi·santárjana, Santána, Nártaka, Ghora, and Asya·módaka as his eighth. Every man pierced by these weapons dies, but when named in succession the weapons also correspond to sins such as lust, anger, greed, folly, pride, arrogance, envy, and selfishness. When struck by these, men writhe about frantically, going out of their

mātsary'|âhaṅ|kṛtī c' âiva kramād eta udāhṛtāḥ.
unmattāś ca viceṣṭante naṣṭa|saṃjñā vicetasaḥ,
96.45 svapanti ca, plavante ca, cchardayanti ca mānavāḥ,
mūtrayante ca satataṃ, rudanti ca hasanti ca.

nirmātā sarva|lokānām īśvaraḥ sarva|karma|vit
yasya Nārāyaṇo bandhur, Arjuno duḥ|saho yudhi.
kas tam utsahate jetuṃ triṣu lokeṣu, Bhārata,
vīraṃ kapi|dhvajaṃ Jiṣṇuṃ? yasya n' âsti samo yudhi.
a|saṃkhyeyā guṇāḥ Pārthe; tad|viśiṣṭo Janārdanaḥ.
tvam eva bhūyo jānāsi Kuntī|putraṃ Dhanañjayam;
Nara|Nārāyaṇau yau tau, tāv ev' Ârjuna|Keśavau
vijānīhi, mahā|rāja, pravīrau puruṣ'|ôttamau.
96.50 yady etad evaṃ jānāsi, na ca māṃ abhiśaṅkase,
āryāṃ matiṃ samāsthāya śāmya, Bhārata, Pāṇḍavaiḥ.
atha cen manyase, ‹śreyo na me bhedo bhaved iti,›
praśāmya, Bharata|śreṣṭha, mā ca yuddhe manaḥ kṛthāḥ.
bhavatāṃ ca, Kuru|śreṣṭha, kulaṃ bahu|mataṃ bhuvi.
tat tath" âiv' âstu! bhadraṃ te, sv'|ârtham ev' ôpacintaya.»

minds, with their wits destroyed. They sleep, jump around, 96.45
vomit, urinate, or cry and laugh incessantly.

Árjuna, whose friend is Naráyana, the lord and creator of all worlds who knows every action, is impossible to withstand in battle. Who in the three worlds would be able to defeat that monkey-bannered hero Jishnu, Bhárata? No one is his match in battle. Partha's virtues are incalculable, though Janárdana excels him. You yourself know him well as Dhanan·jaya, the son of Kunti, but you should realize that Árjuna and Késhava, those supreme heroes, are really Nara and Naráyana, great king.

If you understand this and do not have your doubts 96.50
about me, then come to a noble decision and make peace with the Pándavas, Bhárata. If you believe it is better that there be no division between you, then make peace, greatest of the Bharatas, and don't set your mind on war. Your line is highly respected on earth, best of the Kurus. May it remain so! Bless you, consider what is in your best interest."

97–105

# THE TALE OF MÁTALI

VAIŚAMPĀYANA uvāca:

97.1 JĀMADAGNYA|VACAḤ śrutvā Kaṇvo 'pi bhagavān ṛṣiḥ
Duryodhanam idaṃ vākyam abravīt Kuru|saṃsadi:

KAṆVA uvāca:

a|kṣayaś c' â|vyayaś c' âiva Brahmā loka|pitāmahaḥ
tath" âiva bhagavantau tau Nara|Nārāyaṇāv ṛṣī.
Ādityānāṃ hi sarveṣāṃ Viṣṇur ekaḥ sanātanaḥ,
a|kṣayyaś c' â|vyayaś c' âiva śāśvataḥ prabhur īśvaraḥ.
nimitta|maraṇāś c' ânye: candra|sūryau, mahī, jalam,
vāyur, agnis, tath" ākāśaṃ, grahās, tārā|gaṇās tathā,
97.5 te ca kṣay'|ânte jagato hitvā loka|trayaṃ sadā
kṣayaṃ gacchanti vai sarve, sṛjyante ca punaḥ punaḥ.
muhūrta|maraṇās tv anye: mānuṣā, mṛga|pakṣiṇaḥ,
tairyagyonyaś ca ye c' ânye jīva|loka|carās tathā.
bhūyiṣṭhena tu rājānaḥ śriyaṃ bhuktv" āyuṣaḥ kṣaye
taruṇāḥ pratipadyante bhoktuṃ sukṛta|duṣkṛtam.

sa bhavān Dharma|putreṇa śamaṃ kartum ih' ârhati.
Pāṇḍavāḥ Kuravaś c' âiva pālayantu vasun|dharām.
«balavān aham, ity» eva na mantavyaṃ, Suyodhana,
balavanto balibhyo hi dṛśyante, puruṣa'|rṣabha.
97.10 na balaṃ balināṃ madhye balaṃ bhavati, Kaurava,
balavanto hi te sarve Pāṇḍavā deva|vikramāḥ.

VAISHAMPÁYANA continued:

HAVING LISTENED TO what Jamad·agni's son had to say, 97.1
the blessed sage Kanva also spoke to Duryódhana in
the Kuru assembly.

KANVA said:

Brahma, the world's grandfather, is indestructible and
deathless, and so are that pair of sages, the blessed Nara
and Naráyana. Assuredly, Vishnu is the only one of all the
Adítyas who is eternal, indestructible, and everlasting. He
is the never-ending lord and master. But others, such as
the sun and moon, the earth, water, wind, fire, space, planets, and constellations of stars, are all bound to die. At the 97.5
time of final destruction they always abandon the universe
and the three worlds, going to their end, but they all re-
generate time and again. Others, such as men, animals, and
birds, and indeed all creatures that walk the world of the living, have fleeting lifespans. Kings, having generally enjoyed
their good fortune, begin again at the ends of their lives,
reborn to reap the rewards of their good and bad deeds.

You ought to make peace with the son of Dharma, and
let the Pándavas and Kurus protect the world together. You
should not consider yourself powerful, Suyódhana, for people can always be found who turn out to be more powerful than those previously considered mighty, bull-like man.
Mere physical power in the midst of the powerful is not 97.10
true power, Káurava. All the Pándavas are truly powerful,
for they have the prowess of gods.

atr' âpy udāharant' îmam itihāsaṃ purātanam
Mātaler dātu|kāmasya kanyāṃ mṛgayato varam.
matas tri|loka|rājasya Mātalir nāma sārathiḥ.
tasy' âik" âiva kule kanyā, rūpato loka|viśrutā.
Guṇakeś" îti vikhyātā nāmnā sā deva|rūpiṇī,
śriyā ca vapuṣā c' âiva striyo 'nyāḥ s" âtiricyate.
tasyāḥ pradāna|samayaṃ Mātaliḥ saha bhāryayā
jñātvā vimamṛśe, rājaṃs, tat|paraḥ paricintayan.
97.15 «dhik khalv a|laghu|śīlānām, ucchritānāṃ, yaśasvinām
narāṇāṃ mṛdu|satvānāṃ kule kanyā|prarohaṇam!
mātuḥ kulaṃ, pitṛ|kulaṃ, yatra c' âiva pradīyate—
kula|trayaṃ saṃśayitaṃ kurute kanyakā satām.
deva|mānuṣa|lokau dvau mānuṣeṇ' âiva cakṣuṣā
avagāhy' âiva vicitau, na ca me rocate varaḥ.»

KAṆVA said:

na devān, n' âiva Diti|jān, na gandharvān, na mānuṣān
arocayad vara|kṛte, tath" âiva bahulān ṛṣīn.
bhāryay" ânu sa saṃmantrya saha rātrau Sudharmayā
Mātalir nāga|lokāya cakāra gamane matim.
97.20 «na me deva|manuṣyeṣu Guṇakeśyāḥ samo varaḥ
rūpato dṛśyate kaś cin. nāgeṣu bhavitā dhruvam.»
ity āmantrya Sudharmāṃ sa, kṛtvā c' âbhipradakṣiṇam
kanyāṃ śirasy upāghrāya praviveśa mahī|talam.

It is on this subject that people quote the ancient tale of Mátali, who was looking for a suitor to whom he could willingly give his daughter.

Indra, king of the three worlds, had a charioteer named Mátali, whom he held in high regard. And in Mátali's line was born a girl whose beauty was famed throughout the world. The celestially bewitching girl was known by the name of Guna·keshi, and she outshone other women in her beauty and loveliness. Realizing that the time had come for her to be given away in marriage, Mátali and his wife pondered and considered the matter intensely, my king.

"A curse on daughters who grow up in the lineages of 97.15
powerful, famous, and moderate-natured men of serious conduct! The daughter of good people endangers three families: her mother's, her father's, and the family to which she is given. I have scanned the worlds of both gods and men with my mind's eye, but I have found no one who pleases me as a suitor."

KANVA said:

None of the gods, Daityas, *gandhárvas*, men, or even one of the many sages pleased him as a potential suitor. So, that night, Mátali consulted with his wife Sudhárma and made
up his mind to go to the world of the snakes. Thinking "I 97.20
have seen no potential suitor to match my Guna·keshi in beauty among gods or men, but surely there will be someone among the snakes," he said goodbye to Sudhárma, circled her, kissed his daughter's head, and entered the surface of the earth.

KAṆVA uvāca:

98.1 MĀTALIS TU VRAJAN mārge Nāradena maha”|rṣiṇā
Varuṇaṃ gacchatā draṣṭuṃ samāgacchad yadṛcchayā.
Nārado ’th’ âbravīd enaṃ: «kva bhavān gantum udyataḥ?
svena vā, sūta, kāryeṇa, śāsanād vā Śata|kratoḥ?»
Mātalir Nāraden’ âivaṃ saṃpṛṣṭaḥ pathi gacchatā
yathāvat sarvam ācaṣṭa sva|kāryaṃ Nāradaṃ prati.
tam uvāc’ âtha sa munir, «gacchāvaḥ sahitāv iti.
salil’|ēśa|didṛkṣ”|ârtham aham apy udyato divaḥ;
98.5 ahaṃ te sarvam ākhyāsye darśayan vasudhā|talam.
dṛṣṭvā tatra varaṃ kañ cid rocayiṣyāva, Mātale.»
avagāhya tu tau bhūmim ubhau Mātali|Nāradau
dadṛśāte mah”|ātmānau loka|pālam apāṃ patim.
tatra deva’|ṛṣi|sadṛśīṃ pūjāṃ sa prāpa Nāradaḥ,
Mahendra|sadṛśīṃ c’ âiva Mātaliḥ pratyapdyata.
tāv ubhau prīta|manasau kāryavantau nivedya ha
Varuṇen’ âbhyanujñātau nāga|lokaṃ viceratuḥ.
Nāradaḥ sarva|bhūtānām antar|bhūmi|nivāsinām
jānaṃś cakāra vyākhyānaṃ yantuḥ sarvam a|śeṣataḥ.

NĀRADA uvāca:

98.10 dṛṣṭas te Varuṇaḥ, sūta, putra|pautra|samāvṛtaḥ;
paśy’ ôdaka|pateḥ sthānaṃ sarvato|bhadram ṛddhimat.
eṣa putro mahā|prajño Varuṇasy’ êha go|pateḥ,
eṣa vai śīla|vṛttena śaucena ca viśiṣyate.
eṣo ’sya putro ’bhimataḥ Puṣkaraḥ puṣkar’|ēkṣaṇaḥ,

KANVA continued:

As MÁTALI WENT on his journey, quite by chance he came across the great sage Nárada, who was on his way to visit Váruna. Nárada asked him: "Where are you set on going, sir? Are you on a mission of your own, charioteer, or carrying out the orders of the god of a hundred sacrifices?" Questioned in this manner by Nárada as he was going on his way, Mátali duly told Nárada all about his task. So the sage replied, "Let's go together. I have also left heaven in order to see the lord of the waters, and I will explain everything while I show you the world beneath the surface of the earth. When we see a suitor there, we will both approve him, Mátali." 98.1 98.5

So the two heaven-dwellers both dived into the earth, and high-souled Mátali and Nárada saw the lord of the waters, the defender of the world. Nárada received the honor due to a celestial sage, and Mátali received honor worthy of great Indra. In good spirits, they both explained their task, and so, with Váruna's leave, they traveled through the world of the snakes. As they went, Nárada gave Mátali a complete and thorough account of every creature that lived within the earth, since he knew them all.

NÁRADA said:

You have seen Váruna surrounded by his sons and grand- 98.10
sons, charioteer; now gaze at the lord of water's home, so thoroughly blessed and wealthy. This person here excels in good conduct and purity, and is the highly intelligent son of Váruna, lord of waters. Váruna loves this son here, lotus-eyed, stunningly handsome Púshkara, whom Soma's

rūpavān darśanīyaś ca, Soma|putryā vṛtaḥ patiḥ.
Jyotsnākāl" îti yām āhur dvitīyāṃ rūpataḥ Śriyam,
Adityāś c' âiva yaḥ putro jyeṣṭhaḥ śreṣṭhaḥ kṛtaḥ smṛtaḥ.

bhavanaṃ paśya Vāruṇyaṃ yad etat sarva|kāñcanam,
yat prāpya suratāṃ prāptāḥ surāḥ, sura|pateḥ sakhe.
98.15 etāni hṛta|rājyānāṃ daiteyānāṃ sma, Mātale,
dīpyamānāni dṛśyante sarva|praharaṇāny uta.
a|kṣayāṇi kil' âitāni vivartante sma, Mātale,
anubhāva|prayuktāni surair avajitāni ha.

atra rākṣasa|jātyaś ca Daitya|jātyaś ca, Mātale,
divya|praharaṇāś c' āsan pūrva|daivata|nirmitāḥ.
agnir eṣa mah"|ârciṣmāñ jāgarti Vāruṇe hrade.
Vaiṣṇavaṃ cakram āviddhaṃ vidhūmena haviṣmatā.
eṣa gāṇḍī|mayaś cāpo loka|saṃhāra|saṃbhṛtaḥ
rakṣyate daivatair nityaṃ, yatas tad Gāṇḍivaṃ dhanuḥ.
98.20 eṣa kṛtye samutpanne tat tad dhārayate balam
sahasra|śata|saṃkhyena prāṇena satataṃ dhruvaḥ.

a|śāsyān api śāsty eṣa rakṣo|bandhuṣu rājasu
sṛṣṭaḥ prathamajo daṇḍo† Brahmaṇā brahma|vādinā.
etac chatraṃ nar'|êndrāṇāṃ mahac Chakreṇa bhāsitam
putrāḥ salila|rājasya dhārayanti mah"|ôdayam.
etat salila|rājasya cchatraṃ chatra|gṛhe sthitam
sarvataḥ salilaṃ śītaṃ jīmūta iva varṣati.

daughter chose as her husband. She is called Jyotsna·kali, and people say that she is a second Shri in beauty. It is even reported that she first chose Áditi's eldest and greatest son as her husband before Púshkara.

Just look at that palace, made entirely of gold, and full of Váruni wine—it was by acquiring this wine that the gods became the gods, O friend of the lord of the gods. All these 98.15
blazing weapons that one sees here, Mátali, belonged to the Daityas who lost their kingdom. They still exist because they are in fact indestructible, Mátali; and now that they have been won by the gods, they require great strength of mind to use.

It was here that communities of *rákshasas* and Daityas who had divine weapons once lived, but they were defeated by the gods long ago. Here is the resplendent fire which stays awake in Váruna's sea, and here is Vishnu's discus, pierced by smokeless fire. Here we have the rhinoceros-horn bow that's wielded for the destruction of the world, that's eternally protected by the gods, and from which Árjuna's bow takes the name Gandíva.* When the occasion requir- 98.20
ing it comes, this bow wields the power of a hundred thousand life-breaths, unchanging and forever.

This is the first staff, made by Brahma who spoke the Vedas, which punishes kings who have been otherwise unpunished when they ally themselves to *rákshasas*. This thing here is the huge parasol of lords of men, made brilliant by Shakra; a parasol of great fortune which the sons of the king of the waters carry. Here, in the umbrella stand, is the water-king's umbrella, which rains cold water all around like a stormcloud. The water which falls from this umbrella

etac chatrāt paribhraṣṭaṃ salilaṃ soma|nirmalam
tamasā mūrchitaṃ bhāti, yena n' ārchati darśanam.
98.25 bahūny adbhuta|rūpāṇi draṣṭavyān' îha, Mātale,
tava kāry'|âvarodhas tu, tasmād gacchāva mā ciram.

NĀRADA uvāca:

99.1 ETAT TU NĀGA|LOKASYA nābhi|sthāne sthitaṃ puram
Pātālam iti vikhyātaṃ Daitya|Dānava|sevitam.
idam adbhiḥ samaṃ prāptā ye ke cid bhuvi jaṅgamāḥ,
praviśanto mahā|nādaṃ nadanti bhaya|pīḍitāḥ.
atr' âsuro 'gniḥ satataṃ dīpyate vāri|bhojanaḥ
vyāpāreṇa dhṛt'|ātmānaṃ nibaddhaṃ samabudhyata.
atr' âmṛtaṃ suraiḥ pītvā nihitaṃ nihat'|âribhiḥ;
ataḥ somasya hāniś ca vṛddhiś c' âiva pradṛśyate.
99.5 atr' Âdityo haya|śirāḥ kāle parvaṇi parvaṇi
uttiṣṭhati suvarṇ'|ākhyaṃ vāgbhir āpūrayañ jagat.
yasmād alaṃ samastās tāḥ patanti jala|mūrtayaḥ,
tasmāt Pātālam ity eva khyāyate puram uttamam.
Airāvaṇo 'smāt salilaṃ gṛhītvā jagato hitaḥ
megheṣv āmuñcate śītaṃ, yan Mahendraḥ pravarṣati.
atra nānā|vidh'|ākārās timayo n' âika|rūpiṇaḥ
apsu soma|prabhāṃ pītvā vasanti jala|cāriṇaḥ.
atra sūry'|âṃśubhir bhinnāḥ Pātāla|talam āśritāḥ
mṛtā hi divase, sūta, punar jīvanti vai niśi.
99.10 udayan nityaśaś c' âtra candramā raśmi|bāhubhiḥ
amṛtaṃ spṛśya saṃsparśāt sañjīvayati dehinaḥ.

is as brilliantly pure as the moon, but it is smothered by gloom, and so though it gleams it cannot be seen. There are 98.25
numerous wondrous things to be seen here, Mátali, but it would hinder our business, so let's move on without delay.

NÁRADA continued:

THE CITY KNOWN as Patála, inhabited by Daityas and Dá- 99.1
navas, stands here at the navel of the world of the snakes. Any animate creatures on earth which reach it, brought by the waters, howl and screech loudly as they enter, tormented by terror. Here is the *ásura* fire which blazes eternally, consuming the waters; but it understands that it is bound and restrained by its activity. It was here that the gods drank immortal ambrosia when they had killed their enemies, and here that they then placed it, and so this is the place from which the waxing and waning of the moon are
visible. This is the place where horse-headed Vishnu,* son 99.5
of Áditi, rises at every auspicious moment of time and fills the "golden" universe with mantras.

This most excellent city is called Patála because all forms of water, such as the moon and others, fall in this region.* It is here that Airávata, beneficial to the universe, drinks his water, and sprays it up onto the clouds from where great Indra rains the cool water down again. Various species of diversely shaped fabulous sea creatures live in the waters here; aquatic beasts, drinking brilliant moonbeams. Creatures that live here in Patála die in the daytime, pierced by the sun's rays; but they live again at night, charioteer.

atra te ’|dharma|niratā baddhāḥ kālena pīḍitāḥ
Daiteyā nivasanti sma Vāsavena hṛta|śriyaḥ.
atra Bhūtapatir nāma sarva|bhūta|mah”|ēśvaraḥ
bhūtaye sarva|bhūtānām acarat tapa uttamam.
atra go|vratino viprāḥ sv’|âdhyāy’|āmnāya|karśitāḥ
tyakta|prāṇā jita|svargā nivasanti maha”|rṣayaḥ
yatra|tatra|śayo nityaṃ, yena kena cid āśitaḥ,
yena kena cid ācchannaḥ sa go|vrata ih’ ôcyate.
99.15 Airāvaṇo nāga|rājo, Vāmanaḥ, Kumudo, ’ñjanaḥ
prasūtāḥ Supratīkasya vaṃśe vāraṇa|sattamāḥ
paśya yady atra te kaś cid rocate guṇato varaḥ
varayiṣyāmi taṃ gatvā yatnam āsthāya, Mātale.
aṇḍam etaj jale nyastaṃ dīpyamānam iva śriyā
ā prajānāṃ nisargād vai n’ ôdbhidyati na sarpati.
n’ âsya jātiṃ nisargaṃ vā kathyamānaṃ śṛṇomi vai,
pitaraṃ mātaraṃ c’ âpi n’ âsya jānāti kaś cana.
ataḥ kila mahān agnir anta|kāle samutthitaḥ
dhakṣyate, Mātale, sarvaṃ trailokyaṃ sa|car’|âcaram.

For every night, when the moon rises with its many moonbeams, it touches the immortal ambrosia, and it is because of that touch that the embodied creatures live once more. 99.10

The Daityas who delight in immorality live here too, bound and oppressed by time, now that Vásava has taken away their good fortune. It was here that the mighty lord of all creatures, called Bhuta·pati, practiced the most extreme acts of asceticism for the wellbeing of all creatures. Here too live the brahmins who have become emaciated through severe study and recitation of the Veda, who follow the cattle vows; great sages who abandoned their lives, but won heaven. A man is said to practice the vow of a cow when he always lies down wherever he pleases, eats anything, and covers himself with anything. Airávata, the lord 99.15
of elephants, as well as Vámana, Kúmuda, and Ánjana, most distinguished elephants, were born here in the lineage of Supratíka.

Look around. If anyone here pleases you as a suitably virtuous potential suitor, Mátali, I will make an effort, go to him, and choose him as your son-in-law.

There is an egg lying here in the water, blazing with its own magnificence, which has not cracked or rolled away since the dawn of creation. I have not heard anyone discussing its origin or creation, and no one knows its mother or father. Rumor has it, Mátali, that at the end of time an enormous fire will burst from it, and burn all three worlds with their animate and inanimate creatures.

99.20 Mātalis tv abravīc chrutvā Nāradasy' âtha bhāṣitam,
«na me 'tra rocate kaś cid. anyato vraja mā|ciram.»

NĀRADA uvāca:

100.1 HIRAṆYAPURAM ity etat khyātaṃ pura|varaṃ mahat
Daityānāṃ Dānavānāṃ ca māyā|śata|vicāriṇām.
an|alpena prayatnena nirmitaṃ Viśvakarmaṇā,
Mayena manasā sṛṣṭaṃ Pātāla|talam āśritam.
atra māyā|sahasrāṇi vikurvāṇā mah"|âujasaḥ
Dānavā nivasanti sma śūrā datta|varāḥ purā.
n' âite Śakreṇa, n' ânyena—Yamena Varuṇena vā
śakyante vaśam ānetuṃ, tath" âiva Dhanadena ca.
100.5 asurāḥ, Kālakhañjāś ca tathā Viṣṇu|pad'|ôdbhavāḥ,
Nairṛtā, yātudhānāś ca Brahma|pād'|ôdbhavāś ca ye,
daṃṣṭriṇo bhīma|vegāś ca vāta|vega|parākramāḥ
māyā|vīry'|ôpasaṃpannā nivasanty atra, Mātale.
Nivātakavacā nāma Dānavā yuddha|durmadāḥ,
jānāsi ca yathā Śakro n' âitāñ śaknoti bādhitum.
bahuśo, Mātale, tvaṃ ca tava putraś ca Gomukhaḥ
nirbhagno, deva|rājaś ca saha|putraḥ Śacī|patiḥ.

paśya veśmāni raukmāṇi, Mātale, rājatāni ca,
karmaṇā vidhi|yuktena yuktāny upagatāni ca,
100.10 vaidūrya|maṇi|citrāṇi pravāla|rucirāṇi ca
arka|sphaṭika|śubhrāṇi, vajra|sār'|ôjjvalāni ca,
pārthivān' îva c' ābhānti padmarāga|mayāni ca,

When he heard Nárada's story, Mátali said, "No one 99.20
pleases me here. Go somewhere else without delay."

NÁRADA said:

THIS MIGHTY AND excellent city of Daityas and Dánavas 100.1
who wander about with hundreds of magical illusions is
known as Hiránya·pura. Given creation by the mind of the
Dánava Maya, and built by Vishva·karman with no little
effort, it rests on the surface of Patála. Once, having been
granted a favor by Brahma long ago, the heroic and hugely
energetic Dánavas lived here, making use of their thousands
of magical illusions. Shakra could not defeat them, and nor
could anyone else—Yama, or Váruna, or Kubéra the lord
of wealth.

The *ásura*s and Kala·khanjas who were born out of 100.5
Vishnu's footsteps, and the Náirritas and *yatu·dhana*s who
took their birth from Brahma's feet—tusked and terrify-
ingly forceful creatures, as powerful as the strength of the
wind—live here, Mátali, endowed with great prowess in
trickery. The Dánavas known as Niváta·kávachas, insanely
lustful for battle, live here, and you know how Shakra is unable to oppose them. You and your son Go·mukha, along
with Shachi's husband the king of the gods and his son,
have broken before them many times, Mátali.

Look at their gold and silver palaces, Mátali, beautifully
decorated with workmanship of classically styled architec-
ture. They take their color from the cats-eye gems and jew- 100.10
els, they gleam with coral, they flash with bright crystal and
blaze with diamonds. These palaces sparkle as though made
of lotus-hued rubies, and look as though they may be made

śailān' îva ca dṛśyante dāravāṇ' îva c' âpy uta,
sūrya|rūpāṇi c' ābhānti dīpt'|âgni|sadṛśāni ca,
maṇi|jāla|vicitrāṇi prāṃśūni nibiḍāni ca.
n' âitāni śakyaṃ nirdeṣṭum rūpato dravyatas tathā,
guṇataś c' âiva siddhāni pramāṇa|guṇavanti ca.
ākrīḍān paśya Daityānāṃ, tath" âiva śayanāny uta,
ratnavanti mah"|ârhāṇi bhājanāny āsanāni ca,
100.15 jalad'|ābhāṃs tathā śailāṃs, toya|prasravaṇāni ca,
kāma|puṣpa|phalāṃś c' âpi pādapān kāma|cāriṇaḥ.
Mātale, kaś cid atr' âpi ruciras te varo bhavet?
atha v" ânyāṃ diśaṃ bhūmer gacchāva, yadi manyase.
Mātalis tv abravīd enaṃ bhāṣamāṇaṃ tathā|vidham,
«deva'|rṣe, n' âiva me kāryaṃ vipriyaṃ tridiv'|âukasām.
nity'|ânuṣakta|vairā hi bhrātaro deva|Dānavāḥ;
para|pakṣeṇa sambandhaṃ rocayiṣyāmy ahaṃ katham?
anyatra sādhu gacchāva, draṣṭuṃ n' ârhāmi Dānavān.
jānāmi tava c' ātmānaṃ hiṃs'|ātma|kamanaṃ tathā.»

NĀRADA uvāca:

101.1 AYAṂ LOKAḤ su|parṇānāṃ pakṣiṇāṃ pannag'|âśinām.
vikrame gamane bhāre n' âiṣām asti pariśramaḥ.
Vainateya|sutaiḥ, sūta, ṣaḍbhis tatam idaṃ kulam:
Sumukhena, Sunāmnā ca, Sunetreṇa, Suvarcasā,
Surucā pakṣi|rājena, Subalena ca, Mātale.
vardhitāni prasṛtyā vai Vinatā|kula|kartṛbhiḥ
pakṣi|rāj'|âbhijātyānāṃ sahasrāṇi śatāni ca
Kaśyapasya tato vaṃśe jātair bhūti|vivardhanaiḥ.

of marble or rare wood. They are as luminous as the sun, as bright as a blazing fire, studded with gem-ornamented latticework, and towering and sturdy. It is impossible to convey the beauty, material, and caliber of these palaces, so perfect are they in their scale and quality.

Look at the Daityas' amusements, their beds, highly costly jeweled tableware, and seats. Look at their cloud-like 100.15
hills, their water fountains, and their trees, which move as they wish and flower and fruit as they please. So, Mátali, would anyone here make a pleasing suitor? Or, if you think it's a good idea, let's go to another region of the earth.

Mátali replied to his words as follows: "Celestial sage, I shouldn't do anything which would displease the heaven-dwellers. The gods and Dánavas are brothers who are constantly embroiled in quarreling, so how could I wish to make an alliance with the enemy side? Let's go elsewhere. I'd prefer that, for I ought not to inspect Dánavas. I know that your heart is set on creating division."

NÁRADA said:

THIS IS THE WORLD of those beautiful-winged birds who 101.1
eat snakes, and who never weary in battle, in travel, or when burdened. Charioteer, this lineage has sprung from the six sons of Gáruda, the son of Vínata; from Súmukha, Sunáman, Sunétra, Suvárchas, Súruch, king of birds, and Súbala, O Mátali. Hundreds and thousands of birds descended from the king of birds have been born and raised by the patriarchs of the Vínata dynasty, who were themselves born in the lineage of Káshyapa and have augmented its fortune.

101.5 sarve hy ete śriyā yuktāḥ, sarve Śrīvatsa|lakṣaṇāḥ,
sarve śriyam abhīpsanto dhārayanti balāny uta.
karmaṇā kṣatriyāś c' âite nirghṛṇā bhogi|bhojinaḥ;
jñāti|saṃkṣaya|kartṛtvād brāhmaṇyaṃ na labhanti vai.
nāmāni c' âiṣāṃ vakṣyāmi yathā prādhānyataḥ, śṛṇu.
Mātale, ślāghyam etadd hi kulaṃ Viṣṇu|parigraham;
daivataṃ Viṣṇur eteṣāṃ; Viṣṇur eva parāyaṇam.
hṛdi c' âiṣāṃ sadā Viṣṇur, Viṣṇur eva sadā gatiḥ.
Suvarṇacūḍo, Nāgāśī, Dāruṇaś, Caṇḍatuṇḍakaḥ,
Anilaś c', Ânalaś c' âiva, Viśālākṣo, 'tha Kuṇḍalī,
101.10 Paṅkajid, Vajraviṣkambho, Vainateyo, 'tha Vāmanaḥ,
Vātavego, Diśācakṣur, Nimeṣo, 'nimiṣas tathā,
Trirāvaḥ, Saptarāvaś ca, Vālmīkir, Dvīpakas tathā,
Daityadvīpaḥ, Sariddvīpaḥ, Sārasaḥ, Padmaketanaḥ,
Sumukhaś, Citraketuś ca, Citrabarhas, tath" Ânaghaḥ,
Meṣahṛt, Kumudo, Dakṣaḥ, Sarpāntaḥ, Sahabhojanaḥ,
Gurubhāraḥ, Kapotaś ca, Sūryanetraś, Cirāntakaḥ,
Viṣṇurdharmā, Kumāraś ca, Paribarho, Haris tathā,
Susvaro, Madhuparkaś ca, Hemavarṇas tath" âiva ca,
Mālayo, Mātariśvā ca, Niśākara|Divākarau.
101.15 ete pradeśa|mātreṇa may" ôktā Garuḍ'|ātmajāḥ
prādhānyatas te yaśasā kīrtitāḥ prāṇinaś ca ye.
yady atra na ruciḥ kā cid, ehi, gacchāva, Mātale,
taṃ nayiṣyāmi deśaṃ tvāṃ, varaṃ yatr' ôpalapsyase.

NĀRADA uvāca:

102.1 IDAṂ RASĀTALAṂ nāma saptamaṃ pṛthivī|talam,
yatr' āste Surabhir mātā gavām amṛta|saṃbhavā,
kṣarantī satataṃ kṣīraṃ pṛthivī|sāra|saṃbhavam,
ṣaṇṇāṃ rasānāṃ sāreṇa rasam ekam an|uttamam.
amṛten' âbhitṛptasya sāram udgirataḥ purā

They are all quite assuredly endowed with good for- 101.5
tune, all bear the *shri·vatsa** marking, and all wish to attain
prosperity and maintain their power. They are kshatriyas
through their actions, pitilessly devouring snakes, but they
do not attain brahminhood because they destroy their kin.
I will tell you the names of the leading birds, so listen.

Mátali, this lineage is indeed laudable, for they honor
Vishnu. Vishnu is their god; he is their refuge. Vishnu is al-
ways in their hearts, and Vishnu is their constant aim. There
is Suvárna·chuda, Nagáshin, Dáruna, Chanda·túndaka,
Ánila, Ánala, Vishaláksha, Kúndalin, Pánkajit, Vajra·vish- 101.10
kámbha, Vainatéya, Vámana, Vata·vega, Disha·chakshus,
Nimésha, Ánimisha, Tri·rava, Sapta·rava, Valmíki, Dvípaka,
Daitya·dvipa, Sarid·dvipa, Sárasa, Padma·kétana, Súmukha,
Chitra·ketu, Chitra·barha, Ánagha, Méshahrit, Kúmuda,
Daksha, Sarpánta, Saha·bhójana, Guru·bhara, Kapóta,
Surya·netra, Chirántaka, Vishnu·dharman, Kumára, Pari-
bárha, Hari, Súsvara, Madhu·parka, Hema·varna, Málaya,
Mataríshvan, Nishákara, and Divákara.

I have listed Gáruda's sons by way of an example, for they 101.15
are the praised as the foremost in fame and energy. If none
here please you, then come on, let's go, Mátali, and I will
take you to a place where you may find a suitor.

NÁRADA continued:

THIS IS THE SEVENTH level of the earth, called Rasátala, 102.1
the place where Súrabhi lives, the mother of cattle who
was born from ambrosia and produces milk ceaselessly. Her
milk is the source of the earth's riches, and of one supreme
taste derived from the essence of the six tastes. Long ago,

pitā|mahasya vadanād udatiṣṭhad a|ninditā.
yasyāḥ kṣīrasya dhārāyā nipatantyā mahī|tale
hradaḥ kṛtaḥ kṣīra|nidhiḥ pavitraṃ param ucyate.
102.5 puṣpitasy' êva phenena paryantam anuveṣṭitam.
pibanto nivasanty atra phena|pā muni|sattamāḥ.
phena|pā nāma te khyātāḥ phen'|āhārāś ca, Mātale,
ugre tapasi vartante yeṣāṃ bibhyati devatāḥ.

asyāś catasro dhenvo 'nyā dikṣu sarvāsu, Mātale,
nivasanti diśāṃ pālyo, dhārayanto diśaḥ sma tāḥ.
pūrvāṃ diśaṃ dhārayate Surūpā nāma Saurabhī,
dakṣiṇāṃ Haṃsikā nāma dhārayaty aparāṃ diśam,
paścimā Vāruṇī dik ca dhāryate vai Subhadrayā
mah"|ânubhāvayā nityaṃ, Mātale, viśva|rūpayā.
102.10 Sarvakāmadughā nāma dhenur dhārayate diśam
uttarāṃ, Mātale, dharmyāṃ tath" Âilavila|saṃjñitām.

āsāṃ tu payasā miśraṃ payo nirmathya sāgare
manthānaṃ Mandaraṃ kṛtvā devair asura|saṃhitaiḥ
uddhṛtā Vāruṇī, Lakṣmīr, amṛtaṃ c' âpi, Mātale,
Uccaiḥśravāś c' âśva|rājo maṇi|ratnaṃ ca Kaustubham.

sudh"|āhāreṣu ca sudhāṃ, svadhā|bhojiṣu ca svadhām,
amṛtaṃ c' âmṛt'|âśeṣu Surabhī kṣarate payaḥ.
atra gāthā purā gītā Rasātala|nivāsibhiḥ
paurāṇī śrūyate loke, gīyate yā manīṣibhiḥ:
102.15 «na nāga|loke na svarge na vimāne tri|viṣṭape

the grandfather was satisfied with ambrosia, and so he expelled its essence, and thus the blameless cow arose from his mouth.

It was from a flow of her milk falling onto the earth's
surface that the holy and superb Sea of Milk was formed; a
means of purification. The shore of the Milky Sea is encir- 102.5
cled with foam, as though the lake were covered in bloom-
ing flowers; and it is here that those excellent sages, the foam
drinkers, live and drink. They are known as foam drinkers
because they live on that foam, Mátali. They practice rigor-
ous austerity, and even the gods fear them.

Four other cows born from Súrabhi live in the four cardinal directions, each defending and supporting her point of
the compass. Súrabhi's daughter Surúpa supports the east,
and Hánsika supports the south. Váruna's western region is
supported by Subhádra, an ever illustrious cow of universal form, Mátali. A cow named Sarva·kama·dugha supports 102.10
the northern region, Mátali, which is morally upright and
named after Ílavila's son, Kubéra.

The gods and *ásura*s churned the waters of the ocean, mixed with their milk, using Mount Mándara as the churning pole, and they produced Váruna's wine, Lakshmi, ambrosia, Ucchaih·shravas the king of horses, and Káustubha the gem of jewels, O Mátali.

Súrabhi lets her milk flow as *sudha* for those who live on *sudha*, as *svadha* for those who eat *svadha*, and as ambrosia for those who live on ambrosia.* The song that was sung long ago by those who lived in Rasátala—an ancient song which can still be heard in the world, sung by the

parivāsaḥ sukhas tādṛg, Rasātala|tale yathā.»

NĀRADA uvāca:

103.1 IYAṂ BHOGAVATĪ nāma purī Vāsuki|pālitā
yādṛśī deva|rājasya purī|vary" Âmarāvatī.
eṣa Śeṣaḥ sthito nāgo yen' êyaṃ dhāryate sadā
tapasā loka|mukhyena prabhāva|sahitā mahī,
śvet'|âcala|nibh'|ākāro, divy'|ābharaṇa|bhūṣitaḥ,
sahasraṃ dhārayan mūrdhnāṃ, jvālā|jihvo mahā|balaḥ.
iha nānā|vidh'|ākarā nānā|vidha|vibhūṣaṇāḥ
Surasāyāḥ sutā nāgā nivasanti gata|vyathāḥ,
103.5 maṇi|svastika|cakr'|âṅkāḥ kamaṇḍaluka|lakṣaṇāḥ.
sahasra|saṃkhyā, balinaḥ, sarve raudrāḥ sva|bhāvataḥ.
sahasra|śirasaḥ ke cit, ke cit pañca|śat'|ānanāḥ
śata|śīrṣās tathā ke cit, ke cit tri|śiraso 'pi ca,
dvi|pañca|śirasaḥ ke cit, ke cit sapta|mukhās tathā.
mahā|bhogā, mahā|kāyāḥ, parvat'|ābhoga|bhoginaḥ.
bahūn' îha sahasrāṇi, prayutāny arbudāni ca
nāgānām eka|vaṃśānāṃ. yathā|śreṣṭhaṃ tu me śṛṇu.
Vāsukis, Takṣakaś c' âiva, Karkoṭaka|Dhanañjayau,
Kālīyo, Nahuṣaś c' âiva, Kambal'|Âśvatarāv ubhau,

learned—goes as follows: "Not in the world of the snakes, 102.15
not in heaven or in Indra's dwelling is the living as blissful as in the land of Rasátala."

NÁRADA continued:

THIS IS THE CITY of Bhógavati, ruled by Vásuki, like 103.1
the lovely city Amarávati, which belongs to the king of the gods. This is Shesha, the snake who everlastingly supports this earth and her majesty through his austerity, the foremost of its kind in the world. The enormously powerful snake, adorned with celestial ornaments, who resembles the White Mountain, bore a thousand heads and blazing tongues. The snake sons of Súrasa of various form and
adornment live here, free of anxiety, their bodies marked 103.5
with gems, swastikas, and circles, holding gourds as their attributes.

They number thousands and are all powerful and fearsome in nature. Some have a thousand heads, some have five hundred, some have a hundred heads, and some again have three, or ten, or seven. They have vast coils and bodies which spiral like looping mountains. There are a great many thousands, millions, and tens of millions of snakes in a single lineage. Listen to me as I list their leaders.

There is Vásuki, Tákshaka, Karkótaka, Dhanañ·jaya, Kalíya, Náhusha, Kámbala, Áshvatara, Bahya·kunda, the snake

103.10 Bāhyakuṇḍo, Maṇir nāgas, tath" âiv' Āpūraṇaḥ, Khagaḥ,
Vāmanaś c', Âilapatraś ca, Kukuraḥ, Kukuṇas tathā,
Āryako, Nandakaś c' âiva, tathā Kalaśa|Potakau,
Kailāsakaḥ, Piñjarako, nāgaś c' Āirāvatas tathā,
Sumanomukho, Dadhimukhaḥ,
Śaṅkho, Nand'|Ôpanandakau,
Āptaḥ, Koṭarakaś c' âiva,
Śikhī, Niṣṭhūrikas tathā,
Tittirir, Hastibhadraś ca, Kumudo, Mālyapiṇḍakaḥ,
dvau Padmau, Puṇḍarīkaś ca, Puṣpo, Mudgaraparṇakaḥ,
Karavīraḥ, Pīṭharakaḥ, Saṃvṛtto, Vṛtta eva ca,
Piṇḍāro, Bilvapatraś ca, Mūṣikādaḥ, Śirīṣakaḥ,
103.15 Dilīpaḥ, Śaṅkhaśīrṣaś ca, Jyotiṣko, 'th' Âparājitaḥ,
Kauravyo, Dhṛtarāṣṭraś ca, Kuhuraḥ, Kṛśakas tathā,
Virajā, Dhāraṇaś c' âiva, Subāhur, Mukharo, Jayaḥ,
Badhir'|Ândhau, Viśuṇḍiś ca, Virasaḥ, Surasas tathā.
ete c' ânye ca bahavaḥ Kaśyapasy' ātma|jāḥ smṛtāḥ.
Mātale, paśya yady atra kaś cit te rocate varaḥ.

KAṆVA uvāca:

Mātalis tv ekam a|vyagraḥ satataṃ saṃnirīkṣya vai
papraccha Nāradaṃ tatra, prītimān iva c' âbhavat:

MĀTALIR uvāca:

sthito ya eṣa purataḥ Kauravyasy' Āryakasya tu,
dyutimān darśanīyaś ca, kasy' âiṣa kula|nandanaḥ?
103.20 kaḥ pitā jananī c' âsya? katamasy' âiṣa bhoginaḥ?
vaṃśasya kasy' âiṣa mahān ketu|bhūta iva sthitaḥ?
praṇidhānena, dhairyeṇa, rūpeṇa vayasā ca me
manaḥ praviṣṭo, deva'|rṣe, Guṇakeśyāḥ patir varaḥ.

Mani, Apúrana, Khaga, Vámana, Elapátra, Kúkura, Kúku-
na, Áryaka, Nándaka, Kálasha, Pótaka, Kailásaka, Píñja-
raka, the snake Airávata, Súmano·mukha,Dadhi·mukha,
Shankha, Nanda, Upanándaka, Apta, Kótaraka, Shikhin,
Nishthúrika, Títtiri, Hasti·bhadra, Kúmuda, Malya·pínda-
ka, the two Padmas, Pundaríka, Pushpa, Múdgara·párnaka,
Kara·vira, Pítharaka, Samvrítta, Vritta, Pindára, Bilva·patra,
Mushikáda, Shiríshaka, Dilípa, Shankha·shirsha, Jyotíshka, 103.15
Aparájita, Kaurávya, Dhrita·rashtra, Kúhura, Kríshaka,
Vírajas, Dhárana, Subáhu, Múkhara, Jaya, Bádhira, Andha,
Vishúndi, Vírasa, and Súrasa.

These and many others are recounted as being Káshyapa's sons, Mátali, so see if anyone here pleases you as a suitor.

KANVA said:

Mátali stared coolly and unceasingly at one of the snakes, and, seemingly pleased with him, he questioned Nárada.

MÁTALI said:

Who is this one here, the splendid and handsome one
standing in front of Kaurávya and Áryaka? What lineage is
he descended from? Who are his mother and father? Which 103.20
snake is he related to? Of which family is he the magnificent
bright flame? Celestial sage, his endeavor, fortitude, beauty,
and youth have drawn my heart to him as the best possible
husband for Guna·keshi.

KAṆVA uvāca:

Mātaliṃ prīta|manasaṃ dṛṣṭvā Sumukha|darśanāt
nivedayām āsa tadā māhātmyaṃ, janma karma ca.

NĀRADA uvāca:

Airāvata|kule jātaḥ Sumukho nāma nāga|rāṭ,
Āryakasya mataḥ pautro, dauhitro Vāmanasya ca.
etasya hi pitā nāgaś Cikuro nāma, Mātale,
na|cirād Vainateyena pañcatvam upapāditaḥ.
103.25 tato 'bravīt prītamanā Mātalir Nāradaṃ vacaḥ:
«eṣa me rucitas, tāta, jāmātā bhujag'|ôttamaḥ.
kriyatām atra yatno vai, prītimān asmy anena vai,
asmai nāgāya vai dātuṃ priyāṃ duhitaraṃ, mune.»

NĀRADA uvāca:

104.1 SŪTO 'YAṂ MĀTALIR nāma Śakrasya dayitaḥ su|hṛt,
śuciḥ, śīla|guṇ'|ôpetas, tejasvī, vīryavān, balī.
Śakrasy' âyaṃ sakhā c' âiva, mantrī sārathir eva ca,
alp' ântara|prabhāvaś ca Vāsavena raṇe raṇe.
ayaṃ hari|sahasreṇa yuktaṃ Jaitraṃ rath'|ôttamam
dev'|âsureṣu yuddheṣu manas" âiva niyacchati.
anena vijitān aśvair dorbhyāṃ jayati Vāsavaḥ;
anena Bala|bhit pūrvaṃ prahṛte praharaty uta.

KANVA said:

Noticing how delighted Mátali was at seeing Súmukha, Nárada detailed his noble nature, his birth, and his achievements.

NÁRADA replied:

Súmukha is a king of snakes, born in the line of Airávata, the highly regarded paternal grandson of Áryaka and maternal grandson of Vámana. His father is the snake Chíkura, Mátali. He was killed not so long ago, transformed into the five elements by Vínata's son, Gáruda.

At this news Mátali was delighted and said to Nárada: 103.25
"This superb snake would please me as a son-in-law, my friend, so let's do all we can to ensure he accepts our proposal, for I am delighted with the idea of giving my dear daughter to this snake, sage."

NÁRADA said:

THIS IS MÁTALI, Shakra's friend and charioteer. He is 104.1
pure, endowed with virtuous conduct, splendid, courageous, and powerful. This man is Shakra's friend, counselor, and charioteer, and he has proven to be barely inferior to Vásava in battle after battle. He drives the supreme chariot Jaitra, yoked with a thousand horses, by the power of his mind in the battles between the gods and *ásura*s. Vásava defeats his enemies by the power of his arms after this man has conquered them with his horses, and it is only after this man has hit out first that the slayer of Bala kills his enemies.

104.5 asya kanyā var'|ārohā rūpeṇ' â|sadṛśī bhuvi,
satya|śīla|guṇ'|ôpetā, Guṇakeś" îti viśrutā.
tasy' âsya yatnāc caratas trailokyam, amara|dyute,
Sumukho bhavataḥ pautro rocate duhituḥ patiḥ.
yadi te rocate samyag, bhujag'|ôttama, mā|ciram
kriyatām, Āryaka, kṣipraṃ buddhiḥ kanyā|parigrahe.
yathā Viṣṇu|kule Lakṣmīr, yathā Svāhā Vibhāvasoḥ,
kule tava tath" âiv' âstu Guṇakeśī su|madhyamā.

pautrasy' ârthe bhavāṃs tasmād Guṇakeśīṃ pratīcchatu
sadṛśīṃ pratirūpasya, Vāsavasya Sacīm iva.
104.10 pitṛ|hīnam api hy enaṃ guṇato varayāmahe,
bahu|mānāc ca bhavatas tath" âiv' Āirāvatasya ca,
Sumukhaś ca guṇaiś c' âiva śīla|śauca|dam'|ādibhiḥ
abhigamya svayaṃ kanyām ayaṃ dātuṃ samudyataḥ
Mātalis; tasya saṃmānaṃ kartum arho bhavān api.

KAṆVA uvāca:

sa tu dīnaḥ prahṛṣṭaś ca prāha Nāradam Āryakaḥ
vriyamāṇe tathā pautre, putre ca nidhanaṃ gate,
«katham icchāmi, deva'|rṣe, Guṇakeśīṃ snuṣāṃ prati?»

ĀRYAKA uvāca:

na me n' âitad bahu|mataṃ, maha"|rṣe, vacanaṃ tava,
sakhā Śakrasya saṃyuktaḥ kasy' âyaṃ n' ēpsito bhavet?
104.15 kāraṇasya tu daurbalyāc cintayāmi, mahā|mune,
asya deha|karas, tāta, mama putro, mahā|dyute,

His shapely-hipped daughter has no match for her beauty 104.5
on earth. She is endowed with truth, good conduct, and virtue, and she is called Guna·keshi. As he wandered the three worlds in his struggle to find a suitor, immortally resplendent one, your grandson Súmukha caught his eye as a potential husband for his daughter. If this pleases you, greatest of snakes, then do not delay, but rather quickly make up your mind to accept the girl, Áryaka. May slender-waisted Guna·keshi be to your family what Lakshmi is to the line of Vishnu, or Svaha to that of Agni.

So please accept Guna·keshi on your grandson's behalf, for she is his equal in beauty, just as Shachi is a match
for Vásava. Despite the fact that he has lost his father, 104.10
we choose Súmukha because of his quality, and because he respects you and Airávata. It is because of Súmukha's virtues, his good conduct, purity, control, and other qualities that Mátali has come here himself, endeavoring to give his daughter to him; and so you ought to honor him too.

KANVA said:

His son dead but his grandson chosen, Áryaka replied to Nárada feeling both happy and sad at once, saying, "How could I wish for Guna·keshi as my daughter-in-law, celestial sage?"

ÁRYAKA continued:

It is not that I do not respect what you have to say, great sage, for who would not want to be an ally of Shakra's
friend? My pause for thought is due to the weakness of his 104.15
father—my son, who was eaten by Gáruda, O greatly glorious and mighty sage and friend. We are afflicted with mis-

bhakṣito Vainateyena. duḥkh'|ārtās tena vai vayam.
punar eva ca ten' ôktaṃ Vainateyena gacchatā,
«māsen' ânyena Sumukhaṃ bhakṣiyiṣya! iti,» prabho.
dhruvaṃ tathā tad bhavitā, jānīmas tasya niścayam;
tena harṣaḥ pranaṣṭo me Suparṇa|vacanena vai.

KANVA uvāca:

Mātalis tv abravīd enaṃ, «buddhir atra kṛtā mayā,
jāmātṛ|bhāvena vṛtaḥ Sumukhas tava putra|jaḥ.
so 'yaṃ mayā ca sahito Nāradena ca pannagaḥ
tri|lok'|ēśaṃ sura|patiṃ gatvā paśyatu Vāsavam.
104.20 śeṣeṇ' âiv' âsya kāryeṇa prajñāsyāmy aham āyuṣaḥ,
Suparṇasya vighāte ca prayatiṣyāmi, sattama.
Sumukhaś ca mayā sārdhaṃ dev'|ēśam abhigacchatu
kārya|saṃsādhan'|ârthāya; svasti te 'stu, bhujaṅ|gama.»

tatas te Sumukhaṃ gṛhya sarva eva mah"|âujasaḥ
dadṛśuḥ Śakram āsīnaṃ deva|rājaṃ mahā|dyutim.
saṅgatyā tatra bhagavān Viṣṇur āsīc catur|bhujaḥ.
tatas tat sarvam ācakhyau Nārado Mātaliṃ prati.

tataḥ puran|daraṃ Viṣṇur uvāca bhuvan'|ēśvaram:
«amṛtaṃ dīyatām asmai, kriyatām amaraiḥ samaḥ.
104.25 Mātalir, Nāradaś c' âiva, Sumukhaś c' âiva, Vāsava,
labhantāṃ bhavataḥ kāmāt kāmam etaṃ yath" ēpsitam.»
puran|daro 'tha sañcintya Vainateya|parākramam
Viṣṇum ev' âbravīd enaṃ, «bhavān eva dadātv! iti.»

ery on his account. There is also the fact that when Gáruda, the son of Vínata, was leaving, my lord, he said, "Next month I will eat Súmukha!" His words will surely be fulfilled, for we know his resolve. This is the reason that my joy was truly destroyed by Supárna's words.

KANVA said:

But Mátali replied, "I have made up my mind, and I have chosen your grandson Súmukha to be my son-in-law. This snake should accompany me and Nárada to see Vásava, the lord of the three worlds and the lord of the gods. I will dis- 104.20
cover how much of his life remains, and attempt to hinder Supárna, supreme snake. Let Súmukha accompany me to the lord of the gods, and blessings to you, snake, for the sake of accomplishing our task."

So he took Súmukha with him, and all those magnificently energetic men went to see Shakra, the great glorious celestial sovereign, as he sat on his throne. While this was happening, four-armed Lord Vishnu arrived and took his place there. And so it was that Nárada told the whole story about Mátali.

Vishnu spoke to the sacker of cities, the lord of the worlds, saying, "Give ambrosia to him and make him like the immortals.* That way, Vásava, through your will, Má- 104.25
tali, Nárada, and Súmukha could gain their hearts' desire." The sacker of cities contemplated Gáruda's prowess and said to Vishnu: "You give him ambrosia!"

VIṢṆUR uvāca:

«īśas tvaṃ sarva|lokānāṃ carāṇām, a|carāś ca ye;
tvayā dattam a|dattaṃ kaḥ kartum utsahate, vibho?»
prādāc Chakras tatas tasmai pannagāy' āyur uttamam;
na tv enam amṛta|prāśaṃ cakāra Bala|Vṛtra|hā.
labdhvā varaṃ tu Sumukhaḥ sumukhaḥ sambabhūva ha;
kṛta|dāro yathā|kāmaṃ jagāma ca gṛhān prati.
104.30 Nāradas tv Āryakaś c' âiva kṛta|kāryau mudā yutau
abhijagmatur abhyarcya deva|rājaṃ mahā|dyutim.

KAṆVA uvāca:

105.1 GARUḌAS TATRA śuśrāva yathā|vṛttaṃ mahā|balaḥ
āyuḥ|pradānaṃ Śakreṇa kṛtaṃ nāgasya, Bhārata.
pakṣa|vātena mahatā ruddhvā tri|bhuvanaṃ khagaḥ
Suparṇaḥ parama|kruddho Vāsavaṃ samupādravat.

GARUḌA uvāca:

bhagavan, kim avajñānād vṛttiḥ pratihatā mama?
kāma|kāra|varaṃ dattvā punaś calitavān asi?
nisargāt sarva|bhūtānāṃ sarva|bhūt'|ēśvareṇa me
āhāro vihito dhātrā, kim arthaṃ vāryate tvayā?
105.5 vṛtaś c' âiṣa mahā|nāgaḥ, sthāpitaḥ samayaś ca me
anena ca mayā, deva, bhartavyaḥ prasavo mahān!

etasmiṃs tu tathā|bhūte n' ânyaṃ hiṃsitum utsahe.
krīḍase kāma|kāreṇa, deva|rāja, yath" êcchakam.
so' haṃ prāṇān vimokṣyāmi, tathā parijano mama,

VISHNU said:

"You are the lord of all worlds, of mobile and immobile creatures. Who would dare to annul a gift that had been given by you, my lord?" Shakra gave the snake supremely long life, but the slayer of Bala and Vritra did not make him a present of the immortality-granting ambrosia. Súmukha took the gift, and his face truly beamed with joy.* So he got married, and went home when he pleased. And Nárada and 104.30
Áryaka were also pleased, for they had accomplished their task; and so they too went home, after they had worshipped the greatly glorious king of the gods.

KANVA said:

BUT ENORMOUSLY powerful Gáruda heard what had hap- 105.1
pened: that Shakra had given the gift of long life to the snake, Bhárata. So, besieging the three worlds with his mighty wind-like wings, the furious bird Supárna rushed to Vásava.

GÁRUDA said:

My lord, why do you treat me with disrespect? You willingly granted me a favor, so why are you now taking it back and obstructing my meals? At the moment of the creation of all creatures, the creator and lord of all creatures decreed what I should eat, so why do you now renege on the deal? I 105.5
chose this mighty snake—the agreement has been made. O god, I must support my enormous family with this snake!

Since my plan has turned out this way, I do not dare to kill anyone else. You play with matters as you please, following your impulses, king of the gods, so I will end my life, as will my family and the servants in my home. Are

ye ca bhṛtyā mama gṛhe; prītimān bhava, Vāsava!
etac c' âiv' âham arhāmi, bhūyaś ca, Bala|Vṛtra|han,
trailokyasy' ēśvaro yo 'haṃ para|bhṛtyatvam āgataḥ!
tvayi tiṣṭhati, dev'|ēśa, na Viṣṇuḥ kāraṇaṃ mama,
trailokya|rāja, rājyaṃ hi tvayi, Vāsava, śāśvatam.
105.10 mam' âpi Dakṣasya sutā jananī, Kaśyapaḥ pitā;
aham apy utsahe lokān samantād voḍhum añjasā.
a|sahyaṃ sarva|bhūtānāṃ mam' âpi vipulaṃ balam.
may" âpi su|mahat karma kṛtaṃ daiteya|vigrahe!
Śrutaśrīḥ, Śrutasenaś ca, Vivasvān, Rocanāmukhaḥ,
Prasṛtaḥ, Kālakākṣaś ca may" âpi Diti|jā hatāḥ.
yat tu dhvaja|sthāna|gato yatnāt paricarāmy aham,
vahāmi c' âiv' ânujaṃ te, tena mām avamanyase?
ko 'nyo bhāra|saho hy asti? ko 'nyo 'sti balavattaraḥ
mayā? yo 'haṃ viśiṣṭaḥ san, vahām' îmaṃ sa|bāndhavam.
105.15 avajñāya tu yat te 'haṃ bhojanād vyaparopitaḥ,
tena me gauravaṃ naṣṭaṃ tvattaś c' âsmāc ca, Vāsava.
Adityāṃ ya ime jātā bala|vikrama|śālinaḥ,
tvam eṣāṃ kila sarveṣāṃ balena balavattaraḥ;
so 'haṃ pakṣ'|âika|deśena vahāmi tvāṃ gata|klamaḥ.
vimṛśa tvaṃ śanais, tāta, «ko nv atra balavān? iti.»

KAṆVA uvāca:

sa tasya vacanaṃ śrutvā khagasy' ôdarka|dāruṇam,
a|kṣobhyaṃ kṣobhayaṃs Tārkṣyam uvāca ratha|cakra|bhṛt:
«Garutman, manyase "tmānaṃ balavantaṃ su|durbalam.
alam asmat|samakṣaṃ te stotum ātmānam, aṇḍa|ja.

you happy now, Vásava? I deserve this and more, slayer of Bala and Vritra, for I, who am the natural lord of the three worlds, have lowered myself to depend on another for my livelihood!

As long as you abide, celestial sovereign, Vishnu is not the only reason for my low position, for the kingdom rests on you eternally, Vásava, king of the three worlds. I too have 105.10
a daughter of Daksha as my mother and Káshyapa as my father, and I too can bear the worlds without fatigue. My power too is extensive and insurmountable by all creatures. I too have achieved enormous feats in the battle against the Daityas! I too have killed Daityas: Shruta·shri, Shruta·sena, Vivásvat, Róchana·mukha, Prásrita, and Kalakáksha.

Do you treat me contemptuously because I travel industriously at the top of your brother's flag and because I carry him about? Who else is a match for the burden? Who else is stronger than me? Though I am his better, I carry him and his relatives. And now that I am prevented from taking my 105.15
meal and treated contemptuously, I have lost your respect and his as well, Vásava.

You are more powerful in strength than all Áditi's sons, endowed with force and prowess, or so they say, and yet I carry you unwearyingly with a single wing. So, my friend, consider at length who is the stronger.

KANVA said:

The wielder of the chariot wheel listened to the bird's sharp words and spoke to Tarkshya, making the unflappable tremble: "Garútmat, you believe yourself to be strong, though in reality you are very weak. That's enough self-

105.20 trailokyam api me kṛtsnam a|śaktaṃ deha|dhāraṇe.
aham ev' ātman" ātmānaṃ vahāmi, tvāṃ ca dhāraye.
imaṃ tāvan mam' âikaṃ tvaṃ bāhuṃ savy'|êtaraṃ vaha;
yady enaṃ dhārayasy ekaṃ, sa|phalaṃ te vikatthitam.»
tataḥ sa bhagavāṃs tasya skandhe bāhuṃ samāsajat;
nipapāta sa bhār'|ārto vihvalo naṣṭa|cetanaḥ.
yāvān hi bhāraḥ kṛtsnāyāḥ pṛthivyāḥ parvataiḥ saha,
ekasyā deha|śākhāyās tāvad bhāram amanyata.
na tv enaṃ pīḍayām āsa balena balavattaraḥ,
tato hi jīvitaṃ tasya na vyanīnaśad Acyutaḥ.
105.25 vyātt'|āsyaḥ, srasta|kāyaś ca, vicetā, vihvalaḥ khagaḥ
mumoca patrāṇi tadā guru|bhāra|prapīḍitaḥ.
sa Viṣṇuṃ śirasā pakṣī praṇamya Vinatā|sutaḥ
vicetā vihvalo dīnaḥ kiñ cid vacanam abravīt,
«bhagavan, loka|sārasya sadṛśena vapuṣmatā
bhujena svair a|muktena niṣpiṣṭo 'smi mahī|tale.
kṣantum arhasi me, deva, vihvalasy' âlpa|cetasaḥ
bala|dāha|vidagdhasya pakṣiṇo dhvaja|vāsinaḥ.
na hi jñātaṃ balaṃ, deva, mayā te paramaṃ, vibho,
tena manyāmy ahaṃ vīryam ātmano na samaṃ paraiḥ.»
105.30 tataś cakre sa bhagavān prasādaṃ vai Garutmataḥ,
«m" âivaṃ bhūya, iti» snehāt tadā c' âinam uvāca ha.
pād'|âṅguṣṭhena cikṣepa Sumukhaṃ Garuḍ'|ôrasi;
tataḥ prabhṛti, rāj'|êndra, saha sarpeṇa vartate.
evaṃ Viṣṇu|bal'|ākrānto garva|nāśam upāgataḥ
Garuḍo balavān, rājan, Vainateyo mahā|yaśāḥ.

glorification in our presence, egg-born bird! Even the entire 105.20
universe of three worlds cannot support my body. I am the one who supports myself, and I support you too. Carry just this one right arm of mine, and if you manage to bear it then your boasting will prove fruitful."

So the lord put his arm on the bird's shoulder, and, distressed and tormented under the weight, the bird plummeted and lost his mind. He reckoned the burden of that single arm surely matched the entire earth and its mountains. But intensely powerful Áchyuta did not crush him, nor did he take his life from him.

The bird lay stretched out, his body fell pendulously, and 105.25
his mind was gone as he lay tormented. He lost plumage, oppressed by the heavy weight. The feathered son of Vínata bowed his head to Vishnu, and, pained to the point of near senselessness, he said sadly: "My lord, you have pressed me down to the surface of the earth with your arm, like the embodied form of the world's substance, even when only sparingly used. O god, you ought to forgive this small-minded and tormented bird, who lives at the top of your flag, scorched by the fire of power. I really did not understand your supreme strength, lord god, and that is why I believed that no other's could match mine."

The lord showed mercy to Garútmat and spoke to him 105.30
affectionately, saying, "Don't do it again." He kicked Súmukha onto Gáruda's chest with the toe of his foot, and from that moment onwards Gáruda remained friends with the snake, lord of kings. So it was that, afflicted by Vishnu's strength, the powerful and enormously famous Gáruda, son of Vínata, lost his arrogance, my king.

KAṆVA uvāca:

tathā tvam api, Gāndhāre, yāvat Pāṇḍu|sutān raṇe
n' āsādayasi tān vīrāṃs, tāvaj jīvasi, putraka.
Bhīmaḥ praharatāṃ śreṣṭho Vāyu|putro mahā|balaḥ,
Dhanañjayaś c' Êndra|suto na hanyātāṃ tu kaṃ raṇe?
105.35 Viṣṇur, Vāyuś ca, Śakraś ca,
Dharmas, tau c' Âśvināv ubhau—
ete devās tvayā kena
hetunā vīkṣituṃ kṣamāḥ?
tad alaṃ te virodhena. śamaṃ gaccha, nṛp'|ātmaja.
Vāsudevena tīrthena kulaṃ rakṣitum arhasi.
pratyakṣa|darśī sarvasya Nārado 'yaṃ mahā|tapāḥ
māhātmyasya tadā Viṣṇoḥ so 'yaṃ cakra|gadā|dharaḥ.

VAIŚAMPĀYANA uvāca:

Duryodhanas tu tac chrutvā niḥśvasan bhṛkuṭī|mukhaḥ
Rādheyam abhisaṃprekṣya jahāsa svanavat tadā.
kadarthī|kṛtya tad vākyam ṛṣeḥ Kaṇvasya dur|matiḥ
ūruṃ gaja|kar'|âkaraṃ tāḍayann idam abravīt,
105.40 «yath" âiv' ēśvara|sṛṣṭo 'smi, yad bhāvi, yā ca me gatiḥ,
tathā, maha"|rṣe, vartāmi; kiṃ pralāpaḥ kariṣyati?»

KANVA said:

So you too, son of Gandhári, my lad, remain alive only for as long as you do not take on the heroic sons of Pandu in battle. Whom will Bhima, the greatest of warriors and mighty son of the wind, and Dhanan·jaya, the son of Indra,
not destroy in battle? Vishnu, Vayu, Shakra, Dharma, and 105.35
the Twins—you are incapable of even looking at these gods.

Enough feuding. Make peace, prince. You ought to protect your line, taking Vasudéva as your savior. The mighty ascetic Nárada clearly witnessed everything I have described about the magnanimity of Vishnu, the wielder of the mace and discus.

VAISHAMPÁYANA said:

Duryódhana listened, sighing, with a frown on his face; then he glanced at Radhéya and laughed loudly. The wicked-minded man considered Kanva the sage's words to be useless, and, slapping his thigh that was like an elephant's
trunk, he said, "I am just as the lord created me, and my 105.40
future and course is set. I will act accordingly, great sage, so what will this rambling achieve?"

106–119

# THE TALE OF GÁLAVA

JANAMEJAYA uvāca:

106.1 ANARTHE JĀTA|nirbandhaṃ, par'|ârthe lobha|mohitam,
an|āryakeṣv abhiratam, maraṇe kṛta|niścayam,
jñātīnāṃ duḥkha|kartāraṃ, bandhūnāṃ śoka|vardhanam,
su|hṛdāṃ kleśa|dātāraṃ, dviṣatāṃ harṣa|vardhanam,
kathaṃ n' âinaṃ vimārga|sthaṃ vārayant' îha bāndhavāḥ,
sauhṛdād vā su|hṛt snigdho, bhagavān vā pitā|mahaḥ?

VAIŚAMPĀYANA uvāca:

uktaṃ bhagavatā vākyam, uktaṃ Bhīṣmeṇa yat kṣamam,
uktaṃ bahu|vidhaṃ c' âiva Nāraden' âpi—tac chṛṇu.

NĀRADA uvāca:

106.5 dur|labho vai su|hṛc chrotā, dur|labhaś ca hitaḥ su|hṛt;
tiṣṭhate hi su|hṛd yatra na bandhus tatra tiṣṭhate.
śrotavyam api paśyāmi su|hṛdāṃ, Kuru|nandana,
na kartavyaś ca nirbandho, nirbandho hi su|dāruṇaḥ.
atr' âpy udāharant' îmam itihāsaṃ purātanam,
yathā nirbandhataḥ prāpto Gālavena parājayaḥ.

Viśvāmitraṃ tapasyantaṃ Dharmo jijñāsayā purā
abhyagacchat svayaṃ bhūtvā Vasiṣṭho bhagavān ṛṣiḥ
sapta'|rṣīṇām anyatamaṃ veṣam āsthāya, Bhārata,
bubhukṣuḥ kṣubhito, rājann, āśramaṃ Kauśikasya tu.
106.10 Viśvāmitro 'tha saṃbhrāntaḥ śrapayām āsa vai carum
param'|ânnasya yatnena na ca taṃ pratyapālayat.

JANAM·ÉJAYA said:

THIS MAN WAS obstinately set on disaster, confused by his greed for other people's property. He enjoyed the company of ignoble men, and his mind was set on his own death. He was the cause of his relatives' misery, and he augmented their grief yet further. He granted his friends suffering, and increased the joy of his enemies. How is it that for reasons of friendship his relatives did not ward him off his evil path, and neither did the lord Krishna, the Kurus' affectionate friend, or his grandfather? 106.1

VAISHAMPÁYANA said:

Actually, the blessed lord did have something suitable to say, as did Bhishma, and Nárada too had plenty to add. Listen.

NÁRADA said:

A friend who listens is hard to find, and so too is a friend 106.5
who helps, for a friend is in a position that no relative can be in. In my view, friends say things that are really worth hearing, descendant of the Kurus; and you shouldn't be obstinate, for obstinacy's extremely cruel. This is the point of the ancient story, which men quote, of how Gálava's obstinacy wrought his destruction.

Long ago, Dharma took the form of the blessed sage Vasíshtha, and visited Vishva·mitra as he was practicing asceticism, in order to test him. So it was that he came to Káushika's hermitage, dressed in the guise of one of the seven seers, hungry and eager to eat, Bhárata king.
Vishva·mitra excitedly cooked *charu* rice,* but he didn't 106.10
take proper care of his guest because he was making so

annaṃ tena yadā bhuktam anyair dattaṃ tapasvibhiḥ;
atha gṛhy' ânnam atyuṣṇaṃ Viśvāmitro 'py upāgamat.
«bhuktaṃ me, tiṣṭha tāvat tvam,»
ity uktvā bhagavān yayau.
Viśvāmitras tato, rājan,
sthita eva mahā|dyutiḥ
bhaktaṃ pragṛhya mūrdhnā vai bāhubhyāṃ saṃśita|vrataḥ
sthitaḥ sthāṇur iv' âbhyāśe niścesto, mārut'|âśanaḥ.
tasya śuśrūṣaṇe yatnam akarod Gālavo muniḥ
gauravād bahu|mānāc ca hārdena priya|kāmyayā.
106.15 atha varṣa|śate pūrṇe Dharmaḥ punar upāgamat,
Vāsiṣṭhaṃ veṣam āsthāya Kauśikaṃ bhojan'|ēpsayā.
sa dṛṣṭvā śirasā bhaktaṃ dhriyamāṇaṃ maha"|rṣiṇā
tiṣṭhatā vāyu|bhakṣeṇa Viśvāmitreṇa dhīmatā,
pratigṛhya tato Dharmas tath" âiv' ôṣṇaṃ tathā navam,
bhuktvā, «prīto 'smi, vipra'|rṣe,» tam uktvā sa munir gataḥ.
kṣatra|bhāvād apagato brāhmaṇatvam upāgataḥ
Dharmasya vacanāt prīto Viśvāmitras tath" âbhavat.
Viśvāmitras tu śiṣyasya Gālavasya tapasvinaḥ
śuśrūṣayā ca bhaktyā ca prītimān ity uvāca ha,
106.20 «anujñāto mayā, vatsa, yath" êṣṭaṃ gaccha, Gālava.»
ity uktaḥ pratyuvāc' êdaṃ Gālavo muni|sattamam
prīto madhurayā vācā Viśvāmitraṃ mahā|dyutim:
«dakṣiṇāḥ kāḥ prayacchāmi bhavate guru|karmaṇi?
dakṣiṇābhir upetaṃ hi karma sidhyati, māna|da,
dakṣiṇānāṃ hi dātā vai apavargeṇa yujyate.
svarge kratu|phalaṃ tadd hi, dakṣiṇā śāntir ucyate.
kim āharāmi gurv|arthaṃ? bravītu bhagavān iti.»

much effort over the excellent meal. So his guest ate food offered by the other ascetics, until finally Vishva·mitra came out carrying the piping-hot food.

"Wait a while, because I have already eaten," he said; and the blessed lord left. Greatly glorious Vishva·mitra waited, king, holding the food on his head with his hands, faithful to his obligation. He stood near the hermitage, as motionless as a pillar, eating nothing but air, while a sage named Gálava made every effort to serve him out of respect, high regard, affection, and a desire to please him.

A hundred years passed before Dharma returned to Káu- 106.15
shika's hermitage wearing the guise of Vasíshtha, hungry for his meal. He saw wise Vishva·mitra, the mighty sage, supporting the meal on his head as he stood, eating nothing but the wind. So Dharma accepted the hot, fresh food, ate it, and said: "I am pleased, twiceborn sage!" Then the sage left. Dharma's words caused Vishva·mitra to transcend his warrior-class existence and reach brahminhood, and Vishva·mitra was delighted.*

Vishva·mitra was also pleased with the obedience and devotion of his ascetic student Gálava, and he said, "Go with 106.20
my leave as you wish, Gálava, my calf." Addressed in this way, Gálava delightedly replied to the greatest of sages, the illustrious Vishva·mitra, with sweet words, saying: "What presents can I find for you to thank you for having acted as my guru? A sacrifice is only truly accomplished with gifts, granter of honor, and the giver of gifts surely achieves emancipation. The gift is the reward of the sacrifice in heaven, and it is said to be our peace. So what should I fetch for my guru? Tell me, blessed lord!"

jānānas tena bhagavāñ jitaḥ śuśrūṣaṇena vai
Viśvāmitras tam a|sakṛd «gaccha, gacch'! êty» acodayat.
106.25 a|sakṛd «gaccha, gacch'! êti» Viśvāmitreṇa bhāṣitaḥ
«kiṃ dadān'? îti» bahuśo Gālavaḥ pratyabhāṣata.
nirbandhatas tu bahuśo Gālavasya tapasvinaḥ
kiñ cid āgata|saṃrambho Viśvāmitro 'bravīd idam,
«ekataḥ śyāma|karṇānāṃ hayānāṃ candra|varcasām
aṣṭau śatāni me dehi. gaccha, Gālava, mā|ciram!»

NĀRADA uvāca:

107.1 EVAM UKTAS TADĀ tena Viśvāmitreṇa dhīmatā
n' āste, na śete, n' āhāraṃ kurute Gālavas tadā.
tvag|asthi|bhūto, hariṇaś, cintā|śoka|parāyaṇaḥ
śocamāno 'timātraṃ sa, dahyamānaś ca manyunā,
Gālavo duḥkhito duḥkhād vilalāpa, Suyodhana:

«kutaḥ puṣṭāni mitrāṇi? kuto 'rthāḥ? sañcayaḥ kutaḥ?
hayānāṃ candra|śubhrāṇāṃ śatāny aṣṭau kuto mama?
kuto me bhojane śraddhā? sukha|śraddhā kutaś ca me?
śraddhā me jīvitasy' âpi cchinnā. kiṃ jīvitena me?
107.5 ahaṃ pāre samudrasya pṛthivyā vā paraṃ|parāt
gatv" ātmānaṃ vimuñcāmi. kiṃ phalaṃ jīvitena me?
a|dhanasy' â|kṛt'|ârthasya tyaktasya vividhaiḥ phalaiḥ
ṛṇaṃ dhārayamāṇasya kutaḥ sukham an|īhayā?
su|hṛdāṃ hi dhanaṃ bhuktvā, kṛtvā praṇayam īpsitam
pratikartum a|śaktasya jīvitān maraṇaṃ varam.

Lord Vishva·mitra was aware that he had won his victory through Gálava's obedience, so he often urged him on,
saying "Go away, go!" But as often as Vishva·mitra said 106.25
"Go away, leave!" Gálava repeated, "What shall I give you?" Eventually Vishva·mitra became somewhat aggravated with the ascetic Gálava's obstinacy, so he said this: "Give me eight hundred moon-hued horses with a single black ear each. Go without delay, Gálava!"

NÁRADA continued:

ONCE WISE VISHVA·MITRA had given him this order, Gá- 107.1
lava could not sit, sleep, or eat. Mere skin and bones, sallow, filled with worry and grief, he lamented beyond measure, burning with sorrow. So it was, Duryódhana, that wretched Gálava moaned in his misery:

"Where will I find wealthy friends? Where can I find riches? From where will I find a treasure hoard? Where will I find my eight hundred moon-hued horses? Where will I even find an appetite for food? From where can I find any trust in happiness? My faith in life is broken, so what is the point in me living any longer?

I will go to the sea shore or the furthest edge of the earth, 107.5
and then I will end my life, for what does living benefit me? Where can a man find happiness when he is poor, when he has not accomplished his aims, when he is abandoned by every kind of reward and weighed down with debt? For a man who has enjoyed the wealth of friends, which was gladly and affectionately given, but has no means to repay them, death is preferable to life.

pratiśrutya kariṣy' êti kartavyaṃ tad a|kurvataḥ
mithyā|vacana|dagdhasya iṣṭ'|āpūrtaṃ praṇaśyati.
na rūpam an|ṛtasy' âsti, n' ân|ṛtasy' âsti santatiḥ,
n' ân|ṛtasy' ādhipatyaṃ ca, kuta eva gatiḥ śubhā?
107.10 kutaḥ kṛta|ghnasya yaśaḥ? kutaḥ sthānaṃ? kutaḥ sukham?
a|śraddheyaḥ kṛta|ghno hi, kṛta|ghne n' âsti niṣkṛtiḥ.
na jīvaty a|dhanaḥ pāpaḥ; kutaḥ pāpasya tantraṇam?
pāpo dhruvam avāpnoti vināśaṃ, nāśayan kṛtam.
so 'haṃ pāpaḥ kṛta|ghnaś ca, kṛpaṇaś c' ân|ṛto 'pi ca,
guror yaḥ kṛta|kāryaḥ saṃs tat karomi na bhāṣitam.
so 'haṃ prāṇān vimokṣyāmi kṛtvā yatnam an|uttamam.
arthitā na mayā kā cit kṛta|pūrvā div'|âukasām,
mānayanti ca māṃ sarve tri|daśā yajña|saṃstare.
ahaṃ tu vibudha|śreṣṭhaṃ devaṃ tri|bhuvan'|ēśvaram
Viṣṇuṃ gacchāmy ahaṃ Kṛṣṇaṃ gatiṃ gatimatāṃ varam.
107.15 bhogā yasmāt pratiṣṭhante vyāpya sarvān sur'|âsurān,
praṇato draṣṭum icchāmi Kṛṣṇaṃ yoginam a|vyayam.»
evam ukte sakhā tasya Garuḍo Vinat''|ātmajaḥ
darśayām āsa; taṃ prāha saṃhṛṣṭaḥ priya|kāmyayā:
«su|hṛd bhavān mama mataḥ, su|hṛdāṃ ca mataḥ su|hṛt
īpsiten' âbhilāṣeṇa yoktavyo vibhave sati.
vibhavaś c' âsti me, vipra. Vāsav'|âvara|jo, dvija,
pūrvam uktas tvad|arthaṃ ca, kṛtaḥ kāmaś ca tena me.
sa bhavān etu, gacchāva, nayiṣye tvāṃ yathā|sukham

When one fails to do something one should, and something which one has promised one would do, one is burned by one's lies, and one's religious merit is destroyed. A liar has no beauty, nor does he have sons or power; so where can
he find a bright future? Where does an ungrateful man find 107.10
fame? Where can he find rank or happiness? The ungrateful man should not be trusted, for there is no atonement for an ungrateful man.

A destitute sinner does not really live, for where can a sinner find support? An evil man surely finds only destruction if he ruins a good deed done to him. I am evil, ungrateful, wretched, and a liar, for though I have accomplished training, I cannot do what my guru commanded. So I will try my best, and then kill myself.

I have never asked anything from the heaven-dwellers, and all thirty respected me for it at the sacrificial spread. But I will go now to the greatest teacher, the god who is the lord of the three worlds, Vishnu Krishna, the best course
for those who must tread one. I want to see Krishna and 107.15
bow to the eternal yogin through whom pleasures exist, for he pervades all gods and *ásuras*."

When he had said this, his friend Gáruda, the son of Vínata, revealed himself and addressed him with delight, for he wished to do him a favor: "I think of you as my friend, and a friend who is able should help a friend he respects to attain the wish he desires. It just so happens that I have the power to help, twiceborn brahmin, for I spoke to Vásava's younger brother earlier on your behalf, and he complied with my wish. So come on, let's go, sir, and I will bring you

deśaṃ pāraṃ pṛthivyā vā. gaccha, Gālava, mā ciram!»

SUPARṆA uvāca:

108.1 ANUŚIṢṬO 'SMI devena, Gālava, jñāna|yoginā.
brūhi kāmaṃ tu kāṃ yāmi draṣṭuṃ prathamato diśam—
pūrvāṃ vā, dakṣiṇāṃ v" âham, atha vā paścimāṃ diśam,
uttarāṃ vā, dvija|śreṣṭha—kuto gacchāmi, Gālava?
yasyām udayate pūrvaṃ sarva|loka|prabhāvanaḥ
savitā, yatra saṃdhyāyāṃ sādhyānāṃ vartate tapaḥ;
yasyāṃ pūrvaṃ matir yātā yayā vyāptam idaṃ jagat,
cakṣuṣī yatra Dharmasya yatra vai su|pratiṣṭhite;
108.5 kṛtaṃ yato hutaṃ havyaṃ sarpate sarvato|diśam;
etad dvāraṃ, dvija|śreṣṭha, divasasya tath" âdhvanaḥ;
atra pūrvaṃ prasūtā vai Dākṣāyaṇyaḥ prajāḥ striyaḥ;
yasyāṃ diśi pravṛddhāś ca Kaśyapasy' ātma|saṃbhavāḥ;
yato|mūlā surāṇāṃ śrīr, yatra Śakro 'bhyaṣicyata
sura|rājyena, vipra'|rṣe, devaiś c' âtra tapaś citam;
etasmāt kāraṇād, brahman, pūrv" êty eṣā dig ucyate;
yasmāt pūrvatare kāle pūrvam ev' āvṛtā suraiḥ,
ata eva ca sarveṣāṃ pūrvām āśāṃ pracakṣate;
pūrvaṃ sarvāṇi kāryāṇi daivāni sukham īpsatā.
108.10 atra vedāñ jagau pūrvaṃ bhagavān loka|bhāvanaḥ;
atr' âiv' ôktā Savitr" āsīt Sāvitrī brahma|vādiṣu;
atra dattāni sūryeṇa yajūṃṣi, dvija|sattama;
atra labdha|varaḥ Somaḥ suraiḥ kratuṣu pīyate;

smoothly to the far shore of the ocean or the furthest end of the world. Come, Gálava, do not delay!"

SUPÁRNA said:

Gálava, I have been instructed by the god who produces 108.1
knowledge. Tell me, as you wish, Gálava, greatest of brahmins, which direction I should go to see first—the east, the south, the west, or the north? Where shall I go? The sun, the creative force of all worlds, rises in the east, and it is there that the *sadhyas*, celestial beings, perform their asceticism at dawn. That is where the first thought came into being and pervaded the universe. Dharma's two eyes are there,
and it is there that Dharma himself is well established. It 108.5
is from there that the first performed oblation of clarified butter creeps over all directions.

That is the door of the day's course, greatest of brahmins, and it is there that Daksha's daughters first gave birth to their children. It was in that region that Káshyapa's sons prospered, that region where the gods' good fortune has its roots, where Shakra was consecrated as king of the celestials, and where the gods compiled their austerity, brahmin sage. This is the reason this region is called the first region, brahmin, and it is also called the first region of all because in the very early times it was the first to be filled with gods. So the man who desires happiness should perform all his divine rituals here first.

It was here that the blessed lord, creator of the world, 108.10
first sang the Veda, here that the Sávitri was first spoken by Savítri to the Vedic students, here that the sun gave us the Yajur Veda, greatest of brahmins, and here that Soma,

atra tṛptā huta|vahāḥ svāṃ yonim upabhuñjate;
atra Pātālam āśritya Varuṇaḥ śriyam āpa ca;
atra pūrvaṃ Vasiṣṭhasya paurāṇasya, dvija'|rṣabha,
sūtiś c' âiva pratiṣṭhā ca, nidhanaṃ ca prakāśate;
oṃ|kārasy' âtra jāyante sūtayo daśatīr daśa;
pibanti munayo yatra havir|dhūmaṃ sma dhūma|pāḥ;
108.15 prokṣitā yatra bahavo varāh'|ādyā mṛgā vane
Śakreṇa yajña|bhāg'|ârthe daivateṣu prakalpitāḥ;
atr' â|hitāḥ kṛta|ghnāś ca mānuṣāś c' âsurāś ca ye
udayaṃs tān hi sarvān vai krodhādd hanti vibhāvasuḥ;
etad dvāraṃ tri|lokasya, svargasya ca sukhasya ca;
eṣa pūrvo diśāṃ bhāgo. viśāvo 'tra yad' îcchasi,
priyaṃ kāryaṃ hi me tasya yasy' âsmi vacane sthitaḥ.
brūhi, Gālava, yāsyāmi. śṛṇu c' âpy aparāṃ diśam.

SUPARṆA uvāca:

109.1 IYAṂ VIVASVATĀ pūrvaṃ śrautena vidhinā kila
gurave dakṣiṇā dattā, dakṣiṇ" êty ucyate ca dik.
atra loka|trayasy' âsya pitṛ|pakṣaḥ pratiṣṭhitaḥ
atr' Ôṣmapāṇāṃ devānāṃ nivāsaḥ śrūyate, dvija;
atra viśve sadā devāḥ pitṛbhiḥ sārdham āsate
ijyamānāḥ sma lokeṣu saṃprāptās tulya|bhāgatām.

the boon that was won, was drunk by gods at sacrifices. It is here that oblation-eating fires consume their own source when sated by mantras, here that Váruna went to Patála and won his fortune, and here first of all that ancient Vasíshtha's birth, establishment, and demise occurred, bull of the twiceborn.

It was here that the syllable *om* took its birth a thousand times.* It is here that the smoke-drinking sages drink the
smoke of oblations, here that Shakra consecrated numerous 108.15
boars and other animals in the forest and appointed them as the share of the sacrifice for the gods, and here that the rising sun kills all unhelpful, ungrateful men and *ásura*s in his anger. This is the door to the three worlds, to heaven and happiness. This is the eastern region. Let's go there if you wish, for I certainly must do a favor for the man on whose words I rely. Just give me the word, Gálava, and I will be on my way. Now listen to what I have to tell you about another region.

SUPÁRNA continued:

VIVÁSVAT GAVE THIS region to his guru as a gift during a 109.1
*shrauta* ritual, or so they say, and so it is called *dákshina*,* the southern quarter. It is here that the multitude of ancestors of the three worlds exist, and where the Úshmapa gods are said to live, brahmin. The Vishva gods live here eternally with the ancestors, and when they are sacrificed to in the worlds, they gain an equal share here.

etad dvitīyaṃ vedasya dvāram ācakṣate, dvija,
truṭiśo lavaśaś c' âpi gaṇyate kāla|niścayaḥ;
109.5 atra deva'|rṣayo nityaṃ, pitṛ|loka'|rṣayas tathā,
tathā rāja'|rṣayaḥ sarve nivasanti gata|vyathāḥ;
atra dharmaś ca satyaṃ ca, karma c' âtra nigadyate;
gatir eṣā, dvija|śreṣṭha, karmaṇām avasāyinām;
eṣā dik sā, dvija|śreṣṭha, yāṃ sarvaḥ pratipadyate
vṛtā tv an|avabodhena sukhaṃ tena na gamyate;
Nairṛtānāṃ sahasrāṇi bahūny atra, dvija'|rṣabha,
sṛṣṭāni pratikūlāni draṣṭavyāny a|kṛt'|ātmabhiḥ.
atra Mandara|kuñjeṣu vipra'|rṣi|sadaneṣu ca
gāyanti gāthā Gandharvāś citta|buddhi|harā, dvija.
109.10 atra sāmāni gāthābhiḥ śrutvā gītāni Raivataḥ
gata|dāro gat'|âmātyo gata|rājyo vanaṃ gataḥ.
atra Sāvarṇinā c' âiva Yavakrīt'|ātmajena ca
maryādā sthāpitā, brahman, yāṃ sūryo n' âtivartate.
atra rākṣasa|rājena Paulastyena mah"|ātmanā
Rāvaṇena tapaś cīrtvā surebhyo 'maratā vṛtā.
atra vṛttena Vṛtro 'pi Śakra|śatrutvam īyivān;
atra sarv'|āsavaḥ prāptāḥ punar gacchanti pañcadhā.
atra duṣ|kṛta|karmāṇo narāḥ pacyanti, Gālava;
atra Vaitaraṇī nāma nadī vitaraṇair vṛtā.
109.15 atra gatvā sukhasy' ântaṃ duḥkhasy' ântaṃ prapadyate.
atra vṛtto dina|karaḥ su|rasaṃ kṣarate payaḥ,
kāṣṭhāṃ c' āsādya Vāsiṣṭhīṃ himam utsṛjate punaḥ.

They call this the second gate of Vedic law, brahmin,
and time is measured in small divisions of moments and
instants. The celestial sages live here unendingly, as do the 109.5
sages of the ancestral world and the royal sages, free of any
anxiety. This is the place where law, truth, and karma are
said to reside; this is where the results of actions settle, greatest of brahmins. This is the quarter, best of the twiceborn,
where everyone goes, but veiled with ignorance they do not
attain bliss.

There are many thousands of Náirrita demons, bull of the
twiceborn, created to be malicious, whom people with ill-
disciplined souls must face. Here, in the bowers of Mount
Mándara and in the brahmin seers' houses, *gandhárvas* sing
songs which exhilarate the mind and thoughts, brahmin. It 109.10
was here, to the forest, that the Daitya Ráivata came when
he heard the Saman songs in verses, abandoning his wife,
advisors, and kingdom.

It is here that Savárni and Yava·krita's son set the limits, brahmin, which even the sun does not transgress. It was
here that high-souled Rávana, the son of Pulástya and the
king of the *rákshasas*, practiced asceticism and chose invincibility from the gods as his gift. It was here that Vritra's
conduct made him Shakra's enemy, and it is here that every
breathing creature goes back to the five elements.

This is the place where miscreants get cooked, Gálava,
and it is here that the river Váitarani is filled with people
trying to cross. This is the place where one reaches the ex- 109.15
tremes of misery once one has reached the limit of bliss. It is
here that the sun produces sweet dew, and when it reaches
the Vasíshtha quarter it creates frost. This is where I found

atr' âhaṃ, Gālava, purā kṣudh'|ārtaḥ paricintayan
labdhavān yudhyamānau dvau bṛhantau gaja|kacchapau.
atra Cakradhanur nāma sūryāj jāto mahān ṛṣiḥ,
vidur yaṃ Kapilaṃ devaṃ, yen' ārtāḥ Sagar'|ātmajāḥ.
atra siddhāḥ śivā nāma brāhmaṇā veda|pāragāḥ
adhītya sakalān vedāl̃ lobhire mokṣam a|kṣayam.
atra Bhogavatī nāma purī Vāsuki|pālitā,
109.20 Takṣakeṇa ca nāgena, tath" âiv' Āirāvatena ca.
atra niryāṇa|kāle 'pi tamaḥ saṃprāpyate mahat
a|bhedyaṃ bhās|kareṇ' âpi, svayaṃ vā kṛṣṇa|vartmanā.
eṣa tasy' âpi te mārgaḥ paricāryasya, Gālava.
brūhi me yadi gantavyaṃ—pratīcīṃ śṛṇu c' â|parām.

SUPARṆA uvāca:

110.1 IYAṂ DIG DAYITĀ rājño Varuṇasya tu go|pateḥ;
sadā salila|rājasya pratiṣṭhā c' ādir eva ca.
atra paścād ahaḥ sūryo visarjayati gāḥ svayam,
paścim" êty abhivikhyātā dig iyaṃ, dvija|sattama.
yādasām atra rājyena salilasya ca guptaye
Kaśyapo bhagavān devo Varuṇaṃ sm' âbhyaṣecayat.
atra pītvā samastān vai Varuṇasya rasāṃs tu ṣaṭ
jāyate taruṇaḥ somaḥ śuklasy' ādau tamisra|hā.
110.5 atra paścāt kṛtā Daityā vāyunā saṃyatās tadā
niḥśvasanto mahā|vātair arditāḥ suṣupur, dvija.

two enormous creatures battling, an elephant and a tortoise, when I was afflicted with starvation and looking for food long ago, Gálava.

This is the place where Chakra·dhanus was born of the sun. The mighty seer is also known as the god Kápila, and it was he who tormented the sons of Ságara.* Here are the perfect brahmins called *shiva*s who have reached the limits of the Vedas, who have learned the whole Veda in its entirety, and have attained unending release. The city of Bhógavati is here, ruled by Vásuki, the snake Tákshaka, and Airávata. 109.20
This is the place where the thick darkness one experiences as one dies is impenetrable even by the sun or black-pathed fire, and this is the road which even you, worthy of worship though you may be, will have to travel, Gálava. So tell me if we should go there, or listen as I tell you about the another region—the west.

SUPÁRNA continued:

THIS REGION IS the favorite of Váruna the lord of wa- 110.1
ter; it is both the eternal abode of the king of the waters, and his source. This is the place where the sun emits his rays late in the day, and so it is known as the late region,* greatest of brahmins. It was here that blessed god Káshyapa consecrated Váruna as the king of aquatic creatures and the guardian of the sea.

It is here that the moon drinks all Váruna's six liquors and is reborn, young again at the beginning of the bright
fortnight, destroying the gloom. It was here that the winds 110.5
made the Daityas flee and bound them, and where the Daityas sighed, afflicted by the mighty winds, and eventu-

atra sūryaṃ praṇayinaṃ pratigṛhṇāti parvataḥ
Asto nāma yataḥ sandhyā paścimā pratisarpati.
ato rātriś ca nidrā ca nirgatā divasa|kṣaye
jāyate jīva|lokasya hartum ardham iv' āyuṣaḥ.
atra devīṃ Ditiṃ suptām ātma|prasava|dhāriṇīm
vigarbhām akaroc Chakro, yatra jāto Marud|gaṇaḥ.
atra mūlaṃ Himavato Mandaraṃ yāti śāśvatam
api varṣa|sahasreṇa na c' âsy' ânto 'dhigamyate.
110.10 atra kāñcana|śailasya kāñcan'|âṃbu|ruhasya ca
udadhes tīram āsādya Surabhiḥ kṣarate payaḥ.
atra madhye samudrasya kabandhaḥ pratidṛśyate
Svarbhānoḥ sūrya|kalpasya soma|sūryau jighāṃsataḥ;
Suvarṇaśiraso 'py atra hari|romṇaḥ pragāyataḥ
a|dṛśyasy' â|prameyasya śrūyate vipulo dhvaniḥ.
atra Dhvajavatī nāma kumārī Harimedhasaḥ
ākāśe «tiṣṭha tiṣṭh'! êti» tasthau sūryasya śāsanāt.
atra vāyus, tathā vahnir, āpaḥ, khaṃ c' âpi, Gālava,
āhnikaṃ c' âiva, naiśaṃ ca duḥkhaṃ sparśe vimuñcati.
110.15 ataḥ prabhṛti sūryasya tiryag āvartate gatiḥ,
atra jyotīṃṣi sarvāṇi viśanty āditya|maṇḍalam.
aṣṭā|viṃśati|rātraṃ ca caṃkramya saha bhānunā
niṣpatanti punaḥ sūryāt soma|saṃyoga|yogataḥ.

ally slept, brahmin. This is the place where Mount Asta lovingly accepts the sun, and it is from this mountain that the western darkness creeps.*

It is from here that night and sleep emerge, when the day dies, as though to steal half the lifetime of the living world. This is the place where Shakra aborted the child the goddess Diti was carrying while she slept, and from this child the horde of Maruts arose. Here the roots of Mount Himálaya reach the eternal Mount Mándara, and even with a thousand years to look, their limits would not be discovered.

This is the place where Súrabhi came, coming to the bank 110.10
of the sea of golden lotuses by the golden mountain, and
there she let her milk flow. Here in the middle of the ocean,
Svarbhánu the sun-like headless trunk can be seen, eager
to gobble the sun and moon. Green haired, invisible, and
immeasurable Suvárna·shiras can be heard singing the Veda
in a loud voice.

This is the place where Dhvájavati, the noble daughter
of Hari·medhas, was stuck in the ether when the sun commanded her, "Stay there, stay!" In this region, Gálava, wind,
fire, water, and air are all freed from the pain of their touch,
both day and night. It is from here that the sun's course be- 110.15
gins to meander,* and it is here that all constellations enter
the sun's course. Once they have traveled with the sun for
twenty-eight nights, they leave the sun's orbit to join the
moon's once more.

atra nityaṃ sravantīnāṃ prabhavaḥ sāgar'|ôdayaḥ,
atra loka|trayasy' āpas tiṣṭhanti Varuṇ'|ālaye.
atra pannaga|rājasy' âpy Anantasya niveśanam;
an|ādi|nidhanasy' âtra Viṣṇoḥ sthānam an|uttamam.
atr' ânala|sakhasy' âpi pavanasya niveśanam;
maha"|rṣeḥ Kaśyapasy' âtra Mārīcasya niveśanam.
110.20 eṣa te paścimo mārgo dig|dvāreṇa prakīrtitaḥ.
brūhi, Gālava, gacchāvo—buddhiḥ kā, dvija|sattama?

SUPARṆA uvāca:

111.1 YASMĀD UTTĀRYATE pāpād, yasmān niḥśreyaso 'śnute,
asmād uttāraṇa|balād uttar" êty ucyate, dvija.
uttarasya hiraṇyasya
    parivāpaś ca, Gālava,
mārgaḥ paścima|pūrvābhyāṃ
    digbhyāṃ vai madhyamaḥ smṛtaḥ.
asyāṃ diśi variṣṭhāyām uttarāyāṃ, dvija'|rṣabha,
n' â|saumyo, n' â|vidhey'|ātmā, n' â|dharmo vasate janaḥ.
atra Nārāyaṇaḥ Kṛṣṇo, Jiṣṇuś c' âiva nar'|ôttamaḥ
Badaryām āśrama|pade, tathā Brahmā ca śāśvataḥ.
111.5 atra vai Himavat|pṛṣṭhe nityam āste mah"|eśvaraḥ
Prakṛtyā Puruṣaḥ sārdhaṃ yug'|ânt'|âgni|sama|prabhaḥ.
na sa dṛśyo muni|gaṇais, tathā devaiḥ sa|Vāsavaiḥ,
gandharva|yakṣa|siddhair vā, Nara|Nārāyaṇād ṛte.
atra Viṣṇuḥ sahasr'|âkṣaḥ, sahasra|caraṇo, '|vyayaḥ,
sahasra|śirasaḥ śrīmān ekaḥ paśyati māyayā.

This place is the perpetual source of rivers which flow to the ocean, and it is here that the waters of the three worlds rest in Váruna's home. This place is also the home of the snake king Anánta, as well as the supreme dwelling belonging to Vishnu, the god without begnning or end. The homes of wind, the friend of fire, and the mighty seer Káshyapa Marícha are both here, greatest of the twiceborn.
This is the western path, which I have described to you in 110.20
my description of the quarters. Tell me, Gálava, what your plan is. Let's go, greatest of brahmins.

SUPÁRNA continued:

THIS NORTHERN REGION is called the "saving" quarter 111.1
by force of the word *uttárana*,* because through its power men are saved from evil and attain the ultimate good, brahmin. The path to the reservoir of the northern gold, Gálava, runs through this region from east to west, and so it is also known as the "middle" region. No unpleasant, uncontrolled, or lawless people live in this quarter of the supreme north, bull-like brahmin.

Naráyana Krishna, Jishnu, the greatest of men, and eternal Brahma live here in a hermitage at Bádari. Here on the 111.5
back of Mount Himálaya dwells the mighty lord, as glorious as the fire at the end of the age, as Púrusha with Prákriti. He cannot be seen by the hordes of sages, or by the gods led by Vásava, or by the *gandhárvas*, *yakshas*, and *siddhas*, but only by Nara and Naráyana. Only glorious, eternal, thousand-eyed, thousand-legged, and thousand-headed Vishnu could see him through his cunning.

atra rājyena viprāṇāṃ candramāś c' âbhyaṣicyata;
atra Gaṅgāṃ Mahādevaḥ patantīṃ gaganāc cyutām
pratigṛhya dadau loke mānuṣe, brahmavittama.
atra Devyā tapas taptaṃ Maheśvara|parīpsayā.
111.10 atra kāmaś ca roṣaś ca śailaś c' Ômā ca saṃbabhuḥ.
atra rākṣasa|yakṣāṇāṃ gandharvāṇāṃ ca, Gālava,
ādhitpatyena Kailāse dhana|do py abhiṣecitaḥ.
atra Caitrarathaṃ ramyam, atra Vaikhānas'|āśramaḥ,
atra Mandākinī c' âiva, Mandaraś ca, dvija'|rṣabha.
atra Saugandhika|vanaṃ Nairṛtair abhirakṣyate,
śādvalaṃ kadalī|skandham; atra Santānakā nagāḥ.
atra saṃyama|nityānāṃ Siddhānāṃ svaira|cāriṇām
vimānāny anurūpāṇi kāma|bhogyāni, Gālava.
atra te ṛṣayaḥ sapta, devī c' Ârundhatī tathā,
111.15 atra tiṣṭhati vai Svātir, atr' âsyā udayaḥ smṛtaḥ.
atra Yajñaṃ samāsādya dhruvaṃ sthātā pitā|mahaḥ;
jyotīṃṣi candra|sūryau ca parivartanti nityaśaḥ.
atra Gaṅgāṃ mahā|dvāraṃ rakṣanti, dvija|sattama,
Dhāmā nāma mah"|ātmāno munayaḥ satya|vādinaḥ.
na teṣāṃ jñāyate sūtir,† n' ākṛtir, na tapaś citam;
parivarta|sahasrāṇi kāma|bhojyāni, Gālava.

It was here that the moon was consecrated as king of the brahmins, and here that the great god received the river Ganges and then made a gift of her to the human world, as she fell shaken from the sky, most learned Vedic scholar. This is the place where the goddess Uma practiced asceticism, for she was eager to win mighty lord Shiva. This is 111.10
where desire, fury, Mount Himálaya, and Uma united. This is the place where the granter of wealth was consecrated on Mount Kailása as the ruler of the *rákshasa*s, *yaksha*s and *gandhárva*s, Gálava.

This is where the lovely Cháitraratha woods stand, where the hermitage of the Vaikhánasas lies, the river Mandákini runs, and Mount Mándara sits, bull of the twiceborn. The Sugándhika forest is here, guarded by Náirritas, with verdant pastures and banana groves, and so too are the Santánaka mountains. Here one can see the eternally self-disciplined *siddhas*' correspondingly magnificent independently moving chariots, which the *siddha*s enjoy as they wish, Gálava.

Here are the seven sages, the goddess Arúndhati, and the 111.15
constellation Svati, and this is the place it is recorded as rising from. This is where the stationary grandfather Brahma lies, approaching Yajña. This place is home to heavenly bodies and the sun and moon, which perpetually make their journey through the sky. This is where those high-souled and truthful sages who go by the name of Dhama seers guard the mighty floodgates of the Ganges, greatest of the twiceborn. No one knows where they came from, what they

yathā yathā praviśati tasmāt parataraṃ naraḥ,
tathā tathā, dvija|śreṣṭha, pravilīyati, Gālava.
n' âitat kena cid anyena gata|pūrvaṃ, dvija'|rṣabha,
111.20 ṛte Nārāyaṇaṃ devaṃ, Naraṃ vā Jiṣṇum a|vyayam.
atra Kailāsam, ity uktaṃ, sthānam Ailavilasya tat.
atra Vidyutprabhā nāma jajñire 'psaraso daśa.
atra Viṣṇu|padaṃ nāma kramatā Viṣṇunā kṛtam
tri|loka|vikrame, brahmann, uttarāṃ diśam āśritam.

atra rājñā Maruttena yajñen' êṣṭaṃ, dvij'|ôttama,
Uśīrabīje, vipra'|rṣe, yatra jāmbūnadaṃ saraḥ.
Jīmūtasy' âtra vipra'|rṣer upatasthe mah"|ātmanaḥ
sākṣādd Haimavataḥ puṇyo vimalaḥ kanak'|ākaraḥ,
brāhmaṇeṣu ca yat kṛtsnaṃ svantaṃ kṛtvā dhanaṃ mahat
111.25 vavre dhanaṃ maha"|rṣiḥ sa, Jaimūtaṃ tad dhanaṃ tataḥ.

atra nityaṃ diśāṃ|pālāḥ sāyaṃ|prātar, dvija'|rṣabha,
«kasya kāryaṃ kim? iti» vai parikrośanti, Gālava.
evam eṣā, dvija|śreṣṭha, guṇair anyair dig uttarā
uttar" êti parikhyātā, sarva|karmasu c' ôttarā.

etā vistaraśas, tāta, tava saṅkīrtitā diśaḥ
catasraḥ krama|yogena; kām āśāṃ gantum icchasi?
udyato 'haṃ, dvija|śreṣṭha, tava darśayituṃ diśaḥ,
pṛthivīṃ c' âkhilāṃ, brahmaṃs, tasmād āroha māṃ, dvija.

look like, or what asceticism they practice, but their thousands of revolutions of the planets can be enjoyed as one wishes, Gálava.

If a man enters further than this point, Gálava, greatest
of the twiceborn, he melts away. No one else has gone there
before, bull-like brahmin, except for divine Naráyana and 111.20
the eternal Nara Jishnu. This is where Mount Kailása is said
to be, as is the home of Áilavila Kubéra. This is where the
ten *ápsaras*es known as Vidyut·prabha, or Lightning-bright,
were born. Vishnu's footprint lies here in the north, made
as striding Vishnu strode over the three worlds, brahmin.

It was here that King Marútta offered a sacrifice at Ushíra·
bija by the golden lake, supreme twiceborn sage among
brahmins. This is the place where the sacred, pure gold mine
of Mount Himálaya is personified and waits upon the high-
souled brahmin sage Jimúta. The mighty sage gave his entire hoard of great wealth to brahmins, and requested that
it be named after him, and so it is called Jaimúta wealth.* 111.25

This is the place, bull-like brahmin Gálava, where the guardians of the quarters shout morning and evening. "Who needs anything to be done?" they constantly ask. This northern region is renowned as the best* for its other virtues and the best in all acts, greatest of brahmins.

So I have described the four quarters to you, my friend, in detail, at length, and in order. Which one of them do you want to go to? Greatest of the twiceborn, I am prepared to show the quarters and the whole earth to you, brahmin, so climb up onto my back, twiceborn man.

GĀLAVA uvāca:

112.1 GARUTMAN, BHUJAG'|êndr'|âre, Suparṇa, Vinat''|ātmaja,
naya māṃ, Tārkṣya, pūrveṇa yatra Dharmasya cakṣuṣī.
pūrvam etāṃ diśaṃ gaccha yā pūrvaṃ parikīrtitā;
devatānāṃ hi sānnidhyam atra kīrtitavān asi.
atra satyaṃ ca dharmaś ca tvayā samyak prakīrtitaḥ;
iccheyaṃ tu samāgantuṃ samastair daivatair aham,
bhūyaś ca tān surān draṣṭum iccheyam, Aruṇ'|ânuja.

NĀRADA uvāca:

tam āha Vinatā|sūnur: «ārohasv' êti!» vai dvijam.
āruroh' âtha sa munir Garuḍaṃ Gālavas tadā.

GĀLAVA uvāca:

112.5 kramamāṇasya te rūpaṃ dṛśyate, pannag'|âśana,
bhās|karasy' êva pūrv'|âhṇe sahasr'|âṃśor Vivasvataḥ.
pakṣa|vāta|praṇunnānāṃ vṛkṣāṇām anugāminām
prasthitānām iva samaṃ paśyām' îha gatiṃ, kha|ga.
sa|sāgara|vanām urvīṃ sa|śaila|vana|kānanām
ākarṣann iva c' ābhāsi pakṣa|vātena, khe|cara.
sa|mīna|nāga|nakraṃ ca kham iv' āropyate jalam
vāyunā c' âiva mahatā pakṣa|vātena c' ânisam!
tulya|rūp'|ānanān matsyāṃs tathā timi|timiṅgilān,
nāgāṃś ca nara|vaktrāṃś ca paśyāmy unmathitān iva.
112.10 mah''|ârṇavasya ca ravaiḥ śrotre me badhire kṛte!
na śṛṇomi, na paśyāmi, n' ātmano vedmi kāraṇam!

GÁLAVA replied:

O GARÚTMAT, ENEMY of the king of snakes, splendid- 112.1
feathered son of Vínata, take me to the east, Tarkshya,
where Dharma's two eyes reside. Go first to the quarter
which you first described, for you said in your description
that this is the place where the gods are. You talked about
truth and law being there, so take me there so I can meet all
the gods, for I would particularly like to visit the celestials,
brother
of Áruna.

NÁRADA continued:

Vínata's son said to the brahmin, "Climb aboard!" And so Gálava the sage clambered up onto Gáruda.

GÁLAVA said:

Snake-eater, as you travel your beauty resembles that of 112.5
Vivásvat, the thousand-rayed creator of light first thing in
the morning. I see the trees set on your path like an entourage, felled by the force of your wings, sky-traveler. You
blaze, sky-wanderer, through the force of your wings, and
seem to drag the earth with her oceans and forests, mountains, woods, and groves along with you.

The powerful and incessant force of your violent wings
seems to lift the water with its fish, snakes, and crocodiles
to the sky! I see fish with human faces, and whales, and fan-
tastical sea creatures, and snakes with the faces of men—as
though they've become transfused. The mighty ocean's roar 112.10
has deafened my ears! I can't hear anything, I can't see anything, and I don't know what I'm doing here!

śanaiḥ sa tu bhavān yātu brahma|vadhyām anusmaran!
na dṛśyate ravis, tāta, na diśo na ca khaṃ, kha|ga!
tama eva tu paśyāmi, śarīraṃ te na lakṣaye,
maṇī va jātyau paśyāmi cakṣuṣī te 'ham, aṇḍa|ja.
śarīraṃ tu na paśyāmi tava c' âiv' ātmanaś ca ha;
pade pade tu paśyāmi śarīrād agnim utthitam!
sa me nirvāpya sahasā cakṣuṣī śāmyate punaḥ.
tan niyaccha mahā|vegaṃ gamane, Vinat"|ātmaja!
112.15 na me prayojanaṃ kiñ cid gamane, pannag'|âśana.
saṃnivarta, mahā|bhāga, na vegaṃ viṣahāmi te!
gurave saṃśrutān' îha śatāny aṣṭau hi vājinām
ekataḥ śyāma|karṇānāṃ śubhrāṇāṃ candra|varcasām;
teṣāṃ c' âiv' âpavargāya mārgaṃ paśyāmi n', âṇḍa|ja,
tato 'yaṃ jīvita|tyāge dṛṣṭo mārgo may" ātmanaḥ.
n' âiva me 'sti dhanaṃ kiñ cin, na dhanen' ânvitaḥ su|hṛt,
na c' ârthen' âpi mahatā śakyam etad vyapohitum.

NĀRADA uvāca:

evaṃ bahu ca dīnaṃ ca bruvāṇaṃ Gālavaṃ tadā
pratyuvāca vrajann eva prahasan Vinat'|ātmajaḥ:
112.20 «n' âtiprajño 'si, vipra'|rṣe, yo "tmānaṃ tyaktum icchasi.
na c' âpi kṛtrimaḥ kālaḥ, Kālo hi param'|ēśvaraḥ.
kim ahaṃ pūrvam ev' êha bhavatā n' âbhicoditaḥ?
upāyo 'tra mahān asti yen' âitad upapadyate!
tad eṣa Ṛṣabho nāma parvataḥ sāgar'|ântike;
atra viśramya bhuktvā ca nivartiṣyāva, Gālava.»

Please go slowly, sir, and remember the enormity of brahmanicide! The sun has become invisible, my friend, as have the directions and the sky, sky-traveler! I see nothing but darkness and I cannot discern your body, but I can see your eyes, egg-born bird, like two jewels of exquisite quality. I see neither your body, nor even my own, but I do see fire rising from your body with every step you take. It blinds my eyes suddenly and is then extinguished once more, so rein in the excessive speed at which you are going, son of Vínata!

I don't really have any reason to go, snake-eater. Stop, 112.15
illustrious bird, for I cannot stand your pace! I did indeed promise my guru eight hundred radiant, moon-hued horses with one black ear each, but I can't see any way to pay my debt, egg-born bird. I do, however, see a way to forsake my life. I have no wealth of my own, nor even a rich friend. But even with enormous wealth I would be unable to keep my end of the bargain.

NÁRADA continued:

As Gálava kept moaning, going on and on, Vínata's son laughed, and as he sped along he replied to him, saying:
"You are not too wise, brahmin sage, wanting to kill yourself 112.20
as you do. One's time of death cannot be manufactured, for Time is the supreme master. Why did you not tell me this before? There is a great way to achieve a task of this sort right here! We shall rest and eat on this mountain called Ríshabha, here in the middle of the ocean, and then we will turn back, Gálava."

NĀRADA uvāca:

113.1 Ṛṣabhasya tataḥ śṛṅgaṃ nipatya dvija|pakṣiṇau
Śāṇḍilīṃ brāhmaṇīṃ tatra dadṛśāte tapo|'nvitām.
abhivādya Suparṇas tu Gālavaś c', âbhipūjya tām,
tayā ca svāgaten' ôktau, viṣṭare sanniṣīdatuḥ.
siddham annaṃ tayā dattaṃ bali|mantr'|ôpabṛṃhitam.
bhuktvā tṛptāv ubhau bhūmau suptau tāv anumohitau.
muhūrtāt pratibuddhas tu Suparṇo gaman'|ēpsayā
atha bhraṣṭa|tanūj'|âṅgam ātmānaṃ dadṛśe khagaḥ.
113.5 māṃsa|piṇḍ'|ôpamo 'bhūt sa mukha|pād'|ânvitaḥ khagaḥ.
Gālavas taṃ tathā dṛṣṭvā vimanāḥ paryapṛcchata:
«kim idaṃ bhavatā prāptam ih' āgamana|jaṃ phalam?
vāso 'yam iha kālaṃ tu kiyantaṃ nau bhaviṣyati?
kiṃ nu te manasā dhyātam a|śubhaṃ dharma|dūṣaṇam?
na hy ayaṃ bhavataḥ sv|alpo vyabhicāro bhaviṣyati!»
Suparṇo 'th' âbravīd vipraṃ:
«pradhyātaṃ vai mayā, dvija,
imāṃ siddhām ito netuṃ
tatra yatra Prajāpatiḥ,
yatra devo Mahādevo, yatra Viṣṇuḥ sanātanaḥ,
yatra Dharmaś ca, Yajñaś ca, tatr' êyaṃ nivased iti.
113.10 so 'haṃ bhagavatīṃ yāce praṇataḥ priya|kāmyayā:
‹may" âitan nāma pradhyātaṃ manasā śocatā kila.
tad evaṃ bahu|mānāt te may" êh' ân|īpsitaṃ kṛtam;
su|kṛtaṃ duṣ|kṛtaṃ vā tvaṃ māhātmyāt kṣantum arhasi.› »

NÁRADA continued:

THE BRAHMIN AND the bird alighted on a peak of Mount Ríshabha, and there they saw a brahmin woman called Shándili engaged in asceticism. Supárna and Gálava both greeted her and paid her their respects, and when she welcomed them both, they sat on the grass. They ate the food she provided, which had been invigorated with an offering and mantras, and then, both satisfied and overwhelmed, they slept on the ground. 113.1

Presently Supárna awoke and was keen to get going, but the bird saw that his wings were no longer attached to his body as they were supposed to be, but had, in fact, broken off. So it was that the bird had become a mere ball of flesh, 113.5 furnished with only a face and feet. When Gálava saw him, he dejectedly asked: "What happened to you? Is this the result of our coming here? How long will we have to stay here? Have you been entertaining impure thoughts detrimental to moral law? This could certainly not have been any small transgression on your part!"

Supárna told the brahmin: "I had planned to take this lady of accomplished austerity to the place where Praja·pati, the god Maha·deva, and eternal Vishnu live with Dharma and Sacrifice, brahmin, for she should live there. So I will 113.10 beg the lady and bow to her, in my desire for some good to come out of this, and I will admit to her: 'With a grieving heart I did indeed entertain the idea, but it was out of my deep respect for you that I did this thing you disliked, so regardless of whether it was a good or bad thing to do, you ought to forgive me in your magnanimity.'"

sā tau tad" âbravīt tuṣṭā
patag'|êndra|dvija'|rṣabhau:
«na bhetavyaṃ, su|parṇo 'si,
Suparṇa, tyaja saṃbhramam.
nindit" âsmi tvayā, vatsa, na ca nindāṃ kṣamāmy aham.
lokebhyaḥ sapadi bhraśyed yo māṃ nindeta pāpa|kṛt.
hīnay" â|lakṣaṇaiḥ sarvais tath" â|ninditayā mayā
ācāraṃ pratigṛhṇantyā siddhiḥ prāpt" êyam uttamā.
113.15 ācāraḥ phalate dharmam, ācāraḥ phalate dhanam,
ācārāc chriyam āpnoti, ācāro hanty a|lakṣaṇam.
tad, āyuṣman khaga|pate, yath" êṣṭaṃ gamyatām itaḥ;
na ca te garhaṇīy" âhaṃ, garhitavyāḥ striyaḥ kva cit.
bhavit" âsi yathā|pūrvaṃ bala|vīrya|samanvitaḥ.»
babhūvatus tatas tasya pakṣau draviṇavattarau.
anujñātas tu Śāṇḍilyā yath"|āgatam upāgamat;
n' âiva c' āsādayām āsa tathā|rūpāṃs turaṅgamān.
Viśvāmitro 'tha taṃ dṛṣṭvā Gālavaṃ c' âdhvani sthitaḥ;
uvāca vadatāṃ śreṣṭho Vainateyasya sannidhau:
113.20 «yas tvayā svayam ev' ârthaḥ pratijñāto mama, dvija,
tasya kālo 'pavargasya, yathā vā manyate bhavān.
pratīkṣiṣyāmy ahaṃ kālam etāvantaṃ tathā param;
yathā saṃsidhyate, vipra, sa mārgas tu niśamyatām.»
Suparṇo 'th' âbravīd dīnaṃ Gālavaṃ bhṛśa|duḥkhitam:
«pratyakṣaṃ khalv idānīṃ me, Viśvāmitro yad uktavān.
tad āgaccha, dvija|śreṣṭha, mantrayiṣyāva, Gālava.
n' â|datvā gurave śakyaṃ kṛtsnam arthaṃ tvay" āsitum.»

So, satisfied, she said to the bull of brahmins and the king of birds:

"Don't be afraid, Supárna, for you are indeed well-winged.* Abandon your agitation. You insulted me, calf, and I do not endure insult. The evil-doer who abuses me will be lost from his worlds instantly. I have achieved the ultimate ascetic success because I am blameless and devoid of all inauspicious markings, and because of my moral behavior. Good conduct results in law, good conduct results 113.15
in wealth, good conduct gains good fortune, and good conduct destroys anything inauspicious.

So, long-lived lord of birds, go as you please from this place. Though there may be women elsewhere who deserve reproach, I am not one of them. Do not reproach me. You will be as powerful and mighty as before."

His pair of wings grew back even stronger than ever they were. Then, with Shándili's leave, he left just as he had come, though the brahmin had not found any horses of the required appearance.

Vishva·mitra saw Gálava as he was on the road, and the greatest of speakers said to him in the presence of Vínata's
son: "The time has come for you to pay the debt that you 113.20
promised; or do you think otherwise, brahmin? I will wait as long again, so find a way to achieve your aim, brahmin!"

Supárna said to the dejected and excessively pained Gálava: "Now I have indeed clearly heard what Vishva·mitra has said. So come, greatest of brahmins, and let us take counsel, Gálava. You cannot sit and rest until you have given your guru his entire prize."

NĀRADA uvāca:

114.1 ATH' ĀHA GĀLAVAM dīnaṃ Suparṇaḥ patatāṃ varaḥ:
«nirmitaṃ vahninā bhūmau, vāyunā śodhitaṃ tathā,
yasmādd hiraṇmayaṃ sarvaṃ, hiraṇyaṃ tena c' ôcyate.
dhatte dhārayate c' êdam, etasmāt kāraṇād dhanam,
tad etat triṣu lokeṣu dhanaṃ tiṣṭhati śāśvatam.
nityaṃ proṣṭha|padābhyāṃ ca Śukre dhana|patau tathā
manuṣyebhyaḥ samādatte Śukraś citt'|ārjitaṃ dhanam.
Ajaikapād|Ahirbudhnyai rakṣyate, dhana|dena ca;
evaṃ na śakyate labdhum a|labdhavyaṃ, dvija'|rṣabha.
ṛte ca dhanam aśvānāṃ n' âvāptir vidyate tava.
114.5 sa tvaṃ yāc' âtra rājānaṃ kañ cid rāja'|rṣi|vaṃśa|jam,
a|pīḍya rājā paurān hi yo nau kuryāt kṛt'|ârthinau.
asti som'|ânvavāye me jātaḥ kaś cin nṛpaḥ sakhā.
abhigacchāvahe taṃ vai; tasy' âsti vibhavo bhuvi.
Yayātir nāma rāja'|rṣir Nāhuṣaḥ satya|vikramaḥ,
sa dāsyati mayā c' ôkto, bhavatā c' ârthitaḥ svayam.
vibhavaś c' âsya su|mahān āsīd dhana|pater iva;
evaṃ guru|dhanaṃ, vidvan, dānen' âiva viśodhaya.»
tathā tau kathayantau ca cintayantau ca yat kṣamam
Pratiṣṭhāne nara|patiṃ Yayātiṃ pratyupasthitau.
114.10 pratigṛhya ca sat|kārair arghya|pādy'|ādikaṃ varam,
pṛṣṭaś c' āgamane hetum, uvāca Vinatā|sutaḥ.

NÁRADA continued:

SUPÁRNA, THE BEST of birds, then said to the distressed Gálava: "Made in the earth by fire, and made pure by the wind, gold—*hiránya*—is so called because the earth is called *hiránmaya* or golden. Wealth is called *dhana* because it puts men down and supports them,* and that is why wealth exists eternally in the three worlds. Shukra,* the lord of wealth, bestows upon men the wealth which they have earned with their thoughts, under the double constellation known as the 'two feet of the stool.' 114.1

One is not able to attain the unattainable, bull-like brahmin, when it is guarded by Ajáikapad, Ahir·búdhnya, and the lord of wealth. But without wealth you have no chance of obtaining the horses. So beg some king, born into a line 114.5
of royal sages, who could, in fact, help us achieve our aim without doing any harm to his citizens.

There is a certain king—a friend of mine who was born in the lineage of the moon. Let's go to him for he possesses majesty in this world. He is Yayáti, the royal sage and son of Náhusha, and his strength is his truth. He will give if you yourself ask and I command him. He used to have wealth so great that it equaled that of the lord of riches, so purify yourself by paying your debt to your guru through Yayáti's generosity."

As they discussed and contemplated the options, they reached King Yayáti in Pratishtháná. Once they had been 114.10
accepted with hospitality, guest gifts, water, and excellent food, Vínata's son was questioned as to why he had come.

«ayaṃ me, Nāhuṣa, sakhā Gālavas tapaso nidhiḥ
Viśvāmitrasya śiṣyo 'bhūd varṣāṇy ayutaśo, nṛpa.
so 'yaṃ ten' âbhyanujñāta upakār'|ēpsayā dvijaḥ
tam āha bhagavān kāle, ‹dadāni guru|dakṣiṇām?›
a|sakṛt tena c' ôktena kiñ cid āgata|manyunā
ayam uktaḥ ‹prayacch' êti› jānatā vibhavaṃ laghu,
‹ekataḥ śyāma|karṇānāṃ śubhrāṇāṃ śuddha|janmanām
aṣṭau śatāni me dehi hayānāṃ candra|varcasām.
114.15 gurv|artho dīyatām eṣa yadi, Gālava, manyase.›
ity evam āha sa|krodho Viśvāmitras tapo|dhanaḥ.
so 'yaṃ śokena mahatā tapyamāno dvija'|rṣabhaḥ
a|śaktaḥ pratikartuṃ tad bhavantaṃ śaraṇaṃ gataḥ.
pratigṛhya, nara|vyāghra, tvatto bhikṣāṃ gata|vyathaḥ,
kṛtv" âpavargaṃ gurave cariṣyati mahat tapaḥ.
tapasaḥ saṃvibhāgena bhavantam api yokṣyate,
svena rāja'|rṣi|tapasā pūrṇaṃ tvāṃ pūrayiṣyati.
yāvanti romāṇi haye bhavant' îha, nar'|ēśvara,
tāvato vājino lokān prāpnuvanti, mahī|pate.
114.20 pātraṃ pratigrahasy' âyaṃ, dātuṃ pātraṃ tathā bhavān,
śaṅkhe kṣīram iv' āsiktaṃ bhavatv etat tath" ôpamam.»

NĀRADA uvāca:

115.1 EVAM UKTAḤ Suparṇena tathyaṃ vacanam uttamam
vimṛśy' âvahito rājā. niścitya ca punaḥ punaḥ,
yaṣṭā kratu|sahasrāṇāṃ, dātā dāna|patiḥ prabhuḥ
Yayātiḥ sarva|Kāś'|īśa idaṃ vacanam abravīt,
dṛṣṭvā priya|sakhaṃ Tārkṣyaṃ Gālavaṃ ca dvija'|rṣabham,

"Son of Náhusha, this is my friend, the ascetic Gálava. He has been Vishva·mitra's pupil for ten thousand years, king.

When he was given leave to go by his teacher, this blessed brahmin wanted to repay him, so he said to him at that time: 'What should I give as a guru gift?' Being asked repeatedly, the teacher became irritable and said, 'Then give!' And though he understood how pitiful his means were, he continued, 'Give me eight hundred pure-bred, radiant,
moon-hued horses with a single black ear each. Let this be 114.15
the gift for your guru, if you wish, Gálava.' This is how Vishva·mitra, rich in asceticism, spoke to him in his anger.

This bull-like brahmin is burned by his great grief, for he is unable to keep his end of the bargain. And so he has come to you for refuge. Tiger-like man, when he has accepted help from you and his agitation is gone, then he will repay his guru and practice mighty austerity. He will endow you with a share of his asceticism, and fill you with asceticism, full as you are already with your own austerity, that of a royal sage. For he who gives away his horse gains as many worlds as there are hairs on his horse, lord of men and earth.
This man here is as suitable a vessel to receive as you are a 114.20
vessel to give, just like milk poured into a conch shell."

NÁRADA continued:

ADDRESSED BY Supárna in suitable and excellent words, 115.1
generous King Yayáti, the lord who performs a thousand sacrifices, the lord of wealth, and the lord of all the Kashis, contemplated them deeply over and over again, then made up his mind and spoke. He gazed at his dear friend Tarkshya

nidarśanaṃ ca tapasā, bhikṣāṃ ślāghyāṃ ca kīrtitām,
atītya ca nṛpān anyān āditya|kula|saṃbhavān,
mat|sakāśam anuprāptāv etāṃ buddhim avekṣya ca,
115.5 «adya me sa|phalaṃ janma, tāritaṃ c' âdya me kulam,
ady' âyaṃ tārito deśo mama, Tārkṣya, tvayā, 'n|agha.
vaktum icchāmi tu, sakhe, yathā jānāsi māṃ purā,
na tathā vittavān asmi; kṣīṇaṃ vittaṃ ca me, sakhe.
na ca śakto 'smi te kartuṃ mogham āgamanaṃ, khaga,
na c' āśām asya vipra'|rṣer vitathī|kartum utsahe.
tat tu dāsyāmi yat kāryam idaṃ sampādayiṣyati;
abhigamya hat'|āśo hi nivṛtto dahate kulam.

n' âtaḥ paraṃ, Vainateya, kiñ cit pāpiṣṭham ucyate
yath" āśā|nāśanāl loke ‹dehi› ‹n' âst' îti› vā vacaḥ.
115.10 hat'|āśo hy a|kṛt'|ârthaḥ san hataḥ saṃbhāvito naraḥ
hinasti tasya putrāṃś ca pautrāṃś c' â|kurvato hitam.
tasmāc caturṇāṃ vaṃśānāṃ sthāpayitrī sutā mama
iyaṃ sura|suta|prakhyā sarva|dharm'|ôpacāyinī,
sadā deva|manuṣyāṇām asurāṇāṃ ca, Gālava,
kāṅkṣitā rūpato bālā sutā me pratigṛhyatām.

asyāḥ śulkaṃ pradāsyanti nṛpā rājyam api dhruvam,
kiṃ punaḥ śyāma|karṇānāṃ hayānāṃ dve catuḥ|śate!
sa bhavān pratigṛhṇātu mam' âitāṃ Mādhavīṃ sutām;
ahaṃ dauhitravān syāṃ vai, vara eṣa mama, prabho!»

and the bull-like brahmin Gálava, and he considered that the request for help would be renowned as a commendable indication of his asceticism, as he thought on the fact that those two had come to him, ignoring the other kings born into the lineage of the sun. He said:

"Today my birth has borne fruit, today my line is res- 115.5
cued, and today my realm has been saved by you, blameless Tarkshya. I wish to tell you, however, my friend, that
I am not as wealthy as I once was when you knew me, for
my wealth has been depleted, my friend. But I cannot allow your coming here to be in vain, sky-traveler, and nor
do I dare to disappoint this brahmin sage's hopes. So I will
provide the means to achieve your task; for someone who
comes and leaves with his hopes dashed does indeed burn
the lineage.

Son of Vínata, it is claimed that there is nothing more
evil in the world than saying 'I have nothing,' thereby crush-
ing the hopes of the man who says 'Please give me something.' The esteemed man whose hopes are dashed and 115.10
whose aims are unachieved does harm to the sons and
grandsons of the man who failed to help him. And so, accept my daughter who will found four lineages: a woman
who is as beautiful as a celestial child, who acts in accordance with all laws, and who is always desired by gods, men,
and *ásuras* for her beauty, Gálava.

Kings will surely give even their kingdom as a dowry for her, let alone eight hundred black-eared horses! Please accept my daughter Mádhavi, sir, for my wish is to have grandsons, lord!"

115.15 pratighya ca tāṃ kanyāṃ Gālavaḥ saha pakṣiṇā
«punar drakṣyāva, ity» uktvā pratasthe saha kanyayā.
«upalabdham idaṃ dvāram aśvānām, iti» c' âṇḍa|jaḥ
uktvā Gālavam āpṛcchya jagāma bhavanaṃ svakam.
gate pataga|rāje tu Gālavaḥ saha kanyayā
cintayānaḥ kṣamaṃ dāne rājñāṃ vai śulkato 'gamat.
so 'gacchan manas" Êkṣvākuṃ Haryaśvaṃ rāja|sattamam
Ayodhyāyāṃ mahā|vīryaṃ catur aṅga|bal'|ânvitam,
kośa|dhānya|bal'|ôpetaṃ, priya|pauraṃ, dvija|priyam,
praj'|âbhikāmaṃ śāmyantaṃ, kurvāṇaṃ tapa uttamam.
115.20 tam upāgamya vipraḥ sa Haryaśvaṃ Gālavo 'bravīt:
«kany" êyaṃ mama, rāj'|êndra, prasavaiḥ kula|vardhinī.
iyaṃ śulkena bhāry"|ârthaṃ, Haryaśva, pratigṛhyatām.
śulkaṃ te kīrtayiṣyāmi; tac chrutvā saṃpradhāryatām.»

NĀRADA uvāca:

116.1 HARYAŚVAS TV abravīd rājā vicintya bahudhā tataḥ
dīrgham uṣṇaṃ ca niḥśvasya prajā|hetor nṛp'|ôttamaḥ,
«unnateṣ' ûnnatā ṣaṭsu, sūkṣmā sūkṣmeṣu saptasu,
gambhīrā triṣu gambhīreṣv iyaṃ, raktā ca pañcasu.
bahu|dev'|âsur'|ālokā, bahu|gandharva|darśanā,
bahu|lakṣaṇa|sampannā, bahu|prasava|dhāriṇī;
samarth" ēyaṃ janayituṃ cakra|vartinam ātma|jam.

So, having accepted his daughter, Gálava said, "We will see each other again," and left with the bird and the girl. The bird said, "You have found the gate to the horses!" Then he bade Gálava farewell and returned to his own home. 115.15

Once the king of the birds had left, Gálava continued on his way with the girl, pondering the options as to which kings would pay the proper dowry. He made up his mind to go to superb King Hary·ashva Ikshváku of Ayódhya, the great powerful leader of a four-winged army, endowed with treasuries, grain, and strength; a man who was dear to his citizens and kind to brahmins, cared peacefully for his subjects, and practiced the strictest asceticism.

So it was that the brahmin Gálava approached Hary·ashva and said to him: "Please accept this girl of mine as your wife for a dowry, lord of kings, for she will augment lineages with children. I will detail the price, and when you've heard it, ponder my offer." 115.20

NÁRADA continued:

KING HARY·ASHVA thought a great deal, and sighed long, hot sighs for the sake of children, and then the excellent king said, "She is high in the six places a woman should be high. She is slender in the seven places a woman should be slender. She is deep in the three areas a woman should be deep, and crimson in the five areas that she should be crimson. She is a sight to behold for numerous gods and *ásuras*, a vision for many *gandhárvas*, endowed with numerous auspicious markings, and she is a woman who could bear many children. She could give birth to a child who would rule 116.1

brūhi śulkaṃ, dvija|śreṣṭha, samīkṣya vibhavaṃ mama.»

GĀLAVA uvāca:

116.5 ekataḥ śyāma|karṇanāṃ śatāny aṣṭau prayaccha me
hayānāṃ candra|śubhrāṇāṃ deśa|jānāṃ vapuṣmatām.
tatas tava bhavitr" îyaṃ putrāṇāṃ jananī śubhā
araṇ" îva hut'|âśānāṃ yonir āyata|locanā.

NĀRADA uvāca:

etac chrutvā vaco rājā Haryaśvaḥ kāma|mohitaḥ
uvāca Gālavaṃ dīno rāja'|rṣir ṛṣi|sattamam:
«dve me śate saṃnihite hayānāṃ yad|vidhās tava
eṣṭavyā, śataśas tv anye caranti mama vājinaḥ.
so 'ham ekam apatyaṃ vai janayiṣyāmi, Gālava,
asyām; etaṃ bhavān kāmaṃ saṃpādayatu me varam.»
116.10 etac chrutvā tu sā kanyā Gālavaṃ vākyam abravīt:
«mama datto varaḥ kaś cit kena cid brahma|vādinā:
‹prasūty|ante prasūty|ante kany" âiva tvaṃ bhaviṣyasi.›
sa tvaṃ dadasva māṃ rājñe pratigṛhya hay'|ôttamān.
nṛpebhyo hi caturbhyas te pūrṇāny aṣṭau śatāni vai
bhaviṣyanti tathā putrā mama catvāra eva ca.
kriyatām upasaṃhāro gurv|arthaṃ, dvija|sattama,
eṣā tāvan mama prajñā; yathā vā manyase, dvija?»
evam uktas tu sa muniḥ kanyayā Gālavas tadā
Haryaśvaṃ pṛthivī|pālam idaṃ vacanam abravīt:
116.15 «iyaṃ kanyā, nara|śreṣṭha Haryaśva, pratigṛhyatām
catur|bhāgena śulkasya janayasv' âikam ātmajam.»
pratigṛhya sa tāṃ kanyāṃ, Gālavaṃ pratinandya ca,

the world. So tell me the dowry price, greatest of brahmins, and take my circumstances into account."

GÁLAVA replied:

Give me eight hundred native, handsome, moon-hued 116.5
horses with a single black ear each. Then this wide-eyed beautiful lady will bear your children, just as the kindling wood is the source of the oblation-eating fire.

NÁRADA continued:

Hearing these words, King Hary·ashva was confused by lust, but he spoke dejectedly to Gálava as a royal sage to an excellent brahmin sage: "I have two hundred of these horses which I can give you, and hundreds of other desirable horses run in my lands. I want to have one child with this girl, Gálava, so please grant my wish."

When the girl had heard the king speak, she said to Gá- 116.10
lava: "A Vedic reciter once granted me a wish that every time I gave birth I would become a virgin again. So give me to the king and take your fine horses. You will surely get your full eight hundred steeds from four kings, and I will have four sons. This is how you should collect your teacher's gift, greatest of brahmins; or at least that's my idea. Do you think differently, brahmin?"

Thus addressed by the girl, Gálava the sage said to Hary·
ashva, the lord of earth: "Hary·ashva, greatest of men, please 116.15
take this girl and, for a quarter of the dowry, have one child with her." So it was that he accepted the girl and praised Gálava. Then at the due time and place he obtained the son he had longed for, and the son became a wealth-granting

samaye deśa|kāle ca labdhavān sutam īpsitam.
tato Vasumanā nāma Vasubhyo vasumattaraḥ
Vasu|prakhyo nara|patiḥ sa babhūva vasu|pradaḥ.

atha kāle punar dhīmān Gālavaḥ pratyupasthitaḥ,
upasaṅgamya c' ôvāca Haryaśvaṃ prīta|mānasam:
«jāto, nṛpa, sutas te 'yaṃ bālo bhāskara|saṃnibhaḥ.
kālo gantuṃ, nara|śreṣṭha, bhikṣ"|ârtham a|paraṃ nṛpam.»
116.20 Haryaśvaḥ satya|vacane sthitaḥ, sthitvā ca pauruṣe
dur|labhatvādd hayānāṃ ca pradadau Mādhavīṃ punaḥ.
Mādhavī ca punar dīptāṃ parityajya nṛpa|śriyam
kumārī kāmato bhūtvā Gālavaṃ pṛṣṭhato 'nvayāt.
«tvayy eva tāvat tiṣṭhantu hayā, ity» uktavān dvijaḥ
prayayau kanyayā sārdhaṃ Divodāsaṃ praj'|ēśvaram.

GĀLAVA uvāca:

117.1 MAHĀ|VĪRYO mahī|pālaḥ Kāśīnām īśvaraḥ prabhuḥ
Divodāsa iti khyāto Bhaimasenir nar'|âdhipaḥ.
tatra gacchāvahe, bhadre, śanair āgaccha, mā śucaḥ;
dhārmikaḥ, saṃyame yuktaḥ, satye c' âiva jan'|ēśvaraḥ.

NĀRADA uvāca:

tam upāgamya sa munir nyāyatas tena sat|kṛtaḥ
Gālavaḥ prasavasy' ârthe taṃ nṛpaṃ pratyacodayat.

king called Vasu·manas, richer than the Vasus themselves, and equal to a Vasu in appearance.

In time, wise Gálava returned once more, and upon meeting joyful-minded King Hary·ashva, he said to him: "Your son has been born, king, and your child blazes like the sun. So the time has come, greatest of men, for us to go to another king for aid."

So Hary·ashva, who remained true to his word just as he 116.20
remained true to his manliness, returned Mádhavi because he found those horses too difficult to attain. And Mádhavi for her part abandoned her blazing royal glory and became a virgin once more through the force of her will, following behind Gálava. Then, saying "Let the horses stay here with you for a while," the brahmin set out with the girl to see Divo·dasa, the ruler of men.

GÁLAVA said:

THERE IS A GREAT and powerful king in this world known 117.1
as Divo·dasa. He is the lord and king of the Kashis, and Bhima·sena's sovereign son. Let's go there, my dear girl. Come slowly and do not be sad, for that lord of men is moral, and practices self-discipline and truth.

NÁRADA said:

The sage made his way to the king, and was treated well and properly by him. Then Gálava began to encourage the king to have children.

DIVODĀSA uvāca:

«śrutam etan mayā pūrvaṃ; kim uktvā vistaraṃ, dvija?
kāṅkṣito hi may" âiṣo 'rthaḥ śrutv" âiva, dvija|sattama!
117.5 etac ca me bahu|mataṃ yad utsṛjya nar'|âdhipān
mām evam upayāto 'si; bhāvi c' âitad a|saṃśayam.
sa eva vibhavo 'smākam aśvānām api, Gālava,
aham apy ekam ev' âsyāṃ janayiṣyāmi pārthivam.»
tath" êty uktvā dvija|śreṣṭhaḥ prādāt kanyāṃ mahī|pateḥ
vidhi|pūrvāṃ ca tāṃ rājā kanyāṃ pratigṛhītavān.
reme sa tasyāṃ rāja'|rṣiḥ Prabhāvatyāṃ yathā raviḥ,
Svāhāyāṃ ca yathā Vahnir, yathā Śacyāṃ ca Vāsavaḥ;
yathā Candraś ca Rohiṇyāṃ,
yathā Dhūmorṇayā Yamaḥ,
Varuṇaś ca yathā Gauryāṃ,
yathā ca' Rddhyāṃ Dhan'|ēśvaraḥ;
117.10 yathā Nārāyaṇo Lakṣmyāṃ, Jāhnavyāṃ ca yath" Ôdadhiḥ,
yathā Rudraś ca Rudrāṇyāṃ, yathā vedyāṃ pitā|mahaḥ;
Adṛśyantyāṃ ca Vāsiṣṭho, Vasiṣṭhaś c' Âkṣamālayā,
Cyavanaś ca Sukanyāyāṃ, Pulastyaḥ Sandhyayā yathā;
Agastyaś c' âpi Vaidarbhyāṃ, Sāvitryāṃ Satyavān yathā,
yathā Bhṛguḥ Pulomāyām, Adityāṃ Kaśyapo yathā;
Reṇukāyāṃ yath" Ārcīko, Haimavatyāṃ ca Kauśikaḥ,
Bṛhaspatiś ca Tārāyāṃ, Śukraś ca Śataparvayā;
yathā Bhūmyāṃ Bhūmipatir, Urvaśyāṃ ca Purūravāḥ,
Ṛcīkaḥ Satyavatyāṃ ca, Sarasvatyāṃ yathā Manuḥ;
117.15 Śakuntalāyāṃ Duṣyanto, Dhṛtyāṃ Dharmaś ca śāśvataḥ,
Damayantyāṃ Nalaś c' âiva, Satyavatyāṃ ca Nāradaḥ;
Jaratkārur Jaratkārvāṃ, Pulastyaś ca Pratīcyayā
Menakāyāṃ yath" Ōrṇāyus, Tumburuś c' âiva Rambhayā;
Vāsukiḥ Śataśīrṣāyāṃ, Kumāryāṃ ca Dhanañjayaḥ,

DASA replied:

"I have already heard all about this, so why speak further, brahmin? In fact, my heart was set on this matter the
moment I heard about it, greatest of the twiceborn! It is a 117.5
matter of great esteem that you passed over other kings and
came to me, so without a shred of doubt the deal will be
done. I only have an equal wealth of horses, Gálava, so I
too will only have one royal son with her."

Spoken to in this manner, the greatest of brahmins bestowed the girl upon the king, and the king accepted the
girl according to the ancient customs. The royal sage made
love to her like the Sun to Prabhávati, like Fire to Svaha,
like Vásava to Shachi, like the Moon to Róhini, like Yama
to Dhumórna, like Váruna to Gauri, like Kubéra to Riddhi,
like Naráyana to Lakshmi, like the Ocean to the Ganges, 117.10
like Rudra to Rudráni, and like the grandfather to the Altar.

He made love to her like Vasíshtha's son to Adrishyánti, Vasíshtha to Aksha·mala, Chyávana to Sukánya, Pulástya to Sandhya, Agástya to the Vidárbhan princess, like Sátyavat to Sávitri, Bhrigu to Pulóma, Káshyapa to Áditi, Archíka to Rénuka, Káushika to the Himálaya's daughter, Brihas·pati to Tara, Shukra to Shata·parva, like Bhumi·pati to Bhumi, Puru·ravas to Úrvashi, Richíka to Sátyavati, and Manu to Sarásvati.

He made love to her as Dushyánta to Shakúntala, like 117.15
eternal Dharma to Dhriti, like Nala to Damayánti, like
Nárada to Sátyavati, like Jarat·karu to Jarat·karú, like Pulás-
tya to Pratíchya, like Urnáyus to Ménaka, like Túmburu to
Rambha, like Vásuki to Shata·shirsha, like Dhanañ·jaya to
Kumári, like Rama to the Vidéhan princess, and like Janár-

Vaidehyāṃ ca yathā Rāmo, Rukmiṇyāṃ ca Janārdanaḥ.
tathā tu ramamāṇasya Divodāsasya bhū|pateḥ
Mādhavī janayām āsa putram ekaṃ Pratardanam.
 ath' ājagāma bhagavān Divodāsaṃ sa Gālavaḥ
samaye samanuprāpte, vacanaṃ c' êdam abravīt:
117.20 «niryātayatu me kanyāṃ bhavāṃs; tiṣṭhantu vājinaḥ,
yāvad anyatra gacchāmi śulk'|ârthaṃ, pṛthivī|pate.»
Divodāso 'tha dharm'|ātmā samaye Gālavasya tām
kanyāṃ niryātayām āsa sthitaḥ satye mahī|patiḥ.

NĀRADA uvāca:

118.1 TATH" ÂIVA TĀṂ śriyaṃ tyaktvā kanyā bhūtvā yaśasvinī
Mādhavī Gālavaṃ vipram abhyayāt satya|saṅgarā.
Gālavo vimṛśann eva sva|kārya|gata|mānasaḥ
jagāma Bhoja|nagaraṃ draṣṭum Auśīnaraṃ nṛpam.
tam uvāc' âtha gatvā sa nṛ|patiṃ satya|vikramam:
 «iyaṃ kanyā sutau dvau te janayiṣyati pārthivau.
asyāṃ bhavān avāpt'|ârtho bhavitā pretya c' êha ca
som'|ârka|pratisaṃkāśau janayitvā sutau, nṛpa.
118.5 śulkaṃ tu, sarva|dharma|jña, hayānāṃ candra|varcasām
ekataḥ śyāma|karṇānāṃ deyaṃ mahyaṃ catuḥ|śatam.
gurv|arthe 'yaṃ samārambho, na hayaiḥ kṛtyam asti me.
yadi śakyaṃ, mahā|rāja, kriyatām a|vicāritam.
an|apatyo 'si, rāja'|rṣe, putrau janaya, pārthiva,
pitṝn putra|plavena tvam, ātmānaṃ c' âiva tāraya.
na putra|phala|bhoktā hi, rāja'|rṣe, pātyate divaḥ,
na yāti narakaṃ ghoraṃ yathā gacchanty an|ātmajāḥ!»

dana to Rúkmini. So it was that as King Divo·dasa made love to her, Mádhavi gave birth to a single son—Pratárdana.

And the blessed Gálava returned to Divo·dasa when the time had come, and said to him: "Return the girl to me, 117.20
but let the horses remain here while I go elsewhere for the dowry, lord of earth, sir." So righteous-souled King Divo·dasa returned the girl, abiding by his agreement with Gálava, and abiding by truth.

NÁRADA continued:

118.1
SO ONCE AGAIN Mádhavi abandoned her fortune and became the famous virgin once more, and, true to her word, she followed the brahmin Gálava. Gálava, for his part, was lost in thought, his mind set upon his own task, and he went to the city of the Bhojas to see King Aushínara. When he reached him, he addressed the king whose prowess was his truth:

"This girl will bear you two princes, my lord. You will achieve your aims with her both here and in the next life, for she will bear you two sons who blaze like the sun and moon, king.

118.5
The dowry I must be paid is four hundred moon-hued horses with a single black ear each, sage and scholar of all law. This price is for my guru, for I have no need of horses. If you can pay, great king, then please do, and do not waver. You have no children, royal sage, so have two sons, king. Save your ancestors and yourself with a son as your life-raft. The man who reaps the fruits of having sons, royal seer, does not fall from heaven, nor does he go to horrifying hell as do those without children!"

etac c' ânyac ca vividhaṃ śrutvā Gālava|bhāṣitam
Uśīnaraḥ prativaco dadau tasya nar'|âdhipaḥ,
118.10 «śrutavān asmi te vākyaṃ yathā vadasi, Gālava,
vidhis tu balavān, brahman, pravaṇaṃ hi mano mama.
śate dve tu mam' âśvānām īdṛśānāṃ, dvij'|ôttama,
itareṣāṃ sahasrāṇi su|bahūni caranti me.
aham apy ekam ev' âsyāṃ janayiṣyāmi, Gālava,
putraṃ, dvija; gataṃ mārgaṃ gamiṣyāmi parair aham.
mūlyen' âpi samaṃ kuryāṃ tav' âhaṃ, dvija|sattama,
paura|jānapad'|ârthaṃ tu mam' ârtho, n' ātma|bhogataḥ.
kāmato hi dhanaṃ rājā pārakyaṃ yaḥ prayacchati,
na sa dharmeṇa, dharm'|ātman, yujyate, yaśasā na ca.
118.15 so 'haṃ pratigrahīṣyāmi. dadātv etāṃ bhavān mama
kumārīṃ deva|garbh'|ābhām eka|putra|bhavāya me!»
tathā tu bahudhā kanyām uktavantaṃ nar'|âdhipam
Uśīnaraṃ dvija|śreṣṭho Gālavaḥ pratyapūjayat.
Uśīnaraṃ pratigrāhya Gālavaḥ prayayau vanam.
reme sa tāṃ samāsādya kṛta|puṇya iva śriyam,
kandareṣu ca śailānāṃ, nadīnāṃ nirjhareṣu ca,
udyāneṣu vicitreṣu, vaneṣ' ûpavaneṣu ca,
harmyeṣu ramaṇīyeṣu, prāsāda|śikhareṣu ca,
vātāyana|vimāneṣu, tathā garbha|gṛheṣu ca.
118.20 tato 'sya samaye jajñe putro bāla|ravi|prabhaḥ
Śibir nāmn" âbhivikhyāto yaḥ sa pārthiva|sattamaḥ.
upasthāya sa taṃ vipro Gālavaḥ, pratigṛhya ca
kanyāṃ prayātas tāṃ, rājan, dṛṣṭavān Vinat"|ātmajam.

Once King Ushínara had listened to Gálava's varied words, he gave his answer, saying:

"I have heard what you have to say, brahmin Gálava, but 118.10
though my mind is willing, fate has the strong hand, for I only have two hundred horses of this kind, greatest of brahmins, though a great many thousands of other types run in my lands. So I too will have only one son with her, Gálava, and travel the road that others have taken, brahmin.

I will pay you the same amount as well, greatest of brahmins, because my wealth is for the good of my townspeople, not for my own pleasure. A king who spends other people's money on his own lust wins neither law nor good reputation, righteous-souled man. So I will accept her, sir. Give 118.15
me this princess who blazes like a child of the gods, so that I may have a son with her!"

So, Gálava, the greatest of brahmins, paid his respects to King Ushínara, who had said a great deal with great charm. Once Gálava had made Ushínara accept the girl, he went to the forest. In the meanwhile, just as a virtuous man takes pleasure in his good fortune, so the king took his pleasure in the girl, in mountain caves, by river waterfalls, in colorful gardens and forests and woodland groves, in charming mansions, on palace rooftops, in windowed houses and private apartments.

In due time a son, whom they named Shibi, was born. He 118.20
shone like the newly risen sun and was the most excellent of kings. So the brahmin Gálava came back and took the girl, then went on his way to see the son of Vínata, king.

NĀRADA uvāca:

119.1 GĀLAVAṂ VAINATEYO 'tha prahasann idam abravīt:
«diṣṭyā kṛt'|ârthaṃ paśyāmi bhavatam iha vai, dvija.»
Gālavas tu vacaḥ śrutvā Vainateyena bhāṣitam
catur|bhāg'|âvaśiṣṭaṃ tad ācakhyau kāryam asya hi.
Suparṇas tv abravīd enaṃ Gālavaṃ vadatāṃ varaḥ:
«prayatnas te na kartavyo, n' âiṣa saṃpatsyate tava.

purā hi Kānyakubje vai Gādheḥ Satyavatīṃ sutām
bhāry"|ârthe varayat kanyām Ṛcīkas tena bhāṣitaḥ,
119.5 ‹ekataḥ śyāma|karṇānāṃ hayānāṃ candra|varcasām,
bhagavan, dīyatāṃ mahyaṃ sahasram iti,› Gālava.
Ṛcīkas tu ‹tath" êty› uktvā Varuṇasy' ālayaṃ gataḥ
aśva|tīrthe hayān labdhvā dattavān pārthivāya vai.

iṣṭvā te Puṇḍarīkeṇa dattā rājñā dvijātiṣu
tebhyo dve dve śate krītvā prāpte taiḥ pārthivais tadā.
aparāṇy api catvāri śatāni, dvija|sattama,
nīyamānāni santāre hṛtāny āsan Vitastayā.
evaṃ na śakyam a|prāpyaṃ prāptuṃ, Gālava, karhi cit.
imām aśva|śatābhyāṃ vai dvābhyāṃ tasmai nivedaya
119.10 Viśvāmitrāya, dharm'|ātman, ṣaḍbhir aśva|śataiḥ saha.
tato 'si gata|saṃmohaḥ, kṛta|kṛtyo, dvija|sattama.»

Gālavas taṃ «tath" êty» uktvā Suparṇa|sahitas tataḥ
ādāy' âśvāṃś ca kanyāṃ ca Viśvāmitram upāgamat.
«aśvānāṃ kāṅkṣit'|ārthānāṃ ṣaḍ imāni śatāni vai
śata|dvayena kany" êyāṃ bhavatā pratigṛhyatām.
asyāṃ rāja'|rṣibhiḥ putrā jātā vai dhārmikās trayaḥ;

NÁRADA continued:

THE SON OF VÍNATA laughed and said to Gálava: "Congratulations! I see you have achieved your task, brahmin!" But upon hearing Vínata's son speaking these words, Gálava told him that a quarter of his task was, in fact, as yet undone. But Supárna, the greatest of speakers, said to Gálava: 119.1

"No more effort needs to be made in this matter, for it will not work for you.

Long ago Richíka chose Sátyavati, the daughter of Gadhi, for his wife in Kanya·kubja, and he was told, 'Sir, please 119.5
give me a thousand moon-hued horses with a single black ear each,' Gálava. So it was that Richíka said 'So be it,' and went to Váruna's dwelling, where he found the horses at the Horse Ford, and gave them to the king.

The king gave them to the brahmins at the *pundaríka* sacrifice, and then the kings to whom you have rented this girl bought two hundred each from them. The four hundred that were left, greatest of brahmins, were taken by the river Vitásta, when they were being led through at the crossing.
Since they cannot be won back, there are no more to be 119.10
found anywhere, Gálava. So give this lady to Vishva·mitra in place of two hundred horses, along with the six hundred steeds, righteous-souled man, and then your anxiety will be gone, for your job will be done, greatest of the twiceborn."

Gálava replied "So be it," and went to Vishva·mitra with Supárna once he had collected the horses and the girl. He said to Vishva·mitra: "Please accept six hundred horses for the prize you wanted, with this girl in lieu of two hundred. Three moral sons have been born to royal sages by this girl, so let her bear you a fourth, to be the greatest of them all.

caturthaṃ janayatv ekaṃ bhavān api nar'|ôttamam.
pūrṇāny evaṃ śatāny aṣṭau turagāṇāṃ bhavantu te;
bhavato hy an|ṛṇo bhūtvā tapaḥ kuryāṃ yathā|sukham.»
119.15 Viśvāmitras tu taṃ dṛṣṭvā Gālavaṃ saha pakṣiṇā,
kanyāṃ ca tāṃ var'|ārohām, idam ity abravīd vacaḥ:
«kim iyaṃ pūrvam ev' êha na dattā mama, Gālava?
putrā mam' âiva catvāro bhaveyuḥ kula|bhāvanāḥ.
praitgṛhṇāmi te kanyām eka|putra|phalāya vai
aśvāś c' āśramam āsādya carantu mama sarvaśaḥ.»
sa tayā ramamāṇo 'tha Viśvāmitro mahā|dyutiḥ
ātma|jaṃ janayām āsa Mādhavī putram Aṣṭakam.
jāta|mātraṃ sutaṃ taṃ ca Viśvāmitro mahā|muniḥ
saṃyojy' ârthais tathā dharmair aśvais taiḥ samayojayat.
119.20 ath' Âṣṭakaḥ puraṃ prāyāt tadā soma|pura|prabham;
niryātya kanyāṃ śiṣyāya Kauśiko 'pi vanaṃ yayau.
Gālavo 'pi Suparṇena saha niryātya dakṣiṇām,
manas" âtipratītena kanyām idam uvāca ha:
«jāto dāna|patiḥ putras tvayā, śūras tath" â|paraḥ,
satya|dharma|rataś c' ânyo, yajvā c' âpi tath" âparaḥ.
tad āgaccha, var'|ārohe, tāritas te pitā sutaiḥ,
catvāraś c' âiva rājānas, tathā c' âhaṃ, su|madhyame.»
Gālavas tv abhyanujñāya Suparṇaṃ pannag'|âśanam
pitur niryātya tāṃ kanyāṃ prayayau vanam eva ha.

May this fulfill the price of the full eight hundred horses, and may I be freed of my debt so that I can practice asceticism as I wish."

Vishva·mitra gazed at Gálava, and the bird, and the shapely-hipped girl, and said: "Why did you not give me this girl before now, Gálava? I would have had four sons to augment my lineage. I accept this girl of yours for the reward of a single son; and all the horses are to come to my hermitage, and run there." 119.15

So it was that the great sage Vishva·mitra had his fun with her, and Mádhavi gave birth to a son named Áshtaka. As soon as he was born, the great sage Vishva·mitra endowed him with profit and law and transferred the horses to him.
Then Áshtaka went to a city which shone like the city of the 119.20
moon, while Kúshika's son Vishva·mitra returned the girl to his pupil and went to the forest.

Now that Gálava, with Supárna, had paid his debt, he spoke to the girl, his heart brimming with joy: "You have given birth to one son who is a generous king, another who is a hero, another who delights in truth and law, and a fourth who is a sacrificer. So go now, shapely-hipped girl. You have saved your father with sons, saved four kings, and saved me too, slender-waisted girl."

Gálava bade Supárna the snake-eater farewell, then returned the girl to her father and went to the forest.

# 120–123
# YAYÁTI'S FALL

NĀRADA UVĀCA:

120.1 SA TU RĀJĀ PUNAS tasyāḥ kartu|kāmaḥ svayaṃ|varam
upagamy' āśrama|padaṃ Gaṅgā|Yamuna|saṅgame
gṛhīta|mālya|dāmāṃ tāṃ ratham āropya Mādhavīm
Pūrur Yaduś ca bhaginīm āśrame paryadhāvatām.
nāga|yakṣa|manuṣyāṇāṃ gandharva|mṛga|pakṣiṇām
śaila|druma|van'|âukānām āsīt tatra samāgamaḥ.

nānā|puruṣa|deśyānām īśvaraiś ca samākulam
ṛṣibhir brahma|kalpaiś ca samantād āvṛtaṃ vanam.
120.5 nirdiśyamāneṣu tu sā vareṣu vara|varṇinī
varān utkramya sarvāṃs tān varaṃ vṛtavatī vanam.
avatīrya rathāt kanyā, namas|kṛtya ca bandhuṣu
upagamya vanaṃ puṇyaṃ tapas tepe Yayāti|jā.

upavāsaiś ca vividhair, dīkṣābhir niyamais tathā
ātmano laghutāṃ kṛtvā babhūva mṛga|cāriṇī.
vaiḍūry'|âṅkura|kalpāni mṛdūni haritāni ca
carantī ślakṣṇa|śaṣpāṇi tiktāni madhurāṇi ca.
sravantīnāṃ ca puṇyānāṃ su|rasāni śucīni ca
pibantī vārimukhyāni śītāni vimalāni ca.
120.10 vaneṣu mṛga|rājeṣu vyāghra|viproṣiteṣu ca,
dāv'|âgni|viprayukteṣu, śūnyeṣu gahaneṣu ca,
carantī hariṇaiḥ sārdhaṃ mṛg" îva vana|cāriṇī,
cacāra vipulaṃ dharmaṃ brahma|caryeṇa saṃvṛtam.

Yayātir api pūrveṣāṃ rājñāṃ vṛttam anuṣṭhitaḥ
bahu|varṣa|sahasr'|āyur yuyuje kāla|dharmaṇā.
Pūrur Yaduś ca dvau vaṃśe vardhamānau nar'|ôttamau,
tābhyāṃ pratiṣṭhito loke para|loke ca Nāhuṣaḥ.
mahī|pate, nara|patir Yayātiḥ svargam āsthitaḥ

NÁRADA continued:

KING YAYÁTI WISHED to hold a bridegroom choice for his daughter, so he made his way to the hermitage in the place where the Ganges and Yámuna meet, with Mádhavi aboard a chariot wearing garlands of flowers; and Puru and Yadu also came to the hermitage, accompanying their sister. Snakes, *yaksha*s, men, *gandhárva*s, deer, birds, mountains, trees, and forests were gathered there. 120.1

The woods were filled with Brahma-like sages, and brimming with sovereigns of various peoples and regions. But 120.5
when all the suitors had been announced, the flawlessly complexioned girl passed over all the suitors and chose the forest itself as her bridegroom. Yayáti's maiden daughter climbed down from her chariot, bowed to her relatives, went to the holy forest, and practiced asceticism.

By means of fasts, various rites, religious observances, and restraints, she lost a great deal of weight and lived wandering around like a deer. She lived off sweet and bitter soft green grasses like tufts of cats-eye gems, and drank the pure, delicious waters of holy streams, so excellent, cool,
and clear. She wandered in the empty and impenetrable 120.10
forests devoid of forest fires and tigers, where deer were king; and roaming the woods like a doe with the deer, she practiced strict law, furnished with vows of chastity.

In the meantime, Yayáti followed the custom of kings before him, and after living for many thousands of years he succumbed to the law of time. Puru and Yadu, the greatest of men, made their two lineages flourish, and they secured Náhusha's son in this world and the next. O lord of earth,

maha"|rṣi|kalpo nṛ|patiḥ svarg'|âgrya|phala|bhug vibhuḥ.
120.15 bahu|varṣa|sahasr'|ākhye kāle bahu|guṇe gate
rāja'|rṣiṣu niṣaṇṇeṣu mahīyaḥsu maha"|rṣiṣu
avamene narān sarvān, devān, ṛṣi|gaṇāṃs tathā
Yayātir mūḍha|vijñāno vismay'|āviṣṭa|cetanaḥ.
tatas taṃ bubudhe devaḥ Śakro Bala|niṣūdanaḥ,
te ca rāja'|rṣayaḥ sarve «dhig dhig, ity» evam abruvan.
vicāraś ca samutpanno nirīkṣya Nahuṣ'|ātmajam,
«ko 'nv ayaṃ? kasya vā rājñaḥ? kathaṃ vā svargam āgataḥ?
karmaṇā kena siddho 'yaṃ? kva v" ânena tapaś citam?
kathaṃ vā jñāyate svarge? kena vā jñāyate 'py uta?»
120.20 evm vicārayantas te rājānaṃ svarga|vāsinaḥ
dṛṣṭvā papracchur anyonyaṃ Yayātiṃ nṛ|patiṃ prati.
vimāna|pālāḥ śataśaḥ svarga|dvār'|âbhirakṣiṇaḥ
pṛṣṭā āsana|pālāś ca «na jānīm', êty» ath' âbruvan.
sarve te hy āvṛta|jñānā n' âbhyajānanta taṃ nṛpam
sa muhūrtād atha nṛpo hat'|âujāś c' âbhavat tadā.

NĀRADA uvāca:

121.1 ATHA PRACALITAḤ sthānād āsanāc ca paricyutaḥ
kampiten' êva manasā dharṣitaḥ śoka|vahninā,
mlāna|srag|bhraṣṭa|vijñānaḥ prabhraṣṭa|mukuṭ'|âṅgadaḥ
vighūrṇan srasta|sarv'|âṅgaḥ prabhraṣṭ'|ābharaṇ'|âmbaraḥ,
a|dṛśyamānas tān paśyann a|paśyaṃś ca punaḥ punaḥ,
śūnyaḥ śūnyena manasā prapatiṣyan mahī|talam.

King Yayáti reached heaven, and like a great sage the lordly king enjoyed the most exceptional fruits of heaven.

When he had passed great aeons of time—numbering many thousands of years—among royal sages and the great glorious seers who were sittting there, Yayáti, whose judgment had become muddled and whose mind was destroyed by amazement, felt nothing but contempt for all men, gods, and hordes of sages. Then the god Shakra, the slayer of Bala, found him out, and all the royal sages chanted, "Shame! Shame!" 120.15

Now, as they stared at Náhusha's son, doubt arose. "Who is this man? Which king's son is this? How did he reach heaven? What did he do to reach perfection? Where did he learn his ascetic powers? How is he known in heaven, and who actually knows him?" So it was that the heaven-dwellers had their doubts about the king, and questioned each other when they saw King Yayáti. When asked, the hundreds of heaven's doorkeepers, chariot protectors, and seat guards replied, "We don't know him." So it was that everyone's knowledge was veiled, and they did not recognize the king. As a result the king instantly lost his majesty. 120.20

NÁRADA continued:

REMOVED FROM office, shaken from his seat, his mind trembling, overcome by fiery grief, with his garlands shriveled and his wits confused, his crown and armlets fallen, swaying to and fro, with every limb hanging loosely and his robe and adornments fallen into a mess, now invisible and time and again both seeing and yet not seeing anyone around him, hollow and vacant-minded, he was about to 121.1

«kiṃ mayā manasā dhyātam a|śubhaṃ dharma|dūṣaṇam
yen' âhaṃ calitaḥ sthānād? iti» rājā vyacintayat.
121.5 te tu tatr' âiva rājānaḥ siddhāś c' âpsarasas tathā
apaśyanta nirālambaṃ taṃ Yayātiṃ paricyutam.
ath' âitya puruṣaḥ kaś cit kṣīṇa|puṇya|nipātakaḥ
Yayātim abravīd, rājan, deva|rājasya śāsanāt:
«at'|îva mada|mattas tvaṃ na kañ cin n' âvamanyase.
mānena bhraṣṭaḥ svargas te, n' ârhas tvaṃ, pārthiv'|ātmaja;
na ca prajñāyase, gaccha, patasv'! êti» tam abravīt.
«pateyaṃ satsv! iti» vacas trir uktvā Nahuṣ'|ātmajaḥ
patiṣyaṃś cintayām āsa gatiṃ gatimatāṃ varaḥ.
etasminn eva kāle tu Naimiṣe pārthiva'|rṣabhān
121.10 caturo 'paśyata nṛpas, teṣāṃ madhye papāta ha.
Pratardano, Vasumanāḥ, Śibir Auśīnaro, 'ṣṭakaḥ
vājapeyena yajñena tarpayanti sur'|ēśvaram.
teṣām adhvara|jaṃ dhūmaṃ svarga|dvāram upasthitam
Yayātir upajighran vai nipapāta mahīṃ prati,
bhūmau svarge ca sambaddhāṃ nadīṃ dhūma|mayīm iva,
Gaṅgāṃ gām iva gacchantīm ālambya jagatī|patiḥ.
śrīmatsv avabhṛth'|âgryeṣu caturṣu pratibandhuṣu
madhye nipatito rājā loka|pāl'|ôpameṣu saḥ
caturṣu huta|kalpeṣu rāja|siṃha|mah"|âgniṣu
papāta madhye rāja'|rṣir Yayātiḥ puṇya|saṃkṣaye.
121.15 tam āhuḥ pārthivāḥ sarve dīpyamānam iva śriyā:
«ko bhavān? kasya vā bandhur? deśasya nagarasya vā?

fall to the surface of the earth. The king thought to himself, "What impure, law-corrupting ideas did I harbor in my mind, for which I have fallen from my position?"

The kings, *siddhas*, and *ápsarases* in that place watched 121.5
Yayáti, ruined and friendless. Then, my king, a person whose job it was to throw out those whose merit was lost came up to Yayáti, and at the order of the king of the gods he said: "You are too drunk with arrogance, and there is no one you do not treat with contempt. You have now lost heaven because of your pride, for you are no longer worthy of it, prince. You are no longer recognized, so go and fall!" But Náhusha's son repeated three times to the custodian: "Let me fall among good people!"

As he fell, that greatest of travelers gave thought to his 121.10
course, and at that very moment the king saw four bull-like kings in the Náimisha Forest, so he fell in their midst. Pratárdana, Vasu·manas, Shibi Aushínara, and Áshtaka were satisfying the lord of the gods with a *vajapéya* sacrifice. Smelling the smoke which rose from their sacrifice and reached the gates of heaven, Yayáti, the lord of the universe, fell to earth, clinging to the streaming smoke-made river that connected heaven and earth like the river Ganges does.

The king fell into the midst of the four prosperous lead- 121.15
ing sacrificers, who happened to be related to him, and who resembled the cardinal points who defend the earth; those four lion-like kings were like great fires and oblations. So it was that, with his merit lost, the royal sage Yayáti fell in their midst. As he seemed to blaze with glory, all the kings said to him: "Who are you? What family are you descended from? Which land or town do you come from? Are you

yakṣo v" âpy, atha vā devo, gandharvo, rākṣaso 'pi vā?
na hi mānuṣa|rūpo 'si. ko v" ârthaḥ kāṅkṣyate tvayā?»

YAYĀTIR uvāca:

Yayātir asmi rāja'|rṣiḥ, kṣīṇa|puṇyaś cyuto divaḥ.
«pateyaṃ satsv!» iti dhyāyan bhavatsu patitas tataḥ.

RAJĀNA ūcuḥ:

satyam etad bhavatu te kāṅkṣitam, puruṣa'|rṣabha,
sarveṣāṃ naḥ kratu|phalaṃ, dharmaś ca pratigṛhyatām.

YAYĀTIR uvāca:

n' âhaṃ pratigraha|dhano brāhmaṇaḥ, kṣatriyo hy aham!
na ca me pravaṇā buddhiḥ para|puṇya|vināśane.

NĀRADA uvāca:

121.20 etasminn eva kāle tu mṛga|caryā|kram'|āgatām
Mādhavīṃ prekṣya rājānas te 'bhivādy' êdam abruvan:
«kim āgamana|kṛtyaṃ te? kiṃ kurmaḥ śāsanaṃ tava?
ājñāpyā hi vayaṃ sarve tava putrās, tapo|dhane.»
teṣāṃ tad bhāṣitaṃ śrutvā Mādhavī parayā mudā
pitaraṃ samupāgacchad Yayātiṃ sā, vavanda ca.
spṛṣṭā mūrdhani tān putrāṃs tāpasī vākyam abravīt.
«dauhitrās tava, rāj'|ēndra, mama putrā, na te parāḥ.
ime tvāṃ tārayiṣyanti, dṛṣṭam etat purātane.
ahaṃ te duhitā, rājan, Mādhavī mṛga|cāriṇī.
121.25 may" âpy upacito dharmas, tato 'rdhaṃ pratigṛhyatām.
yasmād, rājan, narāḥ sarve apatya|phala|bhāginaḥ,

a *yaksha*, a god, a *gandhárva*, or a *rákshasa*? You certainly don't look human. What profit do you wish to achieve?"

YAYÁTI replied:

I am the royal sage Yayáti. I have fallen from heaven because I lost my religious merit. But I thought to myself, "Let me fall among good people," and I fell among you.

THE KINGS said:

Then may your wish come true, bull-like man. Please accept all our rewards from sacrifice, and our merit.

YAYÁTI replied:

I am not a brahmin who becomes wealthy through taking gifts. I am a member of the warrior class! My mind is not disposed to destroying other people's religious merit.

NÁRADA continued:

At that time the kings caught sight of Mádhavi as she 121.20
came wandering on her way like a doe, and they greeted her and said to her: "What is your reason for coming? What can we do for you at your behest? As your sons, we are indeed all yours to command, lady of rich asceticism." Hearing their words, Mádhavi came up to her father with the greatest delight and greeted Yayáti. Then, touching her sons' heads, the ascetic lady spoke.

"These are your grandsons by your daughter, lord of kings, for they are my sons, not strangers. These men will save you, for this practice is seen to reach back to ancient times. I am Mádhavi, your daughter, king, and I roam free
as a doe. I have also built up law, so please accept half. 121.25
Since all men take a share of their descendants' rewards,

tasmād icchanti dauhitrān, yathā tvaṃ, vasudh"|âdhipa.»

tatas te pārthivāḥ sarve śirasā jananīṃ tadā
abhivādya, namas|kṛtya mātā|maham ath' âbruvan;
uccair an|upamaiḥ snigdhaiḥ svarair āpūrya medinīm
mātā|mahaṃ nṛ|patayas tārayanto divaś cyutam.
atha tasmād upagato Gālavo 'py āha pārthivam:
«tapaso me 'ṣṭa|bhāgena svargam ārohatāṃ bhavān.»

NĀRADA uvāca:

122.1 PRATYABHIJÑĀTA|MĀTRO 'tha sadbhis tair nara|puṅgavaḥ
samāruroha nṛ|patir a|spṛśan vasudhā|talam,
Yayātir divya|saṃsthāno babhūva vigata|jvaraḥ.
divya|māly'|âmbara|dharo, divy'|ābharaṇa|bhūṣitaḥ,
divya|gandha|guṇ'|ôpeto na pṛthvīm aspṛśat padā.

tato Vasumanāḥ pūrvam uccair uccārayan vacaḥ
khyāto dāna|patir loke vyājahāra nṛpaṃ tadā:
«prāptavān asmi yal loke sarva|varṇeṣv a|garhayā,
tad apy atha ca dāsyāmi, tena saṃyujyatāṃ bhavān;
122.5 yat phalaṃ dāna|śīlasya, kṣamā|śīlasya yat phalam,
yac ca me phalam ādhāne, tena saṃyujyatāṃ bhavān.»

they therefore wish for their daughters to have sons, just as you do, lord of earth."

All the kings nodded their heads to their mother, greeted their maternal grandfather by bowing to him, and spoke. So it was that the kings saved their maternal grandfather who had fallen from heaven, filling the earth with their loud, matchless, and affectionate voices. Then Gálava also arrived, and said to the king: "Please ascend to heaven, sir, with an eighth of my ascetic merit."

NÁRADA continued:

As SOON AS bull-like King Yayáti was recognized once 122.1
more by those excellent beings, he ascended to heaven, no longer touching the surface of the earth. He regained his celestial position, and his fever was gone. Decked in celestial garlands and finery, adorned with divine decorations and endowed with heavenly perfume and virtues, his feet never touched the earth again.

Then Vasu·manas, renowned in the world as a king of generosity, first raised his voice loudly and said to the king: "Whatever I have attained in this world by my irreproachable conduct to all classes, that I will give to you, so let
it be attached to you, lord. May whatever fruits I have 122.5
reaped through my generous conduct, whatever fruits I have reaped through my forgiving conduct, and whatever fruits I have won by performing sacrifices be attached to you, lord."

tataḥ Pratardano 'py āha vākyaṃ kṣatriya|puṅgavaḥ,
«yathā dharma|ratir nityaṃ, nityaṃ yuddha|parāyaṇaḥ,
prāptavān asmi yal loke kṣatra|vaṃś'|ôdbhavaṃ yaśaḥ,
vīra|śabda|phalaṃ c' âiva, tena saṃyujyatāṃ bhavān.»

Śibir Auśīnaro dhīmān uvāca madhurāṃ giram,
«yathā bāleṣu, nārīṣu, vaihāryeṣu tath" âiva ca,
saṅgareṣu, nipāteṣu, tathā tad vyasaneṣu ca
an|ṛtaṃ n' ôkta|pūrvaṃ me, tena satyena khaṃ vraja!
122.10 yathā prāṇāṃś ca rājyaṃ ca, rājan, kāma|sukhāni ca
tyajeyaṃ na punaḥ satyaṃ, tena satyena khaṃ vraja!
yathā satyena me dharmo, yathā satyena pāvakaḥ
prītaḥ, śata|kratuś c' âiva, tena satyena khaṃ vraja!»

Aṣṭakas tv atha rāja'|rṣiḥ Kauśiko Mādhavī|sutaḥ
an|eka|śata|yajvānaṃ Nāhuṣaṃ prāha dharma|vit:
«śataśaḥ puṇḍarīkā me, go|savāś caritāḥ, prabho,
kratavo, vāja|peyāś ca; teṣāṃ phalam avāpnuhi.
na me ratnāni, na dhanaṃ, na tath" ânye paricchadāḥ
kratuṣv an|upayuktāni, tena satyena khaṃ vraja!»

122.15 yathā yathā hi jalpanti dauhitrās taṃ nar'|âdhipam,
tathā tathā vasumatīṃ tyaktvā rājā divaṃ yayau.
evaṃ sarve samastais te rājānaḥ su|kṛtais tadā
Yayātiṃ svargato bhraṣṭaṃ tārayām āsur añjasā.
dauhitrāḥ svena dharmeṇa yajña|dāna|kṛtena vai
caturṣu rāja|vaṃśeṣu sambhūtāḥ kula|vardhanāḥ
mātā|mahaṃ mahā|prājñaṃ divam āropayanta te.

Next Pratárdana, the bull-like warrior, also spoke, saying: "May whatever fame I have won, arising from my warrior line in this world, through my constant delight in law and constant dedication to war, and whatever fruits I have won through being named a hero, be applied to you, lord."

Then wise Shibi Aushínara spoke his sweet words: "Go to heaven by virtue of the truth that I have never before told a lie to children, women, in quarrels, battles, disasters,
or calamities! Go to heaven by virtue of the truth that I 122.10
would abandon my life, kingdom, pleasures, and happiness before I would abandon the truth, my king! Go to heaven by virtue of the truth that law, fire, and Shakra, the god of a hundred sacrifices, are pleased with my truth!"

Next law-wise Áshtaka the royal sage, son of Káushika and Mádhavi, spoke to Náhusha's son who had performed many hundreds of sacrifices: "I have accomplished hundreds of *pundaríkas* and *gósavas*, lord, as well as *vajapéya* sacrifices, so take their rewards. Go to heaven by virtue of the truth that I have no jewels or treasure or any other wealth which has not been used for sacrifices!"

As his grandsons spoke to the lord of men, the king made 122.15
his way to heaven, leaving the earth behind him. So it was that through their united good deeds all the kings quickly rescued Yayáti, who had fallen from heaven. His grandsons, augmenters of their families who had been born into four royal lineages, helped their maternal grandfather of great wisdom to ascend to heaven by means of their merit and the sacrifices and generosity they had accomplished.

RĀJĀNA ūcuḥ:

rāja|dharma|guṇ'|ôpetāḥ, sarva|dharma|guṇ'|ânvitāḥ
dauhitrās te vayaṃ, rājan; divam āroha, pārthiva.

NĀRADA uvāca:

123.1 SADBHIR ĀROPITAḤ svargaṃ pārthivair bhūri|dakṣiṇaiḥ
abhyanujñāya dauhitrān Yayātir divam āsthitaḥ.
abhivṛṣṭaś ca varṣeṇa nānā|puṣpa|sugandhinā,
pariṣvaktaś ca puṇyena vāyunā puṇya|gandhinā,
a|calaṃ sthānam āsādya dauhitra|phala|nirjitam,
karmabhiḥ svair upacito jajvāla parayā śriyā.
upagīt'|ôpanṛttaś ca gandharv'|âpsarasāṃ gaṇaiḥ,
prītyā pratigṛhītaś ca svarge dundubhi|niḥsvanaiḥ.
123.5 abhiṣṭutaś ca vividhair deva|rājarṣi|cāraṇaiḥ,
arcitaś c' ôttam'|ârgheṇa daivatair abhinanditaḥ.
prāptaḥ svarga|phalaṃ c' âiva tam uvāca pitā|mahaḥ
nirvṛtaṃ śānta|manasaṃ, vacobhis tarpayann iva:
«catuṣ|pādas tvayā dharmaś cito lokyena karmaṇā,
a|kṣayas tava loko 'yaṃ, kīrtiś c' âiv' â|kṣayā divi.
punas tvay" âiva, rāja'|rṣe, su|kṛtena vighātitam
āvṛtaṃ tamasā cetaḥ sarveṣāṃ svarga|vāsinām.
yena tvāṃ n' âbhijānanti, tato 'jñāto 'si pātitaḥ,
prīty" âiva c' âsi dauhitrais tāritas tvam ih' āgataḥ
123.10 sthānaṃ ca pratipanno 'si karmaṇā svena nirjitam,
a|calaṃ, śāśvataṃ, puṇyam, uttamaṃ, dhruvam, a|vyayam.»

THE KINGS said:

Sovereign, we are your daughter's sons, endowed with royalty, law, virtue, and all morality and virtues; so ascend to heaven, king.

NÁRADA continued:

RAISED UP TO heaven by those excellent kings who be- 123.1
stowed rich gifts, Yayáti took his leave of his grandsons, and took his place in heaven. Showered with a rain of various beautifully fragranced flowers, and embraced by a holy, pure-perfumed breeze, he reached the unchanging position won by his grandsons' rewards and supplemented by his own deeds, and he blazed with the utmost glory.

He was happily accepted back into heaven with songs and dances performed by hosts of *gandhárvas* and *ápsarases*,
and with drum-rolls. Praised by various gods, royal sages, 123.5
and heralds, honored with the finest hospitality, and greeted by gods, he reaped the rewards of heaven. Then the grandfather addressed the tranquil and calm-minded Yayáti, seemingly gladdening him with his words:

"You have achieved the fourfold law by means of your earthly actions, and this world is everlastingly yours. Your good reputation is also imperishable in heaven. However, royal sage, you destroyed what you had won by your good conduct, and so the minds of all heaven-dwellers were veiled with darkness. This was the reason they did not recognize you, and you became unknown and fell. But, lovingly saved
by your grandsons, you returned here; and you have now re- 123.10
taken the unchanging, eternal, holy, supreme, assured, and everlasting position you had won by your own conduct."

YAYĀTIR uvāca:

bhagavan, saṃśayo me 'sti kaś cit, taṃ chettum arhasi;
na hy anyam aham arhāmi praṣṭuṃ, loka|pitāmaha.
bahu|varṣa|sahasr'|ântaṃ prajā|pālana|vardhitam
an|eka|kratu|dān'|âughair arjitaṃ me mahat phalam.
kathaṃ tad alpa|kālena kṣīṇaṃ, yen' âsmi pātitaḥ?
bhagavan, vettha lokāṃś ca śāśvatān mama nirjitān;†
kathaṃ nu mama tat sarvaṃ vipranaṣṭaṃ, mahā|dyute?

PITĀ|MAHA uvāca:

bahu|varṣa|sahasr'|ântaṃ prajā|pālana|vardhitam,
an|eka|kratu|dān'|âughair yat tvay" ôpārjitaṃ phalam,
123.15 tad anen' âiva doṣeṇa kṣīṇaṃ, yen' âsi pātitaḥ;
abhimānena, rāj'|êndra, dhik|kṛtaḥ svarga|vāsibhiḥ.
n' âyaṃ mānena, rāja'|ṛṣe, na balena, na hiṃsayā,
na śāṭhyena, na māyābhir loko bhavati śāśvataḥ.
n' âvamānyās tvayā, rājann, adham'|ôtkṛṣṭa|madhyamāḥ.
na hi māna|pradagdhānāṃ kaś cid asti śamaḥ kva cit.
patan'|ārohaṇam idaṃ kathayiṣyanti ye narāḥ,
viṣamāṇy api te prāptās tariṣyanti na saṃśayaḥ.

NĀRADA uvāca:

eṣa doṣo 'bhimānena purā prāpto Yayātinā,
nirbadhnat" âtimātraṃ ca Gālavena, mahī|pate.
123.20 śrotavyaṃ hita|kāmānāṃ su|hṛdāṃ hitam icchatām,
na kartavyo hi nirbandho; nirbandho hi kṣay'|ôdayaḥ.

YAYÁTI replied:

Blessed lord, I am in some doubt, so please eliminate it. Indeed, there is no one else I should ask, grandfather of the world. My reward had grown great, augmented by my ruling over my subjects for many thousands of years, through the masses of gifts I gave and my numerous sacrifices. How could all that have been depleted in so small a time that I fell? Blessed lord, you know the eternal worlds I had won, so how could all my merit have been destroyed, greatly glorious one?

GRANDFATHER replied:

The fruits you won with your masses of generous gifts
and many sacrifices, augmented by ruling your people for
many thousands of years, were depleted by one sin, and 123.15
that's why you fell. Lord of men, the heaven-dwellers shouted "Shame!" because of your arrogance. This world does not exist eternally with arrogance, force, violence, deceit, or trickery, royal sage. You should not feel contempt for the worst, the best, or the average, king. There is certainly no peace anywhere for the man who is burned by arrogance, but there is no doubt that men who tell this story of your fall and ascension will pass through the dangers they encounter.

NÁRADA continued:

So this is the fault which Yayáti committed long ago with
his arrogance, and Gálava too sinned, earth-lord, because
of his excessive obstinacy. Men who desire what is good for 123.20
them should listen to friends who want only what is best for them, and they should not be obstinate, for obstinacy

tasmāt tvam api, Gāndhāre, mānaṃ krodhaṃ ca varjaya;
sandhatsva Pāṇḍavair, vīra, saṃrambhaṃ tyaja, pārthiva.
dadāti yat, pārthiva, yat karoti,
yad vā tapas tapyati, yaj juhoti,
na tasya nāśo 'sti, na c' âpakarṣo;
n' ânyas tad aśnāti—sa eva kartā.
idaṃ mah"|ākhyānam an|uttamaṃ hitaṃ
bahu|śrutānāṃ gata|roṣa|rāgiṇām
samīkṣya loke bahudhā pradhāritaṃ
tri|varga|dṛṣṭiḥ pṛthivīm upāśnute.

is certainly the means to one's destruction. For this reason, son of Gandhári, you too should avoid pride and anger. Make peace with the Pándavas, hero, and abandon your fury, king.

Whatever one gives, king, whatever one does, whatever austerity one practices, and whatever offerings one makes are never destroyed, nor do they decay, and no one else but the practitioner gains anything from it. When this wonderful and excellent story, approved by men of high learning whose fury and lust has disappeared, is examined in great detail and understood in this world, then their insight into the three subjects of virtue, profit, and desire will take over the world.

as certainly as it leads to one's destruction. For [illegible] sake of [illegible], you too should avoid [illegible] and [illegible] make peace with the Pandavas, [illegible] and abandon your fury, king.

Whatever one gives, [illegible], whatever one does, [illegible] austerity one practices, and whatever offerings one makes [illegible] destroyed [illegible] and no one else but the practitioner gains anything from it. [illegible] [illegible] excellent story, approved by men of high determination whose fury and lust has disappeared, is recounted in great detail and understood in the world, then their insight into the three aspects of virtue, [illegible] and desire will take over the world.

## 124–132

# THE DEBATE CONTINUES

DHṚTARĀṢṬRA uvāca:

124.1 BHAGAVANN, EVAM ev' âitad,
yathā vadasi, Nārada.
icchāmi c' âham apy evaṃ,
na tv īśo, bhagavann, aham.

VAIŚAMPĀYANA uvāca:

evam uktvā tataḥ Kṛṣṇam
abhyabhāṣata Kauravaḥ:
«svargyaṃ lokyaṃ ca mām āttha,
dharmyaṃ nyāyyaṃ ca, Keśava,
na tv ahaṃ sva|vaśas, tāta, kriyamāṇaṃ na me priyam.
aṅga Duryodhanaṃ, Kṛṣṇa, mandaṃ śāstr'|âtigaṃ mama
anunetuṃ, mahā|bāho, yatasva, puruṣ'|ôttama.
na śṛṇoti, mahā|bāho, vacanaṃ sādhu|bhāṣitam
124.5 Gāndhāryāś ca, Hṛṣīkeśa, Vidurasya ca dhīmataḥ,
anyeṣāṃ c' âiva su|hṛdāṃ Bhīṣm'|ādīnāṃ hit'|âiṣiṇām.
sa tvaṃ pāpa|matiṃ, krūraṃ, pāpa|cittam, a|cetanam
anuśādhi dur|ātmānam svayaṃ Duryodhanaṃ nṛpam.
suhṛt|kāryaṃ tu su|mahat kṛtaṃ te syāj, Janārdana.»
tato 'bhyāvṛtya Vārṣṇeyo Duryodhanam a|marṣaṇam
abravīn madhurāṃ vācaṃ
sarva|dharm'|ârtha|tattva|vit:
«Duryodhana, nibodh' êdaṃ
mad|vākyaṃ, Kuru|sattama,
śarm'|ârthaṃ te viśeṣeṇa s'|ânubandhasya, Bhārata.
mahā|prajña, kule jātaḥ sādhv etat kartum arhasi.
124.10 śruta|vṛtt'|ôpasampannaḥ sarvaiḥ samudito guṇaiḥ.
dauṣkuleyā, dur|ātmāno, nṛ|śaṃsā, nirapatrapāḥ,
ta etad īdṛśaṃ kuryur, yathā tvaṃ, tāta, manyase.

DHRITA·RASHTRA said:

LORD NÁRADA, IT is indeed just as you say. I too wish it 124.1
could be this way, but it is not in my power, lord.

VAISHAMPÁYANA said:

Having said this, the Káurava then addressed Krishna: "You have told me about heaven, this world, law, and what is proper, Késhava, but I am not under my own power, my friend, and my wishes are never carried out, so please strive to conciliate my fool of a son Duryódhana, who transgresses my orders, long-armed and greatest of men.

He pays no attention to the eloquently delivered advice of Gandhári, wise Vídura, or his other friends such as 124.5
Bhishma and so on, though they only want what is good for him, Hrishikésha. So command evil-minded, cruel, wicked-acting, senseless, and black-hearted King Duryódhana, and you will have achieved a wonderful service to your friend, Janárdana."

Varshnéya turned to the intolerant Duryódhana and, aware of all law, profit, and truth, he spoke these sweet-natured words to him:

"Duryódhana, greatest of the Kurus, listen to what I have to say, for your protection in particular, and also for your followers' protection, Bhárata. You are born into a great lineage, highly intelligent man, so you ought to do what is
right, for you possess learning and good conduct and are 124.10
endowed with every virtue. It is the ignobly born, wicked-souled, cruel, and shameless who act the way you deem sensible, my friend.

dharm'|ârtha|yuktā loke 'smin pravṛttir lakṣyate satām;
a|satāṃ viparītā tu lakṣyate, Bharata'|ṛṣabha.
viparītā tv iyaṃ vṛttir a|sakṛl lakṣyate tvayi,
a|dharmaś c' ânubandho 'tra ghoraḥ prāṇa|haro mahān.
an|iṣṭaś c' â|nimittaś ca, na ca śakyaś ca, Bhārata.
tam an|arthaṃ pariharann ātma|śreyaḥ kariṣyasi
bhrātṝṇām atha bhṛtyānāṃ, mitrāṇāṃ ca, paran|tapa,
124.15 a|dharmyād a|yaśasyāc ca
karmaṇas tvaṃ pramokṣyase.
prājñaiḥ, śūrair, mah"|ôtsāhair,
ātmavadbhir, bahu|śrutaiḥ
sandhatsva, puruṣa|vyāghra, Pāṇḍavair, Bharata'|ṛṣabha,
tadd hitaṃ ca priyaṃ c' âiva Dhṛtarāṣṭrasya dhīmataḥ
pitā|mahasya Droṇasya, Vidurasya mahā|mateḥ,
Kṛpasya, Somadattasya, Bāhlīkasya ca dhīmataḥ,
Aśvatthāmno, Vikarṇasya, Sañjayasya, Viviṃśateḥ,
jñātīnāṃ c' âiva bhūyiṣṭhaṃ mitrāṇāṃ ca, paraṃ|tapa.
śame śarma bhavet, tāta, sarvasya jagatas tathā.
hrīmān asi, kule jātaḥ, śrutavān, a|nṛśaṃsavān;
tiṣṭha, tāta, pituḥ śāstre, mātuś ca, Bharata'|ṛṣabha.
124.20 etac chreyo hi manyante pitā yac chāsti, Bhārata,
uttam'|āpad|gataḥ sarvaḥ pituḥ smarati śāsanam.
rocate te pitus, tāta, Pāṇḍavaiḥ saha saṅgamaḥ
s'|âmātyasya, Kuru|śreṣṭha; tat tubhyaṃ, tāta, rocatām.
śrutvā yaḥ su|hṛdāṃ śāstraṃ martyo na pratipadyate,
vipāk'|ânte dahaty enaṃ, kiṃpākam iva bhakṣitam.
yas tu niḥśreyasaṃ vākyaṃ mohān na pratipadyate,

In this world, the conduct of good men is distinguished by being endowed with law and profit, but the conduct of evil men is distinguished by being quite the contrary, bull of the Bharatas. Your behavior often appears wrong; your lawless stubbornness is horrifying and extremely lethal. It is undesirable and groundless, and you cannot continue this for long, Bhárata. You will act in your best interest if you 124.15
abandon this profitless course, and you will escape the lawless and infamous actions of your brothers, followers, and friends, enemy-scorcher.

Make peace with those wise, brave, greatly daring, self-controlled, and highly learned Pándavas, tiger-like bull of the Bharatas. This would be beneficial and pleasing to wise Dhrita·rashtra, your grandfather, Drona, highly intelligent Vídura, Kripa, Soma·datta, wise Báhlika, Ashva·tthaman, Vikárna, Sánjaya, and Vivínshati, as well as your relatives and the great bulk of your friends, enemy-scorcher. Peace would ensure protection for the whole universe, my friend. You are modest, born into a good lineage, learned, and non-violent, my friend, so abide by your mother and father's commands, bull of the Bharatas.

It is true that a father's command is considered best, Bhá- 124.20
rata; and when they meet utter disasters, everyone recalls their father's words. Your father likes the idea of an agreement with the Pándavas, my friend, and that should please your advisors too, greatest of the Kurus, my friend. The mortal who listens to his friend's advice but does not take it, suffers the consequences and is burned as though he had eaten a foul-tasting *kimpáka* plant. The man who foolishly

sa dīrgha|sūtro hīn'|ârthaḥ paścāt tāpena yujyate.

yas tu niḥśreyasaṃ śrutvā prāk tad ev' âbhipadyate
ātmano matam utsṛjya, sa loke sukham edhate.

124.25 yo 'rtha|kāmasya vacanaṃ prātikūlyān na mṛṣyate,
śṛṇoti pratikūlāni, dviṣatāṃ vaśam eti saḥ.
satāṃ matam atikramya yo '|satāṃ vartate mate,
śocante vyasane tasya su|hṛdo na cirād iva.
mukhyān amātyān utsṛjya yo nihīnān niṣevate,
sa ghorām āpadaṃ prāpya n' ôttāram adhigacchati.
yo '|sat|sevī vṛth"|ācāro, na śrotā su|hṛdāṃ satām,
parān vṛṇīte, svān dveṣṭi, taṃ gaus tyajati, Bhārata.

sa tvaṃ virudhya tair vīrair anyebhyas trāṇam icchasi
a|śiṣṭebhyo, '|samarthebhyo, mūḍhebhyo, Bharata'|ṛṣabha.
124.30 ko hi Śakra|samāñ jñātīn atikramya mahā|rathān
anyebhyas trāṇam āśaṃset tvad|anyo bhuvi mānavaḥ?
janma|prabhṛti Kaunteyā nityaṃ vinikṛtās tvayā,
na ca te jātu kupyanti; dharm'|ātmāno hi Pāṇḍavāḥ.
mithy"|ôpacaritās, tāta, janma|prabhṛti bāndhavāḥ
tvayi samyaṅ mahā|bāho pratipannā yaśasvinaḥ.

does not follow beneficial advice, but spins his yarn endlessly, loses his profit and then, in the end, he is consumed with sorrow.

But the man who listens to good advice and follows it immediately, ignoring his own opinion, wins happiness in this world. The man who does not tolerate the speech of 124.25
those who wish for his benefit because it seems disagreeable to him, and instead listens to the opposite advice, falls under his enemies' power. The friends of the man who transgresses good men's opinion and turns to the opinion of wicked men will grieve for him before long, when he is sunk in disaster. The man who ignores leading counselors and panders to wretches reaches horrifying disaster, and finds no rescue. The earth abandons the man who serves the wicked, behaves frivolously, and does not listen to his good friends—the man who chooses his enemies and hates his own people, Bhárata.

You have broken allegiance with those heroes, and instead you wish for the protection of others who are untrained, unequal to the task, and idiotic, bull of the Bharatas. What man on earth but you would pass over his Shakra- 124.30
like relatives who are mighty warriors, and would hope for protection from others? From the moment you were born you have always treated the Kauntéyas badly, but the law-souled Pándavas did not get angry. From the moment of their birth you treated your relatives deceitfully, my friend, though those illustrious and long-armed men treated you fairly.

tvay" âpi pratipattavyaṃ tath" âiva, Bharata'|ṛṣabha,
sveṣu bandhuṣu mukhyeṣu mā manyu|vaśam anvagāḥ.
tri|varga|yuktaḥ prājñānām ārambho, Bharata'|ṛṣabha;
dharm'|ârthāv anurudhyante tri|varg'|âsambhave narāḥ;
124.35 pṛthak ca viniviṣṭānāṃ dharmaṃ dhīro 'nurudhyate,
madhyamo 'rthaṃ kaliṃ, bālaḥ kāmam ev' ânurudhyate.
indriyaiḥ prākṛto lobhād dharmaṃ viprajahāti yaḥ,
kām'|ârthāv an|upāyena lipsamāno vinaśyati.
kām'|ârthau lipsamānas tu dharmam ev' āditaś caret,
na hi dharmād apaity arthaḥ kāmo v" âpi kadā cana.
upāyaṃ dharmam ev' āhus tri|vargasya, viśām pate,
lipyamāno hi ten' āśu kakṣe 'gnir iva vardhate.
sa tvaṃ, tāt', ân|upāyena lipsase, Bharata'|ṛṣabha,
ādhirājyaṃ mahad dīptaṃ prathitam sarva|rājasu.
124.40 ātmānaṃ takṣati hy eṣa, vanaṃ paraśunā yathā,
yaḥ samyag vartamāneṣu mithyā, rājan, pravartate.
na tasya hi matiṃ chindyād, yasya n' êcchet parābhavam;
a|vicchinna|mater asya kalyāṇe dhīyate matiḥ.
ātmavān n' âvamanyeta triṣu lokeṣu, Bhārata,
apy anyaṃ prākṛtaṃ kiñ cit, kim u tān Pāṇḍava'|ṛṣabhān.
a|marṣa|vaśam āpanno na kiñ cid budhyate janaḥ.
chidyate hy ātataṃ sarvaṃ—pramāṇaṃ paśya, Bhārata.

You must treat them the same way, bull of the Bharatas. Do not fall under the power of your fury at your greatest relatives. The wise act in accordance with the three pursuits—law, profit, and desire, bull of the Bharatas—but when using all three together is no longer possible, men only use law and profit. The steadfast man acts in accor- 124.35
dance with law on its own when all three are separated; the mediocre man acts in accordance with contentious profit; and the fool acts according to his desire.

The man whose greed ensures he is led by his senses and abandons law, wishing to attain his desire and profit by wicked means, is destroyed. The man who truly wishes to attain his desire and profit should act in accordance with law right from the start, for truly neither profit nor desire ever separate from law. They say that law is the means to all three pursuits, lord of earth, and the man who aims to attain them by this means surely grows quickly like a fire in a dry forest.

You, my friend, want to gain great blazing rule, established over all kings, through the wrong means, bull of the Bharatas. The man who acts deceitfully towards men who 124.40
act properly, king, is like someone who cuts himself down with an axe as if he were a forest. One should not cut down the opinion of the man whose defeat one does not want, for the mind of the man whose opinion is not cut off is set on the good. The self-possessed man would not despise anyone weak in the three worlds, even if they were vulgar, Bhárata, let alone the bull-like Pándavas. An intolerant man does not comprehend anything. Something too stretched must surely be cut—you see all the evidence, Bhárata.

śreyas te dur|janāt, tāta, Pāṇḍavaiḥ saha saṅgatam,
tair hi saṃprīyamāṇas tvaṃ sarvān kāmān avāpsyasi.
Pāṇḍavair nirmitāṃ bhūmiṃ bhuñjāno, rāja|sattama,
124.45 Pāṇḍavān pṛṣṭhataḥ kṛtvā trāṇam āśaṃsase 'nyataḥ.
Duḥśāsane, Durviṣahe, Karṇe c' âpi sa|Saubale—
eteṣv aiśvaryam ādhāya bhūtim icchasi, Bhārata,
na c' âite tava paryāptā jñāne dharm'|ârthayos tathā,
vikrame c' âpy a|paryāptāḥ Pāṇḍavān prati, Bhārata.
na h' îme sarva|rājānaḥ paryāptāḥ sahitās tvayā
kruddhasya Bhīmasenasya prekṣituṃ mukham āhave.
idaṃ sannihitaṃ, tāta, samagraṃ pārthivaṃ balam,
ayaṃ Bhīṣmas, tathā Droṇaḥ, Karṇaś c' âyaṃ, tathā Kṛpaḥ,
Bhūriśravāḥ, Saumadattir, Aśvatthāmā, Jayadrathaḥ
124.50 a|śaktāḥ sarva ev' âite pratiyoddhuṃ Dhanañjayam.
a|jeyo hy Arjunaḥ saṅkhye sarvair api sur'|âsuraiḥ,
mānuṣair, api gandharvair; mā yuddhe ceta ādhithāḥ.
dṛśyatāṃ vā pumān kaś cit samagre pārthive bale
yo 'rjunaṃ samare prāpya svastimān āvrajed gṛhān.
kiṃ te jana|kṣayeṇ' êha kṛtena, Bharata'|rṣabha?
yasmiñ jite jitaṃ tat syāt pumān ekaḥ sa dṛśyatām.
yaḥ sa devān, sa|gandharvān, sa|yakṣ'|âsura|pannagān
ajayat Khāṇḍava|prasthe, kas taṃ yudhyeta mānavaḥ?
tathā Virāṭa|nagare śrūyate mahad adbhutam
ekasya ca bahūnāṃ ca paryāptaṃ tan nidarśanam.

My friend, it is better to join the Pándavas than the wicked, for by befriending them you will obtain all your desires. Greatest of kings, you enjoy the earth which the Pándavas won, but you hope for protection elsewhere, turn- 124.45
ing your back on the sons of Pandu themselves. You wish for prosperity, granting power to Duhshásana, Dúrvishaha, Karna, and Súbala's son, but these men of yours do not match the Pándavas in knowledge of law and profit, and they are no match for the Pándavas in prowess, Bhárata. All these kings united with you are incapable of even looking upon the face of furious Bhima·sena in battle.

The gathered force of earthly kings is right here, my friend, but Bhishma here, Drona, this man Karna, Kripa, Bhuri·shravas, Soma·datta's son, Ashva·tthaman, Jayad·ratha, and all these men are incapable of fighting against 124.50
Dhanan·jaya. Árjuna cannot be defeated in battle by all the gods, *ásura*s, men, and *gandhárva*s. So don't set your mind on battle. Or please look at this assembled force of kings: do you see any man in this group who could take on Árjuna in battle and return home safe and sound?

What use is the destruction of men, bull of the Bharatas? Please show me a single man who could defeat Árjuna to ensure your victory. Which man could fight the man who defeated the gods, *gandhárva*s, *yaksha*s, *ásura*s, and snakes at Khándava·prastha? Then there is the great and incredible tale we hear of what happened at Viráta's city, where one man proved a match for many. That is proof.

124.55 yuddhe yena mahā|devaḥ sākṣāt santoṣitaḥ Śivaḥ,
tam a|jeyam an|ādhṛṣyaṃ vijetuṃ Jiṣṇum Acyutam
āśaṃsas' îha samare vīram Arjunam ūrjitam.
mad|dvitīyaṃ punaḥ Pārthaṃ kaḥ prārthayitum arhati
yuddhe pratīpam āyāntam, api sākṣāt puran|daraḥ?
bāhubhyām udvahed bhūmiṃ, dahet kruddha imāḥ prajāḥ,
pātayet tri|divād devān yo 'rjunaṃ samare jayet.

paśya putrāṃs tathā bhrātṝn, jñātīn sambandhinas tathā.
tvat|kṛte na vinaśyeyur ime Bharata|sattamāḥ.
astu śeṣaṃ Kauravāṇāṃ. mā parābhūd idaṃ kulam;
kula|ghna iti n' ôcyethā naṣṭa|kīrtir, nar'|âdhipa.
124.60 tvām eva sthāpayiṣyanti yauvarājye mahā|rathāḥ,
mahā|rājye 'pi pitaraṃ Dhṛtarāṣṭraṃ jan'|ēśvaram.
mā, tāta, śriyam āyāntīm avamaṃsthāḥ samudyatām;
ardhaṃ pradāya Pārthebhyo mahatīṃ śriyam āpnuhi.
Pāṇḍavaiḥ saṃśamaṃ kṛtvā, kṛtvā ca su|hṛdāṃ vacaḥ,
saṃprīyamāṇo mitraiś ca ciraṃ bhadrāṇy avāpsyasi.»

VAIŚAMPĀYANA uvāca:

125.1 TATAḤ ŚĀNTANAVO Bhīṣmo Duryodhanam a|marṣaṇam
Keśavasya vacaḥ śrutvā provāca, Bharata'|rṣabha:

Despite this, you hope to defeat in battle the unconquer- 124.55
able and undefeatable Jishnu Áchyuta, the powerful hero Árjuna who singlehandedly satisfied the mighty god Shiva in battle. So again, who is worthy to take Partha on, with me as his second, when he comes out to face him in battle, even if it were the sacker of cities himself? The man who could defeat Árjuna in battle could uproot the earth with his arms, he could burn these people if angry, and he could topple the gods from their heaven.

Look at your sons, your brothers, your relatives and followers. Don't allow the destruction of the greatest of the Bharatas, for you will be directly responsible. May the rest of the Káuravas survive. Don't kill your family, lest you be named the destroyer of your lineage and lose your good reputation, lord of men. Those mighty warriors will establish 124.60
you as the young king, with your father Dhrita·rashtra, the lord of men, as the senior king. Don't reject the good fortune that is coming to join you, my friend; for by giving half to the Parthas you will attain great glory. Make peace with the Pándavas and take your friends' advice, for by treating your friends affectionately you will obtain good things for a long time to come."

VAISHAMPÁYANA said:

ONCE HE HAD heard what Késhava had to say, Bhishma, 125.1
the son of Shántanu, then addressed the intolerant Duryódhana:

«Kṛṣṇena vākyam ukto 'si su|hṛdāṃ śamam icchatā.
anvapadyasva tat, tāta, mā manyu|vaśam anvagāḥ.
a|kṛtvā vacanaṃ, tāta, Keśavasya mah"|ātmanaḥ
śreyo na jātu, na sukhaṃ, na kalyāṇam avāpsyasi.
dharmyam arthyaṃ mahā|bāhur āha tvāṃ, tāta, Keśavaḥ
tad artham abhipadyasva; mā, rājan, nīnaśaḥ prajāḥ.
125.5 jvalitāṃ tvam imāṃ lakṣmīṃ Bhāratīṃ sarva|rājasu
jīvato Dhṛtarāṣṭrasya daurātmyād bhraṃśayiṣyasi.
ātmānaṃ ca sah'|âmātyaṃ sa|putra|bhrātṛ|bāndhavam
aham ity anayā buddhyā jīvitād bhraṃśayiṣyasi
atikrāman Keśavasya tathyaṃ vacanam arthavat,
pituś ca, Bharata|śreṣṭha, Vidurasya ca dhīmataḥ.
mā kula|ghnaḥ ku|puruṣo dur|matiḥ kā|pathaṃ gamaḥ,
mātaraṃ pitaraṃ c' âiva mā majjīḥ śoka|sāgare!»

atha Droṇo 'bravīt tatra Duryodhanam idaṃ vacaḥ
a|marṣa|vaśam āpannaṃ niḥśvasantaṃ punaḥ punaḥ:
125.10 «dharm'|ârtha|yuktaṃ vacanam āha tvāṃ, tāta, Keśavaḥ
tathā Bhīṣmaḥ Śāntanavas; taj juṣasva, nar'|âdhipa.
prājñau, medhāvinau, dāntāv, artha|kāmau, bahu|śrutau
āhatus tvāṃ hitaṃ vākyaṃ; taj juṣasva, nar'|âdhipa.
anutiṣṭha, mahā|prājña, Kṛṣṇa|Bhīṣmau yad ūcatuḥ;
Mādhavaṃ buddhi|mohena m" âvamaṃsthāḥ, paraṃ|tapa.

"Krishna has spoken to you because he wishes for peace between his friends. So understand this, my son, and do not give in to the power of your anger. If you do not do what high-souled Késhava has advised, my son, then you will certainly not obtain what is in your best interest, nor happiness, nor good fortune. Long-armed Késhava has spoken to you in terms of law and profit, my son, so act profitably and do not destroy your citizens, king.

Your evil-heartedness will cause you to ruin this Bháratan 125.5
good fortune in Dhrita·rashtra's lifetime, though it is a blazing beacon among all kings. You will deprive yourself, your advisors, and your sons, brothers, and relatives of their lives with this self-centered plan of yours, if you ignore the proper and profitable words of Késhava, as well as those of your father, best of the Bharatas, and those of wise Vídura. Don't take the wrong course as a wicked-minded, contemptible murderer of your family! Don't drown your mother and father in an ocean of grief!"

Then Drona spoke to Duryódhana, as he sighed over and over again, a slave to the power of his irritability:

"My son, Késhava spoke words which complied with law 125.10
and profit, as did Bhishma, son of Shántanu; so be satisfied with them, lord of men. Two wise, prudent, generous men of great learning, whose wish is for your profit, have spoken in your best interest, so happily accept their advice, lord of men. Abide by what Krishna and Bhishma have advised, wise man, and do not disregard Mádhava through foolish-mindedness, enemy-scorcher.

ye tvāṃ protsāhayanty ete, n' âite kṛtyāya karhi cit;
vairaṃ pareṣāṃ grīvāyāṃ pratimokṣyanti saṃyuge.
mā jīghanaḥ prajāḥ sarvāḥ, putrān, bhrātṝṃs tath" âiva ca.
Vāsudev'|Ârjunau yatra viddhy a|jeyaṃ balaṃ hi tat.†
125.15 etac c' âiva mataṃ satyaṃ su|hṛdoḥ Kṛṣṇa|Bhīṣmayoḥ
yadi n' ādāsyase, tāta, paścāt tapsyasi, Bhārata.

yath" ôktaṃ Jāmadagnyena, bhūyān eṣa tato 'rjunaḥ,
Kṛṣṇo hi Devakī|putro devair api su|duḥsahaḥ.
kiṃ te sukha|priyeṇ' êha proktena, Bharata'|rṣabha?
etat te sarvam ākhyātaṃ; yath" êcchasi tathā kuru;
na hi tvām utsahe vaktuṃ bhūyo, Bharata|sattama.»

VAIŚAMPĀYANA uvāca:

tasmin vāky'|ântare vākyaṃ kṣatt" âpi Viduro 'bravīt
Duryodhanam abhiprekṣya Dhārtarāṣṭram a|marṣaṇam:
«Duryodhana, na śocāmi tvām ahaṃ, Bharata'|rṣabha,
imau tu vṛddhau śocāmi—Gāndhārīṃ pitaraṃ ca te.
125.20 yāv a|nāthau cariṣyete tvayā nāthena dur|hṛdā,
hata|mitrau hat'|âmātyau, lūna|pakṣāv iv' âṇḍa|jau,
bhikṣukau vicariṣyete śocantau pṛthivīm imām,
kula|ghnam īdṛśaṃ pāpaṃ janayitvā ku|pūruṣam!»

atha Duryodhanaṃ rājā Dhṛtarāṣṭro 'bhyabhāṣata
āsīnaṃ bhrātṛbhiḥ sārdhaṃ, rājabhiḥ parivāritam:

These men who goad you on will never bring you victory, but in war they will unburden themselves of responsibility, putting the quarrel on the necks of others instead. Do not kill all your subjects and your sons and brothers as well. Understand that where Vasudéva and Árjuna are united, there
is an invincible army. The opinion given by your friends 125.15
Krishna and Bhishma is true, and if you do not accept it, my son, then you will regret it later, Bhárata.

Árjuna is in fact greater than Jamad·agni's son foretold, and Krishna, the son of Dévaki, is surely supremely invincible, even against the gods. But what use is it to talk of your happiness and delight, bull of the Bharatas? Everything has been said before, so do what you want. I do not dare to lecture you again, greatest of the Bharatas."

VAISHAMPÁYANA said:

During this speech, the steward Vídura watched intolerant Duryódhana, son of Dhrita·rashtra, and he said to him: "Duryódhana, I do not grieve for you, bull of the Bharatas, but I do grieve for these two elders—Gandhári and your
father. These two will roam with no protector but you as 125.20
their black-hearted defender, and when their friends and advisors have been killed, like a pair of clipped-winged birds they will sorrowfully wander over this earth like beggars, having produced such a vile and contemptible destroyer of his line as you!"

Next King Dhrita·rashtra spoke to Duryódhana, who was sitting with his brothers and surrounded by kings:

«Duryodhana, nibodh' êdam
Śaurin" ôktam mah"|ātmanā,
ādatsva śivam atyantam,
yoga|kṣemavad a|vyayam.
anena hi sahāyena Kṛṣṇen' â|kliṣṭa|karmaṇā
iṣṭān sarvān abhiprāyān prāpsyāmaḥ sarva|rājasu.
125.25 su|saṃhataḥ Keśavena, tāta, gaccha Yudhiṣṭhiram,
cara svasty|ayanaṃ kṛtsnaṃ Bharatānām an|āmayam.
Vāsudevena tīrthena, tāta, gacchasva saṃśamam
kāla|prāptam idaṃ manye. mā tvaṃ, Duryodhan', âtigāḥ.
śamaṃ ced yācamānaṃ tvaṃ pratyākhyāsyasi Keśavam
tvad|artham abhijalpantaṃ, na tav' âsty a|parābhavaḥ.»

VAIŚAMPĀYANA uvāca:

126.1 DHṚTARĀṢṬRA|VACAḤ śrutvā
Bhīṣma|Droṇau sama|vyathau
Duryodhanam idaṃ vākyam
ūcatuḥ śāsan'|âtigam:
«yāvat Kṛṣṇāv a|sannaddhau, yāvat tiṣṭhati Gāṇḍivam,
yāvad Dhaumyo na medh'|âgnau juhot' îha dviṣad|balam,
yāvan na prekṣate kruddhaḥ senāṃ tava Yudhiṣṭhiraḥ
hrī|niṣevo mah"|êṣv|āsas, tāvac chāmyatu vaiśasam.
yāvan na dṛśyate Pārthaḥ sve 'py anīke vyavasthitaḥ
Bhīmaseno mah"|êṣv|āsas, tāvac chāmyatu vaiśasam.
126.5 yāvan na carate mārgān pṛtanām abhidharṣayan
Bhīmaseno gadā|pāṇis, tāvat saṃśāmya Pāṇḍavaiḥ.
yāvan na śātayaty ājau śirāṃsi gaja|yodhinām
gadayā vīra|ghātinyā, phalān' îva vanas|pateḥ
kālena paripakvāni, tāvac chāmyatu vaiśasam.

"Duryódhana, listen to what high-souled Shauri has said, and accept it, for it is in your interest. It is timeless, has a pious purpose, and is eternal. With Krishna of pure acts here as our ally, we, among all kings, will achieve all our desired plans.

Go to Yudhi·shthira with Késhava's full alliance, my son, 125.25
and do what will bring good luck and complete health to the Bharatas. Go to the meeting, my son, with Vasudéva as your sacred ford, for I believe the time is at hand. Don't let the opportunity pass you by, Duryódhana. If you argue against Késhava as he begs you for peace and tries to help you, then you will never have your victory."

VAISHAMPÁYANA said:

WHEN THEY HAD heard Dhrita·rashtra's words, Bhishma 126.1
and Drona, who sympathized with him, both spoke to Duryódhana, the transgressor of his father's commands:

"For as long as the two Krishnas are not dressed in armor, for as long as the Gandíva lies still, for as long as Dhaumya has not made an offering of the enemy army into the fire of war, for as long as the modest archer Yudhi·shthira does not glance angrily at your army, butchery may be avoided.

For as long as the great archer Bhima·sena Partha does not appear, taking his stand in the army, butchery may be
avoided. For as long as Bhima·sena does not wander on his 126.5
paths, mace in hand, bringing joy to his army, there may be peace with the Pándavas. For as long as he does not knock elephant warriors' heads off on the battlefield with his hero-slaughtering mace as though they were fruits ripened by time plucked from the tree, then butchery may be avoided.

Nakulaḥ, Sahadevaś ca, Dhṛṣṭadyumnaś ca Pārṣataḥ,
Virāṭaś ca, Śikhaṇḍī ca, Śaiśupāliś ca daṃśitāḥ
yāvan na praviśanty ete, nakrā iva mah"|ârṇavam,
kṛt'|âstrāḥ, kṣipram asyantas, tāvac chāmyatu vaiśasam.
yāvan na su|kumāreṣu śarīreṣu mahī|kṣitām
126.10 gārdhra|patrāḥ patanty ugrās, tāvac chāmyatu vaiśasam.
candan'|âguru|digdheṣu, hāra|niṣka|dhareṣu ca
n' ôraḥsu yāvad yodhānāṃ mah"|êṣv|āsair mah"|êṣavaḥ
kṛt'|âstraiḥ kṣipram asyadbhir dūra|pātibhir āyasāḥ
abhilakṣyair nipātyante, tāvac chāmyatu vaiśasam.
abhivādayamānaṃ tvāṃ śirasā rāja|kuñjaraḥ
pāṇibhyāṃ pratigṛhṇātu dharma|rājo Yudhiṣṭhiraḥ!
dhvaj'|âṅkuśa|patāk'|âṅkaṃ dakṣiṇaṃ te su|dakṣiṇaḥ
skandhe nikṣipatāṃ bāhuṃ śāntaye, Bharata'|rṣabha.
ratn'|âuṣadhi|sametena ratn'|âṅguli|talena ca
upaviṣṭasya pṛṣṭhaṃ te pāṇinā parimārjatu.
126.15 śala|skandho mahā|bāhus tvāṃ svajāno Vṛkodaraḥ
sāmn" âbhivadatāṃ c' âpi śāntaye, Bharata'|rṣabha.
Arjunena yamābhyāṃ ca tribhis tair abhivāditaḥ
mūrdhni tān samupāghrāya premṇ" âbhivada, pārthiva.
dṛṣṭvā tvāṃ Pāṇḍavair vīrair bhrātṛbhiḥ saha saṃgatam
yāvad ānanda|j'|âśrūṇi pramuñcantu nar'|âdhipāḥ;
ghuṣyatāṃ rāja|dhānīṣu sarva|saṃpan mahī|kṣitām,
pṛthivī bhrātṛ|bhāvena bhujyatāṃ, vijvaro bhava.»

For as long as Nákula, Saha·deva, Dhrishta·dyumna Párshata, Viráta, Shikhándin, and Shishu·pala's son, armored swift-shooting warriors trained in weaponry, do not invade like crocodiles in the mighty ocean, then butchery may be avoided. For as long as fierce vulture-feathered arrows do 126.10
not land in the tender bodies of our kings, then butchery may be avoided. For as long as no mighty iron shafts—shot by fast-shooting trained archers firing over long distances—hit the warriors' chests smeared with sandal and aloe and decked with gilt ornaments and necklaces, butchery may be avoided.

May Yudhi·shthira, the king of righteousness, an elephant among kings, take you by the hands when you greet him with a bow of your head! May the supremely generous king place his right hand, marked with a banner, elephant hook, and flag, on your shoulder for peace, bull of the Bharatas. May he pat you on the back when you have sat down, with his jeweled, red-painted, and gem-fingered hand.

May long-armed Vrikódara, whose shoulders are like 126.15
*shala* trees, embrace you and greet you in a conciliatory manner for peace, bull of the Bharatas. When greeted by all three—Árjuna and the twins—greet them affectionately in return, kissing them on their heads, king. When they see you united with your hero brothers, the Pándavas, let lords of men weep tears born of joy, let the prosperity of all be announced in shouts in the cities of the kings of this world, let the earth be enjoyed in a brotherly fashion, and let your fever disappear."

VAIŚAMPĀYANA uvāca:

127.1 ŚRUTVĀ DURYODHANO vākyam a|priyaṃ Kuru|saṃsadi
pratyuvāca mahā|bāhuṃ Vāsudevaṃ yaśasvinam:
«prasamīkṣya bhavān etad vaktum arhati, Keśava.
mām eva hi viśeṣeṇa vibhāṣya parigarhase,
bhakti|vādena Pārthānām a|kasmān Madhu|sūdana!
bhavān garhayate nityaṃ kiṃ samīkṣya bal'|âbalam?

bhavān, kṣattā ca, rājā v" âpy, ācāryo vā, pitā|mahaḥ
mām eva parigarhante, n' ânyaṃ kañ cana pārthivam;
127.5 na c' âhaṃ lakṣaye kañ cid vyabhicāram ih' ātmanaḥ;
atha sarve bhavanto māṃ vidviṣanti sa|rājakāḥ!
na c' âhaṃ kañ cid atyartham aparādham, arin|dama,
vicintayan prapaśyāmi su|sūkṣmam api, Keśava.

priy'|âbhyupagate dyūte Pāṇḍavā, Madhu|sūdana,
jitāḥ Śakuninā rājyaṃ—tatra kiṃ mama duṣ|kṛtam?
yat punar draviṇaṃ kiñ cit tatr' âjīyanta Pāṇḍavāḥ,
tebhya ev' âbhyanujñātaṃ tat tadā, Madhu|sūdana.
aparādho na c' âsmākaṃ yat te hy akṣaiḥ parājitāḥ
a|jeyā, jayatāṃ śreṣṭha, Pārthāḥ pravrājitā vanam.
127.10 kena v" âpy apavādena virudhyanty aribhiḥ saha
a|śaktāḥ Pāṇḍavāḥ, Kṛṣṇa, prahṛṣṭāḥ pratyamitravat?
kim asmābhiḥ kṛtaṃ teṣāṃ, kasmin vā punar āgasi
Dhārtarāṣṭrāñ jighāṃsanti Pāṇḍavāḥ Sṛñjayaiḥ saha?
na c' âpi vayam ugreṇa karmaṇā vacanena vā
prabhraṣṭāḥ praṇamām' êha bhayād api śata|kratum!

VAISHAMPÁYANA said:

WHEN HE HAD heard this displeasing speech, Duryódhana addressed long-armed, illustrious Vasudéva in the Kuru assembly: 127.1

"You ought to reflect on matters before you speak, Késhava. Surely you berate me and speak offensively to me in particular because you have groundlessly declared your devotion to the Parthas, Madhu·súdana! But do you examine the strengths and weaknesses of the case before you always blame me?

You, the steward, the king, and even the teacher and the
grandfather blame only me and no other king. I do not no- 127.5
tice any misconduct on my part, but all of you hate me and so too do the kings! Though I ponder the matter, I cannot spot any excessive wrongdoing, enemy-tamer, or even the very slightest offence, Késhava.

The Pándavas gladly took part in the gambling, Madhu·súdana, but lost their kingdom to Shákuni—is that my fault? Whatever wealth the Pándavas lost there, I gave them leave to take back at the time, Madhu·súdana. It is not my fault that the unbeatable Parthas were in fact beaten with dice, greatest of victors, and went into exile into the forest.

Furthermore, on the grounds of what insult do the pow- 127.10
erless Pándavas delightedly quarrel with us inimically, assuming we are their enemies, Krishna? What did we do to them? For what offence done to them do the Pándavas and Srínjayas want to kill the sons of Dhrita·rashtra? We will not bow, terrified, at a fierce deed or word, or even from fear of Shakra, the god of a hundred sacrifices!

na ca taṃ, Kṛṣṇa, paśyāmi kṣatra|dharmam anuṣṭhitam,
utsaheta yudhā jetuṃ yo naḥ, śatru|nibarhaṇa.
na hi Bhīṣma|Kṛpa|Droṇāḥ sa|Karṇā, Madhu|sūdana,
devair api yudhā jetuṃ śakyāḥ, kim uta Pāṇḍavaiḥ?
127.15 sva|dharmam anupaśyanto yadi, Mādhava, saṃyuge
astreṇa nidhanaṃ kāle prāpsyāmaḥ, svargyam eva tat.
mukhyaś c' âiv' âiṣa no dharmaḥ kṣatriyāṇāṃ, Janārdana,
yac chayīmahi saṃgrāme śara|talpa|gatā vayam.
te vayaṃ vīra|śayanaṃ prāpsyāmo yadi saṃyuge,
a|praṇamy' âiva śatrūṇāṃ, na nas tapsyanti, Mādhava.
kaś ca jātu kulaṃ jātaḥ kṣatra|dharmeṇa vartayan
bhayād vṛttiṃ samīkṣy' âivaṃ praṇamed iha karhi cit?
‹udyacched eva, na named; udyamo hy eva pauruṣam;
apy a|parvaṇi bhajyeta, na named iha karhi cit.›
127.20 iti Mātaṅga|vacanaṃ parīpsanti hit'|ēpsavaḥ.
dharmāya c' âiva praṇamed, brāhmaṇebhyaś ca mad|vidhaḥ
a|cintayan kañ cid anyaṃ, yāvaj|jīvaṃ tath" ācaret;
eṣa dharmaḥ kṣatriyāṇāṃ, matam etac ca me sadā.
rājy'|âṃśaś c' âbhyanujñāto yo me pitrā pur" âbhavat,
na sa labhyaḥ punar jātu mayi jīvati, Keśava.
yāvac ca rājā dhriyate Dhṛtarāṣṭro, Janārdana,
nyasta|śastrā vayaṃ te v" âpy upajīvāma, Mādhava.
a|pradeyaṃ purā dattaṃ rājyaṃ paravato mama
a|jñānād vā bhayād v" âpi mayi bāle, Janārdana,

I see no warrior who follows the kshatriya code who could stand against us and defeat us, destroyer of your enemies. The warriors Bhishma, Kripa, Drona, and Karna assuredly cannot be defeated by the gods, Madhu·súdana, so
what hope do the Pándavas have? But if we abide by our 127.15
own duty, Mádhava, and die in battle by the sword when it is our destined time, then we will attain heaven.

This is the foremost law for kshatriyas, Janárdana: that we lie down in battle, fallen on a bed of arrows. We will have no regrets, Mádhava, if we obtain a hero's bed in battle without bowing to our enemies. Which man born into a good line, who lives his life by the warrior code, would ever allow fear to make him bow before his enemy, with his sole consideration being for his own life?

'One ought to rise, not bow, for that is the manly way, and one should break one's joints before one ever bows
down.' This is what Matánga said, and it is held dear by 127.20
those who strive to attain their good. A man of similar values to my own should bow to the law and to brahmins, and he should follow this for as long as he lives, without giving consideration to anyone else. This is the law for kshatriyas, and it has always been my point of view.

While I live, Késhava, they will never get back the part of the kingdom which my father gave them long ago. For as long as King Dhrita·rashtra survives, Janárdana, we should live dependent upon him and put down our weapons, Mádhava. This kingdom was given away long ago, either from ignorance or fear, when I was only a child, Janárdana, and therefore dependent, but it should not be given away again.

na tad adya punar labhyaṃ Pāṇḍavair, Vṛṣṇi|nandana.
127.25 dhriyamāṇe mahā|bāhau mayi samprati, Keśava,
yāvadd hi tīkṣṇāyāḥ sūcyā vidhyed agreṇa, Keśava,
tāvad apy a|parityājyaṃ bhūmer naḥ Pāṇḍavān prati.»

VAIŚAMPĀYANA uvāca:

128.1 TATAḤ PRAŚAMYA Dāśārhaḥ krodha|paryākul'|ēkṣaṇaḥ
Duryodhanam idaṃ vākyam abravīt Kuru|saṃsadi:
«lapsyase vīra|śayanaṃ! kāmam etad avāpsyasi!
sthiro bhava sah'|âmātyo; vimardo bhavitā mahān!
yac c' âivaṃ manyase, mūḍha, ‹na me kaś cid vyatikramaḥ
Pāṇḍaveṣv, iti› tat sarvaṃ nibodhata, nar'|âdhipāḥ!
śriyā santapyamānena Pāṇḍavānāṃ mah"|ātmanām
tvayā dur|mantritaṃ dyūtaṃ Saubalena ca, Bhārata.
128.5 kathaṃ ca jñātayas, tāta, śreyāṃsaḥ sādhu|saṃmatāḥ
ath' â|nyāyyam upasthātuṃ jihmen' â|jihma|cāriṇaḥ?
akṣa|dyūtaṃ, mahā|prājña, satāṃ mati|vināśanam;
a|satāṃ tatra jāyante bhedāś ca vyasanāni ca.
tad idaṃ vyasanaṃ ghoraṃ tvayā dyūta|mukhaṃ kṛtam,
a|samīkṣya sad|ācāraiḥ sārdhaṃ pāp'|ânubandhanaiḥ.
kaś c' ânyo bhrātṛ|bhāryāṃ vai viprakartuṃ tath" ârhati,
ānīya ca sabhāṃ vyaktaṃ, yath" ôktā Draupadī tvayā?
kulīnā, śīla|sampannā, prāṇebhyo 'pi garīyasī
mahiṣī Pāṇḍu|putrāṇāṃ tathā vinikṛtā tvayā.

The Pándavas will not reclaim it any more, joy of the Vrishnis. As long as I live, long-armed Késhava, I will not sur- 127.25
render so much as a sharp pinpoint of land to the Pándavas, Késhava."

VAISHAMPÁYANA said:

EYES FRENZIED IN fury, Dashárha remained calm for a 128.1
moment, but then he replied to Duryódhana in the Kuru assembly:

"You will win your hero's bed! You will get your wish! You and your advisors remain steady, for there will be a great massacre! Do you really believe that you have not offended the Pándavas, you fool? Just listen to all this, kings!

You were scorched by the high-souled Pándavas' good fortune, so you and Sáubala wickedly contrived the gambling match, Bhárata. How could your superior and law- 128.5
fully acting relatives, esteemed by good men, have taken part in such a lawless match with that wicked man, boy? Gambling destroys the devotion of the good, wise man, and breeds division and evil among the wicked.

It was you who thoughtlessly set that horrible and sinful gambling match in motion, associating with evil men rather than consulting men of good conduct. Who else but you would be capable of molesting a brother's wife, bringing Dráupadi to court as you openly did, and speaking to her in such a manner? You molested the well-born, impeccably behaved queen of the Pándavas, held dearer to them than their lives.

128.10 jānanti Kuravaḥ sarve yath" ôktāḥ Kuru|saṃsadi
Duḥśāsanena Kaunteyāḥ pravrajantaḥ paraṃ|tapāḥ.
samyag vṛtteṣv a|lubdheṣu satataṃ dharma|cāriṣu
sveṣu bandhuṣu kaḥ sādhuś cared evam a|sāmpratam?
nṛśaṃsānām an|āryāṇāṃ puruṣāṇāṃ ca bhāṣaṇam
Karṇa|Duḥśāsanābhyāṃ ca tvayā ca bahuśaḥ kṛtam.

saha mātrā pradagdhuṃ tān bālakān Vāraṇāvate
āsthitaḥ paramaṃ yatnaṃ, na samṛddhaṃ ca tat tava.
ūṣuś ca suciraṃ kālaṃ pracchannāḥ Pāṇḍavās tadā
mātrā sah' Âikacakrāyāṃ brāhmaṇasya niveśane,
128.15 viṣeṇa sarpa|bandhaiś ca yatitāḥ Pāṇḍavās tvayā
sarv'|ôpāyair vināśāya, na samṛddhaṃ ca tat tava.

evaṃ buddhiḥ Pāṇḍaveṣu mithyā|vṛttiḥ sadā bhavān;
kathaṃ te n' âparādho 'sti Pāṇḍaveṣu mah"|ātmasu?
yac c' âibhyo yācamānebhyaḥ pitryam aṃśaṃ na ditsasi,
tac ca, pāpa, pradāt" âsi bhraṣṭ'|āiśvaryo nipātitaḥ.
kṛtvā bahūny a|kāryāṇi Pāṇḍaveṣu nṛśaṃsavat,
mithyā|vṛttir an|āryaḥ sann adya vipratipadyase.

mātā|pitṛbhyāṃ, Bhīṣmeṇa, Droṇena Vidureṇa ca,
‹śāmy', êti› muhur ukto 'si, na ca śāmyasi, pārthiva.
128.20 śame hi su|mahāl lābhas tava Pārthasya c' ôbhayoḥ;
na ca rocayase, rājan, kim anyad buddhi|lāghavāt?
na śarma prāpsyase, rājann, utkramya su|hṛdāṃ vacaḥ.
a|dharmyam a|yaśasyaṃ ca kriyate, pārthiva, tvayā!»

All the Kurus know how the enemy-scorching Kauntéyas 128.10
were spoken to in the Kuru assembly by Duhshásana when
they were leaving for their exile. What good man would
behave so improperly towards his own ever law-abiding,
well-behaved, and abstemious relatives? You, Karna, and
Duhshásana often spoke like cruel and ignoble men.

You did your utmost to burn them and their mother
when they were children at Varanávata, but you didn't manage it. The Pándavas then went into hiding for a very long
time, living in a brahmin's house with their mother at Eka·
chakra. You tried every means available to you—poison, 128.15
snakes, and chains—in your attempt to destroy the Pándavas, but still you did not succeed.

With this attitude towards the Pándavas, and your constantly deceitful behavior towards them, how are you not to blame with regard to those high-souled Pándavas? You don't want to give them their paternal share of the kingdom, though they are begging you for it, but you will give it to them, evil man, when you have fallen and your power is lost. Though you have committed many offences towards the Pándavas, cruel and ignoble man of deceptive conduct as you are, you are now at odds with everyone.

Your mother, father, Bhishma, Drona, and Vídura have
told you to make peace, but you have not done so, king.
There is surely enormous gain to be had for both you and 128.20
Partha in peace, but the idea doesn't appeal to you, king—
for any other reason than on a whim? You will find no
refuge, king, if you ignore your friends' advice. What you
are doing is lawless and inglorious, king!"

VAIŚAMPĀYANA uvāca:

evaṃ bruvati Dāśārhe Duryodhanam a|marṣaṇam
Duḥśāsana idaṃ vākyam abravīt Kuru|saṃsadi,
«na cet sandhāsyase, rājan, svena kāmena Pāṇḍavaiḥ,
baddhvā kila tvāṃ dāsyanti Kuntī|putrāya Kauravāḥ!
Vaikartanaṃ, tvāṃ ca, māṃ ca, trīn etān, manuja'|rṣabha,
Pāṇḍavebhyaḥ pradāsyanti Bhīṣmo, Droṇaḥ, pitā ca te.»

128.25 bhrātur etad vacaḥ śrutvā Dhārtarāṣṭraḥ Suyodhanaḥ
kruddhaḥ prātiṣṭhat' ôtthāya, mahā|nāga iva śvasan,
Viduraṃ, Dhṛtarāṣṭraṃ ca,
    mahā|rājaṃ ca Bāhlikam,
Kṛpaṃ ca, Somadattaṃ ca,
    Bhīṣmaṃ, Droṇaṃ, Janārdanam—
sarvān etān an|ādṛtya dur|matir nirapatrapaḥ
a|śiṣṭavad a|maryādo, mānī, māny'|âvamānitā.

tam prasthitam abhiprekṣya bhrātaro manuja'|rṣabham
anujagmuḥ sah'|âmātyā, rājānaś c' âpi sarvaśaḥ.
sabhāyām utthitaṃ kruddhaṃ prasthitaṃ bhrātṛbhiḥ saha
Duryodhanam abhiprekṣya Bhīṣmaḥ Śāntanavo 'bravīt,

128.30 «dharm'|ârthāv abhisantyajya saṃrambhaṃ yo 'numanyate,
hasanti vyasane tasya dur|hṛdo na cirād iva.
dur|ātmā rāja|putro 'yaṃ Dhārtarāṣṭro 'n|upāya|kṛt
mithy"|âbhimānī rājyasya, krodha|lobha|vaś'|ânugaḥ.
kāla|pakvam idaṃ manye sarvaṃ kṣatraṃ, Janārdana,
sarve hy anusṛtā mohāt pārthivāḥ saha mantribhiḥ.»

VAISHAMPÁYANA said:

When Dashárha was talking to irascible Duryódhana, Duhshásana made a speech in the Kuru assembly: "If you do not make peace with the Pándavas of your own accord, king, apparently the Káuravas will tie you up and hand you over to the son of Kunti! Bhishma, Drona, and your father will hand over the three of us—Vaikártana, you, and me—to the Pándavas, bull-like man."

Hearing what his brother had to say, Suyódhana Dhar- 128.25
taráshtra stood up in fury, hissing like a mighty snake, and stormed out, with nothing but contempt for Vídura, Dhrita·rashtra, great King Báhlika, Kripa, Soma·datta, Bhishma, Drona, Janárdana, and all of them. So it was that the wicked-minded, shameless, untrained, and arrogant man transgressed every boundary, scorning men who should be respected.

When his brothers, counselors, and kings on all sides saw him get up and leave, they followed the bull-like man. But when Bhishma son of Shántanu noticed Duryódhana
leaving the court in fury with his brothers, he said: "The 128.30
man who abandons law and profit, with regard only for his anger, will find that before long his enemies laugh at him when he falls on hard times. This evil-souled princely son of Dhartaráshtra, who uses improper means to further his ends, is wrongly arrogant in his kingdom, and he is a slave to the power of his anger and greed. I believe the time has ripened for all warriors, Janárdana, for all the kings and advisors follow him in their idiocy."

Bhīṣmasy' âtha vacaḥ śrutvā Dāśārhaḥ puṣkar'|ēkṣaṇaḥ
Bhīṣma|Droṇa|mukhān sarvān abhyabhāṣata vīryavān:
«sarvēṣāṃ Kuru|vṛddhānāṃ mahān ayam atikramaḥ,
prasahya mandam aiśvarye na niyacchata yan nṛpam.
128.35 tatra kāryam ahaṃ manye kāla|prāptam, arin|damāḥ,
kriyamāṇe bhavec chreyas—tat sarvaṃ śṛṇut', ân|aghāḥ!
pratyakṣam etad bhavatāṃ yad vakṣyāmi hitaṃ vacaḥ
bhavatām ānukūlyena, yadi roceta, Bhāratāḥ.

Bhoja|rājasya vṛddhasya dur|ācāro hy an|ātmavān
jīvataḥ pitur aiśvaryaṃ hṛtvā mṛtyu|vaśaṃ gataḥ.
Ugrasena|sutaḥ Kaṃsaḥ parityaktaḥ sa bāndhavaiḥ
jñātīnāṃ hita|kāmena mayā śasto mahā|mṛdhe.
Āhukaḥ punar asmābhir jñātibhiś c' âpi sat|kṛtaḥ
Ugrasenaḥ kṛto rājā Bhoja|rājanya|vardhanaḥ.
128.40 Kaṃsam ekaṃ parityajya kul'|ârthe sarva|Yādavāḥ
sambhūya sukham edhante Bhārat'|Ândhaka|Vṛṣṇayaḥ.

api c' âpy avadad, rājan, Parameṣṭhī Prajāpatiḥ
vyūḍhe dev'|âsure yuddhe 'bhyudyateṣv āyudheṣu ca,
dvaidhī|bhūteṣu lokeṣu vinaśyatsu ca, Bhārata,
abravīt sṛṣṭimān devo bhagavāl̃ loka|bhāvanaḥ,
‹parābhaviṣyanty asurā, daiteyā Dānavaiḥ saha;
Ādityā, Vasavo, Rudrā bhaviṣyanti div'|âukasaḥ.
dev'|âsura|manuṣyāś ca, gandharv'|ôraga|rākṣasāḥ
asmin yuddhe su|saṃkruddhā haniṣyanti paras|param.›

Having heard Bhishma's words, lotus-eyed heroic Dashárha addressed all who remained, led by Bhishma and Drona:

"It is a great transgression on the part of all the Kuru elders that they do not forcibly restrain that foolish king so drunk on his power. Enemy-tamers, I believe the time has 128.35
come for this to be done, and if it is done then everything may still turn out for the best; so listen, sinless men! What I will say to you will be clear and beneficial, if it appeals to you as suitable, Bháratas.

The ill-disciplined miscreant son of the old Bhoja king was a slave to his anger, and he stole power from his father while he was still alive. Ugra·sena's son Kansa was deserted by his relatives, and I punished him in a great battle, wishing to benefit his relatives. So his relatives and I made Ugra·sena Áhuka king once more, as the augmenter of the Bhoja kings. Forsaking just Kansa for the sake of the whole 128.40
family, all Yádavas, Bháratas, Ándhakas, and Vrishnis prospered and became happy.

When the gods and *ásura*s were lined up in battle with weapons raised, Paraméshthin Praja·pati shouted, king, and while the worlds were divided and devastated, the blessed lord, the creator and architect of the world, spoke, saying, 'The *ásura*s, Daityas, and Dánavas will be destroyed, and the Adítyas, Vasus, and Rudras will live in heaven. Terribly furious gods, *ásura*s, men, *gandhárva*s, snakes, and *rákshasa*s will kill each other in this battle.'

128.45 iti matv" âbravīd Dharmaṃ Parameṣṭhī Prajāpatiḥ:
‹Varuṇāya prayacch' âitān baddhvā daiteya|Dānavān.›
evam uktas tato Dharmo niyogāt Parameṣṭhinaḥ
Varuṇāya dadau sarvān baddhvā daiteya|Dānavān.
tān baddhvā dharma|pāśaiś ca, svaiś ca pāśair jal'|ēśvaraḥ
Varuṇaḥ sāgare yatto nityaṃ rakṣati Dānavān.
tathā Duryodhanaṃ, Karṇaṃ, Śakuniṃ c' âpi Saubalam
baddhvā, Duḥśāsanaṃ c' âpi, Pāṇḍavebhyaḥ prayacchatha.
tyajet kul'|ârthe puruṣaṃ, grāmasy' ârthe kulaṃ tyajet,
grāmaṃ jana|padasy' ârthe, ātm'|ârthe pṛthivīṃ tyajet.
128.50 rājan, Duryodhanaṃ baddhvā, tataḥ saṃśāmya Pāṇḍavaiḥ,
tvat|kṛte na vinaśyeyuḥ kṣatriyāḥ, kṣatriya'|rṣabha!»

VAIŚAMPĀYANA uvāca:

129.1 KṚṢṆASYA TU VACAḤ śrutvā Dhṛtarāṣṭro jan'|ēśvaraḥ
Viduraṃ sarva|dharma|jñaṃ tvaramāṇo 'bhyabhāṣata:
«gaccha, tāta, mahā|prājñāṃ Gāndhārīṃ dīrgha|darśinīm
ānay' êha; tayā sārdham anuneṣyāmi dur|matim.
yadi s" âpi dur|ātmānaṃ śamayed duṣṭa|cetasam,
api Kṛṣṇasya su|hṛdas tiṣṭhema vacane vayam.
api lobh'|âbhibhūtasya panthānam anudarśayet
dur|buddher duḥ|sahāyasya śam'|ârthaṃ bruvatī vacaḥ.
129.5 api no vyasanaṃ ghoraṃ Duryodhana|kṛtaṃ mahat
śamayec cira|rātrāya yoga|kṣemavad a|vyayam.»

Giving this some consideration, Paraméshthin Praja·pati 128.45
said to Dharma: 'Chain up the Daityas and Dánavas and
assign them to Váruna.' When he said this, Dharma tied
up the Daityas and Dánavas and handed them all over to
Váruna, at Paraméshthin's command. So Váruna, lord of
waters, tied them with the bonds of law and with his own
chains, and he guards the Dánavas eternally in the sea.

So, in this way, chain Duryódhana, Karna, Shákuni Sáubala, and Duhshásana, and give them to the Pándavas. One
should abandon a man for the sake of one's family, a family
for the sake of one's village, a village for the sake of one's
people, and the earth for the sake of one's soul. King, re- 128.50
strain Duryódhana and make peace with the Pándavas, so
that the warriors are not destroyed because of your actions,
bull-like warrior!"

VAISHAMPÁYANA said:

WHEN DHRITA·RASHTRA, lord of men, had heard what 129.1
Krishna had to say, he spoke quickly to Vídura, knowledgeable in all matters of law: "Go, my friend, and bring wise
and farsighted Gandhári here, for I will bring that wicked-
minded man round with her help. If she can calm that
wicked-souled and evil-intentioned man, then we could
abide by our friend Krishna's words. She might be able to
show that evil-minded, greed-obsessed man of bad associa-
tions the true path, if she speaks peaceably. She may avert 129.5
the great horrifying disaster that Duryódhana is causing, for
our long lasting and eternal welfare."

rājñas tu vacanaṃ śrutvā Viduro dīrgha|darśinīm
ānayām āsa Gāndhārīṃ Dhṛtarāṣṭrasya śāsanāt.

DHṚTARĀṢṬRA uvāca:

eṣa, Gāndhāri, putras te dur|ātmā śāsan'|âtigaḥ
aiśvarya|lobhād aiśvaryaṃ jīvitaṃ ca prahāsyati.
a|śiṣṭavad a|maryādaḥ pāpaiḥ saha dur|ātmavān
sabhāya nirgato mūḍho vyatikramya suhṛd|vacaḥ.

VAIŚAMPĀYANA uvāca:

sā bhartṛ|vacanaṃ śrutvā rāja|putrī yaśasvinī
anvicchantī mahac chreyo Gāndhārī vākyam abravīt.

GĀNDHĀRY uvāca:

129.10 ānāyaya sutaṃ kṣipraṃ rājya|kāmukam āturam;
na hi rājyam a|śiṣṭena śakyaṃ dharm'|ârtha|lopinā
āptum; āptaṃ tath" âp' îdam a|vinītena sarvathā.
tvaṃ hy ev' âtra bhṛśaṃ garhyo, Dhṛtarāṣṭra, suta|priyaḥ
yo jānan pāpatām asya tat|prajñām anuvartase.
sa eṣa kāma|manyubhyāṃ pralabdho lobham āsthitaḥ
a|śakyo 'dya tvayā, rājan, vinivartayituṃ balāt.

rāṣṭra|pradāne mūḍhasya, bāliśasya, dur|ātmanaḥ,
duḥ|sahāyasya, lubdhasya Dhṛtarāṣṭro 'śnute phalam.
kathaṃ hi sva|jane bhedam upekṣeta mahī|patiḥ?
bhinnaṃ hi sva|janena tvāṃ prasahiṣyanti śatravaḥ.
129.15 yā hi śakyā, mahā|rāja, sāmnā bhedena vā punaḥ

When he had heard the king's words, Vídura brought farsighted Gandhári at Dhrita·rashtra's command.

DHRITA·RASHTRA said:

Gandhári, this wicked-souled son of yours always transgresses my orders. In his greed for power, he laughs at power and at life itself. This untrained and wicked-souled man, who transgresses all boundaries with his evil friends, has left court, and the fool ignores the advice of his friends.

VAISHAMPÁYANA said:

Having listened to her husband's words, the illustrious Gandhári, the daughter of a king, replied, wishing for the greatest benefit.

GANDHÁRI said:

Quickly, fetch my sick son who lusts after kingship, for 129.10
the kingdom certainly cannot be ruled by a badly trained man who violates law and profit. But even so, the ill-behaved man has got his hands on a kingdom, despite his wicked ways, using every means at his disposal. You are largely responsible for this, Dhrita·rashtra, being so fond of your son, since you always give way to his ideas though you know how wicked he is. But now that he is so set on his greed and overwhelmed with his lust and anger, you are no longer able to forcibly turn him back, king.

Dhrita·rashtra reaps the rewards of having given his kingdom to a greedy, childish, evil-souled fool with wicked friends. How could a king overlook division among his own people? Your enemies will overwhelm you if there is division in your ranks. When there is still a possibility of peace 129.15

nistartum āpadaḥ sveṣu, daṇḍaṃ kas tatra pātayet?

VAIŚAMPĀYANA uvāca:

śāsanād Dhṛtarāṣṭrasya Duryodhanam a|marṣaṇam,
mātuś ca vacanāt kṣattā sabhāṃ prāveśayat punaḥ.
sa mātur vacan'|ākāṅkṣī praviveśa punaḥ sabhām
abhitāmr'|ēkṣaṇaḥ krodhān, niḥśvasann iva panna|gaḥ.
taṃ praviṣṭam abhiprekṣya putram utpatham āsthitam
vigarhamāṇā Gāndhārī śam'|ârthaṃ vākyam abravīt.
«Duryodhana, nibodh' êdaṃ vacanaṃ mama, putraka,
hitaṃ te s'|ânubandhasya tath" āyatyāṃ sukh'|ôdayam.
129.20 Duryodhana, yad āha tvāṃ pitā, Bharata|sattama,
Bhīṣmo, Droṇaḥ, Kṛpaḥ, kṣattā, su|hṛdāṃ kuru tad vacaḥ.
Bhīṣmasya tu, pituś c' âiva, mama c' âpacitiḥ kṛtā
bhaved, Droṇa|mukhānāṃ ca, su|hṛdāṃ śāmyatā tvayā.
na hi rājyaṃ, mahā|prājña, svena kāmena śakyate
avāptuṃ, rakṣituṃ v" âpi, bhoktuṃ, Bharata|sattama.
na hy a|vaśy'|êndriyo rājyam aśnīyād dīrgham antaram
vijit'|ātmā tu medhāvī sa rājyam abhipālayet.
kāma|krodhau hi puruṣam arthebhyo vyapakarṣataḥ
tau tu śatrū vinirjitya rājā vijayate mahīm.
129.25 lok'|ēśvara|prabhutvaṃ hi mahad etad dur|ātmabhiḥ
rājyaṃ nām' ēpsitaṃ sthānaṃ na śakyam abhirakṣitum.
indriyāṇi mahat prepsur niyacched artha|dharmayoḥ,
indriyair niyatair buddhir vardhate, 'gnir iv' êndhanaiḥ.

either through conciliation or bribery, who would bring violence upon his own people?

VAISHAMPÁYANA said:

The steward had impatient Duryódhana re-enter the assembly at Dhrita·rashtra's command and at the advice of his mother. So it was that he returned to court expecting his mother's lecture, his eyes red with fury, hissing like a snake. And when she saw her stray son entering, Gandhári reproached him and spoke for peace.

"Duryódhana, my little boy, listen to what I have to say, for my advice is to your benefit and that of your followers, and will bring future happiness. Duryódhana, follow your 129.20
friends' advice—that which your father, Bhishma, Drona, Kripa, and the steward gave you, greatest of the Bharatas. If you make peace, then you would do honor to Bhishma, to your father, and to me, as well as to your friends, led by Drona.

A kingdom cannot be won, protected, or enjoyed by one's own desire, wise and greatest of the Bharatas, for the man who has failed to discipline his senses cannot keep control of his kingdom for long. The self-controlled and wise man, however, can protect his kingdom. Lust and fury drag a man from his interests, and it is in defeating these two enemies that a king conquers the world.

Being lord and master of the world is a great feat, and 129.25
though evil-souled men obviously want to obtain kingdoms, they cannot protect them. The man who wants greatness ought to direct his senses to profit and law, for the mind develops when the senses are kept under control, just

a|vidheyāni h' îmāni vyāpādayitum apy alam,
a|vidheyā iv' â|dāntā hayāḥ pathi ku|sārathim.
a|vijitya ya ātmānam amātyān vijigīṣate,
a|mitrān v" âjit'|âmātyaḥ, so '|vaśaḥ parihīyate.
ātmānam eva prathamaṃ dveṣya|rūpeṇa yojayet,
tato 'mātyān a|mitrāṃś ca na moghaṃ vijigīṣate.
129.30 vaśy'|êndriyaṃ, jit'|âmātyaṃ, dhṛta|daṇḍaṃ vikāriṣu,
parīkṣya|kāriṇaṃ, dhīram atyarthaṃ śrīr niṣevate.
kṣudr'|âkṣeṇ' êva jālena jhaṣāv apihitāv ubhau
kāma|krodhau śarīra|sthau prajñānaṃ tau vilumpataḥ.
yābhyāṃ hi devāḥ svar|yātuḥ svargasya pidadhur mukham
bibhyato 'n|uparāgasya kāma|krodhau sma vardhitau.
kāmaṃ, krodhaṃ ca, lobhaṃ ca,
dambhaṃ, darpaṃ ca bhūmi|paḥ
samyag vijetuṃ yo veda,
sa mahīm abhijāyate.
satataṃ nigrahe yukta indriyāṇāṃ bhaven nṛpaḥ
īpsann arthaṃ ca dharmaṃ ca, dviṣatāṃ ca parābhavam.
129.35 kām'|âbhibhūtaḥ krodhād vā yo mithyā pratipadyate
sveṣu c' ânyeṣu vā, tasya na sahāyā bhavanty uta.
ekī|bhūtair mahā|prājñaiḥ śūrair ari|nibarhaṇaiḥ
Pāṇḍavaiḥ pṛthivīṃ, tāta, bhokṣyase sahitaḥ sukhī.
yathā Bhīṣmaḥ Śāntanavo, Droṇaś c' âpi mahā|rathaḥ
āhatus, tāta, tat satyam—a|jeyau Kṛṣṇa|Pāṇḍavau.
prapadyasva mahā|bāhuṃ Kṛṣṇam a|kliṣṭa|kāriṇam

as a fire grows with kindled wood. If they are sufficiently uncontrolled then they can even destroy the man, just as uncontrolled and unbroken horses throw a bad rider onto the path.

If one cannot discipline oneself but wishes to discipline one's advisors, or wishes to discipline one's enemies without first disciplining one's advisors, one is ruined and made powerless. One should discipline oneself first, as though one were an enemy, and only then can one fruitfully seek
to control one's advisors and enemies. Good fortune visits 129.30
most particularly the man who controls his senses, disciplines his advisors, brings punishment down upon miscreants, acts with forethought, and is resolute.

Like a pair of large fish caught in a finely woven net, desire and fury within the body rip wisdom apart. The gods certainly close the doors of heaven to the man who has passed over and approaches with fully developed lust and fury, for they are afraid of misconduct. The king who understands how to entirely conquer his lust, fury, greed, deceit, and pride, will conquer the world. A king should always concentrate on disciplining his senses if he wishes for
profit, law, and his enemies' defeat. The man who, from 129.35
overwhelming lust or from fury, acts deceitfully towards either his own people or others, will never have any allies.

You will enjoy the earth happily, my son, with the wise and brave Pándavas, the enemy-uprooters who are as one. It is just as Bhishma the son of Shántanu and Drona the mighty warrior said, my boy: Krishna and the son of Pandu are truly invincible. Take refuge with long-armed and pure-

prasanno hi sukhāya syād ubhayor eva Keśavaḥ.
su|hṛdām artha|kāmānāṃ yo na tiṣṭhati śāsane
prājñānāṃ kṛta|vidyānāṃ, sa naraḥ śatru|nandanaḥ.
129.40 na yuddhe, tāta, kalyāṇaṃ,
na dharm'|ârthau, kutaḥ sukham,
na c' âpi vijayo nityaṃ;
mā yuddhe ceta ādhithāḥ.
Bhīṣmeṇa hi, mahā|prajña, pitrā te, Bāhlikena ca
datto 'ṃśaḥ Pāṇḍu|putrāṇāṃ bhedād bhītair, arin|dama.
tasya c' âitat pradānasya phalam ady' ânupaśyasi,
yad bhuṅkṣe pṛthivīṃ kṛtsnāṃ śūrair nihata|kaṇṭakām.
prayaccha Pāṇḍu|putrāṇāṃ yath" ôcitam, arin|dama,
yad' îcchasi sah'|âmātyo bhoktum, ardhaṃ pradīyatām.
alam ardhaṃ pṛthivyās te sah'|âmātyasya jīvitum;
su|hṛdāṃ vacane tiṣṭhan yaśaḥ prāpsyasi, Bhārata.
129.45 śrīmadbhir ātmavadbhis tair buddhimadbhir jit'|êndriyaiḥ
Pāṇḍavair vigrahas, tāta, bhraṃśayen mahataḥ sukhāt.
nigṛhya su|hṛdāṃ manyuṃ śādhi rājyaṃ yath" ôcitam
svam aṃśaṃ Pāṇḍu|putrebhyaḥ pradāya, Bharata'|rṣabha.
alam aṅga nikāro 'yaṃ trayo|daśa samāḥ kṛtaḥ.
śamay' âinaṃ, mahā|prājña, kāma|krodha|samedhitam.
na c' âiṣa śaktaḥ Pārthānāṃ yas tvad|artham abhīpsati†
sūta|putro dṛḍha|krodho, bhrātā Duḥśāsanaś ca te.
Bhīṣme, Droṇe, Kṛpe, Karṇe,
Bhīmasene, Dhanañjaye,
Dhṛṣṭadyumne ca saṃkruddhe
na syuḥ sarvāḥ prajā dhruvam.

acting Krishna, for if Késhava is gracious then both sides will assuredly find happiness.

The man who does not abide by the command of wise and scholarly friends who wish only for his profit, is a joy to his enemies. There is no benefit in war, my son, nor law, 129.40
nor profit; so what happiness will come of it? There is never any victory either, so don't set your thoughts on war.

Bhishma, your father, and Báhlika gave the sons of Pandu their share, for they were afraid of division, my wise, foe-taming son. Now you can see the result of this gift of theirs, for you enjoy the whole earth, with all your rivals having been killed by those brave men. So give the sons of Pandu what they were promised, enemy-tamer. If you and your advisors wish to enjoy your half, then let their half be returned.

Half the earth is sufficient for you and your advisors to live on, and you will attain glory by abiding by your friends' advice, Bhárata. A quarrel with those glorious, self- 129.45
possessed, and intelligent Pándavas of disciplined senses will only serve to deprive you of your great happiness, my son. Do away with your friends' anger, rule your kingdom properly, and return their share to the sons of Pandu, bull of the Bharatas.

Their mistreatment has lasted thirteen years; that's surely enough. Lay to rest this resentment fueled by lust and fury, wise man. He may hope for your success, but the resolutely furious son of the *suta** is no match for the Parthas, and nor is your brother Duhshásana. Once Bhishma, Drona, Kripa, Karna, Bhima·sena, Dhanan·jaya, and Dhrishta·dyumna are angry, then it is assured that no citizens will survive.

129.50 a|marṣa|vaśam āpanno mā Kurūṃs, tāta, jīghanaḥ.
eṣā hi pṛthivī kṛtsnā m" āgamat tvat|kṛte vadham.
yac ca tvaṃ manyase, mūḍha, ‹Bhīṣma|Droṇa|Kṛp'|ādayaḥ
yotsyante sarva|śakty", êti› n' âitad ady' ôpapadyate;
samaṃ hi rājyaṃ, prītiś ca, sthānaṃ hi vidit'|ātmanām
Pāṇḍaveṣv atha yuṣmāsu; dharmas tv abhyadhikas tataḥ.
rāja|piṇḍa|bhayād ete yadi hāsyanti jīvitam,
na hi śakṣyanti rājānaṃ Yudhiṣṭhiram udīkṣitum.
na lobhād artha|sampattir narāṇām iha dṛśyate,
tad alaṃ, tāta, lobhena; praśāmya, Bharata'|rṣabha.»

VAIŚAMPĀYANA uvāca:

130.1 TAT TU VĀKYAM an|ādṛtya so 'rthavan mātṛ|bhāṣitam
punaḥ pratasthe saṃrambhāt sakāśam a|kṛt'|ātmanām.
tataḥ sabhāyā nirgamya mantrayām āsa Kauravaḥ
Saubalena mat'|âkṣeṇa rājñā Śakuninā saha.
Duryodhanasya, Karṇasya, Śakuneḥ Saubalasya ca
Duḥśāsana|caturthānām idam āsīd viceṣṭitam:
«pur" âyam asmān gṛhṇāti kṣipra|kārī Janārdanaḥ
sahito Dhṛtrarāṣṭreṇa rājñā Śāntanavena ca,
130.5 vayam eva Hṛṣīkeśaṃ nigṛhṇīma balād iva
prasahya puruṣa|vyāghram, Indro Vairocaniṃ yathā.
śrutvā gṛhītaṃ Vārṣṇeyaṃ Pāṇḍavā hata|cetasaḥ
nirutsāhā bhaviṣyanti, bhagna|daṃṣṭrā iv' ôragāḥ;
ayaṃ hy eṣāṃ mahā|bāhuḥ sarveṣāṃ śarma varma ca!

Do not become enslaved to your irritability and kill the Kurus, my son. Don't let this whole earth reach its destruction at your hands. You believe that Bhishma, Drona, Kripa and so on will fight with all their power, but it will not turn out that way, you fool. These self-aware men may well hold the Pándavas' kingship, affection, and rank as the same as yours, but law trumps these concerns. 129.50

If these men give up their lives for fear of losing the king's charity, then they will not be able to face King Yudhi·shthira. Greed is not shown to provide men with profit in this world, my son; so don't be greedy, but be calm, bull of the Bharatas."

VAISHAMPÁYANA continued:

DURYÓDHANA DID not take his mother's profitable advice, but instead he once again left in fury for the presence of ill-disciplined men. Having left court, the Káurava took counsel from the gambling addict, King Shákuni, the son of Súbala. Then this idea occurred to Duryódhana, Karna, Shákuni Sáubala, and fourthly to Duhshásana: 130.1

"Before swift-acting Janárdana, King Dhrita·rashtra, and Shántanu's son can seize us we should capture tiger-like 130.5
Hrishikésha just as forcibly as Indra seized Viróchana's son. When the Pándavas hear that Varshnéya has been taken prisoner, they will become senseless and cowardly, like snakes with broken fangs, for that long-armed man is the refuge and defense of them all!

asmin gṛhīte vara|de ṛṣabhe sarva|Sātvatām
nirudyamā bhaviṣyanti Pāṇḍavāḥ Somakaiḥ saha.
tasmād vayam ih' âiv' âinaṃ Keśavaṃ kṣipra|kāriṇam
krośato Dhṛtrāṣṭrasya baddhvā yotsyāmahe ripūn!»
teṣāṃ pāpam abhiprāyaṃ pāpānāṃ duṣṭa|cetasām
130.10 iṅgita|jñaḥ kaviḥ kṣipram anvabudhyata Sātyakiḥ.
tad|artham abhiniṣkramya Hārdikyena sah' āsthitaḥ
abravīt Kṛtavarmāṇaṃ: «kṣipraṃ yojaya vāhinīm,
vyūḍh'|ânīkaḥ sabhā|dvāram upatiṣṭhasva daṃśitaḥ,
yāvad ākhyāmy ahaṃ c' âitat Kṛṣṇāy' â|kliṣṭa|kāriṇe.»
sa praviśya sabhāṃ vīraḥ siṃho giri|guhām iva,
ācaṣṭa tam abhiprāyaṃ Keśavāya mah"|ātmane.
Dhṛtarāṣṭraṃ tataś c' âiva Viduraṃ c' ânvabhāṣata.
teṣām etam abhiprāyam ācacakṣe smayann iva,
«dharmād arthāc ca kāmāc ca karma sādhu|vigarhitam
130.15 mandāḥ kartum ih' êcchanti, na c' âvāpyaṃ kathañ cana.
purā vikurvate mūḍhāḥ pāp'|ātmānaḥ samāgatāḥ
dharṣitāḥ kāma|manyubhyāṃ, krodha|lobha|vaś'|ânugāḥ.
imaṃ hi Puṇḍarīk'|âkṣaṃ jighṛkṣanty alpa|cetasaḥ,
paṭen' âgniṃ prajvalitaṃ yathā bālā yathā jaḍāḥ.»
Sātyakes tad vacaḥ śrutvā Viduro dīrgha|darśivān
Dhṛtarāṣṭraṃ mahā|bāhum abravīt Kuru|saṃsadi:
«rājan, parīta|kālās te putrāḥ sarve, paraṃ|tapa,
a|śakyam a|yaśasyaṃ ca kartuṃ karma samudyatāḥ.
imaṃ hi Puṇḍarīk'|âkṣam abhibhūya prasahya ca
130.20 nigrahītuṃ kil' êcchanti sahitā Vāsav'|ânujam!

When the gift-granting bull of all Sátvatas is captured, the Pándavas and Sómakas will cease all their activity; so we will keep swift-acting Késhava tied up here, despite Dhrita·rashtra's anger, and we will fight our enemies!"

Wise Sátyaki, who could read the signs, quickly realized 130.10
what sinful plan those wicked-minded, evil men were concocting. So it was for this reason that he left with Hardíkya. He said to Krita·varman: "Quickly, draw up the army and wait at the court doors in armor, with forces arrayed, while I speak to pure-acting Krishna." So the hero entered court like a lion entering a mountain cave, and explained their plan to high-souled Késhava. Then he spoke to Dhrita·rashtra and Vídura.

Barely restraining his laughter, he told them about their
plan. "Those fools want to do something prohibited by 130.15
good men who take law, profit, and desire into consideration, but it will never be achieved. Long ago those idiotic, evil-souled men gathered and did mischief, overcome by their lust and fury, as slaves to their greed and anger. But this time they want to overpower lotus-eyed Krishna, small-minded men that they are, like children or idiots trying to catch a blazing fire with cloth."

When farsighted Vídura heard what Sátyaki had to say, he spoke to long-armed Dhrita·rashtra in the Kuru assembly, saying:

"King, time is up for all your sons, enemy-scorcher, for they are prepared to commit an impossible and infamous
sin. In fact, they wish together to tackle and take lotus-eyed 130.20
Krishna here, Vásava's younger brother, prisoner!

imaṃ puruṣa|śārdūlam a|pradhṛṣyaṃ dur|āsadam
āsādya na bhaviṣyanti, pataṅgā iva pāvakam!
ayam icchan hi tān sarvān yudhyamānāñ Janārdanaḥ
siṃho nāgān iva kruddho gamayed Yama|sādanam!
na tv ayaṃ ninditaṃ karma kuryāt pāpaṃ kathañ cana,
na ca dharmād apakrāmed Acyutaḥ puruṣ'|ôttamaḥ.»

Vidureṇ' âivam ukte tu Keśavo vākyam abravīt
Dhṛtarāṣṭram abhiprekṣya su|hṛdāṃ śṛṇvatāṃ mithaḥ:
«rājann, ete yadi kruddhā māṃ nigṛhṇīyur ojasā,
130.25 ete vā mām, ahaṃ v" âinān, anujānīhi, pārthiva,
etān hi sarvān saṃrabdhān niyantum aham utsahe.
na tv ahaṃ ninditaṃ karma kuryāṃ pāpaṃ kathañ cana.
Pāṇḍav'|ârthe hi lubhyantaḥ sv'|ârthān hāsyanti te sutāḥ.

ete ced evam icchanti, kṛta|kāryo Yudhiṣṭhiraḥ.
ady' âiva hy aham enāṃś ca, ye c' âinān anu, Bhārata,
nigṛhya, rājan, Pārthebhyo dadyāṃ. kiṃ duṣ|kṛtaṃ bhavet?
idaṃ tu na pravarteyaṃ ninditaṃ karma, Bhārata,
sannidhau te, mahā|rāja, krodha|jaṃ pāpa|buddhi|jam.
eṣa Duryodhano, rājan, yath" êcchati, tath" âstu tat.
130.30 ahaṃ tu sarvāṃs tanayān anujānāmi te, nṛpa.»

etac chrutvā tu Viduraṃ Dhṛtarāṣṭro 'bhyabhāṣata:
«kṣipram ānaya taṃ pāpaṃ rājya|lubdhaṃ Suyodhanam,
saha|mitraṃ, sah'|âmātyaṃ, sa|sodaryaṃ, mah"|ânugam,
śaknuyāṃ yadi panthānam avatārayituṃ punaḥ.»
tato Duryodhanaṃ kṣattā punaḥ prāveśayat sabhām

If they attack this tiger-like, unassailable, and invincible man then they will die in their attempt, like moths to the flame! If Janárdana here wished it, he could send them to Yama's realm as they all fought, just as a furious lion kills elephants! But this man would not do anything reprehensible, and would never do anything wicked. Áchyuta, the greatest of men, would not transgress the law."

Once Vídura had spoken, Késhava glanced at Dhrita·rashtra, and as his friends listened together he said:

"King, if those furious men attempt to forcibly capture me, then allow them to attack me, or allow me to deal 130.25
with them in return, sovereign, for I am indeed ready to restrain all those angry men. I will, however, perpetrate no censurable act of evil whatsoever. Your sons are greedy for the Pándavas' wealth, but instead they will lose their own treasures.

If this is their wish, then Yudhi·shthira's task is done. I will capture them and their followers today, Bhárata, and hand them over to the Parthas. And what would be wrong with such a course of action, king? I would not do anything reprehensible in your presence, mighty Bhárata sovereign, which is born of fury, or born of wicked intentions. But if this is really what Duryódhana wants, king, then so be it. I 130.30
permit all your sons to try, king."

When he had heard this, Dhrita·rashtra said to Vídura: "Quickly, fetch evil Suyódhana who lusts after kingship, along with his friends, advisors, brothers, and followers, to see if I am able to bring him back to the proper path once more." So the steward brought the unwilling man back to court with his brothers, surrounded by kings. Then King

a|kāmaṃ bhrātṛbhiḥ sārdhaṃ, rājabhiḥ parivāritam.
atha Duryodhanaṃ rājā Dhṛtarāṣṭro 'bhyabhāṣata
Karṇa|Duḥśāsanābhyāṃ ca rājabhiś c' âpi saṃvṛtam:
«nṛśaṃsa pāpa|bhūyiṣṭha, kṣudra|karma|sahāyavān
pāpaiḥ sahāyaiḥ saṃhatya pāpaṃ karma cikīrṣasi—
130.35 a|śakyam, a|yaśasyaṃ ca, sadbhiś c' âpi vigarhitam,
yathā tvādṛśako mūḍho vyavasyet kula|pāṃsanaḥ!
tvam imaṃ Puṇḍarīk'|âkṣam a|pradhṛṣyaṃ dur|āsadaṃ
pāpaiḥ sahāyaiḥ saṃhatya nigrahītuṃ kil' êcchasi.
yo na śakyo balāt kartuṃ devair api sa|Vāsavaiḥ,
taṃ tvaṃ prārthayase, manda, bālaś candramasaṃ yathā!
devair, manuṣyair, gandharvair, asurair, uragaiś ca yaḥ
na soḍhuṃ samare śakyas, taṃ na budhyasi Keśavam!
dur|grāhyaḥ pāṇinā vāyur, duḥ|sparśaḥ pāṇinā śaśī,
dur|dharā pṛthivī mūrdhnā, dur|grāhyaḥ Keśavo balāt!»
130.40 ity ukte Dhṛtarāṣṭreṇa kṣatt" âpi Viduro 'bravīt
Duryodhanam abhipretya Dhārtarāṣṭram a|marṣaṇam:

VIDURA uvāca:

Duryodhana, nibodh' êdaṃ vacanaṃ mama sāmpratam;
Saubha|dvāre vānar'|êndro Dvivido nāma nāmataḥ
śilā|varṣeṇa mahatā chādayām āsa Keśavam.
grahītu|kāmo vikramya sarva|yatnena Mādhavam,
grahītuṃ n' âśakac c' âinaṃ. taṃ tvaṃ prārthayase balāt!
Prāgjyotiṣa|gataṃ Śauriṃ Narakaḥ saha Dānavaiḥ
grahītuṃ n' âśakat tatra. taṃ tvaṃ prārthayase balāt!

Dhrita·rashtra addressed Duryódhana who stood surrounded by Karna, Duhshásana, and other kings, saying:

"Cruel and most evil-natured creature, your allies are men of low deeds, and with these evil friends you plot to commit a wicked act—an impossible, infamous act, forbid- 130.35
den by good men; the type of deed which only some foolish disgrace to his family like you would plan! United with your wicked friends you apparently wish to capture lotus-eyed unassailable and invincible Krishna here!

He cannot be forcibly overpowered by the gods led by Vásava, and yet you, fool, want to capture him, as though you were a child wishing to seize the moon! No one is able to match him in battle—not gods, men, *gandhárva*s, *ásura*s, or snakes. You have no understanding of Késhava! One cannot seize the wind in one's hand. One cannot touch the moon with one's hand. One cannot support the earth on one's head, and one cannot capture Késhava by force!"

When Dhrita·rashtra had said this, the steward Vídura 130.40
addressed Duryódhana, the truculent son of Dhrita·rashtra, staring at him.

VÍDURA said:

Duryódhana, listen to the advice I give you now. The monkey king, named Dvívida, shrouded Késhava with a great downpour of rocks at the gate of Saubha. He made every effort, for he longed to capture Mádhava, but he was unable to do so; and yet you too want to catch him by force! Náraka and the Dánavas found themselves unable to capture Shauri when he went to Prag·jyótisha, and yet you still want to catch him by force! Once Krishna, whose lifetime

an|eka|yuga|varṣ'|āyur nihatya Narakaṃ mṛdhe
nītvā kanyā|sahasrāṇi upayeme yathā|vidhi.
130.45 Nirmocane ṣaṭ|sahasrāḥ pāśair baddhā mah"|âsurāḥ;
grahītuṃ n' âśakaṃś c' âinaṃ. taṃ tvaṃ prārthayase balāt.
anena hi hatā bālye Pūtanā, śakunī tathā,
Govardhano dhāritaś ca gav'|ârthe, Bharata'|rṣabha.
Ariṣṭo, Dhenukaś c' âiva, Cāṇūraś ca mahā|balaḥ,
Aśvarājaś ca nihataḥ, Kaṃsaś c' âriṣṭam ācaran.
Jarāsandhaś ca, Vaktraś ca, Śiśupālaś ca vīryavān,
Bāṇaś ca nihataḥ saṅkhye, rājānaś ca niṣūditāḥ.
Varuṇo nirjito, rājā Pāvakaś c' â|mit'|âujasā,
Pārijātaṃ ca haratā jitaḥ sākṣāc Chacī|patiḥ!
130.50 ek'|ârṇave ca svapatā nihatau Madhu|Kaiṭabhau,
janm'|ântaram upāgamya Hayagrīvas tathā hataḥ.
ayaṃ kartā, na kriyate, kāraṇaṃ c' âpi pauruṣe.
yad yad icched ayaṃ Śauris, tat tat kuryād a|yatnataḥ.
taṃ na budhyasi Govindaṃ ghora|vikramam Acyutam,
āśīviṣam iva kruddhaṃ, tejo|rāśim a|ninditam.
pradharṣayan mahā|bāhuṃ Kṛṣṇam a|kliṣṭa|kāriṇam
pataṅgo 'gnim iv' āsādya s'|âmātyo na bhaviṣyasi!

VAIŚAMPĀYANA uvāca:

131.1 VIDUREṆ' ÂIVAM uktas tu Keśavaḥ śatru|pūga|hā
Duryodhanaṃ Dhārtarāṣṭram abhyabhāṣata vīryavān:
«eko 'ham, iti yan mohān manyase māṃ, Suyodhana,
paribhūya, su|durbuddhe, grahītuṃ māṃ cikīrṣasi!

spans the years of numerous aeons, had killed Náraka in battle, he led a thousand girls away and married them according to the ancient custom.

At Nirmóchana six thousand mighty *ásuras* bound him 130.45
in chains, but were unable to keep hold of him, and yet you still want to catch him by force! When he was only a child he killed Pútana and two bird *ásuras*, and he supported Mount Govárdhana to keep the cattle dry, bull of the Bharatas. He has killed Arísta, Dhénuka, great powerful Chanúra, Ashva·raja, and the miscreant Kansa.

He has killed Jara·sandha, Vaktra, heroic Shishu·pala, and Bana, and he has butchered kings in battle. He defeated Váruna and King Pávaka with his immeasurable energy, and by fetching down the *parijáta* flower he defeated Shachi's husband himself! When sleeping in the single ocean he 130.50
killed Madhu and Káitabha, and once he had reached another birth he killed Haya·griva.

This man is the uncreated creator. He is the very cause of manliness. Shauri here effortlessly achieves whatever he wishes. You have no understanding of Govínda Áchyuta of horrifying prowess, a blameless mass of glory, like a furious poisonous snake. You and your advisors will burn up like a moth to the flame if you attack long-armed, pure-acting Krishna!

VAISHAMPÁYANA continued:

WHEN VÍDURA HAD spoken, Késhava, the heroic slayer 131.1
of enemy hordes, spoke to Duryódhana Dhartaráshtra: "In your foolishness you believe that I am only one man, Suyódhana, and so you eagerly plan to attack me and take me pris-

ih' âiva Pāṇḍavāḥ sarve, tath" âiv' Ândhaka|Vṛṣṇayaḥ,
ih' Ādityāś ca, Rudrāś ca, Vasavaś ca maha"|ṛṣibhiḥ!»

evam uktvā jahās' ôccaiḥ Keśavaḥ para|vīra|hā
tasya saṃsmayataḥ Śaurer vidyud|rūpā mah"|ātmanaḥ
131.5 aṅguṣṭha|mātrās tri|daśā mumucuḥ pāvak'|ārciṣaḥ;
asya Brahmā lalāṭa|stho, Rudro vakṣasi c' âbhavat,
loka|pālā bhujeṣv āsann, Agnir āsyād ajāyata,
Ādityāś c' âiva, sādhyāś ca, Vasavo, 'th' Âśvināv api,
marutaś ca sah' Êndreṇa, Viśvedevās tath" âiva ca
babhūvuś c' âika|rūpāṇi yakṣa|gandharva|rakṣasām.

prādur āstāṃ tathā dorbhyāṃ Saṅkarṣaṇa|Dhanañjayau:
dakṣiṇe 'th' Ârjuno dhanvī, halī Rāmaś ca savyataḥ;
Bhīmo, Yudhiṣṭhiraś c' âiva, Mādrī|putrau ca pṛṣṭhataḥ,
Andhakā, Vṛṣṇayaś c' âiva Pradyumna|pramukhās tataḥ
131.10 agre babhūvuḥ Kṛṣṇasya samudyata|mah"|āyudhā.
śaṅkha|cakra|gadā|śakti|Śārṅga|lāṅgala|Nandakāḥ
adṛśyant' ôdyatāny eva sarva|praharaṇāni ca
nānā|bāhuṣu Kṛṣṇasya dīpyamānāni sarvaśaḥ.

netrābhyāṃ, nastataś c' âiva, śrotrābhyāṃ ca samantataḥ
prādur āsan mahā|raudrāḥ sa|dhūmāḥ pāvak'|ârciṣaḥ,
roma|kūpeṣu ca tathā sūryasy' êva marīcayaḥ.

taṃ dṛṣṭvā ghoram ātmānaṃ Keśavasya mah"|ātmanaḥ
nyamīlayanta netrāṇi rājānas trasta|cetasaḥ,
ṛte Droṇaṃ ca, Bhīṣmaṃ ca, Viduraṃ ca mahā|matim,
131.15 Sañjayaṃ ca mahā|bhāgam, ṛṣīṃś c' âiva tapo|dhanān;

oner, you incredibly ignorant man! But all the Pándavas, all the Ándhakas, Vrishnis, Adítyas, Rudras, Vasus, and mighty sages are here in this very place!"

Saying this, Késhava, the slayer of enemy heroes, laughed loudly, and as high-souled Shauri laughed, all thirty thumb- 131.5
sized gods were released from his body, as dazzling as lightning and flashing like fire. Brahma took up his position on his forehead, Rudra settled on his chest, the protectors of the world settled on his arms, and Agni was born from his mouth. The Adítyas, *sadhyas*, Vasus, and the two Ashvins also materialized. Indra and the Maruts appeared, as did the *vishva·devas*, and the forms of *yakshas*, *gandhárvas*, and *rákshasas*.

Sankárshana and Dhanan·jaya appeared on his arms—the archer Árjuna on his right arm, and Rama the plow-bearer on his left. Bhima, Yudhi·shthira, and Madri's twin sons emerged from his back. The Ándhakas and Vrishnis,
led by Pradyúmna, appeared in front of Krishna, with their 131.10
mighty weapons raised. His conch, discus, mace, spear, the horn-bow named Sharnga, his plow, and the sword named Nándaka appeared, and all Krishna's weapons were raised in his various hands, blazing in all directions.

Great terrifying flames of smoky fire shot all around from his eyes, nose, and ears, and rays of light, like those of the sun, burst forth from the pores of his skin.

As they watched this dread person of great-souled Késhava, the kings closed their eyes and their hearts trembled—all, that is, except Drona, Bhishma, highly wise Vídura,
noble Sánjaya, and the sages of ascetic wealth; for the blessed 131.15
lord Janárdana bestowed the gift of celestial sight upon

prādāt teṣāṃ sa bhagavān divyaṃ cakṣur Janārdanaḥ.
tad dṛṣṭvā mahad āścaryaṃ Mādhavasya sabhā|tale
deva|dundubhayo neduḥ, puṣpa|varṣaṃ papāta ca.
tatr' âdbhutaṃ, mahā|rāja, Dhṛtarāṣṭraḥ sva|cakṣuṣī†
labdhavān Vāsudevāc ca viśva|rūpa|didṛkṣayā.
labdha|cakṣuṣam āsīnaṃ Dhṛtarāṣṭraṃ nar'|âdhipāḥ
vismitā ṛṣibhiḥ sārdhaṃ tuṣṭuvur Madhu|sūdanam.

DHṚTARĀṢṬRA uvāca:

tvam eva, Puṇḍarīk'|âkṣa, sarvasya jagato hitaḥ;
tasmāt tvaṃ, Yādava|śreṣṭha, prasādaṃ kartum arhasi.
131.20 bhagavan, mama netrāṇām antar|dhānaṃ vṛṇe punaḥ,
bhavantaṃdṛṣṭavān asmi.† n' ânyaṃ draṣṭum ih' ôtsahe!
tato 'bravīn mahā|bāhur Dhṛtarāṣṭraṃ Janārdanaḥ:
«a|dṛśyamāne netre dve bhavetāṃ, Kuru|nandana.»
cacāla ca mahī kṛtsnā, sāgaraś c' âpi cukṣubhe;
vismayaṃ paramaṃ jagmuḥ pārthivā, Bharata'|rṣabha.
tataḥ sa puruṣa|vyāghraḥ saṃjahāra vapuḥ svakam,
tāṃ divyām, adbhutāṃ, citrām, ṛddhim āttām arin|damaḥ.
tataḥ Sātyakim ādāya pāṇau, Hārdikyam eva ca,
ṛṣibhis tair anujñāto niryayau Madhu|sūdanaḥ.
131.25 ṛṣayo 'ntar|hitā jagmus tatas te Nārad'|ādayaḥ;
tasmin kolāhale vṛtte tad adbhutam iv' âbhavat.
taṃ prasthitam abhiprekṣya Kauravāḥ saha rājabhiḥ
anujagmur nara|vyāghraṃ devā iva śata|kratum.
a|cintayann a|mey'|ātmā sarvaṃ tad rāja|maṇḍalam
niścakrāma tataḥ Śauriḥ sa|dhūma iva pāvakaḥ.

them. Once they had seen Mádhava's great miracle in court, divine kettledrums boomed, and a rain of flowers fell.

Then an astounding miracle occurred, great king. Dhrita·rashtra regained his eyesight from Vasudéva, for he desired to see Krishna in his varied forms. The kings and sages were amazed as Dhrita·rashtra sat with his sight restored, and they were delighted with Madhu·súdana.

DHRITA·RASHTRA said:

Lotus-eyed and greatest of the Yádavas, you benefit the whole universe and so you ought to do me a kindness.
Blessed lord, please return the blindness of my eyes once 131.20
more, for now I have seen you I dare not look at anything else.

So long-armed Janárdana replied to Dhrita·rashtra: "May your eyes become blind once more, descendant of the Kurus."

The whole earth moved, the ocean shook, and the kings were utterly astonished, bull of the Bharatas. But then the tiger-like enemy-tamer concealed his real form—the celestial, miraculous, and multicolored supernatural power he had taken on—and taking Sátyaki and Hardíkya by the
hand, with the leave of the sages, Madhu·súdana left. Next 131.25
the sages, Nárada and so on, disappeared and vanished; it was yet another wonder in this uproarious state of affairs.

The Káuravas and kings watched him go, then followed the tiger-like man just as the celestials follow the god of a hundred sacrifices. Without giving so much as a thought to the entire circle of kings, immeasurably souled Shauri strode away like a smoky fire. Dáruka appeared on his large,

tato rathena śubhreṇa mahatā, kiṅkiṇīkinā,
hema|jāla|vicitreṇa, laghunā, megha|nādinā,
s'|ûpaskareṇa, śubhreṇa, vaiyāghreṇa, varūthinā,
Śaibya|Sugrīva|yuktena pratyadṛśyata Dārukaḥ.
131.30 tath" âiva ratham āsthāya Kṛtavarmā mahā|rathaḥ
Vṛṣṇīnāṃ saṃmato vīro Hārdikyaḥ samadṛśyata.
upasthita|rathaṃ Śauriṃ prayāsyantam arin|damam
Dhṛtarāṣṭro mahā|rājaḥ punar ev' âbhyabhāṣata:
«yāvad balaṃ me putreṣu paśyatas te, Janārdana,
pratyakṣaṃ te, na te kiñ cit parokṣaṃ, śatru|karśana.
Kurūṇāṃ śamam icchantaṃ yatamānaṃ ca, Keśava,
viditv' âitām avasthāṃ me n' âbhiśaṅkitum arhasi.
na me pāpo 'sty abhiprāyaḥ Pāṇḍavān prati, Keśava,
jñātam eva hitaṃ vākyaṃ yan may" ôktaḥ Suyodhanaḥ.
131.35 jānanti Kuravaḥ sarve, rājānaś c' âiva pārthivāḥ
śame prayatamānaṃ māṃ sarva|yatnena, Mādhava.»

VAIŚAMPĀYANA uvāca:

tato 'bravīn mahā|bāhur
Dhṛtarāṣṭraṃ Janārdanaḥ,
Droṇaṃ, pitā|mahaṃ Bhīṣmaṃ,
kṣattāraṃ, Bāhlikaṃ, Kṛpam:
«pratyakṣam etad bhavatāṃ yad vṛttaṃ Kuru|saṃsadi,
yathā c' â|śiṣṭavan mando roṣād adya samutthitaḥ.
vadaty an|īśam ātmānaṃ Dhṛtarāṣṭro mahī|patiḥ.
āpṛcche bhavataḥ sarvān, gamiṣyāmi Yudhiṣṭhiram.»

gleaming, belled chariot, so brightly hued with golden latticework. It was quick and boomed like thunder, and the well-equipped armored chariot was decked with bright tigerskins and yoked to Shaibya and Sugríva.

Similarly, Krita·varman Hardíkya the mighty warrior and 131.30
esteemed hero of the Vrishnis appeared, standing on a chariot. The mighty sovereign Dhrita·rashtra addressed Shauri the enemy-tamer once more, as he stood on his car, about to set off:

"You have seen the extent of the power I have over my sons, Janárdana. It is clear to you, and nothing is hidden, enemy-plower.

Knowing that I wish and strive for peace among the Kurus, Késhava, and being aware of my circumstances, you should not be suspicious of me. I have no evil plan for the Pándavas, Késhava, and you know what beneficial advice I
gave to Suyódhana. The Kurus and all kings and lords know 131.35
how I have strived for peace with every means at my disposal, Mádhava."

VAISHAMPÁYANA continued:

Long-armed Janárdana replied to Dhrita·rashtra, Drona, grandfather Bhishma, the steward, Báhlika, and Kripa, saying: "It was clear to you what happened in the Kuru assembly; how the untrained fool rose in fury. King Dhrita·rashtra claims he is powerless, so I shall bid you all goodbye and go to Yudhi·shthira."

āmantrya prasthitaṃ Śauriṃ ratha|sthaṃ, puruṣa'|rṣabha
anujagmur mah"|êṣv|āsāḥ pravīrā Bharata'|rṣabhāḥ:
131.40 Bhīṣmo, Droṇaḥ, Kṛpaḥ, kṣattā, Dhṛtarāṣṭro, 'tha Bāhlikaḥ,
Aśvatthāmā, Vikarṇaś ca, Yuyutsuś ca mahā|rathaḥ.
tato rathena śubhreṇa, mahatā, kiṅkiṇīkinā
Kurūṇāṃ paśyatāṃ draṣṭuṃ svasāraṃ sa pitur yayau.

VAIŚAMPĀYANA uvāca:

132.1 PRAVIŚY' ÂTHA GṚHAṂ tasyāś, caraṇāv abhivādya ca
ācakhyau tat samāsena yad vṛttaṃ Kuru|saṃsadi.

VĀSUDEVA uvāca:

uktaṃ bahu|vidhaṃ vākyaṃ grahaṇīyaṃ sa|hetukam
ṛṣibhiś c' âiva ca mayā, na c' âsau tad gṛhītavān.
kāla|pakvam idaṃ sarvaṃ Suyodhana|vaś'|ânugam.
āpṛcche bhavatīṃ śīghraṃ, prayāsye Pāṇḍavān prati.
kiṃ vācyāḥ Pāṇḍaveyās te bhavatyā vacanān mayā?
tad brūhi tvaṃ, mahā|prājñe, śuśrūṣe vacanaṃ tava.

KUNTY uvāca:

132.5 brūyāḥ, Keśava, rājānaṃ dharm'|ātmānaṃ Yudhiṣṭhiram:
«bhūyāṃs te hīyate dharmo; mā, putraka, vṛthā kṛthāḥ.
śrotriyasy' êva te, rājan, mandakasy' â|vipaścitaḥ
anuvāka|hatā|buddhir dharmam ev' âikam īkṣate.
aṅg' âvekṣasva dharmaṃ tvaṃ, yathā sṛṣṭaḥ Svayaṃbhuvā;
bāhubhyāṃ kṣatriyāḥ sṛṣṭā bāhu|vīry'|ôpajīvinaḥ,
krūrāya karmaṇe nityaṃ, prajānāṃ paripālane.
śṛṇu c' âtr' ôpamām ekāṃ yā vṛddhebhyaḥ śrutā mayā:

So, having said his farewells, Shauri set off standing on his chariot, bull-like man, and those mighty archer heroes, the bulls of the Bharatas—Bhishma, Drona, Kripa, the 131.40
steward, Dhrita·rashtra, Báhlika, Ashva·tthaman, Vikárna, and the great chariot warrior Yuyútsu—followed him. Then, on his large, gleaming, and belled chariot he went to see his paternal aunt, while the Kurus watched him go.

VAISHAMPÁYANA said:

KRISHNA ENTERED HER house and greeted her, taking 132.1
hold of her feet, and explained briefly what had taken place in the Kuru assembly.

VASUDÉVA said:

A great variety of valuable and reasonable advice was given by both the sages and myself, but that man would not accept it. Now all who are slaves to Suyódhana's will are cooked by time, so I take my leave of you, and I will quickly return to the Pándavas. What message should I give the Pándavas on your behalf? Tell me, wise lady, for I will obey your words.

KUNTI replied:

Késhava, tell righteous-souled King Yudhi·shthira: 132.5

"Your law has waned a great deal, and so, my dear son, don't go astray. Your mind is lost on mere repetition of the words of the Veda, and so you see only law, just as a man who has merely learned the Veda by heart, and is unable to catch its true meaning, is therefore a fool. So then, please have regard for the law which the self-existent Brahma set for you: the kshatriya was created from his arms, to always rely on the strength of his own arms in cruel deeds and in

Mucukundasya rāja'|rṣer adadat pṛthivīm imām
purā Vaiśravaṇaḥ prīto, na c' âsau tad gṛhītavān.
132.10 ‹bāhu|vīry'|ârjitaṃ rājyam aśnīyām, iti kāmaye.›
tato Vaiśravaṇaḥ prīto vismitaḥ samapadyata.
Mucukundas tato rājā so 'nvaśāsad vasun|dharām
bāhu|vīry'|ârjitāṃ samyak kṣatra|dharmam anuvrataḥ.

yaṃ hi dharmaṃ carant' îha prajā rājñā su|rakṣitāḥ,
caturthaṃ tasya dharmasya rājā vindeta, Bhārata.
rājā carati ced dharmaṃ, devatvāy' âiva kalpate;
sa ced a|dharmaṃ carati, narakāy' âiva gacchati.
daṇḍa|nītiś ca dharmabhyaś cāturvarṇyaṃ niyacchati
prayuktā svāminā samyag a|dharmebhyaś ca yacchati.
132.15 daṇḍa|nītyāṃ yadā rājā samyak kārtsnyena vartate,
tadā Kṛta|yugaṃ nāma kālaḥ śreṣṭhaḥ pravartate.
kālo vā kāraṇaṃ rājño, rājā vā kāla|kāraṇam
iti te saṃśayo mā bhūd; rājā kālasya kāraṇam.
rājā kṛta|yuga|sraṣṭā, tretāyā, dvāparasya ca,
yugasya ca caturthasya rājā bhavati kāraṇam.

kṛtasya karaṇād rājā svargam atyantam aśnute.
tretāyāḥ karaṇād rājā svargaṃ n' âtyantam aśnute.
pravartanād dvāparasya yathā|bhāgam upāśnute;
kaleḥ pravartanād rājā pāpam atyantam aśnute.
132.20 tato vasati duṣ|karmā narake śāśvatīḥ samāḥ;
rāja|doṣeṇa hi jagat spṛśyate; jagataḥ sa ca.

defense of his subjects. Listen to this example which I heard from the elders:

Long ago, Váishravana presented this earth to the royal sage Muchukúnda, for he was pleased with him; but he
would not accept it. 'I wish to win a kingdom earned by 132.10
my strength of arms alone,' he said. So Váishravana was surprised, but pleased, and he left. King Muchukúnda went on to rule the earth, winning it by his strength of arms, abiding completely by the kshatriya law.

When a king's subjects are well defended by their sovereign, then the king certainly wins a quarter of the virtue they practice, Bhárata. If a king practices law he is worthy of divinity, but if he practices lawlessness then he goes to hell. It is the properly conducted policy of punishment by the ruler which reins in the four classes to their respective lawful duties, and prevents them from becoming lawless.

When a king practices a full and complete policy of pun- 132.15
ishment, then the best age, called the *krita yuga*, begins. Do not be in doubt about whether the age causes the king or the king is the cause of the age, for it is the king who causes the age. It is the king who creates the *krita yuga*, the *treta yuga*, and the *dvápara yuga*, and it is the king who is the cause of the fourth *yuga*.

The king who brings about the *krita yuga* wins eternal heaven. The king who brings about the *treta yuga* wins limited heaven. The king who ushers in the *dvápara* age wins his fair reward, and the king who brings about the *kali yuga*
gains only eternal evil. A miscreant king lives in hell for all 132.20
eternity, for the universe is touched by the king's sins, and the king is touched by those of the universe.

rāja|dharmān avekṣasva pitṛ|paitāmah'|ôcitān,
n' âitad rāja'|rṣi|vṛttaṃ hi, yatra tvaṃ sthātum icchasi.
na hi vaiklavya|saṃsṛṣṭa ānṛśaṃsya|vyavasthitaḥ
prajā|pālana|saṃbhūtaṃ phalaṃ kiñ cana labdhavān.
na hy etām āśiṣaṃ Pāṇḍur, na c' âhaṃ, na pitā|mahaḥ
prayuktavantaḥ pūrvaṃ te, yayā carasi medhayā.
yajñe dānaṃ, tapaḥ, śauryaṃ, prajñā, saṃtānam eva ca,
māhātmyaṃ, balam, ojaś ca nityam āśaṃsitaṃ mayā.
132.25 nityaṃ svāhā, svadhā nityaṃ dadyur mānuṣa|devatāḥ,
dīrgham āyur, dhanaṃ, putrān, samyag ārādhitāḥ śubhāḥ.
putreṣv āśāsate nityaṃ, pitaro, daivatāni ca,
dānam, adhyayanaṃ, yajñaḥ, prajānāṃ paripālanam.
etad dharmam a|dharmaṃ vā
janman" âiv' âbhyajāyathāḥ.
te tu vaidyāḥ kule jātā
a|vṛttyā, tāta, pīḍitāḥ.
yatra dāna|patiṃ śūraṃ kṣudhitāḥ pṛthivī|carāḥ
prāpya tuṣṭāḥ pratiṣṭhante; dharmaḥ ko 'bhyadhikas tataḥ?
dānen' ânyaṃ, balen' ânyaṃ, tathā sūnṛtayā param,
sarvataḥ pratigṛhṇīyād rājyaṃ prāpy' êha dhārmikaḥ.
132.30 brāhmaṇaḥ pracared bhaikṣaṃ, kṣatriyaḥ paripālayet,
vaiśyo dhan'|ârjanaṃ kuryāc, chūdraḥ paricarec ca tān.
bhaikṣaṃ vipratiṣiddhaṃ te, kṛṣir n' âiv' ôpapadyate;
kṣatriyo 'si kṣatā|trātā bāhu|vīry'|ôpajīvitā.

Look to the royal lawful duties which befitted your fathers and forefathers, for the behavior by which you wish to abide is not that of a royal sage. The king who is born feeble-minded, and does not settle on cruelty, does not gain any of the rewards won by the defense of his subjects. When we were making our wishes for you in the past, neither Pandu, nor I, nor your grandfather ever wished for you to have the intelligence by which you act. Rather, sacrifice, generosity, austerity, bravery, wisdom, children, greatness of soul,
strength, and energy were what I always wished for. With 132.25
constant *svaha* and constant *svadha* the ancestors and gods were completely propitiated, and they kindly granted long life, wealth, and sons. Parents and gods always hope for generosity, learning, sacrifice, and defense of their subjects in their sons.

Regardless of whether or not it is righteous, you were born to it by your birth. Now, though learned and born into a good family, my son, your incorrect behavior causes you to suffer. Men who are hungry in this world remain and are happy where they find a brave and generous king. What greater law is there? Once a lawful man has attained kingship, he should attach all men to himself, one through
bribery, another by force, and another by kindness. A brah- 132.30
min should make a living by begging. A kshatriya should protect his people. A vaishya should work by accumulating wealth, and a *shudra* should serve the others. You are forbidden to beg, and agriculture is not appropriate for you. You are a kshatriya, a rescuer of the downtrodden, and you live by the strength of your arms.

pitryam aṃśaṃ, mahā|bāho, nimagnaṃ punar uddhara
sāmnā, bhedena, dānena, daṇḍen', âtha nayena vā.
ito duḥkhataraṃ kiṃ nu, yad ahaṃ dīna|bāndhavā
para|piṇḍam udīkṣe vai, tvāṃ sūtv", âmitra|nandana?
yudhyasva rāja|dharmeṇa, mā nimajjīḥ pitā|mahān!
mā gamaḥ kṣīṇa|puṇyas tvaṃ s'|ânujaḥ pāpikāṃ gatim!»

Raise up your sunken paternal share of the kingdom once more, long-armed man, either by conciliation, by causing division, or by bribery, punishment, or political acumen. Is there anything more wretched than that I am seperated from my family, looking for handouts from others, when I have given birth to you, joy of your enemies? Fight with the law of kings, and don't drown your ancestors! Don't tread an evil path with your brothers now that your merit is depleted!"

# 133–139

# THE TALE OF VÍDULA

KUNTY uvāca:

133.1 ATR' ÂPY UDĀHARANT' îmam itihāsaṃ purātanam
Vidulāyāś ca saṃvādaṃ putrasya ca, paraṃ|tapa.
tataḥ śreyaś ca bhūyaś ca yathāvad vaktum arhasi.
yaśasvinī, manyumatī, kule jātā, vibhāvarī,
kṣatra|dharma|ratā, dāntā, vidulā, dīrgha|darśinī,
viśrutā rāja|saṃsatsu, śruta|vākyā, bahu|śrutā,
Vidulā nāma rājanyā jagarhe putram aurasam
nirjitaṃ Sindhu|rājena, śayānaṃ dīna|cetasam.

VIDUL" ôvāca:

133.5 a|nandana mayā jāta, dviṣatāṃ harṣa|vardhana!
na mayā tvaṃ, na pitrā ca jātaḥ, kv' âbhyāgato hy asi?
nirmanyuś c' âpy a|saṃkhyeyaḥ puruṣaḥ klība|sādhanaḥ!
yāvaj|jīvaṃ nirāśo 'si? kalyāṇāya dhuraṃ vaha!
m" ātmānam avamanyasva, m" âinam alpena bībharaḥ!
manaḥ kṛtvā su|kalyāṇaṃ mā bhais tvaṃ, pratisaṃhara!
uttiṣṭha he, kā|puruṣa, mā śeṣv' âivaṃ parājitaḥ!
a|mitrān nandayan sarvān nirmāno, bandhu|śoka|daḥ!
su|pūrā vai ku|nadikā, su|pūro mūṣik'|âñjaliḥ,
su|saṃtoṣaḥ kā|puruṣaḥ, sv|alpaken' âiva tuṣyati.
133.10 apy aher ārujan daṃṣṭrām āśv eva nidhanaṃ vraja,
api vā saṃśayaṃ prāpya jīvite 'pi parākrameḥ.
apy areḥ śyenavac chidraṃ paśyes tvaṃ viparikraman

KUNTI continued:

IT IS IN SITUATIONS like these that people quote the ancient tale of the conversation between Vídula and her son, enemy-scorcher. You ought to advise Yudhi·shthira with the best and most suitable points of this story. There was an illustrious and splendid, but irritable, nobly born lady of foresight, discipline, and prudence, who took delight in the law of royalty. She was famous among the courts of kings, as a very scholarly lady who gave educated advice. This royal lady by the name of Vídula once admonished her own son as he lay around in low spirits—for he had been defeated by the king of the Sindhus. 133.1

VÍDULA said:

You are no son of mine, augmenter of your enemies' joy! 133.5
Your father and I did not produce you, so where have you come from? You cannot be counted as a man when you are so dispassionate. It rather denotes you as a eunuch! Are you going to be hopeless all your life? Carry the burden, if you want prosperity! Don't despise yourself, and don't be content with only a little. Have ideas for great success, and don't give in to fear! Oh get up, you coward, and don't just lie about defeated! Without pride you bring joy to all your enemies, and bring nothing but sorrow to your family!

A pitiful little stream is easily full, a mouse's paws are soon filled, and a coward is easily pleased and satisfied with
the bare minimum. Better to die quickly, pulling out the 133.10
snake's fangs! Find your prowess, even if you must risk your life to do so. Would you watch for an opportunity against

vivadan v", âthavā tūṣṇīṃ, vyomn' îv' â|pariśaṅkitaḥ?
tvam evaṃ pretavac cheṣe kasmād, vajra|hato yathā?
uttiṣṭha he, kā|puruṣa, mā svāpsīḥ śatru|nirjitaḥ!
m" âstaṃ gamas tvaṃ kṛpaṇo,
viśrūyasva sva|karmaṇā!
mā madhye, mā jaghanye tvaṃ,
m" âdho bhūs, tiṣṭha garjitaḥ!
alātaṃ tindukasy' êva, muhūrtam api hi jvala!
mā tuṣ'|âgnir iv' ân|arcir dhūmāyasva jijīviṣuḥ!
133.15 muhūrtaṃ jvalitaṃ śreyo, na ca dhūmāyitaṃ ciram.
mā ha sma kasya cid gehe jani rājñaḥ kharo mṛduḥ.
kṛtvā mānuṣyakaṃ karma, sṛtv" ājiṃ yāvad uttamam,
dharmasy' ānṛṇyam āpnoti, na c' ātmānaṃ vigarhate.
a|labdhvā yadi vā labdhvā n' ânuśocati paṇḍitaḥ,
ānantaryaṃ c' ārabhate, na prāṇānāṃ dhanāyate.
udbhāvayasva vīryaṃ vā, tāṃ vā gaccha dhruvāṃ gatim.
dharmaṃ, putr', âgrataḥ kṛtvā kiṃ nimittaṃ hi jīvasi?
iṣṭ'|āpūrtaṃ hi te, klība, kīrtiś ca sakalā hatā!
vicchinnaṃ bhoga|mūlaṃ te, kiṃ nimittaṃ hi jīvasi?
133.20 śatrur nimajjatā grāhyo jaṅghāyāṃ prapatiṣyatā;
viparicchinna|mūlo 'pi na viṣīdet kathañ cana.
udyamya dhuram utkarṣed ājāneya|kṛtaṃ smaran;
kuru satvaṃ ca mānaṃ ca, viddhi pauruṣam ātmanaḥ!

your enemy like a shrieking or silent and unhesitant hawk circling in the sky?

Why do you lie there like a corpse as though you've been struck by lightning? Oh get up, coward, and don't sleep when you've been defeated by your enemies! Don't vanish wretchedly like the setting sun, but be famed for your exploits! Don't stay among the average or lower or right at the bottom, but stand tall, being vaunted! Blaze, even if it is only for a moment, like a firebrand of *tínduka* wood! Don't
just smoke, desperate to live, like a flameless chaff fire! It 133.15
is better to blaze for a moment than to smoke for a long time. May such a soft mule of a prince never be born into a king's house.

If he pursues battle and reaches the limit of manly exploits, then a man wins freedom from the debt to his duty, and does not bring reproach upon himself. The wise man does not grieve, regardless of whether he achieves his objectives or not. Instead he immediately undertakes his next task and does not take his own life into consideration. Show some courage, or go down the certain path of death. What is the point of living when you have put your duty first, my son?

My castrated son, the religious merit you accumulated has been destroyed, as has all your fame! When the roots of one's pleasure are cut, then what is the point of living?
A sinking man who is about to fall should grab hold of his 133.20
enemy by the calves and drag him down with him, and if his roots are cut out from under him he should never be melancholy. One should raise the yoke and become peerless, remembering the achievements of well-bred horses. So

udbhāvaya kulaṃ magnaṃ tvat|kṛte svayam eva hi;
yasya vṛttaṃ na jalpanti mānavā mahad adbhutam,
rāśi|vardhana|mātraṃ sa, n' âiva strī na punaḥ pumān.
dāne, tapasi satye ca yasya n' ôccaritaṃ yaśaḥ,
vidyāyām artha|lābhe vā, mātur uccāra eva saḥ
śrutena, tapasā v" âpi, śriyā vā, vikrameṇa vā,
133.25 janān yo 'bhibhavaty anyān karmaṇā hi, sa vai pumān.

na tv eva jālmīṃ kāpālīṃ vṛttim eṣitum arhasi
nṛśaṃsyām a|yaśasyāṃ ca, duḥkhāṃ, kāpuruṣ'|ôcitām.
yam enam abhinandeyur amitrāḥ puruṣaṃ kṛśam,
lokasya samavajñātaṃ, nihīn'|āsana|vāsasam,
aho|lābha|karaṃ, hīnam, alpa|jīvanam, alpakam,
n' ēdṛśaṃ bandhum āsādya bāndhavaḥ sukham edhate!

a|vṛtty" âiva vipatsyāmo vayaṃ rāṣṭrāt pravāsitāḥ,
sarva|kāma|rasair hīnāḥ, sthāna|bhraṣṭā a|kiñ|canāḥ!
a|valgu|kāriṇaṃ satsu, kula|vaṃśasya nāśanam,
133.30 Kaliṃ putra|pravādena, Sañjaya, tvām ajījanam!
niramarṣaṃ, nirutsāhaṃ, nirvīryam, ari|nandanam
mā sma sīmantinī kā cij janayet putram īdṛśam!

act true, win honor, and understand the extent of your own manliness!

Elevate your lineage, sunk down by your exploits, for if men do not gossip about a man's conduct, describing it as a great wonder, then he is merely one more on the heap of humanity, neither man nor woman any more. The man whose fame does not grow from his generosity, austerity,
truth, learning, and the gains he has won, is nothing more 133.25
than his mother's excrement. One becomes a man by excelling other men in learning, austerity, glory, prowess, or accomplishment.

You ought not to make a living out of the base, inglorious, wretched, and contemptible practice of begging—something only cowards practice. No man will ever live happily if he is related to the sort of person who is emaciated, the sort of person whom enemies welcome, whom the world treats with contempt, who has vile food and clothing, who earns only the minimum daily subsistence, who is destitute, survives on little, and is himself next to worthless!

We will die, for we have no livelihood now that we have
been exiled from our kingdom, deprived of every pleasure 133.30
and delight, and demoted from our rank—we are nobodies! I gave birth to Kali, merely disguised as my son, Sánjaya, for you are the destruction of your family lineage, and you misbehave in the presence of good men! May no pregnant woman ever give birth to a son like you—a passive, cowardly, and unheroic man who brings delight to his enemies!

mā dhūmāya, jval' âtyantam! ākramya jahi śātravān!
jvala mūrdhany amitrāṇāṃ muhūrtam api vā kṣaṇam!
etāvān eva puruṣo, yad a|marṣī, yad a|kṣamī.
kṣamāvān niramarṣaś ca n' âiva strī, na punaḥ pumān;
santoṣo vai śriyaṃ hanti, tath" ânukrośa eva ca;
anutthāna|bhaye c' ôbhe nirīho n' āśnute mahat.
ebhyo nikṛti|pāpebhyaḥ pramuñc' ātmānam ātmanā.
133.35 āyasaṃ hṛdayaṃ kṛtvā mṛgayasva punaḥ svakam.

paraṃ viṣahate yasmāt, tasmāt puruṣa ucyate;
tam āhur vyartha|nāmānaṃ, strīvad ya iha jīvati
śūrasy' ôrjita|sattvasya siṃha|vikrānta|cāriṇaḥ
diṣṭa|bhāvaṃ gatasy' âpi viṣaye modate prajā.
ya ātmanaḥ priya|sukhe hitvā mṛgayate śriyam
amātyānām atho harṣam ādadhāty a|cireṇa saḥ.

PUTRA uvāca:

kiṃ nu te mām a|paśyantyāḥ pṛthivyā api sarvayā?
kim ābharaṇa|kṛtyaṃ te? kiṃ bhogair jīvitena vā?

MĀT" ôvāca:

133.40 kim|adyakānāṃ ye lokā, dviṣantas tān avāpnuyuḥ;
ye tv ādṛt'|ātmanāṃ lokāḥ, su|hṛdas tān vrajantu naḥ!
bhṛtyair vihīyamānānāṃ, para|piṇḍ'|ôpajīvinām,
kṛpaṇānām, a|sattvānāṃ mā vṛttim anuvartithāḥ!
anu tvāṃ, tāta, jīvantu brāhmaṇāḥ, su|hṛdas tathā,

Don't just smoke, but blaze! Attack ceaselessly, and destroy your enemies! Blaze on the head of your enemies even if only for a moment, or just an instant! It is one's truculence and mercilessness that makes one a man. A forgiving and tolerant person is neither a man nor a woman, for satisfaction destroys good fortune, as do sympathy and both laziness and fear. A man without ambition achieves nothing of consequence. Free yourself from these sins of deceit through
your own effort. Make your heart as steel, and search for 133.35
what is yours once more.

A man is called *púrusha* because he is able to match his enemy.* They say that a man who lives like a woman, as in this case, is incorrectly named a man. When a brave man of true power, who moves with a lion-like stride, meets his end, then the subjects in his realm still rejoice. The man who ignores his own pleasure and happiness and hunts down good fortune, quickly brings joy to his counselors.

HER SON replied:

If you could no longer even see me then what good would the whole world be to you? What good would it be to be decked in ornaments? What good would the pleasures of life be to you?

HIS MOTHER said:

Let your enemies win the worlds of men who cry "What 133.40
now?" But may you and your friends reach the worlds of respected souls! Don't follow the lifestyle of wicked and wretched men who have lost their servants and scratch a living from the charity of others! Instead, may brahmins and friends take their living from you, my son, just as creatures

parjanyam iva bhūtāni, devā iva śata|kratum.
yam ājīvanti puruṣaṃ sarva|bhūtāni, Sañjaya,
pakvaṃ drumam iv' āsādya, tasya jīvitam arthavat.
yasya śūrasya vikrāntair edhante bāndhavāḥ sukham,
tri|daśā iva Śakrasya, sādhu tasy' êha jīvitam.
133.45 sva|bāhu|balam āśritya yo 'bhyujjīvati mānavaḥ,
sa loke labhate kīrtiṃ, paratra ca śubhāṃ gatim.

VIDUL" ôvāca:

134.1 ATH' ÂITASYĀM avasthāyāṃ pauruṣaṃ hātum icchasi,
nihīna|sevitaṃ mārgaṃ gamiṣyasy a|cirād iva.
yo hi tejo yathā|śakti na darśayati vikramāt
kṣatriyo jīvit'|ākāṅkṣī, stena ity eva taṃ viduḥ.
arthavanty upapannāni vākyāni, guṇavanti ca,
n' âiva saṃprāpnuvanti tvāṃ, mumūrṣum iva bheṣajam.
santi vai Sindhu|rājasya santuṣṭā na tathā janāḥ
daurbalyād āsate mūḍhā vyasan'|âugha|pratīkṣiṇaḥ.
134.5 sahāy'|ôpacitiṃ kṛtvā, vyavasāyya tatas tataḥ,
anuduṣyeyur apare paśyantas tava pauruṣam.
taiḥ kṛtvā saha saṅghātaṃ giri|durg'|ālayaṃ cara,
kāle vyasanam ākāṅkṣan; n' âiv' âyam a|jar'|â|maraḥ.

survive by relying on the rains and gods survive by relying upon Indra, the god of a hundred sacrifices.

The man upon whom all creatures rely for support for their lives has a profitable life, Sánjaya, like a tree whose fruit has ripened. A hero has a good life if his relatives live happily because of his heroic exploits, just as the thirty gods do because of Shakra's. The man who preserves his life by 133.45
relying on the strength of his own arms wins fame in this world, and obtains a splendid course in the hereafter.

VÍDULA continued:

IF YOU WISH TO put an end to your manliness in the 134.1
present circumstances, then before long you will travel the path frequented by those who have sunk low. If a kshatriya does not reveal his splendor through prowess to the best of his ability, because he hopes to live, then men know him as a thief. But even though my advice is significant, fitting, and excellent, it is not getting through to you, like medicine given to a man on his deathbed.

The Sindhu king's men are contented, but they can be dismissed, for their weakness ensures they sit around foolishly, just waiting for the floods of calamity. Once you have 134.5
restored the resolve of your growing number of allies, and others see your manliness, they will become demoralized as a result. So join with them for battle, and stalk the wildernesses and abodes in the mountains, awaiting the time of his destruction, for he is neither ageless nor immortal.

Sañjayo nāmataś ca tvaṃ, na ca paśyāmi tat tvayi.
anvartha|nāmā bhava, me putra, mā vyartha|nāmakaḥ!
samyag|dṛṣṭir mahā|prājño bālaṃ tvāṃ brāhmaṇo 'bravīt,
«ayaṃ prāpya mahat kṛcchraṃ punar vṛddhiṃ gamiṣyati.»
tasya smarantī vacanam āśaṃse vijayaṃ tava;
tasmāt, tāta, bravīmi tvāṃ, vakṣyāmi ca punaḥ punaḥ.
134.10 yasya hy arth'|âbhinirvṛttau bhavanty āpyāyitāḥ pare
tasy' ârtha|siddhir niyatā nayeṣv arth'|ânusāriṇaḥ.
samṛddhir a|samṛddhir vā pūrveṣāṃ mama, Sañjaya,
evaṃ vidvān yuddha|manā bhava, mā pratyupāharaḥ.
n' ātaḥ pāpīyasīṃ kāñ cid avasthāṃ Śambaro 'bravīt,
yatra n' âiv' âdya na prātar bhojanaṃ pratidṛśyate.
pati|putra|vadhād etat paramaṃ duḥkham abravīt,
dāridryam iti yat proktaṃ, paryāya|maraṇaṃ hi tat.

aham mahā|kule jātā, hradādd hradam iv' āgatā,
īśvarī sarva|kalyāṇī, bhartrā parama|pūjitā.
134.15 mah"|ârha|māly'|ābharaṇāṃ, su|mṛṣṭ'|âmbara|vāsasam
purā hṛṣṭaḥ suhṛd|vargo mām apaśyat su|hṛd|gatām.
yadā māṃ c' âiva bhāryāṃ ca draṣṭ" âsi bhṛśa|durbalām,
na tadā jīviten' ârtho bhavitā tava, Sañjaya.

dāsa|karma|karān bhṛtyān, ācārya'|rtvik|puro|hitān
a|vṛtty" âsmān prajahato dṛṣṭvā kiṃ jīvitena te?
yadi kṛtyaṃ na paśyāmi tav' âdy' âhaṃ yathā purā,
ślāghanīyaṃ yaśasyaṃ ca, kā śāntir hṛdayasya me?

You are Sánjaya in name alone, for I see no victory within you.* Embody your name, my son, and do not prove to have been named in vain! An all-seeing, highly astute brahmin said of you while you were a child, "This one will meet great calamity, but he will become great once more." I remember his prophecy and I have hopes for your victory, and that, my son, is why I nag you time and time again.

The man who allows others to thrive as a result of the 134.10
aims he achieves, is guaranteed to be successful in his aims when he pursues his goals in line with good policy. Sánjaya, become a warrior and do not retreat; be aware that my ancestors too faced success or failure. Shámbara has said there is no condition more evil than not being able to tell where one's food will come from from one day to the next. He called poverty the ultimate evil, worse than the death of one's husband and son, for he claimed it was perpetual death.

I was born into a great lineage and I came from one lake to another.* I was supremely honored by my husband, and
I was the mistress of all good things. In the past, my happy 134.15
circle of friends saw me in the company of my companions, decked in expensive garlands and ornaments, well dressed and well washed; but when you see me and your wife made so very weak, then you will find no meaning to your life, Sánjaya.

When you see our servants who do all our menial tasks, our teachers, priests, and family priests leave us because we cannot pay them, what will be the point of your living? If I am now no longer to see your praiseworthy and famous exploits, as I did in the past, then what peace will my heart

«n' êti» ced brāhmaṇaṃ brūyāṃ, dīryeta hṛdayaṃ mama;
na hy ahaṃ na ca me bhartā «n' êti» brāhmaṇam uktavān.
134.20 vayam āśrayaṇīyāḥ sma, n' āśritāraḥ† parasya ca;
s" ânyam āsādya jīvantī parityakṣyāmi jīvitam.

a|pāre bhava naḥ pāram, a|plave bhava naḥ plavaḥ,
kuruṣva sthānam a|sthāne, mṛtān sañjīvayasva naḥ.
sarve te śatravaḥ śakyā na cej jīvitum arhasi.
atha ced īdṛśīṃ vṛttiṃ klībām abhyupapadyase,
nirviṇṇ'|ātmā hata|manā muñc' âitāṃ pāpa|jīvikām!

eka|śatru|vadhen' âiva śūro gacchati viśrutim.
Indro Vṛtra|vadhen' âiva Mahendraḥ samapadyata,
Māhendraṃ ca grahaṃ lebhe, lokānāṃ c' ēśvaro 'bhavat.
134.25 nāma viśrāvya vai saṃkhye, śatrūn āhūya daṃśitān,
sen"|âgraṃ c' âpi vidrāvya, hatvā vā puruṣaṃ varam,
yad" âiva labhate vīraḥ su|yuddhena mahad yaśaḥ,
tad" âiva pravyathante 'sya śatravo, vinamanti ca.

tyaktv" ātmānaṃ raṇe dakṣaṃ śūraṃ kā|puruṣā janāḥ
a|vaśās tarpayanti sma sarva|kāma|samṛddhibhiḥ;
rājyaṃ c' âpy ugra|vibhraṃśaṃ, saṃśayo jīvitasya vā,
na labdhasya hi śatror vai śeṣaṃ kurvanti sādhavaḥ.
svarga|dvār'|ôpamaṃ rājyam, atha v" âpy amṛt'|ôpamam,
ruddham ek'|āyanaṃ matvā pat' ôlmuka iv' âriṣu!

ind? If I were to deny the brahmins, my heart would tear apart, for neither I nor my husband have ever told the brahmins "No." People should depend on us, but we are no one's 134.20
dependants, and if I should live to see the day when I am reliant on another person, then I will abandon my life.

Be our shore when we have none, be our ship when we are without. Create a refuge when we have none, and bring us back to life now that we are dead. You can take on all your enemies if you do not long to live. But if you continue practicing this castrated course, then, depressed and despondent, free yourself from this life of evil!

A brave man wins renown by killing even a single enemy. It was by killing Vritra that Indra became great Indra. He took great Indra's Soma cup and became lord of the
worlds. When he shouts his name in battle and challenges 134.25
his armored enemies, routing an excellent army or killing an excellent fighter, the hero wins great fame through his skilled fighting, and his enemies tremble in fear and bow to him.

The cowardly powerlessly sate a skilled hero who is prepared to risk his life in battle by fulfilling his every desire. Even if it means the fierce destruction of the kingdom, or if it is a risk to their own lives, excellent warriors do not leave their captured enemy alive. Kingship is like the door to heaven, or even like ambrosia itself. Understand that it is your only path, and that it is shut to you. Fall upon your enemies like a firebrand!

134.30 jahi śatrūn raṇe, rājan, sva|dharmam anupālaya.
mā tvādṛśaṃ su|kṛpaṇaṃ, śatrūṇāṃ bhaya|vardhanam,
asmadīyaiś ca śocadbhir, nadadbhiś ca parair vṛtam
api tvāṃ n' ânupaśyeyaṃ dīnā dīnam iv' āsthitam!
hṛṣya Sauvīra|kanyābhiḥ ślāghasv' ârthair yathā purā!
mā ca Saindhava|kanyānām avasanno vaśaṃ gamaḥ!

yuvā rūpeṇa saṃpanno, vidyay" âbhijanena ca,
yat tvādṛśo vikurvīta yaśasvī, loka|viśrutaḥ
a|dhuryavac ca voḍhavye, manye maraṇam eva tat.
yadi tvām anupaśyāmi parasya priya|vādinam,
134.35 pṛṣṭhato 'nuvrajantaṃ vā, kā śāntir hṛdayasya me?
n' âsmiñ jātu kule jāto gacched yo 'nyasya pṛṣṭhataḥ.
na tvaṃ parasy' ânucaras, tāta, jīvitum arhasi.

ahaṃ hi kṣatra|hṛdayaṃ veda yat pariśāśvatam,
pūrvaiḥ pūrvataraiḥ proktaṃ, paraiḥ paratarair api,
śāśvataṃ c' â|vyayaṃ c' âiva Prajāpati|vinirmitam.
yo vai kaś cid ih' ājātaḥ kṣatriyaḥ kṣatra|karma|vit
bhayād vṛtti|samīkṣo vā na named iha kasya cit.
udyacched eva, na named; udyamo hy eva pauruṣam
apy a|parvaṇi bhajyeta, na namet' êha kasya cit!
134.40 mātaṅgo matta iva ca parīyāt sa mahā|manāḥ,
brāhmaṇebhyo namen nityaṃ, dharmāy' âiva ca, Sañjaya,
niyacchann itarān varṇān, vinighnan sarva|duṣkṛtaḥ,
sa|sahāyo '|sahāyo vā yāvaj|jīvaṃ tathā bhavet.

Kill your enemies in battle, king, and defend your own 134.30
law. I pray I see you like this no longer—so horribly wretched, though you are the augmenter of your enemies' fear, surrounded by us as we grieve and your enemies as they rejoice! Don't force me to witness you in this wretched state when I too am wretched! Boast of your treasure as you did once, enjoying yourself with the Suvíran girls! Don't despondently fall under the power of the Sindhu girls!

When a handsome, learned, nobly born, renowned, and world-famous youth like you misbehaves as though you were a yokeless beast forced to carry his yoke, then I believe it is like death. If I see you speaking sycophantically to
your enemy or following behind him, then what peace can 134.35
my heart find? Certainly no one born in this family should walk shadowing another. You ought not to live as another man's follower, my boy.

I do indeed know the eternal heart of the kshatriya class, as laid down by my fathers and forefathers as well as our descendants and theirs in turn. It is eternal and unending, set by Praja·pati himself. No kshatriya born in this world who knows his warrior duties would ever bow to anyone here, either from fear, or on the lookout for a livelihood. One should stand tall, not bow, for uprightness is manliness. One should even break one's joints before one bows
to anyone in this world! One should be proud, and charge 134.40
about like a rutting elephant, though one should always bow to brahmins and to the law, Sánjaya. Reining the other classes in and destroying all miscreants, one should remain just so for as long as one lives, either with allies or without.

PUTRA uvāca:

135.1 KṚṢṆ'|ĀYASASY' êva ca te saṃhatya hṛdayaṃ kṛtam
mama mātas tv, a|karuṇe vīra|prājñe hy a|marṣaṇe.
aho kṣatra|samācāro yatra mām itaraṃ yathā
niyojayasi yuddhāya, para|māt" êva māṃ tathā
īdṛśaṃ vacanaṃ brūyād bhavatī putram eka|jam!
kiṃ nu te mām a|paśyantyāḥ pṛthivyā api sarvayā?
kim ābharaṇa|kṛtyena? kiṃ bhogair jīvitena vā?
mayi vā saṅgara|hate, priya|putre viśeṣataḥ?

MĀT" ôvāca:

135.5 sarv'|âvasthā hi viduṣāṃ, tāta, dharm'|ârtha|kāraṇāt.
tāv ev' âbhisamīkṣy' âhaṃ, Sañjaya, tvām acūcudam.
sa samīkṣya kram'|ôpeto mukhyaḥ kālo 'yam āgataḥ.
asmiṃś ced āgate kāle kāryaṃ na pratipadyase,
a|saṃbhāvita|rūpas tvam ānṛśaṃsyaṃ kariṣyasi.
taṃ tvām a|yaśasā spṛṣṭaṃ na brūyāṃ yadi, Sañjaya,
kharī|vātsalyam āhus tan niḥsāmarthyam a|hetukam.

sadbhir vigarhitaṃ mārgaṃ tyaja mūrkha|niṣevitam;
a|vidyā vai mahaty asti yām imāṃ saṃśritāḥ prajāḥ.
tava syād yadi sad|vṛttaṃ, tena me tvaṃ priyo bhaveḥ;
135.10 dharm'|ârtha|guṇa|yuktena, n' êtareṇa kathañ cana,
daiva|mānuṣa|yuktena, sadbhir ācaritena ca.

HER SON replied:

YOUR HEART IS black iron merely beaten into shape, O 135.1
merciless, war-wise, and impatient mother of mine. Damn the warriors' conduct, with which you force me to war as though I were some stranger and as though you were someone else's mother. Damn the warrior's conduct, for which you would say such words to me—and I your only son! If you could really no longer see me, then what good would the whole world do you? What good would it be to be decked in ornaments? What good would luxuries or life itself do you? What would you have to compare when I, your dear son, have been killed in battle?

HIS MOTHER said:

All the undertakings of the wise are for the sake of law 135.5
and profit, my son. It is with regard to these two things, Sánjaya, that I have urged you. Now that the pivotal time has arrived, you must consider what course you will take. If you do not begin your task now that this time has come, then you will be dishonored and commit an act of cruelty. If I were to hold my tongue when you were touched by infamy, Sánjaya, then my love for you would be what men call a she-mule's love: useless and pointless.

Abandon the road forbidden by good men and frequented by fools, for it is the great ignorance to which people adhere. If yours should be the right way then you will
become dear to me, for it is none other than that which 135.10
complies with law, profit, and virtue, allows for both fate and human actions, and is taken by good men.

yo hy evam a|vinītena ramate putra|naptṛṇā
an|utthānavatā c' âpi, dur|vinītena dur|dhiyā,
ramate yas tu putreṇa, mogham tasya prajā|phalam.
a|kurvanto hi karmāṇi, kurvanto ninditāni ca,
sukhaṃ n' âiv' êha n' âmutra labhante puruṣ'|âdhamāḥ.

yuddhāya kṣatriyaḥ sṛṣṭaḥ, Sañjay', êha, jayāya ca.
jayan vā vadhyamāno vā prāpnot' Îndra|salokatām.
na Śakra|bhavane puṇye divi tad vidyate sukham,
yad amitrān vaśe kṛtvā kṣatriyaḥ sukham edhate.
135.15 manyunā dahyamānena puruṣeṇa manasvinā,
nikṛten' êha bahuśaḥ, śatrūn pratijigīṣayā,
ātmānaṃ vā parityajya, śatruṃ vā vinipātya ca,
ato 'nyena prakāreṇa śāntir asya kuto bhavet?

iha prājño hi puruṣaḥ sv|alpam a|priyam icchati;
yasya svalpaṃ priyaṃ loke dhruvaṃ tasy' âlpam a|priyam.
priy'|âbhāvāc ca puruṣo n' âiva prāpnoti śobhanam,
dhruvaṃ c' â|bhāvam abhyeti, gatvā Gaṅg" êva sāgaram.

PUTRA uvāca:

n' êyaṃ matis tvayā vācyā, mātaḥ, putre viśeṣataḥ;
kāruṇyam ev' âtra paśya bhūtv" êha jaḍa|mūkavat.

The man who takes delight in his ill-behaved, ill-mannered, weak-minded and unenergetic son or grandson, enjoys the fruit of his descendants in vain. Low people who do not do their jobs but act reprehensibly, do not gain happiness either in this world or the next.

Kshatriyas were created for war, Sánjaya, and for victory in this world, and regardless of whether he is the victor or is slain, a kshatriya wins Indra's realm. But the happiness a warrior feels when he brings his enemies under his control cannot be found even in Shakra's holy and heavenly abode.
May the spirited man, who burns with anger after being 135.15
cut down many times in this world, bide his time, eager to defeat his enemies. By what other means will he find peace than by taking his life or toppling his enemy?

In this world, a wise man wishes for little discomfort. One who finds comfort in little will certainly find little discomfort. When there are no pleasant matters available, a man does not win radiance and assuredly becomes nothing himself, like the Ganges flowing to the ocean.

THE SON replied:

You ought not to voice such an opinon, mother, and particularly not to your son. Look on him kindly in this situation, as though you had become idiotic and dumb.

MĀT" ôvāca:

135.20 ato me bhūyasī nandir, yad evam anupaśyasi.
codyaṃ māṃ codayasy etad bhṛśaṃ vai codayāmi te!
atha tvāṃ pūjayiṣyāmi hatvā vai sarva|Saindhavān;
ahaṃ paśyāmi vijayaṃ kṛcchra|bhāvitam eva te.

PUTRA uvāca:

a|kośasy' â|sahāyasya kutaḥ siddhir, jayo mama?
ity avasthāṃ viditv" âitām ātman" ātmani dāruṇām,
rājyād bhāvo nivṛtto me, tri|divād iva duṣ|kṛtaḥ.
īdṛśaṃ bhavatī kañ cid upāyam anupaśyati,
tan me, pariṇata|prajñe, samyak prabrūhi pṛcchate.
kariṣyāmi hi tat sarvaṃ yathāvad anuśāsanam.

MĀT" ôvāca:

135.25 putra, n' ātm" âvamantavyaḥ pūrvābhir a|samṛddhibhiḥ.
a|bhūtvā hi bhavanty arthā, bhūtvā naśyanti c' âpare;
a|marṣeṇ' âiva c' âpy arthā n' ārabdhavyāḥ su|bāliśaiḥ.
sarveṣāṃ karmaṇāṃ, tāta, phale nityam a|nityatā;
a|nityam iti jānanto na bhavanti bhavanti ca;
atha ye n' âiva kurvanti, n' âiva jātu bhavanti te.
aikaguṇyam an|īhāyām—a|bhāvaḥ karmaṇāṃ phalam.
atha dvaiguṇyam īhāyāṃ—phalaṃ bhavati vā na vā.
yasya prāg eva viditā sarv'|ârthānām a|nityatā,
nuded vṛddhi|samṛddhī sa pratikūle, nṛp'|ātma|ja.

HIS MOTHER said:

It is a matter of exceeding joy to me that you see it that way. You admonish me, as I should be admonished, but I will admonish you a good deal more besides! I will pay you honor when you have killed all the Sáindhavas, for I see your suffering turned to victory. 135.20

HER SON replied:

Where will my success and victory come from when I have neither treasury nor allies? I am well aware of the cruelty of my situation, and my soul has turned away from kingship just as a criminal's soul turns away from heaven. But if a lady such as yourself sees any means, then I beg you, lady of highly developed wisdom, tell me in detail. I will indeed do all that you command.

HIS MOTHER said:

My son, do not despise yourself for your failures in the past. Wealth comes of nothing, and other wealth disappears. But this does not mean that idiotic men can win treasures through impatience. The result of all actions are merely transitory, my son. Those who understand its transient nature either flourish or do not, but those who do not act certainly do not prosper. Inactivity has only one result which stems from it—nothing. But activity has two results—either one gets the desired result, or one does not. The man who understands the transience of all matters right from the start pushes success and growth away at his peril, prince. 135.25

utthātavyaṃ, jāgṛtavyaṃ, yoktavyaṃ bhūti|karmasu,
135.30 «bhaviṣyat' îty» eva manaḥ kṛtvā satatam a|vyathaiḥ,
maṅgalāni puras|kṛtya, brāhmaṇāṃś c' ēśvaraiḥ saha.
prājñasya nṛ|pater āśu vṛddhir bhavati, putraka,
abhivartati lakṣmīs taṃ, prācīm iva divā|karaḥ.
nidarśanāny upāyāṃś ca bahūny uddharṣaṇāni ca
anudarśita|rūpo 'si, paśyāmi; kuru pauruṣam!

purus'|ârtham abhipretaṃ samāhartum ih' ârhasi,
kruddhān, lubdhān, parikṣīṇān, avaliptān, vimānitān,
spardhinaś c' âiva ye ke cit, tān yukta upadhāraya.
etena tvaṃ prakāreṇa mahato bhetsyase gaṇān,
135.35 mahā|vega iv' ôdbhūto mātari|śvā balāhakān.
teṣām agra|pradāyī syāḥ, kalp'|ôtthāyī priyaṃ|vadaḥ.
te tvāṃ priyaṃ kariṣyanti, purodhāsyanti ca dhruvam.

yad" âiva śatrur jānīyāt sapatnaṃ tyakta|jīvitam,
tad" âiv' âsmād udvijate sarpād veśma|gatād iva.
taṃ viditvā parākrāntaṃ vaśe na kurute yadi,
nirvādair nirvaded enam, antatas tad bhaviṣyati.
nirvādād āspadaṃ labdhvā dhana|vṛddhir bhaviṣyati;
dhanavantaṃ hi mitrāṇi bhajante c' āśrayanti ca.
skhalit'|ârthaṃ punas tāni santyajanti ca bāndhavāḥ,
apy asmin n' āśvasante ca, jugupsante ca tādṛśam.
135.40 śatruṃ kṛtvā yaḥ sahāyaṃ viśvāsam upagacchati,
ataḥ saṃbhāvyam ev' âitad yad rājyaṃ prāpnuyād iti.

Having made up his mind unhesitatingly, thinking, "This 135.30
will happen," a man must always wake up, get up, and set himself to prosperous tasks, once he has first performed auspicious rites with the brahmins and gods. Prosperity comes swiftly to a wise king, my dear boy, and good fortune returns just as the sun returns to the east. I see that you appear to be considering my examples, strategies, and copious encouraging words; so put your manliness to use!

You ought to gain the manly aim you desire, and keep in mind the angry, the greedy, weakened, jealous, humiliated, and the competitive. This is the way you can split mighty
hosts of men, just as a great violent storm scatters clouds. 135.35
Be the first one to bribe, rise at dawn, and speak kindly. They will do you favors and will assuredly put you first.

When an enemy realizes that his enemy is prepared to sacrifice his life, he shies away from him as though he were a snake that had got into his house. If one understands that a man's prowess is such that one won't be able to subdue him, then one should warn him off with abuse, and the same end will be achieved. A man can take a breather and augment his wealth through threats. Friends will turn to a wealthy man and rely on him. But on the other hand, relatives abandon men whose wealth has trickled away again. They do not have confidence in him and are disgusted by such a man.
It is impossible for a man to ever regain his kingdom if he 135.40
makes his enemy an ally and puts his trust in him.

MĀT" ôvāca:

136.1 N' ÂIVA RĀJÑĀ daraḥ kāryo jātu kasyāñ cid āpadi;
atha ced api dīrṇaḥ syān, n' âiva varteta dīrṇavat.
dīrṇaṃ hi dṛṣṭvā rājānaṃ sarvam ev' ânudīryate.
rāṣṭraṃ, balam, amātyāś ca pṛthak kurvanti te matīḥ.
śatrūn eke prapadyante, prajahaty apare punaḥ,
anye tu prajihīrṣanti ye purastād vimānitāḥ.

ya ev' âtyanta|suhṛdas ta enaṃ paryupāsate,
a|śaktayaḥ svasti|kāmā, baddha|vatsā ilā iva.
136.5 śocantam anuśocanti patitān iva bāndhavān.
api te pūjitāḥ pūrvam, api te su|hṛdo matāḥ,
ye rāṣṭram abhimanyante rājño vyasanam īyuṣaḥ.
mā dīdaras tvaṃ, su|hṛdo mā tvāṃ dīrṇaṃ prahāsiṣuḥ.

prabhāvaṃ pauruṣaṃ buddhiṃ jijñāsantyā mayā tava
vidadhatyā samāśvāsam uktaṃ tejo|vivṛddhaye.
yad etat saṃvijānāsi, yadi samyag bravīmy aham,
kṛtv" â|saumyam iv' ātmānaṃ jayāy' ôttiṣṭha, Sañjaya.
asti naḥ kośa|nicayo mahān hy a|viditas tava;
tam ahaṃ veda n' ânyas; tam upasaṃpādayāmi te.
136.10 santi n' âikatamā bhūyaḥ su|hṛdas tava, Sañjaya,
sukha|duḥkha|sahā, vīra, saṅgrāmād a|nivartinaḥ.
tādṛśā hi sahāyā vai puruṣasya bubhūṣataḥ
iṣṭaṃ jihīrṣataḥ kiñ cit sacivāḥ, śatru|karśana.

yasyās tv īdṛśakaṃ vākyaṃ śrutv" âpi sv|alpa|cetasaḥ
tamas tv apāgamat, tasya sucitr'|ârthapad'|âkṣaram.

THE MOTHER continued:

A KING SHOULD certainly never be afraid in any disaster, 136.1
and even if he is scared he should not act as though he were
scared. If people see that their king is frightened, then they
too all become afraid. The kingdom, army, and counselors
each make up their minds in turn. Some go over to the enemy, others merely leave, while others still, who had previously been dishonored, want to hit back.

Only his closest friends stand by him, helpless and wishing for better luck, like a cow whose calf is bound. They 136.5
grieve for his grief, as though for fallen relatives. But even
men who were honored in the past, and were considered
friends, covet the kingdom of a king who has fallen into
calamity. So do not be afraid, lest your friends leave you in
your fear.

What I have said was to encourage you and raise your energy, and to get an idea of your power, manliness, and judgment. If you understand this, and if what I have said is correct, then toughen your soul and rise for victory, Sánjaya. We still have a huge but secret treasury store. I and no one else know about it, and I will give it to you to use.

You still have a great many friends, Sánjaya, who are con- 136.10
stant in good times and bad, and who will not flee from
battle, hero. Allies such as these are good counselors to a
man who wishes for his welfare and strives to win his goals,
enemy-plower.

Once the man of such limited brain-power had heard her speak such varied words of sense, the gloom that had descended over him evaporated.

PUTRA uvāca:

udake bhūr iyaṃ dhāryā, martavyaṃ pravaṇe mayā,
yasya me bhavatī netrī bhaviṣyad|bhūti|darśinī.
ahaṃ hi vacanaṃ tvattaḥ śuśrūṣur a|par'|âparam
kiñ cit kiñ cit prativadaṃs tūṣṇīm āsaṃ muhur|muhuḥ,
136.15 a|tṛpyann amṛtasy' êva kṛcchrāl labdhasya bāndhavāt.
udyacchāmy eṣa śatrūṇāṃ niyam'|ârthaṃ jayāya ca.

KUNTY uvāca:

sad|aśva iva sa kṣiptaḥ praṇunno vākya|sāyakaiḥ,
tac cakāra tathā sarvaṃ yathāvad anuśāsanam.
idam uddharṣaṇaṃ bhīmaṃ tejo|vardhanam uttamam
rājānaṃ śrāvayen mantrī sīdantaṃ śatru|pīḍitam.
Jayo nām' êtihāso 'yaṃ śrotavyo vijigīṣuṇā;
mahīṃ vijayate kṣipraṃ śrutvā, śatrūṃś ca mardati.

idaṃ puṃsavanaṃ c' âiva, vīr'|ājananam eva ca,
abhīkṣṇaṃ garbhiṇī śrutvā dhruvaṃ vīraṃ prajāyate
136.20 vidyā|śūraṃ, tapaḥ|śūraṃ, dāna|śūraṃ, tapasvinam,
brāhmyā śriyā dīpyamānaṃ, sādhu|vāde ca saṃmatam,
arciṣmantaṃ, bal'|ôpetaṃ, mahā|bhāgaṃ, mahā|ratham,
dhṛtimantam, an|ādhṛṣyam, jetāram, a|parājitam,
niyantāram a|sādhūnāṃ, goptāraṃ dharma|cāriṇām,
īdṛśaṃ kṣatiryā sūte vīraṃ satya|parākramam.

HER SON replied:

With you, who sees my future prosperity, as my guide, I will raise this world, currently sunk in the water, or soon die in the attempt. I have indeed listened to your advice, interrupting with some word or other now and then, but I was silent for the most part, for I could not drink my fill of 136.15
your ambrosian words, which I've received from a relative in my time of difficulty. I will strive for control over my enemies, and for victory.

KUNTI continued:

So, rushing like an excellent horse, propelled along by her arrow-sharp words, he did everything, following her command to the letter. An advisor should repeat this rousing but fearful, energy-enhancing, and excellent speech to a king who is sinking into depression and afflicted by his enemies. The man who wishes to win should listen to this story from history, called Victory, and when he has heard it he will soon conquer the earth and crush his enemies.

This story causes a son to be born, it causes the birth of a hero, and if a pregnant lady hears it repeatedly then she will certainly give birth to a valiant hero of learning, a 136.20
hero of asceticism, or an austere hero of generosity, blazing with brahmanic splendor and esteemed with praise. A hero who gleams brightly, endowed with strength; a noble warrior who is resolute, indomitable, and an invincible conquerer; a controller of the wicked and defender of the law-abiding—this is the kind of hero to whom a kshatriya woman will give birth, and his strength will be his truth.

KUNTY uvāca:

137.1 ARJUNAM, KEŚAVA, brūyās: «tvayi jāte sma, sūtake,
upopaviṣṭā nārībhir āśrame parivāritā.
ath' ântarikṣe vāg āsīd dīvya|rūpā mano|ramā,
‹sahasr'|âkṣa|samaḥ, Kunti, bhaviṣyaty eṣa te sutaḥ.
eṣa jeṣyati saṅgrāme Kurūn sarvān samāgatān,
Bhīmasena|dvitīyaś ca lokam udvartayiṣyati.
putras te pṛthivīṃ jetā, yaśaś c' âsya divaṃ spṛśet,
hatvā Kurūṃś ca saṅgrāme Vāsudeva|sahāyavān.
137.5 pitryam aṃśaṃ pranaṣṭaṃ ca punar apy uddhariṣyati,
bhrātṛbhiḥ sahitaḥ śrīmāṃs trīn medhān āhariṣyati.› »
sa satya|sandho Bībhatsuḥ savya|sācī yath", Âcyuta,
tathā tvam eva jānāsi balavantaṃ dur|āsadam;
tathā tad astu, Dāśārha, yathā vāg abhyabhāṣata!
dharmaś ced asti, Vārṣṇeya, tathā satyaṃ bhaviṣyati!
tvaṃ c' âpi tat tathā, Kṛṣṇa, sarvaṃ sampādayiṣyasi,
n' âhaṃ tad abhyasūyāmi, yathā vāg abhyabhāṣata.
namo dharmāya mahate, dharmo dhārayati prajāḥ;
etad Dhanañjayo vācyo nity'|ôdyukto Vṛkodaraḥ:
137.10 «yad|arthaṃ kṣatriyā sūte, tasya kālo 'yam āgataḥ;
na hi vairaṃ samāsādya sīdanti puruṣa'|rṣabhāḥ.»
viditā te sadā buddhir Bhīmasya; na sa śāmyati
yāvad antaṃ na kurute śatrūṇāṃ, śatru|karśana.

KUNTI continued:*

KÉSHAVA, TELL Árjuna: "When you were born, my dear boy, I was sitting in the hermitage, surrounded by women, when a captivating celestial voice appeared in the sky, and it said, 'Kunti, this son of yours will be a match for the god of a thousand eyes. This boy will defeat all the gathered Kurus, and with Bhima·sena as his second he will overturn the world. Your son will conquer the earth, and when he has killed the Kurus in battle with Vasudéva as his ally, his fame will touch heaven. He will win back the lost paternal share of his kingdom once more, and he will offer three glorious sacrifices with his brothers.'" 137.1

137.5

O Áchyuta, you know the mighty and unassailable Bibhátsu, the ambidextrous archer who is true to his vows, so let what the voice foretold come true, Dashárha! If righteousness really does exist, Varshnéya, then may it come true! You, Krishna, will cause everything to happen, so I have no doubts about what the voice prophesied. I bow to the mighty law, for the law supports its subjects. Tell Dhanan·jaya this, and to the ever-prepared Vrikódara, say this:

"The very time for which a kshatriya woman gives birth has arrived, and bull-like men do not sink into despondency when they reach conflict." You have always known Bhima's mind, and he will never be at peace until he has put an end to his enemies, enemy-plower. 137.10

sarva|dharma|viśeṣa|jñāṃ snuṣāṃ Pāṇḍor mah"|ātmanaḥ
brūyā, Mādhava, kalyāṇīṃ, Kṛṣṇa, Kṛṣṇāṃ yaśasvinīm:
«yuktam etan, mahā|bhāge kule jāte yaśasvini,
yan me putreṣu sarveṣu yathāvat tvam avartithāḥ.»

Mādrī|putrau ca vaktavyau kṣatra|dharma|ratāv ubhau:
«vikrameṇ' ârjitān bhogān vṛṇītam jīvitād api;
137.15 vikram'|âdhigatā hy arthāḥ kṣatra|dharmeṇa jīvataḥ
mano manuṣyasya sadā prīṇanti, puruṣ'|ôttama.
yac ca vaḥ prekṣamāṇānāṃ sarva|dharm'|ôpacāyinām
Pāñcālī paruṣāṇy uktā, ko nu tat kṣantum arhati?»

na rājya|haraṇaṃ duḥkhaṃ, dyūte c' âpi parājayaḥ,
pravrājanaṃ sutānāṃ vā na me tad duḥkha|kāraṇam,
yatra sā bṛhatī śyāmā sabhāyāṃ rudatī tadā
aśrauṣīt paruṣā vācas, tan me duḥkhataraṃ mahat.
strī|dharmiṇī var'|ārohā kṣatra|dharma|ratā sadā
n' âdhyagacchat tadā nāthaṃ Kṛṣṇā nāthavatī satī.
137.20 taṃ vai brūhi, mahā|bāho, sarva|śastra|bhṛtāṃ varam
Arjunaṃ puruṣa|vyāghraṃ: «Draupadyāḥ padavīṃ cara!»
viditaṃ hi tav', âtyantaṃ kruddhāv iva Yam'|ântakau,
Bhīm'|Ârjunau nayetāṃ hi devān api parāṃ gatim.
tayoś c' âitad avajñānaṃ, yat sā Kṛṣṇā sabhā|gatā,
Duḥśāsanaś ca yad Bhīmaṃ kaṭukāny abhyabhāṣata,
paśyatāṃ Kuru|vīrāṇāṃ tac ca saṃsmārayeḥ punaḥ.

O Krishna Mádhava, say to illustrious and beautiful Krishná, high-souled Pandu's daughter-in-law, who understands every particular aspect of law: "Illustrious and noble lady born into a good lineage, it is befitting that you have treated all my sons honestly."

You should tell both of Madri's sons who delight in their kshatriya duties: "Choose the pleasures which are won through prowess over life itself, for goals achieved through 137.15
prowess always delight the mind of a man who lives by the kshatriya law, best of men. Who ought to forgive the fact that the Pancháli princess, who had won the merit of every law, was abused with harsh words as you looked on?"

The misery of the theft of our kingdom, the pain of the defeat at dice gambling, and even the misery of my sons going into exile is not the cause of such misery to me as the fact that the tall, dark lady wept in court and was forced to listen to harsh insults—that is more distressing to me by far. Shapely-hipped Krishná, who always delights in kshatriya duties, was bleeding at that time but she could find no one to protect her, though she had husbands to defend her.

Long-armed man, say to tiger-like Árjuna, the greatest 137.20
of all who wield weapons: "Walk in Dráupadi's footsteps!" You certainly know that Bhima and Árjuna are both like Yama when excessively furious, and they could charge even the gods onto the final course of death. It was an affront to them that Krishná was taken to court and that Duhshásana hurled insults at Bhima while the Kuru heroes looked on—remind them of it again.

Pāṇḍavān kuśalaṃ pṛccheḥ sa|putrān Kṛṣṇayā saha,
māṃ ca kuśalinīṃ brūyās teṣu bhūyo, Janārdana.
a|riṣṭaṃ gaccha panthānaṃ, putrān me pratipālaya.

VAIŚAMPĀYANA uvāca:

137.25 abhivādy' âtha tāṃ Kṛṣṇaḥ, kṛtvā c' âpi pradakṣiṇam,
niścakrāma mahā|bāhuḥ siṃha|khela|gatis tataḥ.
tato visarjayām āsa Bhīṣm'|ādīn Kuru|puṅgavān,
āropy' âtha rathe Karṇaṃ prāyāt Sātyakinā saha.
tataḥ prayāte Dāśārhe Kuravaḥ saṃgatā mithaḥ,
jajalpur mahad āścaryaṃ Keśave param'|âdbhutam.
«pramūḍhā pṛthivī sarvā, mṛtyu|pāśa|vaśī|kṛtā,
Duryodhanasya bāliśyān n' âitad ast' îti» c' âbruvan.
tato niryāya nagarāt prayayau puruṣ'|ôttamaḥ,
mantrayām āsa ca tadā Karṇena su|ciraṃ saha.
137.30 visarjayitvā Rādheyaṃ sarva|Yādava|nandanaḥ
tato javena mahatā tūrṇam aśvān acodayat.
te pibanta iv' ākāśaṃ Dārukeṇa pracoditāḥ
hayā jagmur mahā|vegā mano|māruta|raṃhasaḥ.
te vyatītya mah"|âdhvānaṃ kṣipraṃ, śyenā iv' āśu|gāḥ,
uccair jagmur Upaplavyaṃ Śārṅga|dhanvānam āvahan.

VAIŚAMPĀYANA uvāca:

138.1 KUNTYĀS TU vacanaṃ śrutvā
Bhīṣma|Droṇau mahā|rathau
Duryodhanam idaṃ vākyam
ūcatuḥ śāsan'|âtigam:

Enquire after the health of the Pándavas, along with that of their sons and Krishná's, and tell them in reply that I am well, Janárdana. Take a safe path, and defend my sons.

VAISHAMPÁYANA narrated:

Long-armed Krishna bade her farewell and circled her, 137.25
then he strode out, moving like a lion. He sent away the bull-like Kurus, Bhishma and so on, made Karna mount his chariot, and left with Sátyaki. Then, when Dashárha had left, the Kurus gathered together and gossiped about Krishna's great, astonishing, and extraordinary miracle. "The whole earth is bewildered, forced into the power of death's chains," they said, "and Duryódhana's foolishness will cause it all to end!"

So it was that the best of men left, riding away from the
city, and he debated with Karna for a very long while. Then 137.30
the joy of all the Yádavas sent Radhéya away and urged his horses on to enormous speed. And so, incited by Dáruka, those great fleet horses, swift as mind and wind, rode on, seeming to drink down the sky as they ran. Traveling a great distance at speed like swift hawks, they soon carried the mighty Sharnga archer to Upaplávya.

VAISHAMPÁYANA continued:

HAVING LISTENED to what Kunti had to say, the mighty 138.1
warriors Bhishma and Drona said these words to Duryódhana, a man who transgressed his orders:

«śrutaṃ te, puruṣa|vyāghra,
Kuntyāḥ Kṛṣṇasya sannidhau
vākyam arthavad atyugram
uktaṃ, dharmyam an|uttamam.
tat kariṣyanti Kaunteyā Vāsudevasya saṃmatam,
na hi te jātu śāmyerann ṛte rājyena, Kaurava.
kleśitā hi tvayā Pārthā dharma|pāśa|sitās tadā,
sabhāyāṃ Draupadī c' âiva, taiś ca tan marṣitaṃ tava.
138.5 kṛt'|âstraṃ hy Arjunaṃ prāpya, Bhīmaṃ ca kṛta|niścayam,
Gāṇḍīvaṃ c' êṣu|dhī c' âiva, rathaṃ ca dhvajam eva ca,
Nakulaṃ Sahadevaṃ ca bala|vīrya|samanvitau,
sahāyaṃ Vāsudevaṃ ca, na kṣaṃsyati Yudhiṣṭhiraḥ.
pratyakṣaṃ te, mahā|bāho, yathā Pārthena dhīmatā
Virāṭa|nagare pūrvaṃ sarve sma yudhi nirjitāḥ.
Dānavā ghora|karmāṇo Nivātakavacā yudhi
raudram astraṃ samādāya dagdhā vānara|ketunā.
Karṇa|prabhṛtayaś c' ême, tvaṃ c' âpi kavacī rathī,
mokṣito ghoṣa|yātrāyāṃ—paryāptaṃ tan nidarśanam.
praśamya, Bharata|śreṣṭha,
bhrātṛbhiḥ saha Pāṇḍavaiḥ,
138.10 rakṣ' êmāṃ pṛthivīṃ sarvāṃ
mṛtyor daṃṣṭr'|ântaraṃ gatām.
jyeṣṭho bhrātā dharma|śīlo, vatsalaḥ, ślakṣṇa|vāk, kaviḥ;
taṃ gaccha puruṣa|vyāghraṃ vyapanīy' êha kilbiṣam.
dṛṣṭaś ca tvaṃ Pāṇḍavena vyapanīta|śarāsanaḥ,
praśānta|bhru|kuṭiḥ, śrīmān, kṛtā śāntiḥ kulasya naḥ.

"Tiger-like man, you have heard Kunti's very passionate, meaningful, and particularly virtuous speech that was made in Krishna's presence. The Kauntéyas will follow her advice, for Vasudéva respects it; and they will certainly not make peace without their kingdom, Káurava.

You certainly made the Parthas suffer, and you pained 138.5
Dráupadi in court as well, but since they were fettered by
the chains of righteousness they endured it. Yudhi·shthira
will not be forgiving any longer, for he has weapon-trained
Árjuna, resolute Bhima, the Gandíva, his quivers, chariot,
and banner, as well as Nákula and Saha·deva, both possessed
of strength and heroism; and he has Vasudéva as his ally.

It was obvious before, long-armed man, when wise Partha defeated everyone in the battle at Viráta's city. The monkey-bannered man fired his Raudra weapon and burned the Niváta·kávacha Dánavas of fearsome deeds in battle. Karna and the others, and even you yourself, dressed in armor on your chariot, were freed at the herdsmen's procession—this should be adequate proof.

So make peace with your Pándava brothers, greatest of
the Bharatas, and protect this whole earth, fallen into the 138.10
fangs of death. The eldest brother is righteous in his conduct, affectionate, tenderly spoken, and learned, so go to
that tiger-like man and absolve your guilt. When the son of
Pandu sees you putting down your bow, unfurrowing your
brow, and being charming, then peace could yet be made
within our family.

tam abhyetya sah'|âmātyaḥ, pariṣvajya nṛp'|ātma|jam,
abhivādaya rājānaṃ yathā|pūrvam, arin|dama.
abhivādayamānaṃ tvāṃ pāṇibhyāṃ Bhīma|pūrva|jaḥ
pratigṛhṇātu sauhārdāt Kuntī|putro Yudhiṣṭhiraḥ.
siṃha|skandh'|ôru|bāhus tvāṃ vṛtt'|āyata|mahā|bhujaḥ
138.15 pariṣvajatu bāhubhyāṃ Bhīmaḥ praharatāṃ varaḥ.
kambu|grīvo Guḍākeśas tatas tvāṃ puṣkar'|ēkṣaṇaḥ.
abhivādayatāṃ Pārthaḥ Kuntī|putro Dhanañjayaḥ.

Āśvineyau nara|vyāghrau rūpeṇ' â|pratimau bhuvi,
tau ca tvāṃ guruvat premṇā pūjayā pratyudīyatām.
muñcantv ānanda|j'|âśrūṇi
    Dāśārha|pramukhā nṛpāḥ.
saṃgaccha bhrātṛbhiḥ sārdhaṃ,
    mānaṃ saṃtyajya, pārthiva,
praśādhi pṛthivīṃ kṛtsnāṃ tatas tvaṃ bhrātṛbhiḥ saha.
samāliṅgya ca harṣeṇa nṛpā yāntu paras|param.
138.20 alaṃ yuddhena, rāj'|êndra! su|hṛdāṃ śṛṇu vāraṇam,
dhruvaṃ vināśo yuddhe hi kṣatriyāṇāṃ pradṛśyate.

jyotīṃṣi pratikūlāni, dāruṇā mṛga|pakṣiṇaḥ,
utpātā vividhā, vīra, dṛśyante kṣatra|nāśanāḥ.
viśeṣata ih' âsmākaṃ nimittāni niveśane.
ulkābhir hi pradīptābhir bādhyate pṛtanā tava,
vāhanāny a|prahṛṣṭāni rudant' îva, viśām pate.
gṛdhrās te paryupāsante sainyāni ca samantataḥ.
nagaraṃ na yathā|pūrvaṃ, tathā rāja|niveśanam,
śivāś c' â|śiva|nirghoṣā dīptāṃ sevanti vai diśam.

Go to that prince with your advisors, and embrace him. 138.15
Greet the king as before, enemy-tamer, and then let Yudhi·shthira, Kunti's son and Bhima's elder brother, take you by the hands in friendship when saluted. Let Bhima, the greatest of warriors, whose shoulders, thighs, and arms are like those of a lion, embrace you in his long, rounded arms. Let lotus-eyed and conch-necked Guda·kesha, Dhanan·jaya Partha, the son of Kunti, greet you.

Let the tiger-like twin sons of the Ashvins, matchless on earth in beauty, rise up in affection and respect you as befits an elder. Let the kings led by Dashárha weep tears of joy. Unite with your brothers, abandoning your arrogance, king, and then rule the entire earth together with your brothers. Let the kings embrace each other with joy
and then return to their homes. Enough war-mongering, 138.20
lord of kings! Listen to your friends' restraint, for the destruction of kshatriyas is assuredly at hand.

The stars are hostile and the animals and birds are frightful. Various omens are appearing, hero, signifying the destruction of the kshatriyas. The portents are particular to us; the signs are in our homes. Your army is being pressed by blazing meteors and the miserable horses seem to be weeping, lord of earth. Vultures are everywhere, circling your forces. The city and the royal palace don't seem as splendid as they once were, and dangerously howling jackals are skulking on the blazing horizon.

138.25 kuru vākyaṃ pitur, mātur, asmākaṃ ca hit'|âiṣiṇām;
tvayy āyatto, mahā|bāho, śamo vyāyāma eva ca.
na cet kariṣyasi vacaḥ su|hṛdām, ari|karśana,
tapsyase vāhinīṃ dṛṣṭvā Pārtha|bāṇa|prapīḍitām.
Bhīmasya ca mahā|nādaṃ nadataḥ śuṣmiṇo raṇe
śrutvā smart" âsi me vākyaṃ, Gāṇḍīvasya ca niḥsvanaṃ;
yady etad apasavyaṃ te vaco mama bhaviṣyati.»

VAIŚAMPĀYANA uvāca:

139.1 EVAM UKTAS TU vimanās tiryag|dṛṣṭir adho|mukhaḥ
saṃhatya ca bhruvor madhyaṃ na kiṃ cidd hy ājahāra ha.
taṃ vai vimanasaṃ dṛṣṭvā, saṃprekṣy' ânyonyam antikāt,
punar ev' ôttaraṃ vākyam uktavantau nara'|ṛṣabhau.

BHĪṢMA uvāca:

śuśrūṣum, an|asūyaṃ ca, brahmaṇyaṃ, satya|vādinam
pratiyotsyāmahe Pārtham—ato duḥkhataraṃ nu kim?

DROṆA uvāca:

Aśvatthāmni yathā putre, bhūyo mama Dhanañjaye
bahu|mānaḥ paro, rājan, saṃnatiś ca kapi|dhvaje,
139.5 taṃ ca putrāt priyatamaṃ pratiyotsye Dhanañjayam
kṣātraṃ dharmam anuṣṭhāya—dhig astu kṣatra|jīvikām!
yasya loke samo n' âsti kaś cid anyo dhanur|dharaḥ,
mat|prasādāt sa Bībhatsuḥ śreyān anyair dhanur|dharaiḥ.

Take the advice of your mother and father, and take our advice, for we want only what is good for you. Peace and war depend on you, long-armed man. If you do not take the advice of your friends, enemy-plower, then you will be burned by regret as you watch your army tormented by Partha's arrows. When you hear the great thundering bellow of Bhima as he roars in battle, and the whirr of Gandíva, then you will remember what I told you. In fact, if you do remember, then my words will finally make sense to you." 138.25

VAISHAMPÁYANA said:

ADDRESSED IN THIS way, Duryódhana became depressed. His glance fell askance, and his head hung low. He furrowed his brow, but he did not speak. Seeing him despondent, the bull-like men nearby glanced at each other, and they spoke to him again. 139.1

BHISHMA said:

What is more painful than that we will have to fight obedient, unenvious, brahmanic, and truthful Partha?

DRONA said:

My highest respect is for Dhanan·jaya, even over my son Ashva·tthaman, king, for the monkey-bannered man possesses modesty. I will have to fight against Dhanan·jaya who 139.5
is dearer to me than my son, just so that I can abide by a warrior's duty.* Damn a warrior's life! There is no other bowman on earth to match him, and it is through my favor that Bibhátsu is greater than any other archer.

mitra|dhrug, duṣṭa|bhāvaś ca, nāstiko, 'th' ân|ṛjuḥ, śaṭhaḥ
na satsu labhate pūjāṃ, yajñe mūrkha iv' āgataḥ.
vāryamāṇo 'pi pāpebhyaḥ pāp'|ātmā pāpam icchati;
codyamāno 'pi pāpena śubh'|ātmā śubham icchati.
mithy"|ôpacaritā hy ete vartamānā hy anupriye
a|hitatvāya kalpante doṣā, Bharata|sattama.
139.10 tvam uktaḥ Kuru|vṛddhena, mayā ca, Vidureṇa ca,
Vāsudevena ca tathā, śreyo n' âiv' âbhimanyase.

«asti me balam, ity» eva sahasā tvaṃ titīrṣasi,
sa|grāha|nakra|makaraṃ Gaṅgā|vegam iv' ôṣṇage.
vāsas" âiva yathā hi tvaṃ prāvṛṇvāno 'bhimanyase,
srajaṃ tyaktām iva prāpya lobhād Yaudhiṣṭhirīṃ śriyam.
Draupadī|sahitaṃ Pārthaṃ s'|āyudhair bhrātṛbhir vṛtam
vana|stham api rājya|sthaḥ Pāṇḍavaṃ ko vijeṣyati?

nideśe yasya rājānaḥ sarve tiṣṭhanti kiṅkarāḥ,
tam Ailavilam āsādya dharma|rājo vyarājata.
139.15 Kubera|sadanaṃ prāpya, tato ratnāny avāpya ca,
sphītam ākramya te rāṣṭraṃ rājyam icchanti Pāṇḍavāḥ.

dattaṃ, hutam, adhītaṃ ca, brāhmaṇās tarpitā dhanaiḥ,
āvayor gatam āyuś ca; kṛta|kṛtyau ca viddhi nau.
tvaṃ tu hitvā sukhaṃ, rājyaṃ, mitrāṇi ca, dhanāni ca,
vigrahaṃ Pāṇḍavaiḥ kṛtvā mahad vyasanam āpsyasi.

A betrayer of his friends, an evil-natured man, an atheist, and a dishonest trickster win no respect among good men, just like an idiot who comes to a sacrifice. An evil-souled man wants what is wicked, even if he has been warned off evil things, but a pure-souled man wants what is pure even though he is lured by evil. Despite the fact that they have been treated deceitfully, they still behave pleasantly; but your faults will lead to your disadvantage, best of the
Bharatas. The Kuru elder has spoken to you, as have I, as 139.10
well as Vídura and Vasudéva, and yet you still have no conception of what is best for you.

You imagine you have strength, and you seek to cross over your troubles quickly, but it is like trying to cross the powerful Ganges, full of sharks, crocodiles, and monsters, in the rainy season. You believe you are wearing Yudhi·shthira's robe, when in your greed you have appropriated Yudhi·shthira's fortune for yourself as though it were an abandoned garland. Which man could conquer the son of Pandu, even if he had a kingdom and Partha was exiled to the forest, surrounded by his armed brothers and Dráupadi?

The king of righteousness gleamed even when he reached Áilavila, at whose command all kings stand by as servants.
Having now reached Kubéra's home and taken riches, the 139.15
sons of Pandu are marching back to your flourishing kingdom and want kingship.

We have offered our gifts, we have poured our oblations, we have performed our studies, we have satisfied the brahmins with gifts, and we have both lived out our lives, so know that we have done our jobs. But you have ignored happiness, your kingdom, your friends, and your wealth,

Draupadī yasya c' āśāste vijayaṃ satya|vādinī
tapo|ghora|vratā devī, kathaṃ jeṣyasi Pāṇḍavam?
mantrī Janārdano yasya, bhrātā yasya Dhanañjayaḥ
sarva|śastra|bhṛtāṃ śreṣṭhaḥ, kathaṃ jeṣyasi Pāṇḍavam?
139.20 sahāyā brāhmaṇā yasya dhṛtimanto jit'|êndriyāḥ,
tam ugra|tapasaṃ vīraṃ kathaṃ jeṣyasi Pāṇḍavam?

punar uktaṃ ca vakṣyāmi, yat kāryaṃ bhūtim icchatā
su|hṛdā majjamāneṣu su|hṛtsu vyasan'|ârṇave.
alaṃ yuddhena; tair vīraiḥ śāmya tvaṃ Kuru|vṛddhaye.
mā gamaḥ sa|sut'|âmātyaḥ sa|balaś ca parābhavam!

instead putting your energies into your quarrel with the Pándavas, and for this you will win yourself great calamity. How can you wish to defeat the son of Pandu, for whom Dráupadi, a truthful goddess of fearsomely austere vows, hopes for victory? How can you wish to defeat the son of Pandu, who has Janárdana as his advisor and Dhanan·jaya, the best of all who wield weapons, as his brother? How can 139.20
you wish to defeat the fiercely ascetic hero son of Pandu, whose allies are resolute brahmins of disciplined senses?

I will repeat what I have said, as a friend who wants prosperity must do what he can for his friends when they drown in a sea of troubles. Enough war! Make peace with those heroes so that the Kurus can prosper. Don't go to your destruction with your sons and advisors and armies!

140–146

# THE TEMPTATION OF KARNA

DHṚTARĀṢṬRA uvāca:

140.1 RĀJA|PUTRAIḤ parivṛtas tathā bhṛtyaiś ca, Sañjaya,
upāropya rathe Karṇaṃ niryāto Madhu|sūdanaḥ.
kim abravīd a|mey'|ātmā Rādheyaṃ para|vīra|hā?
kāni sāntvāni Govindaḥ sūta|putre prayuktavān?
udyan|megha|svanaḥ kāle Kṛṣṇaḥ Karṇam ath' âbravīt
mṛdu vā yadi vā tīkṣṇaṃ? tan mam' ācakṣva, Sañjaya.

SAÑJAYA uvāca:

ānupūrvyeṇa vākyāni, tīkṣṇāni ca mṛdūni ca,
priyāṇi, dharma|yuktāni, satyāni ca hitāni ca,
140.5 hṛdaya|grahaṇīyāni Rādheyaṃ Madhu|sūdanaḥ
yāny abravīd a|mey'|ātmā, tāni me śṛṇu, Bhārata.

VĀSUDEVA uvāca:

upāsitās te, Rādheya, brāhmaṇā veda|pāragāḥ,
tattv'|ârthaṃ paripṛṣṭāś ca niyaten' ân|asūyayā.
tvam eva, Karṇa, jānāsi veda|vādān sanātanān;
tvam eva dharma|śāstreṣu sūkṣmeṣu pariniṣṭhitaḥ.

kānīnaś ca, sah'|ōḍhaś ca, kanyāyāṃ yaś ca jāyate,
voḍhāraṃ pitaraṃ tasya prāhuḥ śāstra|vido janāḥ.
so 'si, Karṇa, tathā jātaḥ, Pāṇḍoḥ putro 'si dharmataḥ,
nigrahād dharma|śāstrāṇām ehi, rājā bhaviṣyasi.
140.10 pitṛ|pakṣe ca te Pārthā, mātṛ|pakṣe ca Vṛṣṇayaḥ.
dvau pakṣāv abhijānīhi tvam etau, puruṣa'|rṣabha!

DHRITA·RASHTRA said:

SÁNJAYA, BEFORE the slayer of Madhu left, surrounded by princes and servants, he made Karna mount his chariot. What did the immeasurably souled slayer of enemy heroes say to Radhéya? What words of conciliation did Govínda speak to the *suta*'s son? Tell me what Krishna, whose voice roars like a flood or a stormcloud, said to Karna at that time. Did he speak softly or harshly, Sánjaya? 140.1

SÁNJAYA said:

Bhárata, listen as I tell you of the succession of events, of the pointed, gentle, charming, law-abiding, truthful, beneficial, and heart-warming words that immeasurably souled Madhu·súdana spoke to Radhéya. 140.5

VASUDÉVA said:

Radhéya, you have waited upon brahmins who are advanced in the Veda, and you have asked them for truth, with restraint and without envy. Karna, you understand the eternal sayings of the Veda, and you have been taught thoroughly about the finer points of the sciences of law.

People who are learned in the shastras say that a child born to a woman when she is unmarried is just as much the son of the man she marries as the child she bears to her husband. So you, Karna, are lawfully a son of Pandu, for you were born in that manner. Come, bound by the restraints of the shastras on law, and you will become a king.
The Parthas are related to you on your father's side, and the 140.10
Vrishnis on your mother's. Recognize both these sides as yours, bull-like man!

mayā sārdham ito yātam adya tvāṃ, tāta, Pāṇḍavāḥ
abhijānantu Kaunteyaṃ pūrva|jātaṃ Yudhiṣṭhirāt.
pādau tava grahīṣyanti bhrātaraḥ pañca Pāṇḍavāḥ,
Draupadeyās tathā pañca, Saubhadraś c' â|parājitaḥ.
rājāno rāja|putrāś ca Pāṇḍav'|ârthe samāgatāḥ
pādau tava grahīṣyanti, sarve c' Ândhaka|Vṛṣṇayaḥ.

hiraṇ|mayāṃś ca te kumbhān, rājatān, pārthivāṃs tathā,
oṣadhyaḥ, sarva|bījāni, sarva|ratnāni, vīrudhaḥ
140.15 rājanyā rāja|kanyāś c' âpy ānayantv" âbhiṣecanam,
ṣaṣṭhe tvāṃ ca tathā kāle Draupady upagamiṣyati.

agniṃ juhotu vai Dhaumyaḥ saṃśit'|ātmā dvij'|ôttamaḥ;
adya tvām abhiṣiñcantu cāturvaidyā dvijātayaḥ.
purohitaḥ Pāṇḍavānāṃ brahma|karmaṇy avasthitaḥ,
tath" âiva bhrātaraḥ pañca Pāṇḍavāḥ puruṣa'|rṣabhāḥ,
Draupadeyās tathā pañca, Pañcālāś Cedayas tathā,
ahaṃ ca tv" âbhiṣekṣyāmi rājānaṃ pṛthivī|patim.

yuva|rājo 'stu te rājā Dharma|putro Yudhiṣṭhiraḥ.
gṛhītvā vyajanaṃ śvetaṃ dharm'|ātmā saṃśita|vrataḥ
140.20 upānvārohatu rathaṃ Kuntī|putro Yudhiṣṭhiraḥ,
chatraṃ ca te mahā|śvetaṃ Bhīmaseno mahā|balaḥ
abhiṣiktasya Kaunteyo dhārayiṣyati mūrdhani.
kiṅkiṇī|śata|nirghoṣaṃ vaiyāghra|parivāraṇam
rathaṃ śveta|hayair yuktam Arjuno vāhayiṣyati,
Abhimanyuś ca te nityaṃ pratyāsanno bhaviṣyati.

Come with me now, my friend, and the Pándavas will recognize you as the eldest son of Kunti over Yudhi·shthira. Your five Pándava brothers will take you by the feet, as will Dráupadi's five sons and Subhádra's undefeated son. The kings and princes who have united in the Pándava's cause will clasp your feet, and so will all the Ándhakas and Vrishnis.

Queens and princesses will bring gold, silver, and clay vessels, herbs, all seeds, every jewel, and plants for your consecration, and you will make love to Dráupadi one-sixth of the time. 140.15

Let Dhaumya of disciplined soul, the greatest of brahmins, pour the libation onto the fire, and let the brahmins who represent the four Vedas consecrate you today. Let the Pándavas' family priest—a man who abides by brahmanic rituals—and the five bull-like Pándava brothers, Dráupadi's five sons, the Panchálas, the Chedis, and me, consecrate you as a king and a lord of earth.

Yudhi·shthira the son of Dharma will be your junior king. Let righteous-souled and strict-vowed Yudhi·shthira, 140.20 son of Kunti, mount the chariot behind you, holding the white fan. Mighty Bhima·sena Kauntéya will hold a great white umbrella over your head once you are consecrated. Árjuna will drive your chariot yoked with white horses, ringing with hundreds of bells, and covered with tigerskins. Abhimányu too will always be at your command.

Nakulaḥ Sahadevaś ca, Draupadeyāś ca pañca ye,
Pañcālāś c' ânuyāsyanti, Śikhaṇḍī ca mahā|rathaḥ,
ahaṃ ca tv" ânuyāsyāmi, sarve c' Ândhaka|Vṛṣṇayaḥ,
Dāśārhāḥ parivārās te, Dāśārṇāś ca, viśām pate.
140.25 bhuṅkṣva rājyaṃ, mahā|bāho, bhrātṛbhiḥ saha Pāṇḍavaiḥ,
japair homaiś ca saṃyukto, maṅgalaiś ca pṛthag|vidhaiḥ.
purogamāś ca te santu Draviḍāḥ saha Kuntalaiḥ,
Āndhrās, Tālacarāś c' âiva, Cūcupā, Veṇupās tathā.
stuvantu tvāṃ ca bahubhiḥ stutibhiḥ sūta|māgadhāḥ;
vijayaṃ Vasuṣeṇasya ghoṣayantu ca Pāṇḍavāḥ!
sa tvaṃ parivṛtaḥ Pārthair, nakṣatrair iva candramāḥ,
praśādhi rājyaṃ, Kaunteya, Kuntīṃ ca pratinandaya!
mitrāṇi te prahṛṣyantu, vyathantu ripavas tathā;
saubhrātraṃ c' âiva te 'dy' âstu bhrātṛbhiḥ saha Pāṇḍavaiḥ.

KARṆA uvāca:

141.1 A|SAṂŚAYAṂ SAUHṚDĀN me, praṇayāc c' āttha, Keśava,
sakhyena c' âiva, Vāṛṣṇeya, śreyas|kāmatay" âiva ca;
sarvaṃ c' âiv' âbhijānāmi—Pāṇḍoḥ putro 'smi dharmataḥ
nigrahād dharma|śāstrāṇāṃ, yathā tvaṃ, Kṛṣṇa, manyase.
kanyā garbhaṃ samādhatta bhāskarān māṃ, Janārdana,
āditya|vacanāc c' âiva jātaṃ māṃ sā vyasarjayat.
so 'smi, Kṛṣṇa, tathā jātaḥ, Pāṇḍoḥ putro 'smi dharmataḥ
Kuntyā tv aham apākīrṇo, yathā na kuśalaṃ tathā!
141.5 sūto hi mām Adhiratho dṛṣṭv" âiv' âbhyānayad gṛhān,
Rādhāyāś c' âiva māṃ prādāt sauhārdān, Madhu|sūdana,
mat|snehāc c' âiva Rādhāyāṃ sadyaḥ kṣīram avātarat;

Nákula, Saha·deva, Dráupadi's five sons, the Panchálas, and the mighty warrior Shikhándin will follow you, and I too will follow you with all the Ándhakas and Vrishnis, and the Dashárhas and Dashárnas will make up your train, lord of earth. So enjoy your kingdom, long-armed man, with 140.25
your Pándava brothers, with muttered prayers, oblations, and each varied type of auspicious rite.

Let the Drávidas, Kúntalas, Andhras, Tala·charas, Chúchupas, and Vénupas march before you. Let heralds and bards praise you with numerous eulogies, and let the Pándavas shout of Vasu·shena's victory!

Rule your kingdom, Kauntéya, surrounded by the Parthas, as though you were the moon surrounded by stars, and bring joy to Kunti! Let your friends rejoice and your enemies tremble in fear! Today let there be brotherhood between you and your brothers—the Pándavas.

KARNA replied:

DOUBTLESS, KÉSHAVA, you are telling me this out of 141.1
friendship and affection, and as a friend you want what is best for me, Varshnéya. And I know all this—that lawfully according to the Dharma Shastras I am Pandu's son, as you believe, Krishna. An unmarried girl conceived me by the ray-giving sun, Janárdana, and at the sun's advice she abandoned me when I was born.

Indeed, because I was born that way, I am Pandu's lawful son, Krishna, but Kunti rejected me as though I was sickly! But Ádhiratha, a *suta*, had only to look at me and 141.5
he brought me to his home and presented me lovingly to Radha, Madhu·súdana. It was because she loved me that

sā me mūtraṃ purīṣaṃ ca pratijagrāha, Mādhava.

tasyāḥ piṇḍa|vyapanayaṃ kuryād asmad|vidhaḥ katham,
dharma|vid, dharma|śāstrāṇāṃ śravaṇe satataṃ rataḥ?
tathā mām abhijānāti sūtaś c' Âdhirathaḥ sutam,
pitaraṃ c' âbhijānāmi tam ahaṃ sauhṛdāt sadā.

sa hi me jāta|karm'|ādi kārayām āsa, Mādhava,
śāstra|dṛṣṭena vidhinā putra|prītyā, Janārdana!
141.10 nāma vai Vasuṣeṇ' êti kārayām āsa vai dvijaiḥ,
bhāryāś c' ōḍhā mama prāpte yauvane tat|parigrahāt.
tāsu putrāś ca pautrāś ca mama jātā, Janārdana,
tāsu me hṛdayaṃ, Kṛṣṇa, sañjātaṃ kāma|bandhanam!

na pṛthivyā sakalayā, na suvarṇasya rāśibhiḥ,
harṣād bhayād vā, Govinda, mithyā kartuṃ tad utsahe!
Dhṛtarāṣṭra|kule, Kṛṣṇa, Duryodhana|samāśrayāt
mayā trayo|daśa samā bhuktaṃ rājyam a|kaṇṭakam.
iṣṭaṃ ca bahubhir yajñaiḥ saha sūtair may" â|sakṛt,
āvāhāś ca vivāhāś ca saha sūtair mayā kṛtāḥ.
141.15 māṃ ca, Kṛṣṇa, samāsādya kṛtaḥ śastra|samudyamaḥ
Duryodhanena, Vārṣṇeya, vigrahaś c' âpi Pāṇḍavaiḥ.
tasmād raṇe dvairathe māṃ pratyudyātāram, Acyuta,
vṛtavān paramaṃ, Kṛṣṇa, pratīpaṃ savya|sācinaḥ.
vadhād, bandhād, bhayād v" âpi, lobhād v" âpi, Janārdana,
an|ṛtaṃ n' ôtsahe kartuṃ Dhārtarāṣṭrasya dhīmataḥ.

milk soon flowed from Radha and she could accept my urine and feces, Mádhava!

How could someone of my sort take away her ancestors' offerings, when I am a man who understands duty and always delights in obeying the shastras of law? The *suta* Ádhiratha recognized me as his son, and I too will always recognize him as my father, because I feel affection for him.

It was in fact he who had my birth rituals and so on carried out, Mádhava, in accordance with the rules observed in the shastras, and he did it because he loved his son, Janárdana! He had the brahmins name me Vasu·shena, and I 141.10
married my wives when I became a young man at his recommendation. Sons and grandsons have been born to me by these women, Janárdana, and my heart has developed bonds of love to them, Krishna!

I do not dare to treat them deceitfully either from joy or fear, Govínda—not for the whole world or vast piles of gold! I have enjoyed unrivaled kingship in Dhrita·rashtra's lineage for thirteen years by relying on Duryódhana, Krishna. I have often made many sacrificial offerings with *suta*s, and I have performed my family and marital duties with *suta*s.

Duryódhana has raised weapons and waged this war with 141.15
the Pándavas because he relies on me, Krishna Varshnéya. And so he chose me to be the ambidextrous archer's chief adversary, and to go up against him in single chariot combat, Áchyuta. Neither death, capture, nor fear or greed could induce me to treat wise Dhartaráshtra deceitfully, Janárdana. If I do not enter into my single chariot combat

yadi hy adya na gaccheyaṃ dvairathaṃ savya|sācinā,
a|kīrtiḥ syādd, Hṛṣīkeśa, mama Pārthasya c' ôbhayoḥ.
a|saṃśayaṃ hit'|ârthāya brūyās tvaṃ, Madhu|sūdana,
sarvaṃ ca Pāṇḍavāḥ kuryus tvad|vaśitvān, na saṃśayaḥ.
141.20 mantrasya niyamaṃ kuryās tvam atra, Madhu|sūdana,
etad atra hitaṃ manye sarvaṃ, Yādava|nandana.
yadi jānāti māṃ rājā dharm'|ātmā saṃyat'|êndriyaḥ
Kuntyāḥ prathama|jaṃ putraṃ, na sa rājyaṃ grahīṣyati.
prāpya c' âpi mahad rājyaṃ tad ahaṃ, Madhu|sūdana,
sphītaṃ Duryodhanāy' âiva saṃpradadyām, arin|dama.
sa eva rājā dharm'|ātmā śāśvato 'stu Yudhiṣṭhiraḥ,
netā yasya Hṛṣīkeśo, yoddhā yasya Dhanañjayaḥ.
pṛthivī tasya rāṣṭraṃ ca yasya Bhīmo mahā|rathaḥ,
Nakulaḥ Sahadevaś ca, Draupadeyāś ca, Mādhava,
141.25 Dhṛṣṭadyumnaś ca, Pāñcālyaḥ, Sātyakiś ca mahā|rathaḥ,
Uttamaujā, Yudhāmanyuḥ, satya|dharmā ca Saumakiḥ,
Caidyaś ca, Cekitānaś ca, Śikhaṇḍī c' â|parājitaḥ,
indra|gopaka|varṇāś ca Kekayā bhrātaras tathā,
Indr'|āyudha|savarṇaś ca Kuntibhojo mahā|manāḥ,
mātulo Bhimasenasya, Śyenajic ca mahā|rathaḥ,
Śaṅkhaḥ putro Virāṭasya, nidhis tvaṃ ca, Janārdana.
mahān ayaṃ, Kṛṣṇa, kṛtaḥ kṣatrasya samudānayaḥ;
rājyaṃ prāptam idaṃ dīptaṃ prathitaṃ sarva|rājasu.

with the ambidextrous archer, then disgrace will fall upon me and Partha both, Hrishikésha.

Doubtless you spoke meaning only for the best, Madhu·súdana, and doubtless the Pándavas will achieve everything under your command, but you should restrain yourself 141.20
from discussing this debate here, Madhu·súdana. I think that would be in everyone's interest, joy of the Yádavas. If the righteous-souled king of restrained senses knows that I am Kunti's first born son then he will not take the kingdom. But if I win the mighty flourishing kingdom, enemy-taming Madhu·súdana, then I will only present it to Duryódhana.

So let righteous-souled Yudhi·shthira be the eternal king, for he has Hrishikésha as his guide and Dhanan·jaya as his warrior. The earth is his kingdom, for he has the mighty warrior Bhima, Nákula, Saha·deva, and Dráupadi's sons, Mádhava. He has Dhrishta·dyumna and the Panchála king, 141.25
as well as the mighty chariot warrior Sátyaki, Uttamáujas, and Yudha·manyu Sáumaki, whose law is truth. He has the Chedi king, Chekitána, undefeated Shikhándin, the firefly-hued Kékaya brothers, Bhima·sena's uncle the high-minded and rainbow-colored Kunti·bhoja, the mighty warrior Shyénajit, Shankha the son of Viráta, and you as his treasure, Janárdana. A great gathering of kshatriyas has been brought together, Krishna, and this blazing kingdom, celebrated among all kings, has been won already.

Dhārtarāṣṭrasya, Vārṣṇeya, śastra|yajño bhaviṣyati;
asya yajñasya vettā tvaṃ bhaviṣyasi, Janārdana,
141.30 ādhvaryavaṃ ca te, Kṛṣṇa, kratāv asmin bhaviṣyati.
hotā c' âiv' âtra Bībhatsuḥ sannaddhaḥ sa kapi|dhvajaḥ,
Gāṇḍīvaṃ sruk, tathā c' ājyaṃ vīryaṃ puṃsāṃ bhaviṣyati.
Aindraṃ, Pāśupataṃ, Brāhmaṃ,
Sthūṇākarṇaṃ ca, Mādhava,
mantrās tatra bhaviṣyanti
prayuktāḥ savya|sācinā,
anuyātaś ca pitaram, adhiko vā parākrame,
gītaṃ stotraṃ sa Saubhadraḥ samyak tatra bhaviṣyati.
udgāt" âtra punar Bhīmaḥ prastotā su|mahā|balaḥ,
vinadan sa nara|vyāghro nāg'|ânīk'|ânta|kṛd raṇe,
sa c' âiva tatra dharm'|ātmā śaśvad rājā Yudhiṣṭhiraḥ
japair homaiś ca saṃyukto brahmatvaṃ kārayiṣyati.
141.35 śaṅkha|śabdāḥ sa|murajā, bheryaś ca, Madhu|sūdana,
utkṛṣṭa|siṃha|nādāś ca Subrahmaṇyo bhaviṣyati.
Nakulaḥ Sahadevaś ca Mādrī|putrau yaśasvinau
śāmitraṃ tau mahā|vīryau samyak tatra bhaviṣyataḥ.
kalmāṣa|daṇḍā, Govinda, vimalā ratha|paṅktayaḥ
yūpāḥ samupakalpantām asmin yajñe, Janārdana.
karṇi|nālīka|nārācā vatsa|dant'|ôpabṛṃhaṇāḥ,
tomarāḥ soma|kalaśāḥ, pavitrāṇi dhanūṃṣi ca,

Varshnéya, Dhartaráshtra will hold a weapons-sacrifice, and you will be the sacrifice's witness and the *adhváryu* 141.30 priest at the sacrifice, Krishna. Bibhátsu with his monkey banner will be equipped as the sacrificer, and his bow Gandíva will be the ladle. Manly heroism will serve as the clarified butter. The Aindra, Páshupata, Brahma, and Sthuna·karna missiles will serve as the spells delivered by the ambidextrous archer, Mádhava.

Saubhádra, either surpassing him in prowess or at least as excellent, will be the true hymn to be sung. Incredibly powerful Bhima, the tiger-like man who puts an end to armies of elephants as he roars in battle, will be the *udgátri*—the priest who chants the Sama Veda—and *prastótri*—the assistant to the *udgátri* who chants the *prastáva*—and righteous-souled, eternal King Yudhi·shthira will perform the role of brahmin, for he is practiced in muttered prayers and oblations.

The blasts of conch shells, the drums and kettledrums, 141.35 and the lion-like roars that arise will constitute the *subrahmánya*—the invitation to eat the offering. Nákula and Saha·deva, the illustrious and mightily heroic sons of Madri, will be the *shamítri* priest—the priest who kills the sacrificial animal. Rows of spotless chariots with multicolored banner poles will act like the sacrificial stakes to which the animals are tied during the sacrifice, Govínda Janárdana. Iron arrows, spears and shafts, and arrows with heads like calves' teeth will be the spoons used to pour the Soma juice; the javelins will be the Soma jars; and the bows will act as the Soma strainers.

asayo 'tra kapālāni, puro|ḍāśāḥ śirāṃsi ca,
havis tu rudhiraṃ, Kṛṣṇa, tasmin yajñe bhaviṣyati.
141.40 idhmāḥ paridhayaś c' âiva śaktayo, vimalā gadāḥ,
sadasyā Droṇa|śiṣyāś ca, Kṛpasya ca Śaradvataḥ,
iṣavo 'tra paristomā muktā Gāṇḍīva|dhanvanā,
mahā|ratha|prayuktāś ca Droṇa|Drauṇi|pracoditāḥ,
prātiprasthānikaṃ karma Sātyakis tu kariṣyati,
dīkṣito Dhārtarāṣṭro 'tra, patnī c' âsya mahā|camūḥ.
Ghaṭotkaco 'tra śāmitraṃ kariṣyati mahā|balaḥ
atirātre, mahā|bāho, vitate yajña|karmaṇi.
dakṣiṇā tv asya yajñasya Dhṛṣṭadyumnaḥ pratāpavān
vaitānike karma|mukhe jāto yat, Kṛṣṇa, pāvakāt.
141.45 yad abruvam ahaṃ, Kṛṣṇa, kaṭukāni sma Pāṇḍavān,
priy'|ârthaṃ Dhārtarāṣṭrasya, tena tapye hy a|karmaṇā.
yadā drakṣyasi māṃ, Kṛṣṇa, nihataṃ Savyasācinā,
punaś|cittis tadā c' âsya yajñasy' âtha bhaviṣyati.
Duḥśāsanasya rudhiraṃ yadā pāsyati Pāṇḍavaḥ
ānardaṃ nardataḥ samyak, tadā sūyaṃ bhaviṣyati.
yadā Droṇaṃ ca Bhīṣmaṃ ca Pāñcālyau pātayiṣyataḥ,
tadā yajñ'|âvasānaṃ tad bhaviṣyati, Janārdana.
Duryodhanaṃ yadā hantā Bhīmaseno mahā|balaḥ,
tadā samāpsyate yajño Dhārtarāṣṭrasya, Mādhava,
141.50 snuṣāś ca prasnuṣāś c' âiva Dhṛtarāṣṭrasya saṅgatāḥ
hat'|ēśvarā, naṣṭa|putrā, hata|nāthāś ca, Keśava,

Swords will be the cups, the warriors' heads will be the oblation rice-cakes, and the blood will constitute the clarified butter in this sacrifice, Krishna. The spears and spotless 141.40
maces will be the pokers for the fire and the stakes which keep the fire contained. The pupils of Drona and Kripa Sharádvata will be the assisting priests. The arrows released by the Gandíva bowman, as well as those fired by mighty warriors and shot by Drona and his son Ashva·tthaman, will act as Soma ladles. Sátyaki will act as the assistant to the *adhváryu* priest who chants the Yajur Veda. Dhartaráshtra will be the sacrificer, and his mighty army will act as his wife. Powerful Ghatótkacha will perform the role of the slayer of the victims when the nocturnal sacrificial rites commence, long-armed man. Splendid Dhrishta·dyumna, the man born of fire whose mouth was the sacred fire ritual, will be the sacrificial fee.

I do regret my bad behavior—the abuse I gave the Pán- 141.45
davas, Krishna, just to please Dhartaráshtra; and when you see me killed by Savya·sachin, Krishna, then it will be the re-stoking of his sacrifice. When the son of Pandu drinks the blood of Duhshásana, howling his roars, then the Soma will have been duly drunk.

When the pair of Panchála princes topple Drona and Bhishma, then the sacrifice will pause for an interval. When mighty Bhima·sena kills Duryódhana, the Dhartaráshtra's sacrifice will have come to an end, Mádhava. The wives 141.50
of Dhrita·rashtra's sons and grandsons will gather together when their husbands are dead, their sons are destroyed, and their protectors are killed, Késhava; and they will weep with Gandhári on the battlefield infested with dogs, vultures,

rudantyaḥ saha Gāndhāryā śva|gṛdhra|kurar'|ākule,
sa yajñe 'sminn avabhṛtho bhaviṣyati, Janārdana.
vidyā|vṛddhā, vayo|vṛddhāḥ kṣatriyāḥ, kṣatriya'|rṣabha,
vṛthā mṛtyuṃ na kurvīraṃs tvat|kṛte, Madhu|sūdana!
śastreṇa nidhanaṃ gacchet samṛddhaṃ kṣatra|maṇḍalam
Kuru|kṣetre puṇyatame trailokyasy' âpi, Keśava.
tad atra, puṇḍarīk'|âkṣa, vidhatsva yad abhīpsitam,
yathā kārtsnyena, Vārṣṇeya, kṣatraṃ svargam avāpnuyāt.
141.55 yāvat sthāsyanti girayaḥ, saritaś ca, Janārdana,
tāvat kīrti|bhavaḥ śabdaḥ śāśvato 'yaṃ bhaviṣyati.
brāhmaṇāḥ kathayiṣyanti mahā|Bhāratam āhavam
samāgameṣu, Vārṣṇeya, kṣatriyāṇāṃ yaśo|dhanam.
samupānaya Kaunteyaṃ yuddhāya mama, Keśava,
mantra|saṃvaraṇaṃ kurvan nityam eva, paraṃ|tapa.

SAÑJAYA uvāca:

142.1 KARṆASYA VACANAṂ śrutvā Keśavaḥ para|vīra|hā
uvāca prahasan vākyaṃ smita|pūrvam idaṃ yathā:

ŚRĪ|BHAGAVĀN uvāca:

api tvāṃ na labhet, Karṇa, rājya|lambh'|ôpapādanam?
mayā dattāṃ hi pṛthivīṃ na praśāsitum icchasi?
dhruvo jayaḥ Pāṇḍavānām it' îdaṃ,
na saṃśayaḥ kaś cana vidyate 'tra;
jaya|dhvajo dṛśyate Pāṇḍavasya
samucchrito vānara|rāja ugraḥ!
divyā māyā vihitā Bhaumanena
samucchritā Indra|ketu|prakāśā!
divyāni bhūtāni jay'|âvahāni
dṛśyanti c' âiv' âtra bhayānakāni.

and eagles, and then the purification for this sacrifice will be performed, Janárdana.

I pray that the kshatriyas, advanced in wisdom and age, do not die in vain through your doing, Madhu·súdana, bull of the kshatriyas! May the circle of kshatriyas go to their death at Kuru·kshetra, the holiest place in the three worlds, Késhava, by the sword. Arrange matters here as you wish, lotus-eyed Varshnéya, so that the entire kshatriya order may win heaven.

The fame of this story will exist eternally, for as long as 141.55
the mountains stand and the rivers flow, Janárdana. When brahmins are gathered together, they will tell the tale of the great war of the Bharatas, and of the wealth of fame belonging to the warriors, Varshnéya.

So lead the son of Kunti to war with me, Késhava, and keep our discussion secret forever, enemy-scorcher.

SÁNJAYA said:

WHEN KÉSHAVA heard Karna's words, that slaughterer of 142.1
enemy heroes first smiled, then laughed and said this:

THE BLESSED LORD replied:

Does the present of gaining a kingdom not grab you, Karna? Do you really not want to rule the earth I am giving you? The Pándavas' victory is now assured. No doubt remains here. The son of Pandu's victory flag is already visible, the fierce king of monkeys has been raised! Bháumana devised this celestial illusion, and it is raised like Indra's banner itself! Divine creatures bringing victory and fear can be seen depicted on it. It gets caught on neither mountains nor 142.5

142.5 na sajjate śaila|vanaspatibhya
ūrdhvaṃ tiryag yojana|mātra|rūpaḥ
śrīmān dhvajaḥ, Karṇa, Dhanañjayasya
samucchritaḥ pāvaka|tulya|rūpaḥ!
yadā drakṣyasi saṅgrāme śvet'|âśvaṃ Kṛṣṇa|sārathim,
Aindram astraṃ vikurvāṇam, ubhe c' âpy Agni|Mārute
Gāṇḍīvasya ca nirghoṣaṃ visphūrjitam iv' âśaneḥ,
na tadā bhavitā tretā, na kṛtaṃ, dvāparaṃ na ca.
yadā drakṣyasi saṅgrāme Kuntī|putraṃ Yudhiṣṭhiram
japa|homa|samāyuktaṃ svāṃ rakṣantaṃ mahā|camūm,
ādityam iva dur|dharṣaṃ, tapantaṃ śatru|vāhinīm,
na tadā bhavitā tretā, na kṛtaṃ, dvāparaṃ na ca.
142.10 yadā drakṣyasi saṅgrāme Bhīmasenaṃ mahā|balam
Duḥśāsanasya rudhiraṃ pītvā nṛtyantam āhave,
prabhinnam iva mātaṅgaṃ, pratidvirada|ghātinam,
na tadā bhavitā tretā, na kṛtaṃ, dvāparaṃ na ca.
yadā drakṣyasi saṃgrāme Droṇaṃ Śāntanavaṃ, Kṛpam,
Suyodhanaṃ ca rājānaṃ, Saindhavaṃ ca Jayadratham,
yuddhāy' āpatatas tūrṇaṃ vāritān savya|sācinā,
na tadā bhavitā tretā, na kṛtaṃ, dvāparaṃ na ca.
yadā drakṣyasi saṃgrāme Mādrī|putrau mahā|balau
vāhinīṃ Dhārtarāṣṭrāṇāṃ kṣobhayantau gajāv iva,
142.15 vigāḍhe śastra|sampāte para|vīra|rath'|ārujau,
na tadā bhavitā tretā, na kṛtaṃ, dvāparaṃ na ca.
brūyāḥ, Karṇa, ito gatvā Droṇaṃ Śāntanavaṃ, Kṛpam:
«saumyo 'yaṃ vartate māsaḥ suprāpa|yavas'|êndhanaḥ,
sarv'|âuṣadhi|vana|sphītaḥ, phalavān, alpa|makṣikaḥ,
niṣpaṅko, rasavat toyo n', âtyuṣṇa|śiśiraḥ sukhaḥ,

trees, for its form stretches nine miles high and wide. The glorious raised flag of Dhanan·jaya is as beautiful as fire, Karna!

When you see white-horsed Árjuna in battle with Krishna as his charioteer, making use of Indra's weapon and the weapons of both fire and the wind, and you sense Gandíva's bellowing twang like thundering lightning, then the *treta*, *krita*, and *dvápara* ages will be no more. When you see Yudhi·shthira, son of Kunti, intent on prayers and oblations in battle, as unassailable as the sun itself, protecting his enormous army and burning the enemy force, then the *treta*, *krita*, and *dvápara* ages will cease to be.

When you see powerful Bhima·sena in the conflict drink- 142.10
ing Duhshásana's blood and dancing on the battlefield like a tusker with rent temples who has killed an enemy elephant, then the *treta*, *krita*, and *dvápara* ages will be no more. When you see the ambidextrous archer obstructing Drona, the son of Shántanu, Kripa, King Suyódhana, and Jayad·ratha the Sáindhava king as they rush quickly for battle, then the *treta*, *krita*, and *dvápara* ages will cease to be.

When you see the mighty twin sons of Madri in battle, making the army of Dhartaráshtras tremble as though they
were elephants, demolishing enemy heroes' chariots from 142.15
the moment the collision of weapons begins, then the *treta*, *krita*, and *dvápara* ages will be no more.

Go now, Karna, and tell Drona, Shántanu's son, and Kripa: "This is a good month, for food, drink, and fuel are in good supply. All herbs and plants are flourishing, there is no shortage of fruit, and there are few mosquitoes. There

saptamāc c' âpi divasād amāvāsyā bhaviṣyati,
saṃgrāmo yujyatāṃ tasyāṃ, tām āhuḥ Śakra|devatām.»
tathā rājño vadeḥ sarvān ye yuddhāy' âbhyupāgatāḥ:
«yad vo manīṣitaṃ, tad vai sarvaṃ sampādayāmy aham.»
142.20 rājāno rāja|putrāś ca Duryodhana|vaś'|ânugāḥ
prāpya śastreṇa nidhanaṃ prāpsyanti gatim uttamām.

SAÑJAYA uvāca:

143.1 KEŚAVASYA TU TAD vākyaṃ Karṇaḥ śrutv" āhitaḥ śubham
abravīd abhisampūjya Kṛṣṇaṃ taṃ Madhu|sūdanam:
«jānan māṃ kiṃ, mahā|bāho, saṃmohayitum icchasi?
yo 'yaṃ pṛthivyāḥ kārtsneyna vināśaḥ samupasthitaḥ,
nimittaṃ tatra Śakunir, ahaṃ, Duḥśāsanas tathā,
Duryodhanaś ca nṛ|patir Dhṛtarāṣṭra|suto 'bhavat.
a|saṃśayam idaṃ, Kṛṣṇa, mahad yuddham upasthitam
Pāṇḍavānāṃ Kurūṇāṃ ca ghoraṃ, rudhira|kardamam.
143.5 rājāno rāja|putrāś ca Duryodhana|vaś'|ânugāḥ
raṇe śastr'|âgninā dagdhāḥ prāpsyanti Yama|sādanam.
svapnā hi bahavo ghorā dṛśyante, Madhu|sūdana,
nimittāni ca ghorāṇi, tath" ôtpātāḥ su|dāruṇāḥ;
parājayaṃ Dhārtarāṣṭre vijayaṃ ca Yudhiṣṭhire
śaṃsanta iva, Vārṣṇeya, vividhā roma|harṣaṇāḥ.
Prājāpatyaṃ hi nakṣatraṃ grahas tīkṣṇo mahā|dyutiḥ
Śanaiścaraḥ pīḍayati pīḍayan prāṇino 'dhikam.
kṛtvā c' Âṅgārako vakraṃ Jyeṣṭhāyāṃ, Madhu|sūdana,
Anurādhāṃ prārthayate maitraṃ saṃśamayann† iva.

is no mud, the water is delicious, and the weather is pleasant—neither too hot nor cold. In seven days from now it will be the new moon. Let's join for battle on that day, for they call it Indra's day."

Similarly, tell all the kings who have gathered for war: "I will fully accomplish what you wish for." The kings and 142.20
princes who follow under Duryódhana's power will die by the sword, and so they will win their ultimate path.

SÁNJAYA continued:

ONCE HE HAD heard Késhava's splendid and advanta- 143.1
geous words, Karna paid his respects to Krishna, slayer of Madhu, and said to him: "Long-armed man, why do you wish to confuse me when you know everything? This whole earth is on the brink of destruction, and Shákuni, Duhshásana, and I are the reason, along with Duryódhana, Dhrita·rashtras's son.

Doubtless, Krishna, a mighty, horrifying, blood-smeared battle is at hand for the Pándavas and Kurus. The kings and 143.5
princes who follow subject to Duryódhana's will, will be burned by the fire of weaponry in battle, and they will reach Yama's realm. Numerous terrifying dreams are being seen, Madhu·súdana, as well as horrifying omens and likewise particularly disastrous portents. These hair-raising signs are varied, but they indicate that Dhartaráshtra will find defeat and Yudhi·shthira will find victory, Varshnéya.

The brutal great glorious planet Saturn, the slow mover, is pressing the constellation Róhini in order to torment living creatures further. Mars, retrogade to the constellation

143.10 nūnaṃ mahad bhayaṃ, Kṛṣṇa,
Kurūṇāṃ samupasthitam;
viśeṣeṇa hi, Vārṣṇeya,
Citrāṃ pīḍayate grahaḥ.
somasya lakṣma vyāvṛttaṃ, Rāhur arkam upaiti ca.
divaś c' ôlkāḥ patanty etāḥ sa|nirghātāḥ sa|kampanāḥ,
niṣṭananti ca mātaṅgā, muñcanty aśrūṇi vājinaḥ,
pānīyaṃ yavasaṃ c' âpi n' âbhinandanti, Mādhava,
prādur bhūteṣu c' âiteṣu bhayam āhur upasthitam
nimitteṣu, mahā|bāho, dāruṇaṃ prāṇi|nāśanam.
alpe bhukte purīṣaṃ ca prabhūtam iha dṛśyate
vājināṃ vāraṇānāṃ ca, manuṣyāṇāṃ ca, Keśava,
143.15 Dhārtarāṣṭrasya sainyeṣu sarveṣu, Madhu|sūdana.
parābhavasya tal liṅgam iti prāhur manīṣiṇaḥ.
prahṛṣṭaṃ vāhanaṃ, Kṛṣṇa, Pāṇḍavānāṃ pracakṣate,
pradakṣiṇā mṛgāś c' âiva; tat teṣāṃ jaya|lakṣaṇam,
apasavyā mṛgāḥ sarve Dhārtarāṣṭrasya, Keśava,
vācaś c' âpy a|śarīriṇyas; tat parābhava|lakṣaṇam.
mayūrāḥ, puṇyaśakunā, haṃsa|sārasa|cātakāḥ,
jīvaṃjīvaka|saṅghāś c' âpy anugacchanti Pāṇḍavān.
gṛdhrāḥ, kaṅkā, bakāḥ, śyenā, yātudhānās, tathā vṛkāḥ,
makṣikāṇāṃ ca saṅghātā anudhāvanti Kauravān.

Jyeshtha, O Madhu·súdana, approaches the constellation Anurádha, signaling the destruction of friends.

Surely there is enormous danger on the horizon for the 143.10
Kurus, Krishna, for the planet Mahapáta oppresses the constellation Chitra in particular, Varshnéya.* The moon's mark is misshapen, and Rahu is going for the sun. Meteors are falling from the sky, accompanied by whirlwinds and earthquakes. The elephants are trumpeting, the horses weep their tears, and none of them take any pleasure in their food and drink, Mádhava. Long-armed man, when omens such as these appear, they say that cruel danger is at hand which will result in the end of creatures.

The horses, elephants, and men in all Dhartaráshtra's 143.15
armies eat very little, Késhava, and yet the amount of feces they produce seems enormous in comparison, Madhu·súdana. Wise men claim that this is a sign of defeat. They say that the Pándavas' horses are happy and that the wild animals are circling them in a clockwise direction, and that this is a sign of their victory; but all wild beasts circle the Dhartaráshtra's army in an anticlockwise direction, Késhava, and there are disembodied voices which signify his destruction, Késhava.

Auspicious birds follow the Pándavas, such as peacocks, geese, cranes, *chátaka*s and flocks of *jívanjívaka*s. But vultures, herons, cranes, hawks, evil spirits, wolves, and swarms of flies follow the Káuravas.

143.20 Dhārtarāṣṭrasya sainyeṣu bherīṇāṃ n' âsti niḥsvanaḥ,
an|āhatāḥ Pāṇḍavānāṃ nadanti paṭahāḥ kila.
udapānāś ca nardanti yathā go|vṛṣabhās tathā
Dhārtarāṣṭrasya sainyeṣu; tat parābhava|lakṣaṇam.
māṃsa|śoṇita|varṣaṃ ca vṛṣṭaṃ devena, Mādhava,
tathā gandharva|nagaraṃ bhānumat samupasthitam
sa|prākāraṃ, sa|parikhaṃ, sa|vapraṃ, cāru|toraṇam.
kṛṣṇaś ca parighas tatra bhānum āvṛtya tiṣṭhati,
uday'|âstam|aye sandhye vedayantī mahad bhayam.
śivā ca vāśate ghoraṃ; tat parābhava|lakṣaṇam.
143.25 eka|pakṣ'|âkṣi|caraṇāḥ pakṣiṇo, Madhu|sūdana,
utsṛjanti mahad ghoraṃ; tat parābhava|lakṣaṇam.
kṛṣṇa|grīvāś ca śakunā, rakta|pādā, bhayānakāḥ
sandhyām abhimukhā yānti; tat parābhava|lakṣaṇam.
brāhmaṇān prathamaṃ dveṣṭi, gurūṃś ca, Madhu|sūdana,
bhṛtyān, bhaktimataś c' âpi; tat parābhava|lakṣaṇam.
pūrvā dig lohit'|ākārā, śastra|varṇā ca dakṣiṇā,
āma|pātra|pratīkāśā paścimā, Madhu|sūdana,
uttarā śaṅkha|varṇ'|ābhā—diśāṃ varṇā udāhṛtāḥ.
pradīptāś ca diśaḥ sarvā Dhārtarāṣṭrasya Mādhava,
mahad bhayaṃ vedayanti tasminn utpāta|darśane.
143.30 sahasra|pādaṃ prāsādaṃ svapn'|ânte sma Yudhiṣṭhiraḥ
adhirohan mayā dṛṣṭaḥ saha bhrātṛbhir, Acyuta.
śvet'|ôṣṇīṣāś ca dṛśyante sarve vai, śukla|vāsasaḥ,
āsanāni ca śubhrāṇi sarveṣām upalakṣaye.
tava c' âpi mayā, Kṛṣṇa, svapn'|ânte rudhir'|āvilā
astreṇa pṛthivī dṛṣṭā parikṣiptā, Janārdana.
asthi|saṃcayam ārūḍhaś c' â|mit'|âujā Yudhiṣṭhiraḥ
suvarṇa|pātryāṃ saṃhṛṣṭo bhuktavān ghṛta|pāyasam.

In the Dhartaráshtra's armies the drums do not sound, 143.20
but the Pándavas' war drums boom, unimpeded, or so they say. The wells in the Dhartaráshtra's army encampment are roaring like bulls, and this signals his defeat. The god rains down a shower of blood and flesh, Mádhava, and a luminous *gandhárva* city has appeared nearby, with walls, trenches, ramparts, and a lovely arched gateway.

A black line of clouds hangs, blocking the sun, and the twilights at dawn and dusk signify great danger. Jackals
howl horribly, and this is a sign of our defeat. Birds with 143.25
only one wing, one eye, and one leg release cries of great horror, Madhu·súdana, and this is an omen of defeat.

Formidable black-necked and red-footed birds surround our camp and fly into the dusk: this is an omen of the Dhartaráshtra's defeat. First and foremost he hates brahmins, then teachers, Madhu·súdana, and next his devoted servants, and this too is a sign of his defeat. The east has turned blood-red, the south is steely-hued like weapons, the west is the color of clay, like an unfired pot, Madhu·súdana, and the north is said to be shell-like in hue. All the directions blaze around the Dhartaráshtra, Mádhava, and the sight of this portent signals enormous danger.

In my dreams I saw Yudhi·shthira and his brothers climb- 143.30
ing up into a thousand-pillared palace, Áchyuta. They all appeared with white turbans and white clothes, and I noticed that all their seats were gleaming white. In my dreams I also saw you, Krishna Janárdana, scattering the blood-polluted earth with weapons. Immeasurably energetic Yudhi·shthira ascended the pile of bones and happily ate his buttered rice from a golden bowl.

Yudhiṣṭhiro mayā dṛṣṭo grasamāno vasun|dharām;
tvayā dattām imāṃ vyaktaṃ bhokṣyate sa vasun|dharām.
143.35 uccaṃ parvatam ārūḍho bhīma|karmā Vṛkodaraḥ
gadā|pāṇir nara|vyāghro grasann iva mahīm imām;
kṣapayiṣyati naḥ sarvān sa su|vyaktaṃ mahā|raṇe.
viditaṃ me, Hṛṣīkeśa, yato dharmas tato jayaḥ.

pāṇḍuraṃ gajam ārūḍho Gāṇḍivī sa Dhanañjayaḥ
tvayā sārdhaṃ, Hṛṣīkeśa, śriyā paramayā jvalan.
yūyaṃ sarve vadhiṣyadhvaṃ, tatra me n' âsti saṃśayaḥ,
pārthivān samare, Kṛṣṇa, Duryodhana|purogamān.
Nakulaḥ, Sahadevaś ca, Sātyakiś ca mahā|rathaḥ
śukla|keyūra|kaṇṭhatrāḥ, śukla|mäly'|āṃbar'|āvṛtāḥ,
143.40 adhirūḍhā nara|vyāghrā nara|vāhanam uttamam
traya ete mayā dṛṣṭāḥ pāṇḍura|cchatra|vāsasaḥ

śvet'|ōṣṇīṣāś ca dṛśyante traya ete, Janārdana,
Dhārtarāṣṭreṣu sainyeṣu tān vijānīhi, Keśava,
Aśvatthāmā, Kṛpaś c' âiva, Kṛtavarmā ca Sātvataḥ.
rakt'|ōṣṇīṣāś ca dṛśyante sarve, Mādhava, pārthivāḥ.

uṣṭra|prayuktam ārūḍhau Bhīṣma|Droṇau mahā|rathau
mayā sārdhaṃ, mahā|bāho, Dhārtarāṣṭreṇa vā, vibho,
Agastya|śāstāṃ ca diśaṃ prayātāḥ sma, Janārdana,
a|cireṇ' âiva kālena prāpsyāmo Yama|sādanam.
143.45 ahaṃ c' ânye ca rājāno, yac ca tat kṣatra|maṇḍalam,
Gāṇḍīv'|âgnim pravekṣyāma, iti me n' âsti saṃśayaḥ.»

I watched as you gave Yudhi·shthira the earth and he swallowed it, so evidently he will enjoy power over the earth. Vrikódara, the tiger-like man of fearful accomplish- 143.35
ments, ascended a tall mountain, mace in hand, and seemed to gobble down the earth. It is quite clear that he will slaughter us all in the great battle. I am aware that victory appears where there is law, Hrishikésha.

Dhanan·jaya mounted a white elephant, with the Gandíva and with you, Hrishikésha, and he blazed with supreme glory. I have no doubt that all of you will slaughter the kings led by Duryódhana in battle, Krishna. I saw Nákula, Saha·deva, and the mighty warrior Sátyaki, decked with spotless bracelets and necklaces, and covered with gleaming garlands and decorations. The three tiger-like men had 143.40
mounted superb vehicles, carried by men, and were furnished with white umbrellas and white clothes.

Three white-turbaned men also appeared in the Dhartaráshtra's armies, Janárdana Késhava. They were Ashva·tthaman, Kripa, and Krita·varman Sátvata. All the other kings seemed be wearing red turbans, Mádhava.

Bhishma and Drona, that pair of mighty warriors, had mounted a vehicle drawn by camels, and with me and Duryódhana they went to the region ruled by Agástya, long-armed lord Janárdana. Before long we reached Yama's realm. So I have no doubt that I and other kings as well as 143.45
the circle of kshatriyas will enter the Gandíva's fire."

KṚṢṆA uvāca:

upasthita|vināś" êyaṃ nūnam adya vasun|dharā,
yathā hi me vacaḥ, Karṇa, n' ôpaiti hṛdayaṃ tava.
sarveṣāṃ, tāta, bhūtānāṃ vināśe pratyupasthite
a|nayo naya|saṅkāśo hṛdayān n' âpasarpati.

KARṆA uvāca:

api tvāṃ, Kṛṣṇa, paśyāma jīvanto 'smān mahā|raṇāt
samuttīrṇā, mahā|bāho, vīra|kṣatra|vināśanāt,
atha vā saṅgamaḥ, Kṛṣṇa, svarge no bhavitā dhruvam;
tatr' êdānīṃ sameṣyāmaḥ punaḥ sārdhaṃ tvayā, 'n|agha.

SAÑJAYA uvāca:

143.50 ity uktvā Mādhavaṃ Karṇaḥ, pariṣvajya ca pīḍitam,
visarjitaḥ Keśavena rath'|ôpasthād avātarat.
tataḥ sva|ratham āsthāya jāmbūnada|vibhūṣitam
sah' âsmābhir nivavṛte Rādheyo dīnamānasaḥ.
tataḥ śīghrataraṃ prāyāt Keśavaḥ saha|Sātyakiḥ
punar uccārayan vāṇīṃ «yāhi! yāh'! îti» sārathim.

VAIŚAMPĀYANA uvāca:

144.1 A|SIDDH'|ÂNUNAYE Kṛṣṇe Kurubhyaḥ Pāṇḍavān gate
abhigamya Pṛthāṃ kṣattā śanaiḥ śocann iv' âbravīt:
«jānāsi me, jīva|putri, bhāvaṃ nityam a|vigrahe;
krośato na ca gṛhṇīte vacanaṃ me Suyodhanaḥ.
upapanno hy asau rājā Cedi|Pāñcāla|Kekayaiḥ,
Bhīm'|Ârjunābhyāṃ, Kṛṣṇena, Yuyudhāna|yamair api,
Upaplavye niviṣṭo 'pi dharmam eva Yudhiṣṭhiraḥ

KRISHNA replied:

Surely the destruction of the world is now at hand, for my words have not reached your heart, Karna. When the destruction of all creatures is nigh, my friend, bad policy in the guise of good policy refuses to leave one's heart.

KARNA said:

I pray that I see you again, long-armed Krishna, if we survive the mighty battle and the slaughter of kshatriya heroes. Otherwise we will assuredly meet in heaven, Krishna. Indeed, now it seems that it is there that we will meet you again, sinless man.

SÁNJAYA continued:

Once he had said this, Karna embraced Mádhava, squeez- 143.50
ing him tightly, and then, when dismissed by Késhava, he climbed out of the interior of the chariot; and standing on his own car, which glistened with gold from the river Jambu, Radhéya despondently returned with us. Késhava set off speedily with Sátyaki, and he repeatedly urged his charioteer, shouting "Go! Go!"

VAISHAMPÁYANA said:

SINCE KRISHNA's conciliation was unsuccessful and he 144.1
had returned to the Pándavas from the Kurus, the steward went to Pritha and spoke gently to her, grieving:

"You know that my nature always inclines to peace, mother of still living sons, but Suyódhana doesn't accept my advice even when I'm angry. King Yudhi·shthira, living at Upaplávya, who has the Chedis, the Panchálas and Kékayas, Bhima and Árjuna, Krishna, Yuyudhána, and the twins on his side, hopes only for law, for he is led by his

kāṅkṣate jñāti|sauhārdād balavān, dur|balo yathā.
144.5 rājā tu Dhṛtarāṣṭro 'yaṃ vayo|vṛddho na śāmyati
mattaḥ putra|maden' âiva vidharme pathi vartate.
Jayadrathasya, Karṇasya, tathā Duḥśāsanasya ca,
Saubalasya ca dur|buddhyā mitho bhedaḥ prapatsyate.
a|dharmeṇa hi dharmiṣṭhaṃ kṛtaṃ vai kāryam īdṛśam
yeṣāṃ, teṣām ayaṃ dharmaḥ s'|ânubandho bhaviṣyati.
kriyamāṇe balād dharme Kurubhiḥ ko na sañjvaret?
a|sāmnā Keśave yāte samudyokṣyanti Pāṇḍavāḥ;
tataḥ Kurūṇām a|nayo bhavitā vīra|nāśanaḥ.
cintayan na labhe nidrām ahaḥsu ca niśāsu ca.»
144.10 śrutvā tu Kuntī tad vākyam artha|kāmena bhāṣitam
sā niḥśvasantī duḥkh'|ārtā manasā vimamarśa ha.
«dhig astv arthaṃ yat|kṛte 'yaṃ
mahāñ jñāti|vadhaḥ kṛtaḥ;
vartsyate su|hṛdāṃ c' âiva
yuddhe 'smin vai parābhavaḥ!
Pāṇḍavāś, Cedi|Pañcālā, Yādavāś ca samāgatāḥ
Bhārataiḥ saha yotsyanti—kiṃ nu duḥkham ataḥ param?
paśye doṣaṃ dhruvaṃ yuddhe,
tath" â|yuddhe parābhavam;
a|dhanasya mṛtaṃ śreyo,
na hi jñāti|kṣayo jayaḥ.
iti me cintayantyā vai hṛdi duḥkhaṃ pravartate.
pitā|mahaḥ Śāntanava, ācāryaś ca yudhāṃ patiḥ,

friendship towards his relatives like a weak man, though in reality he is strong.

King Dhrita·rashtra here, on the other hand, does not make peace, though he is advanced in age. Intoxicated with his son's arrogance, he travels on a lawless path. The mutual split continues because of Jayad·ratha's, Karna's, and Duhshásana's foolishness. When men treat such a supremely lawful task lawlessly, then the law and its consequences will catch up with them. 144.5

Who would not be fevered when the Kurus are raping law? When Késhava returns without peace, then the Pándavas will prepare for war and the Kurus' poor policy will become the destroyer of heroes. I can't sleep day or night for thinking about it."

As she listened to the words spoken by the well-meaning steward, Kunti sighed, afflicted with misery, and reflected in her mind. 144.10

"Damn the wealth for which a great massacre of kin will ensue, for defeat will be the result in this war between friends! What is worse than that the Pándavas, Chedis, Panchálas, and Yádavas are gathered and on the brink of fighting the Bharatas?

I certainly see the sin in war, but equally I see the defeat in not going to war. Death is best for the man without wealth, but there is no victory in destroying one's relatives. As I think on these things, misery enters my heart. Grandfather Shántanava, the teacher and lord of warriors, and Karna augment my fears for the Dhartaráshtras. The 144.15

144.15 Karṇaś ca Dhārtarāṣṭr'|ârthaṃ vardhayanti bhayaṃ mama.
n' ācāryaḥ kāmavāñ śiṣyair Droṇo yudhyeta jātu cit;
Pāṇḍaveṣu kathaṃ hārdaṃ kuryān na ca pitā|mahaḥ?
ayaṃ tv eko vṛthā|dṛṣṭir Dhārtarāṣṭrasya dur|mateḥ,
moh'|ânuvartī satataṃ, pāpo, dveṣṭi ca Pāṇḍavān.
mahaty an|arthe nirbandhī, balavāṃś ca viśeṣataḥ,
Karṇaḥ sadā Pāṇḍavānāṃ, tan me dahati saṃprati.
āśaṃse tv adya Karṇasya mano 'haṃ Pāṇḍavān prati
prasādayitum, āsādya darśayantī yathā|tatham.
toṣito bhagavān yatra Durvāsā me varaṃ dadau,
144.20 āhvānaṃ mantra|saṃyuktaṃ vasantyāḥ pitṛ|veśmani.
s" âham antaḥpure rājñaḥ Kuntibhoja|puraskṛtā
cintayantī bahu|vidhaṃ hṛdayena vidūyatā,
bal'|âbalaṃ ca mantrāṇāṃ, brāhmaṇasya ca vāg|balam,
strī|bhāvād bāla|bhāvāc ca cintayantī punaḥ punaḥ,
dhātryā visrabdhayā guptā sakhī|jana|vṛtā tadā,
doṣaṃ pariharantī ca, pituś cāritrya|rakṣiṇī,
‹kathaṃ na su|kṛtaṃ me syān, n' âparādhavatī katham
bhaveyam? iti› sañcintya, brāhmaṇaṃ taṃ namasya ca,
kautūhalāt tu taṃ labdhvā bāliśyād ācaraṃ tadā:
kanyā satī devam arkam āsādayam ahaṃ tataḥ.
144.25 yo 'sau kānīna|garbho me putravat parirakṣitaḥ,
kasmān na kuryād vacanaṃ pathyaṃ bhrātṛ|hitaṃ tathā?»

teacher Drona would never fight against his pupils willingly, and why would grandfather not treat the Pándavas affectionately?

There is only this one wicked man who hates the Pándavas and always acts out of foolishness, vainly following the wicked-minded Dhartaráshtra. Powerful Karna is particularly stubborn in his mighty and fruitless cause to constantly destroy the Pándavas, and it burns me now. But today I hope to turn Karna's mind and make him kindly disposed towards the Pándavas, for I will approach him and show him how matters really stand.

When the blessed lord Durvásas was satisfied, he granted me the gift of summoning the gods with mantras while I 144.20
lived in the inner apartments of my father Kunti·bhoja's house. I thought long and hard in my trembling heart about the strength or weakness of the mantras, and about the force of the brahmin's words, and as I thought time and again, as a woman though still as a girl, protected by my faithful nurse and surrounded by my friends, avoiding sin and defending my father's reputation, I thought, 'How can I do something good without committing any transgression?' So it was that I pondered and bowed to the brahmin.

Out of curiosity and childishness I took the mantra with the power to summon, and being just a girl I brought the sun god to me. Why does the man whom I bore as a girl, 144.25
and who is now protected as my son, not follow my advice when it is proper and to his brothers' advantage?"

iti Kuntī viniścitya kārya|niścayam uttamam
kāry'|ârtham abhiniścitya yayau Bhāgīrathīṃ prati.
ātma|jasya tatas tasya ghṛṇinaḥ satya|saṅginaḥ
Gaṅgā|tīre Pṛth" âśrauṣīd ved'|ādhyayana|niḥsvanam.
prāṇ|mukhasy' ōrdhva|bāhoḥ sā paryatiṣṭhata pṛṣṭhataḥ,
japy'|âvasānaṃ kāry'|ârthaṃ pratīkṣantī tapasvinī.

atiṣṭhat sūrya|tāp'|ārtā Karṇasy' ôttara|vāsasi
Kauravya|patnī Vārṣṇeyī, padma|māl" êva śuṣyatī.
144.30 ā pṛṣṭha|tāpāj japtvā sa, parivṛtya yata|vrataḥ,
dṛṣṭvā Kuntīm upātiṣṭhad abhivādya kṛt'|âñjaliḥ.
yathā|nyāyaṃ mahā|tejā, mānī, dharma|bhṛtāṃ varaḥ,
utsmayan praṇataḥ prāha Kuntīṃ Vaikartano Vṛṣaḥ.

KARṆA uvāca:

145.1 RĀDHEYO 'HAM Ādhirathiḥ Karṇas tvām abhivādaye.
prāptā kim arthaṃ bhavatī? brūhi, kiṃ karavāṇi te.

KUNTY uvāca:

Kaunteyas tvaṃ, na Rādheyo, na tav' Ādhirathaḥ pitā.
n' âsi sūta|kule jātaḥ, Karṇa, tad viddhi me vacaḥ.
kānīnas tvaṃ mayā jātaḥ pūrva|jaḥ kukṣiṇā dhṛtaḥ
Kunti|rājasya bhavane. Pārthas tvam asi, putraka.
prakāśa|karmā tapano yo 'yaṃ devo Virocanaḥ,
ajījanat tvāṃ mayy eṣa, Karṇa, śastra|bhṛtāṃ varam.
145.5 kuṇḍalī, baddha|kavaco deva|garbhaḥ śriyā vṛtaḥ

When Kunti had taken this supreme decision on what she had to do, and was settled on her task, she went to the river Bhagírathi. On the bank of the Ganges Pritha heard the sound of her compassionate son, intent on the truth, chanting the Vedas. So the poor lady stood behind him as he faced east with his arms upraised, and she waited for him to finish his task of muttering prayers.

So she, a Vrishni princess and the wife of a Kaurávya,
stood in the shade of Karna's upper garment, afflicted by the
heat of the sun, withering like a lotus garland. The strict- 144.30
vowed man prayed until the heat of the sun touched his
back, and then he turned and saw Kunti, so he greeted
her, folding his hands together. The proud, greatly glorious
man, the greatest of those who practice *dharma*, waited, as
is right; then, smiling, Vrisha Vaikártana bowed to Kunti
and spoke to her.

KARNA said:

I, KARNA, THE SON of Radha and Ádhiratha, greet you. 145.1
Why has your ladyship come? Tell me what I can do for
you.

KUNTI replied:

You are the son of Kunti, not Radha, and your father is
not Ádhiratha. You were not born into a *suta* family, Karna.
Take heed of what I am telling you. You are my firstborn; I
carried you in my womb in the palace of Kunti·bhoja, and
gave birth to you as a girl. You are a Partha, my dear son.
The god Viróchana who creates heat and brings light begot
you upon me, Karna, as the greatest of those who wield
weapons. You were born earringed, bound with armor, and 145.5

jātas tvam asi, dur|dharṣa, mayā, putra, pitur gṛhe.
sa tvaṃ bhrātṝn a|saṃbudhya mohād yad upasevase
Dhārtarāṣṭrān, na tad yuktaṃ tvayi, putra, viśeṣataḥ.
etad dharma|phalaṃ, putra, narāṇāṃ dharma|niścaye,
yat tuṣyanty asya pitaro, mātā c' âpy eka|darśinī.
Arjunen' ârjitāṃ pūrvaṃ, hṛtāṃ lobhād a|sādhubhiḥ,
ācchidya Dhārtarāṣṭrebhyo bhuṅkṣva Yaudiṣṭhirīṃ śriyam.
adya paśyantu Kuravaḥ, Karṇ'|Ârjuna|samāgamam,
saubhrātreṇa samālakṣya saṃnamantām a|sādhavaḥ.
145.10 Karṇ'|Ârjunau vai bhavetāṃ yathā Rāma|Janārdanau;
a|sādhyaṃ kiṃ nu loke syād yuvayoḥ saṃhit'|ātmanoḥ?
Karṇa, śobhiṣyase nūnaṃ pañcabhir bhrātṛbhir vṛtaḥ,
devaiḥ parivṛto Brahmā vedyām iva mah"|âdhvare.
upapanno guṇaiḥ sarvair, jyeṣṭhaḥ śreṣṭheṣu bandhuṣu,
sūta|putr' êti mā śabdaḥ, Pārthas tvam asi vīryavān.

VAIŚAMPĀYANA uvāca:

146.1 TATAḤ SŪRYĀN niścaritāṃ Karṇaḥ śuśrāva bhāratīm
duratyayāṃ, praṇayinīṃ, pitṛvad bhāskar'|eritām,
«satyam āha Pṛthā vākyaṃ, Karṇa; mātṛ|vacaḥ kuru.
śreyas te syān, nara|vyāghra, sarvam ācaratas tathā.»

covered with splendor, as the son of a god in my father's house, invincible son.

It is inappropriate that you foolishly serve the Dhartaráshtras without knowing your brothers, and particularly so for you, my son. In deciding the duties of men, this is the fruit of law, my son, that the father and mother, the only one to display affection, should be pleased with their son. Cut yourself off from the Dhartaráshtras and enjoy Yudhi·shthira's glory, first won by Árjuna then stolen by wicked men in their greed.

Let the Kurus see Karna and Árjuna united, and seeing you together in brotherhood let the wicked men bow to you. Let Karna and Árjuna be like Rama and Janárdana, for 145.10
when you two are joined in spirit then what in the world could you not accomplish? Karna, you will surely shine when surrounded by your five brothers, like Brahma surrounded by the gods at a great Vedic sacrifice. Endowed with every virtue, the eldest of your greatest relatives, don't be called a *suta*'s son, for you are a mighty Partha.

VAISHAMPÁYANA said:

THEN KARNA HEARD an inscrutable and affectionate voice 146.1
coming a great distance from the sun, spoken in a fatherly manner by the sun: "Pritha has told you the truth, Karna, so take your mother's advice. It would be best for you, tiger-like man, to do everything just as she says."

VAIŚAMPĀYANA uvāca:

evam uktasya mātrā ca svayaṃ pitrā ca bhānunā,
cacāla n' âiva Karṇasya matiḥ satya|dhṛtes tadā.

KARṆA uvāca:

na cet tac chraddadhe vākyaṃ, kṣatriye, bhāṣitaṃ tvayā;
dharma|dvāraṃ mam' âitat syān niyoga|karaṇaṃ tava.
146.5 akaron mayi yat pāpaṃ bhavatī su|mah"|âtyayam,
apākīrṇo 'smi yan, mātas, tad yaśaḥ|kīrti|nāśanam.
ahaṃ cet kṣatriyo jāto, na prāptaḥ kṣatra|satkriyām;
tvat|kṛte kiṃ nu pāpīyaḥ śatruḥ kuryān mam' â|hitam?
kriyā|kāle tv anukrośam a|kṛtvā tvam imaṃ mama
hīna|saṃskāra|samayam adya māṃ samacūcudaḥ!
na vai mama hitaṃ pūrvaṃ mātṛvac ceṣṭitaṃ tvayā;
sā māṃ sambodhayasy adya keval'|ātma|hit'|âiṣiṇī.
Kṛṣṇena sahitāt ko vai na vyatheta Dhanañjayāt?
ko 'dya bhītaṃ na māṃ vidyāt Pārthānāṃ samitiṃ gatam?
146.10 a|bhrātā viditaḥ pūrvaṃ, yuddha|kāle prakāśitaḥ,
Pāṇḍavān yadi gacchāmi, kiṃ māṃ kṣatraṃ vadiṣyati?
sarva|kāmaiḥ saṃvibhaktaḥ, pūjitaś ca yathā|sukham
ahaṃ vai Dhārtarāṣṭrāṇāṃ; kuryāṃ tad a|phalaṃ katham?
upanahya parair vairaṃ ye māṃ nityam upāsate
namas|kurvanti ca sadā Vasavo Vāsavaṃ yathā.

VAISHAMPÁYANA continued:

Spoken to in this way by his mother and his father the sun, Karna's mind did not waver, for he remained firmly set on the truth.

KARNA replied:

Even if I did not believe what you tell me, kshatriya lady, my door to law would still lie in carrying out your commands, but you committed a sin against me by abandon- 146.5
ing me at enormous risk to my life, and the reputation and fame I could have had have been destroyed. Though I was born a kshatriya, I have not received the proper treatment due to a kshatriya. What enemy could be more evil and do me more harm than you?

When the time for action had come you did not treat me with the proper compassion. But now, though you denied me my proper sacraments, you are giving me orders! Never before have you acted in my interest like a mother, and yet now here you are, instructing me because you wish purely for your own good.

Who would not tremble before Dhanan·jaya with Krishna as his ally? Who would not assume that I am scared if I join the Parthas now? I was never known as their brother 146.10
in the past, but now on the eve of war I am revealed as such, so if I go to the Pándavas then what would the kshatriyas say about me?

The Dhartaráshtras have presented me with my every desire and honored me as I please, so how could I of all people render their kindness fruitless? Now that they are tied up in a quarrel with their enemies, they always serve me and

mama prāṇena ye śatrūñ śaktāḥ pratisamāsitum,
manyante te kathaṃ teṣām ahaṃ chindyāṃ mano|ratham?
mayā plavena saṅgrāmaṃ titīrṣanti dur|atyayam
a|pāre pāra|kāmā ye, tyajeyaṃ tān ahaṃ katham?

146.15 ayaṃ hi kālaḥ saṃprāpto Dhārtarāṣṭr'|ôpajīvinām;
nirveṣṭavyaṃ mayā tatra prāṇān a|parirakṣatā.
kṛt'|ârthāḥ su|bhṛtā ye hi kṛtya|kāle hy upasthite
an|avekṣya kṛtaṃ pāpā vikurvanty an|avasthitāḥ
rāja|kilbiṣiṇāṃ teṣāṃ bhartṛ|piṇḍ'|âpahāriṇām
n' âiv' âyaṃ na paro loko vidyate pāpa|karmaṇām.

Dhṛtarāṣṭrasya putrāṇām arthe yotsyāmi te sutaiḥ
balaṃ ca śaktiṃ c' āsthāya. na vai tvayy an|ṛtaṃ vade.
ānṛśaṃsyam atho vṛttaṃ rakṣan sat|puruṣ'|ôcitam;
ato 'rtha|karam apy etan na karomy adya te vacaḥ.

146.20 na ca te 'yaṃ samārambho mayi mogho bhaviṣyati;
vadhyān viṣahyān saṃgrāme na haniṣyāmi te sutān
Yudhiṣṭhiraṃ ca Bhīmaṃ ca, yamau c' âiv', Ârjunād ṛte,

Arjunena samaṃ yuddham api Yaudhiṣṭhire bale.
Arjunaṃ hi nihaty' ājau saṃprāptaṃ syāt phalaṃ mayā,
yaśasā c' âpi yujyeyaṃ nihataḥ savya|sācinā.
na te jātu na śiṣyanti putrāḥ pañca, yaśasvini,
nir|Arjunāḥ sa|Karṇā vā, s'|Ârjunā vā hate mayi.

constantly bow to me as the Vasus bow to Vásava. They believe that they will be able to take their enemies on with the help of my power, so how could I shatter their hopes? How could I abandon them when they want to cross the impassable ocean of battle with me as their boat, for they have no other means of reaching the far shore?

The time has indeed come for those who live off the 146.15
Dhartaráshtra, and I must pay my debt, even if it means risking my life. Evil men who have accomplished their goals and been well supported, but have no regard for the help they have been given and undo all that has been done for them when their moment of duty is at hand—those miscreant offenders against their king, thieves of their supporter's riceball, will find neither this world nor the next is theirs.

I will fight against your sons for the sake of Dhrita·rashtra's sons, making full use of my strength and ability. I will not lie to you. I will defend the kindness and good behavior which befits a good man, so, although your advice
may be beneficial, I will not now do as you say. However, 146.20
this enterprise of yours will not be in vain, for I will not kill your sons in battle—not Yudhi·shthira, Bhima, or the twins, though I can both withstand and kill them. Árjuna, however, is the exception.

I will only fight with Árjuna in Yudhi·shthira's army. I will gain my reward if I do indeed kill Árjuna on the battlefield, and I will win fame if I am killed by the ambidextrous archer. That way you will certainly never have fewer than five sons remaining, illustrious lady, either including Karna and without Árjuna, or with Árjuna if I am killed.

iti Karṇa|vacaḥ śrutvā Kuntī duḥkhāt pravepatī
uvāca putram āśliṣya Karṇaṃ dhairyād a|kampanam:

146.25 «evaṃ vai bhāvyam etena—kṣayaṃ yāsyanti Kauravāḥ,
yathā tvaṃ bhāṣase, Karṇa, daivaṃ tu balavattaram.
tvayā caturṇāṃ bhrāṭṝṇām a|bhayaṃ, śatru|karśana,
dattaṃ; tat pratijānīhi saṃgara|patimocanam!
an|āmayaṃ svasti c' êti» Pṛth" âtho Karṇam abravīt.
tāṃ Karṇo 'tha «tath" êty» uktvā tatas tau jagmatuḥ pṛthak.

When she heard what Karna had to say, Kunti trembled with pain, and embracing her son Karna, whose fortitude meant that he did not move so much as a muscle, she said
to him: "So it must be—the Káuravas will go to their de- 146.25
struction just as you have said, Karna, for fate is too powerful. But when you fire your weapons in battle, remember the pledge of safety you gave to your four brothers, enemy-plower! Good health and good luck!" So it was that Pritha spoke to Karna, and Karna replied "So be it" to her, and they each went their separate ways.

# 147–159
# KÉSHAVA RETURNS TO THE PÁNDAVAS

VAIŚAMPĀYANA uvāca:

147.1 ĀGAMYA HĀSTINAPURĀD Upaplavyam arin|damaḥ
Pāṇḍavānāṃ yathā|vṛttaṃ Keśavaḥ sarvam uktavān.
saṃbhāṣya su|ciraṃ kālaṃ, mantrayitvā punaḥ punaḥ,
svam eva bhavanaṃ Śaurir viśrām'|ârthaṃ jagāma ha.
visṛjya sarvān nṛ|patīn Virāṭa|pramukhāṃs tadā
Pāṇḍavā bhrātaraḥ pañca bhānāv astaṃ gate sati
sandhyām upāsya dhyāyantas tam eva gata|mānasāḥ
ānāyya Kṛṣṇaṃ Dāśārhaṃ punar mantram amantrayan.

YUDHIṢṬHIRA uvāca:

147.5 tvayā nāga|puraṃ gatvā sabhāyāṃ Dhṛtarāṣṭra|jaḥ
kim uktaḥ, puṇḍarīk'|âkṣa? tan naḥ śaṃsitum arhasi.

VĀSUDEVA uvāca:

mayā nāga|puraṃ gatvā sabhāyāṃ Dhṛtarāṣṭra|jaḥ
tathyaṃ pathyaṃ hitaṃ c' ôkto na ca gṛhṇāti dur|matiḥ.

YUDHIṢṬHIRA uvāca:

tasminn utpatham āpanne Kuru|vṛddhaḥ pitā|mahaḥ
kim uktavān, Hṛṣīkeśa, Duryodhanam a|marṣaṇam?
ācāryo vā, mahā|bhāga, Bhāradvājaḥ kim abravīt?
pitā vā Dhṛtarāṣṭras taṃ, Gāndhārī vā kim abravīt?
pitā yavīyān asmākaṃ, kṣattā dharma|vidāṃ varaḥ,
putra|śok'|âbhisantaptaḥ kim āha Dhṛtarāṣṭra|jam?
147.10 kiṃ ca sarve nṛ|patayaḥ, sabhāyāṃ ye samāsate,
uktavanto? yathā|tattvaṃ tad brūhi tvaṃ, Janārdana.

VAISHAMPÁYANA said:

WHEN KÉSHAVA THE enemy-tamer reached Upaplávya from Hástina·pura, he told the Pándavas everything that had happened; and having talked and deliberated repeatedly for a very long while, Shauri went to his own dwelling for a rest. The five Pándava brothers then dismissed all the kings, led by Viráta, and once the sun had set they worshipped the twilight. But their minds wandered to Krishna, so they brought Dashárha before them and consulted once again about their plans. 147.1

SHTHIRA said:

What did you say to Dhrita·rashtra's son when you went to the elephant city's court, lotus-eyed Krishna? You ought to repeat it to us. 147.5

VASUDÉVA replied:

When I went to the elephant city's court I gave Dhrita·rashtra's son suitable, proper, and beneficial advice, but the wicked-minded man would not accept it.

SHTHIRA said:

Once he had left the proper path, what did the aged Kuru grandfather say to impatient Duryódhana, Hrishikésha? What did the teacher son of Bharad·vaja say, noble man? Or what did his father Dhrita·rashtra or Gandhári say to him? What did our junior father the steward, the greatest of all who understand law, say to Dhrita·rashtra's son as he burned with grief for us as his sons? What did all the kings 147.10
who sat in court have to say? Tell us exactly what happened, Janárdana.

uktavān hi bhavān sarvaṃ vacanaṃ Kuru|mukhyayoḥ,
Dhārtarāṣṭrasya teṣāṃ hi vacanaṃ Kuru|saṃsadi,
kāma|lobh'|âbhibhūtasya, mandasya, prājña|māninaḥ;
a|priyaṃ hṛdaye mahyaṃ tan na tiṣṭhati, Keśava.
teṣāṃ vākyāni, Govinda, śrotum icchāmy ahaṃ, vibho.
yathā ca n' âbhipadyeta kālas, tāta, tathā kuru.
bhavān hi no gatiḥ, Kṛṣṇa, bhavān nātho, bhavān guruḥ.

VĀSUDEVA uvāca:

śṛṇu, rājan, yathā vākyam ukto rājā Suyodhanaḥ
madhye Kurūṇāṃ, rāj'|êndra, sabhāyāṃ, tan nibodha me.
147.15 mayā viśrāvite vākye jahāsa Dhṛtarāṣṭra|jaḥ.
atha Bhīṣmaḥ su|saṃkruddha idaṃ vacanam abravīt:
«Duryodhana, nibodh' êdaṃ, kul'|ârthe yad bravīmi te;
tac chrutvā, rāja|śārdūla, sva|kulasya hitaṃ kuru.
mama, tāta, pitā, rājañ, Śāntanur loka|viśrutaḥ.
tasy' âham eka ev' āsaṃ putraḥ putravatāṃ varaḥ.
tasya buddhiḥ samutpannā, ‹dvitīyaḥ syāt kathaṃ sutaḥ?›
eka|putram a|putraṃ vai pravadanti manīṣiṇaḥ,
‹na c' ôcchedaṃ kulaṃ yāyād, vistīryec ca kathaṃ yaśaḥ?›
tasy' âham īpsitaṃ buddhvā Kālīṃ mātaram āvaham.
147.20 pratijñāṃ duṣ|karāṃ kṛtvā pitur arthe kulasya ca
a|rājā c' ōrdhva|retāś ca, yathā su|viditaṃ tava,
pratīto nivasāmy eṣa pratijñām anupālayan.

You did indeed tell us everything the leading pair of Kurus said in the Kuru assembly to the Dhartaráshtra, the fool overwhelmed with lust and greed who thinks he is wise; but unpleasant matters do not stay in my heart, Késhava. So I would like to hear their words again, lord Govínda. My friend, act to prevent time passing us by, for you are our path, our protector, and our guru, Krishna.

VASUDÉVA replied:

Listen, king, to what King Suyódhana was told in court in the midst of the Kurus, and pay attention to me, lord of kings. Once I had had my say, Dhrita·rashtra's son laughed, 147.15
and then Bhishma became incredibly furious and said these words:

"Duryódhana, listen to this, for what I will say is for the benefit of the lineage, and once you have heard it, tiger-like king, then act in your own family's interest.

My boy, my father was world-renowned Shántanu, king, and I was his only son, the greatest of those who have sons. But he wondered how he could have a second son, for as the wise say, only one son is no son. 'I pray my line is not cut down, and I pray my fame spreads,' he implored. And because I knew what he desired, I brought Kali to be my mother. As you well know, I made a difficult promise for 147.20
the sake of my father and my line, to be chaste and not to be a king, and so I live here firmly resolved, protecting my vow.

tasyāṃ jajñe mahā|bāhuḥ śrīmān Kuru|kul'|ôdvahaḥ
Vicitravīryo dharm'|ātmā kanīyān mama, pārthiva.
svar|yāte 'haṃ pitari taṃ sva|rājye saṃnyaveśayam
Vicitravīryaṃ rājānaṃ, bhṛtyo bhūtvā hy adhaś|caraḥ.
tasy' âhaṃ sadṛśān dārān, rāj'|êndra, samupāharam,
jitvā pārthiva|saṅghātam—api te bahuśaḥ śrutam.
tato Rāmeṇa samare dvandva|yuddham upāgamam,
sa hi Rāma|bhayād ebhir nāgarair vipravāsitaḥ,
147.25 dāreṣv apy atisaktaś ca yakṣmāṇaṃ samapadyata.
yadā tv a|rājake rāṣṭre na vavarṣa sur'|ēśvaraḥ,
tad" âbhyadhāvan mām eva prajāḥ kṣud|bhaya|pīḍitāḥ.»

PRAJĀ ūcuḥ:

upakṣīṇāḥ prajāḥ sarvā; rājā bhava bhavāya naḥ,
ītīḥ praṇuda, bhadraṃ te, Śāntanoḥ kula|vardhana!
pīḍyante te prajāḥ sarvā vyādhibhir bhṛśa|dāruṇaiḥ
alp'|âvaśiṣṭā, Gāṅgeya; tāḥ paritrātum arhasi.
vyādhīn praṇuda, vīra, tvaṃ, prajā dharmeṇa pālaya.
tvayi jīvati mā rāṣṭraṃ vināśam upagacchatu!

BHĪṢMA uvāca:

prajānāṃ krośatīnāṃ vai n' âiv' âkṣubhyata me manaḥ
pratijñāṃ rakṣamāṇasya sad|vṛttaṃ smaratas tathā.
147.30 tataḥ paurā, mahā|rāja, mātā Kālī ca me śubhā,
bhṛtyāḥ, purohit'|ācāryā, brāhmaṇāś ca bahu|śrutāḥ
mām ūcur bhṛśa|saṃtaptā «bhava rāj" êti» santatam.
«Pratīpa|rakṣitaṃ rāṣṭraṃ tvāṃ prāpya vinaśiṣyati.

Long-armed, glorious, righteous-souled Vichítra·virya was born to that lady, as the enhancer of the Kuru lineage and my younger brother, king. Once my father had gone to heaven I installed Vichítra·virya as king in my kingdom, and I became his servant, lower than him. I brought him suitable wives, lord of kings, defeating gathered sovereigns —but you have heard this many times. Next I was involved in a duel, in conflict with Rama,* for Vichítra·virya was exiled by his townsmen for fear of Rama, and being overly 147.25
attached to his wives he succumbed to consumption. Then when Indra, the lord of gods, no longer rained on their kingless kingdom, the citizens, afflicted by famine and fear, ran to me."

THE CITIZENS said:

All the citizens are in decline, so be our king and help us prosper. Repel our natural disasters, bless you, augmenter of Shántanu's lineage! All the subjects are oppressed by particularly horrible diseases and few remain now, son of the Ganges, so you ought to save us. Drive away disease, hero, and protect the citizens with law. Don't let the kingdom fall into ruin in your own lifetime!

BHISHMA said:

The subjects' lamentation did not disturb my resolve, and so, keeping good conduct in mind, I protected my promise. Great sovereign, the townspeople, my beautiful 147.30
mother Kali, the servants, family priests, teachers, and brahmins of great learning burned intensely, and incessantly they said to me "Be King! The kingdom that was protected

sa tvam asmadd|hit'|ârthaṃ vai rājā bhava, mahā|mate.»
ity uktaḥ prāñjalir bhūtvā duḥkhito, bhṛśam āturaḥ,
tebhyo nyavedayaṃ tatra pratijñāṃ pitṛ|gauravāt
ūrdhvaretā hy a|rājā ca, kulasy' ârthe punaḥ punaḥ,
«viśeṣatas tvad|arthaṃ ca. dhuri mā māṃ niyojaya.»
tato 'haṃ prāñjalir bhūtvā mātaraṃ saṃprasādayam.
«n', âmba, Śāntanunā jātaḥ Kauravaṃ vaṃśam udvahan
147.35 pratijñāṃ vitathāṃ kuryām» iti, rājan, punaḥ punaḥ,
«viśeṣatas tvad|arthaṃ ca pratijñāṃ kṛtavān aham.
ahaṃ preṣyaś ca dāsaś ca tav' âdya, suta|vatsale.»
evaṃ tām anunīy' âhaṃ mātaraṃ, janam eva ca,
ayācaṃ bhrātṛ|dāreṣu tadā Vyāsaṃ mahā|munim,
saha mātrā, mahā|rāja, prasādya tam ṛṣiṃ tadā
apaty'|ârthaṃ, mahā|rāja; prasādaṃ kṛtavāṃś ca saḥ.
trīn sa putrān ajanayat tadā, Bharata|sattama.
andhaḥ karaṇa|hīnatvān na vai rājā pitā tava;
rājā tu Pāṇḍur abhavan mah"|ātmā loka|viśrutaḥ.
147.40 sa rājā, tasya te putrāḥ pitur dāyādya|hāriṇaḥ;
mā, tāta, kalahaṃ kārṣī, rājyasy' ârdhaṃ pradīyatām.
mayi jīvati rājyaṃ kaḥ saṃpraśāset pumān iha?
m" âvamaṃsthā vaco mahyaṃ, śamam icchāmi vaḥ sadā.
na viśeṣo 'sti me, putra, tvayi teṣu ca, pārthiva,
matam etat pitus tubhyaṃ, Gāndhāryā, Vidurasya ca.

by Pratípa will be destroyed now that it has passed to you. For our benefit, become our king, great wise man."

When they said these things to me I miserably put my hands together, intensely pained, and I told them time and again of the vow I made out of respect for my father, to remain chaste and to refuse kingship for the sake of my line. "I did it for you in particular. Do not to compel me to carry this burden," I begged my mother, and putting my hands together again I soothed her, saying, "Mother, I was begotten by Shántanu and carry on the Kuru lineage, but I can- 147.35
not break my vow." So it was that I spoke time and again, king, and I added, "It was for your sake in particular that I made this vow. I am now your servant and slave, affectionate lady to your son."

Once I had pacified my mother and the people, I asked the mighty sage Vyasa to have children with my brother's wives. So it was that I conciliated the sage with my mother, great sovereign, and begged him for children, mighty king. And he granted us the favor and begat three sons, greatest of the Bharatas.

Your father was blind, and it was because of his lack of sight that he could not be king. So high-souled and world-renowned Pandu was king. He was king and his sons must 147.40
take their father's inheritance, so do not quarrel, my son, but give them their half of the kingdom.

Which man in this world deserves to rule while I am alive? Do not ignore my advice, for I always wish for peace. I make no distinction between you, my son, and them, king. This is the opinion of your father, Gandhári, and Vídura. Your elders should indeed be heard, so do not have any

śrotavyam khalu vṛddhānāṃ n' âbhiśaṅkīr vaco mama;
nāśayiṣyasi mā sarvam, ātmānaṃ, pṛthivīṃ tathā.

VĀSUDEVA uvāca:

148.1 BHĪṢMEṆ' ÓKTE tato Droṇo Duryodhanam abhāṣata
madhye nṛpāṇāṃ, bhadraṃ te, vacanaṃ vacana|kṣamaḥ:
«Prātīpaḥ Śāntanus, tāta, kulasy' ârthe yathā sthitaḥ,
yathā Devavrato Bhīṣmaḥ kulasy' ârthe sthito 'bhavat,
tathā Pāṇḍur nara|patiḥ satya|sandho, jit'|êndriyaḥ,
rājā Kurūṇāṃ dharm'|ātmā, suvrataḥ, su|samāhitaḥ
jyeṣṭhāya rājyam adadad Dhṛtarāṣṭrāya dhīmate,
yavīyase tathā kṣattre Kurūṇāṃ vaṃśa|vardhanaḥ.
148.5 tataḥ siṃh'|āsane, rājan, sthāpayitv" âinam a|cyutam,
vanaṃ jagāma Kauravyo bhāryābhyāṃ sahito nṛpaḥ.
nīcaiḥ sthitvā tu Vidura upāste sma vinītavat,
preṣyavat puruṣa|vyāghro vāla|vyajanam utkṣipan.
tataḥ sarvāḥ prajās, tāta, Dhṛtarāṣṭraṃ jan'|ēśvaram
anvapadyanta vidhivad, yathā Pāṇḍuṃ jan'|âdhipam.
visṛjya Dhṛtarāṣṭrāya rājyaṃ sa|Vidurāya ca,
cacāra pṛthivīṃ Pāṇḍuḥ sarvāṃ para|purañ|jayaḥ.
kośa|saṃvanane, dāne, bhṛtyānāṃ c' ânvavekṣaṇe,
bharaṇe c' âiva sarvasya Viduraḥ satya|saṅgaraḥ.
148.10 sandhi|vigraha|saṃyukto rājñāṃ saṃvāhana|kriyāḥ
avaikṣata mahā|tejā Bhīṣmaḥ para|purañ|jayaḥ.
siṃh'|āsana|stho nṛ|patir Dhṛtarāṣṭro mahā|balaḥ

doubts about my advice, lest you destroy everything, yourself and the earth included.

VASUDÉVA said:

ONCE BHISHMA HAD said his piece, eloquently spoken 148.1
Drona addressed Duryódhana amid the kings, bless you, in these words:

"Just as Pratípa's son Shántanu was intent on his family's welfare, so Bhishma Deva·vrata was standing for his lineage's interest. So Pandu, the lord of men of disciplined senses, who was intent on truth, law-souled, strict-vowed, and devoted, was the king of the Kurus. Eventually the augmenter of the Kuru line gave his kingdom to wise Dhrita·
rashtra, his elder, and to the steward Vídura, his junior. And 148.5
once he had established imperishable Dhrita·rashtra on his lion throne, my king, the Kaurávya king went to the forest with his two wives.

Tiger-like Vídura remained below Dhrita·rashtra, waiting on him humbly, serving him, and raising the yak-tailed chowrie. All the subjects duly followed Dhrita·rashtra as their lord, just as they had followed Pandu as king of men. And once he had handed his kingdom over to Dhrita·rashtra and Vídura, Pandu, the conqueror of enemy cities, traveled the whole earth.

Vídura, true to his agreement, dealt with acquisition for the treasury, gifts, overseeing the servants, and general
maintenance. Great splendid Bhishma, the sacker of enemy 148.10
cities, was entrusted with the job of making peace and war, and oversaw the making and taking of kings' gifts, while

anvāsyamānaḥ satataṃ Vidureṇa mah"|ātmanā.
  kathaṃ tasya kule jātaḥ
    kula|bhedaṃ vyavasyasi?
sambhūya bhrātṛbhiḥ sārdhaṃ
    bhuṅkṣva bhogāñ, jan'|âdhipa.
bravīmy ahaṃ na kārpaṇyān, n' ârtha|hetoḥ kathañ cana;
Bhīṣmeṇa dattam icchāmi, na tvayā, rāja|sattama.
n' âhaṃ tvatto 'bhikāṅkṣiṣye vṛtty|upāyaṃ, jan'|âdhipa.
yato Bhīṣmas tato Droṇo. yad Bhīṣmas tv āha tat kuru.
148.15 dīyatāṃ Pāṇḍu|putrebhyo rājy'|ârdham, ari|karśana.
samam ācāryakaṃ, tāta, tava teṣāṃ ca me sadā.
Aśvatthāmā yathā mahyaṃ, tathā śveta|hayo mama.
bahunā kiṃ pralāpena? yato dharmas tato jayaḥ.»

VĀSUDEVA uvāca:

evam ukte, mahā|rāja, Droṇen' âmita|tejasā
vyājahāra tato vākyaṃ Viduraḥ satya|saṅgaraḥ
pitur vadanam anvīkṣya parivṛtya ca dharma|vit:

VIDURA uvāca:

Devavrata, nibodh' êdaṃ vacanaṃ mama bhāṣataḥ
pranaṣṭaḥ Kauravo vaṃśas tvay" âyaṃ punar uddhṛtaḥ.
tan me vilapamānasya vacanaṃ samupekṣase.
ko 'yaṃ Duryodhano nāma kule 'smin kula|pāṃsanaḥ,
148.20 yasya lobh'|âbhibhūtasya matiṃ samanuvartase,
an|āryasy', â|kṛta|jñasya, lobhena hṛta|cetasaḥ,
atikrāmati yaḥ śāstraṃ pitur dharm'|ârtha|darśinaḥ?

powerful King Dhrita·rashtra remained on his lion throne always accompanied by high-souled Vídura.

How is it that you have resolved upon division in the family when you were born in this line? Enjoy your pleasures with your brothers, lord of men. I am not telling you any of this because I am inspired by greed, or for the sake of gain, for I want Bhishma to support me, not you, greatest of kings. I do not hope for any means to support myself from you, lord of men. Where Bhishma goes, Drona follows. Do what Bhishma says, and grant half the king- 148.15
dom to the sons of Pandu, enemy-plower. I have always acted equally as a teacher to both you and them, my son, and white-horsed Árjuna is as dear to me as Ashva·tthaman. What is the point of chattering on at length? Where there is law there is victory."

VASUDÉVA said:

When immeasurably glorious Drona had said this, great sovereign, law-wise Vídura, who was true to his agreements, turned and looked his father Bhishma in the face, and said these words:

VÍDURA said:

Deva·vrata, hear what I have to say. The Káuravan lineage was ruined and you raised it up again, but you ignore what I say when I moan. Who is this man named Duryódhana in our line, the destroyer of his lineage, that you fol- 148.20
low his opinion though he is overwhelmed by greed, even though he is ignoble, ungrateful, greedy, and robbed of his mind, a man who oversteps the command of his father who perceives the meaning of law?

ete naśyanti Kuravo Duryodhana|kṛtena vai.
yathā te na praṇaśyeyur, mahā|rāja, tathā kuru.
māṃ c' âiva Dhṛtarāṣṭraṃ ca pūrvam eva, mahā|mate,
citra|kāra iv' ālekhyaṃ kṛtvā sthāpitavān asi.
Prajāpatiḥ prajāḥ sṛṣṭvā yathā saṃharate, tathā
n' ôpekṣasva, mahā|bāho, paśyamānaḥ kula|kṣayam.
atha te 'dya matir naṣṭā vināśe pratyupasthite,
148.25 vanaṃ gaccha mayā sārdhaṃ, Dhṛtarāṣṭreṇa c' âiva ha,
baddhvā vā nikṛti|prajñaṃ Dhārtarāṣṭraṃ su|durmatim,
śādh' îdaṃ rājyam ady' āśu Pāṇḍavair abhirakṣitam.
prasīda, rāja|śārdūla, vināśo dṛśyate mahān
Pāṇḍavānāṃ Kurūṇāṃ ca rājñām a|mita|tejasām.
virarām' âivam uktvā tu Viduro dīna|mānasaḥ,
pradhyāyamānaḥ sa tadā, niḥśvasaṃś ca punaḥ punaḥ.
tato 'tha rājñaḥ Subalasya putrī
dharm'|ârtha|yuktaṃ kula|nāśa|bhītā
Duryodhanaṃ pāpa|matiṃ nṛśaṃsaṃ
rājñāṃ samakṣaṃ sutam āha kopāt:
«ye pārthivā rāja|sabhāṃ praviṣṭā,
brahma'|rṣayo ye ca sabhā|sado 'nye,
śṛṇavantu, vakṣyāmi tav' âparādhaṃ
pāpasya s'|âmātya|paricchadasya.
148.30 rājyaṃ Kurūṇām anupūrva|bhojyaṃ
kram'|āgato, naḥ kula|dharma eṣaḥ,
tvaṃ, pāpa|buddhe 'tinṛśaṃsa|karman,
rājyaṃ Kurūṇām a|nayād vihaṃsi.

The Kurus are being ruined through Duryódhana's doing. Act to prevent their destruction, great sovereign. In the past you established both me and Dhrita·rashtra in our positions, just as a painter creates a picture, highly wise man, but just as Praja·pati created the creatures, he destroys them. Do not watch the destruction of your line and ignore it, long-armed man.

But now, if your mind is gone on the eve of destruction, go to the forest with me and Dhrita·rashtra. Or tie up the 148.25
utterly evil Dhartaráshtra whose wisdom lies in wrongdoing, and quickly rule this kingdom today, guarded by the Pándavas. Have mercy, tiger-like king, for the great destruction of the immeasurably splendid Pándava and Kuru kings is at hand.

Once he had finished speaking, Vídura felt despondent in his mind, and he sighed over and over again as he reflected on the matter.

Then Súbala's daughter, fearing the destruction of her family, addressed her evil-minded and cruel son Duryódhana angrily and openly before the kings, in words which complied with law and profit.

"Let the kings who have entered the royal court, the brahmin sages, and other courtiers listen, for I will tell of your guilt and that of your evil retinue of advisors. The Ku- 148.30
rus' kingdom is to be enjoyed in succession, for this is our inherited family law, but you, evil-minded and excessively cruel-acting man, destroy the Kurus' kingdom through your bad policy.

rājye sthito Dhṛtarāṣṭro manīṣī,
tasy' ânujo Viduro dīrgha|darśī.
etāv atikramya kathaṃ nṛpatvaṃ,
Duryodhana, prārthayase 'dya mohāt?
rājā ca kṣattā ca mah"|ânubhāvau
Bhīṣme sthite paravantau bhavetām.
ayaṃ tu dharmajñatayā mah"|ātmā
na kāmayed yo nṛ|varo nadī|jaḥ.
rājyaṃ tu Pāṇḍor idam a|pradhṛṣyaṃ
tasy' âdya putrāḥ prabhavanti, n' ânye;
rājyaṃ tad etan nikhilaṃ Pāṇḍavānāṃ
paitāmahaṃ putra|pautr'|ânugāmi.
yad vai brūte Kuru|mukhyo mah"|ātmā
Devavrataḥ satya|sandho, manīṣī,
sarvaṃ tad asmābhir a|hatya kāryaṃ
rājyaṃ sva|dharmān paripālayadbhiḥ.
148.35 anujñayā c' âtha mahā|vratasya
brūyān nṛpo 'yaṃ Viduras tath" âiva.
kāryaṃ bhavet tat su|hṛdbhir niyojyaṃ,
dharmaṃ puras|kṛtya su|dīrgha|kālam.
nyāy'|āgataṃ rājyam idaṃ Kurūṇāṃ
Yudhiṣṭhiraḥ śāstu vai Dharma|putraḥ,
pracodito Dhṛtarāṣṭreṇa rājñā,
puras|kṛtaḥ Śāntanavena c' âiva.»

VĀSUDEVA uvāca:

149.1 EVAM UKTE TU Gāndhāryā Dhṛtarāṣṭro jan'|ēśvaraḥ
Duryodhanam uvāc' êdaṃ rāja|madhye, jan'|âdhipa:
«Duryodhana, nibodh' êdaṃ yat tvāṃ vakṣyāmi, putraka
tathā tat kuru, bhadraṃ te, yady asti pitṛ|gauravam.

Wise Dhrita·rashtra is established in this kingdom, as is his farsighted younger brother Vídura, but you disobey them both. How is it that you strive for kingship in your folly, Duryódhana? Both the powerful king and the steward ought to remain subject to Bhishma while he still stands, but the high-souled son of the Ganges would not desire kingship, for he understands law. This invincible kingdom belonged to Pandu, and so now his sons, and no others, have the power. This kingdom in its entirety belongs to the Pándavas. It is their ancestral kingdom, and it will fall to their sons and grandsons.

We must do everything that the high-souled leading Kuru —the wise Deva·vrata who is true to his word—tells us, without it being diminished, if we are to protect our kingdom and our own laws. And with this strict-vowed man's 148.35
leave, the king and Vídura should speak in a similar manner. This is a task which our friends must undertake, putting the law first for a long time to come. Let Yudhi·shthira, the son of Dharma, rule this lawfully won kingdom of the Kurus, urged on by King Dhrita·rashtra and put first by Shántanu's son."

VASUDÉVA said:

WHEN GANDHÁRI had said this, Dhrita·rashtra, lord of 149.1
his people, spoke to Duryódhana amid the kings, lord of men:

"Duryódhana, listen to what I will say to you, my boy, then act accordingly, bless you, if you have any respect for your father.

Somaḥ Prajāpatiḥ pūrvaṃ Kurūṇāṃ vaṃśa|vardhanaḥ;
Somād babhūva ṣaṣṭho 'yaṃ Yayātir Nahuṣ'|ātmajaḥ.
tasya putrā babhūvur hi pañca rāja'|rṣi|sattamāḥ;
teṣāṃ Yadur mahā|tejā jyeṣṭhaḥ samabhavat prabhuḥ.

149.5 Pūrur yavīyāṃś ca tato yo 'smākaṃ vaṃśa|vardhanaḥ
Śarmiṣṭhayā saṃprasūto duhitrā Vṛṣaparvaṇaḥ.

Yaduś ca, Bharata|śreṣṭha, Devayānyāḥ suto 'bhavat,
dauhitras, tāta, Śukrasya Kāvyasy' â|mita|tejasaḥ.
Yādavānāṃ kula|karo balavān vīrya|sammataḥ,
avamene sa tu kṣatraṃ darpa|pūrṇaḥ su|manda|dhīḥ.
na c' âtiṣṭhat pituḥ śāstre bala|darpa|vimohitaḥ,
avamene ca pitaraṃ, bhrātṝṃś c' âpy a|parājitaḥ.
pṛthivyāṃ catur|antāyāṃ Yadur ev' âbhavad balī,
vaśe kṛtvā sa nṛ|patīn nyavasan nāga|s'|āhvaye.

149.10 taṃ pitā parama|kruddho Yayātir Nahuṣ'|ātmajaḥ
śaśāpa putraṃ, Gāndhāre, rājyāc c' âpi vyaropayat.
ye c' âinam anvavartanta bhrātaro bala|darpitāḥ,
śaśāpa tān abhikruddho Yayātis tanayān atha.
yavīyāṃsaṃ tataḥ Pūruṃ putraṃ sva|vaśa|vartinam
rājye niveśayām āsa vidheyaṃ nṛpa|sattamaḥ.

evaṃ jyeṣṭho 'py ath' ôtsikto na rājyam abhijāyate;
yavīyāṃso 'pi jāyante rājyaṃ vṛddh'|ôpasevayā.

Soma Praja·pati was the first to cause the lineage to thrive, and Yayáti, the son of Náhusha, was the sixth after Soma. He had five sons, exceptional royal sages, the eldest of whom
was the great splendid lord Yadu. The youngest, Puru, who 149.5
augmented our lineage, was the son of Sharmíshtha, the daughter of Vrisha·parvan.

Yadu was the scion of Devayáni, greatest of the Bharatas, and the grandson of immeasurably energetic Shukra Kavya on his mother's side, my son. The mighty founder of the Yádava line, who was esteemed for his heroism, despised the warrior class, for he was full of pride and extremely foolish-minded. Confused by his arrogance in his strength, the undefeated man did not abide by his father's command and had nothing but contempt for his father and brothers. Yadu was powerful throughout the four corners of the world, and once he had brought the kings under his control, he lived in the city of the elephant.

His father Yayáti, son of Náhusha, was absolutely furious 149.10
and cursed his son, O son of Gandhári, exiling him from the kingdom. Enraged Yayáti also cursed those of his sons who followed their brother, proud of his strength. Then Yayáti, the greatest of kings, established his youngest son Puru as king in the kingdom, and he was compliant and obedient to his will.

So it is that even an eldest son is not necessarily born to kingship if he is haughty, and even the youngest can be born to kingship by attending to his elders.

tath" âiva sarva|dharma|jñaḥ pitur mama pitā|mahaḥ
Pratīpaḥ pṛthivī|pālas triṣu lokeṣu viśrutaḥ.
149.15 tasya pārthiva|siṃhasya rājyaṃ dharmeṇa śāsataḥ
trayaḥ prajajñire putrā deva|kalpā yaśasvinaḥ.
Devāpir abhavac chreṣṭho, Bāhlīkas tad|an|antaram,
tṛtīyaḥ Śāntanus, tāta, dhṛtimān me pitā|mahaḥ.
Devāpis tu mahā|tejās tvag|doṣī, rāja|sattamaḥ,
dhārmikaḥ, satya|vādī ca, pituḥ śuśrūṣaṇe rataḥ.
paura|jānapadānāṃ ca sammataḥ, sādhu|satkṛtaḥ,
sarveṣāṃ bāla|vṛddhānāṃ Devāpir hṛdayaṃ|gamaḥ.
vadānyaḥ, satya|sandhaś ca, sarva|bhūta|hite rataḥ,
vartamānaḥ pituḥ śāstre, brāhmaṇānāṃ mah"|ātmanām.
149.20 Bāhlīkasya priyo bhrātā, Śāntanoś ca mah"|ātmanaḥ,
saubhrātraṃ ca paraṃ teṣāṃ sahitānāṃ mah"|ātmanām.

atha kālasya paryāye vṛddho nṛpati|sattamaḥ
sambhārān abhiṣek'|ârthaṃ kārayām āsa śāstrataḥ.
kārayām āsa sarvāṇi maṅgal'|ârthāni vai vibhuḥ.
taṃ brāhmaṇāś ca vṛddhāś ca paura|jānapadaiḥ saha
sarve nivārayām āsur Devāper abhiṣecanam.
sa tac chrutvā tu nṛ|patir abhiṣeka|nivāraṇam
aśru|kaṇṭho 'bhavad rājā, paryaśocata c' ātma|jam.

evaṃ vadānyo, dharma|jñaḥ, satya|sandhaś ca so 'bhavat,
priyaḥ prajānām api saṃs, tvag|doṣeṇa pradūṣitaḥ.
149.25 hīn'|âṅgaṃ pṛthivī|pālaṃ n' âbhinandanti devatāḥ,
iti kṛtvā nṛpa|śreṣṭhaṃ pratyaṣedhan dvija'|rṣabhāḥ.
tataḥ pravyathit'|âṅgo 'sau putra|śoka|samanvitaḥ
nivāritaṃ nṛpaṃ dṛṣṭvā Devāpiḥ saṃśrito vanam.

Similarly, my father's grandfather Pratípa—a scholar of all law, an earth-protector who was famed in the three worlds, and a lion-like illustrious king who ruled his king- 149.15
dom with law—begat three god-like sons. Devápi was the eldest, Báhlika was next, and Shántanu, my firm grandfather, was the third, my son. Great glorious Devápi, the truthful, virtuous, and most excellent of kings, delighted in obeying his father, but he had leprosy. Devápi was esteemed by the townspeople, treated well by good men, and dear to the hearts of all, young and old. He was eloquent, true to his word, took delight in what benefitted all creatures, and abided by the commands of his father as well as those of the high-souled brahmins. He was a dear brother 149.20
to Báhlika and high-souled Shántanu, and the brotherhood of those three high-souled men was exemplary.

In the passage of time his aged father, the greatest of kings, caused the preparations for consecration to be performed according to the sacred writings, and the lord had all the auspicious rites performed. The brahmins, however, and the elders and townspeople all prevented Devápi's consecration. When the king heard that his son's consecration had been prevented, his throat welled with tears and the king grieved for his son.

So it was that although the eloquent scholar of law was true to his word and dear to his subjects, he was polluted by his leprosy. The gods do not rejoice in a king who is 149.25
physically impaired, and so the bull-like brahmins denied the greatest of kings. When Devápi, physically impaired, saw the king filled with grief for his son and with his plans scuppered, he resorted to the forest.

Bāhlīko mātula|kulaṃ tyaktvā rājyaṃ samāśritaḥ,
pitṛ|bhrātṝn parityajya prāptavān puram ṛddhimat.†
Bāhlīkena tv anujñātaḥ Śāntanur loka|viśrutaḥ
pitary uparate, rājan, rājā rājyam akārayat.
tath" âiv' âhaṃ matimatā paricinty' êha Pāṇḍunā
jyeṣṭhaḥ prabhraṃśito rājyādd, hīn'|âṅga iti, Bhārata.
149.30 Pāṇḍus tu rājyaṃ saṃprāptaḥ kanīyān api san nṛpaḥ,
vināśe tasya putrāṇām idaṃ rājyam, arin|dama.
mayy a|bhāgini rājyāya kathaṃ tvaṃ rājyam icchasi?
a|rāja|putro hy a|svāmī para|svaṃ hartum icchasi.
Yudhiṣṭhiro rāja|putro mah"|ātmā;
nyāy'|āgataṃ rājyam idaṃ ca tasya.
sa Kauravasy' âsya kulasya bhartā,
praśāsitā c' âiva mah"|ânubhāvaḥ.
sa satya|sandhaḥ, sa tath" â|pramattaḥ,
śāstre sthito, bandhu|janasya sādhuḥ,
priyaḥ prajānāṃ, su|hṛd" ânukampī,
jit'|êndriyaḥ, sādhu|janasya bhartā.
kṣamā, titikṣā, dama, ārjavaṃ ca,
satya|vratatvaṃ, śrutam, a|pramādaḥ,
bhūt'|ânukampā hy, anuśāsanaṃ ca:
Yudhiṣṭhire rāja|guṇāḥ samastāḥ.
149.35 a|rāja|putras tvam, an|ārya|vṛtto,
lubdhaḥ sadā, bandhuṣu pāpa|buddhiḥ,
kram'|āgataṃ rājyam idaṃ pareṣāṃ
hartuṃ kathaṃ śakṣyasi, dur|vinīta?
prayaccha rājy'|ârdham apeta|mohaḥ
sa|vāhanaṃ tvaṃ sa|paricchadaṃ ca;

Báhlika abandoned his kingdom and resorted to his maternal uncle's family. He abandoned his father and brothers and won an enormously wealthy kingdom, and, with Báhlika's permission, world-famous Shántanu ruled the kingdom as its sovereign when his father died, my king.

Similarly, after wise Pandu gave it some thought, I too
was deprived of my kingdom, though I was the eldest, because I was physically impaired, Bhárata. Pandu acquired 149.30
the kingdom as king although he was younger, and when
he died his kingdom passed to his sons, enemy-tamer. How
is it that you desire the kingdom, when I could not inherit
it? You are not the king's son, and you do not own the kingdom, but you wish to take what belongs to another.

Yudhi·shthira is the high-souled son of the king, and so this kingdom passes rightfully to him. He is the noble sustainer and ruler of the Kuru lineage. He is true to his word and attentive. He is a good man who abides by the command of his relatives. He is popular with his subjects and compassionate to his friends. He has disciplined his senses and supports good men. Yudhi·shthira has all the royal virtues: forgiveness, patience, control, honesty, true adherence to vows, learning, attentiveness, compassion for creatures, and command.

But you are not the king's son. You are ignoble in your 149.35
conduct, ever avaricious and evilly disposed to your relatives, so how is it that you wish to be able to seize this kingdom which has passed to others in succession, ill-behaved
man? Free of your idiocy, bestow half the kingdom upon
the Pándavas along with horses and paraphernalia. Then

tato 'vaśeṣaṃ tava jīvitasya
sah'|ânujasy' âiva bhaven, nar'|êndra.»

VĀSUDEVA uvāca:

150.1 EVAM UKTE TU Bhīṣmeṇa, Droṇena, Vidureṇa ca,
Gāndhāryā, Dhṛtarāṣṭreṇa, na vai mando 'nvabudhyata.
avadhūy' ôtthito mandaḥ krodha|saṃrakta|locanaḥ;
anvadravanta taṃ paścād rājānas tyakta|jīvitāḥ.
ājñāpayac ca rājñas tān
pārthivān naṣṭa|cetasaḥ:
«prayādhvaṃ vai Kurukṣetram,
Puṣyo 'dy' êti» punaḥ punaḥ.
tatas te pṛthivī|pālāḥ prayayuḥ saha|sainikāḥ
Bhīṣmaṃ senā|patiṃ kṛtvā saṃhṛṣṭāḥ, kāla|coditāḥ.
150.5 akṣauhiṇyo daś' âikā ca Kauravāṇāṃ samāgatāḥ;
tāsāṃ pramukhato Bhīṣmas tāla|ketur vyarocata.
yad atra yuktaṃ prāptaṃ ca, tad vidhatsva, viśām pate.
uktaṃ Bhīṣmeṇa yad vākyaṃ, Droṇena Vidureṇa ca,
Gāndhāryā, Dhṛtarāṣṭreṇa, samakṣaṃ mama, Bhārata,
etat te kathitaṃ, rājan, yad vṛttaṃ Kuru|saṃsadi.
sāmyam ādau prayuktaṃ me, rājan, saubhrātram icchatā,
a|bhedāy' âsya vaṃśasya, prajānāṃ ca vivṛddhaye.
punar bhedaś ca me yukto, yadā sāma na gṛhyate,
karm'|ânukīrtanaṃ c' âiva deva|mānuṣa|saṃhitam.
150.10 yadā n' âdriyate vākyaṃ sāma|pūrvaṃ Suyodhanaḥ,
tadā mayā samānīya bheditāḥ sarva|pārthivāḥ,
adbhutāni ca ghorāṇi dāruṇāni ca, Bhārata,
a|mānuṣāṇi karmāṇi darśitāni mayā, vibho.
nirbhartsayitvā rājñas tāṃs, tṛṇī|kṛtya Suyodhanam,

you and your brothers may live out the rest of your lives, lord of men."

VASUDÉVA continued:

THOUGH ADVISED so wisely by Bhishma, Drona, Vídura, 150.1
Gandhári, and Dhrita·rashtra, the fool did not take it in. The idiot shook off their advice and rose in fury, his eyes bloodshot with rage, and the kings who were prepared to sacrifice their lives for him hurried after him. Again and again King Duryódhana ordered those witless kings: "March to Kuru·kshetra, for the Pushya constellation is rising today!" So the earth-lords and their armies set out joyfully, impelled by fate, making Bhishma their army's general. Eleven battalions gathered on the Káurava side, with 150.5
palm-bannered Bhishma shining at their head.

So, then, arrange matters properly in view of the current situation, lord of the people. I have told you what Bhishma, Drona, Vídura, Gandhári, and Dhrita·rashtra said in my presence, Bhárata king, and I have told you what happened in the Kuru assembly. At first I employed conciliatory tactics, for I wished for brotherhood, for unity in this family, and for prosperity for the subjects, king.

I tried again, using divisionary tactics when peace was not accepted, and I mentioned your achievements, human and divine. When Suyódhana did not respect my first words 150.10
of conciliation, I then brought all the kings together and planted dissension among them. I displayed horrifying and terrible miracles: inhuman achievements, lord Bhárata. Threatening the kings, making light of Suyódhana, scaring Radhéya, and putting the blame for the Dhartaráshtras'

Rādheyaṃ bhīṣayitvā ca, Saubalaṃ ca punaḥ punaḥ,
dyūtato Dhārtarāṣṭrāṇāṃ nindāṃ kṛtvā tathā punaḥ,
bhedayitvā nṛpān sarvān vāgbhir mantreṇa c' â|sakṛt,
punaḥ sām'|âbhisaṃyuktaṃ saṃpradānam ath' âbruvam
a|bhedāt Kuru|vaṃśasya, kārya|yogāt tath" âiva ca.
150.15 «te śūrā Dhṛtarāṣṭrasya, Bhīṣmasya, Vidurasya ca
tiṣṭheyuḥ Pāṇḍavāḥ sarve hitvā mānam adhaś|carāḥ;
prayacchantu ca te rājyam, an|īśās te bhavantu ca.
yath" āha rājā Gāṅgeyo, Viduraś ca hitaṃ tava,
sarvaṃ bhavatu te rājyaṃ, pañca grāmān visarjaya;
a|vaśyaṃ bharaṇīyā hi pitus te, rāja|sattama.»
evam ukto 'pi duṣṭ'|ātmā n' âiva bhāgaṃ vyamuñcata.
daṇḍaṃ caturthaṃ paśyāmi teṣu pāpeṣu, n' ânyathā.
niryātāś ca vināśāya Kuru|kṣetraṃ nar'|âdhipāḥ.
etat te kathitaṃ, rājan, yad vṛttaṃ Kuru|saṃsadi.
150.20 na te rājyaṃ prayacchanti vinā yuddhena, Pāṇḍava,
vināśa|hetavaḥ sarve pratyupasthita|mṛtyavaḥ.

VAIŚAMPĀYANA uvāca:

151.1 JANĀRDANA|VACAḤ śrutvā dharma|rājo Yudhiṣṭhiraḥ
bhrātṝn uvāca dharm'|ātmā samakṣaṃ Keśavasya ha:
«śrutaṃ bhavadbhir yad vṛttaṃ sabhāyāṃ Kuru|saṃsadi,
Keśavasy' âpi yad vākyaṃ, tat sarvam avadhāritam;
tasmāt senā|vibhāgaṃ me kurudhvaṃ, nara|sattamāḥ.
akṣauhiṇyaś ca sapt" âitāḥ sametā vijayāya vai.

gambling match on Sáubala over and over again, I spread division among all the kings with my words and repeated counsel.

I employed conciliatory tactics once again, and I spoke of gifts for the sake of unity in the Kuru lineage and similarly to accomplish my task, saying, "All those brave Pán- 150.15
davas will do away with their pride and be at the disposal of Dhrita·rashtra, Bhishma, and Vídura, as their juniors. Let them grant you the kingdom, and let them be masters no more. Let matters be to your benefit, just as the king, Gangéya, and Vídura advise, and let the whole kingdom be yours; just release five villages, for they should certainly be supported by your father, greatest of kings."

But even though I spoke to him kindly, the wicked-souled man did not release your share. So I see no alternative left to us against those evil men but the fourth—punishment. The kings march to Kuru·kshetra for their destruction. I have told you what happened at the Kuru assembly, king. They will not grant you your kingdom with- 150.20
out war, Pándava, and as their deaths rise on the horizon, they are all the orchestrators of their own destruction.

VAISHAMPÁYANA said:

HAVING LISTENED to what Janárdana had told him, law- 151.1
souled Yudhi·shthira, the king of righteousness, addressed his brothers in Késhava's presence, saying:

"You have heard what happened in court in the Kuru assembly, and you have also heard everything Késhava had to say, so, best of men, draw up my army divisions. There are seven battalions assembled for victory.

tāsāṃ ye patayaḥ sapta. vikhyātās tān nibodhata:
Drupadaś ca, Virāṭaś ca, Dhṛṣṭadyumna|Śikhaṇḍino,
151.5 Sātyakiś, Cekitānaś ca, Bhīmasenaś ca vīryavān—
ete senā|praṇetāro vīrāḥ, sarve tanu|tyajaḥ;
sarve veda|vidaḥ śūrāḥ, sarve su|carita|vratāḥ,
hrīmanto, nītimantaś ca, sarve yuddha|viśāradāḥ,
iṣv|astra|kuśalāḥ sarve, tathā sarv'|âstra|yodhinaḥ.
saptānām api yo netā senānāṃ pravibhāga|vit,
taṃ tāvat, Sahadev', âtra prabrūhi, Kuru|nandana,
sva|mataṃ, puruṣa|vyāghra, ko naḥ senā|patiḥ kṣamaḥ.»

SAHADEVA uvāca:

saṃyukta, eka|duḥkhaś ca, vīryavāṃś ca mahī|patiḥ,
yaṃ samāśritya dharma|jñaṃ svam aṃśam anuyuñjmahe,
151.10 Matsyo Virāṭo balavān, kṛt'|âstro, yuddha|durmadaḥ
prasahiṣyati saṃgrāme Bhīṣmaṃ, tāṃś ca mahā|rathān.

VAIŚAMPĀYANA uvāca:

tath" ôkte Sahadevena vākye vākya|viśāradaḥ
Nakulo 'n|antaraṃ tasmād idaṃ vacanam ādade:
«vayasā, śāstrato, dhairyāt, kulen' âbhijanena ca;
hrīmān, bal'|ânvitaḥ, śrīmān, sarva|śāstra|viśāradaḥ;
veda c' âstraṃ Bharadvājād, dur|dharṣaḥ, satya|saṅgaraḥ,
yo nityaṃ spardhate Droṇaṃ Bhīṣmaṃ c' âiva mahā|balam;
ślāghyaḥ pārthiva|vaṃśasya pramukhe vāhinī|patiḥ;

There are seven generals for them. Listen as they are
named: Drúpada, Viráta, Dhrishta·dyumna and Shikhándin, Sátyaki, Chekitána, and heroic Bhima·sena. They are 151.5
all army-leading heroes who risk their lives. They are all
brave men who know the Veda, and they all practice their
vows excellently. They are all modest, good politicians, and
experienced in war. They are all skilled in the science of
archery, and equally all are fighters versed in every field of
weaponry.

So, then, which man with knowledge of the divisions is to be the leader of the seven armies? Tell us, tiger-like Saha·deva, descendant of the Kurus, who—in your opinion—is competent to be our general."

DEVA replied:

The only man who joined us in our misery, the law-wise
and powerful king upon whom we are relying to win back
our share of the kingdom, the mighty Matsyan sovereign 151.10
Viráta, who has mastered all weapons and lusts for war; he
is my choice, for he will be able to withstand Bhishma and
those mighty warriors in battle.

VAISHAMPÁYANA continued:

Once Saha·deva had voiced his opinion, eloquent Nákula immediately offered this advice:

"The man who excels by virtue of his age, his knowledge of scripture, his fortitude, his lineage, and his birth; the man who is modest, filled with strength, splendid, and experienced in every field of knowledge; the near invincible man who is true to his word, who has learned weaponry from Bharad·vaja, who always challenges Drona and the mighty

putra|pautraiḥ parivṛtaḥ, śata|śākha iva drumaḥ;
151.15 yas tatāpa tapo ghoraṃ sa|dāraḥ pṛthivī|patiḥ,
roṣād Droṇa|vināśāya; vīraḥ samiti|śobhanaḥ
pit" êv' âsmān samādhatte yaḥ sadā pārthiva'|ṛṣabhaḥ—
śvaśuro Drupado 'smākaṃ. sen"|âgraṃ sa prakarṣatu!
sa Droṇa|Bhīṣmāv āyātau sahed, iti matir mama;
sa hi divy'|âstra|vid rājā, sakhā c' Âṅgiraso nṛpaḥ.»
Mādrī|sutābhyām ukte tu sva|mate Kuru|nandanaḥ
Vāsavir Vāsava|samaḥ savya|sācy abravīd vacaḥ:
«yo 'yaṃ tapaḥ|prabhāveṇa' ṛṣi|santoṣaṇena ca
divyaḥ puruṣa utpanno jvālā|varṇo, mahā|bhūjaḥ,
151.20 dhanuṣmān, kavacī, khaḍgī, ratham āruhya daṃśitaḥ
divyair haya|varair yuktam, agni|kuṇḍāt samutthitaḥ,
garjann iva mahā|megho ratha|ghoṣeṇa vīryavān,
siṃha|saṃhanano vīraḥ, siṃha|tulya|parākramaḥ,
siṃh'|ôraskaḥ, siṃha|bhujaḥ, siṃha|vakṣā, mahā|balaḥ,
siṃha|pragarjano vīraḥ, siṃha|skandho, mahā|dyutiḥ,
su|bhruḥ, su|daṃṣṭraḥ, su|hanuḥ,
su|bāhuḥ, su|mukho, '|kṛśaḥ,
su|jatruḥ, su|viśāl'|âkṣaḥ,
su|pādaḥ, su|pratiṣṭhitaḥ,

Bhishma; the laudable commander of forces born into a preeminent lineage of kings, the man who is surrounded by
sons and grandsons, like a tree with a hundred branches; the 151.15
king who in anger practiced horrifying austerity with his wife for Drona's destruction; the heroic ornament of battle, the bull-like king who always treats us like a father—our father-in-law Drúpada. Let him lead the vanguard of the army!

It is my opinion that this king can withstand Drona and Bhishma as they rush towards him, for the king is a friend of Ángiras's descendant Drona, and he certainly knows celestial weapons."

Once Madri's sons had added their points of view, the ambidextrous descendant of Kuru, Vásava's son and equal, said this:

"The divine, long-armed, blazing, fire-hued man who because of the power of asceticism and the satisfaction of the
sages sprang up from a fire furnished with a bow, armor, 151.20
and sword, and decked in mail, and who once aboard his chariot yoked with superb celestial horses roared like a great thundercloud with the boom of his chariot; the powerful hero with lion-like muscles, lion-like prowess, a lion-like chest, lion-like arms, and a lion-like breast; the mighty and great glorious hero who roars like a lion and has a lion's shoulders; the handsome-browed, finely toothed, strong-jawed, strong-armed, handsome-faced, strapping, strong-necked, wide-eyed, strong-footed and firmly rooted man, invulnerable to all weapons, like an elephant with rent
temples born for Drona's destruction; the truth-speaking 151.25
Dhrishta·dyumna of disciplined senses is the man I believe

a|bhedyaḥ sarva|śastrāṇāṃ, prabhinna iva vāraṇaḥ,
jajñe Droṇa|vināśāya, satya|vādī, jit'|êndriyaḥ;
151.25 Dhṛṣṭadyumnam ahaṃ manye, sahed Bhīṣmasya sāyakān,
vajr'|âśani|sama|sparśān, dīpt'|âsyān uragān iva,
Yama|dūta|samān vege, nipāte pāvak'|ôpamān,
Rāmeṇ' ājau viṣahitān, vajra|niṣpeṣa|dāruṇān.
puruṣaṃ taṃ na paśyāmi yaḥ saheta mahā|vratam
Dhṛṣṭadyumnam ṛte, rājann. iti me dhīyate matiḥ.
kṣipra|hastaś, citra|yodhī mataḥ senā|patir mama,
a|bhedya|kavacaḥ, śrīmān, mātaṅga iva yūtha|paḥ.»

BHĪMASENA uvāca:

vadh'|ârthaṃ yaḥ samutpannaḥ
Śikhaṇḍī Drupad'|ātmajaḥ,
vadanti siddhā, rāj'|êndra',
ṛṣayaś ca samāgatāḥ,
151.30 yasya saṅgrāma|madhye tu divyam astraṃ prakurvataḥ
rūpaṃ drakṣyanti puruṣā Rāmasy' êva mah"|ātmanaḥ,
na taṃ yuddhe prapaśyāmi, yo bhindyāt tu Śikhaṇḍinam
śastreṇa samare, rājan, sannaddhaṃ, syandane sthitam.
dvairathe samare n' ânyo Bhīṣmaṃ hanyān mahā|vratam
Śikhaṇḍinam ṛte vīraṃ; sa me senā|patir mataḥ.

YUDHIṢṬHIRA uvāca:

sarvasya jagatas, tāta, sār'|âsāraṃ bal'|âbalam
sarvaṃ jānāti dharm'|ātmā, matam eṣāṃ ca Keśavaḥ.
yam āha Kṛṣṇo Dāśārhaḥ, so 'stu senā|patir mama,
kṛt'|âstro 'py a|kṛt'|âstro vā, vṛddho vā yadi vā yuvā.
151.35 eṣa no vijaye mūlam, eṣa, tāta, viparyaye;
atra prāṇāś ca rājyaṃ ca, bhāv'|âbhāvau, sukh'|âsukhe.

could withstand Bhishma's missiles, though they feel like a lightning strike to the touch, though they are like snakes with blazing mouths, though they are like Yama's messengers in speed, and though they fall like fire—missiles which only Rama could endure in battle, as harsh as a lightning strike.

I see no man bar Dhrishta·dyumna who could withstand strict-vowed Bhishma, king. This, at least, is my opinion. To my mind, the general should be the majestic, quick-handed, varied warrior, with inpenetrable armor like an elephant herd-leader."

SENA said:

Lord of kings, Shikhándin, son of Drúpada, was born to kill Bhishma, or so the assembled *siddhas* and sages claim. Men will see his form firing celestial weapons in the 151.30
midst of battle, like that of high-souled Rama. I see no one who could pierce Shikhándin with a weapon in war as he stands armored for battle on his chariot, my king. No one could kill Bhishma of great vows in a chariot duel in battle but Shikhándin; that hero, I believe, should be our army general.

SHTHIRA replied:

My friend, righteous-souled Késhava knows the entirety of this whole universe, its worth and worthlessness, its strength and weakness, and he knows the opinions of the people here. Let whomsoever Krishna Dashárha names be our general, irrespective of whether or not he has mastered weapons, or whether he is old or young. Krishna here is the 151.35

eṣa dhātā vidhātā ca, siddhir atra pratiṣṭhitā.
yam āha Kṛṣṇo Dāśārhaḥ, so 'stu no vāhinī|patiḥ.
bravītu vadatāṃ śreṣṭho, niśā samabhivartate;
tataḥ senā|patiṃ kṛtvā Kṛṣṇasya vaśa|vartinaḥ
rātreḥ śeṣe vyatikrānte prayāsyāmo raṇ'|ājiram
adhivāsita|śastrāś ca, kṛta|kautuka|maṅgalāḥ.

VAIŚAMPĀYANA uvāca:

tasya tad vacanaṃ śrutvā dharma|rājasya dhīmataḥ
abravīt puṇḍarīk'|âkṣo Dhanañjayam avekṣya ha:
151.40 «mam' âpy ete, mahā|rāja, bhavidbhir ya udāhṛtāḥ
netāras tava senāyā matā vikrānta|yodhinaḥ.
sarva eva samarthā hi tava śatruṃ prabādhitum,
Indrasy' âpi bhayaṃ hy ete janayeyur mah"|āhave,
kiṃ punar Dhārtarāṣṭrāṇāṃ lubdhānāṃ pāpa|cetasām!
may" âpi hi, mahā|bāho, tvat|priy'|ârthaṃ mah"|āhave
kṛto yatno mahāṃs tatra, śamaḥ syād iti, Bhārata,
dharmasya gatam ānṛṇyaṃ na sma vācyā vivakṣatām.
kṛt'|âstraṃ manyate bāla ātmānam a|vicakṣaṇaḥ
Dhārtarāṣṭro, bala|sthaṃ ca paśyaty ātmānam āturaḥ.

root of our victory, my friend, and he is the root of our defeat. Our lives, kingdom, success and failure, and happiness and misery are dependent upon him. He is the founder and creator. It is in him that success abides. Let whomsoever Krishna Dashárha names be our general.

Let the greatest of speakers speak, for the night is passing, then once we have appointed our general, following Krishna's will, and once the remainder of the night has passed, we will march out to the battlefield, with our weapons perfumed and the auspicious ceremonies performed.

VAISHAMPÁYANA continued:

Having heard the words of the wise king of righteousness, lotus-eyed Krishna spoke, glancing at Dhanan·jaya, saying:

"I too have high regard for the powerful fighters you 151.40
raised as possible leaders for your army, great sovereign. All are indeed able to drive off your enemies. In fact, they would even breed fear in Indra in a mighty battle, let alone the greedy and evil-minded Dhartaráshtras!

Of course, long-armed Bhárata, I have also made a great effort as a favor to you to bring about peace instead of great war. The debt to law has been paid, and so we cannot be blamed by those who are inclined to do so. The fool Dhartaráshtra believes he has mastered weaponry, but he has no comprehension, and the sick man sees himself as being in a strong position.

151.45 yujyatāṃ vāhinī sādhu; vadha|sādhyā hi me matāḥ.
na Dhārtarāṣṭrāḥ śakṣyanti sthātuṃ dṛṣṭvā Dhanañjayam
Bhīmasenaṃ ca saṃkruddhaṃ, yamau c' âpi Yam'|ôpamau,
Yuyudhāna|dvitīyaṃ ca Dhṛṣṭadyumnam a|marṣaṇam,
Abhimanyuṃ, Draupadeyān, Virāṭa|Drupadāv api,
akṣauhiṇī|patīṃś c' ânyān nar'|êndrān bhīma|vikramān!
sāravad balam asmākaṃ duṣ|pradharṣaṃ, dur|āsadam,
Dhārtarāṣṭra|balaṃ saṃkhye haniṣyati, na saṃśayaḥ.
Dhṛṣṭadyumnam ahaṃ manye senā|patim, arin|dama.»

VAIŚAMPĀYANA uvāca:

evam ukte tu Kṛṣṇena saṃprāhṛṣyan nar'|ôttamāḥ.
151.50 teṣāṃ prahṛṣṭa|manasāṃ nādaḥ samabhavan mahān,
«yoga! ity» atha sainyānāṃ tvaratāṃ saṃpradhāvatām.
haya|vāraṇa|śabdāś ca, nemi|ghoṣāś ca sarvataḥ,
śaṅkha|dundubhi|ghoṣāś ca tumulāḥ sarvato 'bhavan.
tad ugraṃ sāgara|nibhaṃ kṣubdhaṃ bala|samāgamam
ratha|patti|gaj'|ôdagraṃ, mah"|ōrmibhir iv' ākulam,
dhāvatām, āhvayānānāṃ, tanu|trāṇi ca badhnatām,
prayasyatāṃ Pāṇḍavānāṃ sa|sainyānāṃ samantataḥ
Gaṅg" êva pūrṇā dur|dharṣā samadṛśyata vāhinī.
agr'|ânīke Bhīmaseno, Mādrī|putrau ca daṃśitau,
151.55 Saubhadro, Draupadeyāś ca, Dhṛṣṭadyumnaś ca Pārṣataḥ,
Prabhadrakāś ca, Pañcālā Bhīmasena|mukhā yayuḥ.
tataḥ śabdaḥ samabhavat, samudrasy' êva parvaṇi,
hṛṣṭānāṃ saṃprayātānāṃ, ghoṣo divam iv' âspṛśat.

Well then, arrange your army, for I believe they will only 151.45
be truly amenable through murder. The Dhartaráshtras will not be able to stand their ground when they see Dhanan·jaya, furious Bhima·sena, and the Yama-like twins, with Yuyudhána as a second, truculent Dhrishta·dyumna, Abhimányu, Dráupadi's sons, and Viráta and Drúpada too, as well as the other lords of kings of terrifying prowess, the masters of battalions! Our army is powerful, invincible, and dangerous to approach, and it will doubtless destroy the Dhartaráshtras' force in conflict. I believe Dhrishta·dyumna should be the army's general, enemy-tamer."

VAISHAMPÁYANA continued:

When Krishna had spoken in this way, those greatest of
men were delighted, and a huge cry rose up from the joyful- 151.50
minded men. "Draw up the army!" they shouted, as the forces rushed quickly to and fro. The sounds of horses and elephants and the clatter of chariot wheels were everywhere, and the tumultuous booms of conch shells and drums were all around. When the Pándavas were about to set out with their armies on all sides, rushing about, shouting and binding on their armor, the gathered forces were full of chariots, infantry, and elephants like the fierce and choppy ocean teeming with enormous waves. The army resembled the invincible Ganges in full flood.

Bhima·sena and Madri's twin armored sons were
stationed at the front of the army, and Saubhádra, Dráu- 151.55
padi's sons, Dhrishta·dyumna Párshata, and the Prabhádrakas and Panchálas began to march, led by Bhima·sena. Then there came a sound which came from the joyous men as

prahṛṣṭā daṃśitā yodhāḥ par'|ânīka|vidāraṇāḥ;
teṣāṃ madhye yayau rājā Kuntī|putro Yudhiṣṭhiraḥ.
śakaṭ'|āpaṇa|veśāś ca, yāna|yugyaṃ ca sarvaśaḥ,
kośaṃ yantr'|āyudhaṃ c' âiva, ye ca vaidyāś cikitsakāḥ,
phalgu yac ca balaṃ kiñ cid, yac c' âpi kṛśa|durbalam,
tat saṃgṛhya yayau rājā, ye c' âpi paricārakāḥ.
151.60 Upaplavye tu Pāñcālī Draupadī satya|vādinī
saha strībhir nivavṛte dāsī|dāsa|samāvṛtā.
kṛtvā mūla|pratīkāraṃ gulmaiḥ sthāvara|jaṅgamaiḥ
skandh'|āvāreṇa mahatā prayayuḥ Pāṇḍu|nandanāḥ.
dadato gāṃ hiraṇyaṃ ca brāhmaṇair abhisaṃvṛtāḥ
stūyamānā yayū, rājan, rathair maṇi|vibhūṣitaiḥ.

Kekayā, Dhṛṣṭaketuś ca, putraḥ Kāśyasya c' âbhibhuḥ,
Śreṇimān, Vasudānaś ca, Śikhaṇḍī c' â|parājitaḥ
hṛṣṭās, tuṣṭāḥ, kavacinaḥ, sa|śastrāḥ, samalaṅkṛtāḥ
rājānam anvayuḥ sarve parivārya Yudhiṣṭhiram.
151.65 jaghan'|ârdhe Virāṭaś ca, Yājñaseniś ca, Saumakiḥ,
Sudharmā, Kuntibhojaś ca, Dhṛṣṭadyumnasya c' ātmajāḥ
rath'|âyutāni catvāri, hayāḥ pañca|guṇās tathā,
patti|sainyaṃ daśa|guṇaṃ, gajānām ayutāni ṣaṭ.

they marched, like the roar of the sea on the day of the new moon, and the clamor seemed to touch heaven.

So the armored warriors, the breakers of enemy armies, set out on their way elated, and King Yudhi·shthira, the son of Kunti, marched in their midst. The king gathered the wagons and merchandise, the supplies, the cattle to be yoked milling around on all sides, the treasury supply, the machines and weapons, the medics and physicians, the invalids, and any forces who were emaciated and weak, as well as the attendants and camp-followers, and then he began his march.

Truth-telling Dráupadi the Pancháli princess stayed back 151.60
in Upaplávya with the women, surrounded by slave girls and slaves. The descendants of Pandu set up basic provisions for the great royal headquarters, with stationary and mobile military units, and then they left. They handed out cattle and gold to the brahmins who flocked around them, and they were praised as they set out on their jewel-encrusted chariots, my king.

The Kékayas, Dhrishta·ketu, the prince of Kashi, Shrénimat, Vasu·dana, and undefeated Shikhándin all joyfully and gladly followed King Yudhi·shthira in their armor, and with swords and ornaments. Viráta, Yajñaséni, Sáumaki, Sud- 151.65
hárman, Kunti·bhoja, and the sons of Dhrishta·dyumna, forty thousand chariots, five times again more horses, ten times that number of infantry soldiers, and sixty thousand elephants marched in the rear half.

Anādhṛṣṭiś, Cekitāno, Dhṛṣṭaketuś ca, Sātyakiḥ
parivārya yayuḥ sarve Vāsudeva|Dhanañjayau.
āsādya tu Kuru|kṣetraṃ vyūḍh'|ânīkāḥ prahāriṇaḥ
Pāṇḍavāḥ samadṛśyanta nardanto vṛṣabhā iva.
te 'vagāhya Kuru|kṣetraṃ śaṅkhān dadhmur arin|damāḥ;
tath" âiva dadhmatuḥ śaṅkhaṃ Vāsudeva|Dhanañjayau.
151.70 Pāñcajanyasya nirghoṣaṃ visphūrjitam iv' âśaneḥ
niśamya sarva|sainyāni samahṛṣyanta sarvaśaḥ.
śaṅkha|dundubhi|saṃhṛṣṭaḥ siṃha|nādas tarasvinām
pṛthivīṃ c' ântarikṣaṃ ca sāgarāṃś c' ânvanādayat.

VAIŚAMPĀYANA uvāca:

152.1 TATO DEŚE SAME, snigdhe, prabhūta|yavas'|êndhane
niveśayām āsa tadā senāṃ rājā Yudhiṣṭhiraḥ,
parihṛtya śmaśānāni, devat"|āyatanāni ca,
āśramāṃś ca maha"|rṣiṇāṃ, tīrthāny, āyatanāni ca.
madhur'|ân|ūṣare deśe śucau puṇye mahā|matiḥ
niveśaṃ kārayām āsa Kuntī|putro Yudhiṣṭhiraḥ.
tataś ca punar utthāya sukhī, viśrānta|vāhanaḥ,
prayayau pṛthivī|pālair vṛtaḥ śata|sahasraśaḥ.
152.5 vidrāvya śataśo gulmān Dhārtarāṣṭrasya sainikān
paryakrāmat samantāc ca Pārthena saha Keśavaḥ.
śibiraṃ māpayām āsa Dhṛṣṭadyumnaś ca Pārṣataḥ,
Sātyakiś ca rath'|ôdāro, Yuyudhānaś ca vīryavān,
āsādya saritaṃ puṇyāṃ Kuru|kṣetre Hiraṇvatīm,
s'|ûpatīrthāṃ, śuci|jalāṃ, śarkarā|paṅka|varjitām.
khānayām āsa parikhāṃ Keśavas tatra, Bhārata,
gupty|artham api c' ādiśya balaṃ tatra nyaveśayat.

Anadhríshti, Chekitána, Dhrishta·ketu, and Sátyaki all marched surrounding Vasudéva and Dhanan·jaya. As the warrior Pándavas reached Kuru·kshetra drawn up in battle orders, they looked like roaring bulls. The enemy-tamers plunged into Kuru·kshetra, blowing their conch-shells; and Vasudéva and Dhanan·jaya blew their conches too.

When they heard the blare of the conch called Pancha- 151.70
jánya as it rumbled like thunder, all the soldiers rejoiced on every side. The lion-like roars of the energetic men and the joyful conch-shell blares and drums made the earth, sky, and seas resound.

VAISHAMPÁYANA said:

SHUNNING CEMETERIES, sanctuaries of the gods, hermit- 152.1
ages, and the holy places of great sages, King Yudhi·shthira had the army make camp on smooth, flat ground which abounded with grass and fuel. High-minded Yudhi·shthira, son of Kunti, made his camp in a lovely non-saline region which was pure and holy. Then, rising once more when his horses had rested, he happily went on his way again surrounded by hundreds of thousands of earth-protectors.

Késhava and Partha roamed all round, and set hundreds 152.5
of Dhartaráshtra's military units to flight. Dhrishta·dyumna Párshata and the mighty and noble chariot warrior Yuyudhána Sátyaki measured out the royal camp, reaching as far as the holy Hiránvati in Kuru·kshetra, a well-forded river of pure water, free of grit and mud. Késhava had a moat dug in that spot, Bharata, and placed a force there for its protection, issuing their orders.

vidhir yaḥ śibirasy' āsīt Pāṇḍavānāṃ mah"|ātmanām,
tad|vidhāni nar'|êndrāṇāṃ kārayām āsa Keśavaḥ
152.10 prabhūtatara|kāṣṭhāni, dur|ādharṣatarāṇi ca,
bhakṣya|bhojy'|ânna|pānāni śataśo 'tha sahasraśaḥ
śibirāṇi mah"|ârhāṇi rājñāṃ tatra pṛthak pṛthak
vimānān' îva, rāj'|êndra, niviṣṭāni mahī|tale.

tatr' āsañ śilpinaḥ prājñāḥ śataśo datta|vetanāḥ,
sarv'|ôpakaraṇair yuktā, vaidyāḥ śāstra|viśāradāḥ.
jyā|dhanur|varma|śastrāṇāṃ tath" âiva madhu|sarpiṣoḥ
sasarja rasa|pāṃsūnāṃ rāśayaḥ parvat'|ôpamāḥ,
bah'|ûdakaṃ, su|yavasaṃ, tuṣ'|âṅgāra|samanvitam,
śibire śibire rājā sañcakāra Yudhiṣṭhiraḥ,
152.15 mahā|yantrāṇi, nārācās, tomarāṇi, paraśvadhāḥ,
dhanūṃṣi, kavac'|ādīni, ṛṣṭayas tūṇa|saṃyutāḥ.
gajāḥ kaṇṭaka|sannāhā loha|varm'|ôttara|cchadāḥ
dṛśyante tatra giry|ābhāḥ sahasra|śata|yodhinaḥ.

niviṣṭān Pāṇḍavāṃs tatra jñātvā mitrāṇi, Bhārata,
abhisasrur yathā|deśaṃ sa|balāḥ saha|vāhanāḥ.
carita|brahma|caryās te soma|pā bhūri|dakṣiṇāḥ
jayāya Pāṇḍu|putrāṇāṃ samājagmur mahī|kṣitaḥ.

Késhava followed the rules used for the high-souled Pándavas' tents, and had those precepts followed for the kings' tents. Next he had them supplied with ample water and 152.10
fuel, and made too dangerous to attack. So it was that hundreds of thousands of tents with provisions and stores of food and drink, and the expensive tents for each individual king, were encamped on the surface of the earth like celestial vehicles, lord of kings.

There were hundreds of skilled mechanics on regular pay, as well as medics, experienced in their science and equipped with all the tools of their trade. King Yudhi·shthira supplied each and every tent with bowstrings, bows, armor, weapons, honey, clarified butter, mountainous quantities of liquor and sand, great amounts of water and good supplies of grass for cattle, with chaff and charcoal, huge ma- 152.15
chines, iron arrows, lances, axes, bows, armor and so on, spears, and tied-up quivers. Mountainous elephants girded with spikes and covered with fine copper mail could be seen, capable of taking on hundreds of thousands of warriors.

When they discovered that the Pándavas had encamped, Bhárata, their allies flooded to the appointed place with their armies and horses. The kings of the earth who practiced vows of abstinence, drunk soma, and frequently gave out donations, gathered for the sons of Pandu's victory.

JANAMEJAYA uvāca:

153.1 YUDHIṢṬHIRAM sah'|ânīkam upāyāntaṃ yuyutsayā,
sanniviṣṭaṃ Kuru|kṣetre, Vāsudevena pālitam,
Virāṭa|Drupadābhyāṃ ca sa|putrābhyāṃ samanvitam,
Kekayair Vṛṣṇibhiś c' âiva pārthivaiḥ śataśo vṛtam,
Mahendram iva c' Ādityair abhiguptaṃ mahā|rathaiḥ,
śrutvā Duryodhano rājā kiṃ kāryaṃ pratyapadyata?
etad icchāmy ahaṃ śrotuṃ vistareṇa, mahā|mate,
saṃbhrame tumule tasmin yad" āsīt Kuru|jāṅgale.
153.5 vyathayeyur ime devān s'|Êndrān api samāgame
Pāṇḍavā Vāsudevaś ca, Virāṭa|Drupadau tathā,
Dhṛṣṭadyumnaś ca Pāñcālyaḥ, Śikhaṇḍī ca mahā|rathaḥ,
Yudhāmanyuś ca vikrānto devair api dur|āsadaḥ.
etad icchāmy ahaṃ śrotuṃ vistareṇa, tapo|dhana,
Kurūṇāṃ Pāṇḍavānāṃ ca yad yad āsīd viceṣṭitam.

VAIŚAMPĀYANA uvāca:

pratiyāte tu Dāśārhe rājā Duryodhanas tadā
Karṇaṃ Duḥśāsanaṃ c' âiva Śakuniṃ c' âbravīd idam:
«a|kṛten' âiva kāryeṇa gataḥ Pārthān Adhokṣajaḥ,
sa enān manyun" āviṣṭo dhruvaṃ dhakṣyaty a|saṃśayam.
153.10 iṣṭo hi Vāsudevasya Pāṇḍavair mama vigrahaḥ,
Bhīmasen'|Ârjunau c' âiva Dāśārhasya mate sthitau,
Ajātaśatrur atyarthaṃ Bhīmasena|vaś'|ânugaḥ,
nikṛtaś ca mayā pūrvaṃ saha sarvaiḥ sah' ôdaraiḥ.
Virāṭa|Drupadau c' âiva kṛta|vairau mayā saha,
tau ca senā|praṇetārau Vāsudeva|vaś'|ânugau.
bhavitā vigrahaḥ so 'yaṃ tumule loma|harṣaṇaḥ
tasmāt sāṃgrāmikaṃ sarvaṃ kārayadhvam a|tandritāḥ.

ÉJAYA said:

WHAT DID KING Duryódhana set out to do when he heard that Yudhi·shthira was on his way with his army, encamped on Kuru·kshetra and ready to fight, protected by Vasudéva, with Viráta and Drúpada and their sons, as well as the Kékayas and Vrishnis and surrounded by hundreds of kings, like Mahéndra guarded by mighty warrior Adítyas? 153.1

I wish to hear in detail, high-minded man, what went on in the whirling tumultuous jungle of the Kurus. The 153.5
Pándavas with Vasudéva, Viráta and Drúpada, Dhrishta·dyumna Panchálya, the mighty warrior Shikhándin, and powerful Yudha·manyu would make even the gods and Indra tremble in battle, difficult to attack though they are. I want to hear in detail about whatever it was that happened between the Kurus and Pándavas, man of ascetic wealth.

VAISHAMPÁYANA replied:

When Dashárha had returned, King Duryódhana said the following to Karna, Duhshásana, and Shákuni:

"Adhókshaja has gone back to the Parthas without achieving his goal, so doubtless he will set them ablaze,
filled with fury. Vasudéva wishes for war between the Pán- 153.10
davas and me, and Bhima·sena and Árjuna both abide by Dashárha's opinion, and as for Ajáta·shatru, he follows Bhima·sena's will too heavily.

I have treated him and his brothers badly in the past, and Viráta and Drúpada have also quarreled with me. That pair of army commanders follow Vasudéva's will. This hair-raising conflict will happen chaotically, so make all your war preparations untiringly.

śibirāṇi Kuru|kṣetre kriyantāṃ, vasudh"|âdhipāḥ,
sva|paryāpt'|âvakāśāni, dur|ādeyāni śatrubhiḥ,
153.15 āsanna|jala|koṣṭhāni śataśo 'tha sahasraśaḥ,
a|cchedy'|āhāra|mārgāṇi, bandh'|ôcchraya|citāni ca,
vividh'|āyudha|pūrṇāni, patākā|dhvajavanti ca;
samāś ca teṣāṃ panthānaḥ kriyantāṃ nagarād bahiḥ.
prayāṇaṃ ghuṣyatām adya śvo|bhūta iti mā ciram.»

te «tath" êti» pratijñāya śvo|bhūte cakrire tathā
hṛṣṭa|rūpā mah"|ātmāno nivāsāya mahī|kṣitām.
tatas te pārthivāḥ sarve tac chrutvā rāja|śāsanam,
āsanebhyo mah"|ârhebhya udatiṣṭhann a|marṣitāḥ,
bāhūn parigha|saṅkāśān saṃspṛśantaḥ śanaiḥ śanaiḥ,
153.20 kāñcan'|âṅgada|dīptāṃś ca, candan'|âguru|bhūṣitān,
uṣṇīṣāṇi niyacchantaḥ puṇḍarīka|nibhaiḥ karaiḥ,
antarīy'|ôttarīyāṇi bhūṣaṇāni ca sarvaśaḥ.

te rathān rathinaḥ śreṣṭhā, hayāṃś ca haya|kovidāḥ
sajjayanti sma, nāgāṃś ca nāga|śikṣāsv anuṣṭhitāḥ.
atha varmāṇi citrāṇi kāñcanāni bahūni ca,
vividhāni ca śastrāṇi cakruḥ sarvāṇi sarvaśaḥ,
padātayaś ca puruṣāḥ śastrāṇi vividhāni ca
upājahruḥ śarīreṣu hema|citrāṇy an|ekaśaḥ.

tad utsava iv' ôdagraṃ saṃprahṛṣṭa|nar'|āvṛtam
nagaraṃ Dhārtarāṣṭrasya, Bhārat', āsīt samākulam.
153.25 jan'|âugha|salil'|āvarto, ratha|nāg'|âśva|mīnavān,
śaṅkha|dundubhi|nirghoṣaḥ, kośa|sañcaya|ratnavān,

Let the kings of earth pitch their tents on Kuru·kshetra, positioned very spaciously to make them difficult for the
enemy to seize, with water and wood in good supply by 153.15
the hundreds and thousands, and with unbreakable supply roads and secured treasuries full of various weapons and banners and flags. Let the roads which go out from the city be smoothed, and let it be announced now, without delay, that our march will begin tomorrow."

Promising, "So be it," the cheerful and high-souled men began work the next day on the living arrangements of the kings of this world. Then when all the kings had heard the sovereign's command, the impatient men rose from their costly thrones, slowly and gently touching their steely arms
which blazed with golden bracelets and glistened with san- 153.20
dalwood and aloe. They attached their turbans with hands that were like lotus petals, put on their under and outer clothes, and decked themselves in glittering ornamentation all over.

Superb charioteers equipped the chariots, while trained horsemen saddled up their horses and men trained in elephant training equipped their elephants. On all sides they prepared their many variegated and golden sets of armor, and all their various weapons. The infantry donned their assorted weapons, and strapped their numerous types of gold-studded armor onto their bodies.

The Dhartaráshtra's crowded city, teeming with joyful
men, was like a vast festival, Bhárata. With its whirlpools 153.25
of hosts of men, chariots, elephants, and horses for its fish, conch shells and drums as its roar, the heaps of treasure

citr'|ābharaṇa|varm'|ôrmiḥ, śastra|nirmala|phenavān,
prāsāda|māl''|âdri|vṛto, rathy''|āpaṇa|mahā|hradaḥ,
yodha|candr'|ôday'|ôdbhūtaḥ Kuru|rāja|mah''|ârṇavaḥ
vyadṛśyata tadā rājaṃś candr'|ôdaya iv' ôdadhiḥ.

VAIŚAMPĀYANA uvāca:

154.1 VĀSUDEVASYA tad vākyam
anusmṛtya Yudhiṣṭhiraḥ
punaḥ papraccha Vārṣṇeyaṃ:
«kathaṃ mando 'bravīd idam?
asminn abhyāgate kāle kiṃ ca naḥ kṣamam, Acyuta?
kathaṃ ca vartamānā vai sva|dharmān na cyavemahi?
Duryodhanasya, Karṇasya, Śakuneḥ Saubalasya ca,
Vāsudeva, mata|jño 'si, mama sa|bhrātṛkasya ca.
Vidurasy' âpi tad vākyaṃ śrutaṃ, Bhīṣmasya c' ôbhayoḥ,
Kuntyāś ca, vipula|prajña, prajñā kārtsyena te śrutā.
154.5 sarvam etad atikramya, vicārya ca punaḥ punaḥ,
kṣamaṃ yan no, mahā|bāho, tad bravīhy a|vicārayan.»
śrutv'' âitad dharma|rājasya dharm'|ârtha|sahitaṃ vacaḥ
megha|dundubhi|nirghoṣaḥ Kṛṣṇo vākyam ath' âbravīt:

KṚṢṆA uvāca:

uktavān asmi yad vākyaṃ dharm'|ârtha|sahitaṃ hitam,
na tu tan nikṛti|prajñe Kauravye pratitiṣṭhati.
na ca Bhīṣmasya dur|medhāḥ śṛṇoti, Vidurasya vā,
mama vā bhāṣitaṃ kiñ cit, sarvam ev' âtivartate.

as its pearls, waves of ornaments and armor of various colors, foam of bright weapons, circled by garlands of palaces in place of mountains, with roads and shops like huge lakes, the great sea of Kuru kings swelling to that moonrise of warriors resembled the ocean at the rise of the moon, my king.

VAISHAMPÁYANA continued:

REMEMBERING VASUDÉVA's advice, Yudhi·shthira ques- 154.1
tioned Varshnéya once more, saying: "How could the fool say such things? Now that the time has arrived, what befits us, Áchyuta? How should we act so as not to deviate from our duty? You know what Duryódhana, Karna, and Shákuni Sáubala are thinking, as well as knowing both my plans and those of my brothers, Vasudéva. You have heard the words of both Vídura and Bhishma, and you have listened to all Kunti's wisdom, man of extensive wisdom. But ignoring that for a moment, reflect once more on 154.5
what would suit us, long-armed man, and tell us without hesitation."

Having listened to the words of the king of righteousness, which were fraught with law and profit, Krishna then spoke in a voice that boomed like a thunderclap or a kettledrum, saying:

KRISHNA said:

I gave advice to the Kaurávya, wise in deceit, which was beneficial and conformed to law and profit; but it did not take root in him. The wicked-minded man does not listen to anything Bhishma, Vídura, or I have to say, but instead he transgresses everything. The evil-souled man does not

n' âiṣa kāmayate dharmaṃ, n' âiṣa kāmayate yaśaḥ,
jitaṃ sa manyate sarvaṃ dur|ātmā Karṇam āśritaḥ.
154.10 bandham ājñāpayām āsa mama c' âpi Suyodhanaḥ;
na ca taṃ labdhavān kāmaṃ dur|ātmā pāpa|niścayaḥ,
na ca Bhīṣmo, na ca Droṇo yuktaṃ tatr' āhatur vacaḥ;
sarve tam anuvartante ṛte Viduram, Acyuta.
Śakuniḥ Saubalaś c' âiva, Karṇa|Duḥśāsanāv api
tvayy a|yuktāny abhāṣanta mūḍhā mūḍham a|marṣaṇam.

kiṃ ca tena may" ôktena yāny abhāṣata Kauravaḥ?
saṃkṣepeṇa dur|ātm" âsau na yuktaṃ tvayi vartate.
pārthiveṣu na sarveṣu ya ime tava sainikāḥ,
yat pāpaṃ, yan na kalyāṇaṃ, sarvaṃ tasmin pratiṣṭhitam,
154.15 na c' âpi vayam atyarthaṃ parityāgena karhi cit
Kauravaiḥ śamam icchāmas. tatra yuddham an|antaram.

VAIŚAMPĀYANA uvāca:

tac chrutvā pārthivāḥ sarve Vāsudevasya bhāṣitam
a|bruvanto mukhaṃ rājñaḥ samudaikṣanta, Bhārata.
Yudhiṣṭhiras tv abhiprāyam abhilakṣya mahī|kṣitām
yogam ājñāpayām āsa Bhīm'|Ârjuna|yamaiḥ saha.
tataḥ kilakilā|bhūtam anīkaṃ Pāṇḍavasya ha
ājñāpite tadā yoge samahṛṣyanta sainikāḥ.

a|vadhyānāṃ vadhaṃ paśyan dharma|rājo Yudhiṣṭhiraḥ
niḥśvasan Bhīmasenaṃ ca Vijayaṃ c' êdam abravīt:
154.20 «yad|arthaṃ vana|vāsaś ca prāptaṃ, duḥkhaṃ ca yan mayā,
so 'yam asmān upaity eva paro 'n|arthaḥ prayatnataḥ.
tasmin yatnaḥ kṛto 'smābhiḥ, sa no hīnaḥ prayatnataḥ;

desire law; he does not desire glory. He believes he has already won everything by relying on Karna.

Wicked-souled Suyódhana even ordered that I be taken 154.10
prisoner, but the evil-intentioned man did not gain his wish. Neither Bhishma nor Drona said anything about it then and there, for all except Vídura follow him, Áchyuta. The fools Shákuni Sáubala, Karna, and Duhshásana gave that truculent idiot bad advice about you.

What is the point of me repeating what the Káuravas said? To summarize: that wicked-souled man is not treating you properly. Not in all these kings here as your soldiers is there as much evil and so great a deficiency of good as all
that abides in that man. We do not ever want peace with 154.15
the Káuravas if it means excessive sacrifice on our part. War is inevitable now.

VAISHAMPÁYANA said:

When all the kings heard what Vasudéva had to say, they said nothing, watching the king's face, Bhárata. But Yudhi·shthira perceived the intention of the kings, and, with Bhima, Árjuna, and the twins, he ordered the army to be readied. Then, once the order was given to ready the army, the Pándava's force started to cheer and the soldiers were delighted.

But Yudhi·shthira, the king of righteousness, forseeing the slaughter of men who ought not to be slaughtered, sighed and spoke to Bhima·sena and Víjaya as follows:
"Despite our best efforts, and despite the fact that I lived 154.20
in the forest and suffered misery to prevent it, the worst calamity is now upon us. It seems the very fact that we made

a|kṛte tu prayatne 'smān upāvṛttaḥ kalir mahān.
kathaṃ hy a|vadhyaiḥ saṃgrāmaḥ kāryaḥ saha bhaviṣyati?
kathaṃ hatvā gurūn vṛddhān vijayo no bhaviṣyati?»

tac chrutvā dharma|rājasya savya|sācī paraṃ|tapaḥ
yad uktaṃ Vāsudevena, śrāvayām āsa tad vacaḥ:
«uktavān Devakī|putraḥ Kuntyāś ca Vidurasya ca
vacanaṃ; tat tvayā, rājan, nikhilen' âvadhāritam.
154.25 na ca tau vakṣyato '|dharmam, iti me naiṣṭhikī matiḥ.
n' âpi yuktaṃ ca, Kaunteya, nivartitum a|yudhyataḥ!»

tac chrutvā Vāsudevo 'pi savyasāci|vacas tadā
smayamāno 'bravīd vākyaṃ Pārtham: «evam iti» bruvan.
tatas te dhṛta|saṅkalpā yuddhāya saha|sainikāḥ
Pāṇḍaveyā, mahā|rāja, tāṃ rātriṃ sukham āvasan.

VAIŚAMPĀYANA uvāca:

155.1 VYUṢṬĀYĀṂ VAI rajanyāṃ hi rājā Duryodhanas tataḥ
vyabhajat tāny anīkāni daśa c' âikaṃ ca, Bhārata.
nara|hasti|rath'|âśvānāṃ sāraṃk madhyaṃ cak phalgu ca
sarveṣv eteṣv anīkeṣu sandideśa nar'|âdhipaḥ.

s'|ânukarṣāḥ, sa|tūṇīrāḥ, sa|varūthāḥ, sa|tomarāḥ,
s'|ôpāsaṅgāḥ, sa|śaktīkāḥ, sa|niṣaṅgāḥ, saha'|rṣṭayaḥ,
sa|dhvajāḥ sa|patākāś ca, sa|śar'|âsana|tomarāḥ,
rajjubhiś ca vicitrābhiḥ sa|pāśāḥ, sa|paricchadāḥ,
155.5 sa|kaca|graha|vikṣepāḥ, sa|taila|guḍa|vālukāḥ,
s'|âśīviṣa|ghaṭāḥ sarve, sa|sarjarasa|pāṃsavaḥ,

such an effort made the failure of our efforts inevitable, and now great discord has returned to us, though we certainly didn't strive for it. How can a battle be waged against men who should not be killed? How can we have victory if we kill our teachers and elders?"

Hearing the words of the king of righteousness, the enemy-scorching ambidextrous archer Árjuna repeated the words Vasudéva had said. "Dévaki's son has told you what Kunti and Vídura had to say, king, and you have completely understood them. It is my firm belief that those two would 154.25
not speak unlawfully. Furthermore, it is improper to turn back without fighting, Kauntéya!"

Vasudéva had also heard the ambidextrous archer's advice, and, smiling, he said to Partha: "Indeed it is." So the Pandavéyas were resolved in their expectations of war with the soldiers, great king, and they spent the night happily.

VAISHAMPÁYANA continued:

WHEN THE NIGHT had passed, King Duryódhana orga- 155.1
nized his eleven battalions, Bhárata. The lord of men arranged his men, elephants, chariots, and horses into three categories—best, average, and poor—and distributed them among these divisions.

With their spare chariot axle poles, large quivers strapped to vehicles, chariot bumpers, lances, arrow holders strapped to the horses and elephants, javelins, more quivers carried by infantrymen, with lances, banners, flags, long shafts shot from bows, with ropes of various hues, with chains and armor, with short sharp wooden clubs, oil, molasses, sand, 155.5
they all had jars of poisonous snakes, *sarja·rasa*-tree resin

sa|ghaṇṭa|phalakāḥ sarve, s'|âyo|guḍa|jal'|ôpalāḥ,
sa|śāla|bhindipālāś ca, sa|madh'|ûcchiṣṭa|mudgarāḥ,
sa|kāṇa|daṇḍakāḥ sarve, sa|sīra|viṣa|tomarāḥ,
sa|śūrpa|piṭakāḥ sarve, sa|dātr'|âṅkuśa|tomarāḥ,
sa|kīla|kavacāḥ sarve, vāsī|vṛkṣādan'|ânvitāḥ
vyāghra|carma|parīvārā dvīpi|carm'|āvṛtāś ca te,
saha'|rṣṭayaḥ, sa|śṛṅgāś ca, sa|prāsa|vividh'|āyudhāḥ,
sa|kuṭhārāḥ, sa|kuddālāḥ, sa|taila|kṣauma|sarpiṣaḥ,
155.10 rukma|jāla|praticchannā, nānā|maṇi|vibhūṣitāḥ,
citr'|ânīkāḥ, su|vapuṣo, jvalitā iva pāvakāḥ.

tathā kavacinaḥ śūrāḥ, śastreṣu kṛta|niścayāḥ,
kulīnā, haya|yoni|jñāḥ, sārathye viniveśitāḥ,
baddh'|âriṣṭā, baddha|kakṣā, baddha|dhvaja|patākinaḥ,
baddh'|ābharaṇa|niryūhā, baddha|carm'|âsi|paṭṭiśāḥ,
catur|yujo rathāḥ sarve, sarve c' ôttama|vājinaḥ,
saṃhṛṣṭa|vāhanāḥ† sarve, sarve śata|śar'|âsanāḥ.
dhuryayor hayayor ekas, tathā 'nyau pārṣṇi|sārathī,
tau c' âpi rathināṃ śreṣṭhau, rathī ca haya|vit tathā.
155.15 nagarāṇ' îva guptāni, dur|ādharṣāṇi śatrubhiḥ,
āsan ratha|sahasrāṇi hema|mālīni sarvaśaḥ.

and flammable substances, and all had wooden clubs with bells. With iron weapons and devices for catapulting molasses, water, and rocks, with whistling wooden clubs, with beeswax and hammers, they all had wooden clubs with nails drilled through them. With plow poles and poisoned missiles, all had hollow reeds to pour hot molasses, and cane rods with sickles and hooked spears; all had sharp blocks of wood, armor, axes, and sharp iron spikes. With chariot sides covered in tigerskin and leopardskin, with lances, with horns, missiles, and various weapons, hoes, spades, and cloth soaked in linseed and sesame oil, the gloriously 155.10
handsome and colorful armies blazed like fires, dressed in golden latticeworked armor and flashing brightly with various jewels.

Armored heroes, expertly trained in weaponry, nobly born, and knowledgeable in horse breeding, were assigned to charioteer duties. Each and every chariot was bound with auspicious herbs, furnished with horses decked with bells and pearls on their heads, and strapped with flags and banners. Their turrets were embellished with ornaments, and they were decked with hides, swords, and sharp-edged javelins. Each and every chariot was yoked with four of the very finest steeds, bristling with excitement, and each and every horse was supplied with a hundred quivers. Each chariot had one driver for the yoked horses and one driver each for the horses on the wheel; then there were two excellent chariot warriors and a charioteer skilled in horse-lore. There 155.15
were thousands of chariots on all sides, garlanded with gold, like fortified cities unconquerable by their enemies.

yathā rathās tathā nāgā baddha|kakṣāḥ sv|alaṅkṛtāḥ
babhūvuḥ sapta|puruṣā, ratnavanta iv' ādrayaḥ.
dvāv aṅkuśa|dharau tatra, dvāv uttama|dhanur|dharau,
dvau var'|âsi|dharau, rājann, ekaḥ śakti|pināka|dhṛk.
gajair mattaiḥ samākīrṇaṃ sa|varm'|āyudha|kośakaiḥ
tad babhūva balaṃ, rājan, Kauravyasya mah"|ātmanaḥ.
āmukta|kavacair yuktaiḥ sa|patākaiḥ sv|alaṃkṛtaiḥ,
sādibhiś c' ôpapannās tu tathā c' âyutaśo hayāḥ.
155.20 a|saṃgrāhāḥ, su|saṃpannā, hema|bhāṇḍa|paricchadāḥ,
an|eka|śata|sāhasrāḥ sarve sādi|vaśe sthitāḥ.

nanā|rūpa|vikārāś ca, nānā|kavaca|śastriṇaḥ
padātino narās tatra babhūvur hema|mālinaḥ.
rathasy' āsan daśa gajā, gajasya daśa vājinaḥ,
narā daśa hayasy' āsan pāda|rakṣāḥ samantataḥ.
rathasya nāgāḥ pañcāśan, nāgasy' āsañ śataṃ hayāḥ,
hayasya puruṣāḥ sapta bhinna|sandhāna|kāriṇaḥ.
senā pañca|śataṃ nāgā, rathās tāvanta eva ca,
daśa|senā ca pṛtanā, pṛtanā daśa|vāhinī.
155.25 senā ca, vāhinī c' âiva, pṛtanā, dhvajinī, camūḥ,
akṣauhiṇ" îti paryāyair niruktā ca varūthinī.

And as with the chariots, there were exquisitely ornamented elephants: with their caparisons and howdahs
strapped on, and with seven riders each, they looked like
bejeweled mountains. Two men held the whips, two were
superb archers, two were swordsmen, and the final man,
my king, held a spear and flag. The high-souled Kaurávya's
army swarmed with maddened tuskers bearing cases of
weaponry and armor. There were also myriads of horses
equipped with riders girt in armor, beautifully ornamented,
and carrying flags. Many hundreds of thousands of per- 155.20
fectly trained horses, decked in golden bridles, all stood still,
under the complete control of their riders, refraining from
scratching at the ground with their hooves.

There were also golden-garlanded infantrymen of various types, garbed in varied uniforms and supplied with diverse armor and weaponry. Ten elephants were assigned to each chariot, ten horses to each elephant, and ten men on all sides to each horse to protect their legs. In case of a breach, fifty elephants were assigned to each chariot to fill the gap, a hundred horses were assigned to each elephant, and seven men were assigned to each horse. A *sena* army has five hundred elephants and as many chariots again. A *prítana* army has ten *sena*s and a *váhini* contains ten *prítana*s.
However, the terms *sena*, *váhini*, *prítana*, *dhvájini*, *chamu*, 155.25
*aksháuhini*, and *varúthini* are also used to mean precisely
the same thing.

evaṃ vyūḍhāny anīkāni Kauraveyeṇa dhīmatā.<br>
akṣauhiṇyo daś' âikā ca saṅkhyātāḥ, sapta c' âiva ha;<br>
akṣauhiṇyas tu sapt' âiva Pāṇḍavānām abhūd balam;<br>
akṣauhiṇyo daś' âikā ca Kauravāṇām abhūd balam.<br>
narāṇāṃ pañca|pañcāśad, eṣā pattir vidhīyate;<br>
senā|mukhaṃ ca tisras tā, gulma ity abhiśabditam.<br>
trayo gulmā gaṇas tv āsīd, gaṇās tv ayutaśo 'bhavan<br>
Duryodhanasya senāsu yotsyamānāḥ prahāriṇaḥ.<br>
155.30 tatra Duryodhano rājā śūrān buddhimato narān<br>
prasamīkṣya mahā|bāhuś cakre senā|patīṃs tadā.<br>
pṛthag akṣauhiṇīnāṃ ca praṇetṝn nara|sattamān<br>
vidhivat pūrvam ānīya pārthivān abhyabhāṣata<br>
Kṛpaṃ, Droṇaṃ ca, Śalyaṃ ca,<br>
        Saindhavaṃ ca Jayadratham,<br>
Sudakṣiṇaṃ ca Kāmbojaṃ,<br>
        Kṛtavarmāṇam eva ca,<br>
Droṇa|putraṃ ca, Karṇaṃ ca, Bhūriśravasam eva ca,<br>
Śakuniṃ Saubalaṃ c' âiva, Bāhlīkaṃ ca mahā|balam,<br>
divase divase teṣāṃ prativelaṃ ca, Bhārata.<br>
cakre sa vividhāḥ pūjāḥ pratyakṣaṃ ca punaḥ punaḥ.<br>
155.35 tathā viniyatāḥ sarve, ye ca teṣāṃ pad'|ânugāḥ,<br>
babhūvuḥ sainikā rājñāṃ priyaṃ rājñaś cikīrṣavaḥ.

VAIŚAMPĀYANA UVĀCA:

156.1 TATAḤ ŚĀNTANAVAṂ Bhīṣmaṃ prāñjalir Dhṛtarāṣṭra|jaḥ<br>
saha sarvair mahī|pālair idaṃ vacanam abravīt:

So these were the armies arrayed by the wise Káurava. The assembled battalions of both sides numbered eighteen. On the one hand, the Pándavas had assembled only seven to constitute their force, while the Káuravas on the other hand had assembled eleven battalions. It is said that a *patti* constitutes two hundred and fifty men, and that it takes three of these to create a *sena·mukha* or a *gulma*. Three *gulma*s make a *gana*, and there were tens of thousands of *gana*s in Duryódhana's armies, all consisting of champions eager to fight.

Long-armed and wise King Duryódhana inspected his 155.30
heroic men and appointed his army generals. First he had each battalion's leader brought to him in the customary manner, then he spoke to the kings, all excellent men: Kripa, Drona, Shalya, Jayad·ratha Sáindhava, Sudákshina the Kambójan king, Krita·varman, Drona's son Ashva·tthaman, Karna, Bhuri·shravas, Shákuni Sáubala, and mighty Báhlika. He instructed them day after day, at all hours, Bhárata, and he openly paid them various honors,
time and again. And controlled in this manner, all the king's 155.35
soldiers and their followers became keen to do as the king wished.

VAISHAMPÁYANA continued:

THEN DHRITA·RASHTRA'S son put his hands together and 156.1
said these words to Shántanu's son Bhishma and all the kings of earth:

«ṛte senā|praṇetāraṃ pṛtanā su|mahaty api
dīryate yuddham āsādya, pipīlika|puṭaṃ yathā.
na hi jātu dvayor buddhiḥ samā bhavati karhi cit,
śauryaṃ ca bala|netṝṇāṃ spardhate ca paras|param.
śrūyate ca, mahā|prājña, Haihayān a|mit'|âujasaḥ
abhyayur brāhmaṇāḥ sarve samucchrita|kuśa|dhvajāḥ.
156.5 tān abhyayus tadā vaiśyāḥ śūdrāś c' âiva, pitā|maha,
ekatas tu trayo varṇā, ekataḥ kṣatriya'|rṣabhāḥ.
tato yuddheṣv abhajyanta trayo varṇāḥ punaḥ punaḥ,
kṣatriyāś ca jayanty eva bahulaṃ c' âikato balam.
tatas te kṣatriyān eva papracchur dvija|sattamāḥ;
tebhyaḥ śaśaṃsur dharma|jñā yāthātathyaṃ, pitā|maha:
‹vayam ekasya śṛṇvānā mahā|buddhimato raṇe;
bhavantas tu pṛthak sarve sva|buddhi|vaśa|vartinaḥ.›
tatas te brāhmaṇāś cakrur ekaṃ senā|patiṃ dvijam
naye su|kuśalaṃ, śūram; ajayan kṣatriyāṃs tataḥ.
156.10 evaṃ ye kuśalaṃ, śūraṃ, hit'|ēpsitam, a|kalmaṣam
senā|patiṃ prakurvanti, te jayanti raṇe ripūn.
bhavān Uśanasā tulyo, hit'|âiṣī ca sadā mama,
a|saṃhāryaḥ sthito dharme; sa naḥ senā|patir bhava;
raśmivatām iv' āditya, vīrudhām iva candramāḥ,
Kubera iva yakṣāṇāṃ, devānām iva Vāsavaḥ,
parvatānāṃ yathā Meruḥ, Suparṇaḥ pakṣiṇāṃ yathā,
Kumāra iva devānāṃ, Vasūnām iva Havyavāṭ.

"Without an army commander, an army is torn apart in war like an anthill, no matter how large the force may be. It is certainly true that two men never share the same opinion, and two commanders are jealous of each other's bravery.

We have heard that all the brahmins raised their *kusha*-grass banners and encountered the immeasurably energetic
Háihayas in battle, great wise man, and then the vaishyas 156.5
and shudras followed them, grandfather, so that there were three classes on one side, against the bull-like kshatriyas on the other. But during the battles the three classes broke ranks time and time again, whereas the kshatriyas defeated the huge force opposed to them, though they were alone.

Then the most excellent of the twiceborn brahmins asked the kshatriyas why this was, and the kshatriyas, who understood law, told them the truth of the matter, grandfather: 'We listen to a single man of great intelligence in battle, whereas you are all slaves to your individual opinions and are therefore divided.' So the brahmins then made one brave twiceborn, highly trained in policy, their general; and
they defeated the kshatriyas. So it is that men defeat their 156.10
enemies in battle if they appoint a skilled, brave, and pure man, who desires what is in their interest, as their general.

You are the equal of Úshanas, and you always wish for what is beneficial to me. You cannot be bribed, and you abide by the law. Be our general, as the sun among luminous bodies, the lunar lord of plants among herbs, Kubéra among the *yakshas*, Vásava among the gods, Meru among mountains, Supárna among birds, Kumára among the gods, and Fire among the Vasus.

bhavatā hi vayaṃ guptāḥ, Śakreṇ' êva div'|âukasaḥ
an|ādhṛṣyā bhaviṣyāmas tri|daśānām api dhruvam.
156.15 prayātu no bhavān agre, devānām iva Pāvakiḥ;
vayaṃ tvām anuyāsyāmaḥ saurabheyā iva' ṛṣabham.»

BHĪṢMA uvāca:

evam etan, mahā|bāho, yathā vadasi, Bhārata;
yath" âiva hi bhavanto me, tath" âiva mama Pāṇḍavāḥ.
api c' âiva mayā śreyo vācyaṃ teṣāṃ, nar'|âdhipa,
saṃyoddhavyaṃ tav' ârthāya yathā me samayaḥ kṛtaḥ.
na tu paśyāmi yoddhāram ātmanaḥ sadṛśaṃ bhuvi,
ṛte tasmān nara|vyāghrāt Kuntī|putrād Dhanañjayāt.
sa hi veda mahā|buddhir divyāny astrāṇy an|ekaśaḥ;
na tu māṃ vivṛto yuddhe jātu yudhyeta Pāṇḍavaḥ.
156.20 ahaṃ c' âiva kṣaṇen' âiva nirmanuṣyam idaṃ jagat
kuryāṃ śastra|balen' âiva sa|sur'|âsura|rākṣasam.
na tv ev' ôtsādanīyā me Pāṇḍoḥ putrā, jan'|âdhipa,
tasmād yodhān haniṣyāmi prayogeṇ' âyutam sadā.
evam eṣāṃ kariṣyāmi nidhanaṃ, Kuru|nandana,
na cet te māṃ haniṣyanti pūrvam eva samāgame.
senā|patis tv ahaṃ, rājan, samayen' âpareṇa te
bhaviṣyāmi yathā|kāmaṃ; tan me śrotum ih' ârhasi.
Karṇo vā yudhyatāṃ pūrvam, ahaṃ vā, pṛthivī|pate;
spardhate hi sad" âtyarthaṃ sūta|putro mayā raṇe.

KARṆA uvāca:

156.25 n' âhaṃ jīvati Gāṅgeye, rājan, yotsye kathañ cana;
hate Bhīṣme tu yotsyāmi saha Gāṇḍīva|dhanvanā.

For protected by you as the heaven-dwellers are protected by Shakra, we will surely become invincible like the thirty gods. May you march at our head, like Kumára son of Agni 156.15
at the head of the gods, and let us follow you as though we were a herd of cattle following a bull."

BHISHMA replied:

Long-armed Bhárata, it is indeed just as you say, but I hold the Pándavas in the same regard that I hold you. So I must also say what is best for them, lord of men, though I must fight for your cause as I promised. I see no fighter on earth to match me bar Dhanan·jaya, the tiger-like son of Kunti.

That highly intelligent man does indeed possess the secrets of numerous divine weapons, but the Pándava would certainly not fight against me openly. I could rid this uni- 156.20
verse of men, gods, *ásuras*, and *rákshasas* in an instant with the force of my weapons, but I must not destroy the sons of Pandu, lord of men. Therefore I will kill a myriad of soldiers every day. So, if they do not kill me first, I will slaughter their forces in battle, descendant of the Kurus.

I will willingly become your general on another condition, king, so you ought to listen to me. It should either be Karna or I who fights first, lord of earth, for the *suta*'s son always competes with me excessively in battle.

KARNA said:

While the son of the Ganges is alive, king, I will never 156.25
fight; but when Bhishma is dead then I will fight with the Gandíva archer.

VAIŚAMPĀYANA uvāca:

tataḥ senā|patiṃ cakre vidhivad bhūri|dakṣiṇam
Dhṛtarāṣṭr'|ātmajo Bhīṣmaṃ; so 'bhiṣikto vyarocata.
tato bherīś ca śaṅkhāṃś ca śataśo 'tha sahasraśaḥ
vādayām āsur a|vyagrā vādakā rāja|śāsanāt.

siṃha|nādāś ca vividhā, vāhanānām ca niḥsvanāḥ
prādur āsann, an|abhre ca varṣaṃ rudhira|kardamam.
nirghātāḥ, pṛthivī|kampā, gaja|bṛṃhita|niḥsvanāḥ
āsaṃś ca sarva|yodhānāṃ pātayanto manāṃsy uta,
156.30 vācaś c' âpy a|śarīriṇyo, divaś c' ôlkāḥ prapedire,
śivāś ca bhaya|vedinyo nedur dīptatarā bhṛśam.
saināpatye yadā rājā Gāṅgeyam abhiṣiktavān,
tad" âitāny ugra|rūpāṇi babhūvuḥ śataśo, nṛpa.

tataḥ senā|patiṃ kṛtvā Bhīṣmaṃ para|bal'|ârdanam,
vācayitvā dvija|śreṣṭhān gobhir niṣkaiś ca bhūriśaḥ,
vardhamāno jay'|āśīrbhir niryayau sainikair vṛtaḥ
āpageyaṃ puras|kṛtya bhrātṛbhiḥ sahitas tadā;
skandh'|āvāreṇa mahatā Kuru|kṣetraṃ jagāma ha.
156.35 parikramya Kuru|kṣetraṃ Karṇena saha Kauravaḥ
śibiraṃ māpayām āsa same deśe, jan'|âdhipa.
madhur'|ân|ūṣare deśe prabhūta|yavas'|êndhane
yath" âiva Hāstinapuraṃ, tadvac chibiram ābabhau.

VAISHAMPÁYANA said:

Dhrita·rashtra's son duly made munificent Bhishma the army's general, and once he was consecrated in his position, Bhishma glowed. Then, at the king's command, musicians steadily played kettledrums and conch shells by the hundreds and thousands.

Lion roars and various animal cries echoed, and, though the sky was cloudless, a slimy shower of blood rained down. There were hurricanes, earthquakes, and the bellows of trumpeting elephants, and the spirits of all the soldiers fell.
Incorporeal voices and meteors appeared in the heavens, 156.30
and jackals howled fiercely and all too shrilly, signaling danger. So these were the hundreds of fierce-seeming portents which arose, lord, when the king consecrated the son of the Ganges to the rank of general over the army.

Then, once he had made Bhishma, the destroyer of enemy armies, his general, and had—by means of plentiful gifts of cattle and gold—made the greatest of brahmins recite benedictions over him, he set out lifted by their victory cheers, in the company of his brothers and surrounded by his soldiers, with the son of the Ganges in front; and he went to Kuru·kshetra with his great royal headquarters.
Then, once he had marched to Kuru·kshetra with Karna, 156.35
the Káurava measured out his camp on level ground, lord of men. And, on delightful non-saline ground with plenty of grass and fuel, a camp sprung up to rival Hástina·pura.

JANAMEJAYA uvāca:

157.1 ĀPAGEYAṂ MAH"|ātmānaṃ
Bhīṣmaṃ, śastra|bhṛtāṃ varam,
pitā|mahaṃ Bhāratānāṃ,
dhvajaṃ sarva|mahī|kṣitām,
Bṛhaspati|samaṃ buddhyā, kṣamayā pṛthivī|samam,
samudram iva gāmbhīrye, Himavantam iva sthiram,
Prajāpatim iv' âudārye, tejasā bhāskar'|ôpamam,
Mahendram iva śatrūṇāṃ dhvasanaṃ śara|vṛṣṭhibhiḥ,
raṇa|yajñe pravitate, su|bhīme, loma|harṣaṇe
dīkṣitaṃ cira|rātrāya śrutvā tatra Yudhiṣṭhiraḥ,
157.5 kim abravīn mahā|bāhuḥ sarva|śastra|bhṛtāṃ varaḥ,
Bhīmasen'|Ârjunau v" âpi, Kṛṣṇo vā pratyabhāṣata?

VAIŚAMPĀYANA uvāca:

āpad|dharm'|ârtha|kuśalo, mahā|buddhir Yudhiṣṭhiraḥ
sarvān bhrātṝn samānīya, Vāsudevaṃ ca śāśvatam,
uvāca vadatāṃ śreṣṭhaḥ sāntva|pūrvam idaṃ vacaḥ:
«paryākrāmata sainyāni, yattās tiṣṭhata daṃśitāḥ.
pitā|mahena vo yuddhaṃ pūrvam eva bhaviṣyati;
tasmāt saptasu senāsu praṇetṝn mama paśyata.»

KṚṢṆA uvāca:

yath" ârhati bhavān vaktum asmin kāle hy upasthite,
tath" êdam arthavad vākyam uktaṃ te, Bharata'|rṣabha.
157.10 rocate me, mahā|bāho, kriyatāṃ yad an|antaram;
nāyakās tava senāyāṃ kriyantām iha sapta vai.

ÉJAYA said:

WHEN HE HEARD that high-souled Bhishma, son of the Ganges—the greatest of those who wield weapons, the grandfather of the Bharatas, the ornament of all kings, a match for Brihas·pati in wisdom, a match for the earth in patience, deep as the ocean, steady as the Himálaya, a match for Praja·pati in generosity, sun-like in his energy, the man who resembles great Indra destroying his enemies with showers of arrows—had been installed as general for the widespread, utterly terrifying, hair-raising and long-lasting sacrifice of battle, what did long-armed Yudhi·shthira, the greatest of all who wield weapons, say? Or what did Bhima·sena and Árjuna or Krishna have to say? 157.1 157.5

VAISHAMPÁYANA said:

Yudhi·shthira of great intelligence, skilled in the import of the laws for times of disaster, brought all his brothers and eternal Vasudéva together, and the greatest of speakers said these words in a calm voice: "Make the rounds through the soldiers, and stay in your armor. Our first battle will be with our grandfather. So search for the leaders of my seven battalions."

KRISHNA replied:

You have spoken sensibly, just as you ought to speak now that the time is at hand, bull of the Bharatas. I agree, long- 157.10
armed man, so let what needs to be done immediately be done. Let the seven leaders for your armies be appointed here and now.

VAIŚAMPĀYANA uvāca:

tato Drupadam ānāyya, Virāṭaṃ, Śini|puṅgavam,
Dhṛṣṭadyumnaṃ ca Pāñcālyaṃ, Dhṛṣṭaketuṃ ca, pārthiva,
Śikhaṇḍinaṃ ca Pāñcālyaṃ, Sahadevaṃ ca Māgadham—
etān sapta mahā|bhāgān vīrān yuddh'|âbhikāṅkṣiṇaḥ
senā|praṇetṝn vidhivad abhyaṣiñcad Yudhiṣṭhiraḥ;
sarva|senā|patiṃ c' âtra Dhṛṣṭadyumnaṃ cakāra ha,
Droṇ'|ânta|hetor utpanno ya iddhāj jātavedasaḥ.
sarveṣām eva teṣāṃ tu samastānāṃ mah"|ātmanām
157.15 senā|pati|patiṃ cakre Guḍākeśaṃ Dhanañjayam.
Arjunasy' âpi netā ca, saṃyantā c' âiva vājinām,
Saṅkarṣaṇ'|ânujaḥ śrīmān
mahā|buddhir Janārdanaḥ.

tad dṛṣṭv" ôpasthitaṃ yuddhaṃ
samāsannaṃ mah"|âtyayam
prāviśad bhavanaṃ, rājan, Pāṇḍavānāṃ Halāyudhaḥ,
sah' Âkrūra|prabhṛtibhir Gada|Sāmb'|Ôddhav'|ādibhiḥ,
Raukmiṇey'|Âhuka|sutaiś Cārudeṣṇa|purogamaiḥ.
Vṛṣṇi|mukhyair adhigatair vyāghrair iva bal'|ôtkaṭaiḥ,
abhigupto mahā|bāhur marudbhir iva Vāsavaḥ,
nīla|kauśeya|vasanaḥ, Kailāsa|śikhar'|ôpamaḥ,
157.20 siṃha|khela|gatiḥ, śrīmān, mada|rakt'|ânta|locanaḥ.

taṃ dṛṣṭvā dharma|rājaś ca Keśavaś ca mahā|dyutiḥ
udatiṣṭhat, tataḥ Pārtho bhīma|karmā Vṛkodaraḥ,
Gāṇḍīva|dhanvā, ye c' ânye rājānas tatra ke cana.
pūjayāṃ cakrire te vai samāyāntaṃ Halāyudham.
tatas taṃ Pāṇḍavo rājā kare pasparśa pāṇinā;
Vāsudeva|purogās taṃ sarva ev' âbhyavādayan.

VAISHAMPÁYANA continued:

Then, O king, Yudhi·shthira had Drúpada, Viráta, the bull of the Shini race, Dhrishta·dyumna the prince of Panchála, Dhrishta·ketu, Shikhándin the prince of Panchála, and the Mágadhan king Saha·deva—the seven great noble heroes eager for war—brought before him, and he consecrated them duly as commanders of the army. Then as general of the whole army he installed Dhrishta·dyumna, who 157.15
was born from blazing fire for the destruction of Drona. And he made Dhanan·jaya Guda·kesha the overlord general of all those united high-souled men. Highly intelligent glorious Janárdana, Sankárshana's younger brother, was made Árjuna's guide and driver of his horses.

Noticing that the war of total destruction was at hand, plow-weaponed Rama entered the Pándavas' compound, my king, along with Akrúra, Gada, Samba, Úddhava and so on, Rúkmini's son, and Áhuka's sons, led by Charu·deshna. Guarded by these leading Vrishnis making their way like tigers taking pride in their strength, as though he were Vásava guarded by the Maruts, long-armed glorious Rama, dressed in midnight-blue silk, resembling the peak of Mount Kailása, came with the gait of a playful lion and with 157.20
the whites of his eyes reddened through alcohol.

When the king of righteousness and great glorious Késhava spotted him they stood up, as did Vrikódara Partha of fearful exploits, the Gandíva bowman, and some other kings. They paid their respects to Haláyudha as he joined them, and then the Pándava king touched his hand with his own, and everyone greeted him, led by Vasudéva. Haláyudha saluted his elders, Viráta and Drúpada, and then the

Virāṭa|Drupadau vṛddhāv abhivādya Halāyudhaḥ
Yudhiṣṭhireṇa sahita upāviśad arin|damaḥ.
tatas teṣ' ûpaviṣṭeṣu pārthiveṣu samantataḥ
Vāsudevam abhiprekṣya Rauhiṇeyo 'bhyabhāṣata.
157.25 «bhavit" âyaṃ mahā|raudro dāruṇaḥ puruṣa|kṣayaḥ.
diṣṭam etad dhruvaṃ manye, na śakyam ativartitum.
tasmād yuddhāt samuttīrṇān api vaḥ sa|suhṛj|janān
a|rogān a|kṣatair dehair draṣṭ" âsm' îti matir mama.
sametaṃ pārthivaṃ kṣatraṃ, kāla|pakvam a|saṃśayam,
vimardaś ca mahān bhāvī māṃsa|śoṇita|kardamaḥ.
ukto mayā Vāsudevaḥ punaḥ punar upahvare:
‹sambandhiṣu samāṃ vṛttiṃ vartasva, Madhu|sūdana;
Pāṇḍavā hi yath" âsmākaṃ, tathā Duryodhano nṛpaḥ.
tasy' âpi kriyatāṃ sāhyaṃ sapary", êti› punaḥ punaḥ.
157.30 tac ca me n' âkarod vākyaṃ tvad|arthe Madhū|sūdanaḥ,
nirviṣṭaḥ sarva|bhāvena Dhanañjayam avekṣya ha.
dhruvo jayaḥ Pāṇḍavānām, iti me niścitā matiḥ;
tathā hy abhiniveśo 'yaṃ Vāsudevasya, Bhārata,
na c' âham utsahe Kṛṣṇam ṛte lokam udīkṣitum,
tato 'ham anuvartāmi Keśavasya cikīrṣitam.
ubhau śiṣyau hi me vīrau, gadā|yuddha|viśāradau,
tulya|sneho 'smy ato Bhīme tathā Duryodhane nṛpe;
tasmād yāsyāmi tīrthāni Sarasvatyā niṣevitum;
na hi śakṣyāmi Kauravyān naśyamānān upekṣitum.»
157.35 evam uktvā mahā|bāhur anujñātaś ca Pāṇḍavaiḥ
tīrtha|yātrāṃ yayau Rāmo nirvartya Madhu|sūdanam.

enemy-tamer sat down with Yudhi·shthira. And when the kings were all seated, Rauhinéya glanced at Vasudéva and spoke as follows:

"There will be an immensely horrifying and violent 157.25
slaughter of men. It is surely fated, and I believe it is impossible to avert it. I believe I shall see you and your friends again in good health and with your bodies unbroken, when you have survived the war. The warrior-class kings have congregated, doubtlessly cooked by time, and there will be a vast carnage filthy with flesh and blood.

I told Vasudéva privately time and again: 'Act with equal conduct towards your relatives, Madhu·súdana, for King Duryódhana is as much our relative as the Pándavas. Give
him equal help.' So I warned him over and over again, but 157.30
the slayer of Madhu did not act upon my advice for your sake, for he is loyal to you with his whole being, looking to Dhanan·jaya.

I have come to the conclusion that victory is assured for the Pándavas, for this is indeed Vasudéva's determination, Bhárata. I do not dare to look on the world without Krishna, so I follow whatever Késhava wants to do. Bhima and King Duryódhana, both heroes skilled in battles with the mace, have both been my students, and I feel equal affection for them; and so I will go to stay at the pilgrimage sites on the Sarásvati river, for I find myself truly unable to watch the Káuravas being destroyed."

Once he had spoken in this way, long-armed Rama took 157.35
his leave of the Pándavas, and, turning back the slayer of Madhu, he went on his journey of pilgrimage.

VAIŚAMPĀYANA uvāca:

158.1 ETASMINN EVA kāle tu Bhīṣmakasya mah"|ātmanaḥ,
Hiraṇyaromṇo nṛ|pateḥ, sākṣād Indra|sakhasya vai,
Ākūtīnām adhipater, Bhojasy' âtiyaśasvinaḥ,
dākṣiṇātya|pateḥ putro, dikṣu Rukm" îti viśrutaḥ,
yaḥ kiṃ|puruṣa|siṃhasya Gandhamādana|vāsinaḥ
kṛtsnaṃ śiṣyo dhanur|vedaṃ catuṣ|pādam avāptavān,
yo Māhendraṃ dhanur lebhe tulyaṃ Gāṇḍīva|tejasā,
Śārṅgeṇa ca, mahā|bāhuḥ sammitaṃ divya|lakṣaṇam.
158.5 trīṇy ev' âitāni divyāni dhanūṃṣi divi cāriṇām:
Vāruṇaṃ Gāṇḍivaṃ tatra, Māhendraṃ Vijayaṃ dhanuḥ,
Śārṅgaṃ tu Vaiṣṇavaṃ prāhur divyaṃ tejo|mayaṃ dhanuḥ,
dhārayām āsa yat Kṛṣṇaḥ para|senā|bhay'|āvaham.
Gāṇḍīvaṃ pāvakāl lebhe Khāṇḍave Pāka|śāsaniḥ;
Drumād Rukmī mahā|tejā Vijayaṃ pratyapadyata;
saṃchidya Mauravān pāśān, nihatya Murum ojasā,
nirjitya Narakaṃ bhaumam, āhṛtya maṇi|kuṇḍale,
ṣoḍaśa strī|sahasrāṇi, ratnāni vividhāni ca,
pratipede Hṛṣīkeśaḥ Śārṅgaṃ ca dhanur uttamam.
Rukmī tu Vijayaṃ labdhvā dhanur megha|nibha|svanam,
158.10 vibhīṣayann iva jagat Pāṇḍavān abhyavartata.
n' âmṛṣyata purā yo 'sau sva|bāhu|bala|garvitaḥ
Rukmiṇyā haraṇaṃ vīro Vāsudevena dhīmatā,
kṛtvā pratijñāṃ, «n' â|hatvā nivartiṣye Janārdanam.»
tato 'nvadhāvad Vārṣṇeyaṃ sarva|śastra|bhṛtāṃ varaḥ

VAISHAMPÁYANA continued:

AT THIS TIME the son of high-souled Bhíshmaka arrived —Bhíshmaka, also called King Hiránya·roman, a friend of Indra himself, the ruler of the Akútis, an excessively illustrious Bhoja and the lord of the south. His son was famed in the regions of the world as Rukmin. He was the student of a lion-like *kim·púrusha* who lived on the Gandha·mádana mountain, and he learned the entire four-part science of weapons. The long-armed man won great Indra's divinely marked bow, Víjaya, which in splendor equaled Gandíva and Sharnga, Krishna's bow. 158.1

There are three celestial bows which belong to those who roam heaven: Váruna's bow Gandíva, great Indra's bow Víjaya, and Vishnu's bow Sharnga, which they claim is a divine bow fashioned from the power Krishna wielded, bringing fear to enemy armies. Árjuna, the son of the punisher of Paka, took the Gandíva from the fire god in the Khándava forest; vastly energetic Rukmin took Víjaya from Druma; and, breaking Muru's chains and killing him with his might, Hrishikésha defeated Náraka, son of the earth, and stole jewels and gold, sixteen thousand women, and various treasures, and of course he also won the superb bow Sharnga. 158.5

So Rukmin, who had obtained Víjaya, the bow which twangs like booming thunder, approached the Pándavas, 158.10
seeming to fill the universe with terror. That hero, who took pride in the strength of his arms, had not endured his sister Rúkmini being carried off by cunning Vasudéva. Instead, he had made a promise that he would not return until he had killed Janárdana. So the greatest of all who wield

senayā catur|aṅgiṇyā mahatyā dūra|pātayā,
vicitr'|āyudha|varmiṇyā, Gaṅgay" êva pravṛddhayā.
sa samāsādya Vārṣṇeyaṃ yogānām īśvaraṃ prabhum;
vyaṃsito, vrīḍito, rājann, ājagāma sa Kuṇḍinam.

yatr' âiva Kṛṣṇena raṇe nirjitaḥ para|vīra|hā,
158.15 tatra Bhojakaṭaṃ nāma kṛtaṃ nagaram uttamam.
sainyena mahatā tena prabhūta|gaja|vājinā
puraṃ tad bhuvi vikhyātaṃ nāmnā Bhojakaṭaṃ, nṛpa.

sa Bhoja|rājaḥ sainyena mahatā parivāritaḥ
akṣauhiṇyā mahā|vīryaḥ Pāṇḍavān kṣipram āgamat.
tataḥ sa kavacī, dhanvī, talī, khaḍgī, śar'|âsanī,
dhvajen' āditya|varṇena praviveśa mahā|camūm,
viditaḥ Pāṇḍaveyānāṃ Vāsudeva|priy'|ēpśayā.
Yudhiṣṭhiras tu taṃ rājā pratyudgamy' âbhyapūjayat.
sa pūjitaḥ Pāṇḍu|putrair, yathā|nyāyaṃ su|saṃstutaḥ,
158.20 pratigṛhya tu tān sarvān, viśrāntaḥ saha|sainikaḥ,
uvāca madhye vīrāṇāṃ Kuntī|putraṃ Dhanañjayam:

«sahāyo 'smi sthito yuddhe, yadi bhīto 'si, Pāṇḍava,
kariṣyāmi raṇe sāhyam a|sahyaṃ tava śatrubhiḥ.
na hi me vikrame tulyaḥ pumān ast' îha kaś cana;
haniṣyāmi raṇe bhāgaṃ yan me dāsyasi, Pāṇḍava,
api Droṇa|Kṛpau vīrau, Bhīṣma|Karṇāv atho punaḥ!
atha vā sarva ev' âite tiṣṭhantu vasudh"|âdhipāḥ;
nihatya samare śatrūṃs tava dāsyāmi medinīm!»

weapons pursued Varshnéya with a vast, far-shooting, four-divisioned army, with various weapons and armor, and like the Ganges in full flood he attacked Lord Varshnéya, the master of tactics; but he was defeated and humiliated, my king, so he returned to his city of Kúndina.

Then, in the place where the slayer of enemy heroes had
been defeated in battle by Krishna, he built a magnificent 158.15
city called Bhoja·kata. With its enormous army and wealth
of elephants and horses, that city is still renowned on earth
by the name of Bhoja·kata, my king.

The mightily heroic Bhoja king came quickly to the Pándavas, surrounded by his vast battalion of soldiers. Then,
with his armor, bow, armguards, sword, quiver, and sun-
hued flag, he entered the large compound and made himself known to the Pándavas out of a desire to please Vasudéva. King Yudhi·shthira got up and paid honor to him,
and, being honored by the sons of Pandu and duly praised,
he greeted them all and rested with his soldiers. Then he 158.20
addressed Dhanan·jaya, son of Kunti, in the midst of the
heroes:

"I stand as your ally in war if you are afraid, Pándava, and I will give you help in battle which your enemies cannot withstand. There is no man here who is my match for prowess, and I will kill whatever share you apportion me in battle, Pándava, even the heroes Drona and Kripa, and then again Bhishma and Karna! Alternatively, let all these earth-lords stay and rest, and, killing your enemies in battle, I will deliver the earth to you!"

ity ukto dharma|rājasya Keśavasya ca sannidhau,
158.25 śṛṇvatāṃ pārthiv'|êndrāṇām, anyeṣāṃ c' âiva sarvaśaḥ,
Vāsudevam abhiprekṣya, dharma|rājaṃ ca Pāṇḍavam,
uvāca dhīmān Kaunteyaḥ prahasya sakhi|pūrvikam,
«Kauravāṇāṃ kule jātaḥ, Pāṇḍoḥ putro viśeṣataḥ,
Droṇaṃ vyapadiśañ śiṣyo, Vāsudeva|sahāyavān,
bhīto 'sm', îti kathaṃ brūyāṃ dadhāno Gāṇḍivaṃ dhanuḥ?
yudhyamānasya me, vīra, gandharvaiḥ su|mahā|balaiḥ
sahāyo ghoṣa|yātrāyāṃ kas tad" āsīt sakhā mama?
tathā pratibhaye tasmin deva|Dānava|saṃkule
Khāṇḍave yudhyamānasya kaḥ sahāyas tad" âbhavat?
158.30 Nivātakavacair yuddhe, Kālakeyaiś ca Dānavaiḥ,
tatra me yudhyamānasya kaḥ sahāyas tad" âbhavat?
tathā Virāṭa|nagare Kurubhiḥ saha saṅgare
yudhyato bahubhis tatra kaḥ sahāyo 'bhavan mama?
upajīvya raṇe Rudraṃ, Śakraṃ, Vaiśravaṇaṃ, Yamam,
Varuṇaṃ, Pāvakaṃ c' âiva, Kṛpaṃ, Droṇaṃ ca, Mādhavam
dhārayan Gāṇḍivaṃ divyaṃ dhanus tejo|mayaṃ dṛḍham,
a|kṣayya|śara|saṃyukto, divy'|âstra|paribṛṃhitaḥ,
katham asmad|vidho brūyād, ‹bhīto 'sm', îti› yaśo|haram
vacanaṃ, nara|śārdūla, vajr'|āyudham api svayam?
158.35 n' âsmi bhīto, mahā|bāho, sahāy'|ârthaś ca n' âsti me.
yathā|kāmaṃ yathā|yogaṃ gaccha v" ânyatra, tiṣṭha vā.»
vinivartya tato Rukmī senāṃ sāgara|saṃnibhām
Duryodhanam upāgacchat tath" âiva, Bharata'|rṣabha.
tath" âiva c' âbhigamy' âinam uvāca vasudh"|âdhipaḥ
pratyākhyātaś ca ten' âpi sa tadā śūra|māninā.

Addressed in this manner in the presence of Késhava and
the king of righteousness and within the hearing of the 158.25
lords of kings and others all around, the wise son of Kunti glanced at Vasudéva and the Pándava king of righteousness, laughed amicably, and said:

"Born into the Kuru lineage, and as Pandu's son no less, designating Drona as my teacher when I was a student, with Vasudéva as my ally and Gandíva as my bow, how could I say that I am afraid? What friend did I have as my ally when I fought against the incredibly powerful *gandhárvas* at the cattle expedition, hero? Who was my ally when I fought in the terrifying Khándava Forest packed with gods and Dánavas? Who was my ally when I fought in battle against the 158.30
Niváta·kávachas and the Dánavas called Kalakéyas? Who was my ally when I fought great hosts of Kurus in battle at Viráta's city?

Having made use of Rudra, Shakra, Váishravana, Yama, Váruna, Agni, Kripa, Drona, and Mádhava for battle, wielding the celestial and firm bow Gandíva, made of splendor, endowed with an inexhaustible supply of arrows, and armed with divine weapons, how could someone like me utter the fame-robbing words, 'I am afraid,' tiger-like man, even if he stood before thunderbolt-wielding Indra himself?

I am not scared, long-armed man, nor do I have any need 158.35
of an ally, so go or stay as you wish. Do whatever suits you."

So Rukmin turned his ocean-like army back, and went instead to Duryódhana, bull of the Bharatas. And once the earth-lord had reached him, he addressed him in exactly the same manner, but was rejected by him too, for Duryódhana was proud of his own bravery.

dvāv eva tu, mahā|rāja, tasmād yuddhād apeyatuḥ:
Rauhiṇeyaś ca Vārṣṇeyo, Rukmī ca, vasudh"|âdhipa.
gate Rāme tīrtha|yātrāṃ, Bhīṣmakasya sute tathā,
upāviśan Pāṇḍaveyā mantrāya punar eva ca.
158.40 samitir dharma|rājasya sā pārthiva|samākulā
śuśubhe tārakaiś citrā, dyauś candreṇ' êva, Bhārata.

JANAMEJAYA uvāca:

159.1 TATHĀ VYŪḌHEṢV anīkeṣu Kuru|kṣetre, dvija'|rṣabha,
kim akurvaṃś ca Kuravaḥ kālen' âbhipracoditāḥ?

VAIŚAMPĀYANA uvāca:

tathā vyūḍheṣv anīkeṣu yatteṣu, Bharata'|rṣabha,
Dhṛtarāṣṭro, mahā|rāja, Sañjayaṃ vākyam abravīt:
«ehi, Sañjaya, sarvaṃ me ācakṣv' ân|avaśeṣataḥ,
senā|niveśe yad vṛttaṃ Kuru|Pāṇḍava|senayoḥ.
diṣṭam eva paraṃ manye, pauruṣaṃ c' âpy an|arthakam,
yad ahaṃ budhyamāno 'pi yuddha|doṣān kṣay'|ôdayān,
159.5 tath" âpi nikṛti|prajñaṃ putraṃ dur|dyūta|devinam
na śaknomi niyantuṃ vā kartuṃ vā hitam ātmanaḥ.
bhavaty eva hi me, sūta, buddhir doṣ'|ânudarśinī;
Duryodhanaṃ samāsādya punaḥ sā parivartate.
evaṃ|gate vai yad bhāvi tad bhaviṣyati, Sañjaya.
kṣatra|dharmaḥ kila raṇe tanu|tyāgo hi pūjitaḥ.»

So it was that two men withdrew from the war, mighty sovereign: Rauhinéya Rama of the Vrishni line, and Rukmin, O lord of earth. Once Rama had gone on his pilgrimage and Bhíshmaka's son had left in this manner, the Pándavas sat down for yet more consultation. And the meet- 158.40
ing of the king of righteousness, teeming with kings, glittered like the heavens dotted with stars around the moon, Bhárata.

ÉJAYA said:

ONCE THE ARMIES were arrayed on Kuru·kshetra in this 159.1
manner, bull-like brahmin, what did the Kurus do, impelled by time?

VAISHAMPÁYANA said:

Once the armies were ready and arrayed in this manner, bull of the Bharatas, Dhrita·rashtra addressed Sánjaya in these words, mighty sovereign:

"Come on then, Sánjaya, tell me in minute detail what happened in the army encampments of the Kuru and Pándava forces. I believe that fate is ultimate and human effort is useless, for though I understand that the sins of war will
only cause destruction, I am not even able to restrain my 159.5
despicable gambler of a son who counts deception as wisdom, nor can I do anything to my own advantage.

*Suta*, I do indeed have the wit to see faults, but when I approach Duryódhana, this comprehension leaves me again. This being the case, what must be will be, Sánjaya. Sacrificing one's body in battle is the kshatriya's honored law, or so they say."

SAÑJAYA uvāca:

tvad|yukto 'yam anupraśno, mahā|rāja, yath" êcchasi;
na tu Duryodhane doṣam imam ādhātum arhasi.
śṛṇuṣv' ân|avaśeṣeṇa vadato mama, pārthiva.
ya ātmano duś|caritād a|śubhaṃ prāpnuyān naraḥ,
na sa kālaṃ na vā devān enasā gantum arhati.
159.10 mahā|rāja, manuṣyeṣu nindyaṃ yaḥ sarvam ācaret,
sa vadhyaḥ sarva|lokasya ninditāni samācaran.
nikārā, manuja|śreṣṭha, Pāṇḍavais tvat|pratīkṣayā
anubhūtāḥ sah'|âmātyair nikṛtair adhidevane.

hayānāṃ ca gajānāṃ ca rājñāṃ c' âmita|tejasām
vaiśasaṃ samaraṃ vṛttaṃ yat, tan me śṛṇu sarvaśaḥ.
sthiro bhūtvā, mahā|prājña, sarva|loka|kṣay'|ôdayam
yathā bhūtaṃ mahā|yuddhe; śrutvā c' âikamanā bhava:
na hy eva kartā puruṣaḥ karmaṇoḥ śubha|pāpayoḥ.
a|sva|tantro hi puruṣaḥ kāryate dāru|yantravat.
159.15 ke cid īśvara|nirdiṣṭāḥ, ke cid eva yadṛcchayā,
pūrva|karmabhir apy anye: traidham etat pradṛśyate.
tasmād an|artham āpannaḥ sthiro bhūtvā niśāmaya.

SÁNJAYA replied:

The question you wish to raise befits you, great king, but you ought not to assign the blame to Duryódhana alone. Listen to the detailed advice I give you, king. The man who gains unpleasantness through his own misbehavior ought
not to place the fault on fate or the gods. Great sovereign, 159.10
the man who acts entirely reprehensibly among his fellow men should be killed in the sight of the whole world for committing his offences. It was because they looked to you that the Pándavas and their counselors bore their mistreatments when they were deceived at the gambling match, greatest of men.

Listen to everything I have to say about the holocaust of war to come—the holocaust of horses, elephants, and kings of immeasurable splendor. As you hear about the destruction of the whole world wrought in the great war now begun, great wise man, remain calm and be sure of one thing: man is not the author of his actions, be they good or evil. In fact, man is not master of himself, but is made to act, like
a marionette. There are three theories on this matter: some 159.15
people believe fates are predestined by the gods, some say they are the result of free will, and others say that they are predestined by a person's previous deeds. So remain calm as you hear the calamity that has overcome us.

160–164

# ULÚKA'S EMBASSY

SAÑJAYA UVĀCA:

160.1 HIRAṆVATYĀṂ NIVIṢṬEṢU Pāṇḍaveṣu mah"|ātmasu
nyaviśanta, mahā|rāja, Kauraveyā yathā|vidhi.
tatra Duryodhano rājā niveśya balam ojasā,
saṃmānayitvā nṛ|patīn, nyasya gulmāṃs tath" âiva ca,
ārakṣasya vidhiṃ kṛtvā yodhānāṃ tatra, Bhārata;
Karṇaṃ Duḥśāsanaṃ c' âiva, Śakuniṃ c' âpi Saubalam
ānāyya nṛ|patis tatra mantrayām āsa, Bhārata.
tatra Duryodhano rājā Karṇena saha, Bhārata,
160.5 saṃbhāṣitvā ca Karṇena bhrātrā Duḥśāsanena ca,
Saubalena ca, rāj'|êndra, mantrayitvā, nara'|rṣabha,
āhūy' ôpahvare, rājann, Ulūkam idam abravīt:
«Ulūka, gaccha, kaitavya, Pāṇḍavān saha|Somakān;
gatvā mama vaco brūhi Vāsudevasya śṛṇvataḥ:
‹idaṃ tat samanuprāptaṃ varṣa|pūg'|âbhicintitam.
Pāṇḍavānāṃ Kurūṇāṃ ca yuddhaṃ loka|bhayaṅ|karam!
yad etat katthanā|vākyaṃ Sañjayo mahad abravīt
Vāsudeva|sahāyasya garjataḥ s'|ânujasya te,
madhye Kurūṇāṃ, Kaunteya, tasya kālo 'yam āgataḥ!
160.10 yathā vaḥ saṃpratijñātaṃ,
tat sarvaṃ kriyatām iti.›
jyeṣṭhaṃ tath" âiva Kaunteyaṃ
brūyās tvaṃ vacanān mama:
‹bhrātṛbhiḥ sahitaḥ sarvaiḥ, Somakaiś ca sa|Kekayaiḥ
kathaṃ vā dhārmiko bhūtvā tvam a|dharme manaḥ kṛthāḥ?
ya icchasi jagat sarvaṃ naśyamānaṃ nṛśaṃsavat,
a|bhayaṃ sarva|bhūtebhyo dātā tvam iti me matiḥ.

SÁNJAYA said:

ONCE THE HIGH-SOULED Pándavas had set up camp by the Hiránvati river, the Káuravas also encamped according to the precepts, mighty sovereign. King Duryódhana forcibly made his troops set up camp, paid his respects to the kings, set up units of men, and organized groups to guard the soldiers, Bhárata; and then he sent for the kings such as Karna, Duhshásana, and Shákuni Sáubala, and took their counsel, Bhárata. 160.1

King Duryódhana talked first with Karna alone, Bhárata, and then he consulted with Karna and his brother 160.5 Duhshásana and Sáubala together, bull-like lord of kings. Next he summoned Ulúka and spoke to him privately, my king, as follows:

"Ulúka, son of a gambler, go to the Pándavas and Sómakas, and once you have gone there, give them my message within earshot of Vasudéva:

'The war between the Pándavas and Kurus, deliberated for many a year, is now at hand, bringing fear to the world! Act on your great boast which Sánjaya announced in the midst of the Kurus, and which you and your brothers and Vasudéva as your ally roared—the time for it has come, Kauntéya! Do all that you swore you would!' 160.10

Similarly, you should give my message to the eldest son of Kunti:

'If you are really so righteous, how can you set your mind on lawlessness with all your brothers, the Sómakas, and the Kékayas? You cruelly wish for the entire universe to be destroyed, whereas I have always considered you the provider of freedom from fear to all creatures. We have heard this

śrūyate hi purā gītaḥ śloko 'yaṃ, Bharata'|rṣabha,
Prahlāden' âtha, bhadraṃ te, hṛte rājye tu daivataiḥ:
«yasya dharma|dhvajo nityaṃ surā|dhvaja iv' ôcchritaḥ,
pracchannāni ca pāpāni, baiḍālaṃ nāma tad vratam.»

160.15 atra te vartayiṣyāmi ākhyānam idam uttamam,
kathitaṃ Nāraden' êha pitur mama, nar'|âdhipa.
mārjāraḥ kila duṣṭ'|ātmā niśceṣṭaḥ sarva|karmasu
ūrdhvabāhuḥ sthito, rājan, Gaṅgā|tīre kadā cana.
sa vai kṛtvā manaḥ|śuddhiṃ pratyay'|ârthaṃ śarīriṇām,
«karomi dharmam, ity» āha sarvān eva śarīriṇaḥ.

tasya kālena mahatā viśraṃbhaṃ jagmur aṇḍa|jāḥ,
sametya ca praśaṃsanti mārjāraṃ taṃ, viśām pate.
pūjyamānas tu taiḥ sarvaiḥ pakṣibhiḥ pakṣi|bhojanaḥ
ātma|kāryaṃ kṛtaṃ mene, caryāyāś ca kṛtaṃ phalam.

160.20 atha dīrghasya kālasya taṃ deśaṃ mūṣikā yayuḥ,
dadṛśus taṃ ca te tatra dhārmikaṃ vrata|cāriṇam
kāryeṇa mahatā yuktaṃ dambha|yuktena, Bhārata.
teṣāṃ matir iyaṃ, rājann, āsīt tatra viniścaye.

«bahv|amitrā vayaṃ sarve, teṣāṃ no mātulo hy ayam.
rakṣāṃ karotu satataṃ vṛddha|bālasya sarvaśaḥ.»
upagamya tu te sarve biḍālam idam abruvan:
«bhavat|prasādād icchāmaś cartuṃ c' âiva yathā|sukham.
bhavān no gatir a|vyagrā bhavān naḥ paramaḥ su|hṛt.
te vayaṃ sahitāḥ sarve bhavantaṃ śaraṇaṃ gatāḥ.

verse, sung long ago, bull of the Bharatas, by Prahláda, bless you, when his kingdom was seized by the gods: "The man whose flag of law is always flying straight up like a tavern's banner, but whose sins are hidden, is said to have a cat-like observance."

I will repeat this excellent story here for you, which Nára- 160.15
da told to my father, lord of men. Once upon a time, so they say, an evil-souled cat abandoned all acts and stayed on the bank of the Ganges with his paws raised high, king. Pretending that his mind was pure in order to assure the animals, he told every creature he met that he was practicing law.*

After a long time birds came to trust him, and they gathered and praised the cat, lord of earth. Once he was honored by all birds, despite the fact that he ate birds, he believed that his job was done and that the rewards of the austerities to be practiced had arrived. Then, after a long while 160.20
more, mice came to the place and saw that the cat was virtuous, practiced vows, and was engaged in a momentous task, though he did so with deceptive concentration, Bhárata; so a thought occurred to them, king, and they made their decision.

"We have many enemies, so let this cat here be maternal uncle to us all. Let him eternally provide protection for every one of us, old and young." So, going up to the cat, they all said: "We want to wander as we please, by your favor. You are our safe recourse, you are our greatest friend. So we
all come to you as our refuge. You are eternally devoted to 160.25
virtue, and you are intent upon law, so protect us, highly

160.25 bhavān dharma|paro nityaṃ, bhavān dharme vyavasthitaḥ
sa no rakṣa, mahā|prajña, tri|daśān iva vajra|bhṛt.»
evam uktas tu taiḥ sarvair mūṣikaiḥ sa, viśām pate,
pratyuvāca tataḥ sarvān mūṣikān mūṣik'|ânta|kṛt:
«dvayor yogaṃ na paśyāmi tapaso rakṣaṇasya ca,
a|vaśyaṃ tu mayā kāryaṃ vacanaṃ bhavatāṃ hitam.
yuṣmābhir api kartavyaṃ vacanaṃ mama nityaśaḥ,
tapas" âsmi pariśrānto, dṛḍhaṃ niyamam āsthitaḥ;
na c' âpi gamane śaktiṃ kāñ cit paśyāmi cintayan,
so 'smi neyaḥ sadā, tātā, nadī|kūlam itaḥ param.»
160.30 «tath" êti» taṃ pratijñāya mūṣikā, Bharata'|rṣabha,
vṛddha|bālam atho sarvaṃ mārjārāya nyavedayan.
tataḥ sa pāpo duṣṭ'|ātmā mūṣikān atha bhakṣayan
pīvaraś ca su|varṇaś ca dṛḍha|bandhaś ca jāyate.
mūṣikāṇāṃ gaṇaś c' âtra bhṛśaṃ saṃkṣīyate 'tha saḥ,
mārjāro vardhate c' âpi tejo|bala|samanvitaḥ.
tatas te mūṣikāḥ sarve samety' ânyo|'nyam abruvan:
«mātulo vardhate nityaṃ, vayaṃ kṣīyāmahe bhṛśam.»
tataḥ prājñatamaḥ kaś cid Ḍiṇḍiko nāma mūṣikaḥ
abravīd vacanaṃ, rājan, mūṣikāṇāṃ mahā|gaṇam:
160.35 «gacchatāṃ vo nadī|tīraṃ sahitānāṃ viśeṣataḥ
pṛṣṭhato 'haṃ gamiṣyāmi sah' âiva mātulena tu.»
«sādhu! sādhv! iti» te sarve pūjayāṃ cakrire tadā,
cakruś c' âiva yathā|nyāyaṃ Ḍiṇḍikasya vaco 'rthavat.

intelligent cat, just as the thunderbolt-wielder protects the thirty gods."

Addressed in this manner by all the mice, lord of earth, the mouse-killer said to them: "I do not see that these two things, asceticism and protection, have anything in common. However, I am powerless to refuse the favor you ask of me. You must always do what I tell you, and since I am weakened through asceticism, abiding by my harsh restriction, I do not see—though I have given the matter some thought—any way I can possibly travel. So I must always be brought here to the river bank by you, my little friends."

"So be it," promised the mice, bull of the Bharatas, and 160.30
they handed everyone over to the cat, old and young. Then the evil and wicked-souled cat became fat from eating mice, and his fur became glossy and his limbs became strong once more. And as the horde of mice became greatly depleted, the cat grew, endowed with energy and strength. So all the mice gathered and spoke to each other, saying: "Our uncle keeps growing all the time, but our numbers diminish greatly."

Then a particularly intelligent mouse by the name of
Díndika, my king, said to the great horde of mice: "You 160.35
go to the river bank together, and I will go behind with our uncle." "Good idea! Good idea!" they replied, and then they paid their respects and duly followed Díndika's sensible advice.

a|vijñānāt tataḥ so 'tha Ḍiṇḍikaṃ hy upabhuktavān
tatas te sahitāḥ sarve mantrayām āsur añjasā.
tatra vṛddhatamaḥ kaś cit Koliko nāma mūṣikaḥ
abravīd vacanaṃ, rājañ, jñāti|madhye yathā|tatham.
«na mātulo dharma|kāmaś, chadma|mātraṃ kṛtā śikhā;
na mūla|phala|bhakṣasya viṣṭhā bhavati lomaśā!
160.40 asya gātrāṇi vardhante, gaṇaś ca parihīyate;
adya sapt'|âṣṭa|divasān Ḍiṇḍiko 'pi na dṛśyate.»
etac chrutvā vacaḥ sarve mūṣikā vipradudruvuḥ,
biḍālo 'pi sa duṣṭ'|ātmā jagām' âiva yath"|āgatam.

tathā tvam api, duṣṭ'|ātman, baiḍālaṃ vratam āsthitaḥ
carasi jñātiṣu sadā biḍālo mūṣikeṣv iva.
anyathā kila te vākyam, anyathā karma dṛśyate;
dambhan'|ârthāya lokasya vedāś c' ôpaśamaś ca te.
tyaktvā chadma tv idam, rājan, kṣatra|dharmaṃ samāśritaḥ
kuru kāryāṇi sarvāṇi. dharmiṣṭho 'si, nara'|rṣabha?
160.45 bāhu|vīryeṇa pṛthivīṃ labdhvā, Bharata|sattama,
dehi dānaṃ dvijātibhyaḥ, pitṛbhyaś ca yath" ôcitam.
kliṣṭāyā varṣa|pūgāṃś ca mātur mātṛ|hite sthitaḥ
pramārj' âśru raṇe jitvā sammānaṃ param āvaha.
pañca grāmā vṛtā yatnān, asmābhir apavarjitāḥ;
yudhyāmahe kathaṃ saṃkhye kopayema ca Pāṇḍavān?

But, unaware of their suspicions, the cat ate Díndika, and so all the mice quickly consulted together. A very elderly mouse named Kólika spoke in the midst of his relatives, king, as follows, "Our uncle does not desire virtue. He's put on an ascetic's guise merely to deceive us. The feces of an animal that eats roots and fruit doesn't contain fur! His limbs are growing, while our number is diminishing. 160.40
Also, Díndika has not been seen for seven days—today is the eighth day." When they heard these words, all the mice ran away, and the wicked-souled cat went back the way he came.

So, in the same way, you too act like a cat. You always treat your relatives as the cat treats mice. You seem to say one thing but do another. Your Vedic devotion and calm are mere tools to deceive the world. Abandon this disguise of yours, king, and take refuge in the duty of a kshatriya. Do everything that needs to be done, for you are supremely law-abiding, bull-like man, aren't you?

Win the earth by the strength of your arms, greatest of 160.45
the Bharatas, and grant gifts to the twiceborn brahmins and the ancestors as is proper. Be intent upon what would benefit your mother, for she has suffered for many a year. Wipe away her tears, and, by defeating your enemies in battle, bring her the highest honor. You requested five villages with great effort, but we rejected even that, for how else could we enrage the Pándavas and fight them in battle?

tvat|kṛte duṣṭa|bhāvasya saṃtyāgo Vidurasya ca,
jātuṣe ca gṛhe dāhaṃ smara taṃ. puruṣo bhava!
yac ca Kṛṣṇam avocas tvam āyāntaṃ Kuru|saṃsadi:
«ayam asmi sthito, rājañ, śamāya samarāya ca.»
160.50 tasy' âyam āgataḥ kālaḥ samarasya, nar'|âdhipa!
etad|arthaṃ mayā sarvaṃ kṛtam etad, Yudhiṣṭhira.
kiṃ nu yuddhāt paraṃ lābhaṃ kṣatriyo bahu manyate?
kiṃ ca tvaṃ kṣatriya|kule jātaḥ, saṃprathito bhuvi,
Droṇād astrāṇi saṃprāpya, Kṛpāc ca, Bharata'|rṣabha,
tulya|yonau sama|bale Vāsudevaṃ samāśritaḥ?›
brūyās tvaṃ Vāsudevaṃ ca
Pāṇḍavānāṃ samīpataḥ:
‹ātm'|ârthaṃ Pāṇḍav'|ârthaṃ ca
yatto māṃ pratiyodhaya.
sabhā|madhye ca yad rūpaṃ māyayā kṛtavān asi,
tat tath" âiva punaḥ kṛtvā s'|Ârjuno mām abhidrava!
160.55 Indra|jālaṃ ca māyā† vai, kuhakā v" âpi bhīṣaṇā
ātta|śastrasya saṅgrāme vahanti pratigarjanāḥ.
vayam apy utsahema, dyāṃ khaṃ ca gacchema māyayā,
rasā|talaṃ viśāmo 'pi, Aindraṃ vā puram eva tu.
darśayema ca rūpāṇi sva|śarīre bahūny api;
na tu paryāyataḥ siddhir buddhim āpnoti mānuṣīm.
manas" âiva hi bhūtāni dhāt" âiva kurute vaśe!
yad bravīṣi ca, Vārṣṇeya, «Dhārtarāṣṭrān ahaṃ raṇe
ghātayitvā pradāsyāmi Pārthebhyo rājyam uttamam.»
ācacakṣe ca me sarvaṃ Sañjayas tava bhāṣitam.

Remember that wicked-natured Vídura was forsaken because of you, and recall how we tried to burn you in the lac-covered house. Be a man! You had Krishna tell us your message when he came to the Kuru assembly: "I am ready for peace or war, king." Well, the time for battle has come 160.50
now, lord of men! I have made every preparation for this eventuality, Yudhi·shthira.

What but battle does a kshatriya consider the greatest gain? Why, when you were born into a kshatriya lineage, when you are known throughout the earth, when you have obtained your weapons from Drona and Kripa, O bull of the Bharatas, do you take refuge in Vasudéva who is merely your equal in birth and strength?'

You should say to Vasudéva in the presence of the Pándavas:

'Fight me for your own sake, as well as for the sake of the Pándavas. You assumed a guise through magic in the middle of court, now assume that same guise again and charge at me with Árjuna! Sorcery, illusion, and fearsome witchery 160.55
inspire only retaliatory roars of defiance in the man who has taken up his weapons for battle. With our power of sorcery, we too would dare to go to heaven and the sky, or even to enter hell under the surface of the earth, or Indra's city.

We too could reveal many forms in our own body, but magical power does not always defeat human intelligence as a matter of course. Only the creator can bring creatures 160.60
under control by mere mental power! Varshnéya, you say that you will bring about the deaths of the Dhartaráshtras in battle and grant supreme sovereignty to the Parthas. You said that our dispute is with ambidextrous Partha, and that

160.60 «mad|dvitīyena Pārthena vairaṃ vaḥ savya|sācinā.»
sa satya|saṅgaro bhūtvā Pāṇḍav'|ârthe parākramī
yudhyasv' âdya raṇe yattaḥ, paśyāmaḥ, puruṣo bhava!
yas tu śatrum abhijñāya śuddhaṃ pauruṣam āsthitaḥ
karoti dviṣatāṃ śokaṃ, sa jīvati su|jīvitam.
a|kasmāc c' âiva te, Kṛṣṇa, khyātaṃ loke mahad yaśaḥ.
ady' êdānīṃ vijānīmaḥ: santi ṣaṇḍhāḥ sa|śṛṅgakāḥ!
mad|vidho n' âpi nṛ|patis tvayi yuktaḥ kathaṅ cana
sannāhaṃ saṃyuge kartuṃ Kaṃsa|bhṛtye viśeṣataḥ.›
taṃ ca tūbarakaṃ bālaṃ bahv|āśinam a|vidyakam,
160.65 Ulūka, mad|vaco brūhi a|sakṛd Bhīmasenakam:
‹Virāṭa|nagare, Pārtha, yas tvaṃ sūdo hy abhūḥ purā
Ballavo nāma vikhyātas, tan mam' âiva hi pauruṣam!
pratijñātaṃ sabhā|madhye na tan mithyā tvayā purā.
Duḥśāsanasya rudhiraṃ pīyatāṃ yadi śakyate!
yad bravīṣi ca, Kaunteya, «Dhārtarāṣṭrān ahaṃ raṇe
nihaniṣyāmi tarasā,» tasya kālo 'yam āgataḥ.
tvaṃ hi bhojye puraskāryo, bhakṣye peye ca, Bhārata.
kva yuddhaṃ, kva ca bhoktavyaṃ?
yudhyasva, puruṣo bhava!
śayiṣyase hato bhūmau
gadām āliṅgya, Bhārata.
160.70 tad vṛthā ca sabhā|madhye valgitaṃ te, Vṛkodara!›
Ulūka, Nakulaṃ brūhi vacanān mama, ‹Bhārata:
yudhyasv' âdya sthiro bhūtvā, paśyāmas tava pauruṣam,
Yudhiṣṭhir'|ânurāgaṃ ca, dveṣaṃ ca mayi, Bhārata,
Kṛṣṇāyāś ca parikleśaṃ smar' êdānīṃ yathā|tatham!›
brūyās tvaṃ Sahadevaṃ ca rāja|madhye vaco mama:
‹yudhy' êdānīṃ raṇe yattaḥ, kleśān smara ca, Pāṇḍava!›

you will be his second. This is the message Sánjaya passed on to us from you.

So be true to your word. Fight powerfully, and strive for the Pándavas' cause. Show us your manliness! The man who understands his enemies, and breeds grief within them by relying on pure manliness, lives a good life. Your great reputation is renowned on earth, Krishna, but without justification. Sterile men with the mere outward signs of potency will be revealed for what they are now! A king like me should never deck himself in armor to do battle against you, especially since you are a slave to Kansa.'

Repeat my message to the emasculated, childish, gluttinous, and ignorant Bhima·sena over and over again, Ulúka: 160.65

'You were once a cook in Viráta's city, Partha, known by the name of Bállava. This only proves my manliness! Don't falsify the promise you made long ago in the midst of the assembly. Drink Duhshásana's blood if you can!

You claim you will kill the Dhartaráshtras in battle quickly, Kauntéya. Well, the time for it has come. Truly, you deserve honor for the food and drink you prepare, Bhárata. But what has fighting to do with cooking? Fight now, and be a man! You will lie dead on the ground, clasping your mace, Bhárata. Your leaping about in the midst of the 160.70
assembly was in vain, Vrikódara!'

Ulúka, give Nákula my message: 'Fight now, Bhárata. Be firm so that we can see your manliness, your love for Yudhi·shthira, and your hatred for me, Bhárata. Now remember exactly what Krishná suffered!' Next, tell Saha·deva my message in the midst of the kings: 'Try and fight now in battle, and recall your miseries, Pándava!'

Virāṭa|Drupadau c' ôbhau brūyās tvaṃ vacanān mama:
‹na dṛṣṭa|pūrvā bhartāro bhṛtyair api mahā|guṇaiḥ,
tath" ârtha|patibhir bhṛtyā yataḥ sṛṣṭāḥ prajās tataḥ.
«a|ślāghyo 'yaṃ nara|patir yuvayor! iti» c' āgatam.

160.75 te yūyaṃ saṃhitā bhūtvā
tad vadh'|ârthaṃ mam' âpi ca,
ātm'|ârthaṃ, Pāṇḍav'|ârthaṃ ca
prayudhyadhvaṃ mayā saha.›

Dhṛṣṭadyumnaṃ ca Pāñcālyaṃ
brūyās tvaṃ vacanān mama:
‹eṣa te samayaḥ prāpto,
labdhavyaś ca tvay" âpi saḥ.
Droṇam āsādya samare jñāsyase hitam uttamam.
yudhyasva sa|suhṛt pāpaṃ, kuru karma su|duṣkaram.›
Śikhaṇḍinam atho brūhi, Ulūka, vacanān mama:
‹str" îti matvā mahā|bāhur na haniṣyati Kauravaḥ
Gāṅgeyo dhanvināṃ śreṣṭho, yudhy' êdānīṃ su|nirbhayam!
kuru karma raṇe yattaḥ, paśyāmaḥ pauruṣaṃ tava.› »

160.80 evam uktvā tato rājā prahasy' Ôlūkam abravīt:
«Dhanañjayaṃ punar brūhi Vāsudevasya śṛṇvataḥ:
‹asmān vā tvaṃ parājitya praśādhi pṛthivīm imām,
atha vā nirjito 'smābhī raṇe, vīra, śayiṣyasi.
rāṣṭrān nirvāsana|kleśaṃ saṃsmaran puruṣo bhava!
Kṛṣṇāyāś ca parikleśaṃ saṃsmaran puruṣo bhava!

yad arthaṃ kṣatriyā sūte, sarvaṃ tad idam āgatam,
balaṃ, vīryaṃ ca, śauryaṃ ca, paraṃ c' âpy astra|lāghavam,
pauruṣaṃ darśayan yuddhe kopasya kuru niṣkṛtim!
parikliṣṭasya, dīnasya, dīrgha|kāl'|ôṣitaya ca

Tell both Viráta and Drúpada my message: 'Ever since creatures were created, even servants with great virtues have never really seen their masters, and nor have wealthy kings really seen their servants. You two believe, "This king should not be praised!" and that is why you have come. Join to- 160.75
gether and fight me to kill me, for your own sakes and for the sake of the Pándavas.'

Give my message to Dhrishta·dyumna the Panchálan prince: 'Your time has come and you must seize your opportunity. When you approach Drona in battle, you will know what is in your best interest. Fight, and achieve your friend's near impossible and wicked mission.' Then tell Shikhándin what I have to say to him, Ulúka: 'The long-armed Káurava, the greatest of archers and son of the Ganges, will not kill you, for he believes you are a woman, so fight now utterly fearlessly! Carry out your task, striving in battle, so we can see your manliness.'"

Saying this, King Dhartaráshtra laughed and then said 160.80
to Ulúka again:

"Tell Dhanan·jaya one more thing, within the hearing of Vasudéva:

'Either rule this earth by defeating us, or, defeated by us, you will lie dead in battle, hero. Remember the misery of exile from your kingdom, and be a man! Remember Krishná's torment, and be a man!

The whole purpose for which a kshatriya woman gives birth has arrived. So, showing your strength, prowess, bravery, excellent dexterity with weapons, and manliness in battle, make requital for your fury! Whose heart would not be

hṛdayaṃ kasya na sphoṭed, aiśvaryād bhraṃśitasya ca?
160.85 kule jātasya śūrasya para|vitteṣv a|gṛdhyataḥ
āsthitaṃ rājyam ākramya kopaṃ kasya na dīpayet?

yat tad uktaṃ mahad vākyaṃ, karmaṇā tad vibhāvyatām
a|karmaṇā katthitena santaḥ ku|puruṣaṃ viduḥ.
a|mitrāṇāṃ vaśe sthānaṃ rājyaṃ ca punar uddhara;
dvāv arthau yuddha|kāmasya, tasmāt tat kuru pauruṣam.
parājito 'si dyūtena, Kṛṣṇā c' ānāyitā sabhām!
śakyo '|marṣo manuṣyeṇa kartuṃ puruṣa|māninā!

dvā|daś' âiva tu varṣāṇi vane dhiṣṇyād vivāsitaḥ,
saṃvatsaraṃ Virāṭasya dāsyam āsthāya c' ôṣitaḥ.
160.90 rāṣṭrān nirvāsana|kleśaṃ, vana|vāsaṃ ca, Pāṇḍava,
Kṛṣṇāyāś ca parikleśaṃ saṃsmaran puruṣo bhava!
a|priyāṇāṃ ca vacanaṃ prabruvatsu punaḥ punaḥ
a|marṣaṃ darśayasva tvam, a|marṣo hy eva pauruṣam.

krodho, balaṃ, tathā vīryaṃ, jñāna|yogo, 'stra|lāghavam
iha te dṛśyatāṃ, Pārtha, yudhyasva puruṣo bhava.
loh'|âbhisāro nirvṛttaḥ, Kuru|kṣetram a|kardamam,
puṣṭās te 'śvā, bhṛtā yodhāḥ—śvo yudhyasva sa|Keśavaḥ!
a|samāgamya Bhīṣmeṇa saṃyuge kiṃ vikatthase?
āruruksur yathā mandaḥ parvataṃ Gandhamādanam,
160.95 evaṃ katthasi, Kaunteya; a|katthan puruṣo bhava.

torn apart when tormented, depressed, long-lastingly exiled, and deprived of his power? Whose anger would not 160.85
flare up when, having been born as a brave, uncovetous man in a good lineage, his kingdom, which passes down the generations, is attacked?

Let the high and mighty things you say be fulfilled in your actions. Good men know a man to be a coward if he is all talk and no action. Take your kingdom and position back from your enemies once more. These are the two aims of a man who desires war, so make use of your manliness. You were beaten with dice, and Krishná was led into the assembly! A man who prides himself on his manliness should not put up with this!

You have been exiled from your home for twelve years in the forest, and you spent a year living in the service of
Viráta. Remember the torment of exile from your king- 160.90
dom, remember living in the forest, Pándava, remember Krishná's suffering, and be a man! Show your intolerance for the men who spoke such unkind words time and time again, for manliness is surely irascibility.

Let your anger, strength, heroism, discipline of knowledge, and dexterity with weapons be displayed here, Partha. Fight and be a man. The military ceremonies have been performed, Kuru·kshetra is free of mud, the horses are fat, and the soldiers are paid, so fight with Késhava tomorrow! Why do you boast when you have not even come up against Bhishma in battle? You boast like an idiot who boasts of climbing the Gandha·mádana mountain though he has not
done so, Kauntéya; so be a man, and stop boasting. 160.95

sūta|putraṃ su|durdharṣaṃ, Śalyaṃ ca balināṃ varam,
Droṇaṃ ca balināṃ śreṣṭhaṃ Śacī|pati|samaṃ yudhi
a|jitvā saṃyuge, Pārtha, rājyaṃ katham ih' êcchasi?
brāhme dhanuṣi c' ācāryaṃ vedayor anta|gaṃ dvayoḥ,
yudhi dhuryam, a|vikṣobhyam, anīka|caram, a|cyutam
Droṇaṃ mahā|dyutiṃ, Pārtha, jetum icchasi, tan mṛṣā!
na hi śuśruma vātena Merum unmathitaṃ girim;
anilo vā vahen Meruṃ, dyaur v" âpi nipaten mahīm,
yugaṃ vā parivarteta, yady evaṃ syād yath" āttha mām!
160.100 ko hy asti jīvit'|ākāṅkṣī prāpy' êmam ari|mardanam,
Pārtho vā, itaro v" âpi, ko 'nyaḥ svasti gṛhān vrajet?
katham ābhyām abhidhyātaḥ, saṃspṛṣṭo dāruṇena vā
raṇe jīvan pramucyeta padā bhūmim upaspṛśan?
kiṃ darduraḥ kūpa|śayo yath" êmāṃ
na budhyase rāja|camūṃ sametām
dur|ādharṣāṃ, deva|camū|prakāśāṃ,
guptāṃ nar'|êndrais tri|daśair iva dyām,
prācyaiḥ, pratīcyair, atha dākṣiṇātyair,
udīcya|Kāmboja|Śakaiḥ, Khaśaiś ca,
Śālvaiḥ sa|Matsyaiḥ, Kuru|madhya|deśyair,
Mlecchaiḥ, Pulindair, Draviḍ'|Ândhra|Kāñcyaiḥ;
nānā|jan'|âughaṃ yudhi saṃpravṛddhaṃ,
Gāṅgaṃ yathā vegam a|pāraṇīyam,
māṃ ca sthitaṃ nāga|balasya madhye
yuyutsase, manda, kim, alpa|buddhe?

You have not defeated Karna, the *suta*'s invincible son, Shalya, the strongest of the strong, or mighty Drona, a match for Shachi's husband in battle, Partha, so how can you want to regain your kingdom? The teacher of the Veda and archery, the man who has reached the limit of both branches of learning, the most eminent man in battle, the unshakeable eternally mighty leader of armies—great glorious Drona is the man you vainly want to defeat, Partha!

We never hear that the Meru mountain is uprooted by the wind; but the wind will carry Mount Meru away, heaven itself will fall to the earth, or the age will run in reverse if
your boasts to me should really transpire! Who hopes to 160.100
live—be it one Partha or another, or even someone else entirely—who could return home safe and sound after taking on that enemy-crusher? How could anyone whose feet touch the earth escape from battle alive if Bhishma and Drona pay them the slightest attention or so much as graze them with their pitiless violence?

Why, like a frog hidden in a well, do you not understand that a royal, invincible army is gathered against you, like an army of celestials defended by lords of men just as heaven is defended by the thirty gods; an army which is defended by the kings of the east, west, south, and north, by the Kambójas, the Shakas, the Khashas, the Shalvas, the Matsyas, the Kurus from the central lands, foreigners, the Pulíndas, the Drávidas, Andhras, and Kanchis; the army host of various peoples, enhanced for battle, like the uncrossable force of the river Ganges? Why do you wish to fight me, as I stand positioned in the midst of my elephant forces, small-witted fool?

160.105 a|kṣayyāv iṣudhī c' âiva, Agni|dattaṃ ca te ratham
jānīmo hi raṇe, Pārtha, ketuṃ divyaṃ ca, Bhārata!
a|katthamāno yudhyasva. katthase, 'rjuna, kiṃ bahu?
paryāyāt siddhir etasya, n' âitat sidhyati katthanāt.
yad' îdaṃ katthanāl loke sidhyet karma, Dhanañjaya,
sarve bhaveyuḥ siddh'|ârthāḥ; katthane ko hi dur|gataḥ?

jānāmi te Vāsudevaṃ sahāyaṃ,
  jānāmi te Gāṇḍivaṃ tāla|mātram,
jānāmy ahaṃ, tvādṛśo n' âsti yoddhā;
  jānānas te rājyam etadd harāmi!

na tu paryāya|dharmeṇa siddhiṃ prāpnoti mānavaḥ;
manas" âiv' ânukūlāni dhāt" âiva kurute vaśe.
160.110 trayo|daśa samā bhuktaṃ rājyaṃ vilapatas tava;
bhūyaś c' âiva praśāsiṣye tvāṃ nihatya sa|bāndhavam!
kva tadā Gāṇḍivaṃ te 'bhūd, yat tvaṃ dāsa|paṇair jitaḥ?
kva tadā Bhīmasenasya balam āsīc ca, Phālguna?

sa|gadād Bhīmasenād vā Phālgunād vā sa|Gaṇḍivāt
na vai mokṣas tadā vo 'bhūd vinā Kṛṣṇām a|ninditām.
sā vo dāsye samāpannān mocayām āsa Pārṣatī
a|mānuṣyaṃ samāpannān dāsa|karmaṇy avasthitān.

Your inexhaustible quiver, your chariot given to you by 160.105
Agni, Partha, and your celestial ensign, Bhárata, will be discovered for what they really are in battle! Fight without boasting. Why do you boast so much, Árjuna? Success comes from the course of events, and nothing is achieved through boasting. If mere boasting were to lead to the success of actions in this world, Dhanan·jaya, then everyone would achieve their goals, for who cannot boast?

I know that you have Vasudéva as an ally. I know you have Gandíva, tall as a palm tree. I know there is no fighter to match you, but despite knowing all this, I still deprive you of your kingdom!

A man does not gain success through the mere law of successive events, for it is the creator alone who can make creatures well-disposed and bring them under control by mere
strength of mind. I have enjoyed the kingdom for the same 160.110
thirteen years you were weeping, and I will rule it again when I have killed you and your relatives! Where was your Gandíva then, when you were a slave beaten by gaming? Where was Bhima·sena's strength then, Phálguna?

Bhima·sena and his mace did not bring you freedom, nor Phálguna and his Gandíva. Were it not for faultless Krishná you wouldn't have had your freedom at all. It was the descendant of Príshata who had you released from the dire straits in which you found yourselves, fallen into inhuman conditions and intent upon your tasks of servitude.

avocaṃ yat ṣaṇḍha|tilān ahaṃ vas, tathyam eva tat.
dhṛtā hi veṇī Pārthena Virāṭa|nagare tadā!
160.115 sūda|karmaṇi viśrāntaṃ Virāṭasya mahānase
Bhīmasenena, Kaunteya, yat tu tan mama pauruṣam!
evam eva sadā daṇḍaṃ kṣatriyāḥ kṣatriye dadhuḥ!
veṇīṃ kṛtvā ṣaṇḍha|veṣaḥ kanyāṃ nartitavān asi!

na bhayād Vāsudevasya, na c' âpi tava, Phālguna,
rājyaṃ pratipradāsyāmi; yudhyasva saha|Keśavaḥ!
na māyā h' îndra|jālaṃ vā, kuhakā v" âpi bhīṣaṇā
ātta|śastrasya saṅgrāme vahanti pratigarjanāḥ!
Vāsudeva|sahasraṃ vā, Phālgunānāṃ śatāni vā
āsādya mām a|mogh'|êṣuṃ dravisyanti diśo daśā!
160.120 saṃyugaṃ gaccha Bhīṣmeṇa, bhindhi vā śirasā girim,
tarasva vā mahā|gādhaṃ bāhubhyāṃ puruṣ'|ôdadhim,
Śāradvata|mahā|mīnaṃ, Viviṃśati|mah"|ôragam,
Bṛhadbala|mah"|ôdvelaṃ, Saumadatti|timiṅgilam,
Bhīṣma|vegam a|paryantaṃ, Droṇa|grāha|durāsadam,
Karṇa|Śalya|jhaṣ'|āvartaṃ, Kāmboja|vaḍavā|mukham,
Duḥśāsan'|âughaṃ Śala|Śalya|matsyaṃ,
Suṣeṇa|Citrāyudha|nāga|nakram,
Jayadrath'|âdriṃ, Purumitra|gādhaṃ,
Durmarṣaṇ'|ôdaṃ, Śakuni|prapātam!

I called you emasculated—barren sesame seeds—and it was true. Partha did indeed braid his hair in Viráta's city! Bhima·sena was exhausted from his cook's duties in Viráta's 160.115
kitchen, Kauntéya, so this is indeed a sign of my manliness! This is the punishment kshatriyas always inflict upon another kshatriya! And you tied your hair into a plait, and dressed as a eunuch you taught the king's daughter to dance!

I will not hand back the kingdom from fear of Vasudéva, nor from fear of you, Phálguna, so fight together with Késhava! No illusion, sorcery, or tricks inspire fear in the man who has taken up weapons in battle, but rather they bring only roars of defiance in retaliation!* A thousand Vasudévas and hundreds of Phálgunas may attack me with unfailing arrows, but they will flee to the ten directions!

Plunge into battle with Bhishma, split a mountain with 160.120
your head, or cross the vast deep ocean using only the strength of your arms! My army is such an ocean, with Sharádvata as its whale, Vivínshati its mighty snake, Brihad·bala its enormous swell, the son of Soma·datta its monstrous, whale-eating fish, Bhishma its unbounded current, Drona the invincible alligator, Karna and Shalya its fish and whirlpools, the Kambója king its mare's mouth, Duhshásana its flood, Shala and Shalya its fish, Sushéna and Chitráyudha its snakes and crocodiles, Jayad·ratha its reefs, Puru·mitra its depth, Durmárshana its waters, and Shákuni its shore!

śastr'|âugham, a|kṣayyam, abhipravṛddhaṃ
yad" âvagāhya śrama|naṣṭa|cetāḥ
bhaviṣyasi tvaṃ hata|sarva|bāndhavas,
tadā manas te paritāpam eṣyati.
160.125 tadā manas te tri|divād iv' â|śucer
nivartitā, Pārtha, mahī|praśāsanāt.
praśāmya rājyaṃ hi su|durlabhaṃ tvayā
bubhūṣitaḥ svarga iv' â|tapasvinā!› »

SAÑJAYA uvāca:

161.1 SENĀ|NIVEŚAṂ saṃprāptaḥ kaitavyaḥ Pāṇḍavasya ha
samāgataḥ Pāṇḍaveyair Yudhiṣṭhiram abhāṣata:
«abhijño dūta|vākyānāṃ yath" ôktaṃ bruvato mama
Duryodhana|samādeśaṃ śrutvā na kroddhum arhasi.»

YUDHIṢṬHIRA uvāca:

Ulūka, na bhayaṃ te 'sti, brūhi tvaṃ vigata|jvaraḥ,
yan mataṃ Dhārtarāṣṭrasya lubdhasy' â|dīrgha|darśinaḥ.
tato dyutimatāṃ madhye Pāṇḍavānāṃ mah"|ātmanām,
Sṛñjayānāṃ ca Matsyānāṃ, Kṛṣṇasya ca yaśasvinaḥ,
161.5 Drupadasya sa|putrasya, Virāṭasya ca sannidhau,
bhūmi|pānāṃ ca sarveṣāṃ madhye vākyaṃ jagāda ha:

ULŪKA uvāca:

idaṃ tvām abravīd rājā Dhārtarāṣṭro mahā|manāḥ
śṛṇvatāṃ Kuru|vīrāṇāṃ. tan nibodha, Yudhiṣṭhira.

But when you have plunged into that unending, swelling flood of weapons and are senseless from exertion, you will find that all your relatives have been killed, and regret will flood your mind. Then, Partha, your thoughts will turn 160.125
away from ruling the earth, just as the mind of an impure man turns away from heaven. In fact, it is almost as impossible for you to rule this kingdom as it is for a man without asceticism to win heaven!'"

SÁNJAYA continued:

WHEN THE GAMBLER'S son reached the Pándava's army 161.1
encampment, he joined the Pándavas and said to Yudhi·shthira: "You understand the messages envoys give, so you ought not to become angry with me when you hear me speaking just as Duryódhana ordered."

SHTHIRA replied:

You are in no danger, Ulúka, so tell us, free of anxiety, what the greedy and shortsighted son of Dhrita·rashtra is thinking.

So, in the midst of the high-souled and glorious Pándavas, the Sríñjayas, Matsyas, and illustrious Krishna, and 161.5
in the presence of Drúpada and his sons and Viráta, in the midst of all the earth-lords, he said these words:

ULÚKA said:

High-minded King Dhartaráshtra's message to you, in the hearing of the Kuru heroes, runs as follows, so listen, Yudhi·shthira.*

«parājito 'si dyūtena, Kṛṣṇā c' ānāyitā sabhām!
śakyo '|marṣo manuṣyeṇa kartuṃ puruṣa|māninā!
dvā|daś' âiva tu varṣāṇi vane dhiṣṇyād vivāsitaḥ,
saṃvatsaraṃ Virāṭasya dāsyam āsthāya c' ôṣitaḥ.
a|marṣaṃ rājya|haraṇaṃ vana|vāsaṃ ca, Pāṇḍava,
Draupadyāś ca parikleśaṃ saṃsmaran puruṣo bhava!
161.10 a|śaktena ca yac chaptaṃ Bhīmasenena, Pāṇḍava,
Duḥśāsanasya rudhiraṃ pīyatāṃ yadi śakyate!
loh'|âbhisāro nirvṛttaḥ Kuru|kṣetram a|kardamam;
samaḥ panthā, bhṛtās te 'śvāḥ—śvo yudhyasva sa|Keśavaḥ!
a|samāgamya Bhīṣmeṇa saṃyuge kiṃ vikatthase?
āruruksur yathā mandaḥ parvataṃ Gandhamādanam,
evaṃ katthasi, Kaunteya; a|katthan puruṣo bhava!
sūta|putraṃ su|durdharṣaṃ, Śalyaṃ ca balināṃ varam,
Droṇaṃ ca balināṃ śreṣṭhaṃ Śacī|pati|samaṃ yudhi
a|jitvā saṃyuge, Pārtha; rājyaṃ katham ih' êcchasi?
161.15 brāhme dhanuṣi c' ācāryaṃ vedayor anta|gaṃ dvayoḥ,
yudhi dhuryam, a|vikṣobhyam, anīka|caram, a|cyutam:
Droṇaṃ mahā|dyutiṃ, Pārtha, jetum icchasi, tan mṛṣā!
na hi śuśruma vātena Merum unmathitaṃ girim!
anilo vā vahen Meruṃ, dyaur v" âpi nipaten mahīm,
yugaṃ vā parivarteta, yady evaṃ syād yath" āttha mām!
ko hy asti jīvit'|ākāṅkṣī prāpy' êmam ari|mardanam,

"You were defeated at dice and Krishná was led to court. It is quite possible that someone who takes pride in his manliness would be made angry by this! For twelve years you lived in the woods, exiled from your home, and for a year you lived in the service of Viráta.

Remember the theft of your kingdom, your exile in the forest, Dráupadi's suffering, Pándava, and your fury, and be a man! Impotent though he was, Pándava, Bhima·sena 161.10
made a vow, so let him drink Duhshásana's blood if he is able! The military ceremonies have been performed, Kuru·kshetra is free of mud, the roads are level, and your horses are well maintained; so fight tomorrow with Késhava!

Why do you boast when you have not even come up against Bhishma in battle? You boast like an idiot who boasts of climbing the Gandha·mádana mountain though he has not done so, Kauntéya; so be a man and stop boasting.

You have not defeated Karna, the *suta*'s invincible son, Shalya, the strongest of the strong, or mighty Drona, a match for Shachi's husband in battle, Partha; so how can you want to regain your kingdom? The teacher of the Veda 161.15
and archery, the man who has reached the limit of both branches of learning, the most eminent man in battle, the unshakeable eternally mighty leader of armies: great glorious Drona is the man you vainly want to defeat, Partha!

We never hear of the Meru mountain being uprooted by the wind, but the wind will carry Mount Meru away, heaven itself will fall to the earth, or the age will run in reverse if your boasts to me should really transpire! Who hopes to live—be it one Partha or another, or even someone

gajo, vājī, ratho v" âpi punaḥ svasti gṛhān vrajet?
katham ābhyām abhidhyātaḥ, saṃspṛṣṭo dāruṇena vā
raṇe jīvan pramucyeta padā bhūmim upaspṛśan?

161.20 kiṃ darduraḥ kūpa|śayo yath" êmāṃ
na budhyase rāja|camūṃ sametām
dur|ādharṣāṃ, deva|camū|prakāśāṃ,
guptāṃ nar'|êndrais tri|daśair iva dyām,
prācyaiḥ, pratīcyair, atha dākṣiṇātyair,
udīcya|Kāmboja|Śakaiḥ, Khaśaiś ca,
Śālvaiḥ sa|Matsyaiḥ, Kuru|madhya|deśyair,
Mlecchaiḥ, Pulindair, Draviḍ'|Ândhra|Kāñcyaiḥ;
nānā|jan'|âughaṃ yudhi saṃpravṛddhaṃ,
Gāṅgaṃ yathā vegam a|pāraṇīyam,
māṃ ca sthitaṃ nāga|balasya madhye
yuyutsase, manda, kim, alpa|buddhe?»

ity evam uktvā rājānaṃ Dharma|putraṃ Yudhiṣṭhiram
abhyāvṛtya punar Jiṣṇum Ulūkaḥ pratyabhāṣata:
«a|katthamāno yudhyasva. katthase, 'rjuna, kiṃ bahu?
paryāyāt siddhir etasya, n' âitat sidhyati katthanāt.
161.25 yad' îdaṃ katthanāl loke sidhyet karma, Dhanañjaya,
sarve bhaveyuḥ siddh'|ârthāḥ; katthane ko hi dur|gataḥ?
jānāmi te Vāsudevaṃ sahāyaṃ,
jānāmi te Gāṇḍivaṃ tāla|mātram,
jānāmy ahaṃ, tvādṛśo n' âsti yoddhā;
jānānas te rājyam etadd harāmi!

else entirely—who could return home safe and sound after taking on that enemy-crusher? How could anyone whose feet touch the earth escape from battle alive if Bhishma and Drona pay them the slightest attention or so much as graze them with their pitiless violence?

Why, like a frog hidden in a well, do you not understand 161.20
that a royal, invincible army is gathered against you, like an army of celestials defended by lords of men just as heaven is defended by the thirty gods; an army which is defended by the kings of the east, west, south, and north, by the Kambójas, the Shakas, the Khashas, the Shalvas, the Matsyas, the Kurus from the central lands, foreigners, the Pulíndas, the Drávidas, Andhras and Kanchis; the army host of various peoples, enhanced for battle, like the uncrossable force of the river Ganges? Why do you wish to fight me, as I stand positioned in the midst of my elephant forces, small-witted fool?"

Having said these things to King Yudhi·shthira, the son of Dharma, Ulúka turned to Jishnu and spoke again:

"Fight without boasting. Why do you boast so much, Árjuna? Success comes from the course of events, and nothing
is achieved through boasting. If mere boasting were to lead 161.25
to the success of actions in this world, Dhanan·jaya, then everyone would achieve their goals, for who cannot boast?

I know that you have Vasudéva as an ally. I know you have Gandíva, tall as a palm tree. I know there is no fighter to match you; but despite knowing all this, I still deprive you of your kingdom!

na tu paryāya|dharmeṇa siddhiṃ prāpnoti mānavaḥ;
manas” âiv’ ânukūlāni dhāt” âiva kurute vaśe.
trayo|daśa samā bhuktaṃ rājyaṃ vilapatas tava;
bhūyaś c’ âiva praśāsiṣye tvāṃ nihatya sa|bāndhavam!
kva tadā Gāṇḍivaṃ te ’bhūd, yat tvaṃ dāsa|paṇair jitaḥ?
kva tadā Bhīmasenasya balam āsīc ca, Phālguna?
161.30 sa|gadād Bhīmasenād vā Phālgunād vā sa|Gaṇḍivāt
na vai mokṣas tadā vo ’bhūd vinā Kṛṣṇām a|ninditām.
sā vo dāsye samāpannān mocayām āsa Pārṣatī
a|mānuṣyaṃ samāpannān dāsa|karmaṇy avasthitān.
avocaṃ yat ṣaṇḍha|tilān ahaṃ vas, tathyam eva tat.
dhṛtā hi veṇī Pārthena Virāṭa|nagare tadā!
sūda|karmaṇi viśrāntaṃ Virāṭasya mahānase
Bhīmasenena, Kaunteya, yat tu tan mama pauruṣam!
evam eva sadā daṇḍaṃ kṣatriyāḥ kṣatriye dadhuḥ!
veṇīṃ kṛtvā ṣaṇḍha|veṣaḥ kanyāṃ nartitavān asi!
161.35 na bhayād Vāsudevasya, na c’ âpi tava, Phālguna,
rājyaṃ pratipradāsyāmi; yudhyasva saha|Keśavaḥ!
na māyā h’ îndra|jālaṃ vā, kuhakā v” âpi bhīṣaṇā
ātta|śastrasya saṅgrāme vahanti pratigarjanāḥ!
Vāsudeva|sahasraṃ vā, Phālgunānāṃ śatāni vā
āsādya mām a|mogh’|êṣuṃ draviṣyanti diśo daśa!

A man does not gain success through the mere law of successive events, for the creator makes creatures well-disposed and brings them under his control with the force of his mind. I have enjoyed the kingdom for the same thirteen years you were weeping, and I will rule it again when I have killed you and your relatives! Where was your Gandíva then, when you were a slave beaten by gaming? Where was Bhima·sena's strength then, Phálguna?

Bhima·sena and his mace did not bring you freedom, nor 161.30
Phálguna and his Gandíva. Were it not for faultless Krishná you wouldn't have had your freedom at all. It was the descendant of Príshata who had you released from the dire straits in which you found yourselves, fallen into inhuman conditions and intent upon your tasks of servitude.

I called you emasculated—barren sesame seeds—and it was true. Partha did indeed braid his hair in Viráta's city! Bhima·sena was exhausted from his cook's duties in Viráta's kitchen, Kauntéya, so this is indeed a sign of my manliness! This is the punishment kshatriyas always inflict upon another kshatriya! And you tied your hair into a plait, and dressed as a eunuch you taught the king's daughter to dance!

I will not hand back the kingdom from fear of Vasudéva, 161.35
nor from fear of you, Phálguna, so fight together with Késhava! No illusion, sorcery, or tricks inspire fear in the man who has taken up weapons in battle; but rather they bring only roars of defiance in retaliation!* A thousand Vasudévas and hundreds of Phálgunas may attack me with unfailing arrows, but they will flee to the ten directions!

saṃyugaṃ gaccha Bhīṣmeṇa, bhindhi vā śirasā girim,
tarasva vā mahā|gādhaṃ bāhubhyāṃ puruṣ'|ôdadhim,
Śāradvata|mahā|mīnaṃ, Viviṃśati|mah"|ôragam,
Bṛhadbala|mah"|ôdvelaṃ, Saumadatti|timiṅgilam,
161.40 Bhīṣma|vegam a|paryantaṃ, Droṇa|grāha|durāsadam,
Karṇa|Śalya|jhaṣ'|āvartaṃ, Kāmboja|vaḍavā|mukham,
Duḥśāsan'|âughaṃ Śala|Śalya|matsyaṃ,
Suṣeṇa|Citrāyudha|nāga|nakram,
Jayadrath'|âdriṃ, Purumitra|gādhaṃ,
Durmarṣaṇ'|ôdaṃ, Śakuni|prapātam!
śastr'|âugam, a|kṣayyam, abhipravṛddhaṃ
yad" âvagāhya śrama|naṣṭa|cetāḥ
bhaviṣyasi tvaṃ hata|sarva|bāndhavas,
tadā manas te paritāpam eṣyati.
tadā manas te tri|divād iv' â|śucer
nivartitā, Pārtha, mahī|praśāsanāt.
praśāmya rājyaṃ hi su|durlabhaṃ tvayā
bubhūṣitaḥ svarga iv' â|tapasvinā!»

SAÑJAYA uvāca:

162.1 ULŪKAS TV Arjunaṃ bhūyo yath" ôktaṃ vākyam abravīt,
āśī|viṣam iva kruddhaṃ tudan vākya|śalākayā.
tasya tad vacanaṃ śrutvā ruṣitāḥ Pāṇḍavā bhṛśam,
prāg eva bhṛśa|saṃkruddhāḥ, kaitavyen' âpi dharṣitāḥ.
āsaneṣ' ûdatiṣṭhanta, bāhūṃś c' âiva pracikṣipuḥ,
āśī|viṣā iva kruddhā vīkṣāṃ cakruḥ paras|param.

Plunge into battle with Bhishma, split a mountain with your head, or cross the vast deep ocean using only the strength of your arms! My army is such an ocean, with Sharádvata as its whale, Vivínshati its mighty snake, Brihad·bala its enormous swell, the son of Soma·datta its monstrous, whale-eating fish, Bhishma its unbounded current, 161.40
Drona the invincible alligator, Karna and Shalya its fish and whirlpools, the Kambója king its mare's mouth, Duhshásana its flood, Shala and Shalya its fish, Sushéna and Chitráyudha its snakes and crocodiles, Jayad·ratha its reefs, Puru·mitra its depth, Durmárshana its waters, and Shákuni its shore!

But when you have plunged into that unending, swelling flood of weapons and are senseless from exertion, you will find all your relatives have been killed, and regret will flood your mind. Then, Partha, your thoughts will turn away from ruling the earth, just as the mind of an impure man turns away from heaven. In fact, it is almost as impossible for you to rule this kingdom as it is for a man without asceticism to win heaven!"

SÁNJAYA continued:

ULÚKA REPEATED what he had said to Árjuna, goading 162.1
the furious man with words, as though goading a poisonous snake with sticks. The Pándavas were extremely angry the first time they heard his words, but, being reprimanded by a gambler's son, their fury grew still greater. Rising from their seats and flexing their arms, they glanced at each other like enraged posionous snakes.

avāk|śirā Bhīmasenaḥ samudaikṣata Keśavam
netrābhyāṃ lohit'|ântābhyām, āśī|viṣa iva śvasan.
162.5 ārtaṃ vāt'|ātmajaṃ dṛṣṭvā krodhen' âbhihataṃ bhṛśam
utsmayann iva Dāśārhaḥ kaitavyaṃ pratyabhāṣata:
«prayāhi śīghraṃ, kaitavya,
brūyāś c' âiva Suyodhanam:
‹śrutaṃ vākyaṃ, gṛhīto 'rtho.
matam yat te, tath" âstu tat.› »

evam uktvā mahā|bāhuḥ Keśavo, rāja|sattama,
punar eva mahā|prājñaṃ Yudhiṣṭhiram udaikṣata.
Sṛñjayānāṃ ca sarveṣāṃ, Kṛṣṇasya ca yaśasvinaḥ,
Drupadasya sa|putrasya, Virāṭasya ca sannidhau,
bhūmi|pānāṃ ca sarveṣāṃ madhye vākyaṃ jagāda ha.
Ulūko 'py Arjunaṃ bhūyo yath" ôktaṃ vākyam abravīt,
162.10 aśī|viṣam iva kruddhaṃ tudan vākya|śalākayā,
Kṛṣṇ'|ādīṃś c' âiva tān sarvān yath" ôktaṃ vākyam abravīt.

Ulūkasya tu tad vākyaṃ pāpaṃ dāruṇam īritam
śrutvā vicukṣubhe Pārtho, lalāṭaṃ c' âpy amārjayat.
tad|avasthaṃ tadā dṛṣṭvā Pārthaṃ sā samitir, nṛpa,
n' âmṛṣyanta, mahā|rāja, Pāṇḍavānāṃ mahā|rathāḥ.
adhikṣepeṇa Kṛṣṇasya Pārthasya ca mah"|ātmanaḥ
śrutvā te puruṣa|vyāghrāḥ krodhāj jajvalur, a|cyuta.

Dhṛṣṭadyumnaḥ, Śikhaṇḍī ca, Sātyakiś ca mahā|rathaḥ,
Kekayā bhrātaraḥ pañca, rākṣasaś ca Ghaṭotkacaḥ,
162.15 Draupadey", Âbhimanyuś ca, Dhṛṣṭaketuś ca pārthivaḥ,
Bhīmasenaś ca vikrānto, yama|jau ca mahā|rathau
utpetur āsanāt sarve krodha|saṃrakta|locanāḥ,
bāhūn pragṛhya rucirān rakta|candana|rūṣitān,

Bhima·sena hung his head and glanced at Késhava with his bloodshot-rimmed eyes, hissing like a snake. But notic- 162.5
ing that the wind-god's son was pained and heavily struck with rage, Dashárha smirked and said to the gambler's son: "Go quickly, son of a gambler, and give Suyódhana this message: 'Your message has been heard and understood. Let the aim upon which you have set you mind be fulfilled.'"

When he had said this, long-armed Késhava glanced once more at highly wise Yudhi·shthira, O greatest of kings. Then, in the presence of all the Sríñjayas, illustrious Krishna, Drúpada and his sons, and Viráta, and in the midst of all the earth-lords, Ulúka spoke again to Árjuna, repeating what he had said before, goading the angry man with 162.10
his words as though goading a poisonous snake with sticks. And he gave his message to them all, Krishna and the rest, as it was told to him.

Having listened to the wicked and cruel words Ulúka spoke, Partha became agitated and wiped the sweat from his brow. But then, when the assembly saw Partha in such a state, king, the Pándavas' mighty chariot warriors could not tolerate it, mighty sovereign. As they listened, the tiger-like men blazed with anger at the insult to Krishna and high-souled Partha, O unfadingly glorious man.

Dhrishta·dyumna, Shikhándin, the mighty chariot warrior Sátyaki, the five Kékaya brothers, the *rákshasa* Ghatótkacha, Dráupadi's sons, Abhimányu, and King Dhrishta· 162.15
ketu, as well as powerful Bhima·sena and the great chariot-warrior twins, all rose from their seats, their eyes bloodshot with rage, flexing their handsome arms which were smeared

aṅgadaiḥ pārihāryaiś ca, keyūraiś ca vibhūṣitān.
dantān danteṣu niṣpiṣya, sṛkkiṇī parilelihan,
teṣām ākāra|bhāva|jñaḥ Kuntī|putro Vṛkodaraḥ
udatiṣṭhat sa vegena, krodhena prajvalann iva,
udvṛtya sahasā netre, dantān kaṭakaṭāyya ca,
hastaṃ hastena niṣpiṣya Ulūkaṃ vākyam abravīt:
«a|śaktānām iv' âsmākaṃ protsāhana|nimitttakam
162.20 śrutaṃ te vacanaṃ, mūrkha, yat tvāṃ Duryodhano 'bravīt.
tan me kathayato, manda, śṛṇu vākyaṃ dur|āsadam,
sarva|kṣatrasya madhye taṃ yad vakṣyasi Suyodhanam,
śṛṇvataḥ sūta|putrasya, pituś ca tvaṃ dur|ātmanaḥ.
‹asmābhiḥ prīti|kāmais tu bhrātur jyeṣṭhasya nityaśaḥ
marṣitaṃ te, dur|ācāra. tat tvaṃ na bahu manyase?
preṣitaś ca Hṛṣīkeśaḥ śam'|ākāṅkṣī Kurūn prati,
kulasya hita|kāmena dharma|rājena dhīmatā.
tvaṃ kāla|codito, nūnaṃ gantu|kāmo Yama|kṣayam,
gacchasv' āhavam asmābhis; tac ca śvo bhavitā dhruvam.
162.25 may" âpi ca pratijñāto vadhaḥ sa|bhrātṛkasya te;
sa tathā bhavitā, pāpa, n' âtra kāryā vicāraṇā.
velām atikramet sadyaḥ sāgaro Varuṇ'|ālayaḥ,
parvatāś ca viśīryeyur, may" ôktaṃ na mṛṣā bhavet.
sahāyas te yadi Yamaḥ, Kubero, Rudra eva vā,
yathā|pratijñaṃ, dur|buddhe, prakariṣyanti Pāṇḍavāḥ!
Duḥśāsanasya rudhiraṃ pātā c' âsmi yath" ēpsitam!

with red sandalwood paste and ornamented with golden bracelets and bangles.

Grinding his teeth together and licking the corners of his mouth, the wolf-bellied son of Kunti, who understood both their gestures and their nature, rose forcibly, and, almost ablaze with fury, he quickly rolled his eyes and gnashed his teeth, and pounding his hands together he said these words to Ulúka:

"The message Duryódhana gave you, meant to ground- 162.20
lessly incite us as though we were powerless, has now been heard, fool, but now listen to what I have to say, ignorant man, and then repeat it to unapproachable Suyódhana in the midst of all the warriors, within the hearing of Karna, the *suta*'s son, and your wicked-souled father:

'We always wish to do what pleases our older brother, and we put up with you, you miscreant, for that reason. Do you not consider that fortunate? The wise king of righteousness, wishing only for the benefit of his line, sent Hrishikésha to the Kurus, hoping for peace. Surely you are driven by fate and desperate to reach Yama's realm, so go to battle with us, for it is sure to come tomorrow.

I did indeed swear to kill you and your brothers, and 162.25
so it will be, evil man. Have no doubt that it will happen. The ocean and abode of Váruna could suddenly transgress its limits, the very mountains could split apart, but my words could never be spoken vainly. Even if you had Yama, Kubéra, or Rudra as your ally, the Pándavas would still fulfill what they promised, wicked-minded man! I will drink Duhshásana's blood just as I please!

yaś c' êha pratisaṃrabdhaḥ kṣatriyo m" âbhiyāsyati,
api Bhīṣmaṃ puras|kṛtya, taṃ neṣyāmi Yama|kṣamam.
yac c' âitad uktaṃ vacanaṃ mayā kṣatrasya saṃsadi,
yath" âitad bhavitā satyaṃ, tath" âiv' ātmānam ālabhe!› »

162.30 Bhīmasena|vacaḥ śrutvā Sahadevo 'py a|marṣaṇaḥ
krodha|saṃrakta|nayanas tato vākyam uvāca ha,
śauṭīra|śūra|sadṛśam anīka|jana|saṃsadi:
«śṛṇu, pāpa, vaco mahyaṃ yad vācyo hi pitā tvayā:
‹n' âsmākaṃ bhavitā bhedaḥ kadā cit Kurubhiḥ saha,
Dhṛtarāṣṭrasya sambandho yadi na syāt tvayā saha.
tvaṃ tu loka|vināśāya, Dhṛtarāṣṭra|kulasya ca,
utpanno vaira|puruṣaḥ sva|kula|ghnaś ca pāpa|kṛt.›
janma|prabhṛti c' âsmākaṃ pitā te pāpa|pūruṣaḥ
a|hitāni nṛśaṃsāni nityaśaḥ kartum icchati.
162.35 tasya vair'|ânuṣaṅgasya gant" âsmy antaṃ su|durgamam.
aham ādau nihatya tvāṃ Śakuneḥ saṃprapaśyataḥ
tato 'smi Śakuniṃ hantā miṣatāṃ sarva|dhanvinām!»

Bhīmasya vacanaṃ śrutvā, Sahadevasya c' ôbhayoḥ,
uvāca Phālguno vākyaṃ Bhīmasenaṃ smayann iva:
«Bhīmasena, na te santi yeṣāṃ vairaṃ tvayā saha.
mandā gṛheṣu sukhino mṛtyu|pāśa|vaśaṃ gatāḥ.
Ulūkaś ca na te vācyaḥ paruṣaṃ, puruṣ'|ôttama.
dūtāḥ kim aparādhyante yath"|ôktasy' ânubhāṣiṇaḥ?»

I will guide whichever furious kshatriya comes up against me in this world to Yama's realm, even if I must start with Bhishma. The words I spoke in the assembly of kshatriyas will be fulfilled. I swear it on my soul!'"

When he heard Bhima·sena's words, truculent Saha·deva, 162.30
his eyes bloodshot with rage, also spoke in the assembly of the soldiers, in a manner that suited the brave hero:

"Listen to what I have to add, evil man, and repeat it to your father:

'The split between the Kurus and ourselves would never have occurred if you had not been related to Dhrita·rashtra. Murderer of your own lineage and evil-doer that you are, you have sprung up as the personification of hostility for the destruction of the world as well as the line of Dhrita·rashtra.'

From the moment of our birth your father, that evil man,
always wished to do us harm and injury. So I will go to 162.35
the far, almost inaccessible shore of quarrelsome association. First I will kill you within view of Shákuni, then I will kill Shákuni before the eyes of all the archers!"

When he had listened to Bhima and Saha·deva's speeches, Phálguna smilingly spoke to Bhima·sena: "Bhima·sena, men who quarrel with you cannot live. The fools live happily in their houses, but they fall under the power of death's chains. Ulúka should not be spoken to harshly, greatest of men. What transgression do envoys commit when they merely repeat what was said to them?"

evam uktvā mahā|bāhur Bhīmaṃ bhīma|parākramam,
162.40 Dhṛṣṭadyumna|mukhān vīrān su|hṛdaḥ samabhāṣata:
«śrutaṃ vas tasya pāpasya Dhārtarāṣṭrasya bhāṣitam:
kutsanaṃ Vāsudevasya, mama c' âiva viśeṣataḥ.
śrutvā bhavantaḥ saṃrabdhā asmākaṃ hita|kāmyayā.
prabhāvād Vāsudevasya, bhavatāṃ ca prayatnataḥ
samagraṃ pārthivaṃ kṣatraṃ sarvaṃ na gaṇayāmy aham!
bhavadbhiḥ samanujñāto vākyam asya yad uttaram
Ulūke prāpayiṣyāmi, yad vakṣyati Suyodhanam:
‹śvo|bhūte katthitasy' âsya prativākyaṃ camū|mukhe
Gāṇḍīven' âbhidhāsyāmi; klībā hi vacan'|ôttarāḥ!› »
162.45 tatas te pārthivāḥ sarve praśaśaṃsur Dhanañjayam
tena vāky'|ôpacāreṇa vismitā rāja|sattamāḥ.
anunīya ca tān sarvān yathā|mānyaṃ, yathā|vayaḥ,
dharma|rājas tadā vākyaṃ tat|prāpyaṃ pratyabhāṣata:
«ātmānam avamanvāno na hi syāt pārthiv'|ôttamaḥ.
tatr' ôttaraṃ pravakṣyāmi tava śuśrūṣane rataḥ.»
Ulūkaṃ, Bharata|śreṣṭha, sāma|pūrvam ath' ôrjitam
Duryodhanasya tad vākyaṃ niśamya Bharata'|rṣabhaḥ
atilohita|netrābhyām, āśīviṣa iva śvasan,
smayamāna iva krodhāt, sṛkkiṇī parisaṃlihan,
162.50 Janārdanam abhiprekṣya, bhrātṝṃś c' âiv', êdam abravīt,
abhyabhāṣata kaitavyaṃ pragṛhya vipulaṃ bhujam:
«Ulūka, gaccha, kaitavya, brūhi, tāta, Suyodhanam
kṛta|ghnaṃ vaira|puruṣaṃ dur|matiṃ kula|pāṃsanam:

So it was that the long-armed man spoke to Bhima of
fearsome prowess. Then he spoke to his hero friends, led by 162.40
Dhrishta·dyumna:

"You have heard what the evil Dhartaráshtra had to say: the abuse of Vasudéva, and of me in particular. And hearing it you became angry because you wish to do us good. But when compared to Vasudéva's power and your effort, I value the whole kshatriya order of kings in its entirety as nothing! With your leave, I will give Ulúka an answer to give to Suyódhana: 'When tomorrow dawns, I will reply to your boasts at the head of the army with Gandíva; for those who make their response with mere words are the real eunuchs!'"

Then all those superb kings praised Dhanan·jaya, amazed 162.45
by his civil words. Having conciliated all the kings, according to their age and what they deserved, the king of righteousness then addressed Ulúka in suitable words: "An outstanding king should not tolerate insult to himself. I will tell you my reply, now that I have listened intently."

Best of the Bharatas, when the bull-like Bharata had heard Duryódhana's message, which Ulúka had gently relayed, he hissed like a snake, and his eyes were extremely bloodshot as he grimaced in anger and licked the corners
of his mouth. Glancing at Janárdana and his brothers, he 162.50
addressed the gambler's son, raising his large arms:

"Ulúka my friend, son of a gambler, go to Suyódhana—that ungrateful, wicked-minded personification of hostility and defiler of his lineage—and say:

‹Pāṇḍaveṣu sadā, pāpa, nityaṃ jihmaṃ pravartate.
sva|vīryād yaḥ parākramya, pāpa, āhvayate parān
a|bhītaḥ pūrayan vākyam, eṣa vai kṣatriyaḥ pumān.
sa, pāpa, kṣatriyo bhūtvā,
asmān āhūya saṃyuge
māny'|â|mānyān puras|kṛtya
yuddhaṃ mā gāḥ, kul'|âdhama!
ātma|vīryaṃ samāśritya, bhṛtya|vīryaṃ ca, Kaurava,
āhvayasva raṇe Pārthān, sarvathā kṣatriyo bhava!
162.55 para|vīryaṃ samāśritya yaḥ samāhvayate parān,
a|śaktaḥ svayam ādātum, etad eva na|puṃsakam!
sa tvaṃ pareṣāṃ vīryeṇa ātmānaṃ bahu manyase;
katham evam a|śaktas tvam asmān samabhigarjasi?› »

KṚṢṆA uvāca:

mad|vacaś c' âpi bhūyas te vaktavyaḥ sa Suyodhanaḥ:
«śva idānīṃ prapadyethāḥ. puruṣo bhava, dur|mate.
manyase yac ca, mūḍha, tvaṃ, ‹na yotsyati Janārdanaḥ
sārathyena vṛtaḥ Pārthair, iti› tvaṃ na bibheṣi ca.
jaghanya|kālam apy etan na bhavet; sarva|pārthivān
nirdaheyam ahaṃ krodhāt, tṛṇān' îva hut'|âśanaḥ!
162.60 Yudhiṣṭhira|niyogāt tu Phālgunasya mah"|ātmanaḥ
kariṣye yudhyamānasya sārathyaṃ vijit'|ātmanaḥ.
yady utpatasi lokāṃs trīn, yady āviśasi bhū|talam,
tatra tatr' Ârjuna|rathaṃ prabhāte drakṣyase punaḥ.
yac c' âpi Bhīmasenasya manyase mogha|bhāṣitam,
Duḥśāsanasya rudhiraṃ pītam ady' âvadhāraya!
na tvāṃ samīkṣate Pārtho, n' âpi rājā Yudhiṣṭhiraḥ,

'Evil man, you always treat the Pándavas deceitfully. The man who distinguishes himself through his own prowess, evil man, who challenges his enemies and fearlessly fulfills his own promises, is indeed a kshatriya. Be a kshatriya, evil man, and call us out to battle! But don't go to battle putting men we respect before you, worst of your line!

Káurava, rely on your own strength and that of your servants, and challenge the Parthas to battle. Be a kshatriya in
all you do! The man who relies on the strength of others, 162.55
and calls out his enemies to battle though he himself is unable to receive them, is no real man at all! You think a great deal of yourself, though you rely of the strength of others, so how is it that you roar at us, impotent as you are?'"

KRISHNA said:

You should tell Suyódhana my message as well:

"Let tomorrow come now! Be a man, wicked-minded creature. You believe that I, Janárdana, will not fight, fool, and you are not afraid, for the Pándavas chose me to be a charioteer. But should this fail to be the case, even if only for the slightest moment, I could burn up all the kings in anger, like a fire consuming straw!

However, on Yudhi·shthira's orders, I will act only as 162.60
high-souled and self-disciplined Phálguna's charioteer while he fights. If you fly past the three worlds, if you enter within the earth's core, you will still see Árjuna's chariot before you in the morning. You think Bhima·sena's words are in vain, but get it through your head that Duhshásana's blood is already drunk! Despite your nasty threats, neither Partha,

na Bhīmaseno, na yamau pratikūla|prabhāṣiṇam!»

SAÑJAYA uvāca:

163.1 DURYODHANASYA tad vākyaṃ niśamya, Bharata'|rṣabha,
netrābhyām atitāmrābhyāṃ kaitavyaṃ samudaikṣata,
sa Keśavam abhiprekṣya Guḍākeśo mahā|yaśāḥ
abhyabhāṣata kaitavyaṃ pragṛhya vipulaṃ bhujam:
«‹sva|vīryaṃ yaḥ samāśritya samāhvayati vai parān,
a|bhīto yudhyate śatrūn, sa vai puruṣa ucyate.
para|vīryaṃ samāśritya yaḥ samāhvayate parān,
kṣatra|bandhur a|śaktatvāl loke sa puruṣ'|âdhamaḥ.
163.5 sa tvaṃ pareṣāṃ vīryeṇa manyase vīryam ātmanaḥ,
svayaṃ kā|puruṣo, mūḍha, parāṃś ca kṣeptum icchasi!
yas tvaṃ vṛddhaṃ sarva|rājñāṃ,
hita|buddhiṃ, jit'|êndriyam
maraṇāya mahā|prājñaṃ
dīkṣayitvā vikatthase!
bhāvas te vidito 'smābhir, dur|buddhe kula|pāṃsana;
na haniṣyanti Gāṅgeyaṃ Pāṇḍavā ghṛṇay" êti hi.
yasya vīryaṃ samāśritya,
Dhārtarāṣṭra, vikatthase
hant" âsmi prathamaṃ Bhīṣmaṃ
miṣatāṃ sarva|dhanvinām.›
kaitavya, gatvā Bharatān sametya
Suyodhanaṃ Dhārtarāṣṭraṃ vadasva:
‹«tath" êty» uvāc' Ârjunaḥ savya|sācī,
niśā|vyapāye bhavitā vimardaḥ!

King Yudhi·shthira, Bhima·sena, nor the twins have any regard for you!"

SÁNJAYA continued:

ONCE HE HAD heard Duryódhana's message, bull of the Bharatas, great glorious Guda·kesha glanced at the gambler's son with excessively bloodshot eyes, looked at Késhava, and then, raising his large arms, he addressed the gambler's son as follows: 163.1

"'He who relies on his own strength, challenges his enemies, and fights his foes fearlessly, is said to be a man. But the man who challenges his enemies by relying on the strength of others is only a kshatriya by birth. His powerlessness makes him the worst of men on earth. You think 163.5
you are powerful, but you rely on the power of others, and being a coward yourself, fool, you wish to cast down your enemies!

Now that you have consecrated highly wise Bhishma, the eldest of all the kings, whose mind is set on advantage and whose senses are controlled, thereby ensuring his death, you boast! We understand your motive, you evil-minded disgrace of your line! You believe that the Pándavas will not kill the son of the Ganges because they feel affection for him. Bhishma will be the first man I kill in the sight of all the archers, though you rely upon his power as you boast, Dhartaráshtra.'

Go to the Bharatas, gambler's son, and tell Suyódhana, Dhrita·rashtra's son, that 'Árjuna the ambidextrous archer says, "So be it!" Once the night has passed, there will be slaughter! Unfailingly truthful Bhishma, a man true to his 163.10

163.10 yad v" âbravīd vākyam a|dīna|sattvāṃ
madhye Kurūn harṣayan satya|sandhaḥ:
«ahaṃ hantā Sṛñjayānām anīkaṃ,
Śālveyakāṃś c' êti» mam' âiṣa bhāraḥ.›
kaitavya, gatvā Bharatān sametya
Suyodhanaṃ Dhārtarāṣṭraṃ vadasva:
‹«hanyām ahaṃ Droṇam ṛte 'pi lokaṃ.
na te bhayaṃ vidyate Pāṇḍavebhyaḥ!»
tato hi te «labdhatamaṃ ca rājyam,
āpad|gatāḥ Pāṇḍavāś c' êti» bhāvaḥ.
sa darpa|pūrṇo na samīkṣase tvam
an|artham ātmany api vartamānam.
tasmād ahaṃ te prathamaṃ samūhe
hantā samakṣaṃ Kuru|vṛddham eva.
sūry'|ôdaye yukta|senaḥ pratīkṣya
dhvajī rathī rakṣata satya|sandham.
ahaṃ hi vaḥ paśyatāṃ dvīpam enaṃ
Bhīṣmaṃ rathāt pātayiṣyāmi bāṇaiḥ.›
śvo|bhūte katthanā|vākyaṃ vijñāsyati Suyodhanaḥ
ācitaṃ śara|jālena mayā dṛṣṭvā pitā|maham!

163.15 ‹yad uktaś ca sabhā|madhye puruṣo hrasva|darśanaḥ
kruddhena Bhīmasenena bhrātā Duḥśāsanas tava,
a|dharma|jño nitya|vairī pāpa|buddhir nṛśaṃsavat,
satyāṃ pratijñām a|cirād drakṣyase tāṃ, Suyodhana!

word, brought joy to the Kurus as he spoke in their midst, saying: "I will kill the army of Srínjayas and Shalvéyakas!" But this is my task.' Go to the Bharatas, gambler's son, and tell Suyódhana, son of Dhrita·rashtra, my message:

'Bhishma told you, "I could kill the world even without Drona's aid. There is no danger from the Pándavas!" And so you think the kingdom is won outright, and that the Pándavas have fallen into disaster. But, filled with arrogance, you do not see the disaster that lies within yourself. Therefore, I will kill Bhishma, the eldest of the Kurus, in plain view. He will be my first victim in battle. When your army is drawn up at sunrise, protect that man who is true to his word with banners and chariots. From my chariot with my arrows, I will indeed topple Bhishma, your haven, while you watch.'

Suyódhana will understand the meaning of boasting when tomorrow comes and he sees grandfather struck with my shower of arrows!

'The vow that furious Bhima·sena swore in the midst of 163.15
court to your brother, the shortsighted Duhshásana—the eternally hostile, evil-minded, and cruel man, who has no comprehension of law—will soon come true, Suyódhana, and you will see it!

abhimānasya, darpasya, krodha|pāruṣyayos tathā,
naiṣṭhuryasy', âvalepasya, ātma|saṃbhāvanasya ca,
nṛśaṃsatāyās, taikṣṇyasya, dharma|vidveṣaṇasya ca,
a|dharmasy', âtivādasya, vṛddh'|âtikramaṇasya ca,
darśanasya ca vakrasya, kṛtsnasy' âpanayasya ca
drakṣyasi tvaṃ phalaṃ tīvram a|cireṇa, Suyodhana.
163.20 Vāsudeva|dvitīye hi mayi kruddhe, nar'|âdhipa,
āśā te jīvite, mūḍha, rājye vā kena hetunā?
śānte Bhīṣme, tathā Droṇe, sūta|putre ca pātite
nirāśo jīvite, rājye, putreṣu ca bhaviṣyasi.
bhrātṝṇāṃ nidhanaṃ śrutvā, putrāṇāṃ ca, Suyodhana,
Bhīmasenena nihato duṣ|kṛtāni smariṣyasi!›
na dvitīyāṃ pratijñāṃ hi pratijānāmi, kaitava.
satyaṃ bravīmy ahaṃ hy, etat sarvaṃ satyaṃ bhaviṣyati.»
Yudhiṣṭhiro 'pi kaitavyam Ulūkam idam abravīt:
«Ulūka, mad|vaco brūhi gatvā, tāta, Suyodhanam:
163.25 ‹svena vṛttena me vṛttaṃ n' âdhigantuṃ tvam arhasi
ubhayor antaraṃ veda sūnṛt'|ân|ṛtayor api.
na c' âhaṃ kāmaye pāpam api kīṭa|pipīlayoḥ,
kiṃ punar jñātiṣu vadhaṃ kāmayeyaṃ kathañ cana!
etad|arthaṃ mayā, tāta, pañca grāmā vṛtāḥ purā.
kathaṃ tava, su|durbuddhe, na prekṣye vyasanaṃ mahat?
sa tvaṃ kāma|parīt'|ātmā mūḍha|bhāvāc ca katthase!
tath" âiva Vāsudevasya na gṛhṇāsi hitaṃ vacaḥ.
kiñ c' êdānīṃ bah'|ûktena? yudhyasva saha bāndhavaiḥ.›

Before long you will see the horrible results of your pride, arrogance, anger, harshness, severity, haughtiness, self-conceit, baseness, fierceness, hostility to duty, lawlessness, abusive speech, transgression against elders, skewed vision, and all wicked conduct, Suyódhana.

When I, with Vasudéva as my second, am filled with fury, lord of men, then what reason do you have to hope for life, fool, or for the kingdom? When Bhishma and Drona are peaceable and the *suta*'s son is fallen, you will no longer have any hope for your life, kingdom, or sons. You will remember all your wicked exploits when you hear about the destruction of your brothers and sons, and you have been struck by Bhima·sena, Suyódhana!' 163.20

I do not swear twice, gambler's son! I speak the truth. It will indeed all come true."

Yudhi·shthira also spoke to Ulúka, saying:

"Ulúka, my friend, go to Suyódhana and give him my message:

'You ought not to counter my conduct with your own. Know that the difference between the two of us is the difference between truth and falsehood. I do not even wish evil upon insects and ants, let alone desire any slaughter of my relatives! This is the reason that we chose only five villages before, my friend. How is it that you do not see the great disaster that is upon you, you incredibly wicked-minded man? 163.25

Your soul is overcome with lust, and you boast because of your idiotic nature! This too is the reason that you do not accept Vasudéva's beneficial advice. What is the point of all this discussion now? Fight with your relatives.'

mama vipriya|kartāraṃ, kaitavya, brūhi Kauravam,
163.30 śrutaṃ vākyaṃ, gṛhīto 'rtho, mataṃ yat te, tath" âstu tat.»
Bhīmasenas tato vākyaṃ bhūya āha nṛp'|ātmajam:
«Ulūka, mad|vaco brūhi dur|matiṃ pāpa|pūruṣam,
śaṭhaṃ, naikṛtikaṃ, pāpaṃ, dur|ācāraṃ Suyodhanam:
‹gṛdhr'|ôdare vā vastavyaṃ, pure vā nāga|sāhvaye,
pratijñātaṃ mayā yac ca sabhā|madhye, nar'|âdhama,
kart" âhaṃ tad vacaḥ satyaṃ, satyen' âiva śapāmi te,
Duḥśāsanasya rudhiraṃ hatvā pāsyāmy ahaṃ mṛdhe!
sakthinī tava bhaṅktv" âiva, hatvā hi tava s'|ôdarān.
sarveṣāṃ Dhārtarāṣṭrāṇām ahaṃ mṛtyuḥ, Suyodhana,
163.35 sarveṣāṃ rāja|putrāṇām Abhimanyur a|saṃśayam.
karmaṇā toṣayiṣyāmi. bhūyaś c' âiva vacaḥ śṛṇu.
hatvā, Suyodhana, tvāṃ vai sahitaṃ sarva|sodaraiḥ,
ākramiṣye padā mūrdhni dharma|rājasya paśyataḥ!› »
Nakulas tu tato vākyam idam āha, mahī|pate:
«Ulūka, brūhi Kauravyaṃ Dhārtarāṣṭraṃ Suyodhanam:
‹śrutaṃ te gadato vākyaṃ sarvam eva yathā|tatham.
tathā kart" âsmi, Kauravya, yathā tvam anuśāsi mām.› »
Sahadevo 'pi, nṛ|pate, idam āha vaco 'rthavat:
«Suyodhana, matir yā te, vṛth" âiṣā te bhaviṣyati.
163.40 śauciṣyase, mahā|rāja, sa|putra|jñāti|bāndhavaḥ
idaṃ ca kleśam asmākaṃ, hṛṣṭo yat tvaṃ vikatthase.»
Virāṭa|Drupadau vṛddhāv Ulūkam idam ūcatuḥ:
«dāsa|bhāvaṃ niyaccheva sādhor, iti matiḥ sadā;
tau ca dāsāv a|dāsau vā, pauruṣaṃ yasya yādṛśam!»

Gambler's son, tell the Káurava who does what displeases
me that I have heard and accepted his message. Let it be 163.30
just as he plans."

Bhima·sena spoke once more to the prince:

"Ulúka, tell the foul-minded, evil, malignant, deceitful, wicked miscreant Suyódhana my message:

'You must live in the stomach of a vulture, or in Hástina·pura. Vilest of men, I will accomplish the vow I made in the middle of the court. I swear, by the truth, that I will drink Duhshásana's blood once I have killed him in battle!

I will indeed break your thighs and kill your brothers. I
am the death of all the Dhartaráshtras, Suyódhana, just as 163.35
Abhimányu is doubtless the death of all the princes. I will satisfy you with my actions! Listen to me once more. I will kill you and all your brothers, Suyódhana, and then I will kick your head with my foot as the king of righteousness looks on!'"

Nákula then spoke as follows, earth-lord: "Ulúka, tell Suyódhana Dhartaráshtra the Káurava: 'All you said has been heard and properly understood. I will do just as you have commanded me, Kaurávya.'"

Saha·deva too, king, spoke these meaningful words: "Suyódhana, it will be entirely as you wish. You will repent, 163.40
great sovereign, as will your sons, relatives, and family, just as you now boast and rejoice over our calamity."

Next the aged Viráta and Drúpada said to Ulúka: "Our wish is always to attach ourselves to a good man as his slaves, but whether we are slaves or not remains to be seen, as does the quality of manliness each possesses!"

Śikhaṇḍī tu tato vākyam Ulūkam idam abravīt:
«vaktavyo bhavatā rājā pāpeṣv abhirataḥ sadā:
‹paśya tvaṃ māṃ raṇe, rājan, kurvāṇaṃ karma dāruṇam!
yasya vīryaṃ samāsādya manyase vijayaṃ yudhi
tam ahaṃ pātayiṣyāmi rathāt tava pitā|maham!
ahaṃ Bhīṣma|vadhāt sṛṣṭo nūnaṃ dhātrā mah"|ātmanā!
163.45 so 'haṃ Bhīṣmaṃ haniṣyāmi miṣatāṃ sarva|dhanvinām!› »

Dhṛṣṭadyumno 'pi kaitavyam Ulūkam idam abravīt:
«Suyodhano mama vaco vaktavyo nṛ|pateḥ sutaḥ:
‹ahaṃ Droṇaṃ haniṣyāmi sa|gaṇaṃ saha|bāndhavam,
avaśyaṃ ca mayā kāryaṃ pūrveṣāṃ caritaṃ mahat
kartā c' âhaṃ tathā karma yathā n' ânyaḥ kariṣyati!› »

tam abravīd dharma|rājaḥ kāruṇy'|ârthaṃ vaco mahat:
«‹n' âhaṃ jñāti|vadhaṃ, rājan, kāmayeyaṃ kathañ cana;
tav' âiva doṣād, dur|buddhe, sarvam etat tv an|āvṛtam.›
sa gaccha mā|ciraṃ, tāta Ulūka, yadi manyase,
163.50 iha vā tiṣṭha, bhadraṃ te, vayaṃ hi tava bāndhavāḥ.»

Ulūkas tu tato, rājan, Dharma|putraṃ Yudhiṣṭhiram
āmantrya prayayau tatra yatra rājā Suyodhanaḥ.
Ulūkas tata āgamya Duryodhanam a|marṣaṇam
Arjunasya samādeśaṃ yath" ôktaṃ sarvam abravīt.
Vāsudevasya, Bhīmasya, dharma|rājasya pauruṣam,
Nakulasya, Virāṭasya, Drupadasya ca, Bhārata,
Sahadevasya ca vaco, Dhṛṣṭadyumna|Śikhaṇḍinoḥ,
Keśav'|Ârjunayor vākyaṃ yath" ôktaṃ sarvam abravīt.

Shikhándin then said these words to Ulúka: "You must tell the king who is ever intent on evil deeds: 'King, just watch and see what vicious exploit I achieve in battle! I will topple your grandfather from his chariot, though he is the man upon whose heroism you rely, believing you will have victory in war! Surely I was created by the high-souled creator for Bhishma's murder! I will kill Bhishma in clear sight 163.45
of all archers!'"

Dhrishta·dyumna also addressed Ulúka the gambler's son, in these words: "You must also tell prince Suyódhana my message: 'I will kill Drona and his hordes and relatives! Certainly I must match the great adventures of previous generations, and I will achieve a feat to be matched by no other!'"

Then the king of righteousness spoke great words, designed to be compassionate: "'I never desire the slaughter of my relatives, king, but because of your sin, wicked-minded man, it is all unavoidable now.' Go without delay, Ulúka my friend, if you think it best, or stay here, bless you, for 163.50
we too are assuredly your kin."

My king, Ulúka then took his leave of Yudhi·shthira, son of Dharma, and set off for the place where King Suyódhana was waiting. Ulúka reached truculent Duryódhana and gave him the entire message which Árjuna had told him, as instructed. He also told him the manly messages of Vasudéva, Bhima, the king of righteousness, Nákula, Viráta, Drúpada, O Bhárata, Saha·deva, Dhrishta·dyumna, and Shikhándin, as well as relaying everything Késhava and Árjuna had said to him, just as they said it.

kaitavyasya tu tad vākyaṃ niśamya Bharata'|rṣabhaḥ
Duḥśāsanaṃ ca, Karṇaṃ ca, Śakuniṃ c' âpi, Bhārata,
163.55 ājñāpayata rājñaś ca balaṃ, mitra|balaṃ tathā
yathā prāg udayāt sarve yuktās tiṣṭhanty anīkinaḥ.
tataḥ Karṇa|samādiṣṭā dūtāḥ saṃtvaritā rathaiḥ,
uṣṭra|vāmībhir apy anye, sad|aśvaiś ca mahā|javaiḥ
tūrṇaṃ pariyayuḥ senāṃ kṛtsnāṃ Karṇasya śāsanāt,
ājñāpayanto rājñaś ca, «yogaḥ prāg udayād! iti.»

SAÑJAYA uvāca:

164.1 ULŪKASYA VACAḤ śrutvā Kuntī|putro Yudhiṣṭhiraḥ
senāṃ niryāpayām āsa Dhṛṣṭadyumna|purogamām,
padātinīṃ, nāgavatīṃ, rathinīm, aśva|vṛndinīm
catur|vidha|balāṃ, bhīmām, a|kampāṃ pṛthivīm iva,
Bhīmasen'|ādibhir guptām, s'|Ârjunaiś ca mahā|rathaiḥ,
Dhṛṣṭadyumna|vaśāṃ, durgāṃ, sāgara|stimit'|ôpamām.
tasyās tv agre mah"|êṣv|āsaḥ Pāñcālyo yuddha|durmadaḥ
Droṇa|prepsur anīkāni Dhṛṣṭadyumno vyakarṣata.
164.5 yathā|balaṃ, yath"|ôtsāhaṃ rathinaḥ samupādiśat:
Arjunaṃ sūta|putrāya, Bhīmaṃ Duryodhanāya ca,
Dhṛṣṭaketuṃ ca Śalyāya, Gautamāy' Ôttamaujasam,
Aśvatthāmne ca Nakulaṃ, Śaibyaṃ ca Kṛtavarmaṇe,
Saindhavāya ca Vārshneyaṃ Yuyudhānaṃ samādiśat,
Śikhaṇḍinaṃ ca Bhīṣmāya pramukhe samakalpayat,
Sahadevaṃ Śakunaye, Cekitānaṃ Śalāya vai,
Draupadeyāṃs tathā pañca Trigartebhyaḥ samādiśat,

Having heard what the gambler's son told him, the bull 163.55
of the Bharatas ordered Duhshásana, Karna, and Shákuni, O Bhárata, as well as the force of kings and army of allies, to all stand arrayed in battle formation for sunrise. Then messengers, instructed by Karna, rushed with their chariots, camels, and mares, while others went with swift and excellent horses, and quickly made their way through the whole army, at Karna's command, ordering the kings: "Array yourselves for sunrise!"

SÁNJAYA continued:

ONCE HE HAD heard Ulúka's message, Yudhi·shthira the 164.1
son of Kunti had his army, led by Dhrishta·dyumna, set out. And his four-winged force of infantry, elephants, chariots, and hordes of cavalry, as terrifying and unshakeable as the earth, protected by Bhima·sena and others, including mighty warriors led by Árjuna, and controlled by Dhrishta·dyumna, was like the vast and motionless ocean.

At the front was the great Panchálan archer, battle-crazed Dhrishta·dyumna, eager to reach his target Drona, drawing up the armies. He assigned charioteers to their targets 164.5
according to their strength and daring. He assigned Árjuna to Karna the *suta*'s son, Bhima to Duryódhana, Dhrishta·ketu to Shalya, Uttamáujas to Gáutama, Nákula to Ashva·tthaman, Shaibya to Krita·varman, and Vrishni Yuyudhána to the Sáindhava king. He assigned Shikhándin to Bhishma and positioned him at the front, then he assigned Saha·deva to Shákuni, Chekitána to Shala, and the five sons of Dráupadi to the Tri·gartas. He assigned Subhádra's son Abhimányu to Vrisha·sena and then to the remaining kings,

Vṛṣasenāya Saubhadraṃ, śeṣāṇāṃ ca mahī|kṣitām,
sa samarthaṃ hi taṃ mene, Pārthād abhyadhikaṃ raṇe.
164.10 evaṃ vibhajya yodhāṃs tān pṛthak ca saha c' âiva ha,
jvālā|varṇo mah"|êṣv|āso Droṇam aṃśam akalpayat.
Dhṛṣṭadyumno mah"|êṣv|āsaḥ senā|pati|patis tataḥ
vidhivad vyūhya medhāvī yuddhāya dhṛta|mānasaḥ
yath" ôddiṣṭāni sainyāni Pāṇḍavānām ayojayat,
jayāya Pāṇḍu|putrāṇāṃ yattas tasthau raṇ'|âjire.

for he believed that Abhimányu was superior even to Partha in battle.

Having distributed the fighters, both singly and as a whole, the blazing fire-hued mighty archer took Drona as his share. So the powerful archer Dhrishta·dyumna, the commander of army commanders, duly arrayed his troops and then waited for war with a firm mind. Once he had drawn up the Pándavas' soldiers as just described, he stood on the battlefield, striving to bring victory to the sons of Pandu. 164.10

for he believed that Abhimanyu was superior even to [illegible] in that art.

Having [illegible], both [illegible] and [illegible] which the blazing [illegible] clever [illegible] Drona as his stage. So the powerful archer Dhrishta·dyumna, the commander of armies, duly arrayed his troops and then waited for war with a firm mind. Once he had drawn up the Pándava soldiers as [illegible] described, he stood on the battlefield, striving to bring victory to the sons of Pandu.

165–172

# THE COUNT OF CHARIOTS AND GREAT WARRIORS

DHṚTARĀṢṬRA uvāca:

165.1 PRATIJÑĀTE PHĀLGUNENA vadhe Bhīṣmasya saṃyuge
kim akurvata me mandāḥ putrā Duryodhan'|ādayaḥ?
hatam eva hi paśyāmi Gāṅgeyaṃ pitaraṃ raṇe
Vāsudeva|sahāyena Pārthena dṛḍha|dhanvanā!
sa c' â|parimita|prajñas tac chrutvā Pārtha|bhāṣitam
kim uktavān mah"|êṣv|āso Bhīṣmaḥ praharatāṃ varaḥ?
saināpatyaṃ ca saṃprāpya Kauravāṇāṃ dhuran|dharaḥ
kim aceṣṭata Gāṅgeyo mahā|buddhi|parākramaḥ?

VAIŚAMPĀYANA uvāca:

165.5 tatas tat Sañjayas tasmai sarvam eva nyavedayat
yath" ôktaṃ Kuru|vṛddhena Bhīṣmeṇ' â|mita|tejasā.

SAÑJAYA uvāca:

saināpatyam anuprāpya Bhīṣmaḥ Śāntanavo, nṛpa,
Duryodhanam uvāc' êdaṃ vacanaṃ harṣayann iva:
«namas|kṛtya Kumārāya senā|nye śakti|pāṇaye,
ahaṃ senā|patis te 'dya bhaviṣyāmi na saṃśayaḥ!
senā|karmaṇy abhijño 'smi, vyūheṣu vividheṣu ca,
karma kārayituṃ c' âiva, bhṛtān apy a|bhṛtāṃs tathā.
yātrā|yāne ca yuddhe ca, tathā praśamaneṣu ca
bhṛśaṃ veda, mahā|rāja, yathā veda Bṛhaspatiḥ!
165.10 vyūhānāṃ ca samārambhān daiva|gāndharva|mānuṣān;
tair ahaṃ mohayiṣyāmi Pāṇḍavān, vyetu te jvaraḥ.
so 'haṃ yotsyāmi tattvena pālayaṃs tava vāhinīm
yathāvac chāstrato, rājan; vyetu te mānaso jvaraḥ!»

DHRITA·RASHTRA said:

ONCE PHÁLGUNA HAD sworn upon Bhishma's murder in battle, what did my foolish sons, Duryódhana and the others, do? Even now I see my father, the son of the Ganges, killed in battle by Partha, the sure archer with Vasudéva as his ally! And when he heard what Partha had to say, what did the mighty archer Bhishma—the greatest of warriors, a man of boundless wisdom—say? And when he took the position of army commander, what did the son of the Ganges—that man of great intelligence and prowess, bearing the burden of leadership over the Káuravas—do? 165.1

VAISHAMPÁYANA said:

So Sánjaya explained to him in its entirety exactly what the aged Kuru, Bhishma of boundless energy, had said. 165.5

SÁNJAYA replied:

When he took the position of army commander, my king, Bhishma son of Shántanu said these words to Duryódhana, seemingly pleasing him: "Paying obeisance to Kumára, the leader of the celestial forces, with his spear in hand, I will doubtless be your army commander today! I understand army affairs as well as various battle formations, and I know how to make mercenaries and recruits alike do their jobs. I know as fully as Brihas·pati, O great sovereign, about marching, battle, and keeping my men safe!

I know the battle formations used by gods, *gandhárvas*, 165.10
and men, and with these I will baffle the Pándavas, so let your fever subside. I will fight, truly protecting your army, in accordance with military science, king, so let the fever in your mind subside!"

DURYODHANA uvāca:

vidyate me na, Gāṅgeya, bhayaṃ dev'|âsureṣv api
samasteṣu, mahā|bāho, satyam etad bravīmi te!
kiṃ punas tvayi dur|dharṣe saināpatye vyavasthite,
Droṇe ca puruṣa|vyāghre sthite yuddh'|âbhinandini?
bhavadbhyāṃ puruṣ'|âgryābhyāṃ
  sthitābhyāṃ vijaye mama
na dur|labhaṃ, Kuru|śreṣṭha,
  deva|rājyam api dhruvam!
165.15 ratha|saṃkhyāṃ tu kārtsnyena pareṣām ātmanas tathā,
tath" âiv' âtirathānāṃ ca vettum icchāmi, Kaurava.
pitā|maho hi kuśalaḥ pareṣām ātmanas tathā;
śrotum icchāmy ahaṃ sarvaiḥ sah' âibhir vasudh"|âdhipaiḥ.

BHĪṢMA uvāca:

Gāndhāre, śṛṇu, rāj'|êndra, ratha|saṃkhyāṃ svake bale,
ye rathāḥ, pṛthivī|pāla, tath" âiv' âtirathāś ca ye.
bahūn' îha sahasrāṇi, prayutāny arbudāni ca
rathānāṃ tava senāyāṃ. yathā|mukhyaṃ tu me śṛṇu.
bhavān agre rath'|ôdāraḥ saha sarvaiḥ sah'|ôdaraiḥ
Duḥśāsana|prabhṛtibhir bhrātṛbhiḥ śata|saṃmitaiḥ.
165.20 sarve kṛta|praharaṇāś, cheda|bheda|viśāradāḥ,
rath'|ôpasthe, gaja|skandhe, gadā|prās'|âsi|carmaṇi;
saṃyantāraḥ, prahartāraḥ, kṛt'|âstrā, bhāra|sādhanāḥ,
iṣv|astre Droṇa|śiṣyāś ca, Kṛpasya ca Śaradvataḥ.

DURYÓDHANA replied:

I tell you truly, long-armed son of the Ganges, that I have no fear of even gods and *ásuras* gathered together! How much more, then, is that the case when you are stationed as the invincible army commander and tiger-like Drona is also ready and eager for war? Assuredly, with you two, the foremost of men, drawn up for my victory, not even lordship over the gods would prove hard to attain, greatest of the Kurus!

But I want to know the number of chariot warriors, from 165.15
among the whole force of the enemy and my own, and also the number of great chariot warriors, Káurava. You do indeed have experience in both the enemy forces and my own, grandfather, so I and all the lords of earth want to hear from you!

BHISHMA said:

Son of Gandhári, listen to the number of chariot warriors contained in your own army, lord of kings; those who are the chariot warriors, and those who are the great chariot warriors, defender of earth. There are many thousands, many millions, many tens of millions of chariot warriors in your army, but listen as I list the foremost among them. You are the first, with all your hundred excellent warrior brothers, with Duhshásana at the forefront. You are all trained in 165.20
striking, and experienced in cutting and splitting. You are all good drivers when standing within your chariots. You are all good riders when on the shoulders of an elephant. You are all good wielders of the mace, good swordsmen, all trained with weapons and able to bear your burdens,

ete haniṣyanti raṇe Pañcālān yuddha|durmadān
kṛta|kilbiṣāḥ Pāṇḍaveyair Dhārtarāṣṭrā manasvinaḥ.
tath" âham, Bharata|śreṣṭha, sarva|senāpatis tava
śatrūn vidhvaṃsayiṣyāmi kad|arthī|kṛtya Pāṇḍavān;
na tv ātmano guṇān vaktum arhāmi—vidito 'smi te.

Kṛtavarmā tv atiratho Bhojaḥ śastra|bhṛtāṃ varaḥ
165.25 artha|siddhiṃ tava raṇe kariṣyati, na saṃśayaḥ,
śastra|vidbhir an|ādhṛṣyo, dūra|pātī, dṛḍh'|āyudhaḥ,
haniṣyati camūṃ teṣāṃ Mahendro Dānavān iva!

Madra|rājo mah"|êṣv|āsaḥ Śalyo me 'tiratho mataḥ,
spardhate Vāsudevena nityaṃ yo vai raṇe raṇe.
bhāgineyān nijāṃs tyaktvā Śalyas te 'tiratho mataḥ.
eṣa yotsyati saṃgrāme Pāṇḍavāṃś ca mahā|rathān,
sāgar'|ôrmi|samair bāṇaiḥ plāvayann iva śātravān.

Bhūriśravāḥ kṛt'|âstraś ca, tava c' âpi hitaḥ su|hṛt,
Saumadattir mah"|êṣv|āso, ratha|yūthapa|yūthapaḥ,
bala|kṣayam a|mitrāṇāṃ su|mahāntaṃ kariṣyati.

165.30 Sindhu|rājo, mahā|rāja, mato me dvi|guṇo rathaḥ,
yotsyate samare, rājan, vikrānto ratha|sattamaḥ.
Draupadī|haraṇe, rājan, parikliṣṭaś ca Pāṇḍavaiḥ;
saṃsmaraṃs taṃ parikleśaṃ yotsyate para|vīra|hā.
etena hi tadā, rājaṃs, tapa āsthāya dāruṇam

and you are the students of Drona and Kripa Sharádvata in archery.

The spirited Dhartaráshtras, treated offensively by the Pándavas, will kill the war-crazed Panchálas in battle. Similarly I, as your army commander, O greatest of the Bharatas, will annihilate your enemies, the Pándavas. But I ought not to speak of my own virtues—you know me.

Krita·varman, the Bhojan king, the greatest of those who wield weapons, is an exceptional chariot warrior. Doubtless 165.25 he will achieve success in your purpose in battle. Invincible even to those who are experienced with weapons, the far-shooting and firm-weaponed man will kill their army just as great Indra killed the Dánavas!

The king of the Madras, the great bowman Shalya, is an exceptional warrior, in my opinion. He always emulates Vasudéva in every battle. Now that he has abandoned his own sister's sons, Shalya is your exceptional warrior. This man will fight against the mighty Pándava warriors in battle, seemingly flooding his enemies with his arrows, like waves of the sea.

Weapon-trained Bhuri·shravas, Soma·datta's mighty archer son, the leader of leaders of chariot units, and your advantageous friend, will cause enormous destruction among the forces of the enemy.

The Sindhu king, great sovereign, is in my opinion worth 165.30 two chariot warriors, and the greatest of chariot warriors will fight in battle, king, displaying his prowess. He was tormented by the Pándavas for the abduction of Dráupadi, and that slayer of enemy heroes will fight while recalling his pain. Intent on harsh asceticism, king, he then won a

su|durlabho varo labdhaḥ Pāṇḍavān yoddhum āhave.
sa eṣa ratha|śārdūlas tad vairaṃ saṃsmaran raṇe
yotsyate Pāṇḍavais, tāta, prāṇāṃs tyaktvā su|dus|tyajān.

BHĪṢMA uvāca:

166.1 SUDAKṢIṆAS TU Kāmbojo ratha eka|guṇo mataḥ;
tav' ârtha|siddhim ākāṅkṣan yotsyate samare paraiḥ.
etasya ratha|siṃhasya tav' ârthe, rāja|sattama,
parākramaṃ yath" Êndrasya drakṣyanti Kuravo yudhi.
etasya ratha|vaṃśe hi tigma|vega|prahāriṇaḥ
Kāmbojānāṃ, mahā|rāja, śalabhānām iv' āyatiḥ!

Nīlo Māhiṣmatī|vāsī nīla|varmā rathas tava;
ratha|vaṃśena kadanaṃ śatrūṇāṃ vai kariṣyati.
166.5 kṛta|vairaḥ purā c' âiva Sahadevena, māriṣa,
yotsyate satataṃ, rājaṃs, tav' ârthe, Kuru|nandana.

Vind'|Ânuvindāv Āvantyau saṃmatau ratha|sattamau
kṛtinau samare, tāta, dṛḍha|vīrya|parākramau.
etau tau puruṣa|vyāghrau ripu|sainyaṃ pradhakṣyataḥ
gadā|prās'|âsi|nārācais, tomaraiś ca kara|cyutaiḥ.
yuddh'|âbhikāmau samare krīḍantāv iva yūtha|pau
yūtha|madhye, mahā|rāja, vicarantau Kṛtāntavat.

boon which is very hard to attain: to fight against the Pándavas in battle. This tiger-like chariot warrior will remember his hostility in battle and will fight the Pándavas, my friend, abandoning even his life—such a very difficult thing to sacrifice.

BHISHMA continued:

SUDÁKSHINA, THE Kambója king, has the value of a sin- 166.1
gle chariot warrior as far as I am concerned. He will fight against your enemies in battle, hoping for the success of your cause. The Kurus will see that the prowess of this lion-like chariot warrior matches Indra's as he fights for your cause, greatest of kings. The fierce and ferocious Kambójan fighters in his host of chariots are like a swarm of locusts, great sovereign!

Nila, who lives in Mahíshmati and dresses in midnight-blue armor, is your chariot warrior. He will bring about
the slaughter of your enemies with his host of chariots. He 166.5
quarreled with Saha·deva in the past, worthy friend and king, and he will always fight for your cause, descendant of the Kurus.

Vinda and Anuvínda, the Avántyas, are regarded as excellent chariot warriors. My friend, those two are experienced in battle, and firm in their heroism and prowess. Those two tiger-like men will annihilate the enemy army with their maces, spears, swords, iron arrows, and with the lances hurled from their hands. In battle they are like a pair of elephant herd-leaders playing in the midst of their herd, as they long for war, great sovereign, roaming around like Yama.

Trigartā bhrātaraḥ pañca rath'|ôdārā matā mama,
kṛta|vairāś ca Pārthais te Virāṭa|nagare tadā.
166.10 makarā iva, rāj'|êndra, samuddhata|taraṅgiṇīm
Gaṅgāṃ vikṣobhayiṣyanti Pārthānāṃ yudhi vāhinīm.
te rathāḥ pañca, rāj'|êndra, yeṣāṃ Satyaratho mukham.
ete yotsyanti saṅgrāme saṃsmarantaḥ purā kṛtam,
vyalīkaṃ Pāndaveyena Bhīmasen'|ânujena ha
diśo vijayatā, rājañ, śveta|vāhena, Bhārata;
te haniṣyanti Pārthānāṃ tān āsādya mahā|rathān,
varān varān mah"|êṣv|āsān, kṣatriyāṇāṃ dhuran|dharān.

Lakṣmaṇas tava putraś ca, tathā Duḥśāsanasya ca,
ubhau tau puruṣa|vyāghrau saṅgrāmeṣv a|palāyinau.
166.15 taruṇau su|kumārau ca rāja|putrau tarasvinau,
yuddhānāṃ ca viśeṣa|jñau, praṇetārau ca sarvaśaḥ.
rathau tau, Kuru|śārdūla, matau me ratha|sattamau,
kṣatra|dharma|ratau, vīrau, mahat karma kariṣyataḥ.

Daṇḍadhāro, mahā|rāja, ratha eko, nara'|rṣabha,
yotsyate tava saṃgrāme svena sainyena pālitaḥ.
Bṛhadbalas tathā rājā Kausalyo ratha|sattamaḥ
ratho mama matas, tāta, mahā|vega|parākramaḥ.
eṣa yotsyati saṃgrāme svān bandhūn saṃpraharṣayan
ugr'|āyudho mah"|êṣv|āso Dhārtarāṣṭra|hite rataḥ.

The five Tri·garta brothers are lofty chariot warriors, in
my opinion, and they quarreled with the Parthas at Viráta's
city on the occasion of the cattle raid. Like crocodiles stir- 166.10
ring up the river Ganges, they will agitate the army of the
Parthas in battle. They are five chariot warriors, lord of
kings, and their leader is Satya·ratha. These men will fight
in battle, remembering the past offence caused by Bhima·
sena's younger brother, the son of Pandu, when white-
horsed Árjuna was conquering all regions, King Bhárata;
and they will attack the mighty chariot warriors of the
Parthas, the very greatest archers and the leaders of the kshatriyas, and they will kill them.

Your son Lákshmana and similarly Duhshásana's son are
both tiger-like men who do not retreat in battles. Those 166.15
young and very tender princes are bold, they understand the
particulars of wars, and they are leaders in every respect. To
my mind those chariot warriors, tiger-like Kuru, are excellent chariot warriors. The pair of heroes take delight in the
duties of a kshatriya, and they will achieve great exploits.

Danda·dhara, great sovereign, equals a single chariot warrior, bull-like man. He will fight for you in battle, defended by his own force. King Brihad·bala of Kósala is a chariot warrior, whom I believe to be endowed with great power and prowess, my friend. This fierce-weaponed, mighty archer, who takes delight in benefitting the Dhartaráshtras, will fight in battle, bringing joy to his own kin.

166.20 Kṛpaḥ Śāradvato, rājan, ratha|yūthapa|yūthapaḥ
priyān prāṇān parityajya pradhakṣyati ripūṃs tava.
Gautamasya maha"|rṣer ya ācāryasya Śaradvataḥ
Kārtikeya iv' â|jeyaḥ śara|stambāt suto 'bhavat.
eṣa senāḥ su|bahulā vividh'|āyudha|kārmukāḥ
agnivat samare, tāta, cariṣyati vinirdahan.

BHĪṢMA uvāca:

167.1 ŚAKUNIR MĀTULAS te 'sau ratha eko, nar'|âdhipa,
prayujya Pāṇḍavair vairaṃ yotsyate—n' âtra saṃśayaḥ!
etasya senā dur|dharṣā samare pratiyāyinaḥ,
vikṛt'|āyudha|bhūyiṣṭhā, vāyu|vega|samā jave.

Droṇa|putro mah"|êṣv|āsaḥ sarvān ev' âti dhanvinaḥ,
samare citra|yodhī ca, dṛḍh'|âstraś ca mahā|rathaḥ.
etasya hi, mahā|rāja, yathā Gāṇḍīva|dhanvanaḥ,
śar'|âsana|vinirmuktāḥ saṃsaktā yānti sāyakāḥ.
167.5 n' âiṣa śakyo mayā vīraḥ saṃkhyātuṃ ratha|sattamaḥ;
nirdahed api lokāṃs trīn icchann eṣa mahā|rathaḥ!
krodhas tejaś ca tapasā saṃbhṛto "śrama|vāsinā,
Droṇen' ânugṛhītaś ca divyair astrair udāra|dhīḥ,
doṣas tv asya mahān eko, yen' âiva, Bharata'|rṣabha,
na me ratho, n' âtiratho mataḥ pārthiva|sattamaḥ.

Kripa the son of Sharádvat, O king, is the leader of hosts of leaders of hosts of chariots, and he will sacrifice his dear life and annihilate your enemies. He, like Kartikéya, cannot be defeated. He was born from a thicket of reeds as the son of the mighty sage Gáutama, the teacher Sharádvat. This man will consume an enormous number of soldiers with various weapons and bows in battle, like a blazing fire, my friend. 166.20

BHISHMA continued:

YOUR MATERNAL UNCLE, Shákuni here, equals a single chariot warrior, lord of men, and since he began the quarrel with the Pándavas, he will fight—no doubt about it! His army is unassailable when advancing in battle, and, as fully armed with weapons as possible, they match the force of the wind when it comes to speed. 167.1

Drona's son, the mighty archer Ashva·tthaman, exceeds all bowmen. He is a varied fighter in battle, sure-weaponed and a great chariot warrior. Just like those belonging to the Gandíva archer, great sovereign, this man's arrows travel joined together continuously when released from his bow.
I am unable to calculate the worth of this excellent chariot 167.5
warrior hero, for this great chariot warrior could consume the three worlds should he wish to! His anger and splendor have increased through the asceticism he has practiced, living at his hermitage, and Drona favored the highly intelligent man with celestial weapons. But he has one great flaw, bull of the Bharatas, and it is because of this that I do not consider the greatest of kings a chariot warrior or an exceptional chariot warrior.

jīvitaṃ priyam atyartham, āyuṣkāmaḥ sadā dvijaḥ.
na hy asya sadṛśaḥ kaś cid ubhayoḥ senayor api.
hanyād eka|rathen' âiva devānām api vāhinīm,
vapuṣmāṃs tala|ghoṣeṇa sphoṭayed api parvatān.
167.10 a|saṃkhyeya|guṇo vīraḥ, prahantā, dāruṇa|dyutiḥ,
daṇḍa|pāṇir iv' â|sahyaḥ kālavat pracariṣyati.
yug'|ânt'|âgni|samaḥ krodhāt, siṃha|grīvo, mahā|dyutiḥ,
eṣa Bhārata|yuddhasya pṛṣṭhaṃ saṃśamayiṣyati.

pitā tv asya mahā|tejā, vṛddho 'pi yuvabhir varaḥ,
raṇe karma mahat kartā. atra me n' âsti saṃśayaḥ.
astra|veg'|ânil'|ôddhūtaḥ senā|kakṣ'|êndhan'|ôtthitaḥ
Pāṇḍu|putrasya sainyāni pradhakṣyati raṇe dhṛtaḥ.
ratha|yūthapa|yūthānāṃ yūtha|po 'yaṃ nara'|rṣabhaḥ,
Bhāradvāj'|ātmajaḥ, kartā karma tīvraṃ hitaṃ tava.
167.15 sarva|mūrdh'|âbhiṣiktānām ācāryaḥ sthaviro guruḥ
gacched antaṃ Sṛñjayānāṃ; priyas tv asya Dhanañjayaḥ.

n' âiṣa jātu mah"|êṣv|āsaḥ Pārtham a|kliṣṭa|kāriṇam
hanyād, ācāryakaṃ dīptaṃ saṃsmṛtya guṇa|nirjitam.
ślāghate 'yaṃ sadā, vīra, Pārthasya guṇa|vistaraiḥ,
putrād abhyadhikaṃ c' âinaṃ Bhāradvājo 'nupaśyati!

hanyād eka|rathen' âiva deva|gandharva|mānuṣān
ekī|bhūtān api raṇe divyair astraiḥ pratāpavān.
Pauravo, rāja|śārdūlas tava, rājan, mahā|rathaḥ
mato mama rath'|ôdāraḥ para|vīra|rath'|ārujaḥ.

The twiceborn man is always too eager for long life, for his life is excessively dear to him. Indeed, he has no equal in either army and he could kill an army of the gods with a single chariot, splitting even the mountains with the slap of his bowstring, wonderfully built as he is. This hero-killer 167.10
of innumerable virtues and harsh glory will wander like unbearable death, mace in hand. This lion-necked, great glorious Ashva·tthaman will pacify the last sparks of the war of the Bháratas in his fury, like the fire at the end of the age.

Old he may be, but his highly energetic father surpasses young men. He will achieve great feats in battle. I have no doubt of this. He will annihilate the son of Pandu's soldiers as he stands firm in battle. The Pándava's army will catch alight like dry wood and fuel, kindled as though by the wind, by the force of his weapons. This bull-like man leads leaders of hosts of leaders of chariots. The son of Bharad·vaja will accomplish fierce deeds, to your benefit. The ven- 167.15
erable teacher of every consecrated royal could put an end to the Srínjayas, but Dhanan·jaya is dear to him.

This mighty archer certainly could not kill Partha who accomplishes his tasks unwearied, for he would remember his own splendid and undefeated virtue as a teacher. The son of Bharad·vaja here always boasts of Partha's extensive virtues, and looks upon him with greater affection than upon his son, hero!

He could kill gods, *gandhárvas*, and men, even when united, on a single chariot, scorching them with his celestial weapons in battle. The tiger-like king, Páurava sovereign, is a mighty chariot warrior, and in my opinion the breaker of

167.20 svena sainyena mahatā pratapañ śatru|vāhinīm
pradhakṣyati sa Pañcālān kakṣam agni|gatir yathā!
satya|śravā rathas tv eko rāja|putro Bhṛadbalaḥ
tava, rājan, ripu|bale kālavat pracariṣyati.
etasya yodhā, rāj'|êndra, vicitra|kavac'|āyudhāḥ
vicariṣyanti saṅgrāme nighnantaḥ śātravāṃs tava.
Vṛṣaseno rathas te 'gryaḥ Karṇa|putro mahā|rathaḥ
pradhakṣyati ripūṇāṃ te balaṃ tu balināṃ varaḥ.
Jalasandho mahā|tejā, rājan, ratha|varas tava
tyakṣyate samare prāṇān Mādhavaḥ para|vīra|hā.
167.25 eṣa yotsyati saṅgrāme gaja|skandha|viśāradaḥ,
rathena vā mahā|bāhuḥ kṣapayañ śatru|vāhinīm.
ratha eṣa, mahā|rāja, mato me, rāja|sattama,
tvad|arthe tyakṣyate prāṇān saha|sainyo mahā|raṇe.
eṣa vikrānta|yodhī ca, citra|yodhī ca saṅgare,
vīta|bhīś c' âpi te, rājañ, śatrubhiḥ saha yotsyate.
Bāhlīko 'tirathaś c' âiva, samare c' â|nirvartanaḥ
mama, rājan, mato yuddhe śūro Vaivasvat'|ôpamaḥ.
na hy eṣa samaraṃ prāpya nivarteta kathañ cana!
yathā satata|go, rājan, sa hi hanyāt parān raṇe!

enemy heroes' chariots is an exceptional warrior. Consum- 167.20
ing the enemy forces with his own enormous army, he will annihilate the Panchálas like fire burning dry wood!

Truly renowned Prince Brihad·bala is equal to a single chariot warrior, and he will wander among your enemies' army like time itself. His fighters, lord of kings, decked with various suits of armor and various weapons, will roam around in battle, killing your enemies.

Vrisha·sena, the son of Karna, is one of your leading chariot warriors, and he is a great chariot warrior. The greatest of powerful men will annihilate the army of your enemies.

Hugely energetic Jala·sandha, my king, is one of your excellent chariot warriors. This descendant of Madhu, a slayer
of enemy heroes, will sacrifice his life in battle. This long- 167.25
armed man will fight in battle either riding on an elephant's shoulder, experienced as he is, or on a chariot, flinging the enemy army before him. This chariot warrior, in my opinion, mighty sovereign and greatest of kings, will surrender his life for your sake in the great battle, as will his soldiers. This man is a powerful and varied fighter in war, and with his fear evaporated, my king, he will fight with your enemies.

Báhlika never retreats in battle; he is brave in war and like Yama the son of Vivásvat, so, in my opinion, he is an exceptional warrior, my king. Indeed, this man would never retreat from battle once he has reached it! He could destroy your enemies in battle, my king, as though he were the ever-moving wind!

167.30 senā|patir, mahā|rāja, Satyavāṃs te mahā|rathaḥ
raṇeṣv adbhuta|karmā ca rathī para|rath'|ārujaḥ.
etasya samaraṃ dṛṣṭvā na vyath" âsti kathañ cana
utsmayann utpataty eṣa parān ratha|pathe sthitān!
eṣa c' âriṣu vikrāntaḥ karma sat|puruṣ'|ôcitam
kartā vimarde su|mahat tvad|arthe puruṣ'|ôttamaḥ.

Alambuṣo rākṣas'|êndraḥ krūra|karmā mahā|rathaḥ
haniṣyati parān, rājan, pūrva|vairam anusmaran.
eṣa rākṣasa|sainyānāṃ sarveṣāṃ ratha|sattamaḥ
māyāvī dṛḍha|vairaś ca samare vicariṣyati.

167.35 Prāgjyotiṣ'|âdhipo vīro Bhagadattaḥ pratāpavān
gaj'|âṅkuśa|dhara|śreṣṭho rathe c' âiva viśāradaḥ.
etena yuddham abhavat purā Gāṇḍīva|dhanvanaḥ
divasān su|bahūn, rājann, ubhayor jaya|gṛddhino.

tataḥ sakhāyaṃ, Gāndhāre, mānayan Pāka|śāsanam
akarot saṃvidaṃ tena Pāṇḍavena mah"|ātmanā.
eṣa yotsyati saṃgrāme gaja|skandha|viśāradaḥ
Airāvata|gato rājā devānām iva Vāsavaḥ.

Sátyavat, the commander of forces and breaker of enemy chariots, mighty king, is a great chariot warrior who has achieved astounding feats in battles on his chariot. He never feels alarm when he looks upon battle, but rather this man falls upon the enemies who stand in the path of his chariot with a smile upon his face! Showing his prowess to the enemy, this greatest of men will achieve an enormous feat in the fray on your behalf, as befits a true man. 167.30

Alámbusha, the lord of the *rákshasas*, the great chariot warrior of cruel deeds, will kill the enemy, king, remembering his previous quarrel. This man here, the greatest of chariot warriors from among all *rákshasa* soldiers, who possesses powers of sorcery, will roam around in battle, firm in his hostility.

The lord of Prag·jyótisha, the blazing hero Bhaga·datta, is the greatest of those who bear elephant hooks, and he is also experienced on the chariot. There was a fight long ago between this man and the Gandíva archer which lasted many days, king, for both eagerly longed for victory over the other. 167.35

Then, son of Gandhári, Bhaga·datta, who considered Indra the punisher of Paka his ally, made an agreement with the high-souled son of Pandu. This man here, skilled at riding on an elephant's shoulder, will fight in the fray like Vásava, king of the gods, riding on Airávata.

BHĪṢMA uvāca:

168.1 ACALO VṚṢAKAŚ c' âiva sahitau bhrātarāv ubhau
rathau tava dur|ādharṣau śatrūn vidhvaṃsayiṣyataḥ,
balavantau nara|vyāghrau, dṛḍha|krodhau prahāriṇau,
Gāndhāra|mukhyau, taruṇau, darśanīyau, mahā|balau.
sakhā te dayito nityaṃ ya eṣa raṇa|karkaśaḥ
utsāhayati, rājaṃs, tvāṃ vigrahe Pāṇḍavaiḥ saha;
paruṣaḥ katthano nīcaḥ Karṇo Vaikartanas, tava
mantrī, netā ca, bandhuś ca, mānī c' âtyantam ucchritaḥ,
168.5 eṣa n' âiva rathaḥ Karṇo na c' âpy atiratho raṇe.
viyuktaḥ kavacen' âiṣa saha|jena vicetanaḥ,
kuṇḍalābhyāṃ ca divyābhyāṃ viyuktaḥ satataṃ ghṛṇī,
abhiśāpāc ca Rāmasya, brāhmaṇasya ca bhāṣaṇāt,
karaṇānāṃ viyogāc ca tena me 'rdha|ratho mataḥ.
n' âiṣa Phālgunam āsādya punar jīvan vimokṣyate.
tato 'bravīt punar Droṇaḥ sarva|śastra|bhṛtāṃ varaḥ:
«evam etad yath" āttha tvaṃ, na mithy" âsti kadā cana.
raṇe raṇe 'bhimānī ca vimukhaś c' âpi dṛśyate!
ghṛṇī Karṇaḥ, pramādī ca, tena me 'rdha|ratho mataḥ.»
168.10 etac chrutvā tu Rādheyaḥ krodhād utphālya locane
uvāca Bhīṣmaṃ Rādheyas tudan vāgbhiḥ pratodavat:

BHISHMA continued:

THE BROTHERS ÁCHALA and Vríshaka are both your unassailable chariot warriors, and they will destroy your enemies. Those tiger-like leading Gandháras are powerful fighters, they are firm in their hatred, and they are young, handsome, and extremely strong. 168.1

As for your ever-dear friend, this man here who is harsh in battle and encourages you in your hostility with the Pándavas, my king—the low and cowardly boaster Karna, son of the sun, your advisor, guide, and friend, this arrogant and excessively puffed up Karna here—he is not even a chariot 168.5
warrior in battle, let alone an exceptional chariot warrior.

The senseless man is deprived of his inbuilt armor, and the eternally abusive man has also lost his divine earrings. So, due to Rama's curse, the curse the brahmin spoke, and the loss of his special features, in my estimation he is only half a chariot warrior. If he confronts Phálguna, he will not escape alive again.

Then Drona, the greatest of all who wield weapons, added: "It is indeed just as you said. What you say is never wrong. In battle after battle the self-conceited man is seen to run away! Karna is abusive and negligent, and so he is, in my opinion too, only half a chariot warrior."

Having listened to this, Radha's son opened his eyes wide 168.10
in fury and spoke to Bhishma, assaulting him with words as though he were whipping him:

«pitā|maha, yath" êṣṭaṃ māṃ vāk|śarair upakṛntasi
an|āgasaṃ sadā dveṣād evam eva pade pade;
marṣayāmi ca tat sarvaṃ Duryodhana|kṛtena vai.
tvaṃ tu māṃ manyase mandaṃ yathā kāpuruṣaṃ, tathā.
bhavān ardha|ratho mahyaṃ mato vai, n' âtra saṃśayaḥ!

sarvasya jagataś c' âiva Gāṅgeyo na mṛṣā vadet
Kurūṇām a|hito nityaṃ, na ca rāj" âvabudhyate.
ko hi nāma samāneṣu rājas' ûdāra|karmasu
168.15 tejo|vadham imaṃ kuryād vibhedayiṣur āhave,
yathā tvaṃ guṇa|vidveṣād aparāgaṃ cikīrṣasi?

na hāyanair, na palitair, na vittair, na ca bandhubhiḥ
mahā|rathatvaṃ saṃkhyātuṃ śakyaṃ kṣatrasya, Kaurava!
bala|jyeṣṭhaṃ smṛtaṃ kṣatraṃ, mantra|jyeṣṭhā dvijātayaḥ,
dhana|jyeṣṭhāḥ smṛtā vaiśyāḥ, śūdrās tu vayas" âdhikāḥ.
yath" êcchakaṃ svayaṃ brūyā rathān atirathāṃs tathā;
kāma|dveṣa|samāyukto mohāt prakurute bhavān!

Duryodhana mahā|bāho, sādhu samyag avekṣyatām.
tyajyatāṃ duṣṭa|bhāvo 'yaṃ Bhīṣmaḥ kilbiṣa|kṛt tava.
168.20 bhinnā hi senā, nṛ|pate, duḥ|sandheyā bhavaty uta,
maulā hi, puruṣa|vyāghra, kim u nānā|samutthitāḥ!
eṣāṃ dvaidhaṃ samutpannaṃ yodhānāṃ yudhi, Bhārata.
tejo|vadho naḥ kriyate pratyakṣeṇa viśeṣataḥ!

"Grandfather, at each and every step of the way you constantly scold me with your arrow-like words, just as you wish, despite the fact that I am innocent. It is all because of your hatred for me, but I tolerate all this for Duryódhana's sake. You believe I am as foolish as a coward. But there is no doubt in my mind that it is you who is half a chariot warrior!

It is no lie to claim that the son of the Ganges is forever a 168.15
disadvantage to the entire universe and the Kurus, but the king does not realize this. Who would destroy the energy of equally matched kings who have achieved exceptional feats, and cause division on the battlefield, other than you, who wish to spread discontent because of your hatred of quality?

Káurava, it is neither years, gray hairs, money, nor friends which allow a kshatriya to be counted as a great chariot warrior! Tradition tells us that a kshatriya wins distinction through strength, just as brahmins win distinction through mantras, vaishyas through wealth, and shudras through age. But you act foolishly, naming chariot warriors and exceptional chariot warriors according to your own inclinations, led by your favoritism and hatred!

Long-armed Duryódhana, please examine this properly. Let wicked-natured Bhishma here be abandoned, for he
does you only harm. An army of a single heritage is cer- 168.20
tainly hard to unite once divided, king, let alone in our case where it is made up of various peoples, tiger-like man! Uncertainty has already arisen among the soldiers in battle, Bhárata. This man destroys our energy right before our eyes!

rathānāṃ kva ca vijñānaṃ? kva ca Bhīṣmo 'lpa|cetanaḥ?
aham āvārayiṣyāmi Pāṇḍavānām anīkinīm!
āsādya mām a|mogh'|êṣuṃ gamiṣyanti diśo daśa
Pāṇḍavāḥ saha|Pañcālāḥ, śārdūlaṃ vṛṣabhā iva!
kva ca yuddhaṃ, vimardo vā, mantre su|vyāhṛtāni ca?
kva ca Bhīṣmo gata|vayā, mand'|ātmā, kāla|coditaḥ?
168.25 ekākī spardhate nityaṃ sarveṇa jagatā saha,
na c' ânyaṃ puruṣaṃ kañ cin manyate mogha|darśanaḥ!
śrotavyaṃ khalu vṛddhānām, iti śāstra|nidarśanam;
na tv eva hy ativṛddhānāṃ—punar bālā hi te matāḥ.
aham eko haniṣyāmi Pāṇḍavānām anīkinīm
su|yuddhe, rāja|śārdūla; yaśo Bhīṣmaṃ gamiṣyati!
kṛtaḥ senā|patis tv eṣa tvayā Bhīṣmo, nar'|âdhipa,
senā|patau yaśo gantā, na tu yodhān kathañ cana!
n' âham jīvati Gāṅgeye yotsye, rājan, kathañ cana;
hate Bhīṣme tu yoddh" âsmi sarvair eva mahā|rathaiḥ!»

BHĪṢMA UVĀCA:

168.30 samudyato 'yaṃ bhāro me su|mahān sāgar'|ôpamaḥ
Dhārtarāṣṭrasya saṅgrāme varṣa|pūg'|âbhicintitaḥ.
tasminn abhyāgate kāle pratapte loma|harṣaṇe
mitho bhedo na me kāryas, tena jīvasi, sūta|ja!
na hy ahaṃ tv adya vikramya sthaviro 'pi śiśos tava
yuddha|śraddhām ahaṃ chindyām jīvitasya ca, sūta|ja!

Jāmadagnyena Rāmeṇa mah"|âstrāṇi vimuñcatā
na me vyathā kṛtā kā cit; tvaṃ tu me kiṃ kariṣyasi?
kāmaṃ n' âitat praśaṃsanti santaḥ sva|bala|saṃstavam;
vakṣyāmi tu tvāṃ saṃtapto, nihīna|kula|pāṃsana!

Where is true judgment of the chariot warriors? Where is small-minded Bhishma's expertise? I will ward off the Pándavas' army! When they approach me and my unfailing arrows, the Pándavas and Panchálas will disperse to the ten directions, like bulls before a tiger! Where is the chaos of war, or counsel, or good advice? And where is aged, idiotic-souled Bhishma in comparison, who is driven on by fate?

He alone always contends with the entire universe, and 168.25
the foolish-sighted man believes no one else is a man! It is true that one ought to listen to one's elders, as the scriptures teach; but one should not listen to the geriatric, for they are considered to be children again. I will kill the Pándavas' army on my own in a good battle, tiger-like king, but the glory will go to Bhishma! You made Bhishma commander of the army, lord of men, and the glory goes to the army's commander but not to the soldiers! I will never fight while the son of the Ganges still lives, king, but once Bhishma is dead then I will fight with all the great chariot warriors!"

BHISHMA replied:

I have taken up the vast, ocean-wide burden in the Dhar- 168.30
taráshtra's war, and I have considered it for many years. Now that this grievous and hair-raising time has come, I should cause no division, and that is why you still live, son of a *suta*! Otherwise I would shatter your faith in war and life, *suta*'s son, despite my age and your youth!

I didn't even tremble at all when Rama, son of Jamad·agni, hurled his mighty weapons at me; so what could you do? Good men do not praise someone who longs to eulogize

168.35 sametaṃ pārthivaṃ kṣatraṃ Kāśi|rāja|svayaṃvare
nirjity' âika|rathen' âiva, yat kanyās tarasā hṛtāḥ!
īdṛśānāṃ sahasrāṇi, viśiṣṭānām atho punaḥ
may" âikena nirastāni sa|sainyāni raṇ'|âjire!

tvāṃ prāpya vaira|puruṣaṃ Kurūṇām a|nayo mahān
upasthito vināśāya. yatasva! puruṣo bhava!
yudhyasva samare Pārthaṃ yena vispardhase saha!
drakṣyāmi tvāṃ vinirmuktam asmād yuddhāt, su|durmate!

tam uvāca tato rājā Dhārtarāṣṭraḥ pratāpavān:
«māṃ samīkṣasva, Gāṅgeya! kāryaṃ hi mahad udyatam.
168.40 cintyatām idam ek'|âgraṃ mama niḥśreyasaṃ param.
ubhāv api bhavantau me mahat karma kariṣyataḥ.

bhūyaś ca śrotum icchāmi pareṣāṃ ratha|sattamān,
ye c' âiv' âtirathās tatra, ye c' âiva ratha|yūthapāḥ.
bal'|â|balam amitrāṇāṃ śrotum icchāmi, Kaurava,
prabhātāyāṃ rajanyāṃ vai idaṃ yuddhaṃ bhaviṣyati.»

BHĪṢMA uvāca:

169.1 ETE RATHĀS TAV' ākhyātās, tath" âiv' âtirathā, nṛpa,
ye c' âpy ardha|rathā, rājan. Pāṇḍavānām ataḥ śṛṇu.
yadi kautūhalaṃ te 'dya Pāṇḍavānāṃ bale, nṛpa,
ratha|saṃkhyāṃ śṛṇuṣva tvaṃ sah' âibhir vasudh'|âdhipaiḥ.

his own strength, but I have become so enraged that I will tell you, vile disgrace to your line!

I defeated the congregation of kings and warriors at the 168.35
bridegroom choice of the king of Kashi's daughters with a single chariot, and I quickly carried away the girls! I drove away thousands of men of your quality on the battlefield, and thousands again of far superior men, and their soldiers, all on my own!

In you, the living personification of hostility, the Kurus have gained great misfortune! Strive for the destruction of those who stand against us! Be a man! Fight in battle with Partha, against whom you vie! I'd like to see you wriggle out of that fight, extremely wicked-minded man!

Then powerful King Dhartaráshtra said to Bhishma:

"Look at me, son of the Ganges! The current situation
is important. Please think intently about what would be of 168.40
most benefit to me. You will both achieve great feats for me.

I wish to hear from you again about the greatest chariot warriors among the enemy; which are exceptional warriors, and which are leaders of hosts of chariots. I wish to hear about my enemies' strength and weakness, Káurava, for once the night has turned to dawn, there will be war."

BHISHMA said:

I HAVE NAMED the chariot warriors and exceptional char- 169.1
iot warriors in your ranks, lord, as well as those who are half chariot warriors, king; so listen to those in the Pándavas' ranks. If you have any curiosity now about the Pándavas' forces, lord, then listen with these kings to the count of their chariot warriors.

svayaṃ rājā rath'|ôdāraḥ Pāṇḍavaḥ Kunti|nandanaḥ
agnivat samare, tāta, cariṣyati, na saṃśayaḥ!
Bhīmasenas tu, rāj'|êndra, ratho 'ṣṭa|guṇa|saṃmitaḥ.
na tasy' âsti samo yuddhe gadayā sāyakair api.
169.5 nāg'|âyuta|balo, mānī, tejasā na sa mānuṣaḥ!
Mādrī|putrau ca rathinau dvāv eva puruṣa'|rṣabhau,
Aśvināv iva rūpeṇa tejasā ca samanvitau.
ete camūm upagatāḥ smarantaḥ kleśam uttamam
Rudravat pracariṣyanti, tatra me n' âsti saṃśayaḥ!
sarva eva mah"|ātmānaḥ śāla|stambhā iv' ôdgatāḥ,
prādeśen' âdhikāḥ puṃbhir anyais te ca pramāṇataḥ,
siṃha|saṃhananāḥ sarve Pāṇḍu|putrā mahā|balāḥ.
carita|brahma|caryāś ca sarve, tāta, tapasvinaḥ,
hrīmantaḥ, puruṣa|vyāghrā, vyāghrā iva bal'|ôtkaṭāḥ.
169.10 jave, prahāre, saṃmarde sarva ev' âtimānuṣāḥ,
sarvair jitā mahī|pālā dig|jaye, Bharata'|rṣabha.
na c' âiṣāṃ puruṣāḥ ke cid āyudhāni, gadāḥ, śarān
viṣahanti sadā kartum adhijyāny api, Kaurava,
udyatāṃ vā gadā gurvīḥ, śarān vā kṣeptum āhave.
jave, lakṣyasya haraṇe, bhojye, pāṃsu|vikarṣaṇe
bālair api bhavantas taiḥ sarva eva viśeṣitāḥ.
etat sainyaṃ samāsādya sarva eva bal'|ôtkaṭāḥ
vidhvaṃsayiṣyanti raṇe. mā sma taiḥ saha saṅgamaḥ!
ek' âikaśas te saṃmarde hanyuḥ sarvān mahī|kṣitaḥ,
169.15 pratyakṣaṃ tava, rāj'|êndra, rāja|sūye yath" âbhavat.

The king himself, son of Pandu and Kunti, will act like
blazing fire in battle, my friend—no doubt about that!
Bhima·sena is considered to equal eight chariot warriors,
lord of kings. There is no match for him in war with the
mace or even with arrows. He has the strength of ten thou- 169.5
sand elephants, takes pride in his energy, and is barely even
human!

Madri's two sons are bull-like chariot warriors, like the
Ashvins in beauty, and endowed with splendor. Positioned
with their army, they remember their terrible suffering and
will roam around like Rudra, I have no doubt! All the high-souled,
powerful sons of Pandu are tall like the trunks of
*shala* trees—taller than other men by the span of a hand—
and brave as lions.

All, my friend, are ascetics who have practiced Vedic
vows. They are modest, tiger-like men, and just like tigers
they have immense strength. They are all superhuman when 169.10
it comes to speed, hitting, and destroying. They all defeated earth-lords in their conquest of the world, bull of
the Bharatas. No men can ever wield their weapons, maces,
and arrows, or even string their bows, Káurava, or lift their
weighty maces, or shoot their arrows in battle.

In speed, taking aim, eating, and play-fighting in the dirt,
even as children they proved superior to all of you. All those
men of immense strength will approach your army and destroy it in battle. Don't meet them in battle! Each of them
can singlehandedly kill every king in battle. Lord of kings, 169.15
the circumstances that occurred at the royal consecration
took place openly. Remembering Dráupadi's torment and

Draupadyāś ca parikleśaṃ, dyūte ca paruṣā giraḥ
te smarantaś ca saṅgrāme cariṣyanti ca Rudravat.
lohit'|âkṣo Guḍākeśo Nārāyaṇa|sahāyavān
ubhayoḥ senayor vīro; ratho n' âst' îti tādṛśaḥ.
na hi deveṣu vā pūrvaṃ, manuṣyeṣ', ûrageṣu ca,
rākṣaseṣv, atha yakṣeṣu, nareṣu kuta eva tu
bhūto 'tha vā bhaviṣyo vā rathaḥ kaś cin mayā śrutaḥ
samāyukto, mahā|rāja, rathaḥ Pārthasya dhīmataḥ.
Vāsudevaś ca saṃyantā, yoddhā c' âiva Dhanañjayaḥ,
169.20 Gāṇḍīvaṃ ca dhanur divyaṃ, te c' âśvā vāta|raṃhasaḥ,
a|bhedyaṃ kavacaṃ divyam, a|kṣayyau ca mah"|êṣudhī,
astra|grāmaś ca Māhendro, Raudraḥ, Kaubera eva ca,
Yāmyaś ca, Vāruṇaś c' âiva, gadāś c' ôgra|pradarśanāḥ,
vajr'|ādīni ca mukhyāni, nānā|praharaṇāni ca.
Dānavānāṃ sahasrāṇi Hiraṇyapura|vāsinām
hatāny eka|rathen' ājau. kas tasya sadṛśo rathaḥ?
eṣa hanyādd hi saṃrambhī balavān satya|vikramaḥ
tava senāṃ mahā|bāhuḥ, svāṃ c' âiva paripālayan.
ahaṃ c' âinam pratyudiyām, ācāryo vā Dhanañjayam,
169.25 na tṛtīyo 'sti, rāj'|êndra, senayor ubhayor api,
ya enaṃ śara|varṣāṇi varṣantam udiyād rathī,
jīmūta iva gharm'|ânte mahā|vāta|samīritaḥ.
samāyuktas tu Kaunteyo, Vāsudeva|sahāyavān,
taruṇaś ca, kṛtī c' âiva; jīrṇāv āvām ubhāv api.

the harsh insults at the gambling, they will roam around in battle like Rudra.

There is no heroic chariot warrior in either army like red-eyed Guda·kesha, whose ally is Naráyana. In fact, not among the gods, humans, snakes, *rákshasa*s, or *yaksha*s, let alone men, have I ever heard of any chariot warrior, either born in the past or yet to be born, who is as consummate a chariot warrior as wise Partha, O mighty sovereign.

Vasudéva is the driver, Dhanan·jaya is the warrior, Gan- 169.20
díva the celestial bow, the horses fleet as the wind, his divine armor unbreakable, his mighty quivers inexhaustible, and his masses of weapons include great Indra's, Rudra's, Kubéra's, Yama's, and Váruna's missiles. His maces are terrifying to behold, and his various weapons, his discus and so on, are superb.

He killed thousands of Dánavas living in Hiránya·pura with only a single chariot in battle—what chariot warrior could match him? This furious and powerful long-armed man, whose strength is his truth, could indeed kill your army while defending his own. I or the teacher Drona could
stand against Dhanan·jaya, but there is no third man capa- 169.25
ble in either army, lord of kings.

That chariot warrior would rise for battle, raining down showers of arrows like the stormcloud at the end of the rainy season, driven by a great wind. But while Kauntéya is accomplished, young, skilled, and has Vasudéva for his ally, we on the other hand are both aged and decrepit.

SAÑJAYA† uvāca:

etac chrutvā tu Bhīṣmasya rājñāṃ dadhvaṃsire tadā
kāñcan'|âṅgadinaḥ pīnā bhujāś candana|rūṣitāḥ,
manobhiḥ saha|saṃvegaiḥ saṃsmṛtya ca purātanam
sāmarthyaṃ Pāṇḍaveyānāṃ, yathā pratyakṣa|darśanāt.

BHĪṢMA uvāca:

170.1 DRAUPADEYĀ, mahā|rāja, sarve pañca mahā|rathāḥ,
Vairāṭir, Uttaraś c' âiva rath'|ôdāro mato mama.
Abhimanyur mahā|bāhū ratha|yūthapa|yūthapaḥ
samaḥ Pārthena samare, Vāsudevena c' âri|hā.
labdh'|âstraś citra|yodhī ca, manasvī ca dṛḍha|vrataḥ
saṃsmaran vai parikleśaṃ sva|pitur vikramiṣyati.

Sātyakir Mādhavaḥ śūro, ratha|yūthapa|yūthapaḥ;
eṣa Vṛṣṇi|pravīrāṇām a|marṣī, jita|sādhvasaḥ.
170.5 Uttamaujās tathā, rājan, rath'|ôdāro mato mama,
Yudhāmanyuś ca vikrānto rath'|ôdāro mato mama.
eteṣāṃ bahu|sāhasrā rathā, nāgā, hayās tathā
yotsyante te tanūṃs tyaktvā Kuntī|putra|priy'|ēpsayā
Pāṇḍavaiḥ saha, rāj'|êndra, tava senāsu, Bhārata,
agni|mārutavad, rājann, āhvayantaḥ paras|param.

a|jeyau samare vṛddhau Virāṭa|Drupadau tathā
mahā|rathau mahā|vīryau matau me puruṣa'|rṣabhau.
vayo|vṛddhāv api hi tau kṣatra|dharma|parāyaṇau
yatiṣyete paraṃ śaktyā sthitau vīra|gate pathi.

SÁNJAYA said:

When the kings heard Bhishma's words, their strong, golden-braceleted arms, smeared with sandalwood paste, fell ruined as they recalled in their agitated minds the Pándavas' capabilities in times gone by, as though it were on display before their very eyes.

BHISHMA continued:

ALL FIVE SONS OF Dráupadi are great chariot warriors, 170.1
mighty sovereign, and Viráta's son Úttara is a noble chariot warrior, in my opinion. Long-armed Abhimányu is the leader of hosts of leaders of hosts of chariots, and that slayer of enemies is a match for Partha and Vasudéva in battle. Dextrous with weaponry, a varied fighter and spirited man who is firm in his vows, he will display his prowess, remembering his father's suffering.

Sátyaki Mádhava is a brave leader of hosts of leaders of hosts of chariots, and a truculent member of the leading
Vrishni heroes who has conquered his fear. Uttamáujas is 170.5
a great chariot warrior in my opinion, king, and I believe powerful Yudha·manyu is also a great chariot warrior. The Vrishnis have many thousands of chariots, elephants, and horses, and they will fight sacrificing their lives, wishing to do the sons of Pandu a favor. They will fight with the Pándavas, Bhárata lord of kings, against your armies, like fire and wind roaring at each other, king.

The elderly and undefeated Viráta and Drúpada are both greatly heroic bull-like men whom I consider mighty chariot warriors. Despite the fact that they are advanced in years, these two men take refuge in kshatriya duties and they will

170.10 sambandhakena, rāj'|êndra, tau tu vīrya|bal'|ânvayāt
ārya|vṛttau mah"|êṣv|āsau sneha|vīrya|sitāv ubhau.

kāraṇaṃ prāpya tu narāḥ sarva eva mahā|bhujāḥ
śūrā vā kātarā v" âpi bhavanti, Kuru|puṅgava.
ek'|âyana|gatāv etau pārthivau dṛḍha|dhanvinau
prāṇāṃs tyaktvā paraṃ śaktyā ghaṭṭitārau, paraṃ|tapa.
pṛthag akṣauhiṇībhyāṃ tāv ubhau saṃyati dāruṇau
saṃbandhi|bhāvaṃ rakṣantau mahat karma kariṣyataḥ.
loka|vīrau mah"|êṣv|āsau tyakt'|ātmānau ca, Bhārata,
pratyayaṃ parirakṣantau mahat karma kariṣyataḥ.

BHĪṢMA uvāca:

171.1 PAÑCĀLA|RĀJASYA suto, rājan, para|purañ|jayaḥ
Śikhaṇḍī ratha|mukhyo me mataḥ Pārthasya, Bhārata.
eṣa yotsyati saṃgrāme nāśayan pūrva|saṃsthitam
paraṃ yaśo viprathayaṃs tava senāsu, Bhārata.
etasya bahulāḥ senāḥ Pañcālāś ca Prabhadrakāḥ
ten' âsau ratha|vaṃśena mahat karma kariṣyati.

Dhṛṣṭadyumnaś ca senā|nīḥ sarva|senāsu, Bhārata,
mato me 'tiratho, rājan, Droṇa|śiṣyo mahā|rathaḥ.
171.5 eṣa yotsyati saṃgrāme sūdayan vai parān raṇe,
bhagavān iva saṃkruddhaḥ Pinākī yuga|saṃkṣaye.
etasya tad rath'|ânīkaṃ kathayanti raṇa|priyāḥ

strive to the limits of their capacity, standing on the path which heroes tread. Lord of kings, their relationship with 170.10
the Pándavas and their possessing heroism and power mean that these two mighty archers of noble conduct have both been bound with strength born of their affection.

All long-armed men become either heroes or cowards depending on their cause, bull of the Kurus. Going together along a single course, both kings are firm archers who will sacrifice their lives, killing to the limit of their ability, scorcher of the enemy. At the head of their battalions both men, pitiless in war, will accomplish great exploits, protecting the existence of their relationship with the Pándavas. As heroes of the world and great archers who would forsake their lives, O Bhárata, they will achieve great feats while protecting the trust placed in them.

BHISHMA continued:

THE SON OF THE king of the Panchálas, Shikhándin the 171.1
sacker of enemy cities, my king, is Partha's leading chariot warrior, in my opinion, Bhárata. Having destroyed his previous gender, he will fight in battle and win great fame among your troops, Bhárata. His armies of Panchálas and Prabhádrakas are numerous, and with this host of chariots he will accomplish great feats.

Dhrishta·dyumna, the general over all the armies, O Bhárata king, the mighty chariot warrior and pupil of Drona,
is, in my opinion, an exceptional chariot warrior. This man 171.5
will fight in the conflict, killing his enemies in battle like the blessed wielder of the *pináka*—furious Shiva—at the

bahutvāt sāgara|prakhyaṃ devānām iva saṃyuge!

Kṣatradharmā tu, rāj'|êndra, mato me 'rdha|ratho, nṛpa,
Dhṛṣṭadyumnasya tanayo bālyān n' âti|kṛta|śramaḥ.
Śiśupāla|suto vīraś, Cedi|rājo mahā|rathaḥ,
Dhṛṣṭaketur mah"|êṣv|āsaḥ sambandhī Pāṇḍavasya ha.
eṣa Cedi|patiḥ śūraḥ saha putreṇa, Bhārata,
mahā|rathānāṃ su|karaṃ mahat karma kariṣyati!
171.10 kṣatra|dharma|rato mahyaṃ mataḥ para|purañ|jayaḥ
Kṣatradevas tu, rāj'|êndra, Pāṇḍaveṣu rath'|ôttamaḥ.
Jayantaś c', Âmitaujāś ca, Satyajic ca mahā|rathaḥ,
mahā|rathā mah"|ātmānaḥ sarve Pāñcāla|sattamāḥ.
yotsyante samare, tāta, saṃrabdhā iva kuñjarāḥ.
Ajo Bhojaś ca vikrāntau Pāṇḍav'|ârthe mahā|rathau
yotsyete balinau śūrau paraṃ śaktyā kṣayiṣyataḥ,
śīghr'|âstrāś, citra|yoddhāraḥ, kṛtino, dṛḍha|vikramāḥ.

Kekayāḥ pañca, rāj'|êndra, bhrātaro dṛḍha|vikramāḥ,
sarve c' âiva rath'|ôdārāḥ, sarve lohitaka|dhvajāḥ.
171.15 Kāśikaḥ, Sukumāraś ca, Nīlo yaś c' âparo, nṛpa,
Sūryadattaś ca, Śaṅkhaś ca, Madirāśvaś ca nāmataḥ.
sarva eva rath'|ôdārāḥ, sarve c' āhava|lakṣaṇāḥ,
sarv'|âstra|viduṣaḥ sarve, mah"|ātmāno matā mama.

end of the age. Men who are fond of war tell of his chariot army being so big it resembles the ocean of gods in battle!

Kshatra·dharman, the son of Dhrishta·dyumna, O lord of kings, is someone I rate as half a chariot warrior, king, on account of his youth and the incompleteness of his training. The son of Shishu·pala the hero king of the Chedis, Dhrishta·ketu the mighty archer and relative of the son of Pandu, is a great chariot warrior. This brave lord of the Chedis and his son, O Bhárata, will achieve great feats ranking as enormous achievements even for great chariot warriors!

Kshatra·deva, the sacker of enemy cities who takes de- 171.10
light in kshatriya law, O lord of kings, is in my opinion a most excellent chariot warrior for the Pándavas. Jayánta, Amitáujas, and the mighty chariot warrior Sátyajit are all high-souled, excellent, mighty Panchálan chariot warriors. They will fight in battle, my son, like furious elephants. Aja and Bhoja are powerful and mighty chariot warriors who will fight in the Pándavas' cause. Those strong, brave men will fight, killing to the best of their ability. They are nimble with weapons, and varied fighters who are skilled and firm in their prowess.

The five Kékaya brothers, firm in their prowess, are all excellent chariot warriors with blood-red banners, lord of
kings. Their names, O king, are Káshika, Sukumára, Nila— 171.15
a different Nila, that is!—Surya·datta, and Shankha, who's also known as Madiráshva. In my opinion, those high-souled men are all excellent chariot warriors, all possessed of every attribute for war, and all understand every kind of weapon.

Vārdhakṣemir, mahā|rāja, mato mama mahā|rathaḥ,
Citrāyudhaś ca nṛ|patir mato me ratha|sattamaḥ,
sa hi saṃgrāma|śobhī ca bhaktaś c' âpi Kirīṭinaḥ.
Cekitānaḥ, Satyadhṛtiḥ Pāṇḍavānāṃ mahā|rathau
dvāv imau puruṣa|vyāghrau rath'|ôdārau matau mama.
Vyāghradattaś ca, rāj'|êndra, Candrasenaś ca, Bhārata,
matau mama rath'|ôdārau Pāṇḍavānāṃ—na saṃśayaḥ.
171.20 Senābinduś ca, rāj'|êndra, Krodhahantā ca nāmataḥ,
yaḥ samo Vāsudevena Bhīmasenena vā, vibho.
sa yotsyati hi vikramya samare tava sainikaiḥ.
māṃ ca, Droṇaṃ, Kṛpaṃ c' âiva yathā saṃmanyate bhavā
tathā sa samara|ślāghī mantavyo ratha|sattamaḥ.

Kāśyaḥ parama|śīghr'|âstraḥ ślāghanīyo nar'|ôttamaḥ
ratha eka|guṇo mahyaṃ jñeyaḥ para|purañ|jayaḥ.
ayaṃ ca yudhi vikrānto mantavyo 'ṣṭa|guṇo rathaḥ
Satyajit samara|ślāghī Drupadasy' ātmajo yuvā;
gataḥ so 'tirathatvaṃ hi Dhṛṣṭadyumnena saṃmitaḥ.
171.25 Pāṇḍavānāṃ yaśas|kāmaḥ paraṃ karma kariṣyati.
anuraktaś ca śūraś ca ratho 'yam aparo mahān
Pāṇḍya|rājo mahā|vīryaḥ Pāṇḍavānāṃ dhuraṃ|dharaḥ.
Dṛḍhadhanvā mah"|êṣv|āsaḥ Pāṇḍavānāṃ mahā|rathaḥ.
Śreṇimān, Kaurava|śreṣṭha, Vasudānaś ca pārthivaḥ

Mighty sovereign, I rate Vardhakshémi as a mighty chariot warrior, and as far as I am concerned King Chitráyudha is also an excellent chariot warrior, for he gleams in battle and is devoted to diademed Árjuna. Chekitána and Satya·dhriti are both mighty chariot warriors in the Pándavas' army. These two tiger-like men are, in my opinion, excellent chariot warriors. Vyaghra·datta and Chandra·sena, Bhárata lord of kings, are both excellent chariot warriors for the Pándavas as far as I am concerned—and there is no doubt about it.

Sena·bindu, also called Krodha·hantri, lord of kings, 171.20
equals either Vasudéva or Bhima·sena, lord. He will indeed fight in battle against your soldiers. You should regard him just as you regard me, Drona, and Kripa, since that man, who is praised for his achievements in battle, is an excellent chariot warrior.

The king of the Kashis is extremely dextrous with weapons, and that most excellent of men deserves praise. That sacker of enemy cities should be rated as a single chariot warrior as far as I am concerned. Sátyajit displays his prowess in battle and should be rated as worth eight chariot warriors, for he, Drúpada's young son, is praised for his feats in battle and has reached the status of exceptional chariot
warrior, measured as equal with Dhrishta·dyumna. He will 171.25
achieve great feats, for he desires fame for the Pándavas.

There is another great chariot warrior who is devoted and brave: the mightily heroic King Pandya, the leader of the Pándavas. The great archer Dridha·dhanvan is also a mighty chariot warrior for the Pándavas. Greatest of the Káuravas, Shrénimat and King Vasu·dana, both sackers of

ubhāv etāv atirathau matau para|purañ|jayau.

BHĪṢMA uvāca:

172.1 ROCAMĀNO, MAHĀ|rāja, Pāṇḍavānāṃ mahā|rathaḥ
yotsyate 'maravat saṃkhye para|sainyeṣu, Bhārata.
puru|jit Kuntibhojaś ca mah"|êṣv|āso mahā|balaḥ,
mātulo Bhīmasenasya, sa ca me 'tiratho mataḥ.
eṣa vīro mah"|êṣv|āsaḥ, kṛtī ca nipuṇaś ca ha,
citra|yodhī ca śaktaś ca, mato me ratha|puṅgavaḥ.
sa yotsyati hi vikramya Maghavān iva Dānavaiḥ.
yodhā ye c' âsya vikhyātāḥ sarve yuddha|viśāradāḥ.
172.5 bhāgineya|kṛte vīraḥ sa kariṣyati saṅgare
su|mahat karma Pāṇḍūnāṃ sthitaḥ priya|hite rataḥ.

Bhaimasenir, mahā|rāja, Haiḍimbo rākṣas'|ēśvaraḥ
mato me bahu|māyāvī ratha|yūthapa|yūthapaḥ.
yotsyate samare, tāta, māyāvī samara|priyaḥ,
ye c' âsya rākṣasā virāḥ sacivā vaśa|vartinaḥ.

ete c' ânye ca bahavo nānā|janapad'|ēśvarāḥ
sametāḥ Pāṇḍavasy' ârthe Vāsudeva|purogamāḥ.
ete prādhānyato, rājan, Pāṇḍavasya mah"|ātmanaḥ
rathāś c' âtirathāś c' âiva, ye c' ânye 'rdha|rathā, nṛpa.
172.10 neṣyanti samare senāṃ bhīmāṃ Yaudhiṣṭhirīṃ, nṛpa,
Mahendreṇ' êva vīreṇa pālyamānāṃ Kirīṭinā.

enemy cities, are, in my opinion, exceptional chariot warriors.

BHISHMA continued:

MIGHTY SOVEREIGN, the Pándavas' mighty chariot warrior Rochamána will fight in battle against the enemy armies like a god, Bhárata. Powerful Kunti·bhoja, Bhima·sena's maternal uncle, the mighty archer and defeater of many enemies, is also an exceptional warrior, to my mind. This heroic and mighty archer is trained and experienced. I believe this bull-like chariot warrior and varied fighter is perfectly capable. He will fight, displaying his prowess like Mághavat fighting the Dánavas. His fighters are all renowned as experienced in war. The hero will achieve ex- 172.5
traordinary feats for the sake of his nephews as he stands on the side of the Pándavas and takes pleasure in doing what is pleasing and beneficial to them.

The son of Bhima·sena and Hidímba, O mighty sovereign, is a lord of *rákshasas* whom I believe to possess a great deal of sorcery and to be a leader of hosts of leaders of hosts of chariots. He will fight in battle, my son, using sorcery and delighting in conflict. His *rákshasa* heroes and counselors will also fight, following his orders.

These and many other lords of various peoples have gathered, led by Vasudéva, for the sake of the son of Pandu. King, these are the main chariot warriors, exceptional chariot warriors, and other half chariot warriors under the control of the high-souled Pándava, my lord. They will lead 172.10
Yudhi·shthira's terrifying army in battle, lord, protected by the diademed hero Árjuna, as though by great Indra.

tair ahaṃ samare, vīra, māyā|vidbhir jay'|âiṣibhiḥ
yotsyāmi jayam ākāṅkṣann, atha vā nidhanaṃ raṇe.
Vāsudevaṃ ca Pārthaṃ ca cakra|Gāṇḍīva|dhāriṇau
sandhyā|gatāv iv' ârk'|êndū sameṣyete rath'|ôttamau.
ye c' âiva te rath'|ôdārāḥ Pāṇḍu|putrasya sainikāḥ,
saha|sainyān ahaṃ tāṃś ca pratīyāṃ raṇa|mūrdhani.

ete rathāś c' âtirathāś ca tubhyaṃ
yathā|pradhānaṃ, nṛpa, kīrtitā mayā
tath" âpare ye 'rdha|rathāś ca ke cit,
tath" âiva teṣām api, Kaurav'|êndra.

172.15 Arjunaṃ, Vāsudevaṃ ca, ye c' ânye tatra pārthivāḥ,
sarvāṃs tān vārayiṣyāmi yāvad drakṣyāmi, Bhārata.
Pāñcālyaṃ tu, mahā|bāho, n' âhaṃ hanyāṃ Śikhaṇḍinam
udyat'|êṣum atho dṛṣṭvā pratiyudhyantam āhave.

lokas taṃ veda yad ahaṃ pituḥ priya|cikīrṣayā
prāptaṃ rājyaṃ parityajya brahma|carya|vrate sthitaḥ.
Citrāṅgadaṃ Kauravāṇām ādhipatye 'bhyaṣecayam,
Vicitravīryaṃ ca śiśuṃ yauvarājye 'bhyaṣecayam.
deva|vratatvaṃ vijñāpya pṛthivīṃ sarva|rājasu
n' âiva hanyāṃ striyaṃ jātu, na strī|pūrvaṃ kadā cana.
172.20 sa hi strī|pūrvako, rājañ, Śikhaṇḍī, yadi te śrutaḥ.
kanyā bhūtvā pumāñ jāto; na yotsye tena, Bhārata.
sarvāṃs tv anyān haniṣyāmi pārthivān, Bharata'|rṣabha,
yān sameṣyāmi samare, na tu Kuntī|sutān, nṛpa.

It is with these men, who have knowledge of magic and long to win, that I will fight, hero, expecting either victory or death in battle. I will attack Vasudéva and Partha, wielding their discus and Gandíva respectively, those excellent chariot warriors who are like the sun and moon at twilight; and I shall also meet the son of Pandu's excellent chariot warrior soldiers and their armies at the head of battle.

So I have now named the chariot warriors and exceptional chariot warriors for you, according to their preeminence, king, and equally I have named those others who are merely half chariot warriors, both in your army and theirs, lord of the Káuravas.

I will ward off Árjuna and Vasudéva and any other kings 172.15
I see, Bhárata—I will ward off everyone. But, long-amed man, I will not kill Shikhándin the Panchálan prince, even if I see him fighting in battle with his arrows raised.

The world knows how I abandoned my kingdom when I inherited it, abiding instead by my vow of chastity, for I wished to do my father a favor. I installed Chitrángada in the position of lordship over the Káuravas, and consecrated Vichítra·virya as the young king. Now that I have made the entire world aware that I am one who performs a god-like vow, among all kings I will certainly never kill a woman, nor someone who was previously a woman.

Perhaps you have heard, king, that Shikhándin was pre- 172.20
viously a woman. Though he was born as a girl, he became a man, and I will not fight him, Bhárata. I will certainly kill all the other kings I come across in battle, bull of the Bharatas, but I will not kill the sons of Kunti, king.

[illegible] with these men who have knowledge of magic and [illegible] I will fight [illegible] I will attack [illegible] respectively, these excellent [illegible] who are like [illegible] and [illegible] twilight [illegible] excellent chariot warrior soldiers [illegible] at the head of battle.

[illegible] have now named the chariot warriors and excep[illegible] chariot warrior [illegible] according to their potential [illegible] king, and equally I have named those others who are merely half-chariot warriors [illegible] and [illegible] of the Kauravas.

I will ward off [illegible] and any other kings [illegible] Bharata—I will [illegible] everywhere. But, long-armed [illegible] I will not kill Shikhandi [illegible] even [illegible] fighting in battle with his arrows raised.

[illegible] world knows how I abandoned my kingdom when [illegible] instead by my vow of chastity, for I wished to do my father [illegible] favor. I installed [illegible] in [illegible] of lordship over the Kauravas, and consecrated [illegible] as the young king. Now that I have made the [illegible] world aware that I am one who performs a great vow, among all kings I will certainly never kill a woman, nor someone who was previously a woman.

Perhaps you have heard, king, that Shikhandi was previously a woman. Though he was born as a girl, he became a man, and I will not fight him, Bharata. I will certainly kill all the other kings I come across in battle [illegible] of the Bharatas, but I will not kill the sons of Kunti, king.

173–178

# THE TALE OF AMBA

DURYODHANA uvāca:

173.1 KIM ARTHAM, Bharata|śreṣṭha,
n' âiva hanyāḥ Śikhaṇḍinam
udyat'|êṣum atho dṛṣṭvā
samareṣv ātatāyinam?
pūrvam uktvā, mahā|bāho, «Pañcālān saha Somakaiḥ
haniṣyām'! îti,» Gāṅgeya. tan me brūhi, pitā|maha.

BHĪṢMA uvāca:

śṛṇu, Duryodhana, kathāṃ
sah' âibhir vasudh"|âdhipaiḥ,
yad arthaṃ yudhi saṃprekṣya
n' âhaṃ hanyāṃ Śikhaṇḍinam.
mahā|rājo mama pitā Śāntanur loka|viśrutaḥ
diṣṭ'|ântam āpa dharm'|ātmā samaye, Bharata'|rṣabha.
173.5 tato 'haṃ, Bharata|śreṣṭha, pratijñāṃ paripālayan
Citrāṅgadaṃ bhrātaraṃ vai mahārājye 'bhyaṣecayam.
tasmiṃś ca nidhanaṃ prāpte Satyavatyā mate sthitaḥ
Vicitravīryaṃ rājānam abhyaṣiñcaṃ yathā|vidhi.
may" âbhiṣikto, rāj'|êndra, yavīyān api dharmataḥ,
Vicitravīryo dharm'|ātmā mām eva samudaikṣata.
tasya dāra|kriyāṃ, tāta, cikīrṣur aham apy uta
anurūpād iva kulād ity eva ca mano dadhe.
tath" âśrauṣaṃ, mahā|bāho, tisraḥ kanyāḥ svayaṃvarāḥ,
rūpeṇ' â|pratimāḥ sarvāḥ, Kāśi|rāja|sutās tadā,
Ambāṃ c' âiv' Âmbikāṃ c' âiva tath" âiv' Âmbālikām api.
173.10 rājānaś ca samāhūtāḥ pṛthivyāṃ, Bharata'|rṣabha.
Ambā jyeṣṭh" âbhavat tāsām, Ambikā tv atha madhyamā,
Ambālikā ca, rāj'|êndra, rāka|kanyā yavīyasī.

DURYÓDHANA said:

WHAT IS YOUR reason for refusing to kill Shikhándin even if you see him charging you in battle with his arrows upraised, greatest of the Bharatas? In the past, long-armed son of the Ganges, you claimed, "I will kill the Panchálas and Sómakas!" So tell me, grandfather. 173.1

BHISHMA replied:

Well then, listen to the story with these lords of earth. It will explain why I cannot kill Shikhándin even if I see him in war.

My father, the mighty King Shántanu, was famed throughout the world, and the virtuous-souled man reached his appointed end in the fullness of time, bull of the Bharatas. Then I, greatest of the Bharatas, protected my promise 173.5
and installed my brother Chitrángada as mighty sovereign. Once he reached his end, I abided by Sátyavati's wishes and duly consecrated Vichítra·virya as king. Vichítra·virya was young and law-abiding when I consecrated him as king, O lord of kings, so the virtuous-souled man looked to me for advice.

I also wanted to organize his marriage, my son, so I set my mind to finding him a wife from a suitable lineage. Long-armed man, I heard that all three of the king of Kashi's daughters, unrivaled in their beauty, Amba, Ámbika, and Ambálika, were holding their bridegroom choices, and that the kings of earth were invited, bull of the Bharatas. 173.10
Amba was the eldest, Ámbika the middle sister, and Ambálika was the youngest princess, O lord of kings.

so 'ham eka|rathen' âiva gataḥ Kāśi|pateḥ purīm.
apaśyaṃ tā, mahā|bāho, tisraḥ kanyāḥ sv|alaṃkṛtāḥ,
rājñaś c' âiva samāhūtān pārthivān, pṛthivī|pate.
tato 'haṃ tān nṛpān sarvān āhūya samare sthitān
ratham āropayāṃ cakre kanyās tā, Bharata'|rṣabha,
vīrya|śulkāś ca tā jñātvā samāropya rathaṃ tadā.

avocaṃ pārthivān sarvān ahaṃ tatra samāgatān:
«Bhīṣmaḥ Śāntanavaḥ kanyā harat'! îti» punaḥ punaḥ.
173.15 «te yatadhvaṃ paraṃ śaktyā sarve mokṣāya, pārthivāḥ!
prasahya hi harāmy eṣa miṣatāṃ vo, nara'|rṣabhāḥ.»

tatas te pṛthivī|pālāḥ samutpetur udāyudhāḥ,
«yogo! yoga! iti» kruddhāḥ sārathīn abhyacodayan.
te rathair gaja|saṅkāśair, gajaiś ca gaja|yodhinaḥ,
puṣṭaiś c' âśvair mahī|pālāḥ samutpetur udāyudhāḥ.
tatas te māṃ mahī|pālāḥ sarva eva, viśāṃ pate,
ratha|vrātena mahatā sarvataḥ paryavārayan.

tān ahaṃ śara|varṣeṇa samantāt paryavārayam,
sarvān nṛpāṃś c' âpy ajayaṃ deva|rāḍ iva Dānavān!
173.20 apātayaṃ śarair dīptaiḥ prahasan, Bharata'|rṣabha,
teṣām āpatatāṃ citrān dhvajān hema|pariṣkṛtān!
ek'|âikena hi bāṇena bhūmau pātitavān aham
hayāṃs teṣāṃ, gajāṃś c' âiva, sārathīṃś c' âpy ahaṃ raṇe!

So I went to the city of the king of Kashi with a single chariot, and I saw those three beautifully ornamented girls, as well as the kings and lords of earth who had been invited, long-armed lord of earth. I then challenged all the kings who stood there to battle, and I made the girls climb aboard my chariot, bull of the Bharatas—for I understood that their price was heroism—and finally mounted the chariot myself.

Then I called out to all the kings gathered in that place, shouting: "Bhishma son of Shántanu is carrying off the girls!" over and over again. "Kings! All of you endeavor to 173.15
the best of your ability to release them! I am forcibly stealing them away while you, bull-like men, look on!"

In response, those earth-defenders rushed with weapons upraised, screaming "Yoke the horses! Yoke the horses!" in their fury as they urged on their charioteers. The kings of earth rushed out, weapons upraised, some on chariots which looked like elephants, elephant warriors on their elephants, and others on their well-fed horses. Then all those earth-lords surrounded me on all sides, lord of earth, with an enormous host of chariots.

With my shower of arrows I warded them off on all sides, and defeated all those kings like the sovereign of the gods defeating the Dánavas! With my blazing arrows, bull of the 173.20
Bharatas, I felled their multicolored banners decked with gold as the kings flew at me, and I laughed as I did so! In fact, I sent each and every one of their horses, elephants, and charioteers tumbling to the ground in battle with a single arrow!

te nivṛttāś ca bhagnāś ca dṛṣṭvā tal lāghavaṃ mama;
ath' âhaṃ Hāstinapuram āyāṃ jitvā mahī|kṣitaḥ.
tato 'haṃ tāś ca kanyā vai bhrātur arthāya, Bhārata,
tac ca karma, mahā|bāho, Satyavatyai nyavedayam.

BHĪṢMA uvāca:

174.1 TATO 'HAṂ, BHARATA|śreṣṭha, mātaraṃ vīra|mātaram
abhigamy' ôpasaṃgṛhya dāśeyīm idam abruvam:
«imāḥ Kāśi|pateḥ kanyā mayā nirjitya pārthivān
Vicitravīryasya kṛte vīrya|śulkā hṛtā iti.»
tato mūrdhany upāghrāya paryaśru|nayanā, nṛpa,
āha Satyavatī hṛṣṭā «diṣṭyā, putra, jitaṃ tvayā!»
Satyavatyās tv anumate vivāhe samupasthite
uvāca vākyaṃ sa|vrīḍā jyeṣṭhā Kāśi|pateḥ sutā:
174.5 «Bhīṣma, tvam asi dharma|jñaḥ, sarva|śāstra|viśāradaḥ.
śrutvā ca vacanaṃ dharmyaṃ mahyaṃ kartum ih' ârhasi.
mayā Śālva|patiḥ pūrvaṃ manas" âbhivṛto varaḥ,
tena c' âsmi vṛtā pūrvaṃ rahasy a|vidite pituḥ.
kathaṃ māṃ anya|kāmāṃ tvaṃ rāja|dharmam atītya vai
vāsayethā gṛhe, Bhīṣma, Kauravaḥ san viśeṣataḥ?
etad buddhyā viniścitya manasā, Bharata'|rṣabha,
yat kṣamaṃ te, mahā|bāho, tad ih' ārabdhum arhasi.
sa māṃ pratīkṣate vyaktaṃ Śālva|rājo, viśāṃ pate,
tasmān māṃ tvaṃ, Kuru|śreṣṭha, samanujñātum arhasi.

They retreated and broke ranks when they beheld my dexterity, and I returned to Hástina·pura once I had defeated the kings of earth. I then handed over the girls intended for my brother, O long-armed Bhárata, and explained to Sátyavati what I had done.

BHISHMA continued:

I WENT TO MY mother, the mother of heroes but daughter of a fisherman, O greatest of the Bharatas, and grasping her feet I said to her: "I defeated the kings and carried off these girls, the daughters of the king of Kashi, whose price was heroism, for the sake of Vichítra·virya." Sátyavati kissed me on my head, her eyes full of tears, my king, and, delighted, she said to me: "Congratulations on your victory, my son!" 174.1

When, with Sátyavati's permission, the marriages were approaching, the king of Kashi's eldest daughter, Amba, bashfully said to me:

"Bhishma, you understand law and are experienced in every scripture. When you have heard what I have to say, you ought to treat me lawfully in this matter. 174.5

Long before now, in the privacy of my mind, I chose Lord Shalva as my husband, and he too proposed to me before this in private, without the knowledge of my father. O Bhishma, how could you in particular, being a Káurava, transgress royal law and force me to live in your house when I love another man? Now that you know this and debate it in your mind, long-armed bull of the Bharatas, you ought to do what is right. The King Shalva is surely expecting me, lord of earth, and so you ought to allow me to go, best of the Kurus.

174.10 kṛpāṃ kuru, mahā|bāho, mayi, dharma|bhṛtāṃ vara!
tvaṃ hi satya|vrato, vīra, pṛthivyām iti naḥ śrutam.»

BHĪṢMA uvāca:

175.1 TATO 'HAṂ samanujñāpya Kālīṃ Gandhavatīṃ tadā,
mantriṇaś ca' rtvijaś c' âiva, tath" âiva ca purohitān;
samanujñāsiṣaṃ kanyām Ambāṃ jyeṣṭhāṃ, nar'|âdhipa.
anujñātā yayau sā tu kanyā Śālva|pateḥ puram.
vṛddhair dvijātibhir guptā, dhātryā c' ânugatā tadā,
atītya ca tam adhvānam āsādya nṛ|patiṃ tathā.
sā tam āsādya rājānaṃ Śālvaṃ vacanam abravīt:
«āgat" âhaṃ, mahā|bāho, tvām uddiśya, mahā|mate.»
175.5 tām abravīc Chālva|patiḥ smayann iva, viśāṃ pate:
«tvay" ânya|pūrvayā n' âhaṃ bhāry"|ârthī, vara|varṇini.
gaccha, bhadre, punas tatra sakāśaṃ Bhīṣmakasya vai.
n' âham icchāmi Bhīṣmeṇa gṛhītāṃ tvāṃ prasahya vai!
tvaṃ hi Bhīṣmeṇa nirjitya nītā prītimatī tadā
parāmṛśya mahā|yuddhe nirjitya pṛthivī|patīn.
n' âham tvayy anya|pūrvāyāṃ bhāry"|ârthī, vara|varṇini.
katham asmad|vidho rājā para|pūrvāṃ praveśayet
nārīṃ vidita|vijñānaḥ
pareṣāṃ dharmam ādiśan?
yath" êṣṭaṃ gamyatāṃ, bhadre,

Have pity on me, long-armed man, O greatest of the law-abiding! For you are certainly devoted to the truth, hero. It is known throughout the world." 174.10

BHISHMA continued:

I THEN SUBMITTED the matter to my mother Kali, also called Gándhavati, and to our advisors, sacrificial priests, and family priests; then I gave my permission for Amba, the eldest daughter, to leave, lord of men. So the girl went, with my approval, to the city of Lord Shalva. She was protected by elderly brahmins and attended by her nurse, and once she had traveled the whole distance, she approached the king. 175.1

She made her way to King Shalva and said to him: "I have come here for you, long-armed and high-minded man!"
But Lord Shalva almost laughed and replied, lord of earth, 175.5
saying:

"I have no intention of taking you as my wife when you have already been had by another man, flawlessly complexioned lady. Go back to Bhishma's presence, my dear. I do not want you when you have already been forcibly ravished by Bhishma!

You were certainly very happy when Bhishma won you and led you away, having forcibly overcome those kings in the mighty battle. I have no intention of making you my wife, for you have already been taken by another man, flawlessly complexioned lady. How could a king like me allow a woman who is another man's cast-off into his house, when he has knowledge of areas of learning and when he hands

mā tvāṃ kālo 'tyagād ayam.»

175.10 Ambā tam abravīd, rājann, anaṅga|śara|pīḍitā:
«n' âivaṃ vada, mahī|pāla, n' âitad evaṃ kathañ cana.
n' âsmi prītimatī nītā Bhīṣmeṇ', âmitra|karśana!
balān nīt" âsmi rudatī, vidrāvya pṛthivīpatīn!
bhajasva māṃ, Śālva|pate, bhaktāṃ bālām an|āgasam.
bhaktānāṃ hi partityāgo na dharmeṣu praśasyate!

s" âham āmantrya Gāṅgeyaṃ samareṣv a|nivartinam
anujñātā ca ten' âiva, tato 'haṃ bhṛśam āgatā!
na sa Bhīṣmo mahā|bāhur mām icchati, viśām pate!
bhrātṛ|hetoḥ samārambho Bhīṣmasy', êti śrutaṃ mayā.
175.15 bhaginyau mama ye nīte Ambik'|Âmbālike, nṛpa,
prādād Vicitravīryāya Gāṅgeyo hi yavīyase.

yathā, Śālva|pate, n' ânyaṃ varaṃ dhyāmi kathañ cana
tvām ṛte, puruṣa|vyāghra, tathā mūrdhānam ālabhe!
na c' ânya|pūrvā, rāj'|êndra, tvām ahaṃ samupasthitā.
satyaṃ bravīmi, Śālv', âitat satyen' ātmānam ālabhe!
bhajasva māṃ, viśāl'|âkṣa, svayaṃ kanyām upasthitām
an|anya|pūrvāṃ, rāj'|êndra, tvat|prasād'|âbhikāṅkṣiṇīm!»

tām evaṃ bhāṣamāṇāṃ tu Śālvaḥ Kāśi|pateḥ sutām
atyajad, Bharata|śreṣtha, jīrṇāṃ tvacam iv' ôragaḥ.
175.20 evaṃ bahu|vidhair vākyair yācyamānas tayā nṛpaḥ
n' āśraddadhac Chālva|patiḥ kanyāyāṃ, Bharata'|rṣabha.

down the law to others? Please go wherever you wish, my dear, but don't waste your time."

Tormented by the god of love's arrows, Amba said to him, 175.10
my king:

"Don't say such things, earth-lord, for it is not the case at all! I wasn't happy to be led away by Bhishma, enemy-tormentor! I was led away forcibly and weeping, after Bhishma had routed the lords of earth! Love me, Lord Shalva, as I love you, for I am young and sinless. Abandoning those who love you is certainly not commended by law!

I begged the son of the Ganges who does not retreat in battle, and once I won his permission I quickly came here! Long-armed Bhishma doesn't want me, lord of men! I heard
that Bhishma's enterprise was on behalf of his brother. The 175.15
son of the Ganges has given my sisters Ámbika and Ambálika, who were led off with me, king, to Vichítra·virya, his younger brother.

I swear, touching my head, that I never even considered anyone but you to be my husband, tiger-like Lord Shalva! I stand before you, lord of kings, as a woman who has never belonged any other man. I am telling the truth, Shalva! I swear it truly by my soul! Love me, large-eyed man, for I am a girl who stands before you of her own accord, who has never belonged to any other man, lord of kings, and who hopes for your favor!"

But Shalva rejected the princess of Kashi even though she spoke in this way, greatest of the Bharatas, as though he
were a snake sloughing off his worn-out skin. So it was that 175.20
the royal Lord Shalva did not trust the girl, even though she begged him with varied arguments, bull of the Bharatas.

tataḥ sā manyun" āviṣṭā jyeṣṭhā Kāśi|pateḥ sutā
abravīt s'|âśru|nayanā bāṣpa|viplutayā girā:
«tvayā tyaktā gamiṣyāmi yatra yatra, viśām pate,
tatra me gatayaḥ santu santaḥ, satyaṃ yathā dhruvam!»

BHĪṢMA uvāca:

evaṃ tāṃ bhāṣamāṇāṃ tu kanyāṃ Śālva|patis tadā
paritatyāja, Kauravya, karuṇaṃ paridevatīm.
«gaccha! gachh'! êti» tāṃ Śālvaḥ punaḥ punar abhāṣata,
«bibhemi Bhīṣmāt, su|śroṇi, tvaṃ ca Bhīṣma|parigrahaḥ!»
175.25 evam uktā tu sā tena Śālven' â|dīrgha|darśinā
niścakrāma purād dīnā, rudatī kurarī yathā.
niṣkrāmantī tu nagarāc cintayām āsa duḥkhitā:
«pṛthivyāṃ n' âsti yuvatir viṣamasthatarā mayā!
bandhubhir viprahīṇ" âsmi, Śālvena ca nirākṛtā!
na ca śakyaṃ punar gantuṃ mayā vāraṇa|s'|āhvayam
anujñātā tu Bhīṣmeṇa
Śālvam uddiśya kāraṇam!
kiṃ nu garhāmy ath' ātmānam,
atha Bhīṣmaṃ dur|āsadam?
atha vā pitaraṃ mūḍhaṃ, yo me 'kārṣīt svayaṃ|varam?
may" âyaṃ sva|kṛto doṣo, y" âhaṃ Bhīṣma|rathāt tadā
175.30 pravṛtte dāruṇe yuddhe Śālv'|ârthaṃ n' âpataṃ purā.
tasy' êyaṃ phala|nirvṛttir, yad āpann" âsmi mūḍhavat!

And filled with fury, the eldest daughter of the king of Kashi spoke again, her eyes brimming with tears and her voice choked by tearful sobs:

"Wherever I go, now that you have abandoned me, lord of earth, may good men be my refuge, for the truth is eternal!"

BHISHMA continued:

So it was that Lord Shalva rejected the girl who spoke so well and wept so pitifully, Kaurávya. "Go away! Leave!" repeated Shalva, time and time again. "I am afraid of Bhishma, shapely-hipped lady, and you are Bhishma's property!" Addressed this way by Shalva, a man of limited foresight, 175.25
she left the city depressed, crying like a female osprey.

As she left the city, the miserable woman thought to herself:

"There is no young woman on earth in a worse situation than I! Bereft of friends, I am also driven away by Shalva! I cannot return to the elephant-named city of Hástina·pura, for Bhishma permitted me to leave it specifically for Shalva's sake!

Whom then should I blame? Myself? Or then again, unassailable Bhishma? Or perhaps my fool of a father who 175.30
organized my bridegroom choice? The fault was my own doing. I didn't jump down from Bhishma's chariot for Shalva's sake early on while the harsh battle was under way. My current bewilderment is the result of my mistake!

dhig Bhīṣmaṃ! dhik ca me mandaṃ
pitaraṃ mūḍha|cetasam,
yen' âhaṃ vīrya|śulkena
paṇya|str" îva pracoditā!
dhiṅ māṃ! dhik Śālva|rājānaṃ! dhig dhātāram ath' âpi vā,
yeṣāṃ dur|nīta|bhāvena prāpt" âsmy āpadam uttamām!
sarvathā bhāga|dheyāni svāni prāpnoti mānavaḥ,
a|nayasy' âsya tu mukhaṃ Bhīṣmaḥ Śāntanavo mama.
sā Bhīṣme pratikartavyam ahaṃ paśyāmi sāmpratam
tapasā vā yudhā v" âpi; duḥkha|hetuḥ sa me mataḥ!
175.35 ko nu Bhīṣmaṃ yudhā jetum utsaheta mahī|patiḥ?»
evaṃ sā pariniścitya jagāma nagarād bahiḥ
āśramaṃ puṇya|śīlānāṃ tāpasānāṃ mah"|ātmanām.
tatas tām avasad rātriṃ tāpasaiḥ parivāritā,
ācakhyau ca yathā|vṛttaṃ sarvam ātmani, Bhārata,
vistareṇa, mahā|bāho, nikhilena śuci|smitā:
haraṇaṃ ca visargaṃ ca Śālvena ca visarjanam.
tatas tatra mahān āsīd brāhmaṇaḥ saṃśita|vrataḥ
Śaikhāvatyas tapo|vṛddhaḥ, śāstre c' āraṇyake guruḥ.
ārtāṃ tām āha sa muniḥ Śaikhāvatyo mahā|tapāḥ
niḥśvasantīṃ satīṃ bālāṃ duḥkha|śoka|parāyaṇām:
175.40 «evaṃ|gate tu kiṃ, bhadre, śakyaṃ kartuṃ tapasvibhiḥ
āśrama|sthair, mahā|bhāge, tapo|yuktair mah"|ātmabhiḥ?»

Damn Bhishma! Damn my foolish, idiotic-minded father, because of whom I was dispatched as though I were a woman to be bought and sold, with my price an act of heroism! Damn me! Damn King Shalva! Damn the creator too, and those through whose misconduct I have reached such total disaster!

In all respects, human beings gain only what is allotted to them by fate. But the reason for my current misfortune is Bhishma, son of Shántanu. So I see that I should take revenge on Bhishma for the present, either through asceticism or war, for I believe he is the cause of my misery! But 175.35
which earth-lord would dare to defeat Bhishma in war?"

Considering this, she went outside the city to a hermitage of high-souled ascetics of pure conduct. She stayed there that night, surrounded by ascetics, and the sweet-smiling girl told them everything that had happened to her, long-armed Bhárata, in complete detail: all about her abduction, her dismissal, and her rejection by Shalva.

Now there was a mighty brahmin of strict vows, whose asceticism had grown great and who was a teacher of scripture to the forest-dwelling ascetics, named Shaikhavátya. Shaikhavátya, a sage of high austerity, spoke to the tormented but pure girl as she sighed in abject misery and grief: "Well, with this being the case, my dear, what can 175.40
high-souled ascetics practicing austerities do as they live in their hermitage, noble lady?"

sā tv enam abravīd, rājan: «kriyatāṃ mad|anugrahaḥ.
prāvrājyam aham icchāmi. tapas tapsyāmi duś|caram.
may" âiva yāni karmāṇi pūrva|dehe tu mūḍhayā
kṛtāni nūnaṃ pāpāni, teṣām etat phalaṃ dhruvam.
n' ôtsahe tu punar gantuṃ sva|janaṃ prati, tāpasāḥ,
pratyākhyātā, nirānandā, Śālvena ca nirākṛtā.
upadiṣṭam ih' êcchāmi tāpasyaṃ, vīta|kalmaṣāḥ,
yuṣmābhir deva|saṃkāśaiḥ. kṛpā bhavatu vo mayi!»
175.45 sa tām āśvāsayat kanyāṃ dṛṣṭānt'|āgama|hetubhiḥ,
sāntvayām āsa, kāryaṃ ca pratijajñe dvijaiḥ saha.

BHĪṢMA uvāca:

176.1 TATAS TE TĀPASĀḤ sarve kāryavanto 'bhavaṃs tadā
tāṃ kanyāṃ cintayantas te, «kiṃ kāryam? iti» dharmiṇaḥ.
ke cid āhuḥ, «pitur veśma nīyatām iti» tāpasāḥ.
ke cid asmad|upālambhe matiṃ cakrur hi tāpasāḥ.
ke cic Chālva|patiṃ gatvā niyojyam iti menire.
«n' êti» ke cid vyavasyanti, «pratyākhyātā hi tena sā.»
punar ūcuś ca tāṃ sarve tāpasāḥ saṃśita|vratāḥ:
«evaṃ|gate tu kiṃ śakyaṃ, bhadre, kartuṃ manīṣibhiḥ?
176.5 alaṃ pravrajiten' êha, bhadre. śṛṇu hitaṃ vacaḥ.
ito gacchasva, bhadraṃ te, pitur eva niveśanam.
pratipatsyati rājā sa pitā te, yad an|antaram;
tatra vatsyasi, kalyāṇi, sukhaṃ sarva|guṇ'|ânvitā.

She replied, king, saying: "Please grant me a favor. I long for the vagrant existence of an ascetic. I will practice difficult austerities. Surely I must have foolishly committed some sins in a previous body. This is assuredly their fruit. I do not dare to return to my own people, rejected and melancholy, now that I have been driven away by Shalva, ascetics. I want you, god-like as you are, to instruct me in asceticism, sinless men. Please have pity on me!"

He comforted the girl with examples, doctrines, and rea- 175.45
sons, and soothed her by promising to do what was required, as did the other brahmins.

BHISHMA continued:

THEN ALL THE LAWFUL ascetics busied themselves with 176.1
their tasks, pondering over the girl, thinking "What should be done?" Some ascetics said, "She should be brought to her father's house." Some ascetics, in fact, made up their minds that I should be censured. Others believed they should go to the Shalva king and force him to accept her. "No!" others argued, "for he has rejected her."

All the strict-vowed ascetics spoke to her again, saying:

"With the situation being what it is, what can sages do,
my dear? That's enough nonsense about the vagrant life of 176.5
ascetics, my dear. Listen to our helpful advice. Go to your father's house, bless you. The king, your father, will act immediately. You will live there happily, lovely lady, provided with every comfort.

na ca te 'nyā gatir nyāyyā bhaved, bhadre, yathā pitā;
patir v" âpi gatir nāryāḥ, pitā vā, vara|varṇini.
gatiḥ patiḥ samasthāyā, viṣame ca pitā gatiḥ;
pravrajyā hi su|duḥkh" êyaṃ su|kumāryā viśeṣataḥ,
rāja|putryāḥ prakṛtyā ca kumāryās tava, bhāmini.
bhadre, doṣā hi vidyante bahavo, vara|varṇini;
176.10 āśrame vai vasantyās te na bhaveyuḥ pitur gṛhe.»
tatas tv anye 'bruvan vākyaṃ tāpasās tāṃ tapasvinīm:
«tvām ih' âikākinīṃ dṛṣṭvā nirjane gahane vane
prārthayiṣyanti rājānas; tasmān m" âivaṃ manaḥ kṛthāḥ!»

AMB" ôvāca:

na śakyaṃ Kāśi|nagaraṃ punar gantuṃ pitur gṛhān;
avajñātā bhaviṣyāmi bāndhavānāṃ, na saṃśayaḥ.
uṣit" âsmi tathā bālye pitur veśmani, tāpasāḥ,
n' âhaṃ gamiṣye, bhadram vas, tatra yatra pitā mama.
tapas taptum abhīpsāmi tāpasaiḥ parirakṣitā,
yathā pare 'pi me loke
    na syād evaṃ mah"|âtyayaḥ,
daurbhāgyaṃ, tāpasa|śreṣṭhās,
    tasmāt tapsyāmy ahaṃ tapaḥ.

BHĪṢMA uvāca:

176.15 ity evaṃ teṣu vipreṣu cintayatsu yathā|tatham
rāja'|rṣis tad vanaṃ prāptas tapasvī Hotravāhanaḥ.
tatas te tāpasāḥ sarve pūjayanti sma taṃ nṛpam
pūjābhiḥ svāgat'|ādyābhir, āsanen' ôdakena ca.
tasy' ôpaviṣṭasya sato viśrāntasy' ôpaśṛṇvataḥ
punar eva kathāṃ cakruḥ kanyāṃ prati van'|âukasaḥ.

You have no refuge other than your father, my dear. A
woman's refuge is either her husband or her father, flawlessly complexioned lady. The husband is her refuge in good
times, and her father in hard times. The vagrant life is certainly very painful, especially for so tender a girl. You are
by nature a princess, and you are also delicate, passionate
lady. My dear, there are indeed many drawbacks to such a
life, flawlessly complexioned lady, when you live in a her- 176.10
mitage, but there would be none of these in your father's
house." Then other ascetics said to the austere girl: "When
kings see you living alone in the desolate and impenetrable forest, they will proposition you; so don't set your mind
on it!"

AMBA said:

I cannot return to the Kashi city and my father's house, for I will doubtless be insulted by my kin. I lived in my father's city during my childhood, ascetics, but I will not go back to the place where my father lives now, bless you. I want to practice asceticism, defended by ascetics, so that in my next life I may not suffer such great misfortune and bad luck. Greatest of ascetics, I will practice asceticism.

BHISHMA continued:

While the brahmins were pondering her situation in this 176.15
precise manner, the royal sage and ascetic Hotra·váhana
reached the forest. All the ascetics praised the lord with worship, welcoming phrases, and so on, and with a seat and
some water. Once the sage was seated and rested, the forest-
dwellers began to discuss the girl again, within earshot of
the sage.

Ambāyās tāṃ kathāṃ śrutvā, Kāśi|rājñaś ca, Bhārata,
rāja'|rṣiḥ sa mahā|tejā babhūv' ôdvigna|mānasaḥ.
tāṃ tathā|vādinīṃ śrutvā dṛṣṭvā ca sa mahā|tapāḥ
rāja'|rṣiḥ kṛpay" āviṣṭo mah"|ātmā Hotravāhanaḥ.
176.20 sa vepamāna utthāya mātus tasyāḥ pitā tadā
tāṃ kanyām aṅkam āropya paryaśvāsayata, prabho.
sa tām apṛcchat kārtsnyena vyasan'|ôtpattim āditaḥ;
sā ca tasmai yathā|vṛttaṃ vistareṇa nyavedayat.
tataḥ sa rāja'|rṣir abhūd duḥkha|śoka|samanvitaḥ,
kāryaṃ ca pratipede tan manasā su|mahā|tapāḥ.
abravīd vepamānaś ca kanyām ārtāṃ su|duḥkhitaḥ:
«mā gāḥ pitur gṛhaṃ, bhadre, mātus te janako hy aham.
duḥkhaṃ chindyām ahaṃ te vai. mayi vartasva, putrike!
paryāptaṃ te mano, vatse, yad evaṃ pariśuṣyasi!
176.25 gaccha mad|vacanād Rāmaṃ Jāmadagnyaṃ tapasvinam;
Rāmas te su|mahad duḥkhaṃ śokaṃ c' âiv' âpaneṣyati.
haniṣyati raṇe Bhīṣmaṃ, na kariṣyati ced vacaḥ.
taṃ gaccha Bhārgava|śreṣṭhaṃ kāl'|âgni|sama|tejasam!
pratiṣṭhāpayitā sa tvāṃ same pathi mahā|tapāḥ.»
tatas tu su|svaraṃ bāṣpam utsṛjantī punaḥ punaḥ,
abravīt pitaraṃ mātuḥ sā tadā Hotravāhanam
abhivādayitvā śirasā: «gamiṣye tava śāsanāt.
api nām' âdya paśyeyam āryaṃ taṃ loka|viśrutam?
kathaṃ ca tīvraṃ duḥkhaṃ me nāśayiṣyati Bhārgavaḥ?
etad icchāmy ahaṃ jñātuṃ yathā yāsyāmi tatra vai.»

As he listened to the story of Amba and the king of Kashi, Bhárata, the royal sage of great splendor felt sorrowful in his heart. When he saw her and listened to how she spoke, the high-souled royal sage, Hotra·váhana, a man of enormous austerity, was filled with compassion. So her mater- 176.20
nal grandfather rose, trembling, and, making the girl sit on his lap, he comforted her, my lord.

He asked her about the root of her troubles in detail, starting from the beginning, and she explained everything minutely to him, just as it had happened. The royal sage was filled with misery and grief, and the man of extraordinary asceticism undertook the task in his mind. Then, trembling and very miserable, he said to the suffering girl:

"Don't go to your father's house, my dear. I am your mother's father. I will shatter your misery. Turn to me, my little daughter! Your mind must be so very gloomy, withered as you are, my child!

Go, on my advice, to the ascetic Rama, son of Jamad· 176.25
agni. Rama will destroy your vast grief and misery. He will kill Bhishma in battle if he does not do as he is told. Go to the greatest of the Bhrigus, whose energy matches the fire at the end of the age! The great ascetic will set you on the right path."

Then, loudly weeping tears over and over again, she addressed her maternal grandfather, Hotra·váhana, saluting him with her head, saying: "I will go at your command. But will I really see that noble and world-renowned man? How will the descendant of Bhrigu dispel my acute misery? I wish to know this, and to know how I will go to him."

HOTRAVĀHANA uvāca:

176.30 Rāmaṃ drakṣyasi, bhadre,
tvaṃ Jāmadagnyaṃ mahā|vane
ugre tapasi vartantaṃ,
satya|sandhaṃ, mahā|balam.
Mahendraṃ vai giri|śreṣṭhaṃ Rāmo nityam upāsti ha,
ṛṣayo veda|vidvāṃso, gandharv'|âpsarasas tathā.
tatra gacchasva, bhadraṃ te, brūyāś c' âinaṃ vaco mama,
abhivādya ca taṃ mūrdhnā tapo|vṛddhaṃ dṛḍha|vratam.
brūyāś c' âinaṃ punar, bhadre, yat te kāryaṃ manīṣitam.
mayi saṃkīrtite Rāmaḥ sarvaṃ tat te kariṣyati.
mama Rāmaḥ sakhā, vatse, prīti|yuktaḥ su|hṛc ca me
Jamadagni|suto vīraḥ sarva|śastra|bhṛtāṃ varaḥ.
176.35 evaṃ bruvati kanyāṃ tu pārthive Hotravāhane
Akṛtavraṇaḥ prādur āsīd Rāmasy' ânucaraḥ priyaḥ.
tatas te munayaḥ sarve samuttasthuḥ sahasraśaḥ,
sa ca rājā vayo|vṛddhaḥ Sṛñjayo Hotravāhanaḥ.
tato dṛṣṭvā kṛt'|ātithyam anyonyaṃ te van'|âukasaḥ
sahitā, Bharata|śreṣṭha; niṣeduḥ parivārya tam.
tatas te kathayām āsuḥ kathās tās tā mano|ramāḥ,
dhanyā, divyāś ca, rāj'|êndra, prīti|harṣa|mudā|yutāḥ.
tataḥ kath"|ânte rāja'|rṣir mah"|ātmā Hotravāhanaḥ
Rāmaṃ śreṣṭhaṃ maha"|rṣīṇām apṛcchad Akṛtavraṇam:
176.40 «kva samprati, mahā|bāho, Jāmadagnyaḥ pratāpavān,
Akṛtavraṇa, śakyo vai draṣṭuṃ veda|vidāṃ varaḥ?»

HOTRA·VÁHANA replied:

You will see Rama, the son of Jamad·agni, in the great 176.30
forest, my dear, as the great powerful man, true to his promises, is engaged in harsh asceticism. Rama always lives on Mount Mahéndra, the greatest of mountains, where sages who understand the Vedas, *gandhárva*s, and *ápsaras*es also live. Go there, bless you, and tell him what I said. Salute the sage of firm vows and highly developed asceticism by bowing your head to him.

Tell him again what you wish to be done, my dear. If you mention me, then Rama will do all you ask. Rama, the hero son of Jamad·agni and the greatest of all who wield weapons, is my friend, my child, and a friend filled with affection for me at that.

While King Hotra·váhana was telling the girl this, Rama's 176.35
dear companion Ákrita·vrana appeared. Upon his arrival all the sages in their thousands stood up, as did the aged Srínjaya king, Hotra·váhana. When they saw him, the forest-dwellers united together and set up the proper guest hospitality, greatest of the Bharatas; then they sat surrounding him. Filled with delight, joy, and affection, they told charming, captivating, and enchanting tales, lord of kings.

Then, once the storytelling had come to an end, the high-souled royal sage Hotra·váhana asked Ákrita·vrana about
Rama, the greatest of great sages: "Where is it possible to see 176.40
the majestic son of Jamad·agni, the greatest of those who know the Vedas, at this time, long-armed Ákrita·vrana?"

AKṚTAVRAṆA uvāca:

bhavantam eva satataṃ Rāmaḥ kīrtayati, prabho,
«Sṛñjayo me priya|sakho rāja'|rṣir! iti,» pārthiva.
iha Rāmaḥ prabhāte śvo bhavit", êti matir mama;
draṣṭ" âsy enam ih' āyāntaṃ tava darśana|kāṅkṣayā.
iyaṃ ca kanyā, rāja'|rṣe, kim arthaṃ vanam āgatā?
kasya c' êyaṃ? tava ca kā bhavat' îcchāmi veditum!

HOTRAVĀHANA uvāca:

dauhitr" îyaṃ mama, vibho, Kāśi|rāja|sutā priyā!
jyeṣṭhā svayaṃ|vare tasthau bhaginībhyāṃ sah', ân|agha.
176.45 iyam Amb" êti vikhyātā jyeṣṭhā Kāśi|pateḥ sutā;
Ambik'|Âmbālike kanye kanīyasyau, tapo|dhana.
sametaṃ pārthivaṃ kṣatraṃ Kāśi|puryāṃ tato 'bhavat;
kanyā|nimittaṃ, vipra'|rṣe, tatr' āsīd utsavo mahān.
tataḥ kila mahā|vīryo Bhīṣmaḥ Śāntanavo nṛpān
adhikṣipya mahā|tejās tisraḥ kanyā jahāra tāḥ.
nirjitya pṛthivī|pālān atha Bhīṣmo Gaj'|āhvayam
ājagāma viśuddh'|ātmā kanyābhiḥ saha Bhārataḥ.
Satyavatyai nivedy' âtha vivāhaṃ samanantaram
bhrātur Vicitravīryasya samājñāpayata prabhuḥ.
176.50 taṃ tu vaivāhikaṃ dṛṣṭvā kany" êyaṃ samupārjitam
abravīt tatra Gāṅgeyaṃ mantri|madhye, dvija'|rṣabha:
«mayā Śālva|patir vīro manas" âbhivṛtaḥ patiḥ;
na māṃ arhasi, dharma|jña, dātuṃ bhrātre 'nya|mānasām!»
tac chrutvā vacanaṃ Bhīṣmaḥ saṃmantrya saha mantribhiḥ

VRANA replied:

Rama is always mentioning you, my lord. "The royal Srínjaya sage is a dear friend of mine!" he says, king. Rama will be here tomorrow, I believe. You will see him coming here, hoping to see you. But what about this girl here, royal sage? Why has she come to the forest? To whom does she belong? And what has she got to do with you, I would like to know!

VÁHANA said:

This is my daughter's daughter, my lord, and the dear daughter of the king of Kashi! She stood, as the eldest, with
her two sisters at her bridegroom choice, sinless man. This 176.45
girl here, the eldest daughter of the king of Kashi, is called Amba, and the younger two girls are Ámbika and Ambálika, man of ascetic wealth.

Warrior-class kings congregated in the Kashi king's city for the girls, brahmin sage, and there was an enormous festival there. Then incredibly powerful and glorious Bhishma, son of Shántanu, carried the girls off, insulting the kings, or so they say. Once Bhishma had defeated the earth-lords, the pure-souled Bhárata returned to the elephant-named city of Hástina·pura with the girls. He explained everything to Sátyavati, and then the lord ordered their immediate marriage to his brother Vichítra·virya.

But when she saw the wedding preparations getting un- 176.50
derway, this girl here said to the son of the Ganges in the midst of his advisors, O brahmin sage: "I chose the hero Lord Shalva as my husband in my heart. You ought not to give me to your brother when my heart is set on another

niścitya visasarj' êmāṃ Satyavatyā mate sthitaḥ.
anujñātā tu Bhīṣmeṇa Śālvaṃ Saubha|patiṃ tataḥ
kany" êyaṃ muditā tatra kāle vacanam abravīt:
«visarjit" âsmi Bhīṣmeṇa! dharmaṃ māṃ pratipādaya
manas" âbhivṛtaḥ pūrvaṃ mayā tvam, pārthiva'|rṣabha!»
176.55 pratyācakhyau ca Śālvo 'syāś cāritrasy' âbhiśaṅkitaḥ;
s" êyaṃ tapo|vanaṃ prāptā tāpasye 'bhiratā bhṛśam.
mayā ca pratyabhijñātā vaṃśasya parikīrtanāt
asya duḥkhasya c' ôtpattiṃ Bhīṣmam ev' êha manyate.

AMB" ôvāca:

bhagavann, evam ev' êha yath" āha pṛthivī|patiḥ
śarīra|kartā mātur me Sṛñjayo Hotravāhanaḥ.
na hy utsahe sva|nagaraṃ pratiyātuṃ, tapo|dhana,
apamāna|bhayāc c' âiva, vrīḍayā ca, mahā|mune.
yat tu māṃ bhagavān Rāmo vakṣyati, dvija|sattama,
tan me kāryatamaṃ kāryam, iti me, bhagavan, matiḥ.

AKṚTAVRAṆA uvāca:

177.1 DUḤKHA|DVAYAM idaṃ, bhadre. katarasya cikīrṣasi
pratikartavyam, a|bale? tattvaṃ, vatse, vadasva me.
yadi Saubha|patir, bhadre, niyoktavyo matas tava,
niyokṣyati mah"|ātmā sa Rāmas tvadd|hita|kāmyayā.
ath' āpageyaṃ Bhīṣmaṃ tvaṃ Rāmeṇ' êcchasi dhīmatā
raṇe vinirjitaṃ draṣṭuṃ, kuryāt tad api Bhārgavaḥ.
Sṛñjayasya vacaḥ śrutvā, tava c' âiva, śūci|smite,

man, scholar of the law!" When Bhishma heard what she had to say, he consulted with his advisors, made his decision, then let her leave, abiding by Sátyavati's opinion.

So, with Bhishma's permission, this girl here went happily to Shalva, lord of Saubha, and when the time came, she said to him: "Bhishma released me! Ensure I remain law-abiding! I chose you as my husband long ago in my heart, bull-like king!" But Shalva rejected her, for he had his sus- 176.55
picions about her behavior. This is the girl who has come to the ascetics' forest and is so very intent upon practicing asceticism.

I recognized her from her account of her lineage. She believes that Bhishma is in fact the source of her misery.

AMBA said:

My lord, it is indeed just as the Srínjaya king, my mother's father Hotra·váhana, has said. I do not dare to return to my own city, ascetically rich man, for fear of the stigma, and because my shame prevents me, great sage. My most important task, as I see it, lord, is whatever Lord Rama should tell me to do, O greatest of brahmins.

VRANA said:

THERE ARE TWO problems here, my dear. Which of the 177.1
two do you wish to have remedied, powerless lady? Tell me truly, my child. If it is your intention to have the lord of Saubha made to marry you, my dear, then high-souled Rama will indeed make sure he does, wishing to help you. Or if you wish to see wise Rama defeat Bhishma, son of the river, in battle, then Bhárgava would do that too. Once we have heard what Srínjaya has to say on the matter, and, of

yad atra te bhṛśaṃ kāryaṃ tad ady' âiva vicintyatām.

AMB" ôvāca:

177.5 apanīt" âsmi Bhīṣmeṇa, bhagavann, a|vijānatā;
n' âbhijānāti me Bhīṣmo, brahmañ, Śālva|gataṃ manaḥ.
etad vicārya manasā, bhavān etad viniścayam
vicinotu yathā|nyāyaṃ, vidhānaṃ kriyatāṃ tathā.
Bhīṣme vā Kuru|śārdūle, Śālva|rāje 'tha vā punaḥ,
ubhayor eva vā, brahman, yuktaṃ yat tat samācara.
niveditaṃ mayā hy etad duḥkha|mūlaṃ yathā|tatham;
vidhānaṃ tatra, bhagavan, kartum arhasi yuktitaḥ.

AKṚTAVRAṆA uvāca:

upapannam idaṃ, bhadre, yad evaṃ, vara|varṇini,
dharmaṃ prati vaco brūyāḥ; śṛṇu c' êdaṃ vaco mama.
177.10 yadi tvām āpageyo vai na nayed gaja|s'|āhvayam
Śālvas tvāṃ śirasā, bhīru, gṛhṇīyād Rāma|coditaḥ.
tena tvaṃ nirjitā, bhadre, yasmān nīt" âsi, bhāvini,
saṃśayaḥ Śālva|rājasya tena tvayi, su|madhyame!
Bhīṣmaḥ puruṣa|mānī ca, jita|kāśī tath" âiva ca,
tasmāt pratikriyā yuktā Bhīṣme kārayituṃ tava.

course, what you have to say, sweet-smiling girl, then let it be decided today what it is in particular that needs to be done.

AMBA replied:

Bhishma was ignorant when he led me off, lord, for 177.5
Bhishma did not know that my heart was set on Shalva, brahmin. This should be taken into account in your mind. Please come to a decision according to what is proper, and let it be carried out in a like manner. Do whatever befits Bhishma, the Kuru tiger, or again King Shalva, or even both, brahmin. I have explained the root of my misery to you precisely, so, lord, you ought to act in the manner that reason suggests.

VRANA said:

The advice you give about law is worthy of you indeed, my dear flawlessly complexioned girl. Listen to my advice.
If Bhishma, the river's son, had not led you to the elephant- 177.10
named city of Hástina·pura, then Shalva would have accepted you humbly when urged by Rama, timid girl. It is precisely because you were won and led off, my dear beautiful girl, that King Shalva has his doubts about you, slender-waisted girl! Bhishma takes pride in his manliness and behaves like a conqueror, so you must cause your vengeance to be taken upon Bhishma.

AMB" ôvāca:

mam' âpy eṣa sadā, brahman, hṛdi kāmo 'bhivartate,
ghātayeyaṃ yadi raṇe Bhīṣmam, ity eva nityadā.
Bhīṣmaṃ vā Śālva|rājaṃ vā yaṃ vā doṣeṇa gacchasi,
praśādhi taṃ, mahā|bāho, yat|kṛte 'haṃ su|duḥkhitā.

BHĪṢMA uvāca:

177.15 evaṃ kathayatām eva teṣāṃ sa divaso gataḥ,
rātriś ca, Bharata|śreṣṭha, sukha|śīt'|ôṣṇa|mārutā.
tato Rāmaḥ prādur āsīt prajvalann iva tejasā,
śiṣyaiḥ parivṛto, rājañ, jaṭā|cīra|dharo muniḥ.
dhanuṣ|pāṇir, a|dīn'|ātmā, khaḍgaṃ bibhrat, paraśvadhī,
virajā, rāja|śārdūla, Sṛñjayaṃ so 'bhyayān nṛpam.

tatas taṃ tāpasā dṛṣṭvā, sa ca rājā mahā|tapāḥ,
tasthuḥ prāñjalayo, rājan, sā ca kanyā tapasvinī.
pūjayām āsur a|vyagrā madhu|parkeṇa Bhārgavam,
arcitaś ca yathā|nyāyaṃ niṣasāda sah' âiva taiḥ.
177.20 tataḥ pūrva|vyatītāni kathayantau sma tāv ubhau
āsātāṃ Jāmadagnyaś ca Sṛñjayaś c' âiva, Bhārata.

tathā kath"|ânte rāja'|rṣir Bhṛgu|śreṣṭhaṃ mahā|balam
uvāca madhuraṃ kāle Rāmaṃ vacanam arthavat:
«Rām', êyaṃ mama dauhitrī Kāśi|rāja|sutā, prabho.
asyāḥ śṛṇu yathā|tattvaṃ kāryaṃ, kārya|viśārada.»

AMBA replied:

This is the eternal desire in my heart, brahmin. My desire to have Bhishma killed in battle is constant. Regardless of whether you hold the fault to be Bhishma's or King Shalva's, punish the man through whose doing I am so very miserable, long-armed man!

BHISHMA continued:

So it was that the day passed as they spoke in this way, 177.15
best of the Bharatas, and the night passed with a pleasant breeze, neither too hot nor too cold. Then Rama appeared, a Shaiva sage decked with bark rags and matted hair, almost ablaze with splendor, surrounded by his pupils, king. The joyful-spirited and dust-free man held his bow in hand and carried a sword and axe, and he approached the Srínjaya king, O tiger-like sovereign.

Then, when the ascetics and king of great asceticism saw him, they stood, joining their hands together, my king, as did the austere girl. They steadily paid their respects to the Bhárgava with a honey and milk mixture, and once he had been properly honored he sat down with them. So it was 177.20
that Jamad·agni's son and the Srínjaya king both sat and talked about events long past, Bhárata.

Once their conversation came to an end and the right time came, the royal sage spoke sweetly to Rama, the powerful and greatest of the Bhrigus, in meaningful words: "Rama, this girl is my daughter's daughter and the daughter of the king of Kashi, my lord. Listen to exactly what needs to be done for her, O sage of relevant experience."

«paramaṃ kathyatāṃ» c' êti tāṃ Rāmaḥ pratyabhāṣata.
tataḥ s" âbhyavadad Rāmaṃ jvalantam iva pāvakam,
tato 'bhivādya caraṇau Rāmasya śirasā śubhau
spṛṣṭvā padma|tal'|ābhābhyāṃ pāṇibhyām agrataḥ sthitā.
177.25 ruroda sā śokavatī bāṣpa|vyākula|locanā,
prapede śaraṇaṃ c' âiva śaraṇyaṃ Bhṛgu|nandanam.

RĀMA uvāca:

yathā tvaṃ Sṛñjayasy' âsya, tathā me tvaṃ, nṛp'|ātmaje.
brūhi yat te mano|duḥkhaṃ; kariṣye vacanaṃ tava.

AMB" ôvāca:

bhagavañ, śaraṇaṃ tv" âdya prapann" âsmi mahā|vratam.
śoka|paṅk'|ārṇavān magnāṃ ghorād uddhara māṃ, vibho!

BHĪṢMA uvāca:

tasyāś ca dṛṣṭvā rūpaṃ ca, vapuś c' âbhinavaṃ punaḥ,
saukumāryaṃ paraṃ c' âiva, Rāmaś cintā|paro 'bhavat.
«kim iyaṃ vakṣyat'? îty» evaṃ vimamarśa Bhṛg'|ûdvahaḥ,
iti dadhyau ciraṃ Rāmaḥ kṛpay" âbhipariplutaḥ.
177.30 «kathyatām, iti» sā bhūyo Rāmeṇ' ôktā śuci|smitā
sarvam eva yathā|tattvaṃ kathayām āsa Bhārgave.
tac chrutvā Jāmadagnyas tu rāja|putryā vacas tadā
uvāca tāṃ var'|ārohāṃ niścity' ârtha|viniścayam:

"Please tell me the main points," Rama said to her. Then she saluted Rama who blazed like fire. She paid honor to Rama's shining feet with her head, and touched them with her hands that were like lotus petals, and then she stood before him. The sorrowful girl wept, her eyes welling with 177.25
tears, and took refuge with the descendant of Bhrigu, the refuge of all.

RAMA said:

Princess, you are as dear to me as you to are to Srínjaya. Tell me what brings misery to your heart, and I will do as you command.

AMBA replied:

Blessed lord, today I take refuge in you, a man of strict vows. Lord, lift me from the horrifying muddy ocean of grief in which I am sinking!

BHISHMA continued:

As he gazed at her beauty, youth, freshness, and exceptional delicacy, Rama became lost in thought. "What will this girl say?" he wondered, and Rama, Bhrigu's descendant, reflected this way, pondering for a long time, overflowing with pity. Rama addressed the sweet-smiling girl 177.30
once again, saying "Tell me," and she told the whole story, precisely as it happened, to Bhárgava. And when Jamad·agni's son had heard what the princess said, he made his decision about what he would do, and he said to the shapely-hipped girl:

RĀMA uvāca:

preṣayiṣyāmi Bhīṣmāya Kuru|śreṣṭhāya, bhāvini;
kariṣyati vaco mahyaṃ śrutvā ca sa nar'|âdhipaḥ.
na cet kariṣyati vaco may" ôktaṃ Jānhavī|sutaḥ,
dhakṣyāmy ahaṃ raṇe, bhadre, s'|âmātyaṃ śastra|tejasā!
atha vā te matis tatra, rāja|putri, na vartate,
yāvac Chālva|patiṃ vīraṃ yojayāmy atra karmaṇi!

AMB" ôvāca:

177.35 visarjit" âhaṃ Bhīṣmeṇa śrutv" âiva, Bhṛgu|nandana,
Śālva|rāja|gataṃ bhāvaṃ mama pūrvaṃ manīṣitam.
Saubha|rājam upety' âham avocaṃ dur|vacam vacaḥ;
na ca māṃ pratyagṛhṇāt sa cāritrya|pariśaṅkitaḥ.
etat sarvaṃ viniścitya sva|buddhyā, Bhṛgu|nandana,
yad atr' āupayikaṃ kāryaṃ, tac cintayitum arhasi.

mama tu vyasanasy' âsya Bhīṣmo mūlaṃ mahā|vrataḥ,
yen' âhaṃ vaśam ānītā samutkṣipya balāt tadā!
Bhīṣmaṃ jahi, mahā|bāho, yat|kṛte duḥkham īdṛśam
prāpt" âhaṃ, Bhṛgu|śārdūla, carāmy a|priyam uttamam!
177.40 sa hi lubdhaś ca, nīcaś ca, jita|kāśī ca, Bhārgava,
tasmāt pratikriyā kartuṃ yuktā tasmai tvayā, 'n|agha!

eṣa me kriyamāṇāyā Bhāratena tadā, vibho,
abhavadd hṛdi saṃkalpo: ghātayeyaṃ mahā|vratam!
tasmāt kāmaṃ mam' âdy' êmaṃ,
Rāma, sampāday', ân|agha!
jahi Bhīṣmaṃ, mahā|bāho,
yathā Vṛtraṃ puran|daraḥ!

RAMA said:

I will send a message to Bhishma, the greatest of the Kurus, my beautiful girl, and when he hears it that lord of men will do as I tell him. If the son of Jáhnavi does not obey the commands I give him, then I will scorch him and his advisors in battle through the glory of my weapons, my dear! Or, if your intention does not turn in that direction, princess, I will set the hero Lord Shalva to his task!

AMBA replied:

Bhishma released me, descendant of Bhrigu, when he 177.35
heard that my heart had previously gone to King Shalva of its own accord. So I went to the king of Saubha and gave my difficult speech, but he would not accept me, for he had suspicions about my behavior. Having reached a decision on this whole matter by your own wisdom, descendant of Bhrigu, you ought to consider the proper means of action required.

But strict-vowed Bhishma is the root of my troubles, for he brought me under his control, forcibly taking me onto his chariot! Kill Bhishma, long-armed man, for it is through his doing that I have arrived at such misery, tiger of the
Bhrigus, and that I wander in such utter disaster! He is 177.40
greedy, vile, and behaves like a conqueror, Bhárgava, so you ought to wreak vengeance upon him, sinless man!

While Bhárata was treating me this way, lord, my heart's desire was that I might be able to cause the death of the strict-vowed man! Therefore, sinless Rama, grant my desire now! Kill Bhishma, long-armed man, just as Indra, the sacker of cities, killed Vritra!

BHĪṢMA uvāca:

178.1 EVAM UKTAS TADĀ Rāmo «jahi Bhīṣmam! iti,» prabho,
uvāca rudatīṃ kanyāṃ codayantīṃ punaḥ punaḥ:
«Kāśye, na kāmaṃ gṛhṇāmi śastraṃ vai, vara|varṇini,
ṛte brahma|vidāṃ hetoḥ. kim anyat karavāṇi te?
vācā Bhīṣmaś ca Śālvaś ca mama, rājñi, vaś'|ânugau
bhaviṣyato, 'n|avady'|âṅgi, tat kariṣyāmi, mā śucaḥ.
na tu śastraṃ grahīṣyāmi kathañ cid api, bhāvini,
ṛte niyogād viprāṇām, eṣa me samayaḥ kṛtaḥ.»

AMB" ôvāca:

178.5 mama duḥkhaṃ bhagavatā vyapaneyaṃ yatas tataḥ.
tac ca Bhīṣma|prasūtaṃ me; taṃ jah', īśvara, mā|ciram!

RĀMA uvāca:

Kāśi|kanye, punar brūhi, Bhīṣmas te caraṇāv ubhau
śirasā vandan'|ârho 'pi grahīṣyati girā mama.

AMB" ôvāca:

jahi Bhīṣmaṃ raṇe, Rāma, garjantam asuraṃ yathā,
samāhūto raṇe, Rāma, mama ced icchasi priyam.
pratiśrutaṃ ca yad api, tat satyaṃ kartum arhasi.

BHĪṢMA uvāca:

tayoḥ saṃvadator evaṃ, rājan, Rām'|Âmbayos tadā
ṛṣiḥ parama|dharm'|ātmā idaṃ vacanam abravīt:

BHISHMA continued:

TOLD TO KILL Bhishma, my lord, Rama spoke to the weeping girl, as she incessantly urged him, and he said: "Kashi princess, I do not willingly take up weapons, flawlessly complexioned lady, except in the cause of Vedic scholars. What else can I do for you? Bhishma and Shalva will follow the commands I give them, princess. It will happen, entirely faultlessly limbed girl. I will do it, so do not grieve. But I will never take up arms, beautiful girl, except at the command of the brahmins. This is the agreement I have made." 178.1

AMBA replied:

You must eliminate my misery somehow, blessed lord. 178.5
Bhishma was the cause of my pain so kill him, lord, and don't delay!

RAMA said:

Kashi princess, tell me once more and Bhishma will take your feet on his head, despite the fact he deserves worship, at my command.

AMBA replied:

Kill Bhishma in battle, Rama, as he bellows like an *ásura*. Called to battle, Rama, kill him, if you wish to do me a favor. You ought to fulfill your promise!

BHISHMA continued:

While those two, Rama and Amba, were talking together, king, the sage of supremely virtuous soul, Ákrita·vrana, said:

«śaraṇ'|āgatāṃ, mahā|bāho, kanyāṃ na tyaktum arhasi.
yadi Bhīṣmo raṇe, Rāma, samāhūtas tvayā mṛdhe,
178.10 ‹nirjito 'sm' îti› vā brūyāt, kuryād vā vacanaṃ tava,
kṛtam asyā bhavet kāryaṃ kanyāyā, Bhṛgu|nandana,
vākyaṃ satyaṃ ca te, vīra, bhaviṣyati kṛtaṃ, vibho.
iyaṃ c' âpi pratijñā te tadā, Rāma mahā|mune.
jitvā vai kṣatriyān sarvān brāhmaṇeṣu pratiśrutā:
‹brāhmaṇaḥ, kṣatriyo, vaiśyaḥ, śūdraś c' âiva raṇe yadi
brahma|dviḍ bhavitā, taṃ vai haniṣyām' îti,› Bhārgava.
‹śaraṇ'|ârthe prapannānāṃ bhītānāṃ śaraṇ'|ârthinām
na śakṣyāmi parityāgaṃ kartuṃ jīvan kathañ cana;
yaś ca kṛtsnaṃ raṇe kṣatraṃ vijeṣyati samāgatam,
178.15 dīpt'|ātmānam ahaṃ taṃ ca haniṣyām' îti,› Bhārgava.
sa evaṃ vijayī, Rāma, Bhīṣmaḥ Kuru|kul'|ôdvahaḥ;
tena yudhyasva saṅgrāme sametya, Bhṛgu|nandana!»

RĀMA uvāca:

smarāmy ahaṃ pūrva|kṛtāṃ pratijñām, ṛṣi|sattama,
tath" âiva ca cariṣyāmi yathā sāmn" âiva lapsyate.
kāryam etan mahad, brahman, Kāśi|kanyā|mano|gatam.
gamiṣyāmi svayaṃ tatra kanyām ādāya, yatra saḥ.
yadi Bhīṣmo raṇa|ślāghī na kariṣyati me vacaḥ,
haniṣyāmy enam udriktam, iti me niścitā matiḥ.
na hi bāṇā may" ôtsṛṣṭāḥ sajjant' îha śarīriṇām
kāyeṣu. viditaṃ tubhyaḥ purā kṣatriya|saṅgare.

"You ought not to abandon a girl who has come to you for protection, long-armed man. If Bhishma comes to the
fight when you summon him to battle, and declares himself 178.10
defeated, or if he does what you tell him, then the girl's goal will be accomplished, descendant of Bhrigu, and your words will be proved true, lord and hero.

This was also the promise you made, great sage Rama, after you had defeated all kshatriyas. Bhárgava, you vowed to the brahmins: 'I will kill a brahmin, kshatriya, vaishya, or shudra in battle if he should become a hater of brahmins! If any terrified people, seeking protection, come to me for refuge, I will never be able to abandon them as long as I live! If someone should conquer the entire gathered kshatriya
class in battle, I will kill that proud man!' That's what you 178.15
said, Bhárgava. So then, Rama, Bhishma, the propagator of the Kuru lineage, has achieved such a victory; so fight him when you meet him in battle, descendant of Bhrigu!"

RAMA replied:

I remember the promise I made before, greatest of sages. But I will try to fulfill it by negotiation alone. The task that the Kashi king's daughter has set her mind upon is indeed great, brahmin. I will go myself to where Bhishma is, taking the girl with me. If Bhishma trusts in battle and does not comply with my orders then I will kill the haughty man. This is my decision. The arrows I shoot do not stick in embodied creatures, but pass straight through! You know that from my battle against the kshatriyas long ago.

178.20 evam uktvā tato Rāmaḥ saha tair brahma|vādibhiḥ
prayāṇāya matiṃ kṛtvā samuttasthau mahā|tapāḥ.
tatas te tām uṣitvā tu rajanīṃ tatra tāpasāḥ
hut'|âgnayo japta|japyāḥ pratasthur maj|jighāṃsayā.
abhyagacchat tato Rāmaḥ saha tair brahma|vādibhiḥ
Kuru|kṣetraṃ, mahā|rāja, kanyayā saha, Bhārata.
nyaviśanta tataḥ sarve parigṛhya Sarasvatīm
tāpasās te mah"|ātmāno Bhṛgu|śreṣṭha|puraskṛtāḥ.

BHĪṢMA uvāca:

tatas tṛtīye divase saṃdideśa vyavasthitaḥ,
«kuru priyaṃ sa me, rājan, prāpto 'sm', îti» mahā|vrataḥ.
178.25 tam āgatam ahaṃ śrutvā viṣay'|ântaṃ mahā|balam
abhyagacchaṃ javen' āśu prītyā tejo|nidhiṃ prabhum,
gāṃ puras|kṛtya, rāj'|êndra, brāhmaṇaiḥ parivāritaḥ,
ṛtvigbhir deva|kalpaiś ca, tath" âiva ca puro|hitaiḥ.
sa mām abhigataṃ dṛṣṭvā Jāmadagnyaḥ pratāpavān
pratijagrāha tāṃ pūjāṃ, vacanaṃ c' êdam abravīt:

RĀMA uvāca:

Bhīṣma, kāṃ buddhim āsthāya Kāśi|rāja|sutā tadā
a|kāmena tvay" ānītā, punaś c' âiva visarjitā?
vibhraṃśitā tvayā h' îyaṃ dharmād āste yaśasvinī!
parāmṛṣṭāṃ tvayā h' îmāṃ ko hi gantum ih' ârhati?
178.30 pratyākhyātā hi Śālvena, tvay" ānīt" êti, Bhārata,
tasmād imāṃ man|niyogāt pratigṛhṇīṣva, Bhārata.
sva|dharmaṃ, puruṣa|vyāghra, rāja|putrī labhatv iyam.
na yuktas tv avamāno 'yaṃ rājñā† kartuṃ tvayā, 'n|agha!

Having said this, Rama, along with the expounders of 178.20
the Vedas, then turned his mind to leaving, and the great ascetic stood up. The ascetics spent the night there and then made offerings into the fire, said their prayers, and set out wishing to kill me.

Rama went with the expounders of the Vedas and the girl to Kuru·kshetra, mighty Bhárata sovereign. The high-souled ascetics, led by the greatest of the Bhrigus, all set up camp when they came up to the river Sarásvati.

BHISHMA continued:

On the third day after he had settled there, the strict-vowed man sent me a message, saying, "Do what pleases
me, king, for I have arrived." Once I heard that the pow- 178.25
erful lord, an ocean of splendor, had reached the boundary of the land, I set out quickly with pleasure. I placed a cow at the head of the procession, lord of kings, and was surrounded by brahmins, god-like sacrificial priests, and likewise by family priests. When majestic Jamad·agni's son saw me coming, he accepted the honor and said these words:

RAMA said:

Bhishma, what were you thinking when you led off the daughter of the king of Kashi, though you did not desire her, and then let her go again? This illustrious lady has been caused to fall from virtue because of you! Who ought to
marry her now, when she's been touched by you? Shalva 178.30
rejected her because you led her off, Bhárata. So take this lady for yourself, at my command, Bhárata. Let the princess undertake her duties, tiger-like man. It is not proper for you to treat her so disgracefully, and you a king, sinless man!

tatas taṃ vai vimanasam
udīkṣy' âham ath' âbruvam:
«n' âham enāṃ punar dadyāṃ,
brahman, bhrātre kathañ cana.
‹Śālvasy' âham iti› prāha purā mām eva, Bhārgava,
mayā c' âiv' âbhyanujñātā gat" êyaṃ nagaraṃ prati.
na bhayān, n' âpy anukrośān, n' ârtha|lobhān, na kāmyayā
kṣātraṃ dharmam ahaṃ jahyām, iti me vratam āhitam.»
178.35 atha mām abravīd Rāmaḥ krodha|paryākul'|ēkṣaṇaḥ:
«na kariṣyasi ced etad vākyaṃ me, nara|puṅgava,
haniṣyāmi sah'|âmātyaṃ tvām ady'! êti» punaḥ punaḥ
saṃraṃbhād abravīd Rāmaḥ krodha|paryākul'|ēkṣaṇaḥ.
tam ahaṃ gīrbhir iṣṭābhiḥ punaḥ punar, arin|dama,
ayācaṃ Bhṛgu|śārdūlaṃ; na c' âiva praśaśāma saḥ.
praṇamya tam ahaṃ mūrdhnā
bhūyo brāhmaṇa|sattamam
abruvaṃ: «kāraṇaṃ kiṃ tad
yat tvaṃ yuddhaṃ may" êcchasi?
iṣv|astraṃ mama bālasya bhavat" âiva catur|vidham
upadiṣṭaṃ, mahā|bāho. śiṣyo 'smi tava, Bhārgava.»
178.40 tato mām abravīd Rāmaḥ krodha|saṃrakta|locanaḥ:
«jānīṣe māṃ guruṃ, Bhīṣma, gṛhṇās' îmāṃ na c' âiva ha
sutāṃ Kāśyasya, Kauravya, mat|priy'|ârthaṃ, mahā|mate!
na hi te vidyate śāntir anyathā, Kuru|nandana!
gṛhāṇ' êmāṃ, mahā|bāho, rakṣasva kulam ātmanaḥ.
tvayā vibhraṃśitā h' îyaṃ bhartāraṃ n' âdhigacchati.»
tathā bruvantaṃ tam ahaṃ Rāmaṃ para|purañ|jayam
«n' âitad evaṃ punar bhāvi, brahma'|rṣe. kiṃ śrameṇa te?
gurutvaṃ tvayi saṃprekṣya, Jāmadagnya, purātanam,
prasādaye tvāṃ, bhagavaṃs; tyakt" âiṣā tu purā mayā.

Seeing him depressed, I then said: "I will never give her
to my brother again, brahmin. It was she who told me in the
past, 'I belong to Shalva,' Bhárgava, and it was I who gave
her leave to go to the city. I cannot destroy the kshatriya
law from fear, fury, greed for wealth, or lust. This is the vow
I set down."

Then, eyes rolling in fury, Rama said to me: "If you 178.35
do not do as I tell you, bull-like man, I will kill you and
your advisors this very day!" He repeated this over and over
again, his eyes rolling in fury, enraged as he was; and though
I begged the tiger-like Bhrigu time and again with agreeable
speech, enemy-tamer, he was not appeased.

So, bowing my head to him, I spoke to the greatest of
brahmins again: "What is your reason for wanting battle
with me? It was you who taught me the fourfold science of
archery, long-armed Bhárgava. I am your pupil!"

Then Rama, eyes red with fury, said to me: "You know 178.40
I am your guru, Bhishma, and yet you do not accept this
daughter of the king of Kashi in order to please me, high-
minded Kaurávya! I will certainly not make peace with you
any other way, descendant of Kuru. Accept this girl, long-
armed man, and protect your own family. She was disgraced
by you, and she will not find a husband."

I replied to Rama, the sacker of enemy cities who was
commanding me in this way, saying:

"This will never happen, brahmin sage. What is the point
of your exertion? Reflecting on your position as teacher in
years gone by, son of Jamad·agni, I beg you, lord, for I gave
this woman up long ago. Which man who understands the 178.45

178.45 ko jātu para|bhāvāṃ hi nārīṃ vyālīm iva sthitām
vāsayeta gṛhe jānan strīṇāṃ doṣān mah"|âtyayān?
na bhayād Vāsavasy' âpi dharmaṃ jahyāṃ, mahā|vrata.
prasīda, mā vā, yad vā te kāryaṃ, tat kuru mā|ciram.

ayaṃ c' âpi, viśuddh'|ātman, purāṇe śrūyate, vibho,
Maruttena, mahā|buddhe, gītaḥ śloko mah"|ātmanā:
‹guror apy avaliptasya kāry'|â|kāryam a|jānataḥ
utpatha|pratipannasya parityāgo vidhīyate.›
sa tvaṃ gurur iti premṇā mayā saṃmānito bhṛśam;
guru|vṛttiṃ na jānīṣe, tasmād yotsyāmi vai tvayā!

178.50 guruṃ na hanyām samare, brāhmaṇaṃ ca viśeṣataḥ,
viśeṣatas tapo|vṛddham, evaṃ kṣāntaṃ mayā tava.
udyat'|êṣum atho dṛṣṭvā brāhmaṇaṃ kṣatra|bandhuvat
yo hanyāt samare kruddhaṃ yudhyantam a|palāyinam,
brahma|hatyā na tasya syād, iti dharmeṣu niścayaḥ.
kṣatriyāṇāṃ sthito dharme kṣatriyo 'smi, tapo|dhana.

yo yathā vartate yasmiṃs, tathā tasmin† pravartayan
n' â|dharmaṃ samavāpnoti, na c' â|śreyaś ca vindati.
arthe vā yadi vā dharme samartho deśa|kāla|vit
artha|saṃśayam āpannaḥ śreyān niḥsaṃśayo naraḥ.
178.55 yasmāt saṃśayite 'py arthe '|yathā|nyāyaṃ pravartase,
tasmād yotsyāmi sahitas tvayā, Rāma, mah"|āhave.

highly disastrous sins of women would allow a woman who is in love with another man to live in his house, for she is like a snake? Not even from fear of Vásava would I break the law, strict-vowed man. Pardon me or do what you must, without delay.

This *shloka*, pure-souled lord of great wisdom, is handed down in the Puranas, sung by high-souled Marútta: 'The abandonment of a guru is permitted if he is conceited, unaware of what should or should not be done, or if he treads the wrong path.' I honor you a great deal out of affection, because you are my guru. But you do not understand a guru's proper conduct, and so I will fight you!

But I would not kill a teacher in battle, and particularly 178.50
not a brahmin, and even more especially so if he had developed asceticism. This is why I forgive you. The man who sees a brahmin enraged, his arrows raised like a kshatriya, fighting rather than fleeing, and kills him, is not actually guilty of brahmanicide. This is ascertained in the scriptures of law. I am a kshatriya and I abide by the duties of kshatriyas, sage of ascetic wealth.

One does not gain any demerit nor disadvantage by treating someone just as they treat you. When a man who understands the proper occasion and place, and is accomplished in profit or virtue, is filled with doubt over a matter, he
should go for the best option without any hesitation. There- 178.55
fore, since your goal is dubious and you are acting improperly, I will fight with you, Rama, in a mighty battle.

paśya me bāhu|vīryaṃ ca, vikramaṃ c' âtimānuṣam!
evaṃ|gate 'pi tu mayā yac chakyaṃ, Bhṛgu|nandana,
tat kariṣye; Kuru|kṣetre yotsye, vipra, tvayā saha.
dvandve, Rāma, yath" êṣṭaṃ te, sajjī|bhava, mahā|dyute.
tatra tvaṃ nihato, Rāma, mayā śara|śat'|ârditaḥ
prāpsyase nirjitāl̃ lokāñ śastra|pūto mahā|raṇe.
sa gaccha, vinivartasva Kuru|kṣetraṃ, raṇa|priya;
tatr' âiṣyāmi, mahā|bāho, yuddhāya tvāṃ, tapo|dhana.
178.60 api yatra tvayā, Rāma, kṛtaṃ śaucaṃ purā pituḥ,
tatr' âham api hatvā tvāṃ śaucaṃ kart" âsmi, Bhārgava.
tatra, Rāma, samāgaccha tvaritaṃ, yuddha|durmada,
vyapaneṣyāmi te darpaṃ paurāṇaṃ brāhmaṇa|bruvaḥ.
yac c' âpi katthase, Rāma, bahuśaḥ parivatsare,
‹nirjitāḥ kṣatriyā loke may" âiken' êti,› tac chṛṇu.
na tadā jātavān Bhīṣmaḥ; kṣatriyo v" âpi mad|vidhaḥ.
paścāj jātāni tejāṃsi, tṛṇeṣu jvalitaṃ tvayā!
yas te yuddha|mayaṃ darpaṃ kāmaṃ ca vyapanāśayet,
so 'haṃ jāto, mahā|bāho, Bhīṣmaḥ para|purañ|jayaḥ
vyapaneṣyāmi te darpaṃ yuddhe, Rāma, na saṃśayaḥ!»

BHĪṢMA uvāca:

178.65 tato mām abravīd Rāmaḥ prahasann iva, Bhārata:
«diṣṭyā, Bhīṣma, mayā sārdhaṃ yoddhum icchasi saṅgare!
ayaṃ gacchāmi, Kauravya, Kuru|kṣetraṃ tvayā saha.
bhāṣitaṃ te kariṣyāmi; tatr' āgaccha, paraṃ|tapa!
tatra tvāṃ nihataṃ mātā mayā śara|śat'|ācitam

Look at the strength of my arms and my superhuman prowess! This being the case, I will do whatever I can, descendant of Bhrigu. I will fight with you, brahmin, on Kuru·kshetra. Great glorious Rama, equip yourself as you please for the duel. Rama, when you are struck by me and pained by my hundreds of arrows, you will reach those worlds you have won, purified by my weapons in the great battle.

So go. Turn back to Kuru·kshetra, war-crazed man, and I will go there, long-armed sage of ascetic wealth, to fight you. There I will purify you by killing you, Bhárgava, just 178.60
as you purified your father, Rama. Go there quickly, Rama, battle-lusting sage, and I will destroy your legendary pride, brahmin in name alone as you are.

You boasted for many years, Rama, that you defeated all the warriors on earth singlehandedly. But listen. At that time I, Bhishma, was not born; nor was there a warrior like me. Splendid men were born later, and all you scorched was mere straw! The man who could annihilate your pride and love for war has been born. It is I, Bhishma, the sacker of enemy cities, long-armed man. I will destroy your pride in war, Rama. Have no doubt about that!"

BHISHMA continued:

At that point Rama almost laughed, Bhárata, and he said 178.65
to me:

"It is fortunate, Bhishma, that you want to fight me in battle! I will go with you to Kuru·kshetra, Kaurávya. I will do as you say, so go there, enemy-scorcher! Let your mother Jáhnavi gaze at your dead body, covered with my hundreds

Jānhavī paśyatāṃ, Bhīṣma, gṛdhra|kaṅka|bal'|âśanam!

kṛpaṇaṃ tvām abhiprekṣya siddha|cāraṇa|sevitā
mayā vinihataṃ devī rodatām adya, pārthiva,
a|tad|arhā mahā|bhāgā Bhagīratha|sut" ân|aghā,
yā tvām ajījanan mandaṃ yuddha|kāmukam āturam!
178.70 ehi gaccha mayā, Bhīṣma yuddha|kāmuka, dur|mada,
gṛhāṇa sarvaṃ, Kauravya, rath'|ādi, Bharata'|rṣabha!»

iti bruvāṇaṃ tam ahaṃ Rāmaṃ para|purañ|jayam
praṇamya śirasā Rāmam, «evam astv! ity» ath' âbruvam.
evam uktvā yayau Rāmaḥ Kuru|kṣetraṃ yuyutsayā,
praviśya nagaraṃ c' âhaṃ Satyavatyai nyavedayam.

tataḥ kṛta|svasty|ayano, mātrā ca pratinanditaḥ,
dvijātīn vācya puṇy'|âhaṃ svasti c' âiva, mahā|dyute,
ratham āsthāya ruciraṃ rājataṃ pāṇḍurair hayaiḥ,
s'|ûpaskaraṃ, sv|adhiṣṭhānaṃ, vaiyāghra|parivāraṇam,
178.75 upapannaṃ mahā|śastraiḥ, sarv'|ôpakaraṇ'|ânvitam,
tat kulīnena vīreṇa haya|śāstra|vidā raṇe
yattaṃ sūtena śiṣṭena, bahuśo dṛṣṭa|karmaṇā;

daṃśitaḥ pāṇḍureṇ' âhaṃ kavacena vapuṣmatā,
pāṇḍuraṃ kārmukaṃ gṛhya prāyāṃ, Bharata|sattama,
pāṇḍureṇ' ātapa|treṇa dhriyamāṇena mūrdhani,
pāṇḍuraiś c' âpi vyajanair vījyamāno, nar'|âdhipa.
śukla|vāsāḥ, sit'|ôṣṇīṣaḥ, sarva|śukla|vibhūṣaṇaḥ,
stūyamāno jay'|āśīrbhir niṣkramya gaja|s'|āhvayāt

of arrows, Bhishma, as food for vultures and herons and crows!

Let the goddess, worshipped by *siddhas* and *cháranas*, watch you being pitifully killed by me and weep today, king! The noble and sinless river, daughter of Bhagi·ratha, does not deserve to see it, for she gave birth to you, idiotic, battle-lusting, and sick though you may be! Come on 178.70
then, go with me, mad battle-lusting Bhishma, taking all your equipment, chariots and so on, Kaurávya bull of the Bharatas!"

So I bowed my head to Rama, sacker of enemy cities, as he spoke in this way, and said to Rama: "So be it!" Given this answer, Rama went to Kuru·kshetra, ready to fight, and I entered the city and told Sátyavati what had happened.

Once the blessings for success were performed and I had been blessed by my mother, I made the brahmins speak holy beatitudes over me, great glorious king, and then I mounted my gleaming, well-built, well-designed silver chariot covered with tigerskin and yoked with white horses.
It was equipped with fantastic weapons and furnished with 178.75
every tool. It was driven in battle by a well-born hero experienced in horse-lore; a trained charioteer who had witnessed my deeds many times.

I was armored with beautiful white mail, and taking my white bow I set out, greatest of the Bharatas, with my white umbrella held over my head while I was fanned by white fans, lord of men. So, dressed and turbaned in white and decorated entirely with white ornaments, I left the elephant-named city of Hástina·pura, being praised with victory

Kuru|kṣetraṃ raṇa|kṣetram upāyāṃ, Bharata'|rṣabha.
178.80 te hayāś coditās tena sūtena param'|āhave
avahan māṃ bhṛśam, rājan, mano|māruta|raṃhasaḥ.
gatv" âhaṃ tat Kuru|kṣetraṃ, sa ca Rāmaḥ pratāpavān,
yuddhāya sahasā, rājan, parākrāntau parasparam.
tataḥ saṃdarśane 'tiṣṭhaṃ Rāmasy' âtitapasvinaḥ,
pragṛhya śaṅkha|pravaraṃ tataḥ prādhamam uttamam.

tatas tatra dvijā, rājaṃs, tāpasāś ca van'|âukasaḥ
apaśyanta raṇaṃ divyaṃ devāḥ s'|Êndra|gaṇās tadā.
tato divyāni mālyāni prādur āsaṃs tatas tataḥ,
vāditrāṇī ca divyāni, megha|vṛndāni c' âiva ha.
178.85 tatas te tāpasāḥ sarve Bhārgavasy' ânuyāyinaḥ
prekṣakāḥ samapadyanta parivārya raṇ'|âjiram.

tato mām abravīd devī sarva|bhūta|hit'|âiṣiṇī
mātā sva|rūpiṇī, rājan, «kim idaṃ te cikīrṣitam?
gatv" âhaṃ Jāmadagnyaṃ tu prayāciṣye, Kur'|ûdvaha,
‹Bhīṣmeṇa saha mā yotsīḥ śiṣyeṇ' êti› punaḥ punaḥ.
mā m" âivaṃ, putra, nirbandhaṃ kuru vipreṇa, pārthiva,
Jāmadagnyena samare yoddhum ity eva bhartsayat!
kiṃ na vai kṣatriya|haṇo Hara|tulya|parākramaḥ
viditaḥ, putra, Rāmas te, yatas taṃ yoddhum icchasi?»
178.90 tato 'ham abruvaṃ devīm abhivādya kṛt'|âñjaliḥ
sarvaṃ tad, Bharata|śreṣṭha, yathā vṛttaṃ svayaṃvare,
yathā ca Rāmo, rāj'|êndra, mayā pūrvaṃ pracoditaḥ,
Kāśi|rāja|sutāyāś ca yathā karma purātanam.
tataḥ sā Rāmam abhyetya jananī me mahā|nadī

benedictions, and made my way to Kuru·kshetra, the field of battle, bull of the Bharatas.

My horses, fleet as the wind or thought, bore me swiftly 178.80
to that great battle, king, driven on by the charioteer. And once I had arrived at Kuru·kshetra, majestic Rama and I fiercely demonstrated our prowess to each other for the fight, king. Then, standing in view of the exceptional ascetic Rama, I picked up my excellent conch shell and blew it loudly.

The brahmins, forest-dwelling ascetics, and hosts of gods led by Indra were there watching the celestial battle, king. Then at that moment there suddenly appeared divine garlands and heavenly music and cloud clusters. And all the 178.85
ascetics who followed the Bhárgava stood as spectators, surrounding the battlefield.

My mother, the goddess who wishes all creatures well, appeared to me in her own form, king, and said: "What is it that you want to do? I will go to Jamad·agni's son and beg him repeatedly, son of Kuru's line, saying 'Don't fight with your pupil Bhishma!' As for you, my royal son, don't be so stubborn with a brahmin, threatening to fight in battle with Jamad·agni's son! My son, do you not know that Rama, the man who you wish to fight, equals Shiva in prowess and is the destroyer of the kshatriya class?"

I saluted the goddess with joined hands, and told her ev- 178.90
erything just as it had happened at the bridegroom choice, greatest of the Bharatas, how I had previously urged Rama, O lord of kings, and what the daughter of the king of Kashi had done before that. Then my mother, the mighty river,

mad|arthaṃ tam ṛṣiṃ vīkṣya kṣamayām āsa Bhārgavam.
«Bhīṣmeṇa saha mā yotsīḥ śiṣyen'! êti» vaco 'bravīt;
sa ca tām āha yācantīṃ: «Bhīṣmam eva nivartaya!
na ca me kurute kāmam ity ahaṃ tam upāgamam!»

SAÑJAYA† uvāca:

tato Gaṅgā suta|snehād Bhīṣmaṃ punar upāgamat;
na c' âsyāś c' âkarod vākyaṃ krodha|paryākul'|ēkṣaṇaḥ.
178.95 ath' âdṛśyata dharm'|ātmā Bhṛgu|śreṣṭho mahā|tapāḥ,
āhvayām āsa ca tadā yuddhāya dvija|sattamaḥ.

made her way to Rama and began to beg the Bhárgava sage for my sake.

She said to him, "Don't fight with your pupil Bhishma!" But he answered her, as she begged, by saying: "Turn Bhishma back! He refuses to do what I want, so I have confronted him!"

SÁNJAYA said:

So the river Ganges returned to Bhishma once more, out of love for her son, but he would not do as she asked, and his eyes rolled in fury. Then the virtuous-souled mighty as- 178.95
cetic, the best of the Bhrigus, appeared, and the greatest of brahmins challenged him to battle.

179–184

# BHISHMA AND RAMA'S DUEL BEGINS

BHĪṢMA uvāca:

179.1 TAM AHAṂ smayann iva
raṇe pratyabhāṣaṃ vyavasthitam:
«bhūmi|ṣṭhaṃ n' ôtsahe yoddhuṃ
bhavantaṃ ratham āsthitaḥ.
āroha syandanaṃ, vīra, kavacaṃ ca, mahā|bhuja,
badhāna samare, Rāma, yadi yoddhuṃ may" êcchasi.»
tato mām abravīd Rāmaḥ smayamāno raṇ'|âjire:
«ratho me medinī, Bhīṣma, vāhā vedāḥ sad|aśvavat,
sūtaś ca mātariśvā vai, kavacaṃ veda|mātaraḥ.
su|saṃvīto raṇe tābhir yotsye 'haṃ, Kuru|nandana!»
179.5 evaṃ bruvāṇo, Gāndhāre, Rāmo māṃ satya|vikramaḥ
śara|vrātena mahatā sarvataḥ pratyavārayat.
tato 'paśyaṃ Jāmadagnyaṃ ratha|madhye vyavasthitam,
sarv'|āyudha|vare, śrīmaty, adbhut'|ôpama|darśane,
manasā vihite, puṇye, vistīrṇe, nagar'|ôpame,
divy'|âśva|yuji, sannaddhe, kāñcanena vibhūṣite,
kavacena, mahā|bāho,
som'|ârka|kṛta|lakṣmaṇā.
dhanur|dharo, baddha|tūṇo,
baddha|godh'|âṅgulitra|vān,
sārathyaṃ kṛtavāṃs tatra yuyutsor Akṛtavraṇaḥ
sakhā veda|vid, atyantaṃ dayito Bhārgavasya ha.
179.10 āhvayānaḥ sa māṃ yuddhe mano harṣayat' îva me,
punaḥ punar abhikrośann, «abhiyāh'! îti» Bhārgavaḥ,
tam ādityam iv' ôdyantam an|ādhṛṣyaṃ, mahā|balam,
kṣatriy'|ânta|karaṃ Rāmam ekam ekaḥ samāsadam!

BHISHMA continued:

I SMIRKED AT RAMA as he stood stationed for battle, and I said: "I do not dare to fight you when you are standing on the ground and I am standing on a chariot. Mount your car, hero, and attach armor to yourself for battle, long-armed Rama, if you want to fight with me." But Rama smiled on the battlefield and answered me, saying: "The earth is my chariot, Bhishma, and the Vedas, like superb horses, are my steeds. The wind is my charioteer, and the mothers in the Vedas* are my armor. Well covered by these, I will fight you in battle, descendant of Kuru!" 179.1

Saying this, son of Gandhári, Rama, whose strength was his truth, veiled me with an enormous shower of arrows on all sides. I saw Jamad·agni's son stationed in the middle of a glorious and miraculous spectacle of a chariot which was superbly equipped with every weapon. Created by his mind, it was holy and large as a city, yoked with celestial horses, defensively protected, decorated with gold, armored, and branded with a sun and moon, long-armed man. 179.5

Carrying a bow, with a quiver tied to him and his fingers bound in straps, Ákrita·vrana, the law-wise and eternally close friend of the battle-ready Bhárgava, acted as charioteer. Bhárgava kept repeatedly summoning me to battle 179.10
in his fury, saying "Attack!" And by so doing, he seemed to bring joy to my heart. So I singlehandedly attacked the lone, mighty, and unassailable Rama, bringer of death to kshatriyas, like the rising sun!

tato 'haṃ bāṇa|pāteṣu triṣu vāhān nigṛhya vai,
avatīryan dhanur nyasya padātir ṛṣi|sattamam
abhyāgacchaṃ. tadā Rāmam arciṣyan dvija|sattamam,
abhivādya c' âinaṃ vidhivad abruvaṃ vākyam uttamam:
«yotsye tvayā raṇe, Rāma, sadṛśen' âdhikena vā,
guruṇā dharma|śīlena. jayam āśāsva me, vibho.»

RĀMA uvāca:

179.15 evam etat, Kuru|śreṣṭha, kartavyaṃ bhūtim icchatā;
dharmo hy eṣa, mahā|bāho, viśiṣṭaiḥ saha yudhyatām.
śapeyaṃ tvāṃ, na ced evam āgacchethā, viśām pate.
yudhyasva tvaṃ raṇe yatto, dhairyam ālambya, Kaurava.
na tu te jayam āśāse; tvāṃ vijetum ahaṃ sthitaḥ.
gaccha, yudhyasva dharmeṇa! prīto 'smi caritena te.

tato 'haṃ taṃ namas|kṛtya ratham āruhya sa|tvaraḥ
prādhmāpayaṃ raṇe śaṅkhaṃ punar hema|pariṣkṛtam.
tato yuddhaṃ samabhavan mama tasya ca, Bhārata,
divasān su|bahūn, rājan, paraspara|jigīṣayā.
179.20 sa me tasmin raṇe pūrvaṃ prāharat kaṅka|patribhiḥ
ṣaṣṭyā śataiś ca navabhiḥ śarāṇāṃ nata|parvaṇām.
catvāras tena me vāhāḥ, sūtaś c' âiva, viśāṃ pate,
pratiruddhās; tath" âiv' âhaṃ samare daṃśitaḥ sthitaḥ.

namas|kṛtya ca devebhyo, brāhmaṇebhyo viśeṣataḥ,
tam ahaṃ smayann iva raṇe pratyabhāṣaṃ vyavasthitam:
«ācāryatā mānitā me nirmaryāde hy api tvayi,
bhūyaś ca śṛṇu me, brahman, sampadaṃ dharma|saṃgrahe.
ye te vedāḥ śarīra|sthā, brāhmaṇyaṃ yac ca te mahat,

Then, once I was three arrow-flight's distance away from
him, I restrained my horses, put down my bow, and went on
foot to that greatest of sages. Reaching him, I worshipped
Rama, the best of brahmins, and duly saluted him, saying
these fine words to him: "I will fight in battle with you, my
guru of virtuous conduct, regardless of whether you are my
equal or superior. Wish me victory, my lord."

RAMA replied:

The man who wishes for good fortune ought to behave 179.15
just like this, greatest of the Kurus, for this is indeed the
law for those who fight against their superiors, long-armed
man. Had you not approached me in this manner, lord
of earth, I would have cursed you. Fight me in battle and
strive, sustaining your fortitude, Káurava. I do not hope for
your victory, for I am intent on defeating you myself. Go!
Fight justly! I am pleased with your conduct.

I bowed to him, quickly climbed aboard my chariot, and
blew my gilt conch shell once more. Then the battle between us began, Bhárata, and it lasted many days, king, as
we both longed to defeat each other. Rama struck me first 179.20
in the battle with nine hundred and sixty smooth, heron-
feathered arrows. My four horses and my charioteer were
driven back, lord of earth, but I stood my ground, armored
for conflict.

Bowing to the gods and the brahmins in particular, I almost smiled as I addressed Rama, stationed for battle: "I have respected you as my teacher despite your transgressions towards me. Now listen again, brahmin, to what is advantageous in the acquisition of law. I do not hit at you

tapaś ca te mahat taptaṃ, na tebhyaḥ praharāmy aham.
179.25 prahāre kṣatra|dharmasya yaṃ, Rāma, tvaṃ samāśritaḥ,
brāhmaṇaḥ kṣatriyatvaṃ hi yāti śastra|samudyamāt.
paśya me dhanuṣo vīryaṃ! paśya bāhvor balaṃ mama!
eṣa te kārmukaṃ, vīra, cchinadmi niśit'|êṣuṇā!»

tasy' âham niśitaṃ bhallaṃ cikṣepa, Bharata'|rṣabha;
ten' âsya dhanuṣaḥ koṭiṃ chittvā bhūmāv apātayam,
tath" âiva ca pṛṣatkānāṃ śatāni nata|parvaṇām
cikṣepa kaṅka|patrāṇāṃ Jāmadagnya|rathaṃ prati;
kāye viṣaktās tu tadā vāyunā samudīritāḥ
celuḥ kṣaranto rudhiraṃ nāgā iva ca te śarāḥ.
179.30 kṣataj'|ôkṣita|sarv'|âṅgaḥ kṣaran sa rudhiraṃ raṇe
babhau Rāmas tadā, rājan, Merur dhātum iv' ôtsṛjan.
hemant'|ânte 'śoka iva rakta|stabaka|maṇḍitaḥ
babhau Rāmas tathā, rājan, praphulla iva kiṃśukaḥ.

tato 'nyad dhanur ādāya Rāmaḥ krodha|samanvitaḥ
hema|puṅkhān su|niśitāñ śarāṃs tān hi vavarṣa saḥ.
te samāsādya māṃ raudrā bahudhā marma|bhedinaḥ
akampayan mahā|vegāḥ sarp'|ânala|viṣ'|ôpamāḥ!
tam ahaṃ samavaṣṭabhya punar ātmānam āhave
śata|saṃkhyaiḥ śaraiḥ kruddhas tadā Rāmam avākiram.
179.35 sa tair agny|arka|saṅkāśaiḥ śarair āśī|viṣ'|ôpamaiḥ
śitair abhyardito Rāmo manda|cetā iv' âbhavat.

n the Vedas that reside in your body, your great brahminhood, or the great asceticism you have developed. I will hit 179.25
at the kshatriya duties upon which you rely, for a brahmin
eaches kshatriyahood by taking up weapons. Behold the
power of my bow! Behold the strength of my arms! I will
break your bow, hero, with a sharpened arrow!"

I fired a sharp bear-tipped shaft at him, bull of the Bharatas, and having broken off his bow's curved end, I felled it to the ground. I fired hundreds of smooth, spotted, heron-feathered arrows at Jamad·agni's son's chariot. Penetrating his body and carried by the wind, the arrows flew, vomiting blood, like snakes.

With all his limbs dripping from wounds and streaming 179.30
blood in battle, Rama glistened, my king, like Mount Meru
spewing out its elements. Rama glistened like an *ashóka* tree
at the end of winter, adorned with red blossoms, or like a
*kínshuka* tree in bloom, my king.

Filled with rage, Rama took up another bow and showered me with golden-tipped, extremely sharp arrows. The
fierce, vitals-piercing, extremely forceful arrows rushed at
me from all directions, making me shake in terror, like the
fiery poison of snakes! So, holding myself up for battle once
more, I furiously sprayed Rama with hundreds of arrows.
And pierced by those sharp arrows that resembled fire or the 179.35
sun and felt like poisonous snakes, Rama seemed to have
lost his mind.

tato 'haṃ kṛpay" āviṣṭo
viṣṭabhy' ātmānam ātmanā,
«dhig dhig! ity abruvaṃ yuddhaṃ,
kṣatra|dharmaṃ ca,» Bhārata.
a|sakṛc c' âbruvaṃ, rājañ, śoka|vega|pariplutaḥ,
«aho bata! kṛtaṃ pāpaṃ may" êdaṃ kṣatra|dharmaṇā,
gurur dvi|jātir dharm'|ātmā yad evaṃ pīḍitaḥ śaraiḥ!»
tato na prāharaṃ bhūyo Jāmadagnyāya, Bhārata.
ath' âvatāpya pṛthivīṃ pūṣā divasa|saṃkṣaye
jagām' âstaṃ sahasr'|âṃśus; tato yuddham upāramat.

BHĪṢMA uvāca:

180.1 ĀTMANAS TU TATAḤ sūto, hayānāṃ ca, viśām pate,
mama c' âpanayām āsa śalyān kuśala|sammataḥ.
snāt'|âpavṛttais tura|gair labdha|toyair, a|vihvalaiḥ
prabhāte codite sūrye tato yuddham avartata.
dṛṣṭvā māṃ tūrṇam āyāntaṃ
daṃśitaṃ syandane sthitam
akarod ratham atyarthaṃ
Rāmaḥ sajjaṃ pratāpavān.
tato 'haṃ Rāmam āyāntaṃ dṛṣṭvā samara|kāṅkṣiṇam
dhanuḥ|śreṣṭhaṃ samutsṛjya sahas" âvataraṃ rathāt.
180.5 abhivādya tath" âiv' âhaṃ ratham āruhya, Bhārata,
yuyutsur Jāmadagnyasya pramukhe vīta|bhīḥ sthitaḥ.
tato 'haṃ śara|varṣeṇa mahatā samavākiram,
sa ca māṃ śara|varṣeṇa varṣantaṃ samavākirat.
saṃkruddho Jāmadagnyas tu punar eva su|tejitān
sampraiṣīn me śarān ghorān dīpt'|âsyān uragān iva.
tato 'haṃ niśitair bhallaiḥ śataśo 'tha sahasraśaḥ

Then, filled with pity, I stopped myself of my own accord, and said, Bhárata, "Damn war! Damn a kshatriya's duty!" Overwhelmed by the force of my grief, king, I cried out time and again, "Oh! Alas! I have committed a sin through my kshatriya law, for my virtuous-souled brahmin guru is tormented by my arrows!" And I did not strike Jamad·agni's son again, Bhárata.

Eventually the thousand-rayed sun, having heated the earth, set at the end of the day, and our battle came to an end.

BHISHMA continued:

MY CHARIOTEER, highly regarded for his skill, removed 180.1
the arrows from himself, from the horses, and from me, lord of earth. But once the horses had finished bathing, drunk some water, and got back their courage, the battle resumed when the sun rose the next morning.

When majestic Rama saw me coming towards him at speed, standing armored on my car, he made sure his chariot was ready for every eventuality. Then, when I saw Rama approaching, hoping for battle, I let go of my greatest of
bows and quickly jumped out of my chariot. I saluted him 180.5
as before, climbed back onto my chariot, Bhárata, and stationed myself fearlessly before Jamad·agni's son, ready to fight.

I sprayed him with a thick downpour of arrows, and as I did so he sprayed me in return with a shower of shafts. Furious, Jamad·agni's son once again shot highly energetic and horrifying arrows at me, like blazing-mouthed snakes. I countered them with sharp bear-tipped arrows, by the hun-

acchidaṃ sahasā, rājann, antarikṣe punaḥ punaḥ.
tatas tv astrāṇi divyāni Jāmadagnyaḥ pratāpavān
mayi prayojayām āsa; tāny ahaṃ pratyaṣedhayam
180.10 astrair eva, mahā|bāho, cikīrṣann adhikāṃ kriyām.
tato divi mahān nādaḥ prādur āsīt samantataḥ.
tato 'ham astraṃ Vāyavyaṃ Jāmadagnye prayuktavān;
pratyājaghne ca tad Rāmo Guhyak'|âstreṇa, Bhārata.
tato 'ham astram Āgneyam anumantrya prayuktavān;
Vāruṇen' âiva tad Rāmo vārayām āsa me vibhuḥ.
evam astrāṇi divyāni Rāmasy' âham avārayam,
Rāmaś ca mama tejasvī divy'|âstra|vid arin|damaḥ.
tato māṃ savyato, rājan, Rāmaḥ kurvan dvij'|ôttamaḥ
urasy avidhyat saṃkruddho Jāmadagnyaḥ pratāpavān.
180.15 tato 'haṃ, Bharata|śreṣṭha, saṃnyaṣīdaṃ rath'|ôttame.
tato māṃ kaśmal'|āviṣṭaṃ sūtas tūrṇam udāvahat
glāyantaṃ, Bharata|śreṣṭha, Rāma|bāṇa|prapīḍitam.
tato mām apayāntaṃ vai bhṛśaṃ viddham a|cetasam
Rāmasy' ânucarā hṛṣṭāḥ sarve dṛṣṭvā vicukruśuḥ
Akṛtavraṇa|prabhṛtayaḥ, Kāśi|kanyā ca, Bhārata.
tatas tu labdha|saṃjño 'haṃ jñātvā sūtam ath' âbruvam:
«yāhi, sūta, yato Rāmaḥ; sajjo 'haṃ, gata|vedanaḥ.»
tato mām avahat sūto hayaiḥ parama|śobhitaiḥ
nṛtyadbhir iva, Kauravya, māruta|pratimair gatau.
180.20 tato 'haṃ Rāmam āsādya bāṇa|varṣaiś ca, Kaurava,
avākiraṃ su|saṃrabdhaḥ saṃrabdhaṃ ca jigīṣayā.

dred and then by the thousand, splitting them time and again in the sky, my king.

Next Jamad·agni's majestic son aimed superb celestial
weapons at me, but I countered them with my weapons, 180.10
long-armed man, intending to do a better job. A great cacophony arose on all sides in the sky, and I made use of the Vayávya weapon against Jamad·agni's son, but Rama counteracted it with the Gúhyaka missile, Bhárata. Then, chanting, I used the Agnéya missile, but Lord Rama warded it off with the Váruna weapon. So it was that I warded off Rama's celestial weapons, and splendid Rama, the enemy-tamer and scholar of heavenly missiles, did the same to mine.

Next majestic Rama, the greatest of brahmins and son of Jamad·agni, made an attack from the left, my king, and
furiously hit me on the chest. Greatest of the Bharatas, I 180.15
sank down in my superb chariot, and my charioteer quickly carried me off when he saw that I was filled with despair and exhausted, wounded by Rama's arrows, best of the Bharatas. And seeing me leaving, badly wounded and unconscious, Rama's followers, led by Ákrita·vrana, were all delighted and cheered, and so too did the Kashi king's daughter, Bhárata.

However, as soon as I regained consciousness and knew what was happening I said to my charioteer: "Charioteer, go back to where Rama is, for my pain is gone, and I am prepared." So my charioteer took me back with the beautifully gleaming horses that seemed almost to be dancing as they went on their way, swift as the wind, Kaurávya.
And approaching Rama, Káurava, I very angrily sprayed 180.20

tān āpatata ev' âsau Rāmo bāṇān a|jihma|gān
bāṇair ev' âcchinat tūrṇam ek' âikaṃ tribhir āhave.
tatas te sūditāḥ sarve mama bāṇāḥ su|saṃśitāḥ
Rāma|bāṇair dvidhā chinnāḥ śataśo 'tha sahasraśaḥ.
tataḥ punaḥ śaraṃ dīptaṃ su|prabhaṃ kāla|sammitam
asṛjaṃ Jāmadagnyāya Rāmāy' âhaṃ jighāṃsayā.

tena tv abhihato gāḍhaṃ, bāṇa|vega|vaśaṃ gataḥ,
mumoha samare Rāmo, bhūmau ca nipapāta ha.
180.25 tato hāhā|kṛtaṃ sarvaṃ Rāme bhū|talam āśrite
jagad, Bhārata, saṃvignaṃ, yath" ârka|patane bhavet!
tata enaṃ samudvignāḥ sarva ev' âbhidudruvuḥ
tapo|dhanās te sahasā, Kāśyā ca, Kuru|nandana.
tata enaṃ pariṣvajya śanair āśvāsayaṃs tadā
pāṇibhir jala|śītaiś ca jay'|āśirbhiś ca, Kaurava.

tataḥ sa vihvalaṃ vākyaṃ Rāma utthāya c' âbravīt,
«tiṣṭha, Bhīṣma, hato 's'! îti» bāṇaṃ sandhāya kārmuke.
sa mukto nyapatat tūrṇaṃ savye pārśve mah"|āhave,
yen' âhaṃ bhṛśam udvigno, vyāghūrṇita iva drumaḥ.
180.30 hatvā hayāṃs tato Rāmaḥ śīghr'|âstreṇa mah"|āhave,
avākiran māṃ visrabdho bāṇais tair loma|vāhibhiḥ.

tato 'ham api śīghr'|âstraṃ samara|prativāraṇam.
avāsṛjaṃ, mahā|bāho. te 'ntar" âdhiṣṭhitāḥ śarāḥ
Rāmasya mama c' âiv' āśu vyom' āvṛtya samantataḥ.
na sma sūryaḥ pratapati śara|jāla|samāvṛtaḥ,

the furious man with showers of arrows, for I longed to defeat him.

But Rama quickly split my straight-flying arrows before they reached him, by firing three arrows to each of my one in battle. So all my finely sharpened arrows were ruined and split in two by Rama's hundreds and thousands of shafts. But I fired again, shooting a single blazing, brightly gleaming arrow, like fate itself, at Rama, son of Jamad·agni, in order to kill him.

Struck hard, he fell under the power of the force of the
arrow, and Rama fell to the ground, dazed in battle. Then 180.25
cries of "No! Alas!" sprung up on all sides as Rama lay on the surface of the earth, and the universe became agitated, Bhárata, as if the sun were falling! All the sages of ascetic wealth and the Kashi princess ran at speed, in alarm, descendant of the Kurus. They embraced him and soothed him gently with hands cooled by water, and with blessings for his victory, Káurava.

Then Rama got up, attached an arrow to his bow, and spoke to me in annoyance, saying: "Stand still, Bhishma, you are dead!" He shot the arrow quickly, and it struck me in my left side in the mighty battle, and I was extremely
shaken, like a tree being tossed about. When he had killed 180.30
my horses in the great battle, Rama confidently sprayed me with his feathered arrows, with great dexterity.

But I also fired dexterously to ward off weapons in battle, long-armed man. At this point the arrows hung fixed in the firmament, both my arrows and those which Rama fired, and they soon filled the sky as far as the eye could see. The sun did not shine, for it was veiled by the mesh of arrows,

mātariśvā tatas tasmin megha|ruddha iv' âbhavat.
tato vāyoḥ prakampāc ca, sūryasya ca gabhastibhiḥ,
abhighāta|prabhāvāc ca pāvakaḥ samajāyata.
te śarāḥ sva|samutthena pradīptāś citra|bhānunā
180.35 bhūmau sarve tadā, rājan, bhasma|bhūtāḥ prapedire.
tadā śata|sahasrāṇi, prayutāny, arbudāni ca,
ayutāny, atha kharvāṇi, nikharvāṇi ca, Kaurava,
Rāmaḥ śarāṇāṃ saṃkruddho mayi tūrṇaṃ nyapātayat.
tato 'haṃ tān api raṇe śarair āśīviṣ'|ôpamaiḥ
saṃchidya bhūmau, nṛ|pate, 'pātayaṃ pannagān iva.†
evaṃ tad abhavad yuddhaṃ tadā, Bharata|sattama;
sandhyā|kāle vyatīte tu vyapāyāt sa ca me guruḥ.

BHĪṢMA uvāca:

181.1 SAMĀGATASYA Rāmeṇa punar ev' âtidāruṇam
anye|dyus tumulaṃ yuddhaṃ tadā, Bharata|sattama.
tato divy'|âstra|vic chūro divyāny astrāṇy an|ekaśaḥ
ayojayat sa dharm'|ātmā divase divase vibhuḥ.
tāny ahaṃ tat|pratīghātair astrair astrāṇi, Bhārata,
vyadhamamaṃ tumule yuddhe prāṇāṃs tyaktvā su|dus|tyajān.
astrair astreṣu bahudhā hateṣv eva ca, Bhārata,
akrudhyata mahā|tejās tyakta|prāṇaḥ sa saṃyuge.
181.5 tataḥ śaktiṃ prāhiṇod ghora|rūpām
astre ruddhe Jāmadagnyo mah"|ātmā,
kāl'|ôtsṛṣṭāṃ prajvalitām iv' ôlkāṃ
saṃdīpt'|âgrāṃ, tejasā vyāpya lokam.
tato 'haṃ tām iṣubhir dīpyamānāṃ,

and the wind seemed to stop, as though obstructed by the clouds. Next, through the trembling of the wind, the rays of the sun, and the friction of the arrows striking against each other, a fire sprung up. The arrows in the sky blazed in the flickering fire they had created and all fell to earth, 180.35
king, turned to ashes.

Rama quickly fired hundreds, thousands, tens of thousands, millions, tens of millions, and billions of arrows at me in his fury, Káurava. But I split them with my own shafts in battle, as though with poisonous snakes, and I felled his serpent-like arrows to the ground, king.

So it was that the battle progressed, greatest of the Bharatas, but when the twilight had passed, my guru departed.

BHISHMA continued:

WHEN I MET Rama again on the following day, another 181.1
particularly cruel and tumultuous battle took place, greatest of the Bharatas. Day after day, the brave and virtuous-souled lord, who knew heavenly missiles, used numerous celestial weapons. But I hit them using my own missiles to counteract them, Bhárata, risking my life itself, so hard to sacrifice, in the tumultuous battle. As his many missiles were destroyed by my weapons, Bhárata, the highly energetic man became angry, and risked his life in battle.

When his missiles were obstructed, high-souled Jamad·agni's son hurled a horrifying-looking, blazing-tipped spear, 181.5
which pervaded the world with its splendor, as though it were a fiery meteor hurled by time itself. As it hurtled towards me, dazzling and blazing like the sun at the end of

samāyāntīm anta|kāl'|ârka|dīptām,
chittvā tridhā pātayām āsa bhūmau.
tato vavau pavanaḥ puṇya|gandhiḥ.
tasyāṃ chinnāyāṃ krodha|dīpto 'tha Rāmaḥ
śaktīr ghorāḥ prāhiṇod dvā|daś' ânyāḥ.
tāsāṃ rūpaṃ, Bhārata, n' ôta śakyaṃ
tejasvitvāl lāghavāc c' âiva vaktum.
kiṃ tv ev' âhaṃ vihvalaḥ sampradṛśya
digbhyaḥ sarvās tā mah"|ôlkā iv' âgneḥ
nānā|rūpās tejaso 'greṇa dīptā
yath" ādityā dvā|daśa loka|saṃkṣaye!
tato jālaṃ bāṇa|mayaṃ vivṛttaṃ
saṃdṛśya bhittvā śara|jālena, rājan,
dvā|daś'|êṣūn prāhiṇavaṃ raṇe 'haṃ
tataḥ śaktīr vyadhamam† ghora|rūpāḥ.
181.10 tato, rājañ, Jāmadagnyo mah"|ātmā
śaktīr ghorā vyākṣipadd hema|daṇḍāḥ,
vicitritāḥ kāñcana|paṭṭa|naddhā;
yathā mah"|ôlkā jvalitās, tathā tāḥ.
tāś c' âpy ugrāś carmaṇā vārayitvā,
khaḍgen' ājau pātayitvā, nar'|êndra,
bāṇair divyair Jāmadagnyasya saṃkhye
divyān aśvān abhyavarṣaṃ sa|sūtān.

time, I split it into three with my arrows and felled it to the ground, and a holy-scented breeze wafted around me.

When his missile was broken Rama was ablaze with fury, and he hurled another twelve horrifying spears. Their forms cannot be described, Bhárata, because of their brilliance and speed. How could I describe them? I was terrified as I watched those variously formed luminous missiles, all like great meteors of fire from the sky, their points ablaze like the twelve suns at the destruction of the world!

But when I saw the mesh of shafts whirling towards me, I split them with my own net of arrows, king, and shot twelve arrows in battle, with which I destroyed those horri-
fyingly formed spears. Then, king, high-souled Jamad·agni's 181.10
son fired horrifying, multicolored, golden-staffed javelins, bound with golden threads, like great blazing meteors! I warded off those fierce spears with my shield and sword and brought them crashing down onto the battlefield, lord of men, and then I showered Jamad·agni's son's celestial horses and charioteers with my heavenly arrows in battle.

nirmuktānāṃ pannagānāṃ sa|rūpā
dṛṣṭvā śaktīr hema|citrā nikṛttāḥ,
prāduś cakre divyam astraṃ mah"|ātmā
krodh'|āviṣṭo Haihay'|ēśa|pramāthī.
tataḥ śreṇyaḥ śalabhānām iv' ôgrāḥ
samāpetur viśikhānāṃ pradīptāḥ
samācinoc c' âpi bhṛśaṃ śarīraṃ,
hayān, sūtaṃ sa|rathaṃ c' âiva mahyam.
rathaḥ śarair me nicitaḥ sarvato 'bhūt,
tathā vāhāḥ, sārathiś c' âiva, rājan,
yugaṃ, rath'|ēṣāṃ ca tath" âiva cakre,
tath" âiv' âkṣaḥ śara|kṛtto 'tha bhagnaḥ.
181.15 tatas tasmin bāṇa|varṣe vyatīte
śar'|âugheṇa pratyavarṣaṃ guruṃ tam.
sa vikṣato mārgaṇair brahma|rāśir
dehād a|saktaṃ mumuce bhūri raktam.
yathā Rāmo bāṇa|jāl'|âbhitaptas,
tath" âiv' âhaṃ su|bhṛśaṃ gāḍha|viddhaḥ.
tato yuddhaṃ vyaramac c' âpar'|âhṇe,
bhānāv astaṃ prati yāte mahī|dhram.

BHĪṢMA uvāca:

182.1 TATAḤ PRABHĀTE, rāj'|êndra, sūrye vimalatāṃ gate,
Bhārgavasya mayā sārdhaṃ punar yuddham avartata.
tato 'bhrānte rathe tiṣṭhan Rāmaḥ praharatāṃ varaḥ
vavarṣa śara|jālāni mayi, megha iv' â|cale.
tataḥ sūto mama su|hṛc chara|varṣeṇa tāḍitaḥ
apayāto rath'|ôpasthān mano mama viṣādayan.
tataḥ sūto mam' âtyarthaṃ kaśmalaṃ prāviśan mahat,
pṛthivyāṃ ca śar'|āghātān nipapāta mumoha ca.

When he saw that his golden-glistening spears were cut to shreds, like snakes wriggling free of their skins, the high-souled destroyer of King Kartavírya, the lord of Háihaya, was filled with fury and displayed his celestial missile. Blazing hosts of fierce unfeathered arrows, like swarms of locusts, fell heavily and covered my body, horses, charioteer, and chariot.

My chariot was completely heaped with arrows, as were my horses and charioteer, king. The chariot's yoke, pole,
wheels, and axle were broken by the arrows. But when the 181.15
shower of arrows was over I fired back at my guru with a flock of shafts. That mass of brahmanic splendor was wounded by my arrows, and bled profusely and incessantly from his body.

Just as Rama was scorched by my net of arrows, so I too was very seriously and heavily wounded, and the battle ended in the late afternoon as the sun went to the mountain behind which it sets.

BHISHMA continued:

LATER, ONCE THE bright sun had risen in the morning, 182.1
lord of kings, the Bhárgava's battle with me began once more. Rama, the greatest of warriors, standing on his unerring chariot, rained nets of arrows upon me like a cloud showering a mountain. My charioteer and friend was hit by the shower of arrows, and he fell from his position in the chariot, immersing my mind in grief. My charioteer then fell into great and total unconsciousness, and he collapsed to the ground because of his arrow wounds and slipped into
insensibility. Finally, tormented by Rama's arrows, my char- 182.5
ioteer lost his life.

182.5 tataḥ sūto 'jahāt prāṇān Rāma|bāṇa|prapīḍitaḥ.
muhūrtād iva, rāj'|êndra, māṃ ca bhīr āviśat tadā.
tataḥ sūte hate tasmin kṣipatas tasya me śarān
pramatta|manaso Rāmaḥ prāhiṇon mṛtyu|saṃmitam.
tataḥ sūta|vyasaninaṃ viplutaṃ māṃ sa Bhārgavaḥ
śareṇ' âbhyahanad gāḍhaṃ vikṛṣya balavad dhanuḥ.
sa me bhuj'|ântare, rājan, nipatya rudhir'|âśanaḥ
may" âiva saha, rāj'|êndra, jagāma vasudhā|talam.
matvā tu nihataṃ Rāmas tato māṃ, Bharata'|rṣabha,
meghavad vinanād' ôccair, jahṛṣe ca punaḥ punaḥ.
182.10 tathā tu patite, rājan, mayi Rāmo mudā yutaḥ
udakrośan mahā|nādaṃ saha tair anuyāyibhiḥ.
āgatā api yuddhaṃ taj janās tatra didṛkṣavaḥ
ārtiṃ paramikāṃ jagmus te tadā patite mayi.
tato 'paśyaṃ patito, rāja|siṃha,
dvijān aṣṭau sūrya|hut'|âśan'|ābhān.
te māṃ samantāt parivārya tasthuḥ
sva|bāhubhiḥ paridhāry' āji|madhye.
rakṣyamāṇaś ca tair viprair n' âhaṃ bhūmim upāspṛśam,
antarikṣe dhṛto hy asmi tair viprair bāndhavair iva.
śvasann iv' ântarikṣe ca jala|bindubhir ukṣitaḥ
tatas te brāhmaṇā, rājann, abruvan parigṛhya mām:
182.15 «mā bhair! iti» samaṃ sarve, «svasti te 'stv! iti» c' â|sakṛt.
tatas teṣām ahaṃ vāgbhis tarpitaḥ sahas" ôtthitaḥ.
hayāś ca me saṃgṛhītās tay" āsan
mahā|nadyā saṃyati, Kaurav'|êndra.
pādau jananyāḥ pratigṛhya c' âhaṃ,
tathā pitṝṇāṃ, ratham abhyaroham.

Fear momentarily overwhelmed me, lord of kings, and, once my charioteer had been killed, Rama fired death-like arrows at me as I heedlessly shot shafts. Then, as I remained sunk in depression over the death of my charioteer, Bhárgava drew his powerful bow and hit and wounded me with an arrow.

The blood-devouring arrow hit me in the chest, king, and fell beside me on the earth's surface, lord of kings. Thinking he had killed me, bull of the Bharatas, Rama roared loudly and repeatedly, booming like a cloud, and was jubilant. And 182.10
as I lay there, king, Rama was filled with joy and he and his followers roared, bellowing loudly. But the people who had come to watch the battle were extremely distressed when I fell.

Once I had fallen, I saw eight brahmins who gleamed like the sun and the oblation-eating fire, lion-like king. They stood surrounding me on all sides, and they embraced me in their arms in the midst of the battlefield.

Protected by those brahmins I didn't touch the ground, for the brahmins held me in the air, as though they were kin. The brahmins sprinkled me with drops of water as I almost panted in the sky, and as they held me up, repeatedly saying to me in unison, "Don't be afraid! May you have 182.15
good fortune," I was heartened by their words and quickly got up.

I clasped the feet of my mother, the great river who had driven my horses, and, having worshipped my ancestors, I climbed aboard my chariot.

rarakṣa sā māṃ sa|ratham, hayāṃś c' ôpaskarāṇi ca;
tām ahaṃ prāñjalir bhūtvā punar eva vyasarjayam.
tato 'haṃ svayam udyamya hayāṃs tān vāta|raṃhasaḥ
ayudhyaṃ Jāmadagnyena nivṛtte 'hani, Bhārata.

tato 'haṃ, Bharata|śreṣṭha, vegavantaṃ mahā|balam
amuñcaṃ samare bāṇaṃ Rāmāya hṛdaya|cchidam.
182.20 tato jagāma vasudhāṃ mama bāṇa|prapīḍitaḥ
jānubhyāṃ, dhanur utsṛjya Rāmo moha|vaśaṃ gataḥ.
tatas tasmin nipatite Rāme bhūri|sahasrade
āvavrur jaladā vyoma kṣaranto rudhiraṃ bahu,
ulkāś ca śataśaḥ petuḥ sa|nirghātāḥ sa|kampanāḥ.

arkaṃ ca sahasā dīptaṃ Svarbhānur abhisaṃvṛṇot,
vavuś ca vātāḥ paruṣāś, calitā ca vasun|dharā,
gṛdhrā, balāś ca kaṅkāś ca paripetur mudā yutāḥ.
dīptāyāṃ diśi go|māyur dāruṇaṃ muhur unnadat,
an|āhatā dundubhayo vinedur bhṛśa|niḥsvanāḥ.
182.25 etad autpātikaṃ sarvaṃ ghoram āsīd bhayaṃ|karam,
visaṃjña|kalpe dharaṇīṃ gate Rāme mah"|ātmani.

tato vai sahas" ôtthāya Rāmo mām abhyavartata
punar yuddhāya, Kauravya, vihvalaḥ krodha|mūrcchitaḥ.
ādadāno mahā|bāhuḥ kārmukaṃ bala|sannibham
tato mayy ādadānaṃ taṃ Rāmam eva nyavārayan
maha"|rṣayaḥ kṛpā|yuktāḥ. krodh'|āviṣṭo 'tha Bhārgavaḥ
sa me 'harad a|mey'|ātmā śaraṃ kāl'|ânal'|ôpamam.

She had protected me and my chariot, horses, and tools, so, with folded hands, I asked her to leave once more. Then I myself yoked my horses, fleet as the wind, and I fought with Jamad·agni's son until the day passed, Bhárata.

I released a great, powerful, forceful, heart-rending shaft at Rama in battle, O greatest of the Bharatas. Tormented 182.20
by my arrow, Rama fell to the ground on his knees, dropping his bow, and slipped into unconsciousness. When Rama, the granter of many thousands of coins, fell, clouds covered the heavens and poured down great quantities of blood. Hundreds of meteors fell, as thunderstorms and earthquakes raged.

Suddenly Svarbhánu veiled the blazing sun, harsh gale-force winds blew, the earth shook, and vultures, crows, and herons flew overhead, filled with glee. Jackals incessantly howled hideously on the blazing horizon, and drums boomed incredibly loudly without being beaten. All these 182.25
portentous, horrifying, and fear-inspiring omens occurred when high-souled Rama fell to the ground unconscious.

Then Rama suddenly arose, turning to me to fight once more, Kaurávya, agitated and stupefied by rage. The long-armed man took up his powerful bow, but the great sages were filled with pity and warded off Rama as he took up weapons against me. But Bhárgava was overwhelmed with fury, and the man of immeasurable soul severed my arrow which resembled the fire at the end of the age.

tato ravir manda|marīci|maṇḍalo†
jagām' âstaṃ pāṃsu|puñj'|âvagūḍhaḥ.
niśā vyagāhat sukha|śīta|mārutā;
tato yuddhaṃ pratyavahārayāvaḥ
182.30 evaṃ, rājann, avahāro babhūva;
tataḥ punar vimale 'bhūt su|ghoram.
kalyaṃ kalyaṃ viṃśatiṃ vai dināni,
tath" âiva c' ânyāni dināni trīṇi.

BHĪṢMA uvāca:

183.1 TATO 'HAṂ NIŚI, rāj'|êndra, praṇamya śirasā tadā
brāhmaṇānāṃ, pitṝṇāṃ ca, devatānāṃ ca sarvaśaḥ,
naktaṃ|carāṇāṃ bhūtānāṃ rajanyāś ca,† viśām pate
śayanaṃ prāpya rahite manasā samacintayam,
«Jāmadagnyena me yuddham idaṃ parama|dāruṇam
ahāni ca bahūny adya vartate su|mah"|âtyayam.
na ca Rāmaṃ mahā|vīryaṃ śaknomi raṇa|mūrdhani
vijetuṃ samare vipraṃ Jāmadagnyaṃ mahā|balam.
183.5 yadi śakyo mayā jetuṃ Jāmadagnyaḥ pratāpavān
daivatāni prasannāni darśayantu niśāṃ mama.»
tato niśi ca, rāj'|êndra, prasuptaḥ śara|vikṣataḥ
dakṣiṇen' êha pārśvena prabhāta|samaye tadā,
tato 'haṃ vipra|mukhyais tair, yair asmi patito rathāt
utthāpito dhṛtaś c' âiva, «mā bhair! iti» ca sāntvitaḥ,
ta eva māṃ, mahā|rāja, svapna|darśanam etya vai
parivāry' âbruvan vākyaṃ. tan nibodha, Kur'|ûdvaha.
«uttiṣṭha! mā bhair, Gāṅgeya! na bhayaṃ te 'sti kiñ cana!
rakṣāmahe tvāṃ, Kauravya, sva|śarīraṃ hi no bhavān.
183.10 na tvāṃ Rāmo raṇe jetā Jāmadagnyaḥ kathañ cana;
tvam eva samare Rāmaṃ vijetā, Bharata'|rṣabha!

Concealed by masses of dust, the sun's muted circle of rays set in the west. Night fell, pleasantly cooled by the
breeze, and we both retired from battle. So it was, king, that 182.30
hostilities ceased; but when the light returned, the horrifying battle began again. Dawn after dawn it went on, for twenty-three more days.

BHISHMA continued:

IN THE NIGHT, lord of kings, I bowed my head to the 183.1
brahmins, the ancestors, all the gods, the creatures who roam at night, and the night herself, lord of men, and went to my bed. In the privacy of my mind I thought, "This supremely frightful and very pernicious duel between me and Jamad·agni's son has been going for many days now, and I am not able to defeat the powerful and greatly heroic brahmin Rama, son of Jamad·agni, at the frontline of battle. If it is possible for me to beat majestic Jamad·agni's son, 183.5
then may the gods graciously appear to me tonight."

That night, near dawn, lord of kings, as I slept on my right side, wounded by arrows, the leading brahmins—who had lifted me when I fell from my chariot, held me, and soothed me, saying, "Do not be afraid!"—appeared to me in a dream, great king.

Surrounding me, they spoke, son of the Kuru race. Listen to what they said:

"Stand up! Do not be afraid, son of the Ganges! You are in no danger. We will protect you, Kaurávya, for you are
in fact our own body. Rama, son of Jamad·agni, will never 183.10
defeat you in battle, but you will defeat Rama in the fight, bull of the Bharatas!

idam astraṃ su|dayitaṃ pratyabhijñāsyate bhavān,
viditaṃ hi tav' âpy etat pūrvasmin deha|dhāraṇe.
Prājāpatyaṃ Viśva|kṛtaṃ Prasvāpaṃ nāma, Bhārata,
na h' îdaṃ veda Rāmo 'pi, pṛthivyāṃ vā pumān kva cit.
tat smarasva, mahā|bāho, bhṛśaṃ saṃyojayasva ca;
upasthāsyati, rāj'|êndra, svayam eva tav', ân|agha!

yena sarvān mahā|vīryān praśāsiṣyasi, Kaurava,
na ca Rāmaḥ kṣayaṃ gantā ten' âstreṇa, nar'|âdhipa.
183.15 enasā na tu saṃyogaṃ prāpsyase jātu, māna|da.
svapsyate Jāmadagnyo 'sau tvad|bāṇa|bala|pīḍitaḥ.
tato jitvā tvam ev' âinaṃ punar utthāpayiṣyasi
astreṇa dayiten' ājau, Bhīṣma, Saṃbodhanena vai.

evaṃ kuruṣva, Kauravya, prabhāte ratham āsthitaḥ.
prasuptaṃ vā mṛtaṃ v" êti tulyaṃ manyāmahe vayam.
na ca Rāmeṇa martavyaṃ kadā cid api, pārthiva,
tataḥ samutpannam idaṃ Prasvāpaṃ yujyatām iti.»

ity uktv" ântar|hitā, rājan, sarva eva dvij'|ôttamāḥ
aṣṭau sadṛśa|rūpās te sarve bhāsura|mūrtayaḥ.

BHĪṢMA uvāca:

184.1 TATO RĀTRAU vyatītāyāṃ pratibuddho 'smi, Bhārata,
tataḥ sañcintya vai svapnam avāpaṃ harṣam uttamam.
tataḥ samabhavad yuddhaṃ mama tasya ca, Bhārata,
tumulaṃ, sarva|bhūtānāṃ loma|harṣaṇam, adbhutam.
tato bāṇa|mayaṃ varṣaṃ vavarṣa mayi Bhārgavaḥ;
nyavārayam ahaṃ tac ca śara|jālena, Bhārata.

You will recognize this beloved weapon, for you did in fact know it when you wore an earlier body. It is called Prasvápa, the bringer of sleep. It belongs to Praja·pati and was made by Vishva·karman, Bhárata. Even Rama does not know it, nor, in fact, does any man anywhere on earth. Remember it, long-armed man, and use it powerfully. It will come back to you of its own accord, sinless lord of kings!

With it you will rule over all men of great prowess, Káurava. Rama will not meet his end by this weapon, lord of
men, so you will assuredly not attain any sin by its use, 183.15
granter of honor. Jamad·agni's son will fall asleep, afflicted by the power of your arrow. Then, when you have defeated him in battle, you will wake him once more, Bhishma, with your dear weapon called Sambódhana, the awakening missile.

Do this, Kaurávya, when you stand on your chariot in the morning, for we consider a man to be the same regardless of whether he is sleeping or dead. Rama must never die, king, so please use Prasvápa, the bringer of sleep, once you have equipped yourself with it."

Once they had said this, king, all eight of the excellent brahmins with identical radiant bodies disappeared.

BHISHMA continued:

WHEN THE NIGHT had passed I awoke, Bhárata, and 184.1
thinking about the dream I felt utterly joyful. Then the duel between us got underway, Bhárata; a hair-raising scuffle, miraculous for all creatures. The Bhárgava showered a shaft-made rain upon me, but I warded it off with my own net of arrows, Bhárata.

tataḥ parama|saṃkruddhaḥ punar eva mahā|tapāḥ
hyastanena ca kopena śaktiṃ vai prāhiṇon mayi,
184.5 indr'|âśani|sama|sparśāṃ, Yama|daṇḍa|samaprabhām,
jvalantīm agnivat saṃkhye, lelihānāṃ samantataḥ.
tato, Bharata|śārdūla, dhiṣnyam ākāśa|gaṃ yathā,
sa māṃ abhyavadhīt tūrṇaṃ jatru|deśe, Kur'|ûdvaha.
ath' âsram asravad ghoraṃ, girer gairika|dhātuvat
Rāmeṇa, su|mahā|bāho, kṣatasya, kṣataj'|êkṣaṇa.

tato 'haṃ Jāmadagnyāya bhṛśaṃ krodha|samanvitaḥ
cikṣepa mṛtyu|saṃkāśaṃ bāṇaṃ sarpa|viṣ'|ôpamam.
sa ten' âbhihato vīro lalāṭe dvija|sattamaḥ
aśobhata, mahā|rāja, sa|śṛṃga iva parvataḥ.
184.10 sa saṃrabdhaḥ samāvṛtya śaraṃ kāl'|ântak'|ôpamam
sandadhe balavat kṛṣya ghoraṃ śatru|nibarhaṇam.

sa vakṣasi papāt' ôgraḥ śaro vyāla iva śvasan
mahīṃ, rājaṃs; tataś c' âham agamaṃ rudhir'|āvilaḥ.
saṃprāpya tu punaḥ saṃjñāṃ Jāmadagnyāya dhīmate
prāhiṇvaṃ vimalāṃ śaktiṃ jvalantīm aśanīm iva.
sā tasya dvija|mukhyasya nipapāta bhuj'|ântare;
vihvalaś c' âbhavad, rājan, vepathuś c' âinam āviśat.

tata enaṃ pariṣvajya sakhā vipro mahā|tapāḥ
Akṛtavraṇaḥ śubhair vākyair āśvāsayad an|ekadhā.
184.15 samāśvastas tato Rāmaḥ krodh'|âmarṣa|samanvitaḥ
prāduś cakre tadā Brāhmaṃ param'|âstraṃ mahā|vrataḥ.
tatas tat|pratighāt'|ârthaṃ Brāhmam ev' âstram uttamam
mayā prayuktaṃ jajvāla yug'|ântam iva darśayat!

Utterly infuriated by his rage at what had happened the previous day, the mighty ascetic hurled at me a spear which 184.5
was like Indra's thunderbolt to the touch, like Yama's staff in splendor, and which blazed like fire licking all around in battle. Tiger-like Bharata, it hit me quickly on the collar-bone, like a flying fire-altar, son of the Kuru race. As though it were soil tumbling down a mountain, horrifying blood streamed from the wound when I was struck by Rama, O incredibly long-armed man with bloodshot eyes.

Filled with overwhelming rage, I fired my death-like arrow, like a serpent's poison, at Jamad·agni's son; and it hit the heroic finest of brahmins on the forehead. He looked as stunning as a peaked mountain, great sovereign. But 184.10
he spun round, enraged, forcefully drawing his bow, and aimed a horrifying, enemy-annihilating shaft in my direction like death-bringing fate.

Hissing like a snake, the fierce arrow hit me in the chest, king, and, filthy with blood, I fell to the ground. But regaining consciouness once more, I hurled a bright spear, blazing like lightning, at wise Jamad·agni's son. It landed between the foremost of brahmins' arms, on his chest, my king; and he became exhausted and overwhelmed by trembling.

His friend, the brahmin of great asceticism, Ákrita·vrana, embraced him and encouraged him with glowing words of various kinds. And once Rama was soothed—but filled 184.15
with fury and intolerance—the strict-vowed man produced the ultimate missile: the Brahma weapon. So then I too used the same ultimate Brahma missile in order to repel his, and it blazed as though revealing the end of the age!

tayor Brahm'|âstrayor āsīd antarā vai samāgamaḥ,
a|samprāpy' âiva Rāmaṃ ca māṃ ca, Bharata|sattama.
tato vyomni prādur abhūt teja eva hi kevalam,
bhūtāni c' âiva sarvāṇi jagmur ārtiṃ, viśāṃ pate.
ṛṣayaś ca sa|gandharvā, devatāś c' âiva, Bhārata,
santāpaṃ paramaṃ jagmur astra|tejo|'bhipīḍitāḥ.
184.20 tataś cacāla pṛthivī sa|parvata|vana|drumā,
santaptāni ca bhūtāni viṣādaṃ jagmur uttamam.
prajajvāla nabho, rājan, dhūmāyante diśo daśa
na sthātum antarikṣe ca śekur ākāśa|gās tadā.
tato hāhā|kṛte loke sa|dev'|âsura|rākṣase
idam antaram ity evaṃ moktu|kāmo 'smi, Bhārata,
Prasvāpam astraṃ tvarito vacanād brahma|vādinām,
vicitraṃ ca tad astraṃ me manasi pratyabhāt tadā.

The two Brahma missiles collided in mid-air, but did not reach either Rama or me, greatest of the Bharatas. The heavens became nothing but brilliant fire, and all creatures were pained, lord of earth. The sages, *gandhárvas*, and gods, O Bhárata, suffered supreme anguish, tormented by the splendor of the weapons.

The earth shook, with her mountains, forests, and trees, 184.20
and living creatures were scorched and suffered utter despair. The sky was ablaze, king, and the ten directions were smoking, and no airborne creatures could remain in the heavens any longer.

Then, when the world with the gods, *ásuras*, and *rákshasas* screamed in despair, I longed to swiftly release my other weapon, Bhárata, Prasvápa, the bringer of sleep, at the command of the vedic scholars, and my wonderful weapon appeared in my mind at that very moment.

[illegible]

The two Bedouins [illegible] in madness, but did not [illegible] much [illegible] of the [illegible]. [illegible] [illegible] nothing [illegible] [illegible] [illegible] [illegible] [illegible] and [illegible] [illegible] [illegible] by the [illegible] [illegible].

The earth [illegible] with [illegible] forests and trees [illegible] and living creatures were scorched and suffered under the [illegible]. [illegible] and the [illegible] floods were [illegible] [illegible] creatures could [illegible] [illegible] no longer.

Then, when the world [illegible] [illegible] [illegible] screaming [illegible] [illegible] to [illegible] [illegible] [illegible] other weapon, [illegible] [illegible] [illegible] sleep at the [illegible] of [illegible] and [illegible] [illegible] [illegible].

# 185–187

# RAMA IS DEFEATED

BHĪṢMA uvāca:

185.1 TATO HALAHALĀ|śabdo
divi, rājan, mahān abhūt,
«Prasvāpaṃ, Bhīṣma, mā srākṣīr!»
iti Kaurava|nandana.
ayuñjam eva c' âiv' âhaṃ tad astraṃ Bhṛgu|nandane.
Prasvāpaṃ māṃ prayuñjānaṃ Nārado vākyam abravīt:
«ete viyati, Kauravya, divi deva|gaṇāḥ sthitāḥ;
te tvāṃ nivārayanty adya. Prasvāpaṃ mā prayojaya.
Rāmas tapasvī brahmaṇyo, brāhmaṇaś ca, guruś ca te;
tasy' âvamānaṃ, Kauravya, mā sma kārṣīḥ kathañ cana!»
185.5 tato 'paśyaṃ divi|ṣṭhān vai tān aṣṭau brahma|vādinaḥ;
te māṃ smayanto, rāj'|êndra, śanakair idam abruvan:
«yath" āha, Bharata|śreṣṭha, Nāradas, tat tathā kuru.
etadd hi paramaṃ śreyo lokānāṃ, Bharata'|rṣabha.»
tataś ca pratisaṃhṛtya tad astraṃ svāpanaṃ mahat,
Brahm'|âstraṃ dīpayāṃ cakre tasmin yudhi yathā|vidhi.
tato Rāmo hṛṣito, rāja|siṃha,
dṛṣṭvā tad astraṃ vinivartitaṃ vai
«jito 'smi Bhīṣmeṇa su|manda|buddhir!»
ity eva vākyaṃ sahasā vyamuñcat.
tato 'paśyat pitaraṃ Jāmadagnyaḥ,
pitus tathā pitaraṃ c' âsya mānyam.
te tatra c' âinaṃ parivārya tasthur,
ūcuś c' âinaṃ sāntva|pūrvaṃ tadānīm.

BHISHMA continued:

THEN THERE WAS an enormous commotion of cheering in the sky, my king. A voice spoke to me, descendant of the Káurava line, saying, "Don't release Prasvápa, the bringer of sleep, Bhishma!" I aimed the weapon at the descendant of Bhrigu, but Nárada spoke to me as I was aiming Prasvápa, the bringer of sleep, saying: "These hosts of gods are positioned in the vault of the heavens, Kaurávya, and they will prevent you now. Don't use Prasvápa, the bringer of sleep. Rama is a brahmanic ascetic, a brahmin, and he is also your guru. Don't ever treat him with contempt, Kaurávya!" 185.1

Then I looked up and saw the eight Vedic scholars standing in the sky. They smiled at me, lord of kings, and gently said to me: "Do just as Nárada tells you, greatest of the Bharatas. For this is indeed of greatest benefit to the worlds, bull of the Bharatas." So I withdrew my great sleep-inducing weapon and set my Brahma weapon ablaze in the battle, according to the custom. 185.5

Lion-like king Rama bristled when he saw that the weapon had been withdrawn, and he suddenly let these words escape his lips, "I have been beaten by Bhishma! I am very foolish-minded indeed!" Then Jamad·agni's son saw his father, and his father before him, and his honorable father too. They stood there surrounding him, and spoke to him once they had comforted him, saying:

185.10 «mā sm' âivaṃ sāhasaṃ, tāta, punaḥ kārṣīḥ kathañ cana,
Bhīṣmeṇa saṃyugaṃ gantuṃ, kṣatriyeṇa viśeṣataḥ.
kṣatriyasya tu dharmo 'yaṃ,
yad yuddhaṃ, Bhṛgu|nandana;
sv|ādhyāyo vrata|cary" âtha
brāhmaṇānāṃ paraṃ dhanam.
idaṃ nimitte kasmiṃś cid asmābhiḥ prāg udāhṛtam
śastra|dhāraṇam atyugraṃ, tac c' â|kāryaṃ kṛtaṃ tvayā.
vatsa, paryāptam etāvad Bhīṣmeṇa saha saṃyuge
vimardas te, mahā|bāho; vyapayāhi raṇād itaḥ!
paryāptam etad, bhadraṃ te, tava kārmuka|dhāraṇam.
visarjay' âitad, dur|dharṣa, tapas tapyasva, Bhārgava.
185.15 eṣa Bhīṣmaḥ Śāntanavo devaiḥ sarvair nivāritaḥ.
‹nivartasva raṇād asmād! iti› c' âiva prasāditaḥ,
‹Rāmeṇa saha mā yotsīr guruṇ" êti› punaḥ punaḥ,
‹na hi Rāmo raṇe jetuṃ tvayā nyāyyaḥ, Kur'|ûdvaha.
mānaṃ kuruṣva, Gāṅgeya, brāhmaṇasya raṇ'|âjire;
vayaṃ tu guravas tubhyaṃ tasmāt tvāṃ vārayāmahe.›
Bhīṣmo Vasūnām anyatamo. diṣṭyā jīvasi, putraka!
Gāṅgeyaḥ Śāntanoḥ putro Vasur eṣa mahā|yaśāḥ,
kathaṃ śakyas tvayā jetuṃ? nivartasv' êha, Bhārgava.
Arjunaḥ Pāṇḍava|śreṣṭhaḥ puran|dara|suto balī,
185.20 Naraḥ Prajāpatir vīraḥ, pūrva|devaḥ sanātanaḥ,
savya|sāc" îti vikhyātas triṣu lokeṣu vīryavān,
Bhīṣma|mṛtyur yathā|kālaṃ vihito vai svayaṃ|bhuvā.»

"Don't ever be so rash again, my son, as to go to battle 185.10
with Bhishma, especially since he is a kshatriya. Battle like this is the duty of a kshatriya, descendant of Bhrigu, but the highest wealth of brahmins is hard Vedic study and the practice of vows. In the past, for some reason, we told you to take up your weapons, and you performed that excessively fierce task which should not be done.

Calf, this is enough battle with Bhishma. You have been crushed, long-armed man. Withdraw from this battle! This is enough bow wielding, bless you. Let it go, unassailable
Bhárgava, and practice asceticism. Bhishma here, the son of 185.15
Shántanu, is being restrained by all the gods.

'Turn from this battle!' they say, soothing him. 'Don't fight against Rama, your guru,' they keep telling him over and over again, 'It is not right for you defeat Rama in battle, son of the Kuru race. Pay your respects to the brahmin on the battlefield, son of the Ganges. We are your gurus and so we are preventing you.'

Bhishma is one of the foremost Vasus. You are lucky to be alive, little son! How can you here defeat the son of the Ganges and Shántanu, who is a great glorious Vasu? Turn away, Bhárgava. Árjuna, the powerful son of Indra the
sacker of cities, the greatest of the Pándavas, the hero Nara 185.20
Praja·pati, the eternal and ancient god, the heroic man who is known as the ambidextrous archer throughout the three worlds—he has been ordained by the self-incarnate Brahma to be the death of Bhishma at the appropriate time."

BHĪṢMA uvāca:

evam uktaḥ sa pitṛbhiḥ pitṝn Rāmo 'bravīd idam:
«n' âhaṃ yudhi nivarteyam iti me vratam āhitam.
na nivartita|pūrvaś ca kadā cid raṇa|mūrdhani.
nivartyatām āpageyaḥ kāmaṃ yuddhāt, pitāmahāḥ,
na tv ahaṃ vinivartiṣye yuddhād asmāt kathañ cana!»

tatas te munayo, rājann, Ṛcīka|pramukhās tadā,
Nāraden' âiva sahitāḥ samāgamy' êdam abruvan:
«nivartasva raṇāt, tāta, mānayasva dvij'|ôttamam.»
185.25 ity avocam ahaṃ tāṃś ca kṣatra|dharma|vyapekṣayā:
«mama vratam idaṃ loke: n' âhaṃ yuddhāt kadā cana
vimukho vinivarteyaṃ pṛṣṭhato 'bhyāhataḥ śaraiḥ!
n' âhaṃ lobhān, na kārpaṇyān, na bhayān, n' ârtha|kāraṇāt
tyajeyaṃ śāśvataṃ dharmam, iti me niścitā matiḥ.»

tatas te munayaḥ sarve Nārada|pramukhā, nṛpa,
Bhāgirathī ca me mātā raṇa|madhyaṃ prapedire.
tath" âiv' ātta|śaro dhanvī, tath" âiva dṛḍha|niścayaḥ,
sthiro 'ham āhave yoddhuṃ. tatas te Rāmam abruvan
sametya sahitā bhūyaḥ samare Bhṛgu|nandanam:
«nāvanītaṃ hi hṛdayaṃ viprāṇāṃ. śāmya, Bhārgava.
185.30 Rāma, Rāma, nivartasva yuddhād asmād, dvij'|ôttama!
a|vadhyo vai tvayā Bhīṣmas, tvaṃ ca Bhīṣmasya, Bhārgava!»

evaṃ bruvantas te sarve pratirudhya raṇ'|âjiram
nyāsayāṃ cakrire śastraṃ pitaro Bhṛgu|nandanam.

BHISHMA continued:

Addressed in this manner by his ancestors, Rama replied to his forefathers: "I vowed that I would not turn my back on battle. Never before have I withdrawn from the front of the fray. Please turn the son of the river from battle if you wish, grandfathers, but I will never withdraw from this duel!"

So the sages, led by Richíka, my king, gathered with Nárada and said to me: "Turn away from battle, my lad. Pay
honor to the greatest of brahmins." So I replied to them, 185.25
with a view to my kshatriya duty, saying: "My vow in this world is that I would never turn away and withdraw from battle, only to be hit in the back by arrows! Not from greed, compassion, fear, or to achieve my goals would I ever abandon eternal law. My mind is made up."

All the sages, led by Nárada, my king, as well as my mother Bhagírathi went to the center of battle, but I stood, firmly determined, bow in hand and arrow taken up, ready to fight in battle. So they spoke to Rama, the descendant of Bhrigu, all together once more in battle, saying: "The hearts
of brahmins are soft as butter, Bhárgava. Rama, Rama, 185.30
withdraw from this duel, finest of brahmins! You certainly can't kill Bhishma, and Bhishma can't kill you, Bhárgava!"

So saying, they all shut off the field of battle, and Rama's ancestors made the descendant of Bhrigu put down his weapons.

tato 'haṃ punar ev' âtha tān aṣṭau brahma|vādinaḥ
adrākṣaṃ dīpyamānān vai, grahān aṣṭāv iv' ôditān.
te māṃ sa|praṇayaṃ vākyam abruvan samare sthitam:
«praihi Rāmaṃ, mahā|bāho, guruṃ, loka|hitaṃ kuru.»
dṛṣṭvā nivartitaṃ Rāmaṃ suhṛd|vākyena tena vai,
lokānāṃ ca hitaṃ kurvann aham apy ādade vacaḥ.

185.35 tato 'haṃ Rāmam āsādya vavande bhṛśa|vikṣataḥ;
Rāmaś c' âbhyutsmayan premṇā mām uvāca mahā|tāpāḥ:
«tvat|samo n' âsti loke 'smin
kṣatriyaḥ pṛthivī|caraḥ.
gamyatāṃ, Bhīṣma, yuddhe 'smiṃs
toṣito 'haṃ bhṛśaṃ tvayā.»
mama c' âiva samakṣaṃ tāṃ kanyām āhūya Bhārgavaḥ
uktavān dīnayā vācā madhye teṣāṃ mah"|ātmanām.

RĀMA uvāca:

186.1 PRATYAKṢAM ETAL lokānāṃ sarveṣām eva, bhāvini:
yathā|śaktyā mayā yuddhaṃ, kṛtaṃ vai pauruṣaṃ param.
na c' âivam api śaknomi Bhīṣmaṃ śastra|bhṛtāṃ varam
viśeṣayitum atyartham uttam'|âstrāṇi darśayan.
eṣā me paramā śaktir, etan me paramaṃ balam.
yath" êṣṭaṃ gamyatāṃ, bhadre, kim anyad vā karomi te?
Bhīṣmam eva prapadyasva, na te 'nyā vidyate gatiḥ.
nirjito hy asmi Bhīṣmeṇa mah"|âstrāṇi pramuñcatā.

186.5 evam uktvā tato Rāmo viniḥśvasya mahā|manāḥ
tūṣṇīm āsīt. tataḥ kanyā provāca Bhṛgu|nandanam:
«bhagavann, evam ev' âitad, yath" āha bhagavāṃs, tathā.
a|jeyo yudhi Bhīṣmo 'yam api devair udāra|dhīḥ.

Then I saw the eight Vedic scholars once more, luminous as eight rising planets. They spoke to me charmingly as I stood in battle: "Go to your guru Rama, long-armed man, and do what benefits the world." Seeing that Rama had withdrawn and was following the advice of his friends, I too accepted the advice given to me and acted in the interest of the worlds.

So I approached Rama, seriously wounded though I was, 185.35
and Rama of great asceticism smiled at me affectionately and said to me: "There is no kshatriya walking the earth in the world to match you. Please go, Bhishma. You have satisfied me greatly in battle."

Then the Bhárgava summoned the girl into my presence, and spoke sad words in the midst of those high-souled men.

RAMA said:

OPENLY BEFORE all worlds, beautiful girl, I have fought 186.1
the duel to the best of my ability and used supreme prowess. But I am unable to win the upper hand over Bhishma, the greatest of those who wield weapons, even by displaying my finest weapons. This is the limit of my capabilities and my greatest strength. So please be on your way to wherever you wish, my dear. Or is there something else I can do for you? Go to Bhishma for help, for no other course is left open to you. I have indeed been beaten by Bhishma, shooting his great missiles.

Having spoken in this manner, high-minded Rama 186.5
sighed, and there was silence. Then the girl replied to the descendant of Bhrigu, saying: "Blessed lord, it is just as you say. Noble-minded Bhishma is invincible in battle, even to

yathā|śakti, yath"|ôtsāhaṃ mama kāryaṃ kṛtaṃ tvayā,
a|nivāryaṃ raṇe vīryam, astrāṇi vividhāni ca.
na c' âiva śakyate yuddhe viśeṣayitum antataḥ,
na c' âham enaṃ yāsyāmi punar Bhīṣmaṃ kathañ cana!
gamiṣyāmi tu tatr' âhaṃ yatra Bhīṣmaṃ, tapo|dhana,
samare pātayiṣyāmi svayam eva, Bhṛg'|ûdvaha!»

186.10 evam uktvā yayau kanyā roṣa|vyākula|locanā
tāpasye dhṛta|saṃkalpā sā me cintayatī vadham.
tato Mahendraṃ sahitair munibhir Bhṛgu|sattamaḥ
yath" āgataṃ tathā so 'gān mām upāmantrya, Bhārata.
tato rathaṃ samāruhya, stūyamāno dvijātibhiḥ,
praviśya nagaraṃ mātre Satyavatyai nyavedayam
yathā|vṛttaṃ, mahā|rāja, sā ca māṃ pratyanandata.
  puruṣāṃś c' ādiśaṃ prājñān kanyā|vṛttānta|karmaṇi.
divase divase hy asyā gati|jalpita|ceṣṭitam
pratyāharaṃś ca me yuktāḥ, sthitāḥ priya|hite sadā.
186.15 yad" âiva hi vanaṃ prāyāt sā kanyā tapase dhṛtā,
tad" âiva vyathito dīno gata|cetā iv' âbhavam.
  na hi māṃ kṣatriyaḥ kaś cid vīryeṇa vyajayad yudhi
ṛte brahma|vidas, tāta, tapasā saṃśita|vratāt,
api c' âitan mayā, rājan, Nārade 'pi niveditam,
Vyāse c' âiva tathā kāryaṃ; tau c' ôbhau mām avocatām:
«na viṣādas tvayā kāryo, Bhīṣma, Kāśi|sutāṃ prati.
daivaṃ puruṣa|kāreṇa ko nivartitum utsahet?»

the gods. You have accomplished my task to the best of your ability and energy, without restraining your heroism or various weapons in battle. And he was finally unable to be excelled in battle, but I will certainly never return again to Bhishma! I will go where I can fell Bhishma in battle myself, son of Bhrigu's line rich in asceticism!"

Having said this, the girl set off, her eyes rolling in fury 186.10
and her intentions set on asceticism, and she contemplated murder. The greatest of the Bhrigus took his leave of me and went to Mount Mahéndra with the sages, going back to where he had come from, Bhárata. Then, lauded by the brahmins, I climbed onto my chariot and entered my city. And when I told my mother Sátyavati what had happened, great king, she too lavished me with praise.

I charged intelligent men with discovering what the girl was doing. My men, intent and devoted to me, for I always wished only for their benefit, reported to me every day
about her course, comments, and behavior. But as soon as 186.15
the girl went to the forest, set on asceticism, I became perturbed and depressed, and I almost lost my mind.

Certainly no kshatriya can defeat me in battle with his prowess except the man who knows the Vedas and whose vows are whetted by asceticism, my lad. I even explained her activities to Nárada, my king, and to Vyasa; but they both said to me: "Bhishma, do not be depressed about the king of Kashi's daughter. For who would dare to avert fate through human exertion?"

sā kanyā tu, mahā|rāja, praviśy' āśrama|maṇḍalam
Yamunā|tīram āśritya tapas tepe 'timānuṣam.
186.20 nirāhārā, kṛśā, rūkṣā, jaṭilā, mala|paṅkinī,
ṣaṇ māsān vāyu|bhakṣā ca, sthāṇu|bhūtā tapo|dhanā.
Yamunā|jalam āśritya saṃvatsaram ath' âparam
udavāsaṃ nirāhārā pārayām āsa bhāvinī.
śīrṇa|parṇena c' âikena pārayām āsa sā param
saṃvatsaraṃ tīvra|kopā, pād'|âṅguṣṭh'|âgra|dhiṣṭhitā.
evaṃ dvā|daśa varṣāṇi tāpayām āsa rodasī;
nivartyamān" âpi ca sā jñātibhir n' âiva śakyate.

tato 'gamad Vatsabhūmiṃ siddha|caraṇa|sevitām,
āśramaṃ puṇya|śīlānāṃ tāpasānāṃ mah"|ātmanām.
186.25 tatra puṇyeṣu tīrtheṣu s" āplut'|âṅgī divā|niśam
vyacarat Kāśi|kanyā sā yathā|kāma|vicāriṇī
Nand'|āśrame, mahā|rāja, tath" Ôlūk'|āśrame śūbhe,
Cyavanasy' āśrame c' âiva, Brahmaṇaḥ sthāna eva ca,
Prayāge, deva|yajane, dev'|âraṇyeṣu c' âiva ha,
Bhogavatyāṃ, mahā|rāja, Kauśikasy' āśrame tathā,
Māṇḍavyasy' āśrame, rājan, Dilīpasy' āśrame tathā,
Rāma|hrade ca, Kauravya, Pailagargasya c' āśrame.
eteṣu tīrtheṣu tadā Kāśi|kanyā, viśām pate,
āplāvayata gātrāṇi vratam āsthāya duṣ|karam.

As for the girl, great sovereign, she entered a circle of hermitages, resorting to the bank of the river Yámuna, and
practiced superhuman asceticism. Without food, emaci- 186.20
ated, dried out, with matted hair, and covered in filth, the girl of ascetic wealth remained motionless, living on air for six months. Resorting to the Yámuna river, the beautiful girl spent another year living in the water, staying alive without food. She spent the next year acutely angry, standing on the tips of her toes, sustained by a single withered leaf. So, in this way, she scorched heaven and earth for twelve years, and she could not be turned away from it by her relatives.

Then she went to Vatsa·bhumi, worshipped by *siddhas* and *cháranas*, the hermitage of high-souled ascetics of holy
conduct. She plunged her limbs into the sacred bathing 186.25
fords day and night. The daughter of the king of Kashi wandered wherever she liked, roaming to Nanda's hermitage, great sovereign, to Ulúka's shining hermitage, to Chyávana's hermitage, and to the sites of Brahma. She went to Prayága,* the gods' sacrificial land, to the celestial forests, to Bhógavati, great sovereign, and to Káushika's hermitage. She went to Mandávya's hermitage, king, to Dilípa's hermitage, to Rama's lake, Kaurávya, and to Paila·garga's hermitage. The daughter of the king of Kashi immersed her limbs at these sacred spots, lord of earth, and abided by difficult vows.

186.30 tām abravīc ca, Kauravya, mama mātā jal'|ôtthitā:†
«kim arthaṃ kliśyase, bhadre? tathyam eva vadasva me.»
s" âinām ath' âbravīd, rājan, kṛt'|âñjalir a|ninditā:
«Bhīṣmeṇa samare Rāmo nirjitaś, cāru|locane,
ko 'nyas tam utsahej jetum udyat'|êṣuṃ mahī|patiḥ?
s" âhaṃ Bhīṣma|vināśāya tapas tapsye su|dāruṇam.
vicarāmi mahīṃ, devi, yathā hanyām ahaṃ nṛpam.
etad vrata|phalaṃ, devi, param asmin yathā hi me.»

tato 'bravīt sāgara|gā, «jihmaṃ carasi, bhāvini.
n' âiṣa kāmo, 'n|avady'|âṅgi, śakyaḥ prāptuṃ tvay", â|bale.
186.35 yadi Bhīṣma|vināśāya, Kāśye, carasi vai vratam,
vrata|sthā ca śarīraṃ tvaṃ yadi nāma vimokṣyasi,
nadī bhaviṣyasi, śubhe, kuṭilā, vārṣik'|ôdakā,
dus|tīrthā, na tu vijñeyā, vārṣikī, n' âṣṭa|māsikī,
bhīma|grāhavatī ghorā, sarva|bhūta|bhayaṅ|karī!»

evam uktvā tato, rājan, Kāśi|kanyāṃ nyavartata
mātā mama mahā|bhāgā, smayamān" êva bhāvinī.

kadā cid aṣṭame māsi, kadā cid daśame tathā
na prāśnīt' ôdakam api punaḥ sā vara|varṇinī.
sā Vatsabhūmiṃ, Kauravya, tīrtha|lobhāt tatas tataḥ
patitā paridhāvantī punaḥ Kāśi|pateḥ sutā.

Eventually my mother rose from the water, Kaurávya, and asked her: "Why do you make yourself suffer, my dear? Tell me exactly." The blameless lady put her hands together, king, and replied to her: "Lovely-eyed lady, Rama was defeated by Bhishma in battle, so what other king of earth would dare to defeat him when he has his weapons upraised? I am performing such horribly harsh asceticism for Bhishma's destruction. I wander the earth so that I can kill the king, goddess. This is the ultimate fruit of my vows in whatever I do, goddess." 186.30

Then the ocean-going river said, "You are going off course, beautiful woman. This wish of yours cannot be fulfilled, flawlessly limbed lady. If you practice vows for 186.35
Bhishma's destruction, Kashi lady, even if you abide by your vows and by so doing release yourself from your body, you will become like a crooked river, beautiful woman, dry in all but the rainy season, difficult to ford and unrecognizable; a monsoon river only, dry for eight months of the year, horrifying with terrifying crocodiles and a cause of fear to all creatures!"

Saying this and smirking, my noble and beautiful mother tried to restrain the Kashi king's daughter.

But again the flawlessly complexioned girl sometimes went without food and water for eight months, and sometimes for ten. In her greed for sacred fords, Kaurávya, the Kashi princess wandered here and there and fell once again into the Vatsa·bhumi river.

186.40 sā nadī Vatsabhūmyāṃ tu prathit" Âmb" êti, Bhārata,
vārṣikī, grāha|bahulā, dus|tīrthā, kuṭilā tathā.
sā kanyā tapasā tena deh'|ârdhena vyajāyata,
nadī ca, rājan, Vatseṣu, kanyā c' âiv' âbhavat tadā.

BHĪṢMA uvāca:

187.1 TATAS TE TĀPASĀḤ sarve tapase dhṛta|niścayām
dṛṣṭvā nyavartayaṃs, tāta, «kiṃ kāryam? iti» c' âbruvan.
tān uvāca tataḥ kanyā tapo|vṛddhān ṛṣīṃs tadā:
«nirākṛt" âsmi Bhīṣmeṇa, bhraṃśitā pati|dharmataḥ.
vadh'|ârthaṃ tasya dīkṣā me, na lok'|ârthaṃ, tapo|dhanāḥ.
nihatya Bhīṣmaṃ gaccheyaṃ śāntim, ity eva niścayaḥ,
yat|kṛte duḥkha|vasatim imāṃ prāpt" âsmi śāśvatīm,
pati|lokād vihīnā ca, n' âiva strī na pumān iha!
187.5 n' â|hatvā yudhi Gāṅgeyaṃ nivartiṣye, tapo|dhanāḥ.
eṣa me hṛdi saṃkalpo yad idaṃ kathitaṃ mayā.
strī|bhāve parinirviṇṇā, puṃstv'|ârthe kṛta|niścayā,
Bhīṣme praticikīrṣāmi n' âsmi vāry" êti» vai punaḥ.

tāṃ devo darśayām āsa śūla|pāṇir Umā|patiḥ
madhye teṣāṃ maha"|rṣīṇāṃ svena rūpeṇa tāpasīm.
chandyamānā varen' âtha sā vavre mat|parājayam;
«haniṣyas'! îti» tāṃ devaḥ pratyuvāca manasvinīm.
tataḥ sā punar ev' âtha kanyā Rudram uvāca ha:

She became a river in Vatsa·bhumi, known as the river Amba, Bhárata. She was a monsoon river, full of numerous crocodiles, difficult to cross, and crooked. So, through her asceticism, the girl became the river in Vatsa·bhumi with half her body, king, and remained a girl with the other half. 186.40

BHISHMA continued:

ALL THE ASCETICS tried to stop her when they saw her firmly resolved upon asceticism, my son, saying, "What are you trying to do?" The girl answered the sages of developed asceticism, saying: 187.1

"I have been driven away by Bhishma and I have been deprived of a lawful husband, so I am consecrated for his destruction rather than for another world, ascetics. Once I have killed Bhishma I may find peace. This is my resolve. For it is through his actions that I have found myself in this eternally painful life, deprived of the world of having a husband. I am neither woman nor man in these circumstances! So I will not stop before I have killed the son of the 187.5
Ganges in battle, ascetics. This is my heart's intention and this is what I vowed. I am thoroughly disgusted with being a woman, so I have made up my mind to become a man. I want to take my revenge upon Bhishma and I cannot be prevented from doing so," she repeated again.

Uma's divine husband appeared to the ascetic girl, wielding his trident, among the great sages, in his own form. When asked to choose a boon, she chose my defeat. The god replied to the spirited woman: "You will kill him!" Then the girl spoke to Rudra again, saying:

«upapadyet katham̩, deva, striyā yudhi jayo mama?
187.10 strī|bhāvena ca me gāḍham̩ manaḥ śāntam, Umā|pate,
pratiśrutaś ca, bhūt'|ēśa, tvayā Bhīṣma|parājayaḥ.
yathā sa satyo bhavati, tathā kuru, vṛṣa|dhvaja—
yathā hanyām̩ samāgamya Bhīṣmam̩ Śāntanavam̩ yudhi!»
tām uvāca mahā|devaḥ kanyām̩ kila vṛṣa|dhvajaḥ:
«na me vāg an|ṛtam̩ prāha, satyam̩, bhadre, bhaviṣyati.
haniṣyasi raṇe Bhīṣmam̩, puruṣatvam̩ ca lapsyase,
smariṣyasi ca tat sarvam̩ deham anyam̩ gatā satī.
Drupadasya kule jātā bhaviṣyasi mahā|rathaḥ
śīghr'|âstraś citra|yodhī ca, bhaviṣyasi su|sam̩mataḥ.
187.15 yath" ôktam eva, kalyāṇi, sarvam etad bhaviṣyati;
bhaviṣyasi pumān paścāt kasmāc cit kāla|paryayāt.»
evam uktvā mahā|devaḥ Kapardī vṛṣabha|dhvajaḥ
paśyatām eva viprāṇām̩ tatr' âiv' ântar|adhīyata.
tataḥ sā paśyatām̩ teṣām̩ maha"|rṣīṇām a|ninditā
samāhṛtya vanāt tasmāt kāṣṭhāni vara|varṇinī,
citām̩ kṛtvā su|mahatīm̩, pradāya ca hut'|âśanam,
pradīpte 'gnau, mahā|rāja, roṣa|dīptena cetasā
uktvā «Bhīṣma|vadhāy'! êti» praviveśa hut'|âśanam
jyeṣṭhā Kāśi|sutā, rājan, Yamunām abhito nadīm.

"God, how could it happen that I will have victory in battle when I am a woman? By the very fact that I am a woman 187.10
my heart is extremely calm, husband to Uma. Lord of evil creatures, you promised Bhishma's defeat, so act in such a manner that it may come true, bull-bannered god—so that I can meet Bhishma, son of Shántanu, in battle and kill him!"

The great bull-bannered god apparently said to the girl: "The words I say are not false. It will come true, my dear. You will kill Bhishma in battle once you have attained manhood. You will remember everything once you have gone to another body. You will be born in Drúpada's lineage and become a great chariot warrior. You will be deft with weaponry, and a highly respected and varied fighter. Every- 187.15
thing will be just as I have told you, lovely lady. You will become a man later, once some time has passed."

When he had said this, the great bull-bannered god Kapárdin disappeared there and then, before the eyes of the brahmins.

Then, in the view of those great sages, the blameless and flawlessly complexioned woman gathered wood from the forest. Once she had built an enormous pyre, she set fire to it, and when the fire was blazing, great sovereign, and her mind too was ablaze with fury, she said, "For Bhishma's death!" and the king of Kashi's eldest daughter entered the flames, my king, by the river Yámuna.

188–196

# SHIKHÁNDINI BECOMES SHIKHÁNDIN

DURYODHANA uvāca:

188.1 KATHAṂ ŚIKHAṆḌĪ, Gāṅgeya,
kanyā bhūtvā purā tadā
puruṣo 'bhūd, yudhi śreṣṭha?
tan me brūhi, pitā|maha.

BHĪṢMA uvāca:

bhāryā tu tasya, rāj'|êndra, Drupadasya mahī|pateḥ
mahiṣī dayitā hy āsīd, a|putrā ca, viśāṃ pate.
etasminn eva kāle tu Drupado vai mahī|patiḥ
apaty'|ârthe, mahā|rāja, toṣayām āsa Śaṅkaram.
asmad|vadh'|ârthaṃ niścitya tapo ghoraṃ samāsthitaḥ,
«ṛte kanyāṃ, mahā|deva, putro me syād! iti» bruvan.
188.5 «bhagavan, putram icchāmi Bhīṣmaṃ praticikīrṣayā!»
ity ukto deva|devena «strī|pumāṃs te bhaviṣyati.
nivartasva, mahī|pāla, n' âitaj jātv anyathā bhavet.»
sa tu gatvā ca nagaraṃ bhāryām idam uvāca ha:
«kṛto yatno mayā, devi, putr'|ârthe tapasā mahān†
‹kanyā bhūtvā pumān bhāvī, iti› c' ôkto 'smi Śambhunā.
punaḥ punar yācyamāno ‹diṣṭam, ity› abravīc Chivaḥ;
‹na tad|anyac ca bhavitā, bhavitavyaṃ hi tat tathā.› »
tataḥ sā niyatā bhūtvā ṛtu|kāle manasvinī
patnī Drupada|rājasya Drupadaṃ praviveśa ha.
188.10 lebhe garbhaṃ yathā|kālaṃ vidhi|dṛṣṭena karmaṇā
Pārṣatasya, mahī|pāla, yathā māṃ Nārado 'bravīt.
tato dadhāra sā devī garbhaṃ rājīva|locanā;
tāṃ sa rājā priyāṃ bhāryāṃ Drupadaḥ, Kuru|nandana,
putra|snehān mahā|bāhuḥ sukhaṃ paryacarat tadā.

DURYÓDHANA said:

How did Shikhándin, born originally as a girl, then become a man, son of the Ganges, greatest fighter in war? Tell me, grandfather. 188.1

BHISHMA replied:

Lord of kings and earth, King Drúpada's beloved queen had no sons. During this time King Drúpada appeased Shánkara for the sake of children, great sovereign, and, resolved upon my destruction, he practiced horrifying asceticism and prayed, "Great god, may I have a son rather than
a daughter! Blessed lord, I want a son to take revenge upon 188.5
Bhishma!"

But he was told by the god of gods, "You will have a child who is male and female. Go back, earth-protector, for it will certainly not be otherwise." So he went back to his city and told his wife: "I have made great effort for a son though asceticism, my queen, and Shambhu told me that I will have a daughter who will become a man. I begged Shiva over and over again, but he said, 'It is fated. What must be will be just so, and not otherwise.'"

The spirited wife of King Drúpada purified herself properly when her time came, and went to Drúpada. She con- 188.10
ceived a child by Párshata, king, at the proper time in the manner prescribed by custom, so Nárada told me. The lotus-eyed queen bore her child in the womb, and long-armed King Drúpada happily fussed over his dear wife, descendant of the Kurus, out of affection for his son.

sarvān abhiprāya|kṛtān bhāry" âlabhata, Kaurava,
a|putrasya sato rājño Drupadasya mahī|pateḥ.
yathā|kālaṃ tu sā devī mahiṣī Drupadasya ha
kanyāṃ pravara|rūpāṃ tu prājāyata, nar'|âdhipa.
a|putrasya tu rājñaḥ sā Drupadasya manasvinī
188.15 khyāpayām āsa, rāj'|êndra, «putro hy eṣa mam' êti» vai.
tataḥ sa rājā Drupadaḥ pracchannāyā, nar'|âdhipa,
putravat putra|kāryāṇi sarvāṇi samakārayat,
rakṣaṇaṃ c' âiva mantrasya mahiṣī Drupadasya sā
cakāra sarva|yatnena, bruvāṇā putra ity uta,
na ca tāṃ veda nagare kaś cid anyatra Pārṣatāt.
śraddadhāno hi tad vākyaṃ devasy' âcyuta|tejasaḥ,
chādayām āsa tāṃ kanyāṃ, pumān iti ca so 'bravīt.
jāta|karmāṇi sarvāṇi kārayām āsa pārthivaḥ
puṃvad vidhāna|yuktāni; Śikhaṇḍ" îti ca tāṃ viduḥ.
188.20 aham ekas tu cāreṇa, vacanān Nāradasya ca,
jñātavān deva|vākyena, Ambāyās tapasā tathā.

BHĪṢMA uvāca:

189.1 CAKĀRA YATNAṂ Drupadaḥ sutāyāḥ sarva|karmasu,
tato lekhy'|ādiṣu tathā, śilpeṣu ca, paraṃ|tapa;
iṣv|astre c' âiva, rāj'|êndra, Droṇa|śiṣyo babhūva ha.
tasya mātā, mahā|rāja, rājānaṃ vara|varṇinī
codayām āsa bhāry"|ârthaṃ kanyāyāḥ putravat tadā.
tatas tāṃ Pārṣato dṛṣṭvā kanyāṃ saṃprāpta|yauvanām
striyaṃ matvā tataś cintāṃ prapede saha bhāryayā.

Káurava, the wife of sonless King Drúpada, the lord of earth, had her every wish granted, and when the time came, Drúpada's goddess queen gave birth to a beautiful daughter, lord of men. Sonless King Drúpada's spirited wife an- 188.15
nounced that her child was a son, lord of kings. King Drúpada, O lord of men, arranged to have all the necessary ceremonies for sons perfomed for his secret daughter as though she were a son, and Drúpada's wife protected her counsels, making every effort and proclaiming that her daughter was in fact a son. And no one in the city, barring Párshata, knew that the child was a girl.

Trusting in the word of the eternally glorious god, the king concealed his daughter and claimed she was male. The king had all the proper and customary birth rites for a boy performed, and people knew her as Shikhándin. I alone 188.20
knew, through a spy, Nárada's words, the god's words, and Amba's asceticism.

BHISHMA continued:

DRÚPADA TOOK trouble over every matter concerning his 189.1
daughter, such as writing and so on and the arts, enemy-scorcher, and she was even a pupil of Drona's in archery, lord of kings. The child's flawlessly complexioned mother, great sovereign, urged the king to see about getting a wife for his daughter, as though she were a boy. Then, when Párshata saw that his daughter was reaching full maturity, it dawned on him that she was, in fact, a woman; and he and his wife became anxious.

DRUPADA uvāca:

kanyā mam' êyaṃ saṃprāptā yauvanaṃ śōka|vardhinī;
mayā pracchāditā c' êyaṃ vacanāc chūla|pāṇinaḥ.

BHĀRY" ôvāca:

189.5 na tan mithyā, mahā|rāja, bhaviṣyati kathañ cana;
trailokya|kartā kasmādd hi vṛthā vaktum ih' ârhati?
yadi te rocate, rājan, vakṣyāmi. śṛṇu me vacaḥ.
śrutv" êdānīṃ prapadyethāḥ svāṃ matiṃ, Pṛṣat'|ātmaja.
kriyatām asya yatnena vidhivad dāra|saṃgrahaḥ.
bhavitā tad|vacaḥ satyam, iti me niścitā matiḥ.

tatas tau niścayaṃ kṛtvā tasmin kārye 'tha daṃpatī
varayāṃ cakratuḥ kanyāṃ Daśārṇ'|âdhipateḥ sutām.
tato rājā Drupado rāja|siṃhaḥ
sarvān rājñaḥ kulataḥ sanniśāmya
Dāśārṇakasya nṛ|pates tanū|jāṃ
Śikhaṇḍine varayām āsa dārān.

189.10 Hiraṇyavarm" êti nṛpo yo 'sau Dāśārṇakaḥ smṛtaḥ,
sa ca prādān mahī|pālaḥ kanyāṃ tasmai Śikhaṇḍine,
sa ca rājā Daśārṇeṣu mahān āsīt su|durjayaḥ
Hiraṇyavarmā dur|dharṣā, mahā|seno, mahā|manāḥ.
kṛte vivāhe tu tadā sā kanyā, rāja|sattama,
yauvanaṃ samanuprāptā sā ca kanyā Śikhaṇḍinī.

kṛta|dāraḥ Śikhaṇḍī ca Kāmpilyaṃ punar āgamat.
tataḥ sā veda tāṃ kanyāṃ kañ cit kālaṃ striyaṃ kila.
Hiraṇyavarmaṇaḥ kanyā jñātvā tāṃ tu Śikhaṇḍinīm,
dhātrīṇāṃ ca sakhīnāṃ ca vrīḍayānā nyavedayat
kanyāṃ Pañcāla|rājasya sutāṃ tāṃ vai Śikhaṇḍinīm.

DRÚPADA said:

My daughter has matured into a woman, increasing my grief, and I have concealed her at the command of Shiva who carries his trident in hand.

HIS WIFE replied:

It can in no way whatsoever be wrong, great king, for why would the creator of the three worlds speak deceitfully? If it pleases you, king, I will speak. Listen to what I have to say, and when you have heard it you should then do what you think right, son of Príshata. Let our child's marriage duly and carefully be arranged. The god's words will come true. I am sure of it in my heart. 189.5

So, when those two, the master and mistress of the house, had made up their minds on this task, they chose the maiden daughter of the king of Dashárna. Lion-like King Drúpada found out about the lineages of all kings, and chose the daughter of the king of Dashárna to be Shikhándin's bride.

Now, the Dashárnaka king was called Hiránya·varman, 189.10
and the earth-protector bestowed his daughter upon Shikhándin. King Hiránya·varman was a mighty king in the Dashárna lands: invincible, unassailable, possessed of an enormous army, and high-minded. Once the marriage had taken place, greatest of kings, the girl reached full maturity, as did the lady Shikhándini.

Once he had married, Shikhándin returned once more to Kampílya, and the wife, so they say, found out after a while that her husband was in fact a woman. When the daughter of Hiránya·varman realized that Shikhándin was in fact Shikhándini, she ashamedly revealed to her nurses

189.15 tatas tā, rāja|śārdūla, dhātryo Dāśārnikās tadā
jagmur ārtiṃ parāṃ preṣyāḥ, preṣayām āsur eva ca.
tato Daśārṇ'|âdhipateḥ preṣyāḥ sarvā nyavedayan
vipralambhaṃ yathā|vṛttaṃ; sa ca cukrodha pārthivaḥ.
Śikhaṇḍy api, mahā|rāja, puṃvad rāja|kule tadā
vijahāra mudā yuktaḥ, strītvaṃ n' âiv' âtirocayan.
tataḥ katipay'|âhasya tac chrutvā, Bharata'|rṣabha,
Hiraṇyavarmā, rāj'|êndra, roṣād ārtiṃ jagāma ha.
tato Dāśārṇako rājā tīvra|kopa|samanvitaḥ
dūtaṃ prasthāpayām āsa Drupadasya niveśanam.
189.20 tato Drupadam āsādya dūtaḥ Kāñcanavarmaṇaḥ
eka ek'|ântam utsārya raho vacanam abravīt:
«Dāśārṇa|rājo, rājaṃs, tvām idaṃ vacanam abravīt,
abhiṣaṅgāt prakupito, vipralabdhas tvayā, 'n|agha:
‹avamanyase māṃ, nṛ|pate, nūnaṃ dur|mantritaṃ tava,
yan me kanyāṃ sva|kany"|ârthe mohād yācitavān asi!
tasy' âdya vipralambhasya phalaṃ prāpnuhi, dur|mate!
eṣa tvāṃ sa|jan'|âmātyam uddharāmi! sthiro bhava!› »

BHĪṢMA uvāca:

190.1 EVAM UKTASYA dūtena Drupadasya tadā, nṛpa,
corasy' êva gṛhītasya na prāvartata bhāratī.
sa yatnam akarot tīvraṃ sambandhiny anumānane,
dūtair madhura|saṃbhāṣair «na tad ast' îti» saṃdiśan.

and friends that the child of the Panchála king was in fact a girl, Shikhándini. Tiger-like king, the Dashárnika nurses 189.15
were then extremely distressed, and they sent word of the subterfuge.

The messengers all explained the whole deception, just as it had occurred, to the Dashárna king; and he became furious. For his part, O great king, Shikhándin happily behaved like a man in the royal palace, and did not overly highlight his womanhood. But when Hiránya·varman heard a few days later, bull of the Bharatas, he was terribly afflicted with fury, lord of kings.

The Dashárnaka king, filled with acute rage, assigned a messenger to Drúpada's house. Hiránya·varman's messen- 189.20
ger approached Drúpada alone, and, taking him aside, he said these words privately:

"The Dashárna king has been deceived by you and is furious about his humiliation, so he sends this message to you, sinless sovereign:

'You have insulted me, king, and I surely received bad advice from you, for you foolishly begged me for my daughter for the sake of what turns out to be your own daughter! Now reap the fruit of your subterfuge, wicked-minded man! I will annihilate you and your family and advisors! Be ready!'"

BHISHMA continued:

ADDRESSED BY the messenger in this way, Drúpada didn't 190.1
say a word, king, as though he were a thief caught red-handed. Instead, he made a great effort to conciliate his relation by sending sweet-speaking messengers to assure him

sa rājā bhūya ev' âtha jñātvā tattvam ath' āgamat,
kany" êti Pāñcāla|sutāṃ tvaramāṇo viniryayau.
tataḥ saṃpreṣayām āsa mitrāṇām a|mit'|âujasām
duhitur vipralambhaṃ taṃ dhātrīṇāṃ vacanāt tadā.
190.5 tataḥ samudayaṃ kṛtvā balānāṃ rāja|sattamaḥ,
abhiyāne matiṃ cakre Drupadaṃ prati, Bhārata.
tataḥ saṃmantrayām āsa mantribhiḥ sa mahī|patiḥ
Hiraṇyavarmā, rāj'|êndra, Pāñcālyaṃ pārthivaṃ prati.
tatra vai niścitaṃ teṣām abhūd rājñāṃ mah"|ātmanām:
«tathyaṃ bhavati ced etat, kanyā, rājañ, Śikhaṇḍinī,
baddhvā Pañcāla|rājānam ānayiṣyāmahe gṛham
anyaṃ rājānam ādhāya Pañcāleṣu nar'|ēśvaram
ghātayiṣyāma nṛ|patiṃ Pāñcālaṃ sa|Śikhaṇḍinam.»
190.10 tat tad" ân|ṛtam ājñāya punar dūtān nar'|âdhipaḥ
prāsthāpayat Pārṣatāya, «nihanm' îti sthiro bhava!»

BHĪṢMA uvāca:

sa hi prakṛtyā vai bhītaḥ, kilbiṣī ca nar'|âdhipaḥ,
bhayaṃ tīvram anuprāpto Drupadaḥ pṛthivī|patiḥ.
visṛjya dūtān Dāśārṇe Drupadaḥ śoka|mūrcchitaḥ
sametya bhāryāṃ rahite vākyam āha nar'|âdhipaḥ
bhayena mahat" āviṣṭo, hṛdi śokena c' āhataḥ
Pāñcāla|rājo dayitāṃ mātaraṃ vai Śikhaṇḍinaḥ:
«abhiyāsyati māṃ kopāt sambandhī su|mahā|balaḥ
Hiraṇyavarmā nṛ|patiḥ karṣamāṇo varūthinīm!
190.15 kim idānīṃ kariṣyāvo mūḍhau kanyām imāṃ prati?
Śikhaṇḍī kila putras te kany" êti pariśaṅkitaḥ.

that it was not true. But when the king had the truth confirmed again—that the Panchála prince was in fact a girl—he set out in a hurry.

He sent word to his immeasurably energetic friends about the subterfuge played upon his daughter, trusting the testimony of her nurses. Then, raising his troops, the greatest 190.5
of kings resolved to attack Drúpada, O Bhárata, and King Hiránya·varman debated with his advisors over means with which to deal with the Panchála king, lord of kings.

Finally the high-souled kings came to a decision: "If Shikhándin really is a girl, king, then we will tie up the Panchála king and lead him home. We will install another king to be lord over the Panchálas, and we will kill the Panchála king and Shikhándin."

When he was made aware of their true decision, the lord 190.10
of men sent messengers to Párshata once more, saying, "I will kill you! Be ready!"

BHISHMA continued:

Since King Drúpada was both fearful by nature and, in this instance, culpable, the lord of earth was exceptionally scared. King Drúpada, stupefied by grief, sent messengers to Dashárna, and meeting his wife privately the Panchála king, filled with great fear and crushed by the grief in his heart, said to his dear wife, the mother of Shikhándin:

"My incredibly powerful in-law, King Hiránya·varman, is marching against me in fury, dragging an army with him! What will we do about this girl now, fools that we are? Ru- 190.15
mor has it that it is suspected that your son Shikhándin is really a girl. Apparently Hiránya·varman, with his allies,

iti sañcintya yatnena sa|mitraḥ sa|bal'|ânugaḥ
‹vañcito 'sm' îti› manvāno māṃ kil' ôddhartum icchati!
kim atra tathyaṃ, su|śroṇi, mithyā kiṃ? brūhi, śobhane.
śrutvā tvattaḥ śubhaṃ vākyaṃ saṃvidhāsyāmy ahaṃ tathā.
ahaṃ hi saṃśayaṃ prāpto, bālā c' êyaṃ Śikhándinī,
tvaṃ ca, rājñi, mahat kṛcchraṃ samprāptā, vara|varṇini.
sā tvaṃ sarva|vimokṣāya tattvam ākhyāhi pṛcchataḥ;
tathā vidadhyāṃ, su|śroṇi, kṛtyam āśu, śuci|smite.
190.20 Śikhaṇḍini ca mā bhais tvaṃ, vidhāsye tatra tattvataḥ
kṛpay" âhaṃ, var'|ārohe, vañcitaḥ putra|dharmataḥ;
mayā Dāśārṇako rājā vañcitaḥ sa mahī|patiḥ.
tad ācakṣva, mahā|bhāge, vidhāsye tatra yadd hitam.»
jānatā hi nar'|êndreṇa khyāpan'|ârthaṃ parasya vai
prakāśaṃ coditā devī pratyuvāca mahī|patim.

BHĪṢMA uvāca:

191.1 TATAḤ ŚIKHAṆḌINO mātā yathā|tattvaṃ, nar'|âdhipa,
ācacakṣe, mahā|bāho, bhartre kanyāṃ Śikhaṇḍinīm.
«a|putrayā mayā, rājan, sa|patnīnāṃ bhayād idam
kanyā Śikhaṇḍinī jātā puruṣo vai niveditā.
tvayā c' âiva, nara|śreṣṭha, tan me prīty" ânumoditam,
putra|karma kṛtaṃ c' âiva kanyāyāḥ, pārthiva'|rṣabha.
bhāryā c' ōḍhā tvayā, rājan, Daśārṇ'|âdhipateḥ sutā,
mayā ca pratyabhihitaṃ deva|vāky'|ârtha|darśanāt,

forces, and followers, is utterly convinced and wants to kill me, believing that he has been tricked!

What is true and what is false, shapely-hipped lady? Tell me, beautiful lady. When I have heard your fine words I will implement your advice. I am certainly in danger, and so too is the child Shikhándini. You, my queen, are also plunged into great misfortune, flawlessly complexioned lady.

Tell me the truth when asked, so that everyone may escape their doom. I will do what must swiftly be done,
shapely-hipped and sweet-smiling lady. Don't worry about 190.20
Shikhándin, for I will act upon the truth of the matter, and with compassion. I was deceived by means of the lawful rights performed for a son, shapely-hipped lady, and so I inadvertently deceived the Dashárnaka king and earth-lord. So tell me, noble lady, how I may act for the good."

Though the lord of men did, in fact, know, he urged her publicly in order to denounce someone else. The queen answered the king.

BHISHMA continued:

SHIKHÁNDIN'S MOTHER told her husband the precise 191.1
truth about her daughter Shikhándin, long-armed lord of men.

"Since I had no sons, king, and I was afraid of the other wives, I had it made known that Shikhándin of dubious gender was a boy, though she was born a girl. You approved this because you loved me, greatest of men, and the rituals for a son were performed on a daughter, bull-like king. You married her to the Dashárna king's daughter, and I ap-

‹kanyā bhūtvā pumān bhāv" îty› evaṃ c' âitad upekṣitam.»
191.5 etac chrutvā Drupado Yajñasenaḥ
sarvaṃ tattvaṃ mantravidbhyo nivedya
mantraṃ rājā mantrayām āsa, rājan,
yathā|yuktaṃ rakṣaṇe vai prajānām.
sambandhakaṃ c' âiva samarthya tasmin
Dāśārṇake vai nṛ|patau, nar'|êndra,
svayaṃ kṛtvā vipralambhaṃ yathāvan
mantr'|âik'|âgro niścayaṃ vai jagāma.

sva|bhāva|guptaṃ nagaram āpat|kāle tu, Bhārata,
gopayām āsa, rāj'|êndra, sarvataḥ samalaṃkṛtam,
ārtiṃ ca paramāṃ rājā jagāma saha bhāryayā
Daśārṇa|patinā sārdhaṃ virodhe, Bharata'|rṣabha.
«kathaṃ sambandhinā sārdhaṃ
na me syād vigraho mahān?»
iti sañcintya manasā
devatām arcayat tadā.

191.10 taṃ tu dṛṣṭvā tadā, rājan, devī deva|paraṃ tadā
arcāṃ prayuñjānam atho, bhāryā vacanam abravīt:
«devānāṃ pratipattiś ca satyaṃ sādhu|matā satām.
kim u duḥkh'|ârṇavaṃ prāpya? tasmād arcayatāṃ gurūn,
daivatāni ca sarvāṇi pūjyantāṃ bhūri|dakṣiṇam,
agnayaś c' âpi hūyantāṃ Dāśārṇa|pratiṣedhane.
a|yuddhena nivṛttiṃ ca manasā cintaya, prabho.
devatānāṃ prasādena sarvam etad bhaviṣyati.
mantribhir mantritaṃ sārdhaṃ tvayā, pṛthula|locana,
purasy' âsy' â|vināśāya yac ca, rājaṃs, tathā kuru.
191.15 daivaṃ hi mānuṣ'|ôpetaṃ bhṛśaṃ sidhyati, pārthiva,

proved it, looking to the meaning of Rudra's prophecy that the girl would become a man. I overlooked the problem."

Having heard this, King Drúpada Yajña·sena explained 191.5
the entire truth of the matter to his advisors and took counsel, my king, as to the best course for the protection of his citizens. Lord of kings, he judged that the tie of kinship with the Dashárnaka king remained intact, despite the fact that he himself had cheated him, so he came to a decision, singlemindedly set on his counsel.

Though the city had natural protection for times of disaster, Bhárata, he defended it by girding it all round, lord of kings. The king and his wife fell into the deepest depression over their quarrel with the king of Dashárna, bull of the Bharatas. Drúpada worshipped the gods in his mind as he pondered how he could avoid large-scale hostilities against a relative.

As the queen watched him absorbed with the gods and 191.10
busy worshipping them, his wife addressed him, king, saying:

"Good men certainly regard observances for the gods as excellent. How much more so when sunk in an ocean of troubles? Therefore worship your gurus, honor all the gods with rich rewards, and make offerings into the fire to ward off Dashárna.

Lord, ponder in your mind how to keep him back without resorting to war. Everything will turn out fine, by the grace of the gods. Large-eyed king, act according to your counsels with your advisors, to prevent the destruction of
the city. Certainly, when fate is assisted by human exertion, 191.15
success is great, king, but when the two are in opposition

parasparaǀvirodhādd hi siddhir asti na c' âitayoḥ.
tasmād vidhāya nagare vidhānaṃ sacivaiḥ saha
arcayasva yathāǀkāmaṃ daivatāni, viśāṃ pate!»
  evaṃ saṃbhāṣamāṇau tau dṛṣṭvā śokaǀparāyaṇau
Śikhaṇḍinī tadā kanyā vrīḍit" êva tapasvinī.
tataḥ sā cintayām āsa, «matǀkṛte duḥkhitāv ubhau
imāv, iti» tataś cakre matiṃ prāṇaǀvināśane.
evaṃ sā niścayaṃ kṛtvā bhṛśaṃ śokaǀparāyaṇā
nirjagāma gṛhaṃ tyaktvā gahanaṃ nirjanaṃ vanam
191.20 yakṣeṇa' rddhimatā, rājan, Sthūṇākarṇena pālitam.
tadǀbhayād eva ca jano visarjayati tad vanam.
tatra ca Sthūṇaǀbhavanaṃ sudhāǀmṛttikaǀlepanam,
lāj'ǀôllāpikaǀdhūm'ǀāḍhyam, uccaǀprākāraǀtoraṇam.
tat praviśya Śikhaṇḍī sā Drupadasy' ātmajā, nṛpa,
anǀaśnātā bahuǀtithaṃ śarīram udaśoṣayat.
  darśayām āsa tāṃ yakṣaḥ Sthūṇo mārdavaǀsaṃyutaḥ,
«kim artho 'yaṃ tav' āraṃbhaḥ? kariṣye. brūhi mā|ciram!»
«aǀśakyam, iti» sā yakṣaṃ punaḥ punar uvāca ha.
«kariṣyām' îti» vai kṣipraṃ pratyuvāc' âtha guhyakaḥ.
191.25 «dhan'ǀēśvarasy' ânucaro varado 'smi, nṛp'ǀātmaje,
aǀdeyam api dāsyāmi. brūhi yat te vivakṣitam.»
  tataḥ Śikhaṇḍī tat sarvam akhilena nyavedayat
tasmai yakṣaǀpradhānāya Sthūṇākarṇāya, Bhārata.

to each other then there is assuredly no success. Therefore, worship the gods as much as you wish, lord of earth; but also act appropriately in the best interest of the city with your advisors!"

When the maiden Shikhándini saw her parents talking, filled with grief, the austere girl was ashamed. Thinking it was her fault that they were both miserable, she made up her mind to end her life. With her decision made, she was greatly occupied with her grief, and she left her home and went to the dense, uninhabited forest.

It was protected by a rich *yaksha* named Sthuna·karna, 191.20
king, and people deserted the forest for fear of him. Sthuna's house stood there, smeared with whitewashed clay, with a high wall and gateway, and rich with smoke from toasted rice cakes. Shikhándin, Drúpada's daughter, entered the forest, king, and, fasting for many days, she desiccated her body.

The *yaksha* Sthuna, filled with kindness, revealed himself to the girl, saying, "What goal are you trying to achieve? I will accomplish it. Tell me immediately!" But she kept replying to the *yaksha*, time and time again, saying: "It is
impossible." The *gúhyaka* quickly insisted, "I will do it! I am 191.25
a follower of Kubéra the lord of wealth, and I am a granter of wishes, princess. I will grant the ungrantable. Tell me what you want to say."

So Shikhándin explained everything in detail to that chief *yaksha*, Sthuna·karna, O Bhárata.

ŚIKHAṆḌY uvāca:

a|putro me pitā, yakṣa, na cirān nāśam eṣyati,
abhiyāsyati sa|krodho Daśārṇ'|âdhipatir hi tam,
mahā|balo, mah"|ôtsāhaḥ, sa|hema|kavaco nṛpaḥ.
tasmād rakṣasva māṃ, yakṣa, mātaraṃ pitaraṃ ca me.
pratijñāto hi bhavatā duḥkha|pratiśamo mama
bhaveyaṃ puruṣo, yakṣa, tvat|prasādād a|ninditaḥ!
191.30 yāvad eva sa rājā vai n' ôpayāti puraṃ mama,
tāvad eva, mahā|yakṣa, prasādaṃ kuru, guhyaka!

BHĪṢMA uvāca:

192.1 ŚIKHAṆḌI|VĀKYAṂ śrutv" âtha sa yakṣo, Bharata'|rṣabha,
provāca manasā cintya daiven' ôpanipīḍitaḥ,
bhavitavyaṃ tathā tadd hi mama duḥkhāya, Kaurava,
«bhadre, kāmaṃ kariṣyāmi; samayaṃ tu nibodha me.
kiñ cit kāl'|ântare dāsye puṃl|liṅgaṃ svam idaṃ tava.
āgantavyaṃ tvayā kāle. satyaṃ c' âiva vadasva me.
prabhuḥ saṃkalpa|siddho 'smi, kāma|cārī vihaṅ|gamaḥ!
mat|prasādāt puraṃ c' âiva trāhi, bandhūṃś ca kevalam!
192.5 strī|liṅgaṃ dhārayiṣyāmi tad evam, pārthiv'|ātmaje.
satyaṃ me pratijānīhi; kariṣyāmi priyaṃ tava!»

ŚIKHAṆḌY uvāca:

pratidāsyāmi, bhagavan, puṃl|liṅgaṃ tava, su|vrata,
kiñ cit kāl'|ântaraṃ strītvaṃ dhārayasva, niśā|cara.
pratiyāte Daśārṇe tu pārthive hema|varmaṇi

SHIKHÁNDIN said:

My father has no son, *yaksha*, and his destruction will come soon. The Dashárna king is furiously marching to attack him. Hiránya·varman, the golden-armored king, is very powerful and vigorous. Therefore, protect me, *yaksha*, and protect my mother and father. You have promised to soothe my pain, so let me become a blameless man through your grace, *yaksha*! Treat me graciously, great *gúhyaka yak-* 191.30
*sha*, before the king attacks my city!

BHISHMA continued:

HAVING LISTENED to Shikhándin's words, bull of the 192.1
Bharatas, the *yaksha* pondered the matter in his mind; and then, because he was pressed by fate and it certainly was destined to happen—much to my sorrow, Káurava!—he replied:

"My dear, I will grant your wish, but there is a catch, so listen to me. I will grant you my own male organs for a certain period of time. But you must return to me at the right time. Swear this truthfully.

I am a lord whose intentions are successful. I am a creature of the sky who goes where he pleases! Through my
grace, save your city and your entire family! I will wear your 192.5
signs of womanhood, princess. So swear to me truthfully, and I will do what you want!"

SHIKHÁNDIN replied:

I will give back your male genitalia, blessed and strict-vowed lord. Wear my womanhood for a while, night-walker. Once the golden-armored Dashárna king, Hiránya·varman,

kany" âiva hi bhaviṣyāmi, puruṣas tvaṃ bhaviṣyasi.

BHĪṢMA uvāca:

ity uktvā samayaṃ tatra cakrāte tāv ubhau, nṛpa,
anyo|'nyasy' âbhisaṃdehe tau saṃkrāmayatāṃ tataḥ.
strī|liṅgaṃ dhārayām āsa Sthūṇā|yakṣo 'tha, Bhārata,
yakṣa|rūpaṃ ca tad dīptaṃ Śikhaṇḍī pratyapadyata.
192.10 tataḥ Śikhaṇḍī Pāñcālyaḥ puṃstvam āsādya, pārthiva,
viveśa nagaraṃ hṛṣṭaḥ, pitaraṃ ca samāsadat.
yathā|vṛttaṃ tu tat sarvam ācakhyau Drupadasya tat.
Drupadas tasya tac chrutvā harṣam āhārayat param,
sa|bhāryas tac ca sasmāra mah"|ēśvara|vacas tadā.
tataḥ saṃpreṣayām āsa Daśārṇ'|âdhipater nṛpaḥ:
«puruṣo 'yaṃ mama sutaḥ. śraddhattāṃ me bhavān iti.»
atha Dāśārṇako rājā sahas" âbhyāgamat tadā
Pañcāla|rājaṃ Drupadaṃ duḥkha|śoka|samanvitaḥ.
tataḥ Kāmpilyam āsādya Daśārṇ'|âdhipatis tataḥ
192.15 preṣayām āsa sat|kṛtya dūtaṃ brahma|vidāṃ varam.
«brūhi mad|vacanād, dūta, Pāñcālyaṃ taṃ nṛp'|âdhamam:
‹yan me kanyāṃ sva|kany"|ârthe vṛtavān asi, dur|mate,
phalaṃ tasy' âvalepasya drakṣyasy adya, na saṃśayaḥ!› »
evam uktaś ca ten' âsau brāhmaṇo, rāja|sattama,
dūtaḥ prayāto nagaraṃ Dāśārṇa|nṛpa|coditaḥ.
tata āsādayām āsa purodhā Drupadaṃ pure.
tasmai Pāñcālako rājā gām arghyaṃ ca su|satkṛtam
prāpayām āsa, rāj'|êndra, saha tena Śikhaṇḍinā.

has gone, then I will certainly become a woman, and you will become a man again.

BHISHMA continued:

Having spoken in this way, they both made the agreement, king, and each handed their sex organs over to the other. The *yaksha* Sthuna wore the distinguishing marks of womanhood, and Shikhándin took the *yaksha*'s blazing form. Shikhándin, the Panchála prince, entered his city ju- 192.10
bilantly, king, now that he had obtained manhood, and he approached his father.

He told Drúpada everything that had happened, and upon hearing the tale Drúpada was absolutely delighted, recalling the great god's words with his wife. So the king sent a message to the Dashárna king, saying: "My son is a man. Please believe me."

But the Dashárnaka king marched vehemently against Drúpada the Panchála king, for he was filled with pain and grief. As he approached Kampílya, the lord of Dashárna sent the greatest of Vedic scholars as his messenger, with 192.15
the proper rites. "Envoy, tell my message to the Panchála lord, the vilest of kings: 'Wicked-minded man, you chose my daughter for your own daughter, but today you will doubtless witness the fruit of your pride!'"

Given these instructions, the brahmin envoy went to the city, urged by the Dashárna king, O greatest of sovereigns. The priest approached Drúpada in his city, and once the Panchála king and Shikhándin had received him properly, offering him a cow and the customary guest reception,

tāṃ pūjāṃ n' âbhyanandat sa, vākyaṃ c' êdam uvāca ha.
192.20 «yad uktaṃ tena vīreṇa rājñā kāñcana|varmaṇā:
‹yat te 'ham, adham'|ācāra, duhitr" âsmy abhivañcitaḥ,
tasya pāpasya karaṇāt phalaṃ prāpnuhi, dur|mate!
dehi yuddhaṃ, nara|pate, mam' âdya raṇa|mūrdhani!
uddhariṣyāmi te sadyaḥ s'|âmātya|suta|bāndhavam!› »
tad upālaṃbha|saṃyuktaṃ śrāvitaḥ kila pārthivaḥ
Daśārṇa|patinā c' ôkto mantri|madhye purodhasā,
abhavad, Bharata|śreṣṭha, Drupadaḥ praṇay'|ānataḥ.
«yad āha māṃ bhavān, brahman, sambandhi|vacanād vacaḥ
asy' ôttaraṃ prativaco dūto rājñe vadiṣyati.»
192.25 tataḥ saṃpreṣayām āsa Drupado 'pi mah"|ātmane
Hiraṇya|varmaṇe dūtaṃ brāhmaṇaṃ veda|pāragam.
tam āgamya tu rājānaṃ Daśārṇ'|âdhipatiṃ tadā
tad vākyam ādade, rājan, yad uktaṃ Drupadena ha.
«āgamaḥ kriyatāṃ vyaktaḥ. kumāro 'yaṃ suto mama!
mithy" âitad uktaṃ ken' âpi, tad a|śraddheyam ity uta.»
tataḥ sa rājā Drupadasya śrutvā
vimarṣa|yukto yuvatīr variṣṭhāḥ
saṃpreṣayām āsa su|cāru|rūpāḥ
Śikhaṇḍinaṃ strī, pumān v" êti vettum.
tāḥ preṣitās tattva|bhāvaṃ viditvā
prītyā rājñe tac chaśaṃsur hi sarvam;
Śikhaṇḍinaṃ puruṣaṃ, Kaurav'|êndra,
Dāśārṇa|rājāya mah"|ânubhāvam.

lord of kings, the envoy refused the honor, simply giving his message.

"The heroic, golden-armored King Hiránya·varman 192.20
sends you this message: 'Vilest miscreant, you have deceived me about your daughter! Reap the reward of your wickedness on her account, wicked-minded man! Give me a fight today, lord of men, at the head of battle! I will kill you, your counselors, and your children and kin!'"

They say that when the priest forced him to listen to words of such abuse relayed from the Dashárna king in the midst of his ministers, King Drúpada was affectionate in his conduct, greatest of the Bharatas. "Brahmin, my own envoy will give the king my reply to the message you have given me from my brother-in-law."

So Drúpada sent a brahmin who had reached the limit 192.25
of Vedic learning as a messenger to high-souled Hiránya·varman, the golden-armored king. And going to the lord and king of Dashárna he gave him the message Drúpada had given him, king. "Please conduct an examination. My son is clearly a young man! Someone gave you false testimony, and their words are not to be trusted."

When the king heard Drúpada's message, he spent time deliberating, and then he sent the finest and most attractive-looking young women to discover whether Shikhándin was a woman or a man. The women he sent learned the truth of the matter and delightedly told the king everything. They informed the Dashárna king that Shikhándin was in fact a powerful male, lord of the Káuravas.

192.30 tataḥ kṛtvā tu rājā sa āgamaṃ prītimān atha
sambandhinā samāgamya hṛṣṭo vāsam uvāsa ha.
Śikhaṇḍine ca muditaḥ prādād vittaṃ jan'|ēśvaraḥ
hastino, 'śvāṃś ca, gāś c' âiva, dāsyo 'tha bahulās tathā.
pūjitaś ca pratiyayau nirbhartsya tanayāṃ kila.
vinīta|kilbiṣe prīte Hemavarmaṇi pārthive
pratiyāte Daśārṇe tu hṛṣṭa|rūpā Śikhaṇḍinī.
kasya cit tv atha kālasya Kubero nara|vāhanaḥ
loka|yātrāṃ prakurvāṇaḥ Sthūṇasy' āgān niveśanam.
sa tad|gṛhasy' ôpari vartamāna
ālokayām āsa dhan'|âdhigoptā.
Sthūṇasya yakṣasya viveśa veśma
sv|alaṃkṛtaṃ mālya|guṇair vicitraiḥ,
192.35 lājyaiś ca gandhaiś ca tathā vitānair
abhyarcitaṃ, dhūpana|dhūpitaṃ ca,
dhvajaiḥ patākābhir alaṃ|kṛtaṃ ca,
bhakṣy'|ânna|pey'|āmiṣa|datta|homam.
tat sthānaṃ tasya dṛṣṭvā tu sarvataḥ samalaṅkṛtam,
maṇi|ratna|suvarṇānāṃ mālābhiḥ paripūritam,
nānā|kusuma|gandh'|āḍhyaṃ, sikta|saṃmṛṣṭa|śobhitam,
ath' âbravīd yakṣa|patis tān yakṣān anugāṃs tadā:
«sv|alaṃkṛtam idaṃ veśma Sthūṇasy', â|mita|vikramāḥ;
n' ôpasarpati māṃ c' âiva kasmād adya sa manda|dhīḥ?
yasmāj jānan sa mand'|ātmā mām asau n' ôpasarpati;
tasmāt tasmai mahā|daṇḍo dhāryaḥ syād iti me matiḥ.»

With his investigation complete the king was delighted, 192.30
and he happily stayed with his brother-in-law for a visit. The jubilant lord of men presented Shikhándin with wealth, elephants, horses, cattle, and numerous slaves. He was honored, and having censured his daughter, or so they claim, he left. Once the golden-armored Dashárna King Hiránya·varman had left delightedly, with the offence wiped out, Shikhándin appeared joyful.

Some time later, Kubéra, driving his human vehicle, made his way to Sthuna's home on his world tour.

The protector of wealth inspected the house as he floated in the air above it. He took himself to Sthuna the *yaksha*'s house, which was beautifully decorated with wonderful multicolored garlands, rice cakes, perfumes, and cano- 192.35
pies. It was purified and scented with incense smoke, ornamented with banners and flags, and fully stocked with food, drink, meat, and offerings.

When he saw the home, beautifully decorated all over, furnished with garlands of gems, jewels, and gold, perfumed by the fragrance of various flowers, and gleaming, well watered, and swept as it was, the lord of the *yakshas* said to the *yaksha*s in his entourage: "Sthuna's house is beautifully embellished, immeasurably powerful *yaksha*s, but why does the foolish-minded *yaksha* not approach me? The idiotic-souled *yaksha* is well aware that I am here, but he does not approach me; so I believe he should be made to suffer great punishment."

YAKṢĀ ūcuḥ:

192.40 Drupadasya sutā, rājan, rājño jātā Śikhaṇḍinī;
tasyā nimitte kasmimś cit prādāt puruṣa|lakṣaṇam.
agrahīl lakṣaṇaṃ strīṇāṃ, strī|bhūto tiṣṭhate gṛhe.
n' ôpasarpati ten' âsau sa|vrīḍaḥ strī|svarūpavān;
etasmāt kāraṇād, rājan, Sthūṇo na tv" âdya sarpati.
śrutvā kuru yathā|nyāyaṃ. vimānam iha tiṣṭhatām.
«ānīyatāṃ Sthūṇa! iti» tato yakṣ'|âdhipo 'bravīt.
«kart" âsmi nigrahaṃ tasya!» pratyuvāca punaḥ punaḥ.
so 'bhyagacchata yakṣ'|êndram āhutaḥ, pṛthivī|pate,
strī|svarūpo, mahā|rāja, tasthau vrīḍā|samanvitaḥ.
192.45 taṃ śaśāp' âtha saṃkruddho dhana|daḥ, Kuru|nandana,
«evam eva bhavatv adya strītvaṃ pāpasya, guhyakāḥ!»
tato 'bravīd yakṣa|patir mah"|ātmā
«yasmād adās tv avamany' êha yakṣān
Śikhaṇḍino lakṣaṇaṃ pāpa|buddheḥ,
strī|lakṣaṇaṃ c' âgrahīḥ, pāpa|karman,
a|pravṛttaṃ, su|durbuddhe, yasmād etat tvayā kṛtam,
tasmād adya prabhṛty eva strī tvaṃ, sā puruṣas tathā!»
tataḥ prasādayām āsur yakṣā Vaiśravaṇaṃ kila,
«Sthūṇasy' ârthe kuruṣv' ântaṃ śāpasy'! êti» punaḥ punaḥ.
tato mah"|ātmā yakṣ'|êndraḥ pratyuvāc' ânugāminaḥ
sarvān yakṣa|gaṇāṃs, tāta, śāpasy' ânta|cikīrṣayā:
192.50 «Śikhaṇḍini hate, yakṣāḥ, svaṃ rūpaṃ pratipatsyate.

THE YAKSHAS replied:

King Drúpada has a daughter named Shikhándini, king, 192.40
and for some reason Sthuna gave her the distinguishing marks of his manhood. He took on a female appearance, and now that he has become a woman, he stays inside the house. He isn't coming out to see you because he is ashamed and bears a woman's appearance. This is the reason that Sthuna has not approached you today, king. So, now that you have heard the story, do what is right. The chariot will wait here.

"Bring Sthuna out!" commanded the *yaksha* lord. He repeated time and time again, "I will punish him!" Sthuna came out to the *yaksha* lord when summoned, earth-lord, and stood in his female form, filled with shame, great king.
The enraged granter of wealth cursed him then, descendant 192.45
of Kuru, saying, "Let this evil creature remain a woman as he is now, *gúhyakas*!"

The high-souled *yaksha* lord said, "Since you have disgraced the *yakshas*, given your signs of manhood to Shikhándin, evil-minded creature, and taken her feminine attributes, miscreant—since you have committed an act never before performed, incredibly wicked-minded *yaksha*, you will be a woman from this moment onwards, and she will be a man!"

The *yakshas* soothingly begged Váishravana, or so they say, pleading over and over again: "Make an end to Sthuna's curse!" The high-souled *yaksha* lord answered his followers—all his hordes of *yakshas*—my son, wishing to set a
limit to his curse, saying: "When Shikhándin is dead, *yak-* 192.50

Sthūṇo yakṣo nirudvego bhavatv, iti, mahā|manāḥ.»
ity uktvā bhagavān devo yakṣa|rājaḥ su|pūjitaḥ
prayayau sahitaḥ sarvair nimeṣ'|ântara|cāribhiḥ.
Sthūṇas tu śāpaṃ samprāpya tatr' âiva nyavasat tadā;
samaye c' āgamat tūrṇaṃ Śikhaṇḍī taṃ kṣapā|caram.
so 'bhigamy' âbravīd vākyaṃ,
«prāpto 'smi, bhagavann iti.»
tam abravīt tataḥ Sthūṇaḥ,
«prīto 'sm'! îti» punaḥ punaḥ.
ārjaven' āgataṃ dṛṣṭvā rāja|putraṃ Śikhaṇḍinam
sarvam eva yathā|vṛttam ācacakṣe Śikhaṇḍine.

YAKṢA uvāca:

192.55 śapto Vaiśravaṇen' âhaṃ tvat|kṛte, pārthiv'|ātmaja,
gacch' êdānīṃ yathā|kāmaṃ, cara lokān yathā|sukham.
diṣṭam etat purā manye, na śakyam ativartitum;
gamanaṃ tava c' êto hi, Paulastyasya ca darśanam.

BHĪṢMA uvāca:

evam uktaḥ Śikhaṇḍī tu Sthūṇa|yakṣeṇa, Bhārata,
pratyājagāma nagaraṃ harṣeṇa mahatā vṛtaḥ.
pūjayām āsa vividhair gandha|mālyair mahā|dhanaiḥ
dvijātīn devatāś c' âiva, caityān atha catuṣ|pathān.
Drupadaḥ saha putreṇa siddh'|ârthena Śikhaṇḍinā
mudaṃ ca paramāṃ lebhe Pāñcālyaḥ saha bāndhavaiḥ.
192.60 śiṣy'|ârthaṃ pradadau c' âtha Droṇāya, Kuru|puṅgava,
Śikhaṇḍinaṃ, mahā|rāja, putraṃ strī|pūrviṇaṃ tathā.
pratipede catuṣ|pādaṃ dhanur|vedaṃ nṛp'|ātmajaḥ

*shas*, he will win back his own form. So, let the high-minded *yaksha* Sthuna be free of his anxiety."

Having spoken, the highly honored blessed god and lord of the *yakshas* went on his way with his whole entourage, traveling in the blink of an eye. But Sthuna stayed at home now that he had sustained a curse, and at the arranged time Shikhándin came quickly to see the night-walker.

When he reached him, he said "I have arrived, blessed lord." And Sthuna repeatedly replied: "I am pleased!" When he saw that Prince Shikhándin had returned honestly, he told Shikhándin everything, just as it had happened.

THE YAKSHA said:

I have been cursed by Váishravana because of you, prince. 192.55
Go now, as you wish, and travel the worlds as you please. I believe this was fated long ago—your coming here, and the appearance of Paulástya—and it is impossible to overcome it.

BHISHMA continued:

Spoken to in this way by the *yaksha* Sthuna, Shikhándin returned to his city filled with great joy, Bhárata. He paid homage to the brahmins, gods, sacred places, and crossroads with various perfumed garlands and great wealth. Now that he had achieved his aim, Drúpada the Panchála king, and his relatives and son Shikhándin, felt blissfully happy.

He handed his previously female son Shikhándin over to 192.60
Drona as a pupil, great bull-like Kuru king. Prince Shikhándin and Dhrishta·dyumna Párshata learned the fourfold science of archery with you. And the spies whom I had sent

Śikhaṇḍī saha yuṣmābhir, Dhṛṣṭadyumnaś ca Pārṣataḥ.
mama tv etac carās, tāta, yathāvat pratyavedayan
jaḍ'|ândha|badhir'|ākārā ye muktā Drupade mayā.
evam eṣa, mahā|rāja, strī|pumān Drupad'|ātmajaḥ
sa saṃbhūtaḥ, Kuru|śreṣṭha, Śikhaṇḍī ratha|sattamaḥ.
jyeṣṭhā Kāśi|pateḥ kanyā Ambā|nām' êti viśrutā
Drupadasya kule jātā Śikhaṇḍī, Bharata'|ṛṣabha.
192.65 n' âham enaṃ dhanuṣ|pāṇiṃ yuyutsuṃ samupasthitam
muhūrtam api paśyeyaṃ; prahareyaṃ na c' âpy uta.
vratam etan mama sadā pṛthivyām api viśrutam:
striyāṃ, strī|pūrvake c' âiva, strī|nāmni, strī|svarūpiṇi
na muñceyam ahaṃ bāṇam iti, Kaurava|nandana.
na hanyām aham etena kāraṇena Śikhaṇḍinam.
etat tattvam ahaṃ veda janma, tāta, Śikhaṇḍinaḥ;
tato n' âinaṃ haniṣyāmi samareṣv ātatāyinam.
yadi Bhīṣmaḥ striyaṃ hanyāt, santaḥ kuryur vigarhaṇam,
n' âinaṃ tasmādd haniṣyāmi dṛṣṭv" âpi samare sthitam.

SAÑJAYA uvāca:

192.70 etac chrutvā tu Kauravyo rājā Duryodhanas tadā
muhūrtam iva sa dhyātvā Bhīṣme yuktam amanyata.

SAÑJAYA uvāca:

193.1 PRABHĀTĀYĀṂ TU śarvaryāṃ punar eva sutas tava
madhye sarvasya sainyasya pitā|maham apṛcchata:

to Drúpada, disguised as the senseless, the blind, and the deaf, told me exactly what was happening, my son.

So that is the tale, great king, of Drúpada's male and female child Shikhándin, who became a superb chariot warrior, greatest of the Kurus. The king of Kashi's eldest daughter, renowned by the name of Amba, was born into Drúpada's lineage as Shikhándin, bull of the Bharatas. I will not 192.65
look at him—not even glance at him for a second!—when he stands before me bow in hand and ready to fight; and I will not strike at him.

This is my constant vow, famed throughout the earth: that I will not release an arrow at a woman, someone who was previously a woman, someone with a woman's name, or someone who looks like a woman, descendant of the Kurus. This is why I cannot kill Shikhándin. I know the true story of Shikhándin's birth, my son, so I will not kill him when he draws his bow to kill me in battle. If Bhishma were to kill a woman in battle, good men would reproach him, and so I will not kill this man, even if I see him stationed in battle.

SÁNJAYA said:

Having listened to all this, Duryódhana the Kaurávya 192.70
king spent a moment lost in thought, and believed that this course of action was right for Bhishma.

SÁNJAYA continued:

WHEN THE NIGHT had passed and dawn came, your son 193.1
questioned his grandfather once again in the midst of the whole army, saying:

«Pāṇḍaveyasya, Gāṅgeya, yad etat sainyam udyatam
prabhūta|nara|nāg'|âśvaṃ, mahā|ratha|samākulam,
Bhīm'|Ârjuna|prabhṛtibhir mah"|êṣv|āsair mahā|balaiḥ
lokapāla|samair guptaṃ Dhṛṣṭadyumna|purogamaiḥ,
a|pradhṛṣyam, an|āvāryam, uddhūtam iva sāgaram,
senā|sāgaram a|kṣobhyam api devair mah"|āhave,
193.5 kena kālena, Gāṅgeya, kṣapayethā, mahā|dyute,
ācāryo vā mah"|êṣv|āsaḥ, Kṛpo vā su|mahā|balaḥ,
Karṇo vā samara|ślāghī, Drauṇir vā dvija|sattamaḥ?
divy'|âstra|viduṣaḥ sarve bhavanto hi bale mama.
etad icchāmy ahaṃ jñātuṃ, paraṃ kautūhalaṃ hi me
hṛdi nityaṃ, mahā|bāho; vaktum arhasi tan mama.»

BHĪṢMA uvāca:

«anurūpaṃ, Kuru|śreṣṭha, tvayy etat, pṛthivī|pate,
bal'|âbalam a|mitrāṇāṃ teṣāṃ yad iha pṛcchasi.
śṛṇu, rājan, mama raṇe yā śaktiḥ paramā bhavet,
śastra|vīrye raṇe yac ca, bhujayoś ca, mahā|bhuja.
193.10 ‹ārjaven' âiva yuddhena yoddhavya itaro janaḥ,
māyā|yuddhena māyāvī, ity› etad dharma|niścayaḥ.
hanyām ahaṃ, mahā|bhāga, Pāṇḍavānām anīkinīm
divase divase kṛtvā bhāgaṃ prāg|āhnikaṃ mama
yodhānāṃ daśa|sāhasraṃ kṛtvā bhāgaṃ, mahā|dyute,
sahasraṃ rathinām ekam—eṣa bhāgo mato mama.
anen' âhaṃ vidhānena sannaddhaḥ satat'|ôtthitaḥ

"Son of the Ganges, the Pándava's trained army, with its hosts of men, elephants, and horses, teeming with mighty chariot warriors, is protected by powerful and magnificent archers, Bhima and Árjuna and so on, led by Dhrishta·dyumna, as though protected by the defenders of the worlds themselves. It is unassailable, unstoppable, and churns like the ocean, and the ocean-like army cannot even be rocked by the gods in fierce battle!

How long would it take you, great glorious son of the 193.5
Ganges, or the great archer and teacher, Drona, or extraordinarily powerful Kripa, or Karna, famed in war, or the greatest of brahmins, Drona's son Ashva·tthaman, to destroy it? You are all assuredly experts in celestial weapons in my army. I wish to know this, for my heart is always extremely curious, long-armed man, so please tell me."

BHISHMA replied:

"It is fitting for you to ask about the strengths and weaknesses of your allies, greatest of the Kurus and lord of earth. Long-armed king, listen to the extent of my ability in battle, in the power of my weapons and in the strength of my arms in war. A normal person should be fought with honest 193.10
war, and a sorcerer with magical war. This is the decision of the law.

I could kill the army of the Pándavas, noble man, taking my quota each and every day before noon—making my quota ten thousand normal soldiers and a thousand chariot warriors, which I reckon is my measure, great glorious man—I could annihilate the great army in this manner, armored and always exerting myself, over some time, Bhá-

kṣapayeyaṃ mahat sainyaṃ kālen' ânena, Bhārata.
muñceyaṃ yadi v" âstrāṇi mahānti samare sthitaḥ
śata|sāhasra|ghātīni, hanyāṃ māsena, Bhārata.»

SAÑJAYA uvāca:

193.15 śrutvā Bhīṣmasya tad vākyaṃ rājā Duryodhanas tataḥ
paryapṛcchata, rāj'|êndra, Droṇam Aṅgirasāṃ varam:
«ācārya, kena kālena Pāṇḍuputrasya sainikān
nihanyā? iti.» taṃ Droṇaḥ pratyuvāca hasann iva:
«sthaviro 'smi, mahā|bāho, manda|prāṇa|viceṣṭitaḥ.
śastr'|âgninā nirdaheyaṃ Pāṇḍavānām anīkinīm,
yathā Bhīṣmaḥ Śāntanavo, māsen', êti matir mama.
eṣa me paramā śaktir, etan me paramaṃ balam.»
«dvābhyām eva tu māsābhyāṃ,» Kṛpaḥ Śāradvato 'bravīt.

Drauṇis tu daśa|rātreṇa pratijajñe bala|kṣayam.
193.20 Karṇas tu pañca|rātreṇa pratijajñe mah"|âstra|vit.
tac chrutvā sūta|putrasya vākyaṃ sāgaragā|sutaḥ
jahāsa sa|svanaṃ hāsaṃ, vākyaṃ c' êdam uvāca ha,
«na hi yāvad raṇe Pārthaṃ bāṇa|śaṅkha|dhanur|dharam
Vāsudeva|samāyuktaṃ rathen' āyāntam āhave
samāgacchasi, Rādheya, ten' âivam abhimanyase!
śakyam evaṃ ca bhūyaś ca tvayā vaktuṃ yath" êṣṭataḥ!»

rata. If I fire my great weapons which destroy hundreds of thousands at a time, standing in battle, then I could kill the army in a month, Bhárata."

SÁNJAYA continued:

When he had heard Bhishma's assessment, lord of kings, 193.15
King Duryódhana asked Drona, the greatest of the Ángirasa line: "Teacher, how long would it take you to kill the son of Pandu's armies?" To which Drona replied, smirking: "I am elderly, long-armed man, and my energy and breath have been lost. I could consume the Pándavas' army with the fire of my weapons in a month, just like Bhishma. That is my estimation. This is the limit of my ability and the extent of my strength."

Kripa, son of Sharádvat, claimed he could do it in two 193.20
months, and Drona's son promised the destruction of the army in ten days. But Karna, skilled in great weapons, promised their destruction in merely five days. When the river's son heard what the *suta*'s son was saying, he laughed loudly and said,

"As long as you do not encounter Partha, bearing his arrows, conch, and bow, with Vasudéva beside him as he charges towards you in battle on his chariot, Radhéya, then you may well believe it! You are capable of saying anything —whatever you please!"

VAIŚAMPĀYANA uvāca:

194.1 ETAC CHRUTVĀ TU Kaunteyaḥ sarvān bhrātṝn upahvare
āhūya, Bharata|śreṣṭha, idaṃ vacanam abravīt:

YUDHIṢṬHIRA uvāca:

Dhārtarāṣṭrasya sainyeṣu ye cāra|puruṣā mama,
te pravṛttiṃ prayacchanti mam' êmāṃ vyuṣitāṃ niśām.
Duryodhanaḥ kil' âpṛcchad āpageyaṃ mahā|vratam:
«kena kālena Pāṇḍūnāṃ hanyāḥ sainyam iti, prabho?»
«māsen' êti» ca ten' ôkto Dhārtarāṣṭraḥ su|durmatiḥ,
tāvatā c' âpi kālena Droṇo 'pi pratijajñivān.
194.5 Gautamo dvi|guṇaṃ kālam uktavān, iti naḥ śrutam.
Drauṇis tu daśa|rātreṇa pratijajñe mah"|âstra|vit.
tathā divy'|âstra|vit Karṇaḥ saṃpṛṣṭaḥ Kuru|saṃsadi
pañcabhir divasair hantuṃ sa sainyaṃ pratijajñivān.
tasmād aham ap' îcchāmi śrotum, Arjuna, te vacaḥ.
kālena kiyatā śatrūn kṣapayer iti, Phālguna?
evam ukto Guḍākeśaḥ Pārthivena Dhanañjayaḥ
Vāsudevaṃ samīkṣy' êdaṃ vacanaṃ pratyabhāṣata:
«sarva ete mah"|ātmānaḥ kṛt'|âstrāś, citra|yodhinaḥ;
a|saṃśayaṃ, mahā|rāja, hanyur eva, balaṃ tava.†
194.10 apaitu te manas|tāpo, yathā satyaṃ bravīmy aham.

VAISHAMPÁYANA said:

WHEN YUDHI·SHTHIRA the son of Kunti had heard this, he secretly summoned all his brothers, best of the Bharatas, and said this to them: 194.1

SHTHIRA said:

My spies among Dhartaráshtra's armies brought me news in the morning. Duryódhana apparently asked the strict vowed son of the Ganges: "How long it would take you to kill the Pándavas' army, lord?" And he replied to the extremely wicked-minded Dhartaráshtra, "One month."
Drona promised the same length of time, but we heard that 194.5
Gáutama said it would take him twice as long. Drona's son Ashva·tthaman, an expert in mighty missiles, promised ten days; and when Karna, an expert in celestial weapons, was asked in the Kuru assembly, he promised to kill us and our army in five days.

Therefore, I want to hear what you have to say, Árjuna. How long would it take for you to annihilate our enemies, Phálguna?

Addressed in this manner by the son of Pritha, Dhanan·jaya Guda·kesha glanced at Vasudéva and answered as follows:

"Without a shadow of a doubt, great king, they are all high-souled experts in weaponry and varied fighters who
could doubtless destroy your army. But let the worries of 194.10
your mind evaporate, for I speak the truth.

hanyām eka|rathen' âiva Vāsudeva|sahāyavān
s'|âmarān api lokāṃs trīn sarvān sthāvara|jaṅgamān,
bhūtaṃ bhavyaṃ bhaviṣyaṃ ca nimeṣād, iti me matiḥ.
yat tad ghoraṃ Paśupatiḥ prādād astraṃ mahan mama
kairāte dvandva|yuddhe tu, tad idaṃ mayi vartate.
yad yug'|ânte Paśupatiḥ sarva|bhūtāni saṃharan
prayuṅkte, puruṣa|vyāghra, tad idaṃ mayi vartate!
tan na jānāti Gāṅgeyo, na Droṇo, na ca Gautamaḥ,
na ca Drona|suto, rājan, kuta eva tu sūta|jaḥ.
194.15 na tu yuktaṃ raṇe hantuṃ divyair astraiḥ pṛthag|janam.
ārjaven' âiva yuddhena vijeṣyāmo vayaṃ parān.
tath" ême puruṣa|vyāghrāḥ sahāyās tatra, pārthiva,
sarve divy'|âstra|vidvāṃsaḥ, sarve yuddh'|âbhikāṅkṣiṇaḥ,
Vedānt'|âvabhṛtha|snātāḥ sarva ete '|parājitāḥ,
nihanyuḥ samare senāṃ devānām api, Pāṇḍava!
Śikhaṇḍī, Yuyudhānaś ca, Dhṛṣṭadyumnaś ca Pārṣataḥ,
Bhīmaseno, yamau c' ôbhau, Yudhāmany'|Ûttamaujasau,
Virāṭa|Drupadau c' ôbhau Bhīṣma|Droṇa|samau yudhi,
Śaṅkhaś c' âiva mahā|bāhur, Haiḍimbaś ca mahā|balaḥ,
194.20 putro 'sy' Âñjanaparvā tu mahā|bala|parākramaḥ,
Śaineyaś ca mahā|bāhuḥ sahāyo raṇa|kovidaḥ,
Abhimanyuś ca balavān, Draupadyāḥ pañca c' ātma|jāḥ,
svayaṃ c' âpi samartho 'si trailoky'|ôtsādane 'pi ca.
krodhād yaḥ puruṣaṃ paśyes tathā, Śakra|sama|dyute,
sa kṣipraṃ na bhaved vyaktam, iti tvāṃ vedmi, Kaurava.»

With Vasudéva as my ally and a single chariot, I could kill all three worlds with the immortals, and all inhabitants, static and mobile—whatever once existed, exists now, or will ever exist—in the mere twinkling of an eye. That is my opinion. Pashu·pati gave me a powerful and horrifying weapon when I fought a duel against him as a man of the mountains, and I still have it. The weapon which Pashu·pati uses to kill all creatures at the end of the age resides in me, tiger-like man! The son of the Ganges does not know it, nor does Drona, Gáutama, Drona's son, or even Karna the *suta*'s son, my king.

But it is not right to kill normal people with celestial mis- 194.15
siles. We will defeat our enemies with honest warfare. These men, whom I will list, are all your tiger-like allies, king. They are all experts in celestial weapons, and all eagerly hoping for battle. They are all invincible and have bathed in the purification of the Vedánta. They would destroy even an army of gods, Pándava!

They are Shikhándin, Yuyudhána, Dhrishta·dyumna Párshata, Bhima·sena and the twins, Yudha·manyu, Uttamáujas, and Viráta and Drúpada, both equal to Bhishma and Drona in war. Then there is long-armed Shankha and powerful Hidímba's son Ghatótkacha, as well as his son Ánjana· 194.20
parvan of enormously strong prowess, and your ally, the long-armed descendant of Shini, who is experienced in battle. There is mighty Abhimányu and the five sons of Dráupadi, and of course you yourself, capable of destroying the three worlds. I know you, and it is obvious, Káurava of glory to match Shakra, that the man you would look upon in fury will quickly be destroyed."

VAIŚAMPĀYANA uvāca:

195.1 TATAḤ PRABHĀTE vimale Dhārtarāṣṭreṇa coditāḥ
Duryodhanena rājānaḥ prayayuḥ Pāṇḍavān prati.
āplāvya śucayaḥ sarve, sragviṇaḥ, śukla|vāsasaḥ,
gṛhīta|śastrā, dhvajinaḥ, svasti|vācya|hut'|âgnayaḥ,
sarve brahma|vidaḥ śūrāḥ, sarve su|carita|vratāḥ,
sarve kāma|kṛtaś c' âiva, sarve c' āhava|lakṣaṇāḥ,
āhaveṣu parāl̐ lokāñ jigīṣanto mahā|balāḥ
ek'|âgra|manasaḥ sarve śraddadhānāḥ parasparam.
195.5 Vind'|Ânuvindāv Avantyau, Kekayā Bāhlikaiḥ saha
prayayuḥ sarva ev' âite Bhāradvāja|purogamāḥ.
Aśvatthāmā, Śāntanavaḥ, Saindhavo 'tha Jayadrathaḥ,
dākṣiṇātyāḥ, pratīcyāś ca, pārvatīyāś ca ye nṛpāḥ,
Gāndhāra|rājaḥ Śakuniḥ, prācy'|ôdīcyāś ca sarvaśaḥ,
Śakāḥ, Kirātā, Yavanāḥ, Śibayo, 'tha Vasātayaḥ
svaiḥ svair anīkaiḥ sahitāḥ parivārya mahā|ratham
ete mahā|rathāḥ sarve dvitīye niryayur bale.

Kṛtavarmā sah'|ânīkas, Trigartaś ca mahā|rathaḥ,
Duryodhanaś ca nṛ|patir bhrātṛbhiḥ parivāritaḥ,
195.10 Śalo, Bhūriśravāḥ, Śalyaḥ, Kausalyo 'tha Bṛhadrathaḥ,
ete paścād anugatā Dhārtarāṣṭra|purogamāḥ.
te sametya yathā|nyāyaṃ Dhārtarāṣṭrā mahā|balāḥ
Kuru|kṣetrasya paśc'|ârdhe vayvātiṣṭhanta daṃśitāḥ.

VAISHAMPÁYANA said:

In the clear-skied morning, the kings marched against 195.1
the Pándavas, driven on by Duryódhana the son of Dhrita·
rashtra. All had washed and purified themselves. They were
all garlanded and dressed in white clothes, and all had taken
up their weapons and were flying their flags. They had all
made oblations into the fire and had benedictions pro-
nounced. All were brave Vedic scholars, and all practiced
their vows properly. All had performed favors, and all bore
battle insignia. The powerful men hoped to reach other
worlds through battle. They were all singlemindedly focused and trusted one another.

The two Avántyas Vinda and Anuvínda, the Kékayas, 195.5
and Báhlikas all marched off, led by Bharad·vaja's son.
Ashva·tthaman, the son of Shántanu, the King Jayad·ratha
of the Sindhus, and kings from the south and west and
mountainous regions came, with Shákuni the Gandhára
king, and the kings from all over the east and north. All
the mighty chariot-warrior Shakas, Kirátas, Yávanas, Shibis,
and Vasátis, each with their own armies surrounding the
great chariot warriors, set out in the second division.

Then came Krita·varman and his army, and the mighty
Tri·gartan chariot-warrior king, along with King Duryódhana surrounded by his brothers. Shala too, and Bhuri· 195.10
shravas, Shalya, and Brihad·ratha the Kósalan king followed
behind, led by the Dhartaráshtras. Then all Dhrita·rashtra's
powerful armored forces gathered in proper fashion on the
far end of Kuru·kshetra, taking their positions.

Duryodhanas tu śibiraṃ kārayām āsa, Bhārata,
yath" âiva Hāstinapuraṃ dvitīyaṃ samalaṃkṛtam;
na viśeṣaṃ vijānanti purasya śibirasya vā
kuśalā api, rāj'|êndra, narā nagara|vāsinaḥ.
tādṛśāny eva durgāṇi rājñām api mahī|patiḥ
kārayām āsa Kauravyaḥ śataśo 'tha sahasraśaḥ.
195.15 pañca|yojanam utsṛjya maṇḍalaṃ tad raṇ'|âjiram
senā|niveśās te, rājann, āviśañ chata|saṅghaśaḥ.
tatra te pṛthivī|pālā yath"|ôtsāhaṃ yathā|balam
viviśuḥ śibirāṇy atra dravyavanti sahasraśaḥ.
teṣāṃ Duryodhano rājā sa|sainyānāṃ mah"|ātmanām
vyādideśa sa|bāhyānāṃ bhakṣya|bhojyam anuttamam,
sa|nāg'|âśva|manuṣyāṇāṃ; ye ca śilp'|ôpajīvinaḥ,
ye c' ânye 'nugatās tatra sūta|māgadha|bandinaḥ,
vaṇijo, gaṇikāś, cārā, ye c' âiva prekṣakā janāḥ,
sarvāṃs tān Kauravo rājā vidhivat pratyavaikṣata.

VAIŚAMPĀYANA uvāca:

196.1 TATH" ÂIVA RĀJĀ Kaunteyo Dharma|putro Yudhiṣṭhiraḥ
Dhṛṣṭadyumna|mukhān vīrāṃś codayām āsa, Bhārata.
Cedi|Kāśi|Karūṣāṇāṃ netāraṃ dṛḍha|vikramam
senā|patim amitra|ghnaṃ Dhṛṣṭaketum ath' ādiśat,
Virāṭaṃ, Drupadaṃ c' âiva, Yuyudhānaṃ, Śikhaṇḍinam,
Pāñcālyau ca mah"|êṣv|āsau, Yudhāmany'|Ûttamaujasau.
te śūrāś citra|varmāṇas tapta|kuṇḍala|dhāriṇaḥ
ājy'|âvasiktā, jvalitā, dhiṣṇyeṣv iva hut'|âśanāḥ,
196.5 aśobhanta mah"|êṣv|āsā grahāḥ prajvalitā iva.

Duryódhana had had a camp built, Bhárata, which was ornamented so as to be a second Hástina·pura. Experienced men who lived in the city, lord of kings, could not distinguish between the city and the camp. The Kaurávya king also had similar but inaccessible camps built for the other kings, numbering hundreds and thousands.

The armies' encampments, grouped in their settled hun- 195.15
dreds, stretched for forty-five miles on the ring of the battlefield, king, and earth-lords in their thousands entered their tents which were well supplied according to their energy and strength. King Duryódhana commanded the finest food to be provided for the high-souled kings with their extra soldiers and their troops of elephants, horses, and men. Mechanics and other followers in the camp—bards, minstrels, singers, traders, courtesans, spies, and spectators—for all these the Káurava king made proper provisions.

VAISHAMPÁYANA continued:

So too, Bhárata, King Yudhi·shthira, son of Kunti and 196.1
Dharma, drove on his heroes led by Dhrishta·dyumna. He issued orders to the firmly powerful leader of the Chedis, to the leader of the Kashis, to the leader of the Karúshas, to the enemy-slaughtering army leader Dhrishta·ketu, to Viráta and Drúpada, as well as to Yuyudhána, Shikhándin, and the two mighty Panchálya archers Yudha·manyu and Uttamáujas.

Those heroes, dressed in their variously hued armor and decked in golden earrings, gleamed like oblation-devouring
fires sprinkled with clarified butter on altars. The mighty 196.5
archers shone like luminous planets.

atha sainyaṃ yathā|yogaṃ pūjayitvā nara'|rṣabhaḥ
dideśa tāny anīkāni prayāṇāya mahī|patiḥ.
teṣāṃ Yudhiṣṭhiro rājā sa|sainyānāṃ mah"|ātmanām
vyādideśa sa|bāhyānāṃ bhakṣya|bhojyam anuttamam,
sa|gaj'|âśva|manuṣyāṇāṃ, ye ca śilp'|ôpajīvinaḥ.

Abhimanyuṃ, Bṛhantaṃ ca, Draupadeyāṃś ca sarvaśaḥ,
Dhṛṣṭadyumna|mukhān etān prāhiṇot Pāṇḍu|nandanaḥ,
Bhīmaṃ ca, Yuyudhānaṃ ca, Pāṇḍavaṃ ca Dhanañjayam
dvtīyaṃ preṣayām āsa bala|skandhaṃ Yudhiṣṭhiraḥ.
196.10 bhāṇḍaṃ samāropayatāṃ, caratāṃ, saṃpradhāvatām,
hṛṣṭānāṃ tatra yodhānāṃ śabdo divam iv' âspṛśat.
svayam eva tataḥ paścād Virāṭa|Drupad'|ânvitaḥ
ath' âparair mahī|pālaiḥ saha prāyān mahī|patiḥ.

bhīma|dhanvāyanī senā Dhṛṣṭadyumnena pālitā
Gaṅg" êva pūrṇā stimitā syandamānā vyadṛśyata.
tataḥ punar anīkāni nyayojayata buddhimān,
mohayan Dhṛtarāṣṭrasya putrāṇāṃ buddhi|niścayam.

Draupadeyān mah"|êṣv|āsān, Abhimanyuṃ ca Pāṇḍavaḥ,
Nakulaṃ Sahadevaṃ ca, sarvāṃś c' âiva Prabhadrakān,
196.15 daśa c' âśva|sahasrāṇi, dvi|sahasrāṇi dantināṃ,
ayutaṃ ca padātīnāṃ, rathāḥ pañca|śataṃ tathā,
Bhīmasenasya dur|dharṣaṃ prathamaṃ prādiśad balam;
madhyame ca Virāṭaṃ ca, Jayatsenaṃ ca Pāṇḍavaḥ,
mahā|rathau ca Pāñcālyau Yudhāmany'|Ûttamaujasau
vīryavantau, mah"|ātmānau, gadā|kārmuka|dhāriṇau;
anvayātāṃ tadā madhye Vāsudeva|Dhanañjayau.

The bull-like king paid honor to the army in due fashion, then ordered the troops to their march. King Yudhi·shthira assigned the finest delicacies as meals for the high-souled kings with their extra soldiers, troops of elephants, horses, infantry, and mechanics.

The son of Pandu first ordered Abhimányu, Brihánta,
and all Dráupadi's sons to go ahead, led by Dhrishta·
dyumna. In the second division of his army Yudhi·shthira
sent Bhima, Yuyudhána, and Pandu's son Dhanan·jaya. The 196.10
sound of excited warriors hoisting harnesses onto their
mounts and wandering and running about seemed to touch
the heavens. Then the lord of earth set off at the rear, with
Viráta, Drúpada, and the other kings.

The army of fearful bows, defended by Dhrishta·dyumna, resembled the Ganges when full: now tranquil, now flowing. The wise king rearranged his armies once more, thereby throwing the previously resolved minds of the sons of Dhrita·rashtra into confusion.

The son of Pandu ordered the mighty archer sons of
Dráupadi, Abhimányu, Nákula, Saha·deva, and all the Prabhádrakas, ten thousand horses, two thousand elephants, 196.15
ten thousand infantry soldiers, five hundred chariots, and
Bhima·sena's unassailable force to the front. The son of
Pandu placed Viráta and Jayat·sena in the middle with
the two Panchályan high-souled heroes Yudha·manyu and
Uttamáujas, wielding their maces and bows; and Vasudéva
and Dhanan·jaya also followed in the middle.

babhūvur atisaṃrabdhāḥ kṛta|praharaṇā narāḥ,
teṣāṃ viṃśati|sāhasrā hayāḥ śūrair adhiṣṭhitāḥ,
pañca nāga|sahasrāṇi, ratha|vaṃśāś ca sarvaśaḥ,
196.20 padātayaś ca ye śūrāḥ kārmuk'|âsi|gadā|dharā
sahasraśo 'nvayuḥ paścād agrataś ca sahasraśaḥ.

Yudhiṣṭhiro yatra sainye svayam eva bal'|ârṇave,
tatra te pṛthivī|pālā bhūyiṣṭhaṃ paryavasthitāḥ,
tatra nāga|sahasrāṇi, hayānām ayutāni ca,
tathā ratha|sahasrāṇi, padātīnāṃ ca, Bhārata.

Cekitānaḥ sva|sainyena mahatā, pārthiva'|rṣabha,
Dhṛṣṭaketuś ca Cedīnāṃ praṇetā pārthivo yayau,
Sātyakiś ca mah"|êṣv|āso Vṛṣṇīnāṃ pravaro rathaḥ
vṛtaḥ śata|sahasreṇa rathānāṃ praṇudan balī.
196.25 Kṣatradeva|Brahmadevau ratha|sthau puruṣa'|rṣabhau
jaghanaṃ pālayantau ca pṛṣṭhato 'nuprajagmatuḥ.

śakaṭā|paṇa|veśāś ca, yānaṃ yugyaṃ ca sarvaśaḥ,
tatra nāga|sahasrāṇi, hayānām ayutāni ca,
phalgu sarvaṃ kalatraṃ ca, yat kiñ cit kṛśa|durbalam,
kośa|sañcaya|vāhāṃś ca, koṣṭh'|āgāraṃ tath" âiva ca,
gaj'|ânīkena saṃgṛhya śanaiḥ prāyād Yudhiṣṭhiraḥ.

tam anvayāt satya|dhṛtiḥ Saucittir yuddha|durmadaḥ,
Śreṇimān, Vasudānaś ca, putraḥ Kāśyasya vā Vibhuḥ.
rathā viṃśati|sāhasrā, ye teṣām anuyāyinaḥ,
hayānāṃ daśa koṭyaś ca mahatāṃ kiṅkiṇīkinām,

In the ranks were utterly enraged and experienced fighters, among whom stood twenty thousand horses ridden by brave men, five thousand elephants, and hosts of chariots
in all areas, with brave infantry soldiers following, wielding 196.20
maces, swords and bows; thousands going in the rear, and thousands in the front.

The majority of kings were positioned where Yudhi·shthira had taken his stand in the ocean of the army's forces, and thousands of elephants, tens of thousands of horses, and as many thousands again of chariots and infantry also took their places, Bhárata.

Chekitána marched in their midst with his own enormous army, bull-like king, and so did Dhrishta·ketu, the leader and king of the Chedis. Sátyaki, the great archer and powerful leading Vrishni chariot warrior, drove on the hundreds of thousands of chariots that surrounded him.
Kshatra·deva and Brahma·deva, those two bull-like men, 196.25
took their position on their chariots, protecting the rear and traveling at the back.

The wagons, wages, clothes, vehicles, and beasts of burden were all around at the rear, as were thousands of elephants and tens of thousands of horses. And taking all the feeble, the women, some weak or sick, the animals carrying the treasury stores, and the stores of grain, Yudhi·shthira advanced slowly, with his elephant division.

Sauchítti, battle-crazed and firm to the truth, followed him, as did Shrénimat, Vasu·dana, and Vibhu the prince of Kashi. They had twenty thousand chariots and a hundred
million mighty horses decked in bells following them, as 196.30

196.30 gajā viṃśati|sāhasrā īṣā|dantāḥ, prahāriṇaḥ,
kulīnā, bhinna|karaṭā, meghā iva visarpiṇaḥ.
ṣaṣṭir nāga|sahasrāṇī, daś' ânyāni ca, Bhārata,
Yudhiṣṭhirasya yāny āsan yudhi senā mah"|ātmanaḥ.
kṣaranta iva jīmūtāḥ prabhinna|karaṭā|mukhāḥ
rājānam anvayuḥ paścāc, calanta iva parvatāḥ.
evaṃ tasya balaṃ bhīmaṃ Kuntī|putrasya dhīmataḥ,
yad āśrity' âtha yuyudhe Dhārtarāṣṭraṃ Suyodhanam.
tato 'nye śataśaḥ paścāt sahasr'|âyutaśo narāḥ
nardantaḥ prayayus teṣām anīkāni sahasraśaḥ.
196.35 tatra bherī|sahasrāṇi, śaṅkhānām ayutāni ca
nyavādayanta saṃhṛṣṭāḥ sahasr'|âyutaśo narāḥ!

well as twenty thousand well-bred fighting elephants like gliding clouds, with plow-like tusks and rent temples.

High-souled Yudhi·shthira had seventy thousand elephants which made up his force for battle, their faces and foreheads streaming as though they were rainclouds. They followed behind the king, like mountains on the move.

So this was the fearful army of the wise son of Kunti; the force upon which he relied and fought Suyódhana, son of Dhrita·rashtra. And apart from those listed, there were men in their hundreds, thousands, and tens of thousands coming after, in myriads of battalions, roaring as they followed.
And the thousands upon tens of thousands of jubilant men 196.35
beat their thousands of drums and blew their tens of thousands of conch shells!

# NOTES

**Bold** *references are to the English text;* ***bold italic*** *references are to the Sanskrit text. An asterisk (*) in the body of the text marks the word or passage being annotated.*

86.12 **Yójanas**: roughly 126 miles.

90.28 **Thousand-armed Árjuna**: son of Krita·virya, king of the Hái-hayas. He worshipped Dattatréya and won many boons including a thousand arms.

90.71 **Shraddha rites**: these rites are not strictly funeral rites, but offerings given by relatives in homage to the dead. Water and sometimes riceballs are offered to give the dead nutriment.

98.19 **Rhinoceros-horn ... from which Árjuna's bow takes the name Gandíva**: the Sanskrit word ***gāṇḍī*** means rhinoceros.

99.5 **Horse-headed Vishnu**: a reference to Vishnu's horse-necked incarnation.

99.6 **Patála** is here punned on the root √*pat* meaning to fall.

101.5 **Shri·vatsa**: this marking is often associated with Vishnu or Krishna, though it is also used for all divine beings. It is a curl of hair on the breast, often represented by a symbol resembling a cruciform flower.

102.13 **Sudha**: nectar and beverage of the gods. **Svadha**: oblation fluid of clarified butter offered to the dead.

104.24 This verse (**Vishnu spoke to the sacker of cities...**) is preceded by *Vaiśampāyana uvāca*, "Vaishampáyana said" in K, but this passage is clearly a continuation of Kanva's speech, and the introductory line is omitted from CE, so we have removed it from here.

104.29 **Súmukha**: *su/mukha* literally means "fair-faced" and therefore cheerful.

106.10 **Charu** is a dish of rice boiled with milk and butter.

106.18 **Caused Vishva·mitra to … reach brahminhood**: this is the most famous instance in the Hindu corpus of someone managing to become a brahmin without being born one. Vishva·mitra, the son of Kúshika, was a king who battled with the brahmin Vasíshtha but could not defeat him, no matter how hard he tried. Even when Shiva granted him mastery over all weaponry he could not defeat Vasíshtha. So he retired to the forest to practice austerities, hoping to become a brahmin. Thousands of years later he succeeded, as depicted here.

108.14 **The syllable om took its birth a thousand times**: Nila·kantha suggests that this refers to the Vedas, Upanishads, and many *śrutis* and *smṛtis*.

109.1 **So it is called dákshina**: the word ***dakṣiṇā*** in the feminine is the name of the fee given to an officiating priest at sacrifices.

109.18 **It was he who tormented the sons of Ságara**: this story is related in the "Ramáyana" and also in the "Maha·bhárata," 'The Forest' (CE III.107.30–34).

110.2 **So it is known as the late region**: the word ***paścima*** means both western and later.

110.6 **Mount Asta**: the idiom *astaṃ gam* means the sun sets, hence the mountain where the sun sets is named Mount Asta.

110.15 I.e., the winter solstice.

111.1 **Uttárana** means rescuing, ***uttārayate*** is a verb meaning to rescue, and ***uttara*** means high and north.

111.25 The Sanskrit ***vavre dhanaṃ*** is a little terse and unclear, but the translation is taken from a fuller explanation given in the commentary.

111.27 **This northern region is renowned as the best**: this is a pun, as ***uttara*** means both north and best.

113.12 **Supárna** literally means well-winged.

114.2 **Puts men down and supports them**: ***dhatte dhārayate ca*** plays on the verbal similarities to *dhana*.

114.3 **Shukra**: the planet Venus.

129.48 The word **suta** literally means charioteer or herald. Here it refers to Karna's adoptive father.

133.35 **A man is called púrusha because he is able to match his enemy**: the word for enemy being ***para***.

134.7 **Sánjaya** means total victory or triumphant.

134.14 **I came from one lake to another**: this is an idiomatic phrase referring to women leaving their own family to join another. Cf. 90.92

Canto 137 This canto is almost identical in parts to Pritha's speech at 90.65.

139.5 **So that I can abide by a warrior's duty**: Drona is in fact a brahmin.

143.10 **The planet Mahapáta** is named in the commentary, but does not appear directly in the Sanskrit printed here.

147.24 The story of Bhishma's conflict with Rama is explained later in this book, at 178.35.

160.17 The story of a cat practicing asceticism to lure prey into a false sense of security also appears in the "Five Discourses on Worldly Wisdom" (*Pañcatantra*, published by the CSL as OLIVELLE 2006). In Mamallapuram, a small coastal town in Tamil Nadu, one can see a carving of an ascetic cat in the position described here on the relief known as 'Árjuna's penance.'

160.118 This verse is almost an exact repeat of 160.55.

161.6–43 The rest of this canto is a repeat of 160.88 to the end of that canto. Ulúka repeats Duryódhana's words verbatim, only serving to demonstrate how lowly an ambassador he is. In comparison to the earlier embassies, this is shown to be entirely powerless. Ulúka is merely a gambler's son, a far cry from Drúpada's priest, the first messenger sent to the Kurus. A messenger of such lowly position is an insult to the Pándavas. He has no power to negotiate like Sánjaya or Krishna, and his function is merely to be a mouthpiece.

161.36 This verse is almost an exact repeat of 160.55.

179.4 Examples of the **mothers in the Vedas** are Gayátri, Sávitri, and Sarásvati.

186.27 **Prayága**: modern-day Allahabad.

# EMENDATIONS TO THE SANSKRIT TEXT

89.26 ***viduṣo*** em. CE : *viduro* K

90.60 ***na*** em. CE : *naḥ* K

90.62 ***sattvaṃ*** em. CE : *sarvaṃ* K

95.12 ***icchasi*** em. CE : *ditsasi* K

98.21 ***prathamajo daṇḍo*** em. CE : *prathamataś caṇḍo* K

111.17 ***sūtir*** em. CE : *mūrtir* K

123.13 ***nirjitān*** em. CE : *nirmitān* K

125.14 ***a|jeyaṃ balaṃ hi tat*** em. CE : *a|jeyānalaṃ hi tān* K

129.48 ***tvad|artham abhīpsati*** em. CE : *tvam artham abhīpsasi* K

131.17 ***Dhṛtarāṣṭraḥ sva|cakṣuṣī*** em. CE : *Dhṛtarāṣṭraś ca cakṣuṣī* K

131.20 ***dṛṣṭavān asmi*** em. CE : *draṣṭum icchāmi* K

134.20 ***n' āśritāraḥ*** em. CE : *na śrotāraḥ* K

143.9 ***saṃśamayann*** em. CE : *saṃgamayann* K

149.27 ***puram ṛddhimat*** em. CE : *parama'|rddhimat* K

155.13 ***saṃhṛṣṭa|vāhanāḥ*** em. CE : *sa|prāsarṣṭikāḥ* K

160.55 ***māyā*** em. conj. : *māyāṃ* K, *māyāṃ* CE

After 169.26 ***Sañjaya*** em. CE : *Vaiśampāyana* K

178.31 ***rājñā*** em. CE : *rājñāṃ* K

178.53 ***tathā tasmin*** em. CE : *tasminn eva* K

After 178.93 ***Sañjaya*** em. CE : *Vaiśampāyana* K

180.37 ***'pātayaṃ pannagān iva*** em. CE : *pātayeyaṃ nagān iva* K

181.9 ***vyadhamam*** em. CE : *apy adhamaṃ* K

182.29 ***manda|*** em. CE : *maṃtra|* K

183.2 ***rajanyāś ca*** em. CE : *rājanyānām* K

186.30 ***jal'|ôtthitā*** em. CE : *jale sthitā* K

188.7 ***mayā devi putr'|ârthe tapasā mahān*** em. CE : *mahā|devas tapas" ārādhito mayā* K

194.9 ***balaṃ tava*** em. CE : *na saṃśayaḥ* K

# GLOSSARY OF COMMON NAMES AND EPITHETS

ABHIMÁNYU Árjuna's son by Subhádra.

ÁCHALA Gandhára warrior allied to Duryódhana

ÁDHIRATHA Karna's adopted father

ADHÓKSHAJA Krishna

ÁDITI Daughter of Daksha, wife of Káshyapa, and mother of the Adítyas.

ADHÓKSHAJA Krishna

ADRISHYÁNTI Daughter-in-law of Vasíshtha

AGÁSTYA A famous sage who reputedly composed some Vedic hymns

AGNI The god Fire

AHIR·BÚDHNYA A minor deity of the Vedic pantheon who by the time of the "Maha·bhárata" had sunk into obscurity

ÁHUKA 1. Name of a tribe. 2. Krishna's great-grandfather

ÁILAVILA Kubéra

AIRÁVATA 1. Indra's elephant. 2. A snake

AJA Ally of the Pándavas

AJÁIKAPAD A minor deity of the Vedic pantheon who by the time of the "Maha·bhárata" had sunk into obscurity

AJA·MIDHA A distant Bhárata ancestor of the Káuravas and Pándavas

ÁKRITA·VRANA Name of a teacher, and friend of Rama son of Jamad·agni

AKRÚRA Krishna's paternal uncle

AKSHA·MALA Wife of Vasíshtha, also called Arúndhati

AKÚTI Name of a tribe

ALÁMBUSHA A *rákshasa* leader allied to Duryódhana

AMARÁVATI Indra's residence

AMBA Eldest daughter of the Kashi king, later reborn and transformed into Shikhándin

AMBÁLIKA Youngest daughter of the king of Kashi; sister to Amba and Ámbika

AMBARÍSHA A royal sage

ÁMBIKA Middle daughter of the king of Kashi; sister to Amba and Ambálika

AMITÁUJAS Panchálan warrior, allied to the Pándavas

ANADHRÍSHTI Yádava general and son of Ugra·sena

ANÁNTA A snake king

ÁNDHAKA Name of a tribe descended originally from Yayáti's son Yadu

ANDHRA Name of a tribe

ÁNJANA A noble elephant

ÁNJANA·PARVAN Son of Ghatótkacha

ANUVÍNDA Avántya king, loyal to Duryódhana

ÁPSARAS Celestial nymphs, companions of the *gandhárvas*

ARCHÍKA Patronymic of Jamad·agni

ARÍSHTA A Daitya who attacked Krishna in the form of a bull, but was killed by him

ARÍSHTA·NEMI Gáruda's brother

ÁRJUNA Third of the Pándava bothers. Known as Dhanan·jaya, Partha, Phálguna, Savya·sachin, Jishnu, Bibhátsu, Kirítin, Víjaya, and Krishna.

ÁRUNA Brother of Gáruda

ARÚNDHATI The star Alcor, wife of Vasíshtha and a paragon of conjugal fidelity

ÁRYAKA A snake, grandfather of Súmukha the serpent king. Name also used for Súmukha himself

ÁSHTAKA Son of Vishva·mitra by Mádhavi

ASHVA·RAJA Ucchaih·shravas

ASHVA·TTHAMAN The son of Drona and Kripi. He is a great warrior and an ally of the sons of Dhrita·rashtra

ASHVINS Divine twins and the fathers of Nákula and Saha·deva

AUSHÍNARA Patronymic of Shibi

AYÓDHYA Capital city of many kings descended from Ikshváku, including Rama (of the "Ramáyana")

BÁDARI A source of the Ganges

BÁHLIKA King of the Báhlikas, brother of Shántanu, allied to the sons of Dhrita·rashtra

BALA·RAMA Brother of Krishna, also known as Rama, Haláyudha, and Rauhinéya

BÁLLAVA Name Bhima·sena adopted when disguised as a cook in Viráta's city

BANA A Daitya who was defeated by Krishna

BHAGA·DATTA Prince of Prag·jyótisha

BHAGÍRATHI A name of the river Ganges

BHÁRATA Descendant of Bharata

BHÁRGAVA Descendant of Bhrigu; patronymic often of Rama, son of Jamad·agni

BHÁUMANA Name of Vishva·karman, the divine architect

BHIMA Second of the Pándava brothers. Known as Bhima·sena, Vrikódara, and Partha.

BHIMA·SENA 1. Bhima. 2. Father of Divo·dasa

BHISHMA Son of King Shántanu and the Ganges river. He is renowned for his wisdom and fidelity, and fights for the sons of Dhrita·rashtra. He is also known as Gangéya, Shántanava, Deva·vrata, and simply "the grandfather" (a label which he shares with the god Brahma)

BHÓGAVATI City ruled by Vásuki

BHOJA 1. Name of a people descended from Maha·bhoja. 2. A warrior allied to the Pándavas

BHOJA·KATA City built and ruled by Rukmin

BHRIGU Ancient sage who gave his name to a line of brahmins

BHURI·SHRAVAS Ally of Duryódhana and son of Soma·datta

BHUTA·PATI ŚivaShiva

BRAHMA·DEVA A king loyal to Yudhi·shthira

BRIHAD·BALA King allied to Duryódhana

BRIHAD·RATHA The king of Kósala, who is loyal to Duryódhana

BRIHÁNTA A king loyal to Yudhi·shthira

BRIHAS·PATI The priest of the gods

CHANDRA·SENA A king allied to the Pándavas

CHANÚRA A wrestler who served Kansa and was killed by Krishna

CHÁRANAS Celestial singers

CHARU·DESHNA Son of Krishna

CHEDI The name of a people

CHEKITÁNA A prince allied to the Pándavas

CHÍKURA Serpent father of Súmukha

CHITRÁNGADA A son of King Shántanu and younger half-brother of Bhishma. Briefly king before being killed by a *rákshasa* of the same name.

CHITRA·SENA A son of Dhrita·rashtra

CHITRÁYUDHA 1. A son of Dhrita·rashtra. 2. A king allied to the Pándavas

CHÚCHUPA Name of a tribe

CHYÁVANA Name of a Bhárgava sage

DAKSHA 1. A son of Brahma. 2. Gáruda's son

DAMAYÁNTI Princess of Vidárbha and wife of Nala

DAMBHÓDBHAVA An ancient king who fought Nara and Naráyana, but lost

DÁNAVA One of a group of antigods, descendants of Danu

DANDA·DHARA A warrior allied to Duryódhana

DÁRUKA Krishna's charioteer

DASHÁRHA 1. Name of a tribe. 2. A name of Krishna

DASHÁRNA 1. Name of a tribe. 2. Land ruled by King Hiránya·varman

DÉVAKI Krishna's mother and Vasu·deva's wife

DEVÁPI Son of Pratípa and eldest brother of Shántanu

DEVA·VRATA Bhishma

DHANAN·JAYA 1. A name of Árjuna. 2. A snake

DHARMA The divine personification of the Law (*dharma*) and Yudhi·shthira's genitor

DHAUMYA Family priest of the Pándavas

DHÉNUKA A demon whom Krishna and Bala·rama killed when children

DHRISHTA·DYUMNA Son of Drúpada, born to kill Drona

DHRISHTA·KETU A king loyal to Yudhi·shthira

DHRITA·RASHTRA 1. The blind Kuru king, father of the hundred Káuravas including Duryódhana, and uncle of the Pándavas. 2. A snake

DHRITI Personification of resolve and wife of Dharma

DHRUVA The Pole Star

DHUMÓRNA Wife of Yama

DHVÁJAVATI Daughter of Hari·medhas

DILÍPA 1. An ancestor of Rama (of the "Ramáyana"). 2. A sage. 3. A snake

DITI Ancestress of the Daityas

DIVO·DASA King of the Kashis and son of Bhima·sena

DRÁUPADI Wife of the five Pándava brothers and daughter of Drúpada. Known as Krishná and Pancháli

DRÁVIDA Name of a tribe

DRIDHA·DHANVAN Renowned archer allied to the Pándavas

DRONA 1. A brahmin warrior and teacher of the Káuravas and Pándavas. He is the father of Ashva·tthaman and the son of Bharad·vaja. 2. Name of a *kim·púrusha*

DRUMA 1. Son of Krishna and Rúkmini. 2. A prince of the *kim·púrushas*

DRÚPADA King of the Panchálas and father of Dhrishta·dyumna, Shikhándin, and Dráupadi

DUHSHÁSANA A son of Dhrita·rashtra, famous for his manhandling of Dráupadi

DURMÁRSHANA A son of Dhrita·rashtra

DÚRMUKHA A son of Dhrita·rashtra

DURVÁSAS A famously irascible sage who granted Kunti her boon to have children with the gods

DÚRVISHAHA A son of Dhrita·rashtra

DURYÓDHANA Eldest son of of Dhrita·rashtra and king of the Káuravas. Also known as Suyódhana and Dhartaráshtra

DUSHYÁNTA Kuru ancestor, father of Bharata, husband of Shakúntala

DVÍVIDA A monkey whom Krishna killed

GADHI Father of Vishva·mitra, and king of Kanya·kubja

GÁLAVA A sage and brahmin pupil of Vishva·mitra

GANDHÁRA The name of a north-western people

GANDHÁRI Dhrita·rashtra's wife and Duryódhana's mother

GANDHÁRVA Celestial beings, companions of the *ápsarases*

GANDÍVA Árjuna's bow

GÁRUDA A bird deity who is KṛṣṇaKrishna's vehicle. He is the son of Vínata

GARÚTMAT Gáruda

GAURI Wife of Váruna

GÁUTAMA Patronymic of Kripa (and his father)

GHATÓTKACHA A *rákshasa*, the son of Bhima and Hidimbá

GO·MUKHA Mátali's son

GOVÍNDA Krishna

GÚHYAKA A class of *yakshas*

GUDA·KESHA Árjuna

GUNA·KESHI Daughter of Mátali and eventual wife of Súmukha

HÁIHAYA Place and name of a tribe ruled by Kartavírya

HALÁYUDHA Name meaning plow-weaponed, used of Bala·rama

HÁNSIKA The cow who supports the southern region, daughter of Súrabhi

HARDÍKYA Patronymic of Krita·varman

HARI·MEDHAS Name of KṛṣṇaKrishna

HARY·ASHVA Name of Ikshváku

HÁSTINA·PURA City of the Kurus

HAYA·GRIVA A Daitya who stole the Veda and was killed by Vishnu

HIDÍMBA A *rákshasa* cannibal killed by Bhima

HIDIMBÁ Sister of the *rákshasa* Hidímba; brief wife of Bhima, and mother of Ghatótkacha

HIRÁNYA·PURA Underworld city inhabited by Daityas and Dánavas

HIRÁNYA·ROMAN King of the Akútis also known as Bhíshmaka

HIRÁNYA·VARMAN King of Dashárna and father-in-law to Shikhándin

HRISHIKÉSHA Krishna

IKSHVÁKU First king of the royal dynasty (sometimes called "solar") based in Ayódhya

INDRA King of the gods and father of Árjuna. Also known as Shakra, Vásava, and Mághavat

JALA·SANDHA A warrior allied to Duryódhana

JAMAD·AGNI Descendant of Bhrigu and father of the sage Rama.

JANAM·ÉJAYA A king directly descended from the Pándavas. The "Maha·bhárata" is recited to him by Vaishampáyana

JANÁRDANA Krishna

JÁHNAVI Patronymic of the Ganges river

JARA·SANDHA Son of Brihad·ratha and king of Mágadha who was a long-term enemy of Krishna

JARAT·KARU A sage, father of Astíka who halts Janam·éjaya's snake sacrifice

JARAT·KARÚ Wife of Jarat·karu and sister of the snake Vásuki

JAYAD·RATHA Sindhu-Sauvíra king who fights for the Káuravas. He is Duryódhana's brother-in-law

JAYÁNTA A Panchálan warrior allied to the Pándavas

JAYAT·SENA King of Mágadha

JIMÚTA An ancient sage

JYOTSNA·KALI Daughter of Soma and wife of Púshkara

KAILÁSA Mountain on which Kubéra and Shiva dwell

KÁITABHA A demon who tried to kill Brahma but was killed by Vishnu instead

KALAKÁKSHA A Daitya killed by Gáruda

KALAKÉYA Name of a race of demons

KALA·KHANJA Name of a race of demons

KALI 1. Bhishma's stepmother, Shántanu's second wife, also known as Gándhavati and Sátyavati. 2. Personification of misfortune and the name of the final and worst cosmic age

KALÍNGA Name of a people on the east coast

KAMBÓJA Land ruled by Sudákshina

KAMPÍLYA King Drúpada's city

KANCHI Name of a tribe

KANSA Krishna's maternal uncle and enemy

KANYA·KUBJA City of great importance in the north-west of India, sitting on the Ganges and ruled by Gadhi

KAPÁRDIN Rudra

KÁPILA Identified as Chakra·dhanus

KARNA Ally of Duryódhana and the Pándavas' older half brother. He is the son of Kunti and the sun, and the foster-son of the *suta* Ádhiratha and his wife Radha. He is also known as Radhéya, Vrisha, Vaikártana, and Vasu·shena

KARTAVÍRYA Árjuna, the son of King Krita·virya of the Háihayas.

KARTIKÉYA The god of war and son of Shiva

KARÚSHA The name of a people

KASHI The name of a people

KÁSHIKA Name of one of the five Kékayan princes

KAUNTÉYA Son of Kunti

KÁURAVA Descendant of Kuru. The patronymic can refer to both the sons of Dhrita·rashtra and the sons of Pandu, but it is more commonly used for the former side.

KAURÁVYA 1. Káurava. 2. Name of a snake

KÁUSHIKA Patronymic often used to refer to Vishva·mitra

KÁUSTUBHA Celebrated gem worn on Krishna's chest

KÉKAYA The name of a people

KÉSHAVA Krishna

KHÁNDAVA A forest (burned by Árjuna and Krishna) on the banks of the Yámuna river

KHASHA Name of a tribe

KÍCHAKA General of Viráta's army and brother of Queen Sudéshna of Matsya

KIM·PÚRUSHA Attendants of Kubéra

KIRÁTA The name of a people

KIRÍTIN Árjuna

KÓLIKA An elderly mouse

KÓSALA Region ruled by Brihad·ratha

KRIPA Son of sage Sharádvat. Raised by King Shántanu, he was a tutor of the Káuravas and Pándavas. He is also known as Sharádvata and Gáutama

KRISHNÁ Dráupadi, "the dark one"

KRISHNA An avatar of the god Vishnu who is allied to the Pándavas. He is also known as Vasudéva, Madhu·súdana, Upéndra, Mádhava, Govínda, Hari, Pundarikáksha, Sátvata, Vrishabhékshana, Adhókshaja, Purushóttama, Anánta, Varshnéya, Janárdana, Vishvak·sena, Shauri, Dashárha, Hrishikésha, Késhava, and Áchyuta

KRITA·VARMAN Son of Hrídika

KRODHA·HANTRI A king also known as Sena·bindu, allied to the Pándavas

KRODHA·VASHA Name of a race of demons

KSHATRA·DEVA A king loyal to Yudhi·shthira

KSHATRA·DHARMAN Son of Dhrishta·dyumna

KUBÉRA Lord of riches, leader of the *yakshas*. He is also known as Váishravana

KUMÁRA 1. Kartikéya. 2. One of the birds of noble lineage descended from Gáruda

KUMÁRI Consort of the snake Dhanan·jaya

KÚMUDA 1. A bird. 2. A snake. 3. A noble elephant

KÚNDINA Rukmin's city

KÚNTALA Name of a tribe

KUNTI Wife of Pandu; mother of the three eldest Pándava brothers, and, by the sun, of Karna

KUNTI·BHOJA Kunti's adoptive father

KURU·KSHETRA The plain (near present-day Delhi) which was the site of the Bharatan war

KURU Ancestor of the heroes of the "Maha·bhárata"

KURUS Descendants of Kuru: Káuravas

LÁKSHMANA Duryódhana's son

LAKSHMI Goddess of good fortune and wife of Vishnu

MÁDHAVI Daughter of Yayáti who was granted the boon of renewable virginity

MADHU A demon killed by Krishna

MADHU·SÚDANA Krishna

MADIRÁSHVA Name of one of the five Kékayan princes, also known as Shankha

MADRI Pandu's second wife, mother of the Pándava twins Nákula and Saha·deva

MAHA·DEVA Name of ŚivaShiva

MAHÍSHMATI A city ruled by Nila

MANDHÁTRI A king in the lineage of Ikshváku

MANU The first man, progenitor of the human race

MARÍCHA Patronymic of Káshyapa

MARUTS Indra's storm gods

MARÚTTA A great king of yore

MÁTALI Indra's charioteer

MATÁNGA Legendary figure brought up as a brahmin but really a *chandála* (the most despised of the mixed castes, with a shudra father and a brahmin mother)

MATSYA A people and the land where they reside

MÉNAKA An *ápsaras* and the wife of Mount Himálaya

NÁHUSHA 1. Father of Yayáti and briefly king of the gods. 2. A snake

NÁIRRITA A type of *rákshasa*

NÁKULA One of the Pándava twins (brother of Saha·deva), son of Madri and the Ashvins

NALA Níshadhan king and husband of Damayánti

NANDA 1. Name of a sage. 2. A snake

NARA The Primeval Man, always associated with Naráyana.

NÁRADA A semidivine figure who circulates widely amongst the inhabitants of the cosmos, telling tales and often making mischief

NÁRAKA Son of the earth and the personification of hell, who lives in Prag·jyótisha

NARÁYANA Supreme deity often associated with Nara and/or identified with Vishnu

NILA 1. A king resident in Mahíshmati. 2. One of the five Kékayan princes

NIVÁTA·KÁVACHA A race of Dánavas

PAKA A Daitya killed by Indra

PANCHÁLA The land ruled by Drúpada

PANDU Son of Vichítra·virya (genitor Vyasa), brother of Dhrita·rashtra and Vídura, and father of the Pándavas

PANDYA A king allied to the Pándavas

PARAMÉSHTHIN Title of Praja·pati, meaning "supreme"

PÁRSHATA Patronymic of Drúpada and Dhrishta·dyumna

PASHU·PATI "Lord of creatures," also known as Rudra

PATÁLA City in the underworld, inhabited by Daityas and Dánavas

PAULÁSTYA Patronymic of Kubéra

PÁURAVA Descendant of Puru

PÁVAKA Agni

PRABHÁDRAKA Name of a people allied to the Pándavas

PRABHÁVATI Wife of the sun

PRADYÚMNA Krishna's son by Rúkmini

PRAG·JYÓTISHA City ruled by Bhaga·datta

PRAHLÁDA A Daitya king

PRAJA·PATI The secondary creator or demiurge

PRÁKRITI Goddess personifying the objective basis of phenomena

PRÁSRITA A Daitya killed by Gáruda

PRATÁRDANA Sometime king of Kashi

PRATISHTHÁNA A city at the confluence of the Ganges and the Yámuna; Yayáti's capital city

PRAYÁGA Name of the confluence of the Ganges and Yámuna (present-day Allahabad)

PRÍSHATA Father of Drúpada

PULÁSTYA An ancient sage

PULÍNDA Name of a tribe

PULÓMA Consort of Bhrigu

PURU·MITRA A warrior allied to Duryódhana

PÚRUSHA god personifying the subjective basis of phenomena [in the text this is in a pair with Prákriti]

PURU·RAVAS An ancient king, ancestor of Yayáti and lover of Úrvashi

PÚSHKARA Son of Váruna

PÚTANA Female demon who tried and failed to kill Krishna when he was a baby

RADHÉYA Metronymic of Karna

RAHU A Daitya who causes eclipses by seizing the sun or moon

RÁIVATA King of Anárta and builder of Dváraka

RAMA 1. A brahmin warrior sage, son of Jamad·agni. 2. Bala·rama, brother of Krishna. 3. Hero of the "Ramáyana," husband of the Vidéhan princess Sita.

RAMBHA A celebrated *ápsaras*

RASÁTALA One of the seven hells beneath the earth

RAUHINÉYA Metronymic of Bala·rama

RÁVANA Famous *rákshasa* ruler of Lanka

RÉNUKA Wife of Jamad·agni

RICHÍKA Father of Jamad·agni

RIDDHI Good fortune personified as Kubéra's wife

ROCHAMÁNA A king allied to the Pándavas

RÓCHANA·MUKHA A Daitya killed by Gáruda

RÓHINI A constellation; the moon's favorite wife

RUDRA 1. (pl.) Storm deities. 2. (sg.) Shiva

RUDRÁNI Wife of Rudra

RUKMIN Son of Bhíshmaka and enemy of Krishna (after Krishna carried off his sister Rúkmini)

RÚKMINI Sister of Rukmin who was abducted by Krishna

SAHA·DEVA One of the Pándava twins (brother of Nákula), son of Madri and the Ashvins

SANDHYA Personification of twilight

SÁNJAYA 1. King Dhrita·rashtra's factotum, son of Gaválgana. 2. Son of Vídula

SANKÁRSHANA Name of Bala·rama (also known as Haláyudha)

SARÁSVATI 1. Goddess of speech. 2. A river

SARVA·KAMA·DUGHA The cow who supports the northern region, daughter of Súrabhi

SÁTVATA Name of the followers of Krishna

SATYA·DHRITI A king allied to the Pándavas

SÁTYAJIT A king allied to the Pándavas

SÁTYAKI Patronymic of Yuyudhána

SATYA·RATHA Leader of five Tri·garta princes allied to Duryódhana

SÁTYAVAT Son of Dyumat·sena and husband of Sávitri

SÁTYAVATI 1. Daughter of King Gadhi and wife to the sage Richíka. She was the mother of Jamad·agni and grandmother of Rama Bhárgava. 2. Shántanu's second wife, stepmother of Bhishma

SAUBHA The city ruled by Shalva

SAUBHÁDRA Metronymic of Abhimányu

SAUCHÍTTI A king loyal to Yudhi·shthira

SÁUMAKI Patronymic from Sómaka

SAVÍTRI Name of the sun

SENA·BINDU King allied to the Pándavas; also known as Krodha·hantri

SHACHI Indra's wife

SHAIBYA 1. Name for the king of the Shibi people. 2. One of Krishna's horses

SHAIKHAVÁTYA A brahmin sage

SHAKRA Indra

SHÁKUNI Son of Súbala and brother-in-law of Dhrita·rashtra. Also known as Sáubala

SHAKÚNTALA Daughter of Vishva·mitra who was raised by the sage Kanva and married King Dushyánta

SHALA A king loyal to Duryódhana

SHALI·BHÁVANA A town between Upaplávya and Hástina·pura

SHALVA King of Saubha

SHALVÉYAKA A tribe of people

SHALYA Brother of Madri; uncle of the Pándavas; king of the Madras. Fights for Duryódhana

SHÁMBARA A demon killed by Indra

SHÁNDILI A female ascetic

SHÁNKARA Shiva

SHANKHA 1. Name of one of the five Kékayan princes, also known as Madiráshva. 2. A son of Viráta. 3. A snake

SHÁNTANU Bhárata king, father of Bhishma

SHARÁDVATA Patronymic of Kripa

SHARMÍSHTHA Mother of Puru and daughter of Vrisha·parvan the king of *ásuras*

SHARNGA Krishna's bow

SHATA·PARVA Wife of Shukra

SHATA·SHIRSHA Wife of Vásuki

SHAURI Patronymic of Vasu·deva and hence of Krishna

SHIBI 1. The name of a people. 2. A king, son of Ushínara and Mádhavi

SHIKHÁNDIN Son of Drúpada, born female to kill Bhishma

SHIKHÁNDINI Shikhándin before his sex-change

SHISHU·PALA King of Chedi, killed by Krishna; father of Dhrishta·ketu

SHIVA Supreme deity, often associated with asceticism and/or destruction

SHRÉNIMAT A king loyal to Yudhi·shthira

SHRUTA·SENA A Daitya killed by Gáruda

SHRUTA·SHRI A Daitya killed by Gáruda

SHUKRA The planet Venus; Yayáti's father-in-law; priest of the *ásuras*; husband of Shata·parva. Also known as Kavya and Úshanas

SHYÉNAJIT A warrior allied to the Pándavas

SOMA 1. The deified drink of victory. 2. The moon (occasionally identified as a Bhárata ancestor)

SOMA·DATTA Son of Báhlika

SRÍNJAYA A people allied to the Panchálas

SÚBALA 1. King of Gandhára, father of Shákuni and of Dhrita·rashtra's wife Gandhári. 2. One of Gáruda's six sons

SUBHÁDRA 1. Wife of Árjuna, sister of Krishna, and mother of Abhimányu. 2. The cow who supports the western region, daughter of Súrabhi

SUDÁKSHINA King of Kambója, allied to Duryódhana

SUDHÁRMAN An ally of the Pándavas

SUDHÁRMA Wife of Mátali

SUKÁNYA The kshatriya wife of the sage Chyávana Bhárgava

SUKUMÁRA Name of one of the five Kékayan princes

SÚMUKHA 1. One of Gáruda's six sons. 2. A serpent chosen by Mátali to marry his daughter

SUNÁMAN One of Gáruda's six sons

SUNÉTRA One of Gáruda's six sons

SUPÁRNA Gáruda

SUPRATÍKA An elephant, descendant of Airávata and others

SÚRABHI Celestial cow, daughter of Daksha and wife of Káshyapa

SÚRUCH One of Gáruda's six sons

SURÚPA The cow who supports the eastern region, daughter of Súrabhi

SURYA·DATTA Name of one of the five Kékayan princes

SUSHÉNA A son of Dhrita·rashtra

SUVÁRCHAS One of Gáruda's six sons

SUVÁRNA·SHIRAS A mythical being

SVAHA Personification of the oblation; wife of Agni

SVARBHÁNU Eclipse demon, also known as Rahu

TÁKSHAKA A royal snake, assassin of Janam·éjaya Bhárata's father Paríkshit

TARA Wife of Brihas·pati

TARKSHYA Gáruda

UCCHAIH·SHRAVAS Indra's white horse

ÚDDHAVA A Yádava friend of Krishna's

UGRA·SENA Father of Kansa whom Krishna reestablished as king of Máthura

ULÚKA Son of Shákuni

UMA Párvati, Shiva's wife

UPAPLÁVYA A city in Viráta's kingdom, where the Pándavas live through most of this volume

URNÁYUS Lover of Ménaka

ÚRVASHI An *ápsaras* who married the Bhárata ancestor Puru·ravas

ÚSHANAS Shukra

USHÍNARA The king of a people of the same name in central India; father of Shibi

USHÍRA·BIJA A mountain

ÚSHMAPA A class of gods

UTTAMÁUJAS A king loyal to Yudhi·shthira

ÚTTARA Prince of Matsya, son of Viráta. Also known as Bhumiñ·jaya

VAICHITRAVÍRYA son of Vichítra·virya, usually referring to Dhrita·rashtra

VAIKÁRTANA Karna

VAIKHÁNASA A class of ascetics

VAISHAMPÁYANA Brahmin pupil of Vyasa; recites the story of the Pándavas to King Janam·éjaya

VÁISHRAVANA Kubéra

VAIVÁSVATA Yama

VÁMANA 1. A celestial elephant. 2. A serpent and the maternal grandfather of Súmukha. 3. A son of Gáruda

VARANÁVATA A city in which the Pándavas live briefly in the first book of the "Maha·bhárata"

VARDHAKSHÉMI A king allied to the Pándavas

VARSHNÉYA Clan name of Krishna

VÁRUNA God of the ocean

VASÁTI The name of a people

VÁSAVA Indra

VASÍSHTHA A sage who owns the cow Nándini and whose identity Dharma assumes. Traditional rival of Vishva·mitra

VASU·DANA A king loyal to Yudhi·shthira

VÁSUKI King of the snakes

VASU·MANAS Son of King Hary·ashva

VASU·SHENA Karna

VIBHU Prince of the Kashi, loyal to Yudhi·shthira

VICHÍTRA·VIRYA Bhárata king; son of Shántanu; younger half-brother of Bhishma; nominal father of Dhrita·rashtra and Pandu

VIDÁRBHA A country (now called Berar) which was home to Dama·yánti

VIDÉHA Name of a country in modern Tirhut, in Bihar

VÍDULA Kshatriya mother of Sánjaya (not to be confused with King Dhrita·rashtra's factotum Sánjaya)

VÍDURA Younger half-brother of Dhrita·rashtra and Pandu

VIKÁRNA A son of Dhrita·rashtra

VÍNATA Mother of Gáruda

VINDA Avántya king loyal to Duryódhana

VIRÁTA King of Matsya, ally of the Pándavas

VIRÓCHANA God of the sun and Karna's father

VISHNU Supreme deity

VISHVA·KARMAN The divine architect, also known as Bháumana

VISHVAK·SENA Krishna

VISHVA·MITRA Legendary sage, born a kshatriya but became a brahmin through asceticism

VIVÁSVAT 1. The sun, father of Yama. 2. A Daitya killed by Gáruda

VIVÍNSHATI A son of Dhrita·rashtra

VRIKA·STHALA A village requested by the Pándavas

VRISHA Karna

VRISHA·SENA Karna's son

VRISHNI A tribe from whom Krishna is descended

VRITRA Archetypical demon, the instigator of a universal drought; killed by Indra

VYAGHRA·DATTA A King allied to the Pándavas

VYASA Pre-marital son of Shántanu's second wife Sátyavati; genitor of Vichítra·virya's sons Dhrita·rashtra, Pandu, and Vídura; seer and composer of the story of the Pándavas

YAKSHA Chthonic nature spirit, able to assume any shape

YÁDAVAS Descendants of Yadu

YAJÑA·SENA Drúpada

YAJÑA Sacrifice personified

YAJÑASÉNI Son of Drúpada

YAMA The god who rules over the spirits of the dead

YAVA·KRITA Son of sage Bharad·vaja

YÁVANA A people (the Greeks)

YAYÁTI Bhárata ancestor, son of King Náhusha

YUDHA·MANYU A king loyal to Yudhi·shthira

YUDHI·SHTHIRA Eldest of the Pándavas. Known as Bhárata, Partha, best of the Kurus, the king of righteousness, and Ajáta·shatru.

YUYUDHÁNA A king loyal to Yudhi·shthira

YUYÚTSU A half-caste son of Dhrita·rashtra

# INDEX

*Sanskrit words are given in the English alphabetical order, according to the accented CSL pronuncuation aid. They are followed by the conventional diacritics in brackets.*

# THE CLAY SANSKRIT LIBRARY

The volumes in the series are listed here in order of publication.
Titles marked with an asterisk* are also available in the Digital Clay Sanskrit Library (eCSL).
For further information visit www.claysanskritlibrary.org

1. The Emperor of the Sorcerers (*Bṛhatkathāślokasaṃgraha*) (vol. 1 of 2) by *Budhasvāmin*. SIR JAMES MALLINSON
2. Heavenly Exploits (*Divyāvadāna*). JOEL TATELMAN
3. Maha·bhárata III: The Forest (*Vanaparvan*) (vol. 4 of 4)* WILLIAM J. JOHNSON
4. Much Ado about Religion (*Āgamaḍambara*) by *Bhaṭṭa Jayanta*. CSABA DEZSŐ
5. The Birth of Kumára (*Kumārasaṃbhava*) by *Kālidāsa*. DAVID SMITH
6. Ramáyana I: Boyhood (*Bālakāṇḍa*) by *Vālmīki*. ROBERT P. GOLDMAN
7. The Epitome of Queen Lilávati (*Līlāvatīsāra*) (vol. 1 of 2) by *Jinaratna*. R.C.C. FYNES
8. Ramáyana II: Ayódhya (*Ayodhyākāṇḍa*) by *Vālmīki*. SHELDON I. POLLOCK
9. Love Lyrics (*Amaruśataka, Śatakatraya & Caurapañcāśikā*) by *Amaru, Bhartṛhari & Bilhaṇa*. GREG BAILEY & RICHARD GOMBRICH
10. What Ten Young Men Did (*Daśakumāracarita*) by *Daṇḍin*. ISABELLE ONIANS
11. Three Satires (*Kaliviḍambana, Kalāvilāsa & Bhallaṭaśataka*) by *Nīlakaṇṭha, Kṣemendra & Bhallaṭa*. SOMADEVA VASUDEVA
12. Ramáyana IV: Kishkíndha (*Kiṣkindhākāṇḍa*) by *Vālmīki*. ROSALIND LEFEBER
13. The Emperor of the Sorcerers (*Bṛhatkathāślokasaṃgraha*) (vol. 2 of 2) by *Budhasvāmin*. SIR JAMES MALLINSON
14. Maha·bhárata IX: Shalya (*Śalyaparvan*) (vol. 1 of 2)* JUSTIN MEILAND

15. Rákshasa's Ring (*Mudrārākṣasa*)*
by *Viśākhadatta*. Michael Coulson

16. Messenger Poems (*Meghadūta, Pavanadūta & Haṃsadūta*)
by *Kālidāsa, Dhoyī & Rūpa Gosvāmin*. Sir James Mallinson

17. Ramáyana III: The Forest (*Araṇyakāṇḍa*)
by *Vālmīki*. Sheldon I. Pollock

18. The Epitome of Queen Lilávati (*Līlāvatīsāra*) (vol. 2 of 2)
by *Jinaratna*. R.C.C. Fynes

19. Five Discourses on Worldly Wisdom (*Pañcatantra*)*
by *Viṣṇuśarman*. Patrick Olivelle

20. Ramáyana V: Súndara (*Sundarakāṇḍa*) by *Vālmīki*.
Robert P. Goldman & Sally J. Sutherland Goldman

21. Maha·bhárata II: The Great Hall (*Sabhāparvan*)
Paul Wilmot

22. The Recognition of Shakúntala (*Abhijñānaśākuntala*) (Kashmir Recension) by *Kālidāsa*. Somadeva Vasudeva

23. Maha·bhárata VII: Drona (*Droṇaparvan*) (vol. 1 of 4)*
Vaughan Pilikian

24. Rama Beyond Price (*Anargharāghava*)
by *Murāri*. Judit Törzsök

25. Maha·bhárata IV: Viráta (*Virāṭaparvan*)
Kathleen Garbutt

26. Maha·bhárata VIII: Karna (*Karṇaparvan*) (vol. 1 of 2)
Adam Bowles

27. "The Lady of the Jewel Necklace" & "The Lady who Shows her Love" (*Ratnāvalī & Priyadarśikā*) by *Harṣa*.*
Wendy Doniger

28. The Ocean of the Rivers of Story (*Kathāsaritsāgara*) (vol. 1 of 7)
by *Somadeva*. Sir James Mallinson

29. Handsome Nanda (*Saundarananda*)*
by *Aśvaghoṣa*. Linda Covill

30. Maha·bhárata IX: Shalya (*Śalyaparvan*) (vol. 2 of 2)*
Justin Meiland

31. Rama's Last Act (*Uttararāmacarita*) by *Bhavabhūti*.
Sheldon Pollock. Foreword by Girish Karnad

32. "Friendly Advice" (*Hitopadeśa*) by *Nārāyaṇa* &
"King Víkrama's Adventures" (*Vikramacarita*). JUDIT TÖRZSÖK
33. Life of the Buddha (*Buddhacarita*)
by *Aśvaghoṣa*. PATRICK OLIVELLE
34. Maha·bhárata V: Preparations for War (*Udyogaparvan*) (vol. 1 of 2)
KATHLEEN GARBUTT. Foreword by GURCHARAN DAS
35. Maha·bhárata VIII: Karna (*Karṇaparvan*) (vol. 2 of 2)
ADAM BOWLES
36. Maha·bhárata V: Preparations for War (*Udyogaparvan*) (vol. 2 of 2)
KATHLEEN GARBUTT
37. Maha·bhárata VI: Bhishma (*Bhīṣmaparvan*) (vol. 1 of 2)*
Including the "Bhagavad Gita" in Context
ALEX CHERNIAK. Foreword by RANAJIT GUHA
38. The Ocean of the Rivers of Story (*Kathāsaritsāgara*) (vol. 2 of 7)
by *Somadeva*. SIR JAMES MALLINSON
39. "How the Nagas were Pleased" (*Nāgānanda*) by *Harṣa* &
"The Shattered Thighs" (*Ūrubhaṅga*) by *Bhāsa*.*
ANDREW SKILTON
40. Gita·govínda: Love Songs of Radha and Krishna (*Gītagovinda*)*
by *Jayadeva*. LEE SIEGEL. Foreword by SUDIPTA KAVIRAJ
41. "Bouquet of Rasa" & "River of Rasa" (*Rasamañjarī & Rasataraṅgiṇī*) by *Bhānudatta*. SHELDON POLLOCK
42. Garland of the Buddha's Past Lives (*Jātakamālā*) (vol. 1 of 2)*
by *Āryaśūra*. JUSTIN MEILAND
43. Maha·bhárata XII: Peace (*Śāntiparvan*) (vol. 3 of 5)*
"The Book of Liberation" (*Mokṣadharma*). ALEXANDER WYNNE
44. The Little Clay Cart (*Mṛcchakaṭikā*) by *Śūdraka*.
DIWAKAR ACHARYA. Foreword by PARTHA CHATTERJEE
45. Bhatti's Poem: The Death of Rávana (*Bhaṭṭikāvya*)*
by *Bhaṭṭi*. OLIVER FALLON

46. "Self-Surrender," "Peace," "Compassion," and "The Mission of the Goose": Poems and Prayers from South India (*Ātmārpaṇastuti, Śāntivilāsa, Dayāśataka & Haṃsasaṃdeśa*) by *Appayya Dīkṣita, Nīlakaṇṭha Dīkṣita & Vedānta Deśika.* YIGAL BRONNER & DAVID SHULMAN
Foreword by GIEVE PATEL
47. Maha·bhárata VI: Bhishma (*Bhīṣmaparvan*) (vol. 2 of 2)* ALEX CHERNIAK
48. How Úrvashi Was Won (*Vikramorvaśīya*) by *Kālidāsa* VELCHERU NARAYANA RAO & DAVID SHULMAN
49. The Quartet of Causeries (*Caturbhāṇī*) by *Śūdraka, Śyāmilaka, Vararuci & Īśvaradatta.* CSABA DEZSŐ & SOMADEVA VASUDEVA
50. Garland of the Buddha's Past Lives (*Jātakamālā*) (vol. 2 of 2)* by *Āryaśūra.* JUSTIN MEILAND
51. Princess Kadámbari (*Kādambarī*) (vol. 1 of 3) by *Bāṇa.* DAVID SMITH
52. The Rise of Wisdom Moon (*Prabodhacandrodaya*)* by *Kṛṣṇamiśra.* MATTHEW T. KAPSTEIN
Foreword by J.N. MOHANTY
53. Maha·bhárata VII: Drona (*Droṇaparvan*) (vol. 2 of 4)* VAUGHAN PILIKIAN
54. Maha·bhárata X & XI: Dead of Night & The Women (*Sauptikaparvan & Strīparvan*).* KATE CROSBY
55. Seven Hundred Elegant Verses (*Āryāsaptaśatī*)* by *Govardhana.* FRIEDHELM HARDY
56. Málavika and Agni·mitra (*Mālavikāgnimitram*) by *Kālidāsa.* DÁNIEL BALOGH & ESZTER SOMOGYI